The Modern Tradition

THE MODERN TRADITION

An Anthology of Short Stories

FOURTH EDITION

EDITED BY

Daniel F. Howard

RUTGERS UNIVERSITY

Scott, Foresman and Company

Glenview, Illinois London, England

Library of Congress Catalog Card No. 78-71866

ISBN 0-673-39219-8

1011121314151617l8-KPF-97969594939291908 9

Printed in the United States of America

ACKNOWLEDGMENTS

John Barth. "Lost in the Funhouse," copyright © 1967 by The Atlantic Monthly Company. "Life-Story," copyright © 1968 by John Barth. Both reprinted from *Lost in the Funhouse* by John Barth, by permission of Doubleday & Company, Inc.

Donald Barthelme. "Me and Miss Mandible," copyright © 1961 by Donald Barthelme. Reprinted from *Come Back, Dr. Caligari* by Donald Barthelme, by permission of Little, Brown and Co. "The Indian Uprising" reprinted with the permission of Farrar, Straus & Giroux, Inc. from *Unspeakable Practices, Unnatural Acts* by Donald Barthelme. Copyright © 1964, 1965, 1966, 1967, 1968 by Donald Barthelme. "The Indian Uprising" appeared originally in *The New Yorker.*

Jorge Luis Borges. "Funes, The Memorious," copyright © 1967 by Grove Press, Inc. Reprinted from *A Personal Anthology* by Jorge Luis Borges, by permission of Grove Press, Inc. "The Secret Miracle," copyright © 1962 by New Directions Publishing Corporation. Reprinted from *Labyrinths* by Jorge Luis Borges, by permission of New Directions.

Willa Cather. "Paul's Case" is reprinted from *Youth and the Bright Medusa* by Willa Cather, courtesy of Alfred A. Knopf, Inc.

Anton Chekhov. "Misery" from *The School Mistress and Other Stories* by Anton Chekhov, translated from the Russian by Constance Garnett. Copyright 1921 by Macmillan Publishing Co., Inc., renewed 1949 by David Garnett. Reprinted by permission of Macmillan Publishing Co., Inc., Chatto & Windus Ltd., and the Estate of Constance Garnett.

Joseph Conrad. "The Secret Sharer," copyright 1910 by Harper Brothers. Reprinted from *Twixt Land and Sea* by Joseph Conrad, by permission of Doubleday & Company, Inc.

Ralph Ellison. "Battle Royal," copyright 1947 by Ralph Ellison. Reprinted from *Invisible Man* by Ralph Ellison, by permission of Random House, Inc. "Flying Home," copyright 1944 (renewed) by Ralph Ellison. Reprinted by permission of William Morris Agency, Inc., on behalf of the author.

William Faulkner. "Dry September," copyright 1930 and renewed 1958 by William Faulkner. "Barn Burning," copyright 1939 and renewed 1967 by Estelle Faulkner and Jill Faulkner Summer. Both reprinted from *Selected Short Stories of William Faulkner,* by permission of Random House, Inc.

F. Scott Fitzgerald. "Babylon Revisited" by F. Scott Fitzgerald is reprinted with the permission of Charles Scribner's Sons from *Taps at Reveille.* Copyright 1931 Curtis Publishing Company.

Ernest Hemingway. "Big Two-Hearted River" by Ernest Hemingway is reprinted with the permission of Charles Scribner's Sons from *In Our Time.* Copyright 1925 Charles Scribner's Sons.

James Joyce. "Araby" and "The Dead" from *Dubliners* by James Joyce. Originally published by B. W. Huebsch, Inc., in 1916. Copyright © 1967 by the Estate of James Joyce. All rights reserved. Reprinted by permission of The Viking Press.

Franz Kafka. "The Metamorphosis" and "A Hunger Artist" are reprinted by permission of Schocken Books, Inc. from *The Penal Colony* by Franz Kafka. Copyright 1948 by Schocken Books, Inc. Copyright renewed © 1975 by Schocken Books, Inc.

D. H. Lawrence. "The Prussian Officer" and "Odour of Chrysanthemums" from *The Complete Short Stories of D. H. Lawrence,* Volumes I & II. All rights reserved. Reprinted by permission of The Viking Press.

Doris Lessing. "He," copyright © 1957 by Doris Lessing. Reprinted from *The Habit of Loving* by Doris Lessing (T. Y. Crowell), by permission of Harper & Row, Publishers, Inc. "To Room Nineteen" from *A Man and Two Women* by Doris Lessing. Copyright © 1958, 1962, 1963 by Doris Lessing. Reprinted by permission of Simon & Schuster, a Division of Gulf & Western Corporation, and James Brown Associates, Inc.

Bernard Malamud. "Black Is My Favorite Color" from *Idiots First* by Bernard Malamud. Copyright © 1963 by Bernard Malamud. "The Magic Barrel" from *The Magic Barrel* by Bernard Malamud. Copyright © 1954, 1958 by Bernard Malamud. Both reprinted with the permission of Farrar, Straus & Giroux, Inc.

Guy de Maupassant. "The Necklace" from *Short Stories* by Guy de Maupassant, translated by Marjorie Laurie. Translation copyright 1934 by Marjorie Laurie. An Everyman's Library Edition. Published in the United States by E. P. Dutton & Co. and reprinted with their permission.

Toni Morrison. "1919" from *Sula* by Toni Morrison. Copyright © 1973 by Toni Morrison. Reprinted by permission of Alfred A. Knopf, Inc.

Vladimir Nabokov. "That in Aleppo Once . . ." copyright 1943 by The Atlantic Monthly Company. "First Love," copyright 1948 by Vladimir Nabokov. Both reprinted from *Nabokov's Dozen* by permission of Doubleday & Company, Inc.

Joyce Carol Oates. "Where Are You Going, Where Have You Been?" and "In the Region of Ice," copyright © 1970, 1969, 1968, 1967, 1966, 1965 by Joyce Carol Oates. Reprinted from *The Wheel of Love* by Joyce Carol Oates, by permission of the publisher, Vanguard Press, Inc.

Flannery O'Connor. "Everything That Rises Must Converge" from *Everything That Rises Must Converge* by Flannery O'Connor. Copyright © 1961, 1965 by the Estate of Mary Flannery O'Connor. Reprinted with the permission of Farrar, Straus & Giroux, Inc. "Good Country People" from *A Good Man is Hard to Find and Other Stories* by Flannery O'Connor. Copyright © 1955 by Flannery O'Connor. Reprinted by permission of Harcourt Brace Jovanovich, Inc.

Tillie Olsen. "Tell Me a Riddle" excerpted from the book *Tell Me a Riddle* by Tillie Olsen. Copyright © 1961, 1960 by Tillie Olsen. "I Stand Here Ironing" excerpted from the book *Tell Me a Riddle* by Tillie Olsen. Copyright © 1956 by Tillie Olsen. Originally appeared in *Pacific Spectator.* Both reprinted by permission of Delacorte Press/Seymour Lawrence.

Grace Paley. "A Conversation with My Father" and "Enormous Changes at the Last Minute" from *Enormous Changes at the Last Minute* by Grace Paley. Copyright © 1972, 1974 by Grace Paley. Reprinted with the permission of Farrar, Straus & Giroux, Inc.

Katherine Anne Porter. "Flowering Judas" from *Flowering Judas and Other Stories* by Katherine Anne Porter. Copyright 1930, 1958 by Katherine Anne Porter. "The Grave" from *The Leaning Tower and Other Stories* by Katherine Anne Porter. Copyright 1944, 1972 by Katherine Anne Porter. Both reprinted by permission of Harcourt Brace Javanovich, Inc.

John Updike. "A & P" from *Pigeon Feathers and Other Stories* by John Updike. Copyright © 1962 by John Updike. "Tomorrow and Tomorrow and So Forth" from *The Same Door* by John Updike. Copyright © 1955 by John Updike. Both originally appeared in *The New Yorker* and are reprinted by permission of Alfred A. Knopf, Inc.

Eudora Welty. "Why I Live at the P.O." and "Death of a Travelling Salesman," copyright 1941, 1969 by Eudora Welty. Reprinted from her volume *A Curtain of Green and Other Stories* by permission of Harcourt Brace Jovanovich, Inc.

Richard Wright. "Big Boy Leaves Home" from *Uncle Tom's Children* by Richard Wright. Copyright 1936 by Richard Wright; renewed 1966 by Ellen Wright. "The Man Who Lived Underground" from *Eight Men* by Richard Wright (World). Copyright © 1961, 1940 by Richard Wright. Copyright 1944 by L. B. Fischer Publishing Corp. Both reprinted by permission of Harper & Row, Publishers, Inc.

PHOTO CREDITS

Photographs of *Jorge Luis Borges, Ralph Ellison, Doris Lessing, Toni Morrison, Vladimir Nabokov, Joyce Carol Oates, Tillie Olsen, Grace Paley, Katherine Anne Porter,* and *Eudora Welty* used by permission of the photographer, Jill Krementz.

John Barth. Photograph used courtesy of Lurton Blassingame. *Donald Barthelme.* Photograph used courtesy of Jerry Dantzic. *Willa Cather.* Photograph used by permission of The Granger Collection, New York. *Anton Chekhov.* Photograph used by permission of Novosti Press Agency. *Joseph Conrad.* Photograph used by permission of The Bettman Archive Inc. *William Faulkner.* Photograph used by permission of Black Star. *F. Scott Fitzgerald.* Photograph used courtesy of Charles Scribner's Sons. *Nathaniel Hawthorne.* Photograph used by permission of Brown Brothers. *Ernest Hemingway.* Photograph used courtesy of Charles Scribner's Sons. *Henry James.* Photograph used by permission of Brown Brothers. *James Joyce.* Photograph by Ruth Asch used courtesy of The Viking Press, Inc. *Franz Kafka.* Photograph used courtesy of Schocken Books, Inc. *D. H. Lawrence.* Photograph used by permission of The Bettman Archive Inc. *Bernard Malamud.* Photograph used courtesy of the photographer, Janna Malamud. *Guy de Maupassant.* Photograph used by permission of The Bettman Archive Inc. *Flannery O'Connor.* Photograph used courtesy of Farrar, Straus & Giroux, Inc. *Edgar Allan Poe.* Photograph used by permission of The Bettman Archive Inc. *John Updike.* Photograph by Peter Simon used courtesy of Alfred A. Knopf, Inc. *Richard Wright.* Photograph used courtesy of Harper & Row, Publishers.

Preface

Two distinct principles motivate this book. The first is that a reader of fiction should have as much opportunity as possible to build up a sensitivity to one writer's range of appeals before moving on to another's. There are of course practical considerations: perhaps ideally one should read all of Joyce's *Dubliners,* at least five or six stories by D. H. Lawrence, etc.; but such concentration is rarely desirable in introductory courses designed to stimulate interests in various authors—some of whose works as presented in the limited form of an anthology may inspire the student to further study in more specialized courses. Thus there are here not The Forty-nine Best Stories of Modern Times but excellent, representative stories by twenty-nine major writers who represent the modern tradition in short fiction. Of course these twenty-nine haven't fashioned the tradition alone; others could be included to round out the picture. But there can be no doubt about the originality and influence of those here. With two stories by each writer who is of the twentieth century (except Fitzgerald and Morrison, because of copyright restrictions), and one for contrast by the older founders of the form, the reader has the chance to put to use, as he reads a second story, the perceptions gained from having read and discussed the first. There is no attempt to furnish mere variety, for it is the editor's view that concepts of "variety" and "difference" among works of literature have little meaning unless one understands exactly what the story read today is supposed to be different from—and unless he is moved to pay special attention to today's story because he knows that it will enrich his reading of tomorrow's.

Stories are grouped by individual authors (rather than by such abstractions as "theme," "technique," "the urban experience," "growing up," etc.) in order to emphasize a multitude of integral connections among shorter works that are part of a whole shaped by a particular imaginative organization: the writer's selection of detail, his projection of voices, his development of theme, his relating of environment to character. Because the stories of any one writer are the products of a single distinctive imagination, this arrangement encourages the reader to make meaningful comparisons and contrasts within each writer's stories and, having developed a set of reactions to one writer, to measure more intelligently the different achievement of the next. It is then finally on the basis of his own experience of particular short stories that the reader can develop a sense of what the "modern tradition" is.

The second principle of this book is that a reader benefits most not from an editor's supposedly definitive analysis of a given writer but from information about each author and a few suggestions about what to look for as he reads. A serious reader wants to learn how to generate his own reactions, to be able to say something about what he has read. To give him a framework in which to do so at that crucial time when he is ready to reflect upon the story before him is the intention of the introductions to the selections from each writer. The introductions are directed toward the disclosure of ranges of possible reaction to an author, not toward making a statement that encapsulates everything that might be said.

The format consists of a general introduction to ways of thinking about short fiction, and one essay on each of the authors.

Contents

Introduction

As one reads the stories in this book it is well to keep in mind the principle of organization that underlies them all: each story's characters, events, scenes, props, are pulled together by being parts of a *short* story—"short" not in terms of an absolute maximum length (which can in exceptional cases extend to a hundred pages or so) but in terms of the writer's assumption that his reader is available for an uninterrupted period of time. This concentration of attention is the source of the short story's unity. In the novel, the assumption is different: that the reader will pick up the novel, read what he can, put it down, come back to it, and so in stages get through it. Thus the novel is available in episodes, perhaps for leisurely reading aloud evening after evening, or serialized for monthly consumption in a magazine (which, in the heyday of serialization of novels, might take almost two years to publish all of a single work). Sure, there may be people who read a Dickens novel straight through from page 1 to page 800 in a single sitting, as certainly as there are people who of necessity interrupt their reading of a short story, but what counts is the assumption of either a continuous or a discontinuous experience on the part of the reader. Dickens wrote novels for an audience that picked up the parts month by month, gradually acclimatizing themselves to his fictional terrain. Short stories have to work faster: there is no time to stroll through the countryside getting to know one family after another. A more intense central focus is required, and this changes the quality of the world of the short story.

The short-story form became popular during the same period—the mid- and late nineteenth century—in which the taste for serialized novels was at its height, and the large English-reading public fond of novels-in-parts influenced the short-story writer. It was a post-Romantic public that more and more preferred prose to poetry but, having lived under the influence of two generations of Romantic poets, also longed for the emotional intensity and metaphorical expansiveness of poetry: its preference for fiction was combined with a taste for poetic intensity. Thus the short-story writer confronted audiences which, though they appreciated the multiple plots of huge Victorian novels, also yearned for a literary form more gripping—one that would carry them off into a more immediately emotional world. The short story's compactness made it potentially more thrilling than the novel; under the pressure of time, it could elevate the reader into intense states of fear, terror, and joy. The tacit agreement between writer and reader that the story's spell was not to be broken by interruptions in the reading made all the difference. For example, the famous horror stories of Edgar Allan Poe, written in the 1840s, use a heightened mood to fuse details into a single powerful impression. Poe's fictional technique in these stories has much in common with his creation of an all-enveloping mood in poems like "Annabel Lee" and "The Raven."

America proved fertile ground for the early development of the short story because of its new and growing population of middle-class citizens trained in the three R's. The thinly settled American countryside did not foster the development of lending libraries to serve this new literate public, as the cities and towns of England did, so a great many monthly magazines, which could be bought cheaply and passed around, sprang up. They created a demand for relatively short pieces of fiction, complete in one issue, that could be put together with articles of general interest in the familiar format of *Harper's, The Atlantic Monthly,* and hundreds of others.

A more speculative explanation for the rapid and concentrated development of the short story in America, versus a much later and less popularly supported development in England, lies in the nature of the form. It is ideally suited to expressing the individual's special case, that of someone alone or at least drastically isolated from the web of ordinary society and tradition. Though the generalization has many exceptions, the greatest writers in England in the nineteenth century participated in the intellectual effort that has come to typify their times, of relating their thinking to biological, religious, political, and cultural history. American writers, on the other hand, tended to search for an individuality apart from the doctrines, the habits, the deceptions of the old world.

What are some of the implications of the special time relationship between the short story and the reader? One certainly is that because the short story has room for but a small fraction of the data of life, the writer must not only select his facts carefully but must choose those which suggest more than themselves—facts that have a kind of radiance that extends the limited area of the story, giving the illusion not only of life but of superintense life. Of course all art is selective. Even a massive novel does not report everything; and though a novelist may offer elaborate information about hats, shoes, dresses, and jewelry, and may thereby encourage the reader to imagine that he sees all, it is all just an *illusion* of inclusiveness. The most elaborately specific novel excludes, necessarily, more details of experience than it includes—despite the fact that the novelist, as opposed to the short-story writer, can afford to indulge many interests, and so may represent his characters' shoes as indicative of this, their hats and gloves as suggestive of that, and so on, weaving these indications into the fabric of his novel. The range of concern of the short story, on the other hand, is so sharply narrowed that a character must be summed up by details that naturally, within the context of the story, must simultaneously give a sense of real life and expand metaphorically to connect the character to everything else in his fictional world.

Take as an example the apparently casual gesture of Gabriel in Joyce's "The Dead" when he arrives at the Misses Morkan's party. There is snow on his shoes, and he flicks at them. There is nothing especially odd in his doing so: it is typical of Gabriel to be ill at ease and to look for some gesture to relieve his self-consciousness, and perhaps it is also typical of him to reveal his fastidiousness by trying to keep his shoes neat. But in the context of the story this casual flicking of snow is much more than a merely natural-seeming action: it takes its place in a pattern of meaning involving Gabriel's dissociation from nature, from Ireland, and finally even from his wife. Thus the gesture joins other facts that define Gabriel's distaste for and yet participation in a kind of death, the physical locus of which is the snow that descends on Ireland. A pattern like this, generated by perfectly chosen details, raises Gabriel's apparently casual flicking away of a bit of snow to a super-lifelike act. To put it another way: we can imagine that if Gabriel were a real person, rather than a character in a short story, he might as he came in have also straightened his tie, hiked up his pants, and rubbed his itchy nose; but Joyce, the short-story writer, invents a gesture that both suggests something that a real person might do *and* connects Gabriel with an evolving synthesis of the people and the things around him.

The snow on Gabriel's shoes is of course a "symbol," but not a static or simple one. In reading "The Dead," or any of the other stories in this book, we will do well not to hunt for symbols that unequivocally "mean" something else (snow equals death, for instance). The world of a short story is an organic one in which words are under pressure and, being under pressure, suggest more than they do in the loose context of everyday life. But instead of labeling them symbols specifically meaning something else, we do better to become aware of the way in which a story's details form a whole. The whole is often made credible by the development of a strong mood, a dominant emotion—such as Gabriel's fevered desire for his wife, which at the end of "The Dead" sustains the Hell-like details of the setting through which he moves, and then his mood of depression, which justifies the cosmic significance of the snow falling over all of Ireland.

The reader will find it rewarding to be aware of the relation established in these stories between people and things. Because the form of the short story is so intense, the things that surround characters serve as components of emotional states. In Lawrence's "Odour of Chrysanthemums," for example, the creaking engine, the coal dust brought back from the mine, the texture of the dead man's body, are sensory facts indistinguishable from the wife's total existence, just as the burnt-over forest and the depths of the swamp represent parts of Hemingway's narrator in "Big Two-Hearted River." They are not merely elements of the story that express his character but integral parts of his identity.

Many of the narrators in these stories attempt to impose imaginary connections between themselves and objects, connections outside the reality otherwise represented in the story. The boy in Joyce's "Araby," for example, is so saturated with the romantic literature of the Arabian Nights (as well as with the ceremonies of the Roman Catholic Church) that as he walks with his aunt through downtown Dublin he transforms the details of the scene before him—the groceries, the smells, the sounds—into an imagined romantic-religious quest. Joyce temporarily lets us participate in the vision the boy is creating for himself. We find the boy's naive world as lovely as it is unreal, though we see that, regrettably, it does not correspond to the solid Dublin that Joyce reveals behind him. Our understanding of the story "Araby" grows as we become aware of the difference between the boy's imagination of the facts of Dublin and what the rest of the story establishes is really Dublin. We are very sympathetic to his illusion, and thus at the end, when he too perceives reality, we feel very close to him. Still, there is a distance between us, created both by our *sympathy* for his burning disappointment (rather than our participation in it) and by our closer association with the gentle older narrator who is no longer the boy he once was. The narrowing but never closed distance between us and the boy makes the story.

Moods and emotions belong to people, and the short story is a form well suited to intensity of expression. So it is not surprising to find that short-story writers, in utilizing the possibilities of their form, often put their readers in the presence of characters who are obsessed, and furthermore whose obsessions are contagious. The character may be the narrator, who wants to tell us his story because it seems to have a special significance that he thinks he understands; or because he is disturbed by something he has heard about or seen in the lives of other people, and is trying in the very act of telling his story to work out its significance. An obsessed character often offers a focus for whatever emotion or mood dominates the story and connects its details.

Maybe in a pure thriller the reader is asked to identify completely with a character who is obsessed by, say, a series of terrors leading to some final horror that presumably both character and reader will thrill to together. In such a pure thriller (if it exists) there is no divergence between the reader and the character. The identification is complete, as it occasionally is in real life when we identify completely with an intimate friend who is telling us what happened to him. In good fiction such a complete identification is impossible. A good story demands of the reader the active role that makes fiction interesting, whereas a pure thriller merely asks the reader to *accept* a character's response.

In good short stories there are elaborate variations of the distance between the reader and the characters. Often, for example, a narrator does not see the meaning of his own story, and by not seeing it acts as a foil to the reader, who has the fun of finding significance *in spite of* the narrator's lack of understanding. The reader is encouraged to play fictionmaker, entering the artificial world of the story as an all-seeing detectivelike observer. His excitement, unlike the narrator's, builds up from his growing apprehension of a reality more complicated than the one understood by those who live it. Then there are tricky narrators out to mesmerize us and force us to agree that their world is exactly what they imagine it to be; there are others who would limit our seeing so that they can convince us that the events of the story are to be understood as merely logical—or emotional, or social—phenomena; and there are apparently dumb narrators who cannot find their story in the facts that go into it, and so seem to leave the matter to us. But sometimes the dominant mood of a story comes not from a particular character or narrator at all but from what we might call a "focus of sensibility," an unlocatable voice, an arrangement of details that invests the events being narrated with emotion. Since there are no pure thrillers in this book, the reader is never expected to identify completely with the characters or to accept uncritically the focus of sensibility: we have to be actively engaged in establishing the terms of our relationship to the characters and to the special feeling of the story.

If we begin to question the appeal made to our imaginations by a story's focus of sensibility or by its viewpoint, we find ourselves involved in helping the author to make his fiction; we accept our position as mature readers, different from, say, schoolchildren accepting the story of Little Red Riding Hood as a report of a real happening rather than a deliberately created story. As mature readers we create our own story out of materials presented. The author is guiding us—by arranging his details in a particular way, by balancing one character against another, by choosing language that reveals unrecognized levels of feeling—but for his guidance to work we must actively seek our position with respect to the characters and/or the focus of sensibility in the story.

The short story, then, is intense, much more so than the novel. All its details and actions must fit, and fit in a special way that suggests the complexity of a world that is perhaps a superworld in the sense of being so perfectly connected in all its parts. The language of a short story tends toward metaphor, because metaphor offers one way of connecting separate facts in a unified, complicated experience. Characters are identified, metaphorically or by pure selection of detail, with things and actions. The metaphor itself is integrated into the story, made to seem natural and appropriate to realistic-seeming fiction, by being made to derive from the personality of an emotionally charged character, often the narrator.

The short story, in short, has a special "singleness"—a singleness of action, character, and effect. However many separate problems and issues it may seem to raise, it drives relentlessly toward a unification of all into a single (albeit complicated) synthesis. This synthesis is accomplished under a pressure not common in daily life, and justified in realistic terms by the presence of some extraordinary mood in which human beings make and accept connections that are neither strictly logical nor limited by ordinary standards of relevance. For this mood to work, the short-story writer has to solicit his reader's participation in making the fiction, in "being there," in feeling for the characters' circumstances at the same level of intensity, even though always rather differently. Thus, more than many other kinds of art, short stories are for participants rather than for spectators.

The Modern Tradition

NATHANIEL HAWTHORNE

1804–1864

Hawthorne was born on the Fourth of July, 1804, in Salem, Massachusetts, a town preoccupied with its witch-hunting past and left in the wake of a more vigorous, secular America. His life reveals a pattern of brooding isolation and retreat interspersed with periods of conventional, nonliterary employment. As a youth he read widely in romantic works and cultivated a taste for wilderness and natural scenery. Following his graduation from Bowdoin in 1825, he retired to his family home for twelve years, preparing for a literary career that began with his first published collection of stories, *Twice-Told Tales* (1837), followed by a series of works that culminated in novels like *The Scarlet Letter* (1850) and *The House of the Seven Gables* (1851). Hawthorne's marriage to Sophia Peabody in 1842 rescued him from gloomier moments of introspection. He was a friend of the great literary figures of his time: Emerson, Thoreau, and Melville. And fortunately for his financial well-being, he was also a classmate and friend of Franklin Pierce, the fourteenth president of the United States, whose influence secured him positions at the Boston Custom House and as United States consul in Liverpool.

When Henry James looked back at this distinguished American predecessor, he saw a writer who to his mind had wasted a remarkable talent on too narrow a society—one lacking in variety, in opportunities for the interplay of personality and society that James so loved. Hawthorne seemed to him burdened by a "sombre lineage" of Puritanism in which a writer had to see right and wrong as always unambiguously evident, and people as either good or bad, honest or dishonest, truthful or lying. James, as we can see from his story in this book, considered such absolutes abhorrent; nothing was farther from his mind than labeling complicated human beings according to any rigid system. He could not, for example, have dealt with the first view that we have of Hester Prynne in Hawthorne's *The Scarlet Letter:* a woman whose whole identity apparently is contained in the letter *A* that she is forced to wear on her breast. True, Hester Prynne is indeed what the *A* declares that she is, an adulteress, and that identity is not irrelevant; but the announcement of it is too crude for James. He preferred to deal with characters who generate their identities as they engage the world—constantly changing as nuances of light and shadow play upon them, not measured against some Puritan caricature of themselves.

So James pitied Hawthorne, confined in his "simpler" America by such coarse conceptions. But his pity was misplaced, for Hawthorne deliberately set out to make use of that simpler America, which did not, after all, exist in his time any more than it did in James'. Hawthorne saw that he could use a colonial world fully two generations behind him, and therefore imaginatively reconstructed it. He recognized in Puritan moral absolutism a background against which he could establish his special kind of complicated experience; for him Puritanism defined the extreme ends of a scale of conceptions of people, all of which he perceived could be valid simultaneously. Always at issue in Hawthorne's stories is the way in which characters can or cannot transcend the limitations of labels, of which Hester's *A* stands as an extreme example; always there is a more or less successful effort to break out of whatever conception society uses to encapsulate the individual. Not that society's conception is ever all wrong: it does point to one area of the individual's personality; but it is never valid alone.

James' appreciative amazement that Hawthorne could have had even partial success with such materials ("[he] transmuted this heavy moral burden into the very substance of the imagination," James says in wonder) points us to the difference between the way a James story generates, out of an interaction of all its materials, the standards by which its action is to be measured, and the way in which a Hawthorne story characteristically sets up polarities that are *not* resolved in some middle ground but are simultaneously valid throughout. If we "listen" to a Hawthorne story we hear an authoritative voice, the voice of history almost, that assures us that the issues in the story are perfectly clear-cut, the facts certain, the attitude to be adopted obvious to all reasonable people. What this voice assures us of is not wrong, but we soon become conscious that other interpretations (even seemingly contradictory ones) are simultaneously right. By contrast, when James in his fiction brushes with Puritan certitudes (as in his novel *The Europeans*), the reader knows at once that they are to be regarded as grotesque extremes, and that to have any value at all they will have to be qualified by a broader, more sophisticated Europeanism. Consequently, in James a dialogue ensues between "simpler America" and Europe, out of which a flexible view emerges. The extreme positions, which constituted one side of the dialogue but were never believed in, are then discarded. In Hawthorne there is no blending: In "Young Goodman

Brown'' Faith *is* faithful, but as a human being she is also complicit in the evil that the Young Goodman Brown perceives so dramatically in the Witches' Sabbath.

To watch Hawthorne construct a world in which even opposing views can be valid, we should strain to hear voices other than that of the authoritative speaker, and to catch, even within his voice, human dimensions which the confident speaker's rationality may unconsciously be excluding. What Hawthorne is constantly doing is adding dimension to rigid conceptions of life, whether about moral matters or about what constitutes reality. As he says,

> We who are born into the world's artificial system can never adequately know how little in our present state and circumstances is natural, and how much is merely the interpolation of the perverted mind and heart of man. . . . It is only through the medium of the imagination that we can loosen those iron fetters, which we call truth and reality, and make ourselves even partially sensible what prisoners we are.
>
> —''The New Adam and Eve''

The psychological state that best expresses the desired freedom from the ''world's artificial system'' and an awareness of the truth that lies in opposing views is a half-waking, half-sleeping state, often as in ''Young Goodman Brown'' intensifying into nightmare. The characters are then perceived halfway between the literalness of the waking day and the uncontrolled creativity of the imagination; and the reader becomes aware of the continuousness of the spectrum from pure naturalism to pure imagination. Thus he is not moved to ask the question that the ''world's artificial system'' prompts: ''Is it a dream or is it real?'' For it is both: the naturalistic world working upon the imagination, and the imagination upon the world, to weave the mysterious and wonderful fabric that is Hawthorne's reality.

Young Goodman Brown

Young Goodman Brown came forth at sunset into the street of Salem village; but put his head back, after crossing the threshold, to exchange a parting kiss with his young wife. And Faith, as the wife was aptly named, thrust her own pretty head into the street, letting the wind play with the pink ribbons of her cap while she called to Goodman Brown.

"Dearest heart," whispered she, softly and rather sadly, when her lips were close to his ear, "prithee put off your journey until sunrise and sleep in your own bed to-night. A lone woman is troubled with dreams and such thoughts that she's afeared of herself sometimes. Pray tarry with me this night, dear husband, of all nights in the year."

"My love and my Faith," replied young Goodman Brown, "of all nights in the year, this one night must I tarry away from thee. My journey, as thou callest it, forth and back again, must needs be done 'twixt now and sunrise. What, my sweet, pretty wife, dost thou doubt me already, and we but three months married?"

"Then God bless you!" said Faith, with the pink ribbons; "and may you find all well when you come back."

"Amen!" cried Goodman Brown. "Say thy prayers, dear Faith, and go to bed at dusk, and no harm will come to thee."

So they parted; and the young man pursued his way until, being about to turn the corner by the meeting-house, he looked back and saw the head of Faith still peeping after him with a melancholy air, in spite of her pink ribbons.

"Poor little Faith!" thought he, for his heart smote him. "What a wretch am I to leave her on such an errand! She talks of dreams, too. Methought as she spoke there was trouble in her face, as if a dream had warned her what work is to be done tonight. But no, no; 't would kill her to think it. Well, she's a blessed angel on earth; and after this one night I'll cling to her skirts and follow her to heaven."

With this excellent resolve for the future, Goodman Brown felt himself justified in making more haste on his present evil purpose. He had taken a dreary road, darkened by all the gloomiest trees of the forest, which barely stood aside to let the narrow path creep through, and closed immediately behind. It was all as lonely as could be; and there is this peculiarity in such a solitude, that the traveller knows not who may be concealed by the innumerable trunks and the thick boughs overhead; so that with lonely footsteps he may yet be passing through an unseen multitude.

"There may be a devilish Indian behind every tree," said Goodman Brown to himself; and he glanced fearfully behind him as he added, "What if the devil himself should be at my very elbow!"

His head turned back, he passed a crook of the road, and, looking forward again, beheld the figure of a man, in grave and decent attire, seated at the foot of an old tree. He arose at Goodman Brown's approach and walked onward side by side with him.

"You are late, Goodman Brown," said he. "The clock of the Old South was striking as I came through Boston, and that is full fifteen minutes agone."

"Faith kept me back a while," replied the young man, with a tremor in his voice, caused by the sudden appearance of his companion, though not wholly unexpected.

It was now deep dusk in the forest, and deepest in that part of it where these two were journeying. As nearly as could be discerned, the second traveller was about fifty years old, apparently in the same rank of life as Goodman Brown, and bearing a considerable resemblance to him, though perhaps more in expression than features. Still they might have been taken for father and son. And yet, though the elder person was as simply clad as the younger, and as simple in manner too, he had an indescribable air of one who knew the world, and who would not have felt abashed at the governor's dinner table or in King William's court, were it possible that his affairs should call him thither. But the only thing about him that could be fixed upon as remarkable was his staff, which bore the likeness of a great black snake, so curiously wrought that it might almost be seen to twist and wriggle itself like a living serpent. This, of course, must have been an ocular deception, assisted by the uncertain light.

"Come, Goodman Brown," cried his fellow-traveller, "this is a dull pace for the beginning of a journey. Take my staff, if you are so soon weary."

"Friend," said the other, exchanging his slow pace for a full stop, "having kept covenant by meeting thee here, it is my purpose now to return whence I came. I have scruples touching the matter thou wot'st of."

"Sayest thou so?" replied he of the serpent, smiling apart. "Let us walk on, nevertheless, reasoning as we go; and if I convince thee not thou shalt turn back. We are but a little way in the forest yet."

"Too far! too far!" exclaimed the goodman, unconsciously resuming his walk. "My father never went into the woods on such an errand, nor his father before him. We have been a race of honest men and good Christians since the days of the martyrs; and shall I be the first of the name of Brown that ever took this path and kept—"

"Such company, thou wouldst say," observed the elder person, interpreting his pause. "Well said, Goodman Brown! I have been as well acquainted with your family as with ever a one among the Puritans; and that's no trifle to say. I helped your grandfather, the constable, when he lashed the Quaker woman so smartly through the streets of Salem; and it was I that brought your father a pitch-pine knot, kindled at my own hearth, to set fire to an Indian village, in King Philip's war. They were my good friends, both; and many a pleasant walk have we had along this path, returned merrily after midnight. I would fain be friends with you for their sake."

"If it be as thou sayest," replied Goodman Brown, "I marvel they never spoke of these matters; or, verily, I marvel not, seeing that the least rumor of the sort would have driven them from New England. We are a people of prayer, and good works to boot, and abide no such wickedness."

"Wickedness or not," said the traveller with the twisted staff, "I have a very general acquaintance here in New England. The deacons of many a church have drunk the communion wine with me; the selectmen of divers towns make me their chairman; and a majority of the Great and General Court are firm supporters of my interest. The governor and I, too — But these are state secrets."

"Can this be so?" cried Goodman Brown, with a stare of amazement at his undisturbed companion. "Howbeit, I have nothing to do with the governor and council; they have their own ways, and are no rule for a simple husbandman like me. But, were I to go on with thee, how should I meet the eye of that good old man, our minister, at Salem village? Oh, his voice would make me tremble both Sabbath day and lecture day."

Thus far the elder traveller had listened with due gravity; but now burst into a fit of irrepressible mirth, shaking himself so violently that his snake-like staff actually seemed to wriggle in sympathy.

"Ha! ha! ha!" shouted he again and again; then composing himself, "Well, go on, Goodman Brown, go on; but, prithee, don't kill me with laughing."

"Well, then, to end the matter at once," said Goodman Brown, considerably nettled, "there is my wife, Faith. It would break her dear little heart; and I'd rather break my own."

"Nay, if that be the case," answered the other, "e'en go thy ways, Goodman Brown. I would not for twenty old women like the one hobbling before us that Faith should come to any harm."

As he spoke he pointed his staff at a female figure on the path, in whom Goodman Brown recognized a very pious and exemplary dame, who had taught him his catechism in youth, and was still his moral and spiritual adviser, jointly with the minister and Deacon Gookin.

"A marvel, truly, that Goody Cloyse should be so far in the wilderness at nightfall," said he. "But with your leave, friend, I shall take a cut through the woods until we have left this Christian woman behind. Being a stranger to you, she might ask whom I was consorting with and whither I was going."

"Be it so," said his fellow-traveller. "Betake you to the woods, and let me keep the path."

Accordingly the young man turned aside, but took care to watch his companion, who advanced softly along the road until he had come within a staff's length of the old dame. She, meanwhile, was making the best of her way, with singular speed for so aged a woman, and mumbling some indistinct words

—a prayer, doubtless—as she went. The traveller put forth his staff and touched her withered neck with what seemed the serpent's tail.

"The devil!" screamed the pious old lady.

"Then Goody Cloyse knows her old friend?" observed the traveller, confronting her and leaning on his writhing stick.

"Ah, forsooth, and is it your worship indeed?" cried the good dame. "Yea, truly is it, and in the very image of my old gossip, Goodman Brown, the grandfather of the silly fellow that now is. But—would your worship believe it?—my broomstick hath strangely disappeared, stolen, as I suspect, by that unhanged witch, Goody Cory, and that, too, when I was all anointed with the juice of smallage, and cinquefoil, and wolf's bane—"

"Mingled with fine wheat and the fat of a new-born babe," said the shape of old Goodman Brown.

"Ah, your worship knows the recipe," cried the old lady, cackling aloud. "So, as I was saying, being all ready for the meeting, and no horse to ride on, I made up my mind to foot it; for they tell me there is a nice young man to be taken into communion to-night. But now your good worship will lend me your arm, and we shall be there in a twinkling."

"That can hardly be," answered her friend. "I may not spare you my arm, Goody Cloyse; but here is my staff, if you will."

So saying, he threw it down at her feet, where, perhaps, it assumed life, being one of the rods which its owner had formerly lent to the Egyptian magi. Of this fact, however, Goodman Brown could not take cognizance. He had cast up his eyes in astonishment, and, looking down again, beheld neither Goody Cloyse nor the serpentine staff, but his fellow-traveller alone, who waited for him as calmly as if nothing had happened.

"That old woman taught me my catechism," said the young man; and there was a world of meaning in this simple comment.

They continued to walk onward, while the elder traveller exhorted his companion to make good speed and persevere in the path, discoursing so aptly that his arguments seemed rather to spring up in the bosom of his auditor than to be suggested by himself. As they went, he plucked a branch of maple to serve for a walking stick, and began to strip it of the twigs and little boughs, which were wet with evening dew. The moment his fingers touched them they became strangely withered and dried up as with a week's sunshine. Thus the pair proceeded, at a good free pace, until suddenly, in a gloomy hollow of the road, Goodman Brown sat himself down on the stump of a tree and refused to go any farther.

"Friend," said he, stubbornly, "my mind is made up. Not another step will I budge on this errand. What if a wretched old woman do choose to go to the devil when I thought she was going to heaven: is that any reason why I should quit my dear Faith and go after her?"

"You will think better of this by and by," said his acquaintance, composedly. "Sit here and rest yourself a while; and when you feel like moving again, there is my staff to help you along."

Without more words, he threw his companion the maple stick, and was as speedily out of sight as if he had vanished into the deepening gloom. The young man sat a few moments by the roadside, applauding himself greatly, and thinking with how clear a conscience he should meet the minister in his morning walk, nor shrink from the eye of good old Deacon Gookin. And what calm sleep would be his that very night, which was to have been spent so wickedly, but so purely and sweetly now, in the arms of Faith! Amidst these pleasant and praiseworthy meditations, Goodman Brown heard the tramp of horses along the road, and deemed it advisable to conceal himself within the verge of the forest, conscious of the guilty purpose that had brought him thither, though now so happily turned from it.

On came the hoof tramps and the voices of the riders, two grave old voices, conversing soberly as they drew near. These mingled sounds appeared to pass along the road, within a few yards of the young man's hiding-place; but, owing doubtless to the depth of the gloom at that particular spot, neither the travellers nor their steeds were visible. Though their figures brushed the small boughs by the wayside, it could not be seen that they intercepted, even for a moment, the faint gleam from the strip of bright sky athwart which they must have passed. Goodman Brown alternately crouched and stood on tiptoe, pulling aside the branches and thrusting forth his head as far as he durst without discerning so much as a shadow. It vexed him the more, because he could have sworn, were such a thing possible, that he recognized the voices of the minister and Deacon Gookin, jogging along quietly, as they were wont to do, when bound to some ordination or ecclesiastical council. While yet within hearing, one of the riders stopped to pluck a switch.

"Of the two, reverend sir," said the voice like the deacon's, "I had rather miss an ordination dinner than to-night's meeting. They tell me that some of our community are to be here from Falmouth and beyond, and others from Connecticut and Rhode Island, besides several of the Indian powwows, who, after their fashion, know almost as much deviltry as the best of us. Moreover, there is a goodly young woman to be taken into communion."

"Mighty well, Deacon Gookin!" replied the solemn old tones of the minister. "Spur up, or we shall be late. Nothing can be done, you know, until I get on the ground."

The hoofs clattered again; and the voices, talking so strangely in the empty air, passed on through the forest, where no church had ever been gathered or solitary Christian prayed. Whither, then, could these holy men be journeying so deep into the heathen wilderness? Young Goodman Brown caught hold of a tree for support, being ready to sink down on the ground, faint and overburdened with the heavy sickness of his heart. He looked up to the sky, doubting whether there really was a heaven above him. Yet there was the blue arch, and the stars brightening in it.

"With heaven above and Faith below, I will yet stand firm against the devil!" cried Goodman Brown.

While he still gazed upward into the deep arch of the firmament and had lifted his hands to pray, a cloud, though no wind was stirring, hurried across the zenith and hid the brightening stars. The blue sky was still visible, except directly overhead, where this black mass of cloud was sweeping swiftly northward. Aloft in the air, as if from the depths of the cloud, came a confused and doubtful sound of voices. Once the listener fancied that he could distinguish the accents of towns-people of his own, men and women, both pious and ungodly, many of whom he had met at the communion table, and had seen others rioting at the tavern. The next moment, so indistinct were the sounds, he doubted whether he had heard aught but the murmur of the old forest, whispering without a wind. Then came a stronger swell of those familiar tones, heard daily in the sunshine at Salem village, but never until now from a cloud of night. There was one voice of a young woman, uttering lamentations, yet with an uncertain sorrow, and entreating for some favor, which, perhaps, it would grieve her to obtain; and all the unseen multitude, both saints and sinners, seemed to encourage her onward.

"Faith!" shouted Goodman Brown, in a voice of agony and desperation; and the echoes of the forest mocked him, crying, "Faith! Faith!" as if bewildered wretches were seeking her all through the wilderness.

The cry of grief, rage, and terror was yet piercing the night, when the unhappy husband held his breath for a response. There was a scream, drowned immediately in a louder murmur of voices, fading into far-off laughter, as the dark cloud swept away, leaving the clear and silent sky above Goodman Brown. But something fluttered lightly down through the air and caught on the branch of a tree. The young man seized it, and beheld a pink ribbon.

"My Faith is gone!" cried he, after one stupefied moment. "There is no good on earth; and sin is but a name. Come, devil; for to thee is this world given."

And, maddened with despair, so that he laughed loud and long, did Goodman Brown grasp his staff and set forth again, at such a rate that he seemed to fly along the forest path rather than to walk or run. The road grew wilder and drearier and more faintly traced, and vanished at length, leaving him in the heart of the dark wilderness, still rushing onward with the instinct that guides mortal men to evil. The whole forest was peopled with frightful sounds—the creaking of the trees, the howling of wild beasts, and the yell of Indians; while sometimes the wind tolled like a distant church bell, and sometimes gave a broad roar around the traveller, as if all Nature were laughing him to scorn. But he was himself the chief horror of the scene, and shrank not from its other horrors.

"Ha! ha! ha!" roared Goodman Brown when the wind laughed at him. "Let us hear which will laugh loudest. Think not to frighten me with your deviltry. Come witch, come wizard, come Indian powwow, come devil himself, and here comes Goodman Brown. You may as well fear him as he fear you."

In truth, all through the haunted forest there could be nothing more frightful than the figure of Goodman Brown. On he flew among the black pines, brandishing his staff with frenzied gestures, now giving vent to an inspiration of horrid blasphemy, and now shouting forth such laughter as set all the echoes of the forest laughing like demons around him. The fiend in his own shape is less hideous than when he rages in the breast of man. Thus sped the demoniac on his course, until, quivering among the trees, he saw a red light before him, as when the felled trunks and branches of a clearing have been set on fire, and throw up their lurid blaze against the sky, at the hour of midnight. He paused, in a lull of the tempest that had driven him onward, and heard the swell of what seemed a hymn, rolling solemnly from a distance with the weight of many voices. He knew the tune; it was a familiar one in the choir of the village meeting-house. The verse died heavily away, and was lengthened by a chorus, not of human voices, but of all the sounds of the benighted wilderness pealing in awful harmony together. Goodman Brown cried out, and his cry was lost to his own ear by its unison with the cry of the desert.

In the interval of silence he stole forward until the light glared full upon his eyes. At one extremity of an open space, hemmed in by the dark wall of the forest, arose a rock, bearing some rude, natural resemblance either to an altar or a pulpit, and surrounded by four blazing pines, their tops aflame, their stems untouched, like candles at an evening meeting. The mass of foliage that had overgrown the summit of the rock was all on fire, blazing high into the night and fitfully illuminating the whole field. Each pendent twig and leafy festoon was in a blaze. As the red light arose and fell, a numerous congregation alternately shone forth, then disappeared in shadow, and again grew, as it were, out of the darkness, peopling the heart of the solitary woods at once.

"A grave and dark-clad company," quoth Goodman Brown.

In truth they were such. Among them, quivering to and fro between gloom and splendor, appeared faces that would be seen next day at the council board of the province, and others which, Sabbath after Sabbath, looked devoutly heavenward, and benignantly over the crowded pews, from the holiest pulpits in the land. Some affirm that the lady of the governor was there. At least there were high dames well known to her, and wives of honored husbands, and widows, a great multitude, and ancient maidens, all of excellent repute, and fair young girls, who trembled lest their mothers should espy them. Either the sudden gleams of light flashing over the obscure field bedazzled Goodman Brown, or he recognized a score of the church members of Salem village famous for their especial sanctity. Good old Deacon Gookin had arrived, and waited at the skirts of that venerable saint, his revered pastor. But, irreverently consorting with these grave, reputable, and pious people, these elders of the church, these chaste dames and dewy virgins, there were men of dissolute lives and women of spotted fame, wretches given over to all mean and filthy vice, and suspected even of horrid crimes. It was strange to see that the good shrank not from the wicked, nor were the sinners abashed by the saints. Scattered also among their pale-faced enemies were the Indian priests, or powwows, who had often scared their native forest with more hideous incantations than any known to English witchcraft.

"But where is Faith?" thought Goodman Brown; and, as hope came into his heart, he trembled.

Another verse of the hymn arose, a slow and mournful strain, such as the pious love, but joined to words which expressed all that our nature can conceive of sin, and darkly hinted at far more. Unfathomable to mere mortals is the lore of fiends. Verse after verse was sung; and still the chorus of the desert swelled between like the deepest tone of a mighty organ; and with the final peal of that dreadful anthem there came a sound, as if the roaring wind, the rushing streams, the howling beasts, and every other voice of the unconcerted wilderness were mingling and according with the voice of guilty man in homage to the prince of all. The four blazing pines threw up a loftier flame, and obscurely discovered shapes and visages of horror on the smoke wreaths above the impious assembly. At the same moment the fire on the rock shot redly forth and formed a glowing arch above its base, where now appeared a figure. With reverence be it spoken, the figure bore no slight similitude, both in garb and manner, to some grave divine of the New England churches.

"Bring forth the converts!" cried a voice that echoed through the field and rolled into the forest.

At the word, Goodman Brown stepped forth from the shadow of the trees and approached the congregation, with whom he felt a loathful brotherhood by the sympathy of all that was wicked in his heart. He could have well-nigh sworn that the shape of his own dead father beckoned him to advance, looking downward from a smoke wreath, while a woman, with dim features of despair, threw out her hand to warn him back. Was it his mother? But he had no power to retreat one step, nor to resist, even in thought, when the minister and good old Deacon Gookin seized his arms and led him to the blazing rock. Thither came also the slender form of a veiled female, led between Goody Cloyse, that pious teacher of the catechism, and Martha Carrier, who had received the devil's promise to be queen of hell. A rampant hag was she. And there stood the proselytes beneath the canopy of fire.

"Welcome, my children" said the dark figure, "to the communion of your race. Ye have found thus young your nature and your destiny. My children, look behind you!"

They turned; and flashing forth, as it were, in a sheet of flame, the fiend worshippers were seen; the smile of welcome gleamed darkly on every visage.

"There," resumed the sable form, "are all whom ye have reverenced from youth. Ye deemed them holier than yourselves, and shrank from your own sin, contrasting it with their lives of righteousness and prayerful aspirations heavenward. Yet here are they all in my worshipping assembly. This night it shall be granted you to know their secret deeds; how hoary-bearded elders of the church have whispered wanton words to the young maids of their households; how many a woman, eager for widows' weeds, has given her husband a drink at bedtime and let him sleep his last sleep in her bosom; how beardless youths have made haste to inherit their fathers' wealth; and how fair damsels—blush not, sweet ones—have dug little graves in the garden, and bidden me, the sole guest, to an infant's funeral. By the sympathy of your human hearts for sin ye shall scent out all the places—whether in church, bedchamber, street, field, or forest—where crime has been committed, and shall exult to behold the whole earth one stain of guilt, one mighty blood spot. Far more than this. It shall be yours to penetrate, in every bosom, the deep mystery of sin, the fountain of all wicked arts, and which inexhaustibly supplies more evil impulses than human power—than my power at its utmost—can make manifest in deeds. And now, my children, look upon each other."

They did so; and, by the blaze of the hell-kindled torches, the wretched man beheld his Faith, and the wife her husband, trembling before that unhallowed altar.

"Lo, there ye stand, my children," said the figure, in a deep and solemn tone, almost sad with its despairing awfulness, as if his once angelic nature could yet mourn for our miserable race. "Depending upon one another's hearts, ye had still hoped that virtue were not all a dream. Now are ye undeceived. Evil is the nature of mankind. Evil must be your only happiness. Welcome again, my children, to the communion of your race."

"Welcome," repeated the fiend worshippers, in one cry of despair and triumph.

And there they stood, the only pair, as it seemed, who were yet hesitating on the verge of wickedness in this dark world. A basin was hollowed, naturally, in the rock. Did it contain water, reddened by the lurid light? or was it blood? or, perchance, a liquid flame? Herein did the shape of evil dip his hand and prepare to lay the mark of baptism upon their foreheads, that they might be partakers of the mystery of sin, more conscious of the secret guilt of others, both in deed and thought, than they could now be of their own. The husband cast one look at his pale wife, and Faith at him. What polluted wretches would the next glance show them to each other, shuddering alike at what they disclosed and what they saw!

"Faith! Faith!" cried the husband, "look up to heaven, and resist the wicked one."

Whether Faith obeyed he knew not. Hardly had he spoken when he found himself amid calm night and solitude, listening to a roar of the wind which died heavily away through the forest. He staggered against the rock, and felt it chill and damp; while a hanging twig, that had been all on fire, besprinkled his cheek with the coldest dew.

The next morning young Goodman Brown came slowly into the street of Salem village, staring around him like a bewildered man. The good old minister was taking a walk along the graveyard to get an appetite for breakfast and meditate his sermon, and bestowed a blessing, as he passed, on Goodman Brown. He shrank from the venerable saint as if to avoid an anathema. Old Deacon Gookin was at domestic worship, and the holy words of his prayer were heard through the open window. "What God doth the wizard pray to?" quoth Goodman Brown. Goody Cloyse, that excellent old Christian, stood in the early sunshine at her own lattice, catechizing a little girl who had brought her a pint of morning's milk. Goodman Brown snatched away the child as from the grasp of the fiend himself. Turning the corner by the meeting-house, he spied the head of Faith, with the pink ribbons, gazing anxiously forth, and bursting into such joy at sight of him that she skipped along the street and almost kissed her husband before the whole village. But Goodman Brown looked sternly and sadly into her face, and passed on without a greeting.

Had Goodman Brown fallen asleep in the forest and only dreamed a wild dream of a witch-meeting?

Be it so if you will; but, alas! it was a dream of evil omen for young Goodman Brown. A stern, a sad, a darkly meditative, a distrustful, if not a desperate man did he become from the night of that fearful dream. On the Sabbath day, when the congregation were singing a holy psalm, he could not listen because an anthem of sin rushed loudly upon his ear and drowned all the blessed strain. When the minister spoke from the pulpit with power and fervid eloquence, and, with his hand on the open Bible, of the sacred truths of our religion, and of saint-like lives and triumphant deaths, and of future bliss or misery unutterable, then did Goodman Brown turn pale, dreading lest the roof should thunder down upon the gray blasphemer and his hearers. Often, waking suddenly at midnight, he shrank from the bosom of Faith; and at morning or eventide, when the family knelt down at prayer, he scowled and muttered to himself, and gazed sternly at his wife, and turned away. And when he had lived long, and was borne to his grave a hoary corpse, followed by Faith, an aged woman, and children and grandchildren, a goodly procession, besides neighbors not a few, they carved no hopeful verse upon his tombstone, for his dying hour was gloom.

EDGAR ALLAN POE

1809–1849

There is Poe the human being, and then there is the myth of Poe, which has it that his stories are thinly disguised versions of his own opium and alcoholic experience. True, Poe took both drugs, and his life seemed degenerate to ordinary citizens of the nineteenth century. But the myth obscures the craftsmanship of the stories, which consciously brought the literary possibilities of Romanticism into America. Poe read widely, especially in Scots and English periodical literature, and he adapted to the form of the short story the sensibility of Scott and Byron. He had a taste for the bizarre, his life was punctuated by one scandal after another, but the Gothic element of many of his tales, the detective-story format of others, are adaptations to the short story of forms that appear only in the poem, the drama, the fake-confession—the genres that Poe was learned in. Far from being a naif who wrote only from his own diseased heart, Poe was a sophisticated literary practitioner who made the mainstream of British Romantic literature available to the American short story. His accomplishment naturally was recognized by the Old World, and his writing was influential almost more in France and England than in America, where his notoriety tended to obscure his genius.

Poe was the son of an alcoholic actor and an attractive actress who died when he was three. John Allan, a family friend, undertook to bring up the boy (hence Poe's middle name), and sent him to the University of Virginia, which he left after two years, trailing alcohol fumes and gambling debts. He joined the army, and later attended West Point, ending his career there by being court-martialed. He had by this time written some poems, and he set out to make his living by writing poems and short stories for magazines. His work caught on with the public, and though Poe, partly because of his habits, led a hand-to-mouth existence all his life, he did earn a meager living by writing poems, fiction, and criticism for various magazines.

There are dark corners in Poe's life that defy investigation. Why he married the thirteen-year-old daughter of his aunt we will probably never know. It is likely that Poe did not know himself (he was never very introspective), certain that he did not want us to know. His motive is well covered up in the Gothic trappings of his poems and stories, and there are no personal diaries or letters that reveal his inner life to posterity. When, after his first wife died, he set out to marry again, this time a wealthy widow (a seemingly ideal solution to his impoverishment), he fell in with a group of drinking buddies on the way to his wedding and carried off to his grave the complications of his bizarre psychology.

Considering his dissolute ways, Poe did an enormous amount of work in a short career—all of it well crafted, and marked with an originality that makes him one of the major figures in the tradition of the modern short story.

The Cask of Amontillado

The thousand injuries of Fortunato I had borne as I best could, but when he ventured upon insult I vowed revenge. You, who so well know the nature of my soul, will not suppose, however, that I gave utterance to a threat. *At length* I would be avenged; this was a point definitely settled—but the very definitiveness with which it was resolved precluded the idea of risk. I must not only punish but punish with impunity. A wrong is unredressed when retribution overtakes its redresser. It is equally unredressed when the avenger fails to make himself felt as such to him who has done the wrong.

It must be understood that neither by word nor deed had I given Fortunato cause to doubt my good will. I continued, as was my wont, to smile in his face, and he did not perceive that my smile *now* was at the thought of his immolation.

He had a weak point—this Fortunato—although in other regards he was a man to be respected and even feared. He prided himself on his connoisseurship in wine. Few Italians have the true virtuoso spirit. For the most part their enthusiasm is adopted to suit the time and opportunity, to practise imposture upon the British and Austrian *millionaires.* In painting and gemmary, Fortunato, like his countrymen, was a quack, but in the matter of old wines he was sincere. In this respect I did not differ from him materially;—I was skillful in the Italian vintages myself, and bought largely whenever I could.

It was about dusk, one evening during the supreme madness of the carnival season, that I encountered my friend. He accosted me with excessive warmth, for he had been drinking much. The man wore motley. He had on a tight-fitting parti-striped dress, and his head was surmounted by the conical cap and bells. I was so pleased to see him that I thought I should never have done wringing his hand.

I said to him—"My dear Fortunato, you are luckily met. How remarkably well you are looking to-day. But I have received a pipe of what passes for Amontillado, and I have my doubts."

"How?" said he. "Amontillado? A pipe? Impossible! And in the middle of the carnival!"

"I have my doubts," I replied; "and I was silly enough to pay the full Amontillado price without consulting you in the matter. You were not to be found, and I was fearful of losing a bargain."

"Amontillado!"

"I have my doubts."

"Amontillado!"

"And I must satisfy them."

"Amontillado!"

"As you are engaged, I am on my way to Luchresi. If any one has a critical turn it is he. He will tell me——"

"Luchresi cannot tell Amontillado from Sherry."

"And yet some fools will have it that his taste is a match for your own."

"Come, let us go."

"Whither?"

"To your vaults."

"My friend, no; I will not impose upon your good nature. I perceive you have an engagement. Luchresi——"

"I have no engagement;—come."

"My friend, no. It is not the engagement, but the severe cold with which I perceive you are afflicted. The vaults are insufferably damp. They are encrusted with nitre."

"Let us go, nevertheless. The cold is merely nothing. Amontillado! You have been imposed upon. And as for Luchresi, he cannot distinguish Sherry from Amontillado."

Thus speaking, Fortunato possessed himself of my arm; and putting on a mask of black silk and drawing a *roquelaire* closely about my person, I suffered him to hurry me to my palazzo.

There were no attendants at home; they had absconded to make merry in honor of the time. I had told them that I should not return until the morning, and had given them explicit orders not to stir from the house. These orders were sufficient, I well knew, to insure their immediate disappearance, one and all, as soon as my back was turned.

I took from their sconces two flambeaux, and giving one to Fortunato, bowed him through several suites of rooms to the archway that led into the vaults. I passed down a long and winding staircase, requesting him to be cautious as he followed. We came at length to the foot of the descent, and stood together upon the damp ground of the catacombs of the Montresors.

The gait of my friend was unsteady, and the bells upon his cap jingled as he strode.

"The pipe," he said.

"It is farther on," said I; "but observe the white web-work which gleams from these cavern walls."

He turned towards me, and looked into my eyes with two filmy orbs that distilled the rheum of intoxication.

"Nitre?" he asked at length.

"Nitre," I replied. "How long have you had that cough?"

"Ugh! ugh! ugh!—ugh! ugh! ugh!—ugh! ugh! ugh!—ugh! ugh! ugh!—ugh! ugh! ugh!"

My poor friend found it impossible to reply for many minutes.

"It is nothing," he said at last.

"Come," I said, with decision, "we will go back; your health is precious. You are rich, respected, admired, beloved; you are happy, as once I was. You are a man to be missed. For me it is no matter. We will go back; you will be ill, and I cannot be responsible. Besides, there is Luchresi——"

"Enough," he said; "the cough is a mere nothing; it will not kill me. I shall not die of a cough."

"True—true," I replied; "and, indeed, I had no intention of alarming you unnecessarily—but you should use all proper caution. A draught of this Medoc will defend us from the damps."

Here I knocked off the neck of a bottle which I drew from a long row of its fellows that lay upon the mould.

"Drink," I said, presenting him the wine.

He raised it to his lips with a leer. He paused and nodded to me familiarly, while his bells jingled.

"I drink," he said, "to the buried that repose around us."

"And I to your long life."

He again took my arm, and we proceeded.

"These vaults," he said, "are extensive."

"The Montresors," I replied, "were a great and numerous family."

"I forget your arms."

"A huge human foot d'or, in a field azure; the foot crushes a serpent rampant whose fangs are imbedded in the heel."

"And the motto?"

"*Nemo me impune lacessit.*"[1]

"Good!" he said.

The wine sparkled in his eyes and the bells jingled. My own fancy grew warm with the Medoc. We had passed through long walls of piled skeletons, with casks and puncheons intermingling, into the inmost recesses of the catacombs. I paused again, and this time I made bold to seize Fortunato by an arm above the elbow.

"The nitre!" I said; "see, it increases. It hangs like moss upon the vaults. We are below the river's bed. The drops of moisture trickle among the bones. Come, we will go back ere it is too late. Your cough——"

"It is nothing," he said; "let us go on. But first, another draught of the Medoc."

I broke and reached him a flagon of De Grâve. He emptied it at a breath. His eyes flashed with a fierce light. He laughed and threw the bottle upwards with a gesticulation I did not understand.

I looked at him in surprise. He repeated the movement—a grotesque one.

"You do not comprehend?" he said.

[1]"No one attacks me with impunity."

"Not I," I replied.

"Then you are not of the brotherhood."

"How?"

"You are not of the masons."

"Yes, yes," I said; "yes, yes."

"You? Impossible! A mason?"

"A mason," I replied.

"A sign," he said, "a sign."

"It is this," I answered, producing from beneath the folds of my *roquelaire* a trowel.

"You jest," he exclaimed, recoiling a few paces. "But let us proceed to the Amontillado."

"Be it so," I said, replacing the tool beneath the cloak and again offering him my arm. He leaned upon it heavily. We continued our route in search of the Amontillado. We passed through a range of low arches, descended, passed on, and descending again, arrived at a deep crypt, in which the foulness of the air caused our flambeaux rather to glow than flame.

At the most remote end of the crypt there appeared another less spacious. Its walls had been lined with human remains, piled to the vault overhead, in the fashion of the great catacombs of Paris. Three sides of this interior crypt were still ornamented in this manner. From the fourth side the bones had been thrown down, and lay promiscuously upon the earth, forming at one point a mound of some size. Within the wall thus exposed by the displacing of the bones, we perceived a still interior crypt or recess, in depth about four feet, in width three, in height six or seven. It seemed to have been constructed for no especial use within itself, but formed merely the interval between two of the colossal supports of the roof of the catacombs, and was backed by one of their circumscribing walls of solid granite.

It was in vain that Fortunato, uplifting his dull torch, endeavored to pry into the depth of the recess. Its termination the feeble light did not enable us to see.

"Proceed," I said; "herein is the Amontillado. As for Luchresi——"

"He is an ignoramus," interrupted my friend, as he stepped unsteadily forward, while I followed immediately at his heels. In an instant he had reached the extremity of the niche, and finding his progress arrested by the rock, stood stupidly bewildered. A moment more and I had fettered him to the granite. In its surface were two iron staples, distant from each other about two feet, horizontally. From one of these depended a short chain, from the other a padlock. Throwing the links about his waist, it was but the work of a few seconds to secure it. He was too much astounded to resist. Withdrawing the key I stepped back from the recess.

"Pass your hand," I said, "over the wall; you cannot help feeling the nitre. Indeed, it is *very* damp. Once more let me *implore* you to return. No? Then I must positively leave you. But I must first render you all the little attentions in my power."

"The Amontillado!" ejaculated my friend, not yet recovered from his astonishment.

"True," I replied; "the Amontillado."

As I said these words I busied myself among the pile of bones of which I have before spoken. Throwing them aside, I soon uncovered a quantity of building stone and mortar. With these materials and with the aid of my trowel, I began vigorously to wall up the entrance of the niche.

I had scarcely laid the first tier of the masonry when I discovered that the intoxication of Fortunato had in a great measure worn off. The earliest indication I had of this was a low moaning cry from the depth of the recess. It was *not* the cry of a drunken man. There was a long and obstinate silence. I laid the second tier, and the third, and the fourth; and then I heard the furious vibrations of the chain. The noise lasted for several minutes, during which, that I might hearken to it with the more satisfaction, I ceased my labors and sat down upon the bones. When at last the clanking subsided, I resumed the trowel, and finished without interruption the fifth, the sixth, and the seventh tier. The wall was now nearly upon a level with my breast. I again paused, and holding the flambeaux over the mason-work, threw a few feeble rays upon the figure within.

A succession of loud and shrill screams, bursting suddenly from the throat of the chained form, seemed to thrust me violently back. For a brief moment I hesitated, I trembled. Unsheathing my rapier, I began to grope with it about the recess; but the thought of an instant reassured me. I placed my hand upon the solid fabric of the catacombs, and felt satisfied. I reapproached the wall; I replied to the yells of him who clamoured. I re-echoed, I aided, I surpassed them in volume and in strength. I did this, and the clamourer grew still.

It was now midnight, and my task was drawing to a close. I had completed the eighth, the ninth and the tenth tier. I had finished a portion of the last and the eleventh; there remained but a single stone to be fitted and plastered in. I struggled with its weight; I placed it partially in its destined position. But now there came from out the niche a low laugh that erected the hairs upon my head. It was succeeded by a sad voice, which I had difficulty in recognizing as that of the noble Fortunato. The voice said—

"Ha! ha! ha!—he! he! he!—a very good joke, indeed—an excellent jest. We will have many a rich laugh about it at the palazzo—he! he! he!—over our wine—he! he! he!"

"The Amontillado!" I said.

"He! he! he!—he! he! he!—yes, the Amontillado. But is it not getting late? Will not they be awaiting us at the palazzo, the Lady Fortunato and the rest? Let us be gone."

"Yes," I said, "let us be gone."

"For the love of God, Montresor!"

"Yes," I said, "for the love of God."

But to these words I hearkened in vain for a reply. I grew impatient. I called aloud—

"Fortunato!"

No answer. I called again—

"Fortunato!"

No answer still. I thrust a torch through the remaining aperture and let it fall within. There came forth in return only a jingling of the bells. My heart grew sick; it was the dampness of the catacombs that made it so. I hastened to make an end of my labour. I forced the last stone into its position; I plastered it up. Against the new masonry I re-erected the old rampart of bones. For the half of a century no mortal has disturbed them. *In pace requiescat!*[2]

[2]May he rest in peace!

HENRY JAMES

1843–1916

The circumstances of James' death reveal his character so well that they seem like materials for a last and very personal tale. James reported that as he collapsed from the stroke that within weeks killed him, he heard a voice say, "So here it is at last, the distinguished thing!" A few months before, he had become a British subject, after having lived in England for most of his adult life; in the New Year's Honours List the King conferred the Order of Merit upon him; yet shortly thereafter, in accord with the directions in his will, his ashes were carried across the Atlantic and buried in Cambridge, Massachusetts, where his parents, brothers, and sister lay. A few years before, a visit to their graves had moved him to melancholy reflection on his divided allegiances to an America in which he could not live but that commanded his deepest loyalties. James' divided selves are implicit in the events of the months surrounding his death. One self speaks in that poised voice with its precise understatement, "at last, the distinguished thing." The voice is not identical with the mortally stricken human being, but it is not separate either.

James was fascinated by the way the attempt to understand experience tends to remove one from the possibility of feeling it. He often created narrators who *understand* more than they *feel,* and he often constructed his stories so as to reveal the distance between a strictly objective, esthetic kind of perception and a fuller, more subjective kind that includes emotion. The narrator's presence is necessary if we are to measure the distance that lies beyond merely intellectual perception, just as James, dying, needed that precise voice to register the moment and yet reveal by indirection so much that it does not say.

James remained a bachelor all his life, but he feared the role of the merely disinterested observer, the role that the lack of intimate ties can impose upon one. And fearing it in life he confronted it in fiction. The son of a rich father who devoted himself to philosophical writings, James was born in New York and spent his boyhood in a cosmopolitan atmosphere. The family traveled extensively and was well acquainted with the social and intellectual leaders of the age. His elder brother William became a famous psychologist, a professor at

Harvard, but Henry James' talent was clearly for literature. From the time he abandoned the study of law at Harvard in 1863, he began writing reviews and short stories—and, later, novels and plays—at a prodigious rate. The finest of his early works is the novel *The Portrait of a Lady* (1881), and his later career is marked brilliantly by three major novels, *The Wings of the Dove* (1902), *The Ambassadors* (1903), and *The Golden Bowl* (1904).

Whatever his ostensible subject, James always wrote about education, not the kind carried on in schools and colleges but that which people of an inquisitive turn of mind achieve (or sometimes, tragically, do not achieve) by examining their own experiences. In the story that follows, the nature of the education is different but the issue involved the same: what can one learn from living?

For James, to learn from one's experience is not only to learn something about how one's imagination deals with external reality, but also to achieve morality, to achieve a proper balance between self-assertiveness (the tendency to demand that others yield themselves to you) and those qualities of sympathy and honor and loyalty which require a yielding of oneself. In James this kind of moral integrity must be derived first from an intelligent understanding of one's experience—and his stories reveal to the reader the difficulty within his fictional world of discerning exactly what demands are being made by other people and what demands one makes on them. But even if these demands can be discerned, enormous difficulties attend the characters as they try to act morally.

The trouble is that there is never one moral prescription that can be applied to all circumstances. Like the other late nineteenth- and twentieth-century writers represented here, James insists that morality emerges only from particular contexts. His fiction presents life as constantly evolving, so that when and if one does learn, he does not learn a set of maxims that he can use to control his next personal and social involvement; rather, he learns that every set of human circumstances is unique. And thus the virtues that allow one to live life at its most elevated, noble, and even heroic are those of awareness—both of oneself, and of oneself in relation to the world—and responsibility to other human beings. That is why the continuous shaping and reshaping of context in a James story is such a delicate process. The context is in fact the definition of the moral problem, the only terms in which intellectual and moral education can be carried on.

My Friend Bingham

Conscious as I am of a deep aversion to stories of a painful nature, I have often asked myself whether, in the events here set forth, the element of pain is stronger than that of joy. An affirmative answer to this question would have stood as a veto upon the publication of my story, for it is my opinion that the literature of horrors needs no extension. Such an answer, however, I am unwilling to pronounce; while, on the other hand, I hesitate to assume the responsibility of a decided negative. I have therefore determined to leave the solution to the reader. I may add, that I am very sensible of the superficial manner in which I have handled my facts. I bore no other part in the accomplishment of these facts than that of a cordial observer; and it was impossible that, even with the best will in the world, I should fathom the emotions of the actors. Yet, as the very faintest reflection of human passions, under the pressure of fate, possesses an immortal interest, I am content to appeal to the reader's sympathy, and to assure him of my own fidelity.

Towards the close of summer, in my twenty-eighth year, I went down to the seaside to rest from a long term of work, and to enjoy, after several years of separation, a *tête-à-tête* with an intimate friend. My friend had just arrived from Europe, and we had agreed to spend my vacation together by the side of the sounding sea, and within easy reach of the city. On taking possession of our lodgings, we found that we should have no fellow-idlers, and we hailed joyously the prospect of the great marine solitudes which each of us declared that he found so abundantly peopled by the other. I hasten to impart to the reader the following facts in regard to the man whom I found so good a companion.

George Bingham had been born and bred among people for whom, as he grew to manhood, he learned to entertain a most generous contempt,—people in whom the hereditary possession of a large property—for he assured me that the facts stood in the relation of cause and effect—had extinguished all intelligent purpose and principle. I trust that I do not speak rhetorically when I describe in these terms the combined ignorance and vanity of my friend's progenitors. It was their fortune to make a splendid figure while they lived, and I feel little compunction in hinting at their poverty in certain human essentials. Bingham was no declaimer, and indeed no great talker; and it was only now and then, in an allusion to the past as the field of a wasted youth, that he expressed his profound resentment. I read this for the most part in the severe humility with which he regarded the future, and under cover of which he seemed to salute it as void at least (whatever other ills it might contain) of those domestic embarrassments which had been the bane of his first manhood. I have no doubt that much may be said, within limits, for the graces of that society against which my friend embodied so violent a reaction, and especially for its good-humor,—that home-keeping benevolence which accompanies a sense of material repletion. It is equally probable that to persons of a simple constitution these graces may wear a look of delightful and enduring mystery; but poor Bingham was no simpleton. He was a man of opinions numerous, delicate, and profound. When, with the lapse of his youth, he awoke to a presentiment of these opinions, and cast his first interrogative glance upon the world, he found that in his own little section of it he and his opinions were a piece of melancholy impertinence. Left, at twenty-three years of age, by his father's death, in possession of a handsome property, and absolute master of his actions, he had thrown himself blindly into the world. But, as he afterwards assured me, so superficial was his knowledge of the real world,—the world of labor and inquiry,—that he had found himself quite incapable of intelligent action. In this manner he had wasted a great deal of time. He had travelled much, however; and, being a keen observer of men and women, he had acquired a certain practical knowledge of human nature. Nevertheless, it was not till he was nearly thirty years old that he had begun to live for himself. "By myself," he explained, "I mean something else than this monstrous hereditary faculty for doing nothing and thinking nothing." And he led me to believe, or I should rather say he allowed me to believe, that at this moment he had made a serious attempt to study. But upon this point he was not very explicit; for if he blushed for the manner in which he had slighted his opportunities, he blushed equally for the manner in which he had used them. It is my belief that he had but a limited capacity for study, and I am certain that to the end of his days there subsisted in his mind a very friendly relation between fancies and facts.

Bingham was *par excellence* a moralist, a man of sentiment. I know—he knew himself—that, in this busy Western world, this character represents no recognized avocation; but in the absence of such avocation, its exercise was nevertheless very dear to him. I protest that it was very dear to me, and that, at the end of a long morning devoted to my office-desk, I have often felt as if I had contributed less to the common cause than I have felt after moralizing—or, if you please, sentimentalizing—half an hour with my friend. He was an idler, assuredly; but his candor, his sagacity, his good taste, and, above all, a certain diffident enthusiasm which followed its objects with the exquisite trepidation of an unconfessed and despairing lover,—these things, and a hundred more, redeemed him from vulgarity. For three years before we came together, as I have intimated, my impressions of my friend had rested on his letters; and yet, from the first hour which we spent together, I felt that they had done him no wrong. We were genuine friends. I don't know that I can offer better proof of this than by saying that, as our old personal relations resumed their force, and the time-shrunken outlines of character filled themselves out, I greeted the reappearance of each familiar foible on Bingham's part quite as warmly as I did that of the less punctual virtue. Compared, indeed, with the comrade of earlier years, my actual companion was a well-seasoned man of the world; but with all his acquired humility and his disciplined *bonhomie,* he had failed to divest himself of a certain fastidiousness of mind, a certain formalism of manner, which are the token and the prerogative of one who has not been obliged to address himself to practical questions. The charm bestowed by these facts upon Bingham's conversation—a charm often vainly invoked in their absence—is explained by his honest indifference to their action, and his indisposition to turn them to account in the interest of the picturesque,—an advantage but too easy of conquest for a young man, rich, accomplished, and endowed with good looks and a good name. I may say, perhaps, that to a critical mind my friend's prime distinction would have been his very positive refusal to drape himself, after the current taste, with those brilliant stuffs which fortune had strewn at his feet.

Of course, a great deal of our talk bore upon Bingham's recent travels, adventures, and sensations. One of these last he handled very frankly, and treated me to a bit of genuine romance. He had been in love, and had been cruelly jilted, but had now grown able to view the matter with much of the impartial spirit of those French critics whose works were his favorite reading. His account of the young lady's character and motives would indeed have done credit to many a clever *feuilleton.* I was the less surprised, however, at his severely dispassionate tone, when, in retracing the process of his opinion, I discerned the traces—the ravages, I may almost say—of a solemn act of renunciation. Bingham had forsworn marriage. I made haste to assure him that I considered him quite too young for so austere a resolve.

"I can't help it," said he; "I feel a foreboding that I shall live and die alone."

"A foreboding?" said I. "What's a foreboding worth?"

"Well, then, rationally considered, my marriage is improbable."

"But it's not to be rationally considered," I objected. "It belongs to the province of sentiment."

"But you deny me sentiment. I fall back upon my foreboding."

"That's not sentiment,—it's superstition," I answered. "Your marrying will depend upon your falling in love; and your falling in love will certainly not depend upon yourself."

"Upon whom, then?"

"Upon some unknown fair one,—Miss A, B, or C."

"Well," said Bingham, submissively, "I wish she would make haste and reveal herself."

These remarks had been exchanged in the hollow of a cliff which sloped seaward, and where we had lazily stretched ourselves at length on the grass. The grass had grown very long and brown; and as we lay with our heads quite on a level with it, the view of the immediate beach and the gentle breakers was so completely obstructed by the rank, course herbage, that our prospect was reduced to a long, narrow band of deep blue ocean traversing its black fibres, and to the great vault of the sky. We had strolled out a couple of hours before, bearing each a borrowed shot-gun and accompanied by a friendly water-dog, somewhat languidly disposed towards the slaughter of wild ducks. We were neither of us genuine sportsmen, and it is certain that, on the whole, we meant very kindly to the ducks. It was at all events fated that on that day they should suffer but lightly at our hands. For the half-hour previous to the exchange of the remarks just cited, we had quite forgotten our real business; and, with our pieces lost in the grass beside us, and our dog, weary of inaction, wandering far beyond call, we looked like any straw-picking truants. At last Bingham rose to his feet, with the asseveration that it would never do for us to return empty-handed. "But, behold," he exclaimed, as he looked down across the breadth of the beach, "there is our friend of the cottage, with the sick little boy."

I brought myself into a sitting posture, and glanced over the cliff. Down near the edge of the water sat a young woman, tossing stones into it for the amusement of a child, who stood lustily crowing and clapping his hands. Her title to be called our friend lay in the fact, that on our way to the beach we had observed her issuing from a cottage hard by the hotel, leading by the hand a pale-faced little boy, muffled like an invalid. The hotel, as I have said, was all but deserted, and this young woman had been the first person to engage our idle observation. We had seen that, although plainly dressed, she was young, pretty, and modest; and, in the absence of heavier cares, these facts had sufficed to make her interesting. The question had arisen between us, whether she was a native of the shore, or a visitor like ourselves. Bingham inclined to the former view of the case, and I to the latter. There was, indeed, a certain lowliness in her aspect; but I had contended that it was by no means a rustic lowliness. Her dress was simple, but it was well made and well worn; and I noticed that, as she strolled along, leading her little boy, she cast upon sky and sea the lingering glance of one to whom, in their integrity, these were unfamiliar objects. She was the wife of some small tradesman, I argued, who had brought her child to the seaside by the physician's decree. But Bingham declared that it was utterly illogical to suppose her to be a mother of five years' motherhood; and that, for his part, he saw nothing in her appearance inconsistent with rural influences. The child was her nephew, the son of a married sister, and she a sentimental maiden aunt. Obviously the volume she had in her hand was Tennyson. In the absence on both sides of authentic data, of course the debate was not prolonged; and the subject of it had passed from our memories some time before we again met her on the beach. She soon became aware of our presence, however; and with a natural sense of intrusion, we immediately resumed our walk. The last that I saw of her, as we rounded a turn in the cliff which concealed the backward prospect, was a sudden grasp of the child's arm, as if to withdraw him from the reach of a hastily advancing wave.

Half an hour's further walk led us to a point which we were not tempted to exceed. We shot between us some half a dozen birds; but as our dog, whose talents had been sadly misrepresented, proved very shy of the deep water, and succeeded in bringing no more than a couple of our victims to shore, we resolved to abstain from further destruction, and to return home quietly along the beach, upon which we had now descended.

"If we meet our young lady," said Bingham, "we can gallantly offer her our booty."

Some five minutes after he had uttered these words, a couple of great seagulls came flying landward over our heads, and, after a long gyration in mid-air, boldly settled themselves on the slope of the cliff at some three hundred yards in front of us, a point at which it projected almost into the waves. After a momentary halt, one of them rose again on his long pinions and soared away seaward; the other remained. He sat perched on a jutting boulder some fifteen feet high, sunning his fishy breast.

"I wonder if I could put a shot into him," said Bingham.

"Try," I answered; and, as he rapidly charged and levelled his piece, I remember idly repeating, while I looked at the great bird,

> "God save thee, ancient mariner,
> From the fiends that plague thee thus!
> Why look'st thou so? 'With my cross-bow
> I shot the albatross.' "

"He's going to rise," I added.

But Bingham had fired. The creature rose, indeed, half sluggishly, and yet with too hideous celerity. His movement drew from us a cry which was almost simultaneous with the report of Bingham's gun. I cannot express our relation to what followed it better than by saying that it exposed to our sight, beyond the space suddenly left vacant, the happy figure of the child from whom we had parted but an hour before. He stood with his little hands extended, and his face raised toward the retreating bird. Of the sickening sensation which assailed our common vision as we saw him throw back his hands to his head, and reel downwards out of sight, I can give no verbal account, nor of the rapidity with which we crossed the smooth interval of sand, and rounded the bluff.

The child's companion had scrambled up the rocky bank towards the low ledge from which he had fallen, and to which access was of course all too easy. She had sunk down upon the stones, and was wildly clasping the boy's body. I turned from this spectacle to my friend as to an image of equal woe. Bingham, pale as death, bounded over the stones, and fell on his knees. The woman let him take the child out of her arms, and bent over, with her forehead on a rock, moaning. I have never seen helplessness so vividly embodied as in this momentary group.

"Did it strike his head?" cried Bingham. "What the devil was he doing up there?"

"I told him he'd get hurt," said the young woman, with harrowing simplicity. "To shoot straight at him!—He's killed!"

"Great heavens! Do you mean to say that I saw him?" roared Bingham. "How did I know he was there? Did you see us?"

The young woman shook her head. "Of course I didn't see you. I saw you with your guns before. Oh, he's killed!"

"He's not killed. It was mere duck shot. Don't talk such stuff.—My own poor little man!" cried George. "Charles, where *were* our eyes?"

"He wanted to catch the bird," moaned our companion. "Baby, my boy! open your eyes. Speak to your mother. For God's sake, get some help!"

She had put her hands to take the child from Bingham, who had half angrily lifted him out of her reach. The senseless movement with which, as she disengaged him from Bingham's grasp, he sank into her arms, was clearly the senselessness of death. She burst into sobs. I went and examined the child.

"He *may* not be killed," I said, turning to Bingham; "keep your senses. It's not your fault. We *couldn't* see each other."

Bingham rose stupidly to his feet.

"She must be got home," I said.

"We must get a carriage. Will you go or stay?"

I saw that he had seen the truth. He looked about him with an expression of miserable impotence. "Poor little devil!" he said, hoarsely.

"Will you go for a carriage?" I repeated, taking his hand, "or will you stay?"

Our companion's sobs redoubled their violence.

"I'll stay," said he. "Bring some woman."

I started at a hard run. I left the beach behind me, passed the white cottage at whose garden gate two women were gossiping, and reached the hotel stable, where I had the good fortune to find a vehicle at my disposal. I drove straight back to the white cottage. One of the women had disappeared, and the other was lingering among her flowers,—a middle-aged, keen-eyed person. As I descended and hastily addressed her, I read in her rapid glance an anticipation of evil tidings.

"The young woman, who stays with you—" I began.

"Yes," she said, "my second-cousin. Well?"

"She's in trouble. She wants you to come to her. Her little boy has hurt himself." I had time to see that I need fear no hysterics.

"Where did you leave her?" asked my companion.

"On the beach."

"What's the matter with the child?"

"He fell from a rock. There's no time to be lost." There was a certain antique rigidity about the woman which was at once irritating and reassuring. I was impelled both to quicken her apprehensions and to confide in her self-control. "For all I know, ma'am," said I, "the child is killed."

She gave me an angry stare. "For all you know!" she exclaimed. "Where were your wits? Were you afraid to look at him?"

"Yes, half afraid."

She glanced over the paling at my vehicle. "Am I to get into that?" she asked.

"If you will be so good."

She turned short about, and re-entered the house, where, as I stood out among the dahlias and the pinks, I heard a rapid opening and shutting of drawers. She shortly reappeared, equipped for driving; and, having locked the house door, and pocketed the key, came and faced me, where I stood ready to help her into the wagon.

"We'll stop for the doctor," she began.

"The doctor," said I, "is of no use."

A few moments of hard driving brought us to my starting-point. The tide had fallen perceptibly in my absence; and I remember receiving a strange impression of the irretrievable nature of the recent event from the sight of poor Bingham, standing down at the low-watermark, and looking seaward with his hands in his pockets. The mother of his little victim still sat on the heap of stones where she had fallen, pressing her child to her breast. I helped my companion to descend, which she did with great deliberation. It is my belief that, as we drove along the beach, she derived from the expression of Bingham's figure, and from the patient aversion of his face, a suspicion of his relation to the opposite group. It was not till the elder woman had come within a few steps of her, that the younger became aware of her approach. I merely had time to catch the agonized appeal of her upward glance, and the broad compassion of the other's stooping movement, before I turned my back upon their encounter, and walked down towards my friend. The monotonous murmur of the waves had covered the sound of our wagonwheels, and Bingham stood all unconscious of the coming of relief,—distilling I know not what divine relief from the simple beauty of sea and sky. I had laid my hand on his shoulder before he turned about. He looked towards the base of the cliff. I knew that a great effusion of feeling would occur in its natural order; but how should I help him across the interval?

"That's her cousin," I said at random. "She seems a very capable woman."

"The child is quite dead," said Bingham, for all answer. I was struck by the plainness of his statement. In the comparative freedom of my own thoughts

I had failed to make allowance for the embarrassed movement of my friend's. It was not, therefore, until afterwards that I acknowledged he had thought to better purpose than I; inasmuch as the very simplicity of his tone implied a positive acceptance (for the moment) of the dreadful fact which he uttered.

"The sooner they get home, the better," I said. It was evident that the elder of our companions had already embraced this conviction. She had lifted the child and placed him in the carriage, and she was now turning towards his mother and inviting her to ascend. Even at the distance at which I stood, the mingled firmness and tenderness of her gestures were clearly apparent. They seemed, morever, to express a certain indifference to our movements, an independence of our further interference, which—fanciful as the assertion may look—was not untinged with irony. It was plain that, by whatever rapid process she had obtained it, she was already in possession of our story. "Thank God for strongminded women!" I exclaimed;—and yet I could not repress a feeling that it behooved me, on behalf of my friend, to treat as an equal with the vulgar movement of antipathy which he was destined to encounter, and of which, in the irresistible sequence of events, the attitude of this good woman was an index.

We walked towards the carriage together. "I shall not come home directly," said Bingham; "but don't be alarmed about me."

I looked at my watch. "I give you two hours," I said, with all the authority of my affection.

The new-comer had placed herself on the back seat of the vehicle beside the sufferer, who on entering had again possessed herself of her child. As I went about to mount in front, Bingham came and stood by the wheel. I read his purpose in his face,—the desire to obtain from the woman he had wronged some recognition of his *human* character, some confession that she dimly distinguished him from a wild beast or a thunderbolt. One of her hands lay exposed, pressing together on her knee the lifeless little hands of her boy. Bingham removed his hat, and placed his right hand on that of the young woman. I saw that she started at his touch, and that he vehemently tightened his grasp.

"It's too soon to talk of forgiveness," said he, "for it's too soon for me to think intelligently of the wrong I have done you. God has brought us together in a very strange fashion."

The young woman raised her bowed head, and gave my friend, if not just the look he coveted, at least the most liberal glance at her command,—a look which, I fancy, helped him to face the immediate future. But these are matters too delicate to be put into words.

I spent the hours that elapsed before Bingham's return to the inn in gathering information about the occupants of the cottage. Impelled by that lively intuition of calamity which is natural to women, the housekeeper of the hotel, a person of evident kindliness and discretion, lost no time in winning my confidence. I was not unwilling that the tragic incident which had thus arrested our idleness should derive its earliest publicity from my own lips; and I was forcibly struck with the exquisite impartiality with which this homely creature bestowed her pity. Miss Horner, I learned, the mistress of the cottage, was the last representative of a most respectable family, native to the neighboring town. It had been for some years her practice to let lodgings during the summer. At the close of the present season she had invited her kinswoman, Mrs. Hicks, to spend the autumn with her. That this lady was the widow of a Baptist minister; that her husband had died some three years before; that she was very poor; that her child had been sickly, and that the care of his health had so impeded her exertions for a livelihood, that she had been intending to leave him with Miss Horner for the winter, and obtain a "situation" in town;—these facts were the salient points of the housekeeper's somewhat prolix recital.

The early autumn dusk had fallen when Bingham returned. He looked very tired. He had been walking for several hours, and, as I fancied, had grown in some degree familiar with his new responsibilities. He was very hungry, and made a vigorous attack upon his supper. I had been indisposed to eat, but the sight of his healthy appetite restored my own. I had grown weary of my thoughts, and I found something salutary in the apparent simplicity and rectitude of Bingham's state of mind.

"I find myself taking it very quietly," he said, in the course of his repast. "There is something so absolute in the nature of the calamity, that one is compelled to accept it. I don't see how I could endure to have mutilated the poor little mortal. To kill a human being is, after all, the least injury you can do him." He spoke these words deliberately, with his eyes on mine, and with an expression of perfect candor. But as he paused, and in spite of my perfect assent to their meaning, I could not help mentally reverting to the really tragic phase of the affair; and I suppose my features revealed to Bingham's scrutiny the process of my thoughts. His pale face flushed a burning crimson, his lips trembled. "Yes, my boy!" he cried; "that's where it's damnable." He buried his head in his hands, and burst into tears.

We had a long talk. At the end of it, we lit our cigars, and came out upon the deserted piazza. There was a lovely starlight, and, after a few turns in silence, Bingham left my side and strolled off towards a bend in the road, in the direction of the sea. I saw him stand motionless for a long time, and then I heard him call me. When I reached his side, I saw that he had been watching a light in the window of the white cottage. We heard the village bell in the distance striking nine.

"Charles," said Bingham, "suppose you go down there and make some offer of your services. God knows whom the poor creatures have to look to. She has had a couple of men thrust into her life. She must take the good with the bad."

I lingered a moment. "It's a difficult task," I said. "What shall I say?"

Bingham silently puffed his cigar. He stood with his arms folded, and his head thrown back, slowly measuring the starry sky. "I wish she could come out here and look at that sky," he said at last. "It's a sight for bereaved mothers. Somehow, my dear boy," he pursued, "I never felt less depressed in my life. It's none of my doing."

"It would hardly do for me to tell her that," said I.

"I don't know," said Bingham. "This isn't an occasion for the exchange of compliments. I'll tell you what you may tell her. Tell her that I should like very much to be present."

I set off for the cottage. Its mistress in person introduced me into the little parlor.

"Well, sir?" she said, in hard, dry accents.

"I've come," I answered, "to ask whether I can be of any assistance to Mrs. Hicks."

Miss Horner shook her head in a manner which deprived her negation of half its dignity. "What assistance is possible?" she asked.

"A man," said I, "may relieve a woman of certain cares——"

"O, men are a blessed set! You had better leave Mrs. Hicks to me."

"But will you at least tell me how she is,—if she has in any degree recovered herself?"

At this moment the door of the adjoining room was opened, and Mrs. Hicks stood on the threshold, bearing a lamp—a graceful and pathetic figure. I now had occasion to observe that she was a woman of decided beauty. Her fair hair was drawn back into a single knot behind her head, and the lamplight deepened the pallor of her face and the darkness of her eyes. She wore a calico dressing-gown and a shawl.

"What do you wish?" she asked, in a voice clarified, if I may so express it, by long weeping.

"He wants to know whether he can be of any assistance," said the elder lady.

Mrs. Hicks glanced over her shoulder into the room she had left. "Would you like to look at the child?" she asked, in a whisper.

"Lucy!" cried Miss Horner.

I walked straight over to Mrs. Hicks, who turned and led the way to a little bed. My conductress raised her lamp aloft, and let the light fall gently on the little white-draped figure. Even the bandage about the child's head had not dispelled his short-lived prettiness. Heaven knows that to remain silent was easy enough; but Heaven knows, too, that to break the silence—and to break it as I broke it—was equally easy. "He must have been a very pretty child," I said.

"Yes, he was very pretty. He had black eyes. I don't know whether you noticed."

"No, I didn't notice," said I. "When is he to be buried?"

"The day after to-morrow. I am told that I shall be able to avoid an inquest."

"Mr. Bingham has attended to that," I said. And then I paused, revolving his petition.

But Mrs. Hicks anticipated it. "If you would like to be present at the funeral," she said, "you are welcome to come.—And so is your friend."

"Mr. Bingham bade me ask leave. There is a great deal that I should like to say to you for him," I added, "but I won't spoil it by trying. It's his own business."

The young woman looked at me with her deep, dark eyes. "I pity him from my heart," she said, pressing her hands to her breast. "I had rather have my sorrow than his."

"They are pretty much one sorrow," I answered. "I don't see that you can divide it. You are two to bear it. Bingham is a wise, good fellow," I went on. "I have shared a great many joys with him. In Heaven's name," I cried, "don't bear hard on him!"

"How can I bear hard?" she asked, opening her arms and letting them drop. The movement was so deeply expressive of weakness and loneliness, that, feeling all power to reply stifled in a rush of compassion, I silently made my exit.

On the following day, Bingham and I went up to town, and on the third day returned in time for the funeral. Besides the two ladies, there was no one present but ourselves and the village minister, who of course spoke as briefly as decency allowed. He had accompanied the ladies in a carriage to the graveyard, while Bingham and I had come on foot. As we turned away from the grave, I saw my friend approach Mrs. Hicks. They stood talking beside the freshly-turned earth, while the minister and I attended Miss Horner to the carriage. After she had seated herself, I lingered at the door, exchanging sober commonplaces with the reverend gentleman. At last Mrs. Hicks followed us, leaning on Bingham's arm.

"Margaret," she said, "Mr. Bingham and I are going to stay here awhile. Mr. Bingham will walk home with me. I'm *very* much obliged to you, Mr. Bland," she added, turning to the minister and extending her hand.

I bestowed upon my friend a glance which I felt to be half interrogative and half sympathetic. He gave me his hand, and answered the benediction by its pressure, while he answered the inquiry by his words. "If you are still disposed to go back to town this afternoon," he said, "you had better not wait for me. I may not have time to catch the boat."

I of course made no scruple of returning immediately to the city. Some ten days elapsed before I again saw Bingham; but I found my attention so deeply engrossed with work, that I scarcely measured the interval. At last, one morning, he came into my office.

"I take for granted," I said, "that you have not been all this time at B——."

"No; I've been on my travels. I came to town the day after you came. I found at my rooms a letter from a lawyer in Baltimore, proposing the sale of some of my property there, and I seized upon it as an excuse for making a journey to that city. I felt the need of movement, of action of some kind. But when I reached Baltimore, I didn't even go to see my correspondent. I pushed on to Washington, walked about for thirty-six hours, and came home."

He had placed his arm on my desk, and stood supporting his head on his hand, with a look of great physical exhaustion.

"You look very tired," said I.

"I haven't slept," said he. "I had such a talk with that woman!"

"I'm sorry that you should have felt the worse for it."

"I feel both the worse and the better. She talked about the child."

"It's well for her," said I, "that she was able to do it."

"She wasn't able, strictly speaking. She began calmly enough, but she very soon broke down."

"Did you see her again?"

"I called upon her the next day, to tell her that I was going to town, and to ask if I could be useful to her. But she seems to stand in perfect isolation. She assured me that she was in want of nothing."

"What sort of a woman does she seem to be, taking her in herself?"

"Bless your soul! I can't take her in herself!" cried Bingham, with some vehemence. "And yet, stay," he added; "she's a very pleasing woman."

"She's very pretty."

"Yes; she's very pretty. In years, she's little more than a young girl. In her ideas, she's one of 'the people.' "

"It seems to me," said I, "that the frankness of her conduct toward you is very much to her credit."

"It doesn't offend you, then?"

"Offend me? It gratifies me beyond measure."

"I think that, if you had seen her as I have seen her, it would interest you deeply. I'm at a loss to determine whether it's the result of great simplicity or great sagacity. Of course, it's absurd to suppose that, ten days ago, it could have been the result of anything but a beautiful impulse. I think that tomorrow I shall again go down to B——."

I allowed Bingham time to have made his visit and to have brought me an account of his further impressions; but as three days went by without his reappearance, I called at his lodgings. He was still out of town. The fifth day, however, brought him again to my office.

"I've been at B—— constantly," he said, "and I've had several interviews with our friend."

"Well; how fares it?"

"It fares well. I'm forcibly struck with her good sense. In matters of mind —in matters of soul, I may say—she has the touch of an angel, or rather of a woman. That's quite sufficient."

"Does she keep her composure?"

"Perfectly. You can imagine nothing simpler and less sentimental than her manner. She makes me forget myself most divinely. The child's death colors our talk; but it doesn't confine or obstruct it. You see she has her religion: she can afford to be natural."

Weary as my friend looked, and shaken by his sudden subjection to care, it yet seemed to me, as he pronounced these words, that his eye had borrowed a purer light and his voice a fresher tone. In short, where I discerned it, how I detected it, I know not; but I felt that he carried a secret. He sat poking with his walking-stick at a nail in the carpet, with his eyes dropped. I saw about his mouth the faint promise of a distant smile,—a smile which six months would bring to maturity.

"George," said I, "I have a fancy."

He looked up. "What is it?"

"You've lost your heart."

He stared a moment, with a sudden frown. "To whom?" he asked.

"To Mrs. Hicks."

With a frown, I say, but a frown that was a smile to the effect of my rejoinder. He rose to his feet; all his color deserted his face and rushed to his eyes.

"I beg your pardon if I'm wrong," I said.

Bingham had turned again from pale to crimson. "Don't beg *my* pardon," he cried. "You may say what you please. Beg *hers!*" he added, bitterly.

I resented the charge of injustice. "I've done *her* no wrong!" I answered. "I haven't said," I went on with a certain gleeful sense that I was dealing with massive truths,—"I haven't said that she had lost her heart to you!"

"Good God, Charles!" cried Bingham, "what a horrid imagination you have!"

"I am not responsible for my imagination."

"Upon my soul, I hope *I*'m not!" cried Bingham, passionately. "I have enough without that."

"George," I said, after a moment's reflection, "if I thought I had insulted you, I would make amends. But I have said nothing to be ashamed of. I believe that I have hit the truth. Your emotion proves it. I spoke hastily; but you must admit that, having caught a glimpse of the truth, I couldn't stand indifferent to it."

"The truth! the truth! What truth?"

"Aren't you in love with Mrs. Hicks? Admit it like a man."

"Like a man! Like a brute. Haven't I done the woman wrong enough?"

"Quite enough, I hope."

"Haven't I turned her simple joys to bitterness?"

"I grant it."

"And now you want me to insult her by telling her that I love her?"

"I want you to tell her nothing. What you tell her is your own affair. Remember that, George. It's as little mine as it is the rest of the world's."

Bingham stood listening, with a contracted brow and his hand grasping his stick. He walked to the dusty office-window and halted a moment, watching the great human throng in the street. Then he turned and came towards me. Suddenly he stopped short. "God forgive me!" he cried; "I believe I do love her."

The fountains of my soul were stirred. "Combining my own hasty impressions of Mrs. Hicks with yours, George," I said, "the consummation seems to me exquisitely natural."

It was in these simple words that we celebrated the sacred fact. It seemed as if, by tacit agreement, the evolution of this fact was result enough for a single interview.

A few days after this interview, in the evening, I called at Bingham's lodgings. His servant informed me that my friend was out of town, although he was unable to indicate his whereabouts. But as I turned away from the door a hack drew up, and the object of my quest descended, equipped with a travelling-bag. I went down and greeted him under the gas-lamp.

"Shall I go with you?" I asked; "or shall I go my way?"

"You had better come in," said Bingham. "I have something to say.—I have been down to B——," he resumed, when the servant had left us alone in his sitting-room. His tone bore the least possible tinge of a confession; but of course it was not as a confessor that I listened.

"Well," said I, "how is our friend?"

"Our friend—" answered Bingham. "Will you have a cigar?"

"No, I thank you."

"Our friend—Ah, Charles, it's a long story."

"I sha'n't mind that, if it's an interesting one."

"To a certain extent it's a painful one. It's painful to come into collision with incurable vulgarity of feeling."

I was puzzled. "Has that been your fortune?" I asked.

"It has been my fortune to bring Mrs. Hicks into a great deal of trouble. The case, in three words, is this. Miss Horner has seen fit to resent, in no moderate terms, what she calls the 'extraordinary intimacy' existing between Mrs. Hicks and myself. Mrs. Hicks, as was perfectly natural, has resented her cousin's pretension to regulate her conduct. Her expression of this feeling has led to her expulsion from Miss Horner's house."

"Has she any other friend to turn to?"

"No one, except some relatives of her husband, who are very poor people, and of whom she wishes to ask no favors."

"Where has she placed herself?"

"She is in town. We came up together this afternoon. I went with her to some lodgings which she had formerly occupied, and which were fortunately vacant."

"I suppose it's not to be regretted that she has left B——. She breaks with sad associations."

"Yes; but she renews them too, on coming to town."

"How so?"

"Why, damn it," said Bingham, with a tremor in his voice, "the woman is utterly poor."

"Has she no resources whatever?"

"A hundred dollars a year, I believe,—worse than nothing."

"Has she any marketable talents or accomplishments?"

"I believe she is up to some pitiful needlework or other. Such a woman! O horrible world!"

"Does *she* say so?" I asked.

"She? No indeed. She thinks it's all for the best. I suppose it is. But it seems but a bad best."

"I wonder," said I, after a pause, "whether I might see Mrs. Hicks. Do you think she would receive me?"

Bingham looked at me an instant keenly. "I suppose so," said he. "You can try."

"I shall go, not out of curiosity," I resumed, "but out of—"

"Out of what?"

"Well, in fine, I should like to see her again."

Bingham gave me Mrs. Hicks's address, and in the course of a few evenings I called upon her. I had abstained from bestowing a fine name upon the impulse which dictated this act; but I am nevertheless free to declare that kindliness and courtesy had a large part in it. Mrs. Hicks had taken up her residence in a plain, small house, in a decent by-street, where, upon presenting myself, I was ushered into a homely sitting-room (apparently her own), and left to await her coming. Her greeting was simple and cordial, and not untinged with a certain implication of gratitude. She had taken for granted on my part, all possible sympathy and good-will; but as she had regarded me besides as a man of many cares, she had thought it improbable that we should meet again. It was no long time before I became conscious of that generous charm which Bingham had rigorously denominated her good-sense. Good-sense assuredly was there, but good-sense mated and prolific. Never had I seen, it seemed to me, as the moments elapsed, so exquisitely modest a use of such charming faculties,—and intelligence so sensible of its obligations and so indifferent to its privileges. It was obvious that she had been a woman of plain associations: her allusions were to homely facts, and her manner direct and unstudied; and yet, in spite of these limitations, it was equally obvious that she was a person to be neither patronized, dazzled, nor deluded. O the satisfaction which, in the course of that quiet dialogue, I took in this sweet infallibility! How it effaced her loneliness and poverty, and added dignity to her youth and beauty! It made her, potentially at least, a woman of the world. It was an anticipation of the self-possession, the wisdom, and perhaps even in some degree of the wit, which comes through the experience of society,—the result, on Mrs. Hicks's part, of I know not what hours of suffering, despondency, and self-dependence. With whatever intentions, therefore, I might have come before her, I should have found it impossible to address her as any other than an equal, and to regard her affliction as anything less than an absolute mystery. In fact, we hardly touched upon it; and it was only covertly that we alluded to Bingham's melancholy position. I will not deny that in a certain sense I regretted Mrs. Hicks's reserve. It is true that I had a very informal claim upon her confidence; but I had gone to her with a half-defined hope that this claim would be liberally interpreted. It was not even recognized; my vague intentions of counsel and assistance had lain undivined; and I departed with the impression that my social horizon had been considerably enlarged, but that my charity had by no means secured a pensioner.

Mrs. Hicks had given me permission to repeat my visit, and after the lapse of a fortnight I determined to do so. I had seen Bingham several times in the interval. He was of course much interested in my impressions of our friend; and I fancied that my admiration gave him even more pleasure than he allowed himself to express. On entering Mrs. Hicks's parlor a second time, I found him in person standing before the fireplace, and talking apparently with some vehemence to Mrs. Hicks, who sat listening on the sofa. Bingham turned impatiently to the door as I crossed the threshold, and Mrs. Hicks rose to welcome me with all due composure. I was nevertheless sensible that my entrance was ill-timed; yet a retreat was impossible. Bingham kept his place on the hearth-rug, and mechanically gave me his hand,—standing irresolute, as I thought, between annoyance and elation. The fact that I had interrupted a somewhat passionate interview was somehow so obvious, that, at the prompting of a very delicate feeling, Mrs. Hicks hastened to anticipate my apologies.

"Mr. Bingham was giving me a lecture," she said; and there was perhaps in her accent a faint suspicion of bitterness. "He will doubtless be glad of another auditor."

"No," said Bingham, "Charles is a better talker than listener. You shall have two lectures instead of one." He uttered this sally without even an attempt to smile.

"What is your subject?" said I. "Until I know that, I shall promise neither to talk nor to listen."

Bingham laid his hand on my arm. "He represents the world," he said, addressing our hostess. "You're afraid of the world. There, make your appeal."

Mrs. Hicks stood silent a moment, with a contracted brow and a look of pain on her face. Then she turned to me with a half-smile. "I don't believe you represent the world," she said; "you are too good."

"She flatters you," said Bingham. "You wish to corrupt him, Mrs. Hicks."

Mrs. Hicks glanced for an instant from my friend to myself. There burned in her eyes a far-searching light, which consecrated the faint irony of the smile which played about her lips. "O you men!" she said,—"you are so wise, so deep!" It was on Bingham that her eyes rested last; but after a pause, extending her hand, she transferred them to me. "Mr. Bingham," she pursued, "seems to wish you to be admitted to our counsels. There is every reason why his friends should be my friends. You will be interested to know that he has asked me to be his wife."

"Have you given him an answer?" I asked.

"He was pressing me for an answer when you came in. He conceives me to have a great fear of the judgments of men, and he was saying very hard things about them. But they have very little, after all, to do with the matter. The world may heed it, that Mr. Bingham should marry Mrs. Hicks, but it will care very little whether or no Mrs. Hicks marries Mr. Bingham. You are the world, for me," she cried with beautiful inconsequence, turning to her suitor; "I know no other." She put out her hands, and he took them.

I am at a mere loss to express the condensed force of these rapid words, —the amount of passion, of reflection, of experience, which they seemed to embody. They were the simple utterance of a solemn and intelligent choice; and, as such, the whole phalanx of the Best Society assembled in judgment could not have done less than salute them. What honest George Bingham said, what I said, is of little account. The proper conclusion of my story lies in the highly dramatic fact that out of the depths of her bereavement—out of her loneliness and her pity—this richly gifted woman had emerged, responsive to the passion of him who had wronged her all but as deeply as he loved her. The reader will decide, I think, that this catastrophe offers as little occasion for smiles as for tears. My narrative is a piece of genuine prose.

It was not until six months had elapsed that Bingham's marriage took place. It has been a truly happy one. Mrs. Bingham is now, in the fulness of her bloom, with a single exception, the most charming woman I know. I have assured her

—once too often, possibly—that, thanks to that invaluable good-sense of hers, she is also the happiest. She has made a devoted wife; but—and in occasional moments of insight it has seemed to me that this portion of her fate is a delicate tribute to a fantastic principle of equity—she has never again become a mother. In saying that she has made a devoted wife, it may seem that I have written Bingham's own later history. Yet as the friend of his younger days, the comrade of his *belle jeunesse,* the partaker of his dreams, I would fain give him a sentence apart. What shall it be? He is a truly incorruptible soul; he is a confirmed philosopher; he has grown quite stout.

GUY DE MAUPASSANT

1850–1893

One of the fathers of the short story, Maupassant learned his craft under the tutelage of Flaubert, the famous author of *Madame Bovary,* who strove always for perfection in prose. Maupassant became famous overnight for his story "Boule de Suif" (Ball of Fat), which deals with the patriotism of a young prostitute, in contrast to the hypocrisy of the middle-class world that surrounds her. Having been silent for nearly ten years while he learned to write fiction, Maupassant then burst forth in a torrent of short stories, novels, and plays that made him rich and famous. That was all to the good, since he had luxurious tastes, and must have been from all accounts one of the greatest woman-chasers in history. One story has it that, dining in London with Henry James, Maupassant regretted his inability to speak English and asked James if he would get a certain woman for him. James carefully explained that that was not the way things were done in England. When Maupassant repeated his request, this time for another woman, and James again explained that this was not proper social etiquette, Maupassant accused him of not having a wide acquaintance. In his last years Maupassant went mad from syphilis and eventually died from the disease.

Readers who would know more of both James and Maupassant should read James' criticism of the great Frenchman in the *Fortnightly Review* in 1888 (still the best account of Maupassant in English). He is in effect James' other self in fiction—carnal where James is cerebral, economical where James is expansive—and yet James admired him greatly, often goading himself in his notebooks, "Oh spirit of Maupassant come to my aid."

The Necklace

She was one of those pretty and charming girls who are sometimes, as if by a mistake of destiny, born in a family of clerks. She had no dowry, no expectations, no means of being known, understood, loved, wedded by any rich and distinguished man; and she let herself be married to a little clerk at the Ministry of Public Instruction.

She dressed plainly because she could not dress well, but she was as unhappy as though she had really fallen from her proper station, since with women there is neither caste nor rank: and beauty, grace, and charm act instead of family and birth. Natural fineness, instinct for what is elegant, suppleness of wit, are the sole heirarchy, and make from women of the people the equals of the very greatest ladies.

She suffered ceaselessly, feeling herself born for all the delicacies and all the luxuries. She suffered from the poverty of her dwelling, from the wretched look of the walls, from the worn-out chairs, from the ugliness of the curtains. All those things, of which another woman of her rank would never even have been conscious, tortured her and made her angry. The sight of the little Breton peasant who did her humble housework aroused in her regrets which were despairing, and distracted dreams. She thought of the silent antechambers hung with Oriental tapestry, lit by tall bronze candelabra, and of the two great footmen in knee breeches who sleep in the big armchairs, made drowsy by the heavy warmth of the hot-air stove. She thought of the long *salons*[1] fitted up with ancient silk, of the delicate furniture carrying priceless curiosities, and of the coquettish perfumed boudoirs made for talks at five o'clock with intimate friends, with men famous and sought after, whom all women envy and whose attention they all desire.

When she sat down to dinner, before the round table covered with a tablecloth three days old, opposite her husband, who uncovered the soup tureen and declared with an enchanted air, "Ah, the good *pot-au-feu!*[2] I don't know anything better than that," she thought of dainty dinners, of shining silverware, of tapestry which peopled the walls with ancient personages and with strange birds flying in the midst of a fairy forest; and she thought of delicious dishes served on marvelous plates, and of the whispered gallantries which you listen to with a sphinxlike smile, while you are eating the pink flesh of a trout or the wings of a quail.

She had no dresses, no jewels, nothing. And she loved nothing but that; she felt made for that. She would so have liked to please, to be envied, to be charming, to be sought after.

[1]Drawing rooms
[2]Stew

She had a friend, a former schoolmate at the convent, who was rich, and whom she did not like to go and see any more, because she suffered so much when she came back.

But one evening, her husband returned home with a triumphant air, and holding a large envelope in his hand.

"There," said he. "Here is something for you."

She tore the paper sharply, and drew out a printed card which bore these words:

"The Minister of Public Instruction and Mme. Georges Ramponneau request the honor of M. and Mme. Loisel's company at the palace of the Ministry on Monday evening, January eighteenth."

Instead of being delighted, as her husband hoped, she threw the invitation on the table with disdain, murmuring:

"What do you want me to do with that?"

"But, my dear, I thought you would be glad. You never go out, and this is such a fine opportunity. I had awful trouble to get it. Everyone wants to go; it is very select, and they are not giving many invitations to clerks. The whole official world will be there."

She looked at him with an irritated glance, and said, impatiently:

"And what do you want me to put on my back?"

He had not thought of that; he stammered:

"Why, the dress you go to the theater in. It looks very well, to me."

He stopped, distracted, seeing his wife was crying. Two great tears descended slowly from the corners of her eyes toward the corners of her mouth. He stuttered:

"What's the matter? What's the matter?"

But, by violent effort, she had conquered her grief, and she replied, with a calm voice, while she wiped her wet cheeks:

"Nothing. Only I have no dress and therefore I can't go to this ball. Give your card to some colleague whose wife is better equipped than I."

He was in despair. He resumed:

"Come, let us see, Mathilde. How much would it cost, a suitable dress, which you could use on other occasions. Something very simple?"

She reflected several seconds, making her calculations and wondering also what sum she could ask without drawing on herself an immediate refusal and a frightened exclamation from the economical clerk.

Finally, she replied, hesitatingly:

"I don't know exactly, but I think I could manage it with four hundred francs."

He had grown a little pale, because he was laying aside just that amount to buy a gun and treat himself to a little shooting next summer on the plain of Nanterre, with several friends who went to shoot larks down there, of a Sunday.

But he said:

"All right. I will give you four hundred francs. And try to have a pretty dress."

The day of the ball drew near, and Mme. Loisel seemed sad, uneasy, anxious. Her dress was ready, however. Her husband said to her one evening:

"What is the matter? Come, you've been so queer these last three days."

And she answered:

"It annoys me not to have a single jewel, not a single stone, nothing to put on. I shall look like distress. I should almost rather not go at all."

He resumed:

"You might wear natural flowers. It's very stylish at this time of the year. For ten francs you can get two or three magnificent roses."

She was not convinced.

"No; there's nothing more humiliating than to look poor among other women who are rich."

But her husband cried:

"How stupid you are! Go look up your friend Mme. Forestier, and ask her to lend you some jewels. You're quite thick enough with her to do that."

She uttered a cry of joy:

"It's true. I never thought of it."

The next day she went to her friend and told of her distress.

Mme. Forestier went to a wardrobe with a glass door, took out a large jewel-box, brought it back, opened it, and said to Mme. Loisel:

"Choose, my dear."

She saw first of all some bracelets, then a pearl necklace, then a Venetian cross, gold and precious stones of admirable workmanship. She tried on the ornaments before the glass, hesitated, could not make up her mind to part with them, to give them back. She kept asking:

"Haven't you any more?"

"Why, yes. Look. I don't know what you like."

All of a sudden she discovered, in a black satin box, a superb necklace of diamonds, and her heart began to beat with an immoderate desire. Her hands trembled as she took it. She fastened it around her throat, outside her high-necked dress, and remained lost in ecstasy at the sight of herself.

Then she asked, hesitating, filled with anguish:

"Can you lend me that, only that?"

"Why, yes, certainly."

She sprang upon the neck of her friend, kissed her passionately, then fled with her treasure.

The day of the ball arrived. Mme. Loisel made a great success. She was prettier than them all, elegant, gracious, smiling, and crazy with joy. All the men looked at her, asked her name, endeavored to be introduced. All the attachés of the Cabinet wanted to waltz with her. She was remarked by the minister himself.

She danced with intoxication, with passion, made drunk by pleasure, forgetting all, in the triumph of her beauty, in the glory of her success, in a sort of cloud of happiness composed of all this homage, of all this admiration, of all these awakened desires, and of that sense of complete victory which is so sweet to a woman's heart.

She went away about four o'clock in the morning. Her husband had been sleeping since midnight, in a little deserted anteroom, with three other gentlemen whose wives were having a very good time. He threw over her shoulders the wraps which he had brought, modest wraps of common life, whose poverty contrasted with the elegance of the ball dress. She felt this, and wanted to escape so as not to be remarked by the other women, who were enveloping themselves in costly furs.

Loisel held her back.

"Wait a bit. You will catch cold outside. I will go and call a cab."

But she did not listen to him, and rapidly descended the stairs. When they were in the street they did not find a carriage; and they began to look for one, shouting after the cabmen whom they saw passing by at a distance.

They went down toward the Seine, in despair, shivering with cold. At last they found on the quay one of those ancient noctambulant coupés which, exactly as if they were ashamed to show their misery during the day, are never seen round Paris until after nightfall.

It took them to their door in the Rue des Martyrs, and once more, sadly, they climbed up homeward. All was ended, for her. And as to him, he reflected that he must be at the Ministry at ten o'clock.

She removed the wraps which covered her shoulders, before the glass, so as once more to see herself in all her glory. But suddenly she uttered a cry. She no longer had the necklace around her neck!

Her husband, already half undressed, demanded:

"What is the matter with you?"

She turned madly towards him:

"I have—I have—I've lost Mme. Forestier's necklace."

He stood up, distracted.

"What!—how?—impossible!"

And they looked in the folds of her dress, in the folds of her cloak, in her pockets, everywhere. They did not find it.

He asked:

"You're sure you had it on when you left the ball?"

"Yes, I felt it in the vestibule of the palace."

"But if you had lost it in the street we should have heard it fall. It must be in the cab."

"Yes. Probably. Did you take his number?"

"No. And you, didn't you notice it?"

"No."

They looked, thunderstruck, at one another. At last Loisel put on his clothes.

"I shall go back on foot," said he, "over the whole route which we have taken to see if I can find it."

And he went out. She sat waiting on a chair in her ball dress, without strength to go to bed, overwhelmed, without fire, without a thought.

Her husband came back about seven o'clock. He had found nothing.

He went to Police Headquarters, to the newspaper offices, to offer a reward; he went to the cab companies—everywhere, in fact, whither he was urged by the least suspicion of hope.

She waited all day, in the same condition of mad fear before this terrible calamity.

Loisel returned at night with a hollow, pale face; he had discovered nothing.

"You must write to your friend," said he, "that you have broken the clasp of her necklace and that you are having it mended. That will give us time to turn round."

She wrote at his dictation.

At the end of a week they had lost all hope.

And Loisel, who had aged five years, declared:

"We must consider how to replace that ornament."

The next day they took the box which had contained it, and they went to the jeweler whose name was found within. He consulted his books.

"It was not I, madame, who sold that necklace; I must simply have furnished the case."

Then they went from jeweler to jeweler, searching for a necklace like the other, consulting their memories, sick both of them with chagrin and anguish.

They found, in a shop at the Palais Royal, a string of diamonds which seemed to them exactly like the one they looked for. It was worth forty thousand francs. They could have it for thirty-six.

So they begged the jeweler not to sell it for three days yet. And they made a bargain that he should buy it back for thirty-four thousand francs, in case they found the other one before the end of February.

Loisel possessed eighteen thousand francs which his father had left him. He would borrow the rest.

He did borrow, asking a thousand francs of one, five hundred of another, five louis[3] here, three louis there. He gave notes, took up ruinous obligations,

[3]A louis was worth 20 francs.

dealt with usurers and all the race of lenders. He compromised all the rest of his life, risked his signature without even knowing if he could meet it; and, frightened by the pains yet to come, by the black misery which was about to fall upon him, by the prospect of all the physical privation and of all the moral tortures which he was to suffer, he went to get the new necklace, putting down upon the merchant's counter thirty-six thousand francs.

When Mme. Loisel took back the necklace, Mme. Forestier said to her, with a chilly manner:

"You should have returned it sooner; I might have needed it."

She did not open the case, as her friend had so much feared. If she had detected the substitution, what would she have thought, what would she have said? Would she not have taken Mme. Loisel for a thief?

Mme. Loisel now knew the horrible existence of the needy. She took her part, moreover, all of a sudden, with heroism. That dreadful debt must be paid. She would pay it. They dismissed their servant; they changed their lodgings; they rented a garret under the roof.

She came to know what heavy housework meant and the odious cares of the kitchen. She washed the dishes, using her rosy nails on the greasy pots and pans. She washed the dirty linen, the shirts, and the dishcloths, which she dried upon a line; she carried the slops down to the street every morning, and carried up the water, stopping for breath at every landing. And, dressed like a woman of the people, she went to the fruiterer, the grocer, the butcher, her basket on her arm, bargaining, insulted, defending her miserable money sou by sou.

Each month they had to meet some notes, renew others, obtain more time.

Her husband worked in the evening making a fair copy of some tradesman's accounts, and late at night he often copied manuscript for five sous a page.

And this life lasted for ten years.

At the end of ten years, they had paid everything, everything, with the rates of usury, and the accumulations of the compound interest.

Mme. Loisel looked old now. She had become the woman of impoverished households—strong and hard and rough. With frowsy hair, skirts askew, and red hands, she talked loud while washing the floor with great swishes of water. But sometimes, when her husband was at the office, she sat down near the window, and she thought of that gay evening of long ago, of that ball where she had been so beautiful and so fêted.

What would have happened if she had not lost that necklace? Who knows? Who knows? How life is strange and changeful! How little a thing is needed for us to be lost or to be saved!

But, one Sunday, having gone to take a walk in the Champs Elysées to refresh herself from the labor of the week, she suddenly perceived a woman who was leading a child. It was Mme. Forestier, still young, still beautiful, still charming.

Mme. Loisel felt moved. Was she going to speak to her? Yes, certainly. And now that she had paid, she was going to tell her all about it. Why not?

She went up.

"Good-day, Jeanne."

The other, astonished to be familiarly addressed by this plain goodwife, did not recognize her at all, and stammered:

"But—madam!—I do not know—You must be mistaken."

"No. I am Mathilde Loisel."

Her friend uttered a cry.

"Oh, my poor Mathilde! How you are changed!"

"Yes, I have had days hard enough, since I have seen you, days wretched enough—and that because of you!"

"Of me! How so?"

"Do you remember that diamond necklace which you lent me to wear at the ministerial ball?"

"Yes. Well?"

"Well, I lost it."

"What do you mean? You brought it back."

"I brought you back another just like it. And for this we have been ten years paying. You can understand that it was not easy for us, us who had nothing. At last it is ended, and I am very glad."

Mme. Forestier had stopped.

"You say that you bought a necklace of diamonds to replace mine?"

"Yes. You never noticed it, then! They were very like."

And she smiled with a joy which was proud and naïve at once.

Mme. Forestier, strongly moved, took her two hands.

"Oh, my poor Mathilde! Why, my necklace was paste. It was worth at most five hundred francs!"

JOSEPH CONRAD

1857–1924

Conrad's parents were educated, well-to-do Polish patriots whose land became Russian territory when Poland was partitioned between Russia and Germany. When Conrad was four, his father was arrested for advocating the cause of Polish freedom, and the family followed him into a humiliating exile north of Moscow. The boy's mother died soon thereafter, and seven years later his father succumbed too. Conrad's memories of family life were warm but understandably marked by a deep sense of transitoriness and loss: he came to feel himself a permanent exile and wanderer. The life of a sailor was perhaps an inevitable acting-out of his childhood feeling; at any rate, after a few years of desultory schooling, and without ever having even seen the sea, he went to Marseilles and signed onto a French ship. Like most educated Poles, he had French as a second language; and he got on well in the French merchant marine. He seemed to seek out the most romantic voyages, for in the four years he sailed out of Marseilles he was involved in South American revolutions, in smuggling guns to Carlist plotters in Spain, in an affair with a Basque beauty, and in a duel with an American sea captain (which left him with a bullet wound just over his heart).

In reaction to or in flight from these adventures, Conrad at twenty-two embarked on a career in British ships, which he determined would lead to a captaincy. Because he knew almost no English, to change to the British flag was a brave move, but in eight years he had his master's papers, and in ten his first command. By the time he was thirty-six Conrad was ready for a new career. He put the sea behind him and began to write in his adopted language. A hard and careful worker with an almost inexhaustible store of adventure to draw on, Conrad soon began to be noticed by connoisseurs—though his real fame did not begin till after the publication of *Chance* in 1913. Perhaps because in a sense he was always learning English, he was particularly receptive to various ways in which he could use the language to express the significance of his adventures. Unlike some authors who repeat one or two successful story-telling formulas, Conrad was always experimenting. He was fortunate in being encouraged to do so by brilliantly inventive friends: writers like James, Ford Madox Ford, and Stephen Crane.

Conrad was interested in the way in which ordinary experience can be interpenetrated by psychic revelations of one's secret self. In "The Secret Sharer" the captain's expertise as a mariner, and his concentration on the physical details of the ship, constitute the realistic pole of the story. Set against this realism is a narrative voice charged with a symbolism of the sort announced in the first paragraph: a dream landscape of neither land nor sea, a dark underworld of the unconscious. The story turns on the extent to which the practical captain can descend into this underworld of symbol and confront another dimension of himself. The story is a particularly fine example of Conrad's use of his own adventures to reveal psychological and mythic significance without compromising the realistic surface of things.

The Secret Sharer

I

On my right hand there were lines of fishing stakes resembling a mysterious system of half-submerged bamboo fences, incomprehensible in its division of the domain of tropical fishes, and crazy of aspect as if abandoned forever by some nomad tribe of fishermen now gone to the other end of the ocean; for there was no sign of human habitation as far as the eye could reach. To the left a group of barren islets, suggesting ruins of stone walls, towers, and blockhouses, had its foundations set in a blue sea that itself looked solid, so still and stable did it lie below my feet; even the track of light from the westering sun shone smoothly, without that animated glitter which tells of an imperceptible ripple. And when I turned my head to take a parting glance at the tug which had just left us anchored outside the bar, I saw the straight line of the flat shore joined to the stable sea, edge to edge, with a perfect and unmarked closeness, in one leveled floor half brown, half blue under the enormous dome of the sky. Corresponding in their insignificance to the islets of the sea, two small clumps of trees, one on each side of the only fault in the impeccable joint, marked the mouth of the river Meinam we had just left on the first preparatory stage of our homeward journey; and, far back on the inland level, a larger and loftier mass, the grove surrounding the great Paknam pagoda, was the only thing on which the eye could rest from the vain task of exploring the monotonous sweep of the horizon. Here and there gleams as of a few scattered pieces of silver marked the windings of the great river; and on the nearest of them, just within the bar, the tug steaming right into the land became lost to my sight, hull and funnel and masts, as though the impassive earth had swallowed her up without an effort, without a tremor. My eye followed the light cloud of her smoke, now here, now there, above the plain, according to the devious curves of the stream, but always fainter and farther away, till I lost it at last behind the miter-shaped hill of the great pagoda. And then I was left alone with my ship, anchored at the head of the Gulf of Siam.

She floated at the starting point of a long journey, very still in an immense stillness, the shadows of her spars flung far to the eastward by the setting sun. At that moment I was alone on her decks. There was not a sound in her—and around us nothing moved, nothing lived, not a canoe on the water, not a bird in the air, not a cloud in the sky. In this breathless pause at the threshold of a long passage we seemed to be measuring our fitness for a long and arduous enterprise, the appointed task of both our existences to be carried out, far from all human eyes, with only sky and sea for spectators and for judges.

There must have been some glare in the air to interfere with one's sight, because it was only just before the sun left us that my roaming eyes made out beyond the highest ridges of the principal islet of the group something which did away with the solemnity of perfect solitude. The tide of darkness flowed on swiftly; and with tropical suddenness a swarm of stars came out above the shadowy earth, while I lingered yet, my hand resting lightly on my ship's rail as if on the shoulder of a trusted friend. But, with all that multitude of celestial bodies staring down at one, the comfort of quiet communion with her was gone for good. And there were also disturbing sounds by this time—voices, footsteps forward; the steward flitted along the main-deck, a busily ministering spirit; a hand bell tinkled urgently under the poop deck....

I found my two officers waiting for me near the supper table, in the lighted cuddy. We sat down at once, and as I helped the chief mate, I said:

"Are you aware that there is a ship anchored inside the islands? I saw her mastheads above the ridge as the sun went down."

He raised sharply his simple face, overcharged by a terrible growth of whisker, and emitted his usual ejaculations: "Bless my soul, sir! You don't say so!"

My second mate was a round-cheeked, silent young man, grave beyond his years, I thought; but as our eyes happened to meet I detected a slight quiver on his lips. I looked down at once. It was not my part to encourage sneering on board my ship. It must be said, too, that I knew very little of my officers. In consequence of certain events of no particular significance, except to myself, I had been appointed to the command only a fortnight before. Neither did I know much of the hands forward. All these people had been together for eighteen months or so, and my position was that of the only stranger on board. I mention this because it has some bearing on what is to follow. But what I felt most was my being a stranger to the ship; and if all the truth must be told, I was somewhat of a stranger to myself. The youngest man on board (barring the second mate), and untried as yet by a position of the fullest responsibility, I was willing to take the adequacy of the others for granted. They had simply to be equal to their tasks; but I wondered how far I should turn out faithful to that ideal conception of one's own personality every man sets up for himself secretly.

Meantime the chief mate, with an almost visible effect of collaboration on the part of his round eyes and frightful whiskers, was trying to evolve a theory of the anchored ship. His dominant trait was to take all things into earnest consideration. He was of a painstaking turn of mind. As he used to say, he "liked to account to himself" for practically everything that came in his way, down to a miserable scorpion he had found in his cabin a week before. The why and the wherefore of that scorpion—how it got on board and came to select his room rather than the pantry (which was a dark place and more what a scorpion would be partial to), and how on earth it managed to drown itself in the inkwell of his writing desk—had exercised him infinitely. The ship within the islands was much more easily accounted for; and just as we were about to rise from table he made his pronouncement. She was, he doubted not, a ship from home lately arrived. Probably she drew too much water to cross the bar except at the top of spring tides. Therefore she went into that natural harbor to wait for a few days in preference to remaining in an open roadstead.

"That's so," confirmed the second mate, suddenly, in his slightly hoarse voice. "She draws over twenty feet. She's the Liverpool ship *Sephora* with a cargo of coal. Hundred and twenty-three days from Cardiff."

We looked at him in surprise.

"The tugboat skipper told me when he came on board for your letters, sir," explained the young man. "He expects to take her up the river the day after tomorrow."

After thus overwhelming us with the extent of his information he slipped out of the cabin. The mate observed regretfully that he "could not account for that young fellow's whims." What prevented him telling us all about it at once, he wanted to know.

I detained him as he was making a move. For the last two days the crew had had plenty of hard work, and the night before they had very little sleep. I felt painfully that I—a stranger—was doing something unusual when I directed him to let all hands turn in without setting an anchor watch. I proposed to keep on deck myself till one o'clock or thereabouts. I would get the second mate to relieve me at that hour.

"He will turn out the cook and the steward at four," I concluded, "and then give you a call. Of course at the slightest sign of any sort of wind we'll have the hands up and make a start at once."

He concealed his astonishment. "Very well, sir." Outside the cuddy he put his head in the second mate's door to inform him of my unheard-of caprice to take a five hours' anchor watch on myself. I heard the other raise his voice incredulously—"What? The Captain himself?" Then a few more murmurs, a door closed, then another. A few moments later I went on deck.

My strangeness, which had made me sleepless, had prompted that unconventional arrangement, as if I had expected in those solitary hours of the night to get on terms with the ship of which I knew nothing, manned by men of whom I knew very little more. Fast alongside a wharf, littered like any ship in port with a tangle of unrelated things, invaded by unrelated shore people, I had hardly seen her yet properly. Now, as she lay cleared for sea, the stretch of her main-deck seemed to me very fine under the stars. Very fine, very roomy for her size, and very inviting. I descended the poop and paced the waist, my mind picturing to myself the coming passage through the Malay Archipelago, down the Indian Ocean, and up the Atlantic. All its phases were familiar enough to me, every characteristic, all the alternatives which were likely to face me on the high seas—everything! . . . except the novel responsibility of command. But I took heart from the reasonable thought that the ship was like other ships, the men like other men, and that the sea was not likely to keep any special surprises expressly for my discomfiture.

Arrived at that comforting conclusion, I bethought myself of a cigar and went below to get it. All was still down there. Everybody at the after end of the ship was sleeping profoundly. I came out again on the quarterdeck, agreeably at ease in my sleeping suit on that warm breathless night, barefooted, a glowing cigar in my teeth, and, going forward, I was met by the profound silence of the fore end of the ship. Only as I passed the door of the forecastle I heard a deep, quiet, trustful sigh of some sleeper inside. And suddenly I rejoiced in the great security of the sea as compared with the unrest of the land, in my choice of that untempted life presenting no disquieting problems, invested with an elementary moral beauty by the absolute straightforwardness of its appeal and by the singleness of its purpose.

The riding light in the forerigging burned with a clear, untroubled, as if symbolic, flame, confident and bright in the mysterious shades of the night. Passing on my way aft along the other side of the ship, I observed that the rope side ladder, put over, no doubt, for the master of the tug when he came to fetch away our letters, had not been hauled in as it should have been. I became annoyed at this, for exactitude in some small matters is the very soul of discipline. Then I reflected that I had myself peremptorily dismissed my officers from duty, and by my own act had prevented the anchor watch being formally set and things properly attended to. I asked myself whether it was wise ever to interfere with the established routine of duties even from the kindest of motives. My action might have made me appear eccentric. Goodness only knew how that absurdly whiskered mate would "account" for my conduct, and what the whole ship thought of that informality of their new captain. I was vexed with myself.

Not from compunction certainly, but, as it were mechanically, I proceeded to get the ladder in myself. Now a side ladder of that sort is a light affair and comes in easily, yet my vigorous tug, which should have brought it flying on board, merely recoiled upon my body in a totally unexpected jerk. What the devil! . . . I was so astounded by the immovableness of the ladder that I remained stockstill, trying to account for it to myself like that imbecile mate of mine. In the end, of course, I put my head over the rail.

The side of the ship made an opaque belt of shadow on the darkling glassy shimmer of the sea. But I saw at once something elongated and pale floating very close to the ladder. Before I could form a guess a faint flash of phosphorescent light, which seemed to issue suddenly from the naked body of a man, flickered in the sleeping water with the elusive, silent play of summer lightning in a night sky. With a gasp I saw revealed to my stare a pair of feet, the long legs, a broad livid back immersed right up to the neck in a greenish cadaverous glow. One hand, awash, clutched the bottom rung of the ladder. He was complete but for the head. A headless corpse! The cigar dropped out of my gaping mouth with a tiny plop and a short hiss quite audible in the absolute stillness of all things under heaven. At that I suppose he raised up his face, dimly pale oval in the shadow of the ship's side. But even then I could only barely make out down there the shape of his black-haired head. However, it was enough for the horrid, frost-bound sensation which had gripped me about the chest to pass off. The moment of vain exclamations was past, too. I only climbed on the spare spar and leaned over the rail as far as I could, to bring my eyes nearer to that mystery floating alongside.

As he hung by the ladder, like a resting swimmer, the sea lightning played about his limbs at every stir; and he appeared in it ghastly, silvery, fishlike. He remained as mute as a fish, too. He made no motion to get out of the water, either. It was inconceivable that he should not attempt to come on board, and strangely troubling to suspect that perhaps he did not want to. And my first words were prompted by just that troubled incertitude.

"What's the matter?" I asked in my ordinary tone, speaking down to the face upturned exactly under mine.

"Cramp," it answered, no louder. Then slightly anxious, "I say, no need to call anyone."

"I was not going to," I said.

"Are you alone on deck?"

"Yes."

I had somehow the impression that he was on the point of letting go the ladder to swim away beyond my ken—mysterious as he came. But, for the moment, this being appearing as if he had risen from the bottom of the sea (it was certainly the nearest land to the ship) wanted only to know the time. I told him. And he, down there, tentatively:

"I suppose your captain's turned in?"

"I am sure he isn't," I said.

He seemed to struggle with himself, for I heard something like the low, bitter murmur of doubt. "What's the good?" His next words came out with a hesitating effort.

"Look here, my man. Could you call him out quietly?"

I thought the time had come to declare myself.

"*I* am the captain."

I heard a "By Jove!" whispered at the level of the water. The phosphorescence flashed in the swirl of the water all about his limbs, his other hand seized the ladder.

"My name's Leggatt."

The voice was calm and resolute. A good voice. The self-possession of that man had somehow induced a corresponding state in myself. It was very quietly that I remarked:

"You must be a good swimmer."

"Yes. I've been in the water practically since nine o'clock. The question for me now is whether I am to let go this ladder and go on swimming till I sink from exhaustion, or—to come on board here."

I felt this was no mere formula of desperate speech, but a real alternative in the view of a strong soul. I should have gathered from this that he was young; indeed, it is only the young who are ever confronted by such clear issues. But at the time it was pure intuition on my part. A mysterious communication was established already between us two—in the face of that silent, darkened tropical sea. I was young, too; young enough to make no comment. The man in the water began suddenly to climb up the ladder, and I hastened away from the rail to fetch some clothes. Before entering the cabin I stood still, listening in the lobby at the foot of the stairs. A faint snore came through the closed door of the chief mate's room. The second mate's door was on the hook, but the darkness in there was absolutely soundless. He, too, was young and could sleep like a stone. Remained the steward, but he was not likely to wake up before he was called. I got a sleeping suit out of my room and, coming back on deck, saw the naked man from the sea sitting on the main hatch, glimmering white in the darkness, his elbows on his knees and his head in his hands. In a moment he had concealed his damp body in a sleeping suit of the same gray-stripe pattern as the one I was wearing and followed me like my double on the poop. Together we moved right aft, barefooted, silent.

"What is it?" I asked in a deadened voice, taking the lighted lamp out of the binnacle, and raising it to his face.

"An ugly business."

He had rather regular features; a good mouth; light eyes under somewhat heavy, dark eyebrows; a smooth, square forehead; no growth on his cheeks; a small, brown mustache, and a well-shaped, round chin. His expression was concentrated, meditative, under the inspecting light of the lamp I held up to his face; such as a man thinking hard in solitude might wear. My sleeping suit was just right for his size. A well-knit young fellow of twenty-five at most. He caught his lower lip with the edge of white, even teeth.

"Yes," I said, replacing the lamp in the binnacle. The warm, heavy tropical night closed upon his head again.

"There's a ship over there," he murmured.

"Yes, I know. The *Sephora.* Did you know of us?"

"Hadn't the slightest idea. I am the mate of her——" He paused and corrected himself. "I should say I *was.*"

"Aha! Something wrong?"

"Yes. Very wrong indeed. I've killed a man."

"What do you mean? Just now?"

"No, on the passage. Weeks ago. Thirty-nine south. When I say a man——"

"Fit of temper," I suggested, confidently.

The shadowy, dark head, like mine, seemed to nod imperceptibly above the ghostly gray of my sleeping suit. It was, in the night, as though I had been faced by my own reflection in the depths of a somber and immense mirror.

"A pretty thing to have to own up to for a Conway boy," murmured my double, distinctly.

"You're a Conway boy?"

"I am," he said, as if startled. Then, slowly . . . "Perhaps you too——"

It was so; but being a couple of years older I had left before he joined. After a quick interchange of dates a silence fell; and I thought suddenly of my absurd mate with his terrific whiskers and the "Bless my soul—you don't say so" type of intellect. My double gave me an inkling of his thoughts by saying: "My father's a parson in Norfolk. Do you see me before a judge and jury on that charge? For myself I can't see the necessity. There are fellows that an angel from heaven—— And I am not that. He was one of those creatures that are just simmering all the time with a silly sort of wickedness. Miserable devils that have no business to live at all. He wouldn't do his duty and wouldn't let anybody else do theirs. But what's the good of talking! You know well enough the sort of ill-conditioned snarling cur——"

He appealed to me as if our experiences had been as identical as our clothes. And I knew well enough the pestiferous danger of such a character where there are no means of legal repression. And I knew well enough also that my double there was no homicidal ruffian. I did not think of asking him for details, and he told me the story roughly in brusque, disconnected sentences. I needed no more. I saw it all going on as though I were myself inside that other sleeping suit.

"It happened while we were setting a reefed foresail, at dusk. Reefed foresail! You understand the sort of weather. The only sail we had left to keep the ship running; so you may guess what it had been like for days. Anxious sort of job, that. He gave me some of his cursed insolence at the sheet. I tell you I was overdone with this terrific weather that seemed to have no end to it. Terrific, I tell you—and a deep ship. I believe the fellow himself was half crazed with funk. It was no time for gentlemanly reproof, so I turned round and felled him like an ox. He up and at me. We closed just as an awful sea made for the ship. All hands saw it coming and took to the rigging, but I had him by the throat, and went on shaking him like a rat, the men above us yelling, 'Look out! look out!' Then a crash as if the sky had fallen on my head. They say that for over ten minutes hardly anything was to be seen of the ship—just the three masts and a bit of the forecastle head and of the poop all awash driving along in a smother of foam. It was a miracle that they found us, jammed together behind the forebitts. It's clear that I meant business, because I was holding him by the throat still when they picked us up. He was black in the face. It was too much for them. It seems they rushed us aft together, gripped as we were, screaming 'Murder!' like a lot of lunatics, and broke into the cuddy. And the ship running for her life, touch and go all the time, any minute her last in a sea fit to turn your hair gray only a-looking at it. I understand that the skipper, too, started raving like the rest of them. The man had been deprived of sleep for more than a week, and to have this sprung on him at the height of a furious gale nearly drove him out of his mind. I wonder they didn't fling me overboard after getting the carcass of their precious shipmate out of my fingers. They had rather a job to separate us, I've been told. A sufficiently fierce story to make an old judge and a respectable jury sit up a bit. The first thing I heard when I came to myself was the maddening howling of that endless gale, and on that the voice of the old man. He was hanging on to my bunk, staring into my face out of his sou'wester. " 'Mr. Leggatt, you have killed a man. You can act no longer as chief mate of this ship.' "

His care to subdue his voice made it sound monotonous. He rested a hand on the end of the skylight to steady himself with, and all that time did not stir a limb, so far as I could see. "Nice little tale for a quiet tea party," he concluded in the same tone.

One of my hands, too, rested on the end of the skylight; neither did I stir a limb, so far as I knew. We stood less than a foot from each other. It occurred to me that if old "Bless my soul—you don't say so" were to put his head up the companion and catch sight of us, he would think he was seeing double, or imagine himself come upon a scene of weird witchcraft; the strange captain having a quiet confabulation by the wheel with his own gray ghost. I became very much concerned to prevent anything of the sort. I heard the other's soothing undertone.

"My father's a parson in Norfolk," it said. Evidently he had forgotten he had told me this important fact before. Truly a nice little tale.

"You had better slip down into my stateroom now," I said, moving off stealthily. My double followed my movements; our bare feet made no sound; I let him in, closed the door with care, and, after giving a call to the second mate, returned on deck for my relief.

"Not much sign of any wind yet," I remarked when he approached.

"No sir. Not much," he assented, sleepily, in his hoarse voice, with just enough deference, no more, and barely suppressing a yawn.

"Well, that's all you have to look out for. You have got your orders."

"Yes, sir."

I paced a turn or two on the poop and saw him take up his position face forward with his elbow in the ratlines of the mizzen rigging before I went below. The mate's faint snoring was still going on peacefully. The cuddy lamp was burning over the table on which stood a vase with flowers, a polite attention from the ship's provision merchant—the last flowers we should see for the next three months at the very least. Two bunches of bananas hung from the beam symmetrically, one on each side of the rudder casing. Everything was as before in the ship—except that two of her captain's sleeping suits were simultaneously in use, one motionless in the cuddy, the other keeping very still in the captain's stateroom.

It must be explained here that my cabin had the form of the capital letter L, the door being within the angle and opening into the short part of the letter. A couch was to the left, the bed place to the right; my writing desk and the chronometers' table faced the door. But anyone opening it, unless he stepped right inside, had no view of what I call the long (or vertical) part of the letter. It contained some lockers surmounted by a bookcase; and a few clothes, a thick jacket or two, caps, oilskin coat, and such like, hung on hooks. There was at the bottom of that part a door opening into my bathroom, which could be entered also directly from the saloon. But that way was never used.

The mysterious arrival had discovered the advantage of this particular shape. Entering my room, lighted strongly by a big bulkhead lamp swung on gimbals above my writing desk, I did not see him anywhere till he stepped out quietly from behind the coats hung in the recessed part.

"I heard somebody moving about, and went in there at once," he whispered.

I, too, spoke under my breath.

"Nobody is likely to come in here without knocking and getting permission."

He nodded. His face was thin and the sunburn faded, as though he had been ill. And no wonder. He had been, I heard presently, kept under arrest in his cabin for nearly seven weeks. But there was nothing sickly in his eyes or in his expression. He was not a bit like me, really; yet, as we stood leaning over my bed place, whispering side by side, with our dark heads together and our backs to the door, anybody bold enough to open it stealthily would have been treated to the uncanny sight of a double captain busy talking in whispers with his other self.

"But all this doesn't tell me how you came to hang on to our side ladder," I inquired, in the hardly audible murmurs we used, after he had told me something more of the proceedings on board the *Sephora* once the bad weather was over.

"When we sighted Java Head I had had time to think all those matters out several times over. I had six weeks of doing nothing else, and with only an hour or so every evening for a tramp on the quarter-deck."

He whispered, his arms folded on the side of my bed place, staring through the open port. And I could imagine perfectly the manner of this thinking out —a stubborn if not a steadfast operation; something of which I should have been perfectly incapable.

"I reckoned it would be dark before we closed with the land," he continued, so low that I had to strain my hearing near as we were to each other, shoulder touching shoulder almost. "So I asked to speak to the old man. He always seemed very sick when he came to see me—as if he could not look me in the face. You know, that foresail saved the ship. She was too deep to have run long under bare poles. And it was I that managed to set it for him. Anyway, he came. When I had him in my cabin—he stood by the door looking at me as if I had the halter around my neck already—I asked him right away to leave my cabin door unlocked at night while the ship was going through Sunda Straits. There would be the Java coast within two or three miles, off Angier Point. I wanted nothing more. I've had a prize for swimming my second year in the Conway."

"I can believe it," I breathed out.

"God only knows why they locked me in every night. To see some of their faces you'd have thought they were afraid I'd go about at night strangling people. Am I a murdering brute? Do I look it? By Jove! If I had been he wouldn't have trusted himself like that into my room. You'll say I might have chucked him aside and bolted out, there and then—it was dark already. Well, no. And for the same reason I wouldn't think of trying to smash the door. There would have been a rush to stop me at the noise, and I did not mean to get into a confounded scrimmage. Somebody else might have got killed—for I would not have broken out only to get chucked back, and I did not want any more of that work. He refused, looking more sick than ever. He was afraid of the men, and also of that old second mate of his who had been sailing with him for years—a gray-headed old humbug; and his steward, too, had been with him devil knows how long—seventeen years or more—a dogmatic sort of loafer who hated me like poison, just because I was the chief mate. No chief mate ever made more than one voyage in the *Sephora,* you know. Those two old chaps ran the ship. Devil only knows what the skipper wasn't afraid of (all his nerve went to pieces altogether in that hellish spell of bad weather we had)— of what the law would do to him—of his wife, perhaps. Oh, yes! she's on board. Though I don't think she would have meddled. She would have been only too glad to have me out of the ship in any way. The 'brand of Cain' business, don't you see. That's all right. I was ready enough to go off wandering on the face of the earth—and that was price enough to pay for an Abel of that sort. Anyhow, he wouldn't listen to me. 'This thing must take its course. I represent the law here.' He was shaking like a leaf. 'So you won't?' 'No!' 'Then I hope you will be able to sleep on that.' I said, and turned my back on him. 'I wonder that *you* can,' cries he, and locks the door.

"Well after that, I couldn't. Not very well. That was three weeks ago. We have had a slow passage through the Java Sea; drifted about Carimata for ten days. When we anchored here they thought, I suppose, it was all right. The nearest land (and that's five miles) is the ship's destination; the consul would soon set about catching me; and there would have been no object in bolting to these islets there. I don't suppose there's a drop of water on them. I don't know how it was, but tonight that steward, after bringing me my supper, went out to let me eat it, and left the door unlocked. And I ate it—all there was, too. After I had finished I strolled out on the quarter-deck. I don't know that I meant to do anything. A breath of fresh air was all I wanted, I believe. Then a sudden temptation came over me. I kicked off my slippers and was in the water before I had made up my mind fairly. Somebody heard the splash and they raised an awful hullabaloo. 'He's gone! Lower the boats! He's committed suicide! No, he's swimming.' Certainly I was swimming. It's not so easy for a swimmer like me to commit suicide by drowning. I landed on the nearest islet before the boat left the ship's side. I heard them pulling about in the dark, hailing, and so on, but after a bit they gave up. Everything quieted down and the anchorage became as still as death. I sat down on a stone and began to think. I felt certain they would start searching for me at daylight. There was no place to hide on those stony things—and if there had been, what would have been the good? But now I was clear of that ship, I was not going back. So after a while I took off all my clothes, tied them up in a bundle with a stone inside, and dropped them in the deep water on the outer side of that islet. That was suicide enough for me. Let them think what they liked, but I didn't mean to drown myself. I meant to swim till I sank—but that's not the same thing. I struck out for another of these little islands, and it was from that one that I first saw your riding light. Something to swim for. I went on easily, and on the way I came upon a flat rock a foot or two above water. In the daytime, I dare say, you might make it out with a glass from your poop. I scrambled up on it and rested myself for a bit. Then I made another start. That last spell must have been over a mile."

His whisper was getting fainter and fainter, and all the time he stared straight out through the porthole, in which there was not even a star to be seen. I had not interrupted him. There was something that made comment impossible in his narrative, or perhaps in himself; a sort of feeling, a quality, which I can't find a name for. And when he ceased, all I found was a futile whisper: "So you swam for our light?"

"Yes—straight for it. It was something to swim for. I couldn't see any stars low down because the coast was in the way, and I couldn't see the land, either.

The water was like glass. One might have been swimming in a confounded thousand-feet deep cistern with no place for scrambling out anywhere; but what I didn't like was the notion of swimming round and round like a crazed bullock before I gave out; and as I didn't mean to go back . . . No. Do you see me being hauled back, stark naked, off one of these little islands by the scruff of the neck and fighting like a wild beast? Somebody would have got killed for certain, and I did not want any of that. So I went on. Then your ladder——"

"Why didn't you hail the ship?" I asked, a little louder.

He touched my shoulder lightly. Lazy footsteps came right over our heads and stopped. The second mate had crossed from the other side of the poop and might have been hanging over the rail for all we knew.

"He couldn't hear us talking—could he?" My double breathed into my very ear, anxiously.

His anxiety was an answer, a sufficient answer, to the question I had put to him. An answer containing all the difficulty of that situation. I closed the porthole quietly, to make sure. A louder word might have been overheard.

"Who's that?" he whispered then.

"My second mate. But I don't know much more of the fellow than you do."

And I told him a little about myself. I had been appointed to take charge while I least expected anything of the sort, not quite a fortnight ago. I didn't know either the ship or the people. Hadn't had the time in port to look about me or size anybody up. And as to the crew, all they knew was that I was appointed to take the ship home. For the rest, I was almost as much of a stranger on board as himself, I said. And at the moment I felt it most acutely. I felt that it would take very little to make me a suspect person in the eyes of the ship's company.

He had turned about meantime; and we, the two strangers in the ship, faced each other in identical attitudes.

"Your ladder——" he murmured, after a silence. "Who'd have thought of finding a ladder hanging over at night in a ship anchored out here! I felt just then a very unpleasant faintness. After the life I've been leading for nine weeks, anybody would have got out of condition. I wasn't capable of swimming round as far as your rudder chains. And, lo and behold! there was a ladder to get hold of. After I gripped it I said to myself, 'What's the good?' When I saw a man's head looking over I thought I would swim away presently and leave him shouting—in whatever language it was. I didn't mind being looked at. I—I liked it. And then you speaking to me so quietly—as if you had expected me—made me hold on a little longer. It had been a confounded lonely time—I don't mean while swimming. I was glad to talk a little to somebody that didn't belong to the *Sephora*. As to asking for the captain, that was a mere impulse. It could have been no use, with all the ship knowing about me and the other people pretty certain to be round here in the morning. I don't know—I wanted to be seen, to talk with somebody, before I went on. I don't know what I would have said.... 'Fine night, isn't it?' or something of the sort."

"Do you think they will be round here presently?" I asked with some incredulity.

"Quite likely," he said, faintly.

He looked extremely haggard all of a sudden. His head rolled on his shoulders.

"H'm. We shall see then. Meantime get into that bed," I whispered. "Want help? There."

It was a rather high bed place with a set of drawers underneath. This amazing swimmer really needed the lift I gave him by seizing his leg. He tumbled in, rolled over on his back, and flung one arm across his eyes. And then, with his face nearly hidden, he must have looked exactly as I used to look in that bed. I gazed upon my other self for a while before drawing across carefully the two green serge curtains which ran on a brass rod. I thought for a moment of pinning them together for greater safety, but I sat down on the couch, and once there I felt unwilling to rise and hunt for a pin. I would do it in a moment. I was extremely tired, in a peculiarly intimate way, by the strain of stealthiness, by the effort of whispering and the general secrecy of this excitement. It was three o'clock by now and I had been on my feet since nine, but I was not sleepy; I could not have gone to sleep. I sat there, fagged out, looking at the curtains, trying to clear my mind of the confused sensation of being in two places at once, and greatly bothered by an exasperating knocking in my head. It was a relief to discover suddenly that it was not in my head at all, but on the outside of the door. Before I could collect myself the words "Come in" were out of my mouth, and the steward entered with a tray, bringing in my morning coffee. I had slept, after all, and I was so frightened that I shouted, "This way! I am here, steward," as though he had been miles away. He put down the tray on the table next the couch and only then said, very quietly, "I can see you are here, sir." I felt him give me a keen look, but I dared not meet his eyes just then. He must have wondered why I had drawn the curtains of my bed before going to sleep on the couch. He went out, hooking the door open as usual.

I heard the crew washing decks above me. I knew I would have been told at once if there had been any wind. Calm, I thought, and I was doubly vexed. Indeed, I felt dual more than ever. The steward reappeared suddenly in the doorway. I jumped up from the couch so quickly that he gave a start.

"What do you want here?"

"Close your port, sir—they are washing decks."

"It is closed," I said, reddening.

"Very well, sir." But he did not move from the doorway and returned my stare in an extraordinary, equivocal manner for a time. Then his eyes wavered, all his expression changed, and in a voice unusually gentle, almost coaxingly:

"May I come in to take the empty cup away, sir?"

"Of course!" I turned my back on him while he popped in and out. Then I unhooked and closed the door and even pushed the bolt. This sort of thing could not go on very long. The cabin was as hot as an oven, too. I took a peep at my double, and discovered that he had not moved, his arm was still over his eyes; but his chest heaved; his hair was wet; his chin glistened with perspiration. I reached over him and opened the port.

"I must show myself on deck," I reflected.

Of course, theoretically, I could do what I liked, with no one to say nay to me within the whole circle of the horizon; but to lock my cabin door and take the key away I did not dare. Directly I put my head out of the companion I saw the group of my two officers, the second mate barefooted, the chief mate in long India-rubber boots, near the break of the poop, and the steward halfway down the poop ladder talking to them eagerly. He happened to catch sight of me and dived, the second ran down on the maindeck shouting some order or other, and the chief mate came to meet me, touching his cap.

There was a sort of curiosity in his eye that I did not like. I don't know whether the steward had told them that I was "queer" only, or downright drunk, but I know the man meant to have a good look at me. I watched him coming with a smile which, as he got into point-blank range, took effect and froze his very whiskers. I did not give him time to open his lips.

"Square the yards by lifts and braces before the hands go to breakfast."

It was the first particular order I had given on board that ship; and I stayed on deck to see it executed, too. I had felt the need of asserting myself without loss of time. That sneering young cub got taken down a peg or two on that occasion, and I also seized the opportunity of having a good look at the face of every foremast man as they filed past me to go to the after braces. At breakfast time, eating nothing myself, I presided with such frigid dignity that the two mates were only too glad to escape from the cabin as soon as decency permitted; and all the time the dual working of my mind distracted me almost to the point of insanity. I was constantly watching myself, my secret self, as dependent on my actions as my own personality, sleeping in that bed, behind that door which faced me as I sat at the head of the table. It was very much like being mad, only it was worse because one was aware of it.

I had to shake him for a solid minute, but when at last he opened his eyes it was in the full possession of his senses, with an inquiring look.

"All's well so far," I whispered. "Now you must vanish into the bathroom."

He did so, as noiseless as a ghost, and then I rang for the steward, and facing him boldly, directed him to tidy up my stateroom while I was having my bath—"and be quick about it." As my tone admitted of no excuses, he said, "Yes, sir," and ran off to fetch his dustpan and brushes. I took a bath and did most of my dressing, splashing, and whistling softly for the steward's edification, while the secret sharer of my life stood drawn up bolt upright in that little space, his face looking very sunken in daylight, his eyelids lowered under the stern, dark line of his eyebrows drawn together by a slight frown.

When I left him there to go back to my room the steward was finishing dusting. I sent for the mate and engaged him in some insignificant conversation. It was, as it were, trifling with the terrific character of his whiskers; but my object was to give him an opportunity for a good look at my cabin. And then I could at last shut, with a clear conscience, the door of my stateroom and get my double back into the recessed part. There was nothing else for it. He had to sit still on a small folding stool, half smothered by the heavy coats hanging there. We listened to the steward going into the bathroom out of the saloon, filling the water bottles there, scrubbing the bath, setting things to rights, whisk, bank, clatter—out again into the saloon—turn the key—click. Such was my scheme for keeping my second self invisible. Nothing better could be contrived under the circumstances. And there we sat; I at my writing desk ready to appear busy with some papers, he behind me out of sight of the door. It would not have been prudent to talk in daytime; and I could not have stood the excitement of that queer sense of whispering to myself. Now and then, glancing over my shoulder, I saw him far back there, sitting rigidly on the low stool, his bare feet close together, his arms folded, his head hanging on his breast—and perfectly still. Anybody would have taken him for me.

I was fascinated by it myself. Every moment I had to glance over my shoulder. I was looking at him when a voice outside the door said:

"Beg pardon, sir."

"Well!" . . . I kept my eyes on him, and so when the voice outside the door announced, "There's a ship's boat coming our way, sir." I saw him give a start—the first movement he had made for hours. But he did not raise his bowed head.

"All right. Get the ladder over."

I hesitated. Should I whisper something to him? But what? His immobility seemed to have been never disturbed. What could I tell him he did not know already? . . . Finally I went on deck.

II

The skipper of the *Sephora* had a thin red whisker all round his face, and the sort of complexion that goes with hair of that color; also the particular, rather smeary shade of blue in the eyes. He was not exactly a showy figure; his shoulders were high, his stature but middling—one leg slightly more bandy than the other. He shook hands, looking vaguely around. A spiritless tenacity was his main characteristic, I judged. I behaved with politeness which seemed to disconcert him. Perhaps he was shy. He mumbled to me as if he were ashamed of what he was saying; gave his name (it was something like Archbold —but at this distance of years I hardly am sure), his ship's name, and a few other particulars of that sort, in the manner of a criminal making a reluctant and doleful confession. He had had terrible weather on the passage out—terrible —terrible—wife aboard, too.

By this time we were seated in the cabin and the steward brought in a tray with a bottle and glasses. "Thanks! No." Never took liquor. Would have some water, though. He drank two tumblerfuls. Terrific thirsty work. Ever since daylight had been exploring the islands round his ship.

"What was that for—fun?" I asked, with an appearance of polite interest.

"No!" He sighed. "Painful duty."

As he persisted in his mumbling and I wanted my double to hear every word, I hit upon the notion of informing him that I regretted to say I was hard of hearing.

"Such a young man, too!" he nodded, keeping his smeary blue, unintelligent eyes fastened upon me. "What was the cause of it—some disease?" he inquired, without the least sympathy and as if he thought that, if so, I'd got no more than I deserved.

"Yes; disease," I admitted in a cheerful tone which seemed to shock him. But my point was gained, because he had to raise his voice to give me his tale. It is not worth while to record that version. It was just over two months since all this had happened, and he had thought so much about it that he seemed completely muddled as to its bearings, but still immensely impressed.

"What would you think of such a thing happening on board your own ship? I've had the *Sephora* for these fifteen years. I am a well-known shipmaster."

He was densely distressed—and perhaps I should have sympathized with him if I had been able to detach my mental vision from the unsuspected sharer of my cabin as though he were my second self. There he was on the other side of the bulkhead, four or five feet from us, no more, as we sat in the saloon. I looked politely at Captain Archbold (if that was his name), but it was the other I saw, in a gray sleeping suit, seated on a low stool, his bare feet close together, his arms folded, and every word said between us falling into the ears of his dark head bowed on his chest.

"I have been at sea now, man and boy, for seven-and-thirty years, and I've never heard of such a thing happening in an English ship. And that it should be my ship. Wife on board, too."

I was hardly listening to him.

"Don't you think," I said, "that the heavy sea which, you told me, came aboard just then might have killed the man? I have seen the sheer weight of a sea kill a man very nearly, by simply breaking his neck."

"Good God!" he uttered, impressively, fixing his smeary blue eyes on me. "The sea! No man killed by the sea ever looked like that." He seemed positively scandalized at my suggestion. And as I gazed at him certainly not prepared for anything original on his part, he advanced his head close to mine and thrust his tongue out at me so suddenly that I couldn't help starting back.

After scoring over my calmness in this graphic way he nodded wisely. If I had seen the sight, he assured me, I would never forget it as long as I lived. The weather was too bad to give the corpse a proper sea burial. So next day at dawn they took it up on the poop, covering its face with a bit of bunting; he read a short prayer, and then, just as it was, in its oilskins and long boots, they launched it amongst those mountainous seas that seemed ready every moment to swallow up the ship herself and the terrified lives on board of her.

"That reefed foresail saved you," I threw in.

"Under God—it did," he exclaimed fervently. "It was by a special mercy, I firmly believe, that it stood some of those hurricane squalls."

"It was the setting of that sail which—" I began.

"God's own hand in it," he interrupted me. "Nothing less could have done it. I don't mind telling you that I hardly dared give the order. It seemed impossible that we could touch anything without losing it, and then our last hope would have been gone."

The terror of that gale was on him yet. I let him go on for a bit, then said, casually—as if returning to a minor subject:

"You were very anxious to give up your mate to the shore people, I believe?"

He was. To the law. His obscure tenacity on that point had in it something incomprehensible and a little awful; something, as it were, mystical, quite apart from his anxiety that he should not be suspected of "countenancing any doings of that sort." Seven-and-thirty virtuous years at sea, of which over twenty of immaculate command, and the last fifteen in the *Sephora,* seemed to have laid him under some pitiless obligation.

"And you know," he went on, groping shame-facedly amongst his feelings, "I did not engage that young fellow. His people had some interest with my owners. I was in a way forced to take him on. He looked very smart, very gentlemanly, and all that. But do you know—I never liked him, somehow. I am a plain man. You see, he wasn't exactly the sort for the chief mate of a ship like the *Sephora.*"

I had become so connected in thoughts and impressions with the secret sharer of my cabin that I felt as if I, personally, were being given to understand that I, too, was not the sort that would have done for the chief mate of a ship like the *Sephora.* I had no doubt of it in my mind.

"Not at all the style of man. You understand," he insisted, superfluously, looking hard at me.

I smiled urbanely. He seemed at a loss for a while.

"I suppose I must report a suicide."

"Beg pardon?"

"Sui-cide! That's what I'll have to write to my owners directly I get in."

"Unless you manage to recover him before tomorrow," I assented, dispassionately. . . . "I mean, alive."

He mumbled something which I really did not catch, and I turned my ear to him in a puzzled manner. He fairly bawled:

"The land—I say, the mainland is at least seven miles off my anchorage."

"About that."

My lack of excitement, of curiosity, of surprise, of any sort of pronounced interest, began to arouse his distrust. But except for the felicitous pretense of deafness I had not tried to pretend anything. I had felt utterly incapable of playing the part of ignorance properly, and therefore was afraid to try. It is also certain that he had brought some ready-made suspicions with him, and that he viewed my politeness as a strange and unnatural phenomenon. And yet how else could I have received him? Not heartily! That was impossible for psychological reasons, which I need not state here. My only object was to keep off his inquiries. Surlily? Yes, but surliness might have provoked a point-blank question. From its novelty to him and from its nature, punctilious courtesy was the manner best calculated to restrain the man. But there was the danger of his breaking through my defense bluntly. I could not, I think, have met him by a direct lie, also for psychological (not moral) reasons. If he had only known how afraid I was of his putting my feeling of identity with the other to the test! But, strangely enough—(I thought of it only afterwards)—I believe that he was not a little disconcerted by the reverse side of that weird situation, by something in me that reminded him of the man he was seeking—suggested a mysterious similitude to the young fellow he had distrusted and disliked from the first.

However that might have been, the silence was not very prolonged. He took another oblique step.

"I reckon I had no more than a two-mile pull to your ship. Not a bit more."

"And quite enough, too, in this awful heat," I said.

Another pause full of mistrust followed. Necessity, they say, is mother of invention, but fear, too, is not barren of ingenious suggestions. And I was afraid he would ask me point-blank for news of my other self.

"Nice little saloon, isn't it?" I remarked, as if noticing for the first time the way his eyes roamed from one closed door to the other. "And very well fitted out, too. Here, for instance," I continued, reaching over the back of my seat negligently and flinging the door open, "is my bathroom."

He made an eager movement, but hardly gave it a glance. I got up, shut the door of the bathroom, and invited him to have a look round, as if I were very proud of my accommodation. He had to rise and be shown round, but he went through the business without any raptures whatever.

"And now we'll have a look at my stateroom," I declared, in a voice as loud as I dared to make it, crossing the cabin to the starboard side with purposely heavy steps.

He followed me in and gazed around. My intelligent double had vanished. I played my part.

"Very convenient—isn't it?"

"Very nice. Very comf. . . ." He didn't finish and went out brusquely as if to escape from some unrighteous wiles of mine. But it was not to be. I had been too frightened not to feel vengeful; I felt I had him on the run, and I meant to keep him on the run. My polite insistence must have had something menacing in it, because he gave in suddenly. And I did not let him off a single item; mate's room, pantry, storerooms, the very sail locker which was also under the poop—he had to look into them all. When at last I showed him out on the quarter-deck he drew a long, spiritless sigh, and mumbled dismally that he must really be going back to his ship now. I desired my mate, who had joined us, to see to the captain's boat.

The man of whiskers gave a blast on the whistle which he used to wear hanging round his neck, and yelled, "*Sephora*'s away!" My double down here in my cabin must have heard, and certainly could not feel more relieved than I. Four fellows came running out from somewhere forward and went over the side, while my own men, appearing on deck too, lined the rail. I escorted my visitor to the gangway ceremoniously, and nearly overdid it. He was a tenacious beast. On the very ladder he lingered, and in that unique, guiltily conscientious manner of sticking to the point:

"I say . . . you . . . don't think that——"

I covered his voice loudly:

"Certainly not. . . . I am delighted. Good-by."

I had an idea of what he meant to say, and just saved myself by the privilege of defective hearing. He was too shaken generally to insist, but my mate, close witness of that parting, looked mystified and his face took on a thoughtful cast. As I did not want to appear as if I wished to avoid all communication with my officers, he had the opportunity to address me.

"Seems a very nice man. His boat's crew told our chaps a very extraordinary story, if what I am told by the steward is true. I suppose you had it from the captain, sir?"

"Yes. I had a story from the captain."

"A very horrible affair—isn't it, sir?"

"It is."

"Beats all these tales we hear about murders in Yankee ships."

"I don't think it beats them. I don't think it resembles them in the least."

"Bless my soul—you don't say so! But of course I've no acquaintance whatever with American ships, not I, so I couldn't go against your knowledge. It's horrible enough for me. . . . But the queerest part is that those fellows seemed to have some idea the man was hidden aboard here. They had really. Did you ever hear of such a thing?"

"Preposterous—isn't it?"

We were walking to and fro athwart the quarter-deck. No one of the crew forward could be seen (the day was Sunday), and the mate pursued:

"There was some little dispute about it. Our chaps took offense. 'As if we would harbor a thing like that,' they said. 'Wouldn't you like to look for him in our coalhole?' Quite a tiff. But they made it up in the end. I suppose he did drown himself. Don't you, sir?"

"I don't suppose anything."

"You have no doubt in the matter, sir?"

"None whatever."

I left him suddenly. I felt I was producing a bad impression, but with my double down there it was most trying to be on deck. And it was almost as trying to be below. Altogether a nerve-trying situation. But on the whole I felt less torn in two when I was with him. There was no one in the whole ship whom I dared take into my confidence. Since the hands had got to know his story, it would have been impossible to pass him off for anyone else, and an accidental discovery was to be dreaded now more than ever. . . .

The steward being engaged in laying the table for dinner, we could talk only with our eyes when I first went down. Later in the afternoon we had a cautious try at whispering. The Sunday quietness of the ship was against us; the stillness of air and water around her was against us; the elements, the men were against us—everything was against us in our secret partnership; time itself—for this could not go on forever. The very trust in Providence was, I suppose, denied to his guilt. Shall I confess that this thought cast me down very much? And as to the chapter of accidents which counts for so much in the book of success, I could only hope that it was closed. For what favorable accident could be expected?

"Did you hear everything?" were my first words as soon as we took up our position side by side, leaning over my bed place.

He had. And the proof of it was his earnest whisper, "The man told you he hardly dared to give the order."

I understood the reference to be to that saving foresail.

"Yes. He was afraid of it being lost in the setting."

"I assure you he never gave the order. He may think he did, but he never gave it. He stood there with me on the break of the poop after the main topsail blew away, and whimpered about our last hope—positively whimpered about it and nothing else—and the night coming on! To hear one's skipper go on like that in such weather was enough to drive any fellow out of his mind. It worked me up into a sort of desperation. I just took it into my own hands and went away from him, boiling, and—— But what's the use telling you? *You* know! . . . Do you think that if I had not been pretty fierce with them I should have got the men to do anything? Not I! The bo's'n perhaps? Perhaps! It wasn't a heavy sea—it was a sea gone mad! I suppose the end of the world will be something like that; and a man may have the heart to see it coming once and be done with it—but to have to face it day after day—— I don't blame anybody. I was precious little better than the rest. Only—I was an officer of that old coal wagon, anyhow——"

"I quite understand," I conveyed that sincere assurance into his ear. He was out of breath with whispering; I could hear him pant slightly. It was all very simple. The same strung-up force which had given twenty-four men a chance, at least, for their lives, had, in a sort of recoil, crushed an unworthy mutinous existence.

But I had no leisure to weigh the merits of the matter—footsteps in the saloon, a heavy knock. "There's enough wind to get under way with, sir." Here was the call of a new claim upon my thoughts and even upon my feelings.

"Turn the hands up," I cried through the door. "I'll be on deck directly."

I was going out to make the acquaintance of my ship. Before I left the cabin our eyes met—the eyes of the only two strangers on board. I pointed to the recessed part where the little campstool awaited him and laid my finger on my lips. He made a gesture—somewhat vague—a little mysterious, accompanied by a faint smile, as if of regret.

This is not the place to enlarge upon the sensations of a man who feels for the first time a ship move under his feet to his own independent word. In my case they were not unalloyed. I was not wholly alone with my command; for there was that stranger in my cabin. Or rather, I was not completely and wholly with her. Part of me was absent. That mental feeling of being in two places at once affected me physically as if the mood of secrecy had penetrated my very soul. Before an hour had elapsed since the ship had begun to move, having occasion to ask the mate (he stood by my side) to take a compass bearing of the pagoda, I caught myself reaching up to his ear in whispers. I say I caught myself, but enough had escaped to startle the man. I can't describe it otherwise than by saying that he shied. A grave, preoccupied manner, as though he were in possession of some perplexing intelligence, did not leave him henceforth. A little later I moved away from the rail to look at the compass with such a stealthy gait that the helmsman noticed it—and I could not help noticing the unusual roundness of his eyes. These are trifling instances, though it's to no commander's advantage to be suspected of ludicrous eccentricities. But I was also more seriously affected. There are to a seaman certain words, gestures, that should in given conditions come as naturally, as instinctively, as the winking of a menaced eye. A certain order should spring on to his lips without thinking; a certain sign should get itself made, so to speak, without reflection. But all unconscious alertness had abandoned me. I had to make an effort of will to recall myself back (from the cabin) to the conditions of the moment. I felt that I was appearing an irresolute commander to those people who were watching me more or less critically.

And, besides, there were the scares. On the second day out, for instance, coming off deck in the afternoon (I had straw slippers on my bare feet) I stopped at the open pantry door and spoke to the steward. He was doing something there with his back to me. At the sound of my voice he nearly jumped out of his skin, as the saying is, and incidentally broke a cup.

"What on earth's the matter with you?" I asked, astonished.

He was extremely confused. "Beg your pardon, sir. I made sure you were in your cabin."

"You see I wasn't."

"No, sir. I could have sworn I had heard you moving in there not a moment ago. It's most extraordinary . . . very sorry, sir."

I passed on with an inward shudder. I was so identified with my secret double that I did not even mention the fact in those scanty, fearful whispers we exchanged. I suppose he had made some slight noise of some kind or other. And yet, haggard as he appeared, he looked always perfectly self-controlled, more than calm—almost invulnerable. On my suggestion he remained almost entirely in the bathroom, which upon the whole, was the safest place. There could be really no shadow of an excuse for anyone ever wanting to go in there, once the steward had done with it. It was a very tiny place. Sometimes he reclined on the floor, his legs bent, his head sustained on one elbow. At others I would find him on the campstool, sitting in his gray sleeping suit and with his cropped hair like a patient, unmoved convict. At night I would smuggle him into my bed place, and we would whisper together, with the regular footfalls of the officer of the watch passing and repassing over our heads. It was an infinitely miserable time. It was lucky that some tins of fine preserves were stowed in a locker in my stateroom; hard bread I could always get hold of; and so he lived on stewed chicken, *pâté de foie gras,* asparagus, cooked oyster, sardines—on all sorts of abominable sham delicacies out of tins. My early-morning coffee he always drank; and it was all I dared do for him in that respect.

Every day there was the horrible maneuvering to go through so that my room and then the bathroom should be done in the usual way. I came to hate the sight of the steward, to abhor the voice of that harmless man. I felt that it was he who would bring the disaster of discovery. It hung like a sword over our heads.

The fourth day out, I think (we were then working down the east side of the Gulf of Siam, tack for tack, in light winds and smooth water)—the fourth day, I say, of this miserable juggling with the unavoidable, as we sat at our evening meal, that man, whose slightest movement I dreaded, after putting down the dishes ran up on deck busily. This could not be dangerous. Presently he came down again; and then it appeared that he had remembered a coat of mine which I had thrown over a rail to dry after having been wetted in a shower which had passed over the ship in the afternoon. Sitting stolidly at the head of the table I became terrified at the sight of the garment on his arm. Of course he made for my door. There was no time to lose.

"Steward," I thundered. My nerves were so shaken that I could not govern my voice and conceal my agitation. This was the sort of thing that made my terrifically whiskered mate tap his forehead with his forefinger. I had detected him using that gesture while talking on deck with a confidential air to the carpenter. It was too far to hear a word, but I had no doubt that this pantomime could only refer to the strange new captain.

"Yes, sir," the pale-faced steward turned resignedly to me. It was this maddening course of being shouted at, checked without rhyme or reason, arbitrarily chased out of my cabin, suddenly called into it, sent flying out of his pantry on incomprehensible errands, that accounted for the growing wretchedness of his expression.

"Where are you going with that coat?"

"To your room, sir."

"Is there another shower coming?"

"I'm sure I don't know, sir. Shall I go up again and see, sir?"

"No! never mind."

My object was attained, as of course my other self in there would have heard everything that passed. During this interlude my two officers never raised their eyes off their respective plates; but the lip of that confounded cub, the second mate, quivered visibly.

I expected the steward to hook my coat on and come out at once. He was very slow about it; but I dominated my nervousness sufficiently not to shout after him. Suddenly I became aware (it could be heard plainly enough) that the fellow for some reason or other was opening the door of the bathroom. It was the end. The place was literally not big enough to swing a cat in. My voice died in my throat and I went stony all over. I expected to hear a yell of surprise and terror, and made a movement, but had not the strength to get on my legs. Everything remained still. Had my second self taken the poor wretch by the throat? I don't know what I could have done next moment if I had not seen the steward come out of my room, close the door, and then stand quietly by the sideboard.

"Saved," I thought. "But, no! Lost! Gone! He was gone!"

I laid my knife and fork down and leaned back in my chair. My head swam. After a while, when sufficiently recovered to speak in a steady voice, I instructed my mate to put the ship round at eight o'clock himself.

"I won't come on deck," I went on. "I think I'll turn in, and unless the wind shifts I don't want to be disturbed before midnight. I feel a bit seedy."

"You did look middling bad a little while ago," the chief mate remarked without showing any great concern.

They both went out, and I stared at the steward clearing the table. There was nothing to be read on that wretched man's face. But why did he avoid my eyes, I asked myself. Then I thought I should like to hear the sound of his voice.

"Steward!"

"Sir!" Startled as usual.

"Where did you hang up that coat?"

"In the bathroom, sir." The usual anxious tone. "It's not quite dry yet, sir."

For some time longer I sat in the cuddy. Had my double vanished as he had come? But of his coming there was an explanation, whereas his disappearance would be inexplicable. . . . I went slowly into my dark room, shut the door, lighted the lamp, and for a time, dared not turn round. When at last I did I saw him standing bolt-upright in the narrow recessed part. It would not be true to say I had a shock, but an irresistible doubt of his bodily existence flitted through my mind. Can it be, I asked myself, that he is not visible to eyes other than mine? It was like being haunted. Motionless, with a grave face, he raised his hands slightly at me in a gesture which meant clearly, "Heavens! what a narrow escape!" Narrow indeed. I think I had come creeping quietly as near insanity as any man who has not actually gone over the border. The gesture restrained me, so to speak.

The mate with the terrific whiskers was now putting the ship on the other tack. In the moment of profound silence which follows upon the hands going to their stations I heard on the poop his raised voice: "Hard alee!" and the distant shout of the order repeated on the main-deck. The sails, in that light breeze, made but a faint fluttering noise. It ceased. The ship was coming round slowly: I held my breath in the renewed stillness of expectation; one wouldn't have thought that there was a single living soul on her decks. A sudden brisk shout, "Mainsail haul!" broke the spell, and in the noisy cries and rush overhead of the men running away with the main brace we two, down in my cabin, came together in our usual position by the bed place.

He did not wait for my question. "I heard him fumbling here and just managed to squat myself down in the bath," he whispered to me. "The fellow only opened the door and put his arm in to hang the coat up. All the same——"

"I never thought of that," I whispered back, even more appalled than before at the closeness of the shave, and marveling at that something unyielding in his character which was carrying him through so finely. There was no agitation in his whisper. Whoever was being driven distracted, it was not he. He was sane. And the proof of his sanity was continued when he took up the whispering again.

"It would never do for me to come to life again."

It was something that a ghost might have said. But what he was alluding to was his old captain's reluctant admission of the theory of suicide. It would obviously serve his turn—if I had understood at all the view which seemed to govern the unalterable purpose of his action.

"You must maroon me as soon as ever you can get amongst these islands off the Cambodge shore," he went on.

"Maroon you! We are not living in a boy's adventure tale," I protested. His scornful whispering took me up.

"We aren't indeed! There's nothing of a boy's tale in this. But there's nothing else for it. I want no more. You don't suppose I am afraid of what can be done to me? Prison or gallows or whatever they may please. But you don't see me coming back to explain such things to an old fellow in a wig and twelve respectable tradesmen, do you? What can they know whether I am guilty or no—or of *what* I am guilty, either? That's my affair. What does the Bible say? 'Driven off the face of the earth.' Very well, I am off the face of the earth now. As I came at night so I shall go."

"Impossible!" I murmured. "You can't."

"Can't? . . . Not naked like a soul on the Day of Judgment. I shall freeze on to this sleeping suit. The Last Day is not yet—and . . . you have understood thoroughly. Didn't you?"

I felt suddenly ashamed of myself. I may say truly that I understood—and my hesitation in letting that man swim away from my ship's side had been a mere sham sentiment, a sort of cowardice.

"It can't be done now till next night," I breathed out. "The ship is on the off-shore tack and the wind may fail us."

"As long as I know that you understand," he whispered. "But of course you do. It's a great satisfaction to have got somebody to understand. You seem to have been there on purpose." And in the same whisper, as if we two whenever we talked had to say things to each other which were not fit for the world to hear, he added, "It's very wonderful."

We remained side by side talking in our secret way—but sometimes silent or just exchanging a whispered word or two at long intervals. And as usual he stared through the port. A breath of wind came now and again into our faces. The ship might have been moored in dock, so gently and on an even keel she slipped through the water, that did not murmur even at our passage, shadowy and silent like a phantom sea.

At midnight I went on deck, and to my mate's great surprise put the ship round on the other tack. His terrible whiskers flitted round me in silent criticism. I certainly should not have done it if it had been only a question of getting out of that sleepy gulf as quickly as possible. I believe he told the second mate, who relieved him, that it was a great want of judgment. The other only yawned. That intolerable cub shuffled about so sleepily and lolled against the rails in such a slack, improper fashion that I came down on him sharply.

"Aren't you properly awake yet?"

"Yes, sir! I am awake."

"Well, then, be good enough to hold yourself as if you were. And keep a lookout. If there's any current we'll be closing with some islands before daylight."

The east side of the gulf is fringed with islands, some solitary, others in groups. On the blue background of the high coast they seem to float on silvery patches of calm water, arid and gray, or dark green and rounded like clumps of evergreen bushes, with the larger ones, a mile or two long, showing the outlines of ridges, ribs of gray rock under the dank mantle of matted leafage. Unknown to trade, to travel, almost to geography, the manner of life they harbor is an unsolved secret. There must be villages—settlements of fishermen at least—on the largest of them, and some communication with the world is probably kept up by native craft. But all that forenoon, as we headed for them, fanned along by the faintest of breezes, I saw no sign of man or canoe in the field of the telescope I kept pointing at the scattered group.

At noon I gave no orders for a change of course, and the mate's whiskers became much concerned and seemed to be offering themselves unduly to my notice. At last I said:

"I am going to stand right in. Quite in—as far as I can take her."

The stare of extreme surprise imparted an air of ferocity also to his eyes, and he looked truly terrific for a moment.

"We're not doing well in the middle of the gulf," I continued, casually. "I am going to look for the land breezes tonight."

"Bless my soul! Do you mean, sir, in the dark amongst the lot of all them islands and reefs and shoals?"

"Well—if there are any regular land breezes at all on this coast one must get close inshore to find them, mustn't one?"

"Bless my soul!" he exclaimed again under his breath. All that afternoon he wore a dreamy, contemplative appearance which in him was a mark of perplexity. After dinner I went into my stateroom as if I meant to take some rest. There we two bent our dark heads over a half-unrolled chart lying on my bed.

"There, " I said. "It's got to be Koh-ring. I've been looking at it ever since sunrise. It has got two hills and a low point. It must be inhabited. And on the coast opposite there is what looks like the mouth of a biggish river—with some towns, no doubt, not far up. It's the best chance for you that I can see."

"Anything. Koh-ring let it be."

He looked thoughtfully at the chart as if surveying chances and distances from a lofty height—and following with his eyes his own figure wandering on the blank land of Cochin-China, and then passing off the piece of paper clean out of sight into uncharted regions. And it was as if the ship had two captains to plan her course for her. I had been so worried and restless running up and down that I had not had the patience to dress that day. I had remained in my sleeping suit, with straw slippers and a soft floppy hat. The closeness of the heat in the gulf had been most oppressive, and the crew were used to seeing me wandering in that airy attire.

"She will clear the south point as she heads now," I whispered into his ear. "Goodness only knows when, though, but certainly after dark. I'll edge her in to half a mile, as far as I may be able to judge in the dark——"

"Be careful," he murmured, warningly—and I realized suddenly that all my future, the only future for which I was fit, would perhaps go irretrievably to pieces in any mishap to my first command.

I could not stop a moment longer in the room. I motioned him to get out of sight and made my way on the poop. That unplayful cub had the watch. I walked up and down for a while thinking things out, then beckoned him over.

"Send a couple of hands to open the two quarterdeck ports," I said, mildly.

He actually had the impudence, or else so forgot himself in his wonder at such an incomprehensible order, as to repeat:

"Open the quarter-deck ports! What for, sir?"

"The only reason you need concern yourself about is because I tell you to do so. Have them open wide and fastened properly."

He reddened and went off, but I believe made some jeering remark to the carpenter as to the sensible practice of ventilating a ship's quarter-deck. I know he popped into the mate's cabin to impart the fact to him because the whiskers came on deck, as it were by chance, and stole glances at me from below—for signs of lunacy or drunkenness, I suppose.

A little before supper, feeling more restless than ever, I rejoined, for a moment, my second self. And to find him sitting so quietly was surprising, like something against nature, inhuman.

I developed my plan in a hurried whisper.

"I shall stand in as close as I dare and then put her round. I will presently find means to smuggle you out of here into the sail locker, which communicates with the lobby. But there is an opening, a sort of square for hauling the sails out, which gives straight on the quarterdeck and which is never closed in fine weather, so as to give air to the sails. When the ship's way is deadened in stays and all the hands are aft at the main braces you will have a clear road to slip out and get overboard through the open quarter-deck port. I've had them both fastened up. Use a rope's end to lower yourself into the water so as to avoid a splash—you know. It could be heard and cause some beastly complication."

He kept silent for a while, then whispered, "I understand."

"I won't be there to see you go," I began with an effort. "The rest . . . I only hope I have understood, too."

"You have. From first to last"—and for the first time there seemed to be a faltering, something strained in his whisper. He caught hold of my arm, but the ringing of the supper bell made me start. He didn't though; he only released his grip.

After supper I didn't come below again till well past eight o'clock. The faint, steady breeze was loaded with dew; and the wet, darkened sails held all there was of propelling power in it. The night, clear and starry, sparkled darkly, and the opaque, lightless patches shifting slowly against the low stars were the drifting islets. On the port bow there was a big one more distant and shadowily imposing by the great space of sky it eclipsed.

On opening the door I had a back view of my very own self looking at a chart. He had come out of the recess and was standing near the table.

"Quite dark enough," I whispered.

He stepped back and leaned against my bed with a level, quiet glance. I sat on the couch. We had nothing to say to each other. Over our heads the officer of the watch moved here and there. Then I heard him move quickly. I knew what that meant. He was making for the companion; and presently his voice was outside my door.

"We are drawing in pretty fast, sir. Land looks rather close."

"Very well," I answered. "I am coming on deck directly."

I waited till he was gone out of the cuddy, then rose. My double moved too. The time had come to exchange our last whispers, for neither of us was ever to hear each other's natural voice.

"Look here!" I opened a drawer and took out three sovereigns. "Take this anyhow. I've got six and I'd give you the lot, only I must keep a little money to buy some fruit and vegetables for the crew from native boats as we go through Sunda Straits."

He shook his head.

"Take it," I urged him, whispering desperately. "No one can tell what——"

He smiled and slapped meaningly the only pocket of the sleeping jacket. It was not safe, certainly. But I produced a large old silk handkerchief of mine, and tying the three pieces of gold in a corner, pressed it on him. He was touched, I supposed, because he took it at last and tied it quickly round his waist under the jacket, on his bare skin.

Our eyes met; several seconds elapsed, till, our glances still mingled, I extended my hand and turned the lamp out. Then I passed through the cuddy, leaving the door of my room wide open. . . . "Steward!"

He was still lingering in the pantry in the greatness of his zeal, giving a rub-up to a plated cruet stand the last thing before going to bed. Being careful not to wake up the mate, whose room was opposite, I spoke in an undertone.

He looked round anxiously. "Sir!"

"Can you get me a little hot water from the galley?"

"I am afraid, sir, the galley fire's been out for some time now."

"Go and see."

He flew up the stairs.

"Now," I whispered, loudly, into the saloon—too loudly, perhaps, but I was afraid I couldn't make a sound. He was by my side in an instant—the double captain clipped past the stairs—through a tiny dark passage . . . a sliding door. We were in the sail locker, scrambling on our knees over the sails. A sudden thought struck me. I saw myself wandering barefooted, bareheaded, the sun beating on my dark poll. I snatched off my floppy hat and tried hurriedly in the dark to ram it on my other self. He dodged and fended off silently. I wonder what he thought had come to me before he understood and suddenly desisted. Our hands met gropingly, lingered united in a steady, motionless clasp for a second. . . . No word was breathed by either of us when they separated.

I was standing quietly by the pantry door when the steward returned.

"Sorry, sir. Kettle barely warm. Shall I light the spirit lamp?"

"Never mind."

I came out on deck slowly. It was now a matter of conscience to shave the land as close as possible—for now he must go overboard whenever the ship was put in stays. Must! There could be no going back for him. After a moment I walked over the leeward and my heart flew into my mouth at the nearness of the land on the bow. Under any other circumstances I would not have held on a minute longer. The second mate had followed me anxiously.

I looked on till I felt I could command my voice.

"She will weather," I said then in a quiet tone.

"Are you going to try that, sir?" he stammered out incredulously.

I took no notice of him and raised my tone just enough to be heard by the helmsman.

"Keep her good full."

"Good full, sir."

The wind fanned my cheek, the sails slept, the world was silent. The strain of watching the dark loom of the land grow bigger and denser was too much for me. I had shut my eyes—because the ship must go closer. She must! The stillness was intolerable. Were we standing still?

When I opened my eyes the second view started my heart with a thump. The black southern hill of Koh-ring seemed to hang right over the ship like a towering fragment of the ever-lasting night. On that enormous mass of blackness there was not a gleam to be seen, not a sound to be heard. It was gliding irresistibly towards us and yet seemed already within reach of the hand. I saw the vague figures of the watch grouped in the waist, gazing in awed silence.

"Are you going on, sir?" inquired an unsteady voice at my elbow.

I ignored it. I had to go on.

"Keep her full. Don't check her way. That won't do now," I said, warningly.

"I can't see the sails very well," the helmsman answered me, in strange, quavering tones.

Was she close enough? Already she was, I won't say in the shadow of the land, but in the very blackness of it, already swallowed up as it were, gone too close to be recalled, gone from me altogether.

"Give the mate a call," I said to the young man who stood at my elbow as still as death. "And turn all hands up."

My tone had a borrowed loudness reverberated from the height of the land. Several voices cried out together; "We are all on deck, sir."

Then stillness again, with the great shadow gliding close, towering higher, without a light, without a sound. Such a hush had fallen on the ship that she might have been a bark of the dead floating in slowly under the very gate of Erebus.

"My God! Where are we?"

It was the mate moaning at my elbow. He was thunderstruck, and as it were deprived of the moral support of his whiskers. He clapped his hands and absolutely cried out, "Lost!"

"Be quiet," I said, sternly.

He lowered his tone, but I saw the shadowy gesture of his despair. "What are we doing here?"

"Looking for the land wind."

He made as if to tear his hair, and addressed me recklessly.

"She will never get out. You have done it, sir. I knew it'd end in something like this. She will never weather, and you are too close now to stay. She'll drift ashore before she's round. O my God!"

I caught his arm as he was raising it to batter his poor devoted head, and shook it violently.

"She's ashore already," he wailed, trying to tear himself away.

"Is she? . . . Keep good full there!"

"Good full, sir," cried the helmsman in a frightened, thin, childlike voice.

I hadn't let go the mate's arm and went on shaking it. "Ready about, do you hear? You go forward"—shake—"and stop there"—shake—"and hold your noise"—shake—"and see these head-sheets properly overhauled"—shake, shake—shake.

And all the time I dared not look towards the land lest my heart should fail me. I released my grip at last and he ran forward as if fleeing for dear life.

I wondered what my double there in the sail locker thought of this commotion. He was able to hear everything—and perhaps he was able to understand why, on my conscience, it had to be thus close—no less. My first order "Hard alee!" re-echoed ominously under the towering shadow of Koh-ring as if I had shouted in a mountain gorge. And then I watched the land intently. In that smooth water and light wind it was impossible to feel the ship coming-to. No! I could not feel her. And my second self was making now ready to ship out and lower himself overboard. Perhaps he was gone already . . . ?

The great black mass brooding over our very mastheads began to pivot away from the ship's side silently. And now I forgot the secret stranger ready to depart, and remembered only that I was a total stranger to the ship. I did not know her. Would she do it? How was she to be handled?

I swung the mainyard and waited helplessly. She was perhaps stopped, and her very fate hung in the balance, with the black mass of Koh-ring like the gate of the everlasting night towering over her taffrail. What would she do now? Had she way on her yet? I stepped to the side swiftly, and on the shadowy water I could see nothing except a faint phosphorescent flash revealing the glassy smoothness of the sleeping surface. It was impossible to tell—and I had not learned yet the feel of my ship. Was she moving? What I needed was something easily seen, a piece of paper, which I could throw overboard and watch. I had nothing on me. To run down for it I didn't dare. There was no time. All at once my strained, yearning stare distinguished a white object floating within a yard of the ship's side. White on the black water. A phosphorescent flash passed under it. What was that thing? . . . I recognized my own floppy hat. It must have fallen off his head . . . and he didn't bother. Now I had what I wanted—the saving mark for my eyes. But I hardly thought of my other self, now gone from the ship, to be hidden forever from all friendly faces, to be a fugitive and a vagabond on the earth, with no brand of the curse on his sane forehead to stay a slaying hand . . . too proud to explain.

And I watched the hat—the expression of my sudden pity for his mere flesh. It had been meant to save his homeless head from the dangers of the sun. And now—behold—it was saving the ship, by serving me for a mark to help out the ignorance of my strangeness. Ha! It was drifting forward, warning me just in time that the ship had gathered sternway.

"Shift the helm," I said in a low voice to the seaman standing still like a statue.

The man's eyes glistened wildly in the binnacle light as he jumped round to the other side and spun round the wheel.

I walked to the break of the poop. On the overshadowed deck all hands stood by the forebraces waiting for my order. The stars ahead seemed to be gliding from right to left. And all was so still in the world that I heard the quiet remark, "She's round," passed in a tone of intense relief between two seamen.

"Let go and haul."

The foreyards ran round with a great noise, amidst cheery cries. And now the frightful whiskers made themselves heard giving various orders. Already the ship was drawing ahead. And I was alone with her. Nothing! no one in the world should stand now between us, throwing a shadow on the way of silent knowledge and mute affection, the perfect communion of a seaman with his first command.

Walking to the taffrail, I was in time to make out, on the very edge of a darkness thrown by a towering black mass like the very gateway of Erebus—yes, I was in time to catch an evanescent glimpse of my white hat left behind to mark the spot where the secret sharer of my cabin and of my thoughts, as though he were my second self, had lowered himself into the water to take his punishment: a free man, a proud swimmer striking out for a new destiny.

ANTON CHEKHOV

1860–1904

A doctor by profession, Chekhov trained himself to look at human experience clinically, without betraying in obvious ways his strong emotional involvement with the people observed. Yet he was a man of compassion who felt in his own life the extremes of ecstasy and despair. Long a sufferer from tuberculosis (from which he died at forty-four), he knew the strange alternating states of consciousness—of delirium, euphoria, and tremendous depression—characteristic of that disease. The result in his writing is a detached view of extraordinary experience. Obsessed, maddened, or profoundly miserable characters are set in relief by the matter-of-factness of the narration. Chekhov feels deeply for these characters, but he wants to show them as they really exist: living among people who are too taken up with their own concerns to pay attention to others' agony.

In the work of Tolstoy and Dostoyevsky, Chekhov's older Russian contemporaries, the characters' extraordinarily intense emotionalism drives the world around them toward a quasi-religious pitch of intensity. In Chekhov's fiction the sufferer or the ecstatic typically produces *no* effect on his environment. He is dismissible, always understood by others as merely queerly apart from the unmelodramatic life that Chekhov's cool narration establishes. Iona's misery, for example, is finally communicable only to his horse.

Outside of Russia Chekhov is best known for the four plays that have become classics of modern drama: *The Seagull, Uncle Vanya, Three Sisters,* and *The Cherry Orchard.* In all of these plays the characters are sympathetically seen as caught in a web of relationships in which their passions, oddities, and traditional allegiances are ineffective. They call out beautifully and movingly, but nobody except the audience leaves his own little world long enough to listen. Events go their own way, without respect to the characters' desires or aspirations.

One can see how suitable a medium the drama was for this vision of reality: characters pour out their private concerns to others on the stage who either ignore them or appropriate them into their own concerns. In productions of his plays, Chekhov always insisted on realistic costumes and sets. Against these modes of realism, his characters revealed the styles of their illusions about themselves and their roles in the world.

Despite his affinity for the theater, Chekhov was successful in it only late in his life, after he had long been famous in Russia for his short stories. As a student he wrote short comic sketches for Moscow newspapers, thereby supporting a desperately poor household consisting of his parents and five brothers and sisters. His father had failed as a grocer in Taganrog, a town in southern Russia, and had fled from his creditors to the obscurity of Moscow's slums. His wife and children moved to a different quarter of the city, and much of the burden of their support then fell on Chekhov. As a writer for the newspapers Chekhov developed a reporter's knack of catching moods in a few words and spotting character-revealing detail. These qualities he began to develop further in the more self-contained form of the short story. Though as he grew more famous he could afford to write longer stories that did not fit the newspaper format, with some notable exceptions his finest works are no more than about fifteen pages long.

Chekhov's fame as a short-story writer brought him enough money to buy his family a small house and some land in the countryside outside Moscow. There he participated in rural life as a landowner and as a doctor, and made use of his observations in his stories and later in his plays. As his tuberculosis grew worse he was forced to leave the severe climate of Moscow and take up residence in Yalta. His last years were brightened to some extent by his marriage to one of the actresses in the Moscow company that produced his plays, but there was inevitably some strain introduced into the marriage by the husband's having to remain in Yalta while the wife was acting in Moscow. The accounts of Chekhov's last days in a German health resort under the care of German doctors (whom he despised) reveal the cynical yet compassionate sensibility that informs all of his writing. After his death Chekhov was given a great public funeral in Moscow, which by one of those peculiar ironies of history was conducted as he might have imagined it in fiction. The corpse arrived from Germany in a box labeled "Lard." After that error was straightened out, most of the people who had assembled to honor the great writer mistakenly followed to the graveyard the cortege of a military officer that happened to be passing by.

Misery

"To Whom Shall I Tell My Grief?"

The twilight of evening. Big flakes of wet snow are whirling lazily about the street lamps, which have just been lighted, and lying in a thin soft layer on roofs, horses' backs, shoulders, caps. Iona Potapov, the sledge-driver, is all white like a ghost. He sits on the box without stirring, bent as double as the living body can be bent. If a regular snowdrift fell on him it seems as though even then he would not think it necessary to shake it off. . . . His little mare is white and motionless too. Her stillness, the angularity of her lines, and the stick-like straightness of her legs make her look like a halfpenny gingerbread horse. She is probably lost in thought. Anyone who has been torn away from the plough, from the familiar gray landscapes, and cast into the slough, full of monstrous lights, of unceasing uproar and hurrying people, is bound to think.

It is a long time since Iona and his nag have budged. They came out of the yard before dinner-time and not a single fare yet. But now the shades of evening are falling on the town. The pale light of the street lamps changes to a vivid color, and the bustle of the street grows noisier.

"Sledge to Vyborgskaya!" Iona hears. "Sledge!"

Iona starts, and through his snow-plastered eyelashes sees an officer in a military overcoat with a hood over his head.

"To Vyborgskaya," repeats the officer. "Are you asleep? To Vyborgskaya!"

In token of assent Iona gives a tug at the reins which sends cakes of snow flying from the horse's back and shoulders. The officer gets into the sledge. The sledge-driver clicks to the horse, cranes his neck like a swan, rises in his seat, and more from habit than necessity brandishes his whip. The mare cranes her neck, too, crooks her stick-like legs, and hesitatingly sets off. . . .

"Where are you shoving, you devil?" Iona immediately hears shouts from the dark mass shifting to and fro before him. "Where the devil are you going? Keep to the r-right!"

"You don't know how to drive! Keep to the right," says the officer angrily.

A coachman driving a carriage swears at him; a pedestrian crossing the road and brushing the horse's nose with his shoulder looks at him angrily and shakes the snow off his sleeve. Iona fidgets on the box as though he were sitting on thorns, jerks his elbows, and turns his eyes about like one possessed, as though he did not know where he was or why he was there.

"What rascals they all are!" says the officer jocosely. "They are simply doing their best to run up against you or fall under the horse's feet. They must be doing it on purpose."

Iona looks at his fare and moves his lips.... Apparently he means to say something, but nothing comes but a sniff.

"What?" inquires the officer.

Iona gives a wry smile, and straining his throat, brings out huskily: "My son ... er ... my son died this week, sir."

"H'm! What did he die of?"

Iona turns his whole body round to his fare, and says:

"Who can tell! It must have been from fever.... He lay three days in the hospital and then he died.... God's will."

"Turn round, you devil!" comes out of the darkness. "Have you gone cracked, you old dog? Look where you are going!"

"Drive on! drive on! ..." says the officer. "We shan't get there till tomorrow going on like this. Hurry up!"

The sledge-driver cranes his neck again, rises in his seat, and with heavy grace swings his whip. Several times he looks round at the officer, but the latter keeps his eyes shut and is apparently disinclined to listen. Putting his fare down at Vyborgskaya, Iona stops by a restaurant, and again sits huddled up on the box.... Again the wet snow paints him and the horse white. One hour passes, and then another....

Three young men, two tall and thin, one short and hunchbacked, come up, railing at each other and loudly stamping on the pavement with their goloshes.

"Cabby, to the Police Bridge!" the hunchback cries in a cracked voice. "The three of us, ... twenty kopecks!"

Iona tugs at the reins and clicks to his horse. Twenty kopecks is not a fair price, but he has no thoughts for that. Whether it is a rouble or whether it is five kopecks does not matter to him now so long as he has a fare.... The three young men, shoving each other and using bad language, go up to the sledge, and all three try to sit down at once. The question remains to be settled: Which are to sit down and which one is to stand? After a long altercation, ill-temper, and abuse, they come to the conclusion that the hunchback must stand because he is the shortest.

"Well, drive on," says the hunchback in his cracked voice, settling himself and breathing down Iona's neck. "Cut along! What a cap you've got, my friend! You wouldn't find a worse one in all Petersburg ..."

"He-he! ... he-he! ..." laughs Iona. "It's nothing to boast of!"

"Well, then, nothing to boast of, drive on! Are you going to drive like this all the way? Eh? Shall I give you one in the neck?"

"My head aches," says one of the tall ones. "At the Dukmasovs' yesterday Vaska and I drank four bottles of brandy between us."

"I can't make out why you talk such stuff," says the other tall one angrily. "You lie like a brute."

"Strike me dead, it's the truth! ..."

"It's about as true as that a louse coughs."

"He-he!" grins Iona. "Me-er-ry gentlemen!"

"Tfoo! the devil take you!" cries the hunchback indignantly. "Will you get on, you old plague, or won't you? Is that the way to drive? Give her one with the whip. Hang it all, give it her well."

Iona feels behind his back the jolting person and quivering voice of the hunchback. He hears abuse addressed to him, he sees people, and the feeling of loneliness begins little by little to be less heavy on his heart. The hunchback swears at him, till he chokes over some elaborately whimsical string of epithets and is overpowered by his cough. His tall companions begin talking of a certain Nadyezhda Petrovna. Iona looks round at them. Waiting till there is a brief pause, he looks round once more and says:

"This week . . . er . . . my . . . er . . . son died!"

"We shall all die . . ." says the hunchback with a sigh, wiping his lips after coughing. "Come, drive on! drive on! My friends, I simply cannot stand crawling like this! When will he get us there?"

"Well, you give him a little encouragement . . . one in the neck!"

"Do you hear, you old plague? I'll make you smart. If one stands on ceremony with fellows like you one may as well walk. Do you hear, you old dragon? Or don't you care a hang what we say?"

And Iona hears rather than feels a slap on the back of his neck.

"He-he! . . ." he laughs. "Merry gentlemen. . . . God give you health!"

"Cabman, are you married?" asks one of the tall ones.

"I? He-he! Me-er-ry gentlemen. The only wife for me now is the damp earth. . . . He-ho-ho! . . . The grave that is! . . . Here my son's dead and I am alive. . . . It's a strange thing, death has come in at the wrong door. . . . Instead of coming for me it went for my son. . . ."

And Iona turns round to tell them how his son died, but at that point the hunchback gives a faint sigh and announces that, thank God! they have arrived at last. After taking his twenty kopecks, Iona gazes for a long while after the revelers, who disappear into a dark entry. Again he is alone and again there is silence for him. . . . The misery which has been for a brief space eased comes back again and tears his heart more cruelly than ever. With a look of anxiety and suffering Iona's eyes stray restlessly among the crowds moving to and fro on both sides of the street: can he not find among those thousands someone who will listen to him? But the crowds flit by heedless of him and his misery. . . . His misery is immense, beyond all bounds. If Iona's heart were to burst and his misery to flow out, it would flood the whole world, it seems, but yet it is not seen. It has found a hiding-place in such an insignificant shell that one would not have found it with a candle by daylight. . . .

Iona sees a house-porter with a parcel and makes up his mind to address him.

"What time will it be, friend?" he asks.

"Going on for ten. . . . Why have you stopped here? Drive on!"

Iona drives a few paces away, bends himself double, and gives himself up to his misery. He feels it is no good to appeal to people. But before five minutes have passed he draws himself up, shakes his head as though he feels a sharp pain, and tugs at the reins. . . . He can bear it no longer.

"Back to the yard!" he thinks. "To the yard!"

And his little mare, as though she knew his thoughts, falls to trotting. An hour and a half later Iona is sitting by a big dirty stove. On the stove, on the floor, and on the benches are people snoring. The air is full of smells and stuffiness. Iona looks at the sleeping figures, scratches himself, and regrets that he has come home so early. . . .

"I have not earned enough to pay for the oats, even," he thinks. "That's why I am so miserable. A man who knows how to do his work, . . . who has had enough to eat, and whose horse has had enough to eat, is always at ease. . . ."

In one of the corners a young cabman gets up, clears his throat sleepily, and makes for the waterbucket.

"Want a drink?" Iona asks him.

"Seems so."

"May it do you good. . . . But my son is dead, mate. . . . Do you hear? This week in the hospital. . . . It's queer business. . . ."

Iona looks to see the effect produced by his words, but he sees nothing. The young man has covered his head over and is already asleep. The old man sighs and scratches himself. . . . Just as the young man had been thirsty for water, he thirsts for speech. His son will soon have been dead a week, and he has not really talked to anybody yet. . . . He wants to talk of it properly, with deliberation. . . . He wants to tell how his son was taken ill, how he suffered, what he said before he died, how he died. . . . He wants to describe the funeral, and how he went to the hospital to get his son's clothes. He still has his daughter Anisya in the country. . . . And he wants to talk about her too. . . . Yes, he has plenty to talk about now. His listener ought to sigh and exclaim and lament. . . . It would be even better to talk to women. Though they are silly creatures, they blubber at the first word.

"Let's go out and have a look at the mare," Iona thinks. "There is always time for sleep. . . . You'll have sleep enough, no fear. . . ."

He puts on his coat and goes into the stables where his mare is standing. He thinks about oats, about hay, about the weather. . . . He cannot think about his son when he is alone. . . . To talk about him with someone is possible, but to think of him and picture him is insufferable anguish. . . .

"Are you munching?" Iona asks the mare, seeing her shining eyes. "There, munch away, munch away. . . . Since we have not earned enough for oats, we will eat hay. . . . Yes, . . . I have grown too old to drive. . . . My son ought to be driving, not I. . . . He was a real cabman. . . . He ought to have lived. . . ."

Iona is silent for a while, and then he goes on:

"That's how it is, old girl. . . . Kuzma Ionitch is gone. . . . He said good-by to me. . . . He went and died for no reason. . . . Now, suppose you had a little colt, and you were own mother to that little colt. . . . And all at once that same little colt went and died. . . . You'd be sorry, wouldn't you? . . ."

The little mare munches, listens, and breathes on her master's hands. Iona is carried away and tells her all about it.

WILLA CATHER

1873–1947

It has been too easy to categorize Willa Cather as a regional writer, a master of "local color." Just as Faulkner is said to be the southern author, Frost the New England poet, so is she the voice of the pioneers, those hardy people who settled the prairies. Such categories, though they contain a grain of truth, almost always falsify; the nearer they come to accounting for the artist, the weaker the artist. The greater the artists' insights, the more they use their subjects to frame the eternal issues of life; so their art is finally not about the South, or New England, or Nebraska.

The move of Cather's family from Virginia (where she was born) to Nebraska when she was about nine supplied her with her central subject: the people who endured terrible winters and impossible summers to make their mark on the land that stretched endlessly around them; and the pressures upon the more imaginative of them produced by the isolation and cultural thinness of the environment. Her leading characters are often sensitive to the beauty of the earth yet unsatisfied, yearning for some ultimate consummation of the desires and possibilities within them. They live among those who have cut back such yearnings—or perhaps they never had them—good people who are practical, the savers, the acceptors of routine or conformity. Cather's most interesting characters imagine beyond the vast distances that separate the farms and small towns of the prairie from the coasts of America. They dream of the fulfillment of a human dream that transcends the petty and the local, yet they are punished for their extravagance, tortured by romantic vistas.

Like Maupassant, Cather was an admirer of Flaubert, whose precision of language was matched with a detestation of the bourgeois and a simultaneous attraction to and criticism of the romantic vision—typically that of his most famous character, Madame Bovary. Something of that mixture of attitudes is easy to see in "Paul's Case," in which Paul, who delights in apprehending the world through sensual textures, contrasts his hemmed-in life in Pittsburgh, epitomized by "the cold bathroom with the grimy zinc tub, the cracked mirror, the dripping spigots," with the imagined magic of the Waldorf: "the lights, the chatter, the perfumes, the bewildering medley of color—he had, for a moment, the feeling of not being able to stand it."

Paul is of course not Cather, as the precise objective narrative (as well as the clinical title) makes clear, but just as in Joyce's portrayal of the boy in "Araby," there is a great sympathy with his yearnings. They may be tawdry —cheap snatches of operas, textures, "scenes"—but at his age and with his limited opportunities for experience, they are all he can be expected to have, and they set Paul apart from his Cordelia-Street environment, making the reader regret and yet admire his final decision. Whereas Oates clearly despises the romantic illusions of her heroine in "Where Have I Been, Where Am I Going?" and Welty finds her hero's too narrow, Cather reveals a great attachment to Paul's.

Far from a western rustic, Cather was extremely intellectual. As a child she learned the classics from her grandmother, and she had a distinguished career at the University of Nebraska. The great influence on her early life was Virgil, whose elegaic mood continued to be apparent in her work throughout her career. She always felt alone, separated from those around her yet sympathetic to their lives. When she moved to Pittsburgh at the age of twenty-three, she entered a sophisticated world that she had only dreamed and read about. The wealth of the great steel and banking families was being poured into cultural and artistic channels. For a while Cather interviewed visiting performers of opera, music, and the theater, whose seemingly glamorous existence contrasted her mundane life in a boarding house. She later moved into the house of an extremely wealthy friend—the contrast between her new style of life and her old serving to reinforce the disparity she saw between the great industrialists and bankers of Pittsburgh and those struggling to establish themselves. It was not the social disparity that attracted her, but the lack of imaginative opportunity that the lower-middle class experienced—the constriction of their possibilities.

Although she was the exponent of the life of the artist, she worried (as her admired Henry James did) whether the perspective of art entailed her removal from participation in the realities of everyday life. After the money earned from her writing allowed her to stop doing such jobs as magazine writer, editor, and teacher of classics and English in a Pittsburgh high school, she lived in New York (where she at first worked as editor-in-chief of *McClure's Magazine*)—summoning up in her books the remembrances of the young girl that beheld life on the prairie.

Though her genius was best expressed by pioneer life, Cather did not write exclusively about it. Her best novels include *O Pioneers!, My Ántonia, A Lost Lady, Death Comes for the Archbishop,* and, perhaps her darkest work, the remarkable *My Mortal Enemy.*

Paul's Case

It was Paul's afternoon to appear before the faculty of the Pittsburgh High School to account for his various misdemeanors. He had been suspended a week ago, and his father had called at the Principal's office and confessed his perplexity about his son. Paul entered the faculty room suave and smiling. His clothes were a trifle outgrown, and the tan velvet on the collar of his open overcoat was frayed and worn; but for all that there was something of the dandy about him, and he wore an opal pin in his neatly knotted black four-in-hand, and a red carnation in his buttonhole. This latter adornment the faculty somehow felt was not properly significant of the contrite spirit befitting a boy under the ban of suspension.

Paul was tall for his age and very thin, with high, cramped shoulders and a narrow chest. His eyes were remarkable for a certain hysterical brilliancy, and he continually used them in a conscious, theatrical sort of way, peculiarly offensive in a boy. The pupils were abnormally large, as though he were addicted to belladonna, but there was a glassy glitter about them which that drug does not produce.

When questioned by the Principal as to why he was there, Paul stated, politely enough, that he wanted to come back to school. This was a lie, but Paul was quite accustomed to lying; found it, indeed, indispensable for overcoming friction. His teachers were asked to state their respective charges against him, which they did with such a rancour and aggrievedness as evinced that this was not a usual case. Disorder and impertinence were among the offences named, yet each of his instructors felt that it was scarcely possible to put into words the real cause of the trouble, which lay in a sort of hysterically defiant manner of the boy's; in the contempt which they all knew he felt for them, and which he seemingly made not the least effort to conceal. Once, when he had been making a synopsis of a paragraph at the blackboard, his English teacher had stepped to his side and attempted to guide his hand. Paul had started back with a shudder and thrust his hands violently behind him. The astonished woman could scarcely have been more hurt and embarrassed had he struck at her. The insult was so involuntary and definitely personal as to be unforgettable. In one way and another, he had made all his teachers, men and women alike, conscious of the same feeling of physical aversion. In one class he habitually sat with his hand shading his eyes; in another he always looked out of the window during the recitation; in another he made a running commentary on the lecture, with humorous intent.

His teachers felt this afternoon that his whole attitude was symbolized by his shrug and his flippantly red carnation flower, and they fell upon him without mercy, his English teacher leading the pack. He stood through it smiling, his pale lips parted over his white teeth. (His lips were continually twitching, and he had a habit of raising his eyebrows that was contemptuous and irritating to the last degree.) Older boys than Paul had broken down and shed tears under that ordeal, but his set smile did not once desert him, and his only sign of discomfort was the nervous trembling of the fingers that toyed with the buttons of his overcoat, and an occasional jerking of the other hand which held his hat. Paul was always smiling, always glancing about him, seeming to feel that people might be watching him and trying to detect something. This conscious expression, since it was as far as possible from boyish mirthfulness, was usually attributed to insolence or "smartness."

As the inquisition proceeded, one of his instructors repeated an impertinent remark of the boy's, and the Principal asked him whether he thought that a courteous speech to make to a woman. Paul shrugged his shoulders slightly and his eyebrows twitched.

"I don't know," he replied. "I didn't mean to be polite or impolite, either. I guess it's a sort of way I have, of saying things regardless."

The Principal asked him whether he didn't think that a way it would be well to get rid of. Paul grinned and said he guessed so. When he was told that he could go, he bowed gracefully and went out. His bow was like a repetition of the scandalous red carnation.

His teachers were in despair, and his drawing-master voiced the feeling of them all when he declared there was something about the boy which none of them understood. He added: "I don't really believe that smile of his comes altogether from insolence; there's something sort of haunted about it. The boy is not strong, for one thing. There is something wrong about the fellow."

The drawing-master had come to realize that, in looking at Paul, one saw only his white teeth and the forced animation of his eyes. One warm afternoon the boy had gone to sleep at his drawing-board, and his master had noted with amazement what a white, blue-veined face it was; drawn and wrinkled like an old man's about the eyes, the lips twitching even in his sleep.

His teachers left the building dissatisfied and unhappy; humiliated to have felt so vindictive toward a mere boy, to have uttered this feeling in cutting terms, and to have set each other on, as it were, in the gruesome game of intemperate reproach. One of them remembered having seen a miserable street cat set at bay by a ring of tormentors.

As for Paul, he ran down the hill whistling the Soldiers' Chorus from "Faust," looking behind him now and then to see whether some of his teachers were not there to witness his light-heartedness. As it was now late in the afternoon and Paul was on duty that evening as usher at Carnegie Hall, he decided that he would not go home to supper.

When he reached the concert hall, the doors were not yet open. It was chilly outside, and he decided to go up into the picture gallery—always deserted at this hour—where there were some of Raffelli's gay studies of Paris streets and an airy blue Venetian scene or two that always exhilarated him. He was delighted to find no one in the gallery but the old guard, who sat in the corner, a newspaper on his knee, a black patch over one eye and the other closed. Paul possessed himself of the place and walked confidently up and down, whistling under his breath. After a while he sat down before a blue Rico and lost himself. When he bethought him to look at his watch, it was after seven o'clock, and he rose with a start and ran downstairs, making a face at Augustus Caesar, peering out from the cast-room, and an evil gesture at the Venus of Milo as he passed her on the stairway.

When Paul reached the ushers' dressing-room, half a dozen boys were there already, and he began excitedly to tumble into his uniform. It was one of the few that at all approached fitting, and Paul thought it very becoming —though he knew the tight, straight coat accentuated his narrow chest, about which he was exceedingly sensitive. He was always excited while he dressed, twanging all over to the tuning of the strings and the preliminary flourishes of the horns in the music-room; but tonight he seemed quite beside himself, and he teased and plagued the boys until, telling him that he was crazy, they put him down on the floor and sat on him.

Somewhat calmed by his suppression, Paul dashed out to the front of the house to seat the early comers. He was a model usher. Gracious and smiling he ran up and down the aisles. Nothing was too much trouble for him; he carried messages and brought programmes as though it were his greatest pleasure in life, and all the people in his section thought him a charming boy, feeling that he remembered and admired them. As the house filled, he grew more and more vivacious and animated, and the colour came to his cheeks and lips. It was very much as though this were a great reception and Paul were the host. Just as the musicians came out to take their places, his English teacher arrived with cheques for the seats which a prominent manufacturer had taken for the season. She betrayed some embarrassment when she handed Paul the tickets, and a hauteur which subsequently made her feel very foolish. Paul was startled for a moment, and had the feeling of wanting to put her out; what business had she here among all these fine people and gay colours? He looked her over and decided that she was not appropriately dressed and must be a fool to sit downstairs in such togs. The tickets had probably been sent her out of kindness, he reflected, as he put down a seat for her, and she had about as much right to sit there as he had.

When the symphony began, Paul sank into one of the rear seats with a long sigh of relief, and lost himself as he had done before the Rico. It was not that symphonies, as such, meant anything in particular to Paul, but the first sight of the instruments seemed to free some hilarious spirit within him; something that struggled there like the Genius in the bottle found by the Arab fisherman.

He felt a sudden zest of life; the lights danced before his eyes and the concert hall blazed into unimaginable splendour. When the soprano soloist came on, Paul forgot even the nastiness of his teacher's being there, and gave himself up to the peculiar intoxication such personages always had for him. The soloist chanced to be a German woman, by no means in her first youth, and the mother of many children; but she wore a satin gown and a tiara, and she had that indefinable air of achievement, that world-shine upon her, which always blinded Paul to any possible defects.

After a concert was over, Paul was often irritable and wretched until he got to sleep—and to-night he was even more than usually restless. He had the feeling of not being able to let down; of its being impossible to give up this delicious excitement which was the only thing that could be called living at all. During the last number he withdrew and, after hastily changing his clothes in the dressing-room, slipped out to the side door where the singer's carriage stood. Here he began pacing rapidly up and down the walk, waiting to see her come out.

Over yonder the Schenley, in its vacant stretch, loomed big and square through the fine rain, the windows of its twelve stories glowing like those of a lighted cardboard house under a Christmas tree. All the actors and singers of any importance stayed there when they were in Pittsburgh, and a number of the big manufacturers of the place lived there in the winter. Paul had often hung about the hotel, watching the people go in and out, longing to enter and leave schoolmasters and dull care behind him forever.

At last the singer came out, accompanied by the conductor, who helped her into her carriage and closed the door with a cordial *auf wiedersehen*—which set Paul to wondering whether she were not an old sweetheart of his. Paul followed the carriage over to the hotel, walking so rapidly as not to be far from the entrance when the singer alighted and disappeared behind the swinging glass doors which were opened by a Negro in a tall hat and a long coat. In the moment that the door was ajar, it seemed to Paul that he, too, entered. He seemed to feel himself go after her up the steps, into the warm, lighted building, into an exotic, a tropical world of shiny, glistening surfaces and basking ease. He reflected upon the mysterious dishes that were brought into the dining-room, the green bottles in buckets of ice, as he had seen them in the supper-party pictures of the Sunday supplement. A quick gust of wind brought the rain down with sudden vehemence, and Paul was startled to find that he was still outside in the slush of the gravel driveway; that his boots were letting in the water and his scanty overcoat was clinging wet about him; that the lights in front of the concert hall were out, and that the rain was driving in sheets between him and the orange glow of the windows above him. There it was, what he wanted—tangibly before him, like the fairy world of a Christmas pantomime; as the rain beat in his face, Paul wondered whether he were destined always to shiver in the black night outside, looking up at it.

He turned and walked reluctantly toward the car tracks. The end had to come sometime; his father in his night-clothes at the top of the stairs, explanations that did not explain, hastily improvised fictions that were forever tripping him up, his upstairs room and its horrible yellow wallpaper, the creaking bureau with the greasy plush collar-box, and over his painted wooden bed the pictures of George Washington and John Calvin, and the framed motto, 'Feed my Lambs,' which had been worked in red worsted by his mother, whom Paul could not remember.

Half an hour later, Paul alighted from the Negley Avenue car and went slowly down one of the side streets off the main thoroughfare. It was a highly respectable street, where all the houses were exactly alike, and where business men of moderate means begot and reared large families of children, all of whom went to Sabbath School and learned the shorter catechism, and were interested in arithmetic; all of whom were as exactly alike as their homes, and of a piece with the monotony in which they lived. Paul never went up Cordelia Street without a shudder of loathing. His home was next the house of the Cumberland minister. He approached it to-night with the nerveless sense of defeat, the hopeless feeling of sinking back forever into ugliness and commonness that he had always had when he came home. The moment he turned into Cordelia Street he felt the waters close above his head. After each of these orgies of living, he experienced all the physical depression which follows a debauch; the loathing of respectable beds, of common food, of a house permeated by kitchen odours; a shuddering repulsion for the flavourless, colourless mass of every-day existence; a morbid desire for cool things and soft lights and fresh flowers.

The nearer he approached the house, the more absolutely unequal Paul felt to the sight of it all: his ugly sleeping chamber; the old bathroom with the grimy zinc tub, the cracked mirror, the dripping spigots; his father, at the top of the stairs, his hairy legs sticking out from his nightshirt, his feet thrust into carpet slippers. He was so much later than usual that there would certainly be enquiries and reproaches. Paul stopped short before the door. He felt that he could not be accosted by his father to-night; that he could not toss again on that miserable bed. He would not go in. He would tell his father that he had no car-fare, and it was raining so hard he had gone home with one of the boys and stayed all night.

Meanwhile, he was wet and cold. He went around to the back of the house and tried one of the basement windows, found it open, raised it cautiously, and scrambled down the cellar wall to the floor. There he stood, holding his breath, terrified by the noise he had made; but the floor above him was silent, and there was no creak on the stairs. He found a soap-box, and carried it over to the soft ring of light that streamed from the furnace door, and sat down. He was horribly afraid of rats, so he did not try to sleep, but sat looking distrustfully at the dark, still terrified lest he might have awakened his father.

In such reactions, after one of the experiences which made days and nights out of the dreary blanks of the calendar, when his senses were deadened, Paul's head was always singularly clear. Suppose his father had heard him getting in at the window and had come down and shot him for a burglar? Then, again, suppose his father had come down, pistol in hand, and he had cried out in time to save himself, and his father had been horrified to think how nearly he had killed him? Then again, suppose a day should come when his father would remember that night, and wish there had been no warning cry to stay his hand? With this last supposition Paul entertained himself until daybreak.

The following Sunday was fine; the sodden November chill was broken by the last flash of autumnal summer. In the morning Paul had to go to church and Sabbath School, as always. On seasonable Sunday afternoons the burghers of Cordelia Street usually sat out on their front "stoops," and talked to their neighbours on the next stoop, or called to those across the street in neighbourly fashion. The men sat placidly on gay cushions placed upon the steps that led down to the sidewalk, while the women, in their Sunday "waists," sat in rockers on the cramped porches, pretending to be greatly at their ease. The children played in the streets; there were so many of them that the place resembled the recreation grounds of a kindergarten. The men on the steps, all in their shirt-sleeves, their vests unbuttoned, sat with their legs well apart, their stomachs comfortably protruding, and talked of the prices of things, or told anecdotes of the sagacity of their various chiefs and overlords. They occasionally looked over the multitude of squabbling children, listened affectionately to their high-pitched, nasal voices, smiling to see their own proclivities reproduced in their offspring, and interspersed their legends of the iron kings with remarks about their sons' progress at school, their grades in arithmetic, and the amounts they had saved in their toy banks.

On this last Sunday of November, Paul sat all the afternoon on the lowest step of his "stoop," staring into the street, while his sisters, in their rockers, were talking to the minister's daughters next door about how many shirtwaists they had made in the last week, and how many waffles someone had eaten at the last church supper. When the weather was warm, and his father was in a particularly jovial frame of mind, the girls made lemonade, which was always brought out in a red-glass pitcher, ornamented with forget-me-nots in blue enamel. This the girls thought very fine, and the neighbours joked about the suspicious colour of the pitcher.

To-day Paul's father, on the top step, was talking to a young man who shifted a restless baby from knee to knee. He happened to be the young man who was daily held up to Paul as a model, and after whom it was his father's dearest hope that he would pattern. This young man was of a ruddy complexion, with a compressed, red mouth, and faded, nearsighted eyes, over which he wore thick spectacles, with gold bows that curved about his ears. He was clerk to one of the magnates of a great steel corporation, and was looked upon in Cordelia Street as a young man with a future. There was a story that, some five years ago—he was now barely twenty-six—he had been a trifle "dissipated," but in order to curb his appetites and save the loss of time and strength that a sowing of wild oats might have entailed, he had taken his chief's advice, oft reiterated to his employees, and at twenty-one had married the first woman whom he could persuade to share his fortunes. She happened to be an angular schoolmistress, much older than he, who also wore thick glasses, and who had now borne him four children, all nearsighted like herself.

The young man was relating how his chief, now cruising in the Mediterranean, kept in touch with all the details of the business, arranging his office hours on his yacht just as though he were at home, and "knocking off work enough to keep two stenographers busy." His father told, in turn, the plan his corporation was considering, of putting in an electric railway plant at Cairo. Paul snapped his teeth; he had an awful apprehension that they might spoil it all before he got there. Yet he rather liked to hear these legends of the iron kings, that were told and retold on Sundays and holidays; these stories of palaces in Venice, yachts on the Mediterranean, and high play at Monte Carlo appealed to his fancy, and he was interested in the triumphs of cash-boys who had become famous, though he had no mind for the cash-boy stage.

After supper was over, and he had helped to dry the dishes, Paul nervously asked his father whether he could go to George's to get some help in his geometry, and still more nervously asked for car-fare. This latter request he had to repeat, as his father, on principle, did not like to hear requests for money, whether much or little. He asked Paul whether he could not go to some boy who lived nearer, and told him that he ought not to leave his school work until Sunday; but he gave him the dime. He was not a poor man, but he had a worthy ambition to come up in the world. His only reason for allowing Paul to usher was that he thought a boy ought to be earning a little.

Paul bounded upstairs, scrubbed the greasy odour of the dishwater from his hands with the ill-smelling soap he hated, and then shook over his fingers a few drops of violet water from the bottle he kept hidden in his drawer. He left the house with his geometry conspicuously under his arm, and the moment he got out of Cordelia Street and boarded a downtown car, he shook off the lethargy of two deadening days, and began to live again.

The leading juvenile of the permanent stock company which played at one of the downtown theatres was an acquaintance of Paul's, and the boy had been invited to drop in at the Sunday-night rehearsals whenever he could. For more than a year Paul had spent every available moment loitering about Charley Edwards's dressing-room. He had won a place among Edwards's following not only because the young actor, who could not afford to employ a dresser, often found him useful, but because he recognized in Paul something akin to what churchmen term "vocation."

It was at the theatre and at Carnegie Hall that Paul really lived; the rest was but a sleep and a forgetting. This was Paul's fairy tale, and it had for him all the allurement of a secret love. The moment he inhaled the gassy, painty, dusty odour behind the scenes, he breathed like a prisoner set free, and felt within him the possibility of doing or saying splendid, brilliant things. The moment the cracked orchestra beat out the overture from "Martha," or jerked at the serenade from "Rigoletto," all stupid and ugly things slid from him, and his senses were deliciously, yet delicately fired.

Perhaps it was because, in Paul's world, the natural nearly always wore the guise of ugliness, that a certain element of artificiality seemed to him necessary in beauty. Perhaps it was because his experience of life elsewhere was so full of Sabbath-School picnics, petty economies, wholesome advice as to how to succeed in life, and the unescapable odours of cooking, that he found this existence so alluring, these smartly clad men and women so attractive, that he was so moved by these starry apple orchards that bloomed perennially under the limelight. It would be difficult to put it strongly enough how convincingly the stage entrance of that theatre was for Paul the actual portal of Romance. Certainly none of the company ever suspected it, least of all Charley Edwards. It was very like the old stories that used to float about London of fabulously rich Jews, who had subterranean halls, with palms, and fountains, and soft lamps and richly apparelled women who never saw the disenchanting light of London day. So, in the midst of that smoke-palled city, enamoured of figures and grimy toil, Paul had his secret temple, his wishing-carpet, his bit of blue-and-white Mediterranean shore bathed in perpetual sunshine.

Several of Paul's teachers had a theory that his imagination had been perverted by garish fiction; but the truth was he scarcely ever read at all. The books at home were not such as would either tempt or corrupt a youthful mind, and as for reading the novels that some of his friends urged upon him —well, he got what he wanted much more quickly from music; any sort of music, from an orchestra to a barrel-organ. He needed only the spark, the indescribable thrill that made his imagination master of his senses, and he could make plots and pictures enough of his own. It was equally true that he was not stage-struck—not, at any rate, in the usual acceptation of that expression. He had no desire to become an actor, any more than he had to become a musician. He felt no necessity to do any of these things; what he wanted was to see, to be in the atmosphere, float on the wave of it, to be carried out, blue league after league, away from everything.

After a night behind the scenes, Paul found the schoolroom more than ever repulsive; the bare floors and naked walls; the prosy men who never wore frock coats, or violets in their buttonholes; the women with their dull gowns, shrill voices, and pitiful seriousness about prepositions that govern the dative. He could not bear to have the other pupils think, for a moment, that he took these people seriously; he must convey to them that he considered it all trivial, and was there only by way of a joke, anyway. He had autographed pictures of all the members of the stock company which he showed his classmates, telling them the most incredible stories of his familiarity with these people, of his acquaintance with the soloists who came to Carnegie Hall, his suppers with them and the flowers he sent them. When these stories lost their effect, and his audience grew listless, he would bid all the boys goodbye, announcing that he was going to travel for a while; going to Naples, to California, to Egypt. Then, next Monday, he would slip back, conscious and nervously smiling; his sister was ill, and he would have to defer his voyage until spring.

Matters went steadily worse with Paul at school. In the itch to let his instructors know how heartily he despised them, and how thoroughly he was appreciated elsewhere, he mentioned once or twice that he had no time to fool with theorems; adding—with a twitch of the eyebrows and a touch of that nervous bravado which so perplexed them—that he was helping the people down at the stock company; they were old friends of his.

The upshot of the matter was that the Principal went to Paul's father, and Paul was taken out of school and put to work. The manager at Carnegie Hall was told to get another usher in his stead; the doorkeeper at the theatre was warned not to admit him to the house; and Charley Edwards remorsefully promised the boy's father not to see him again.

The members of the stock company were vastly amused when some of Paul's stories reached them—especially the women. They were hard-working women, most of them supporting indolent husbands or brothers, and they laughed rather bitterly at having stirred the boy to such fervid and florid inventions. They agreed with the faculty and with his father, that Paul's was a bad case.

The east-bound train was ploughing through a January snowstorm; the dull dawn was beginning to show grey when the engine whistled a mile out of Newark. Paul started up from the seat where he had lain curled in uneasy slumber, rubbed the breath-misted window-glass with his hand, and peered out. The snow was whirling in curling eddies above the white bottom lands, and the drifts lay already deep in the fields and along the fences, while here and there the tall dead grass and dried weed stalks protruded black above it. Lights shone from the scattered houses, and a gang of labourers who stood beside the track waved their lanterns.

Paul had slept very little, and he felt grimy and uncomfortable. He had made the all-night journey in a day coach because he was afraid if he took a Pullman he might be seen by some Pittsburgh business man who had noticed him in Denny and Carson's office. When the whistle woke him, he clutched quickly at his breast pocket, glancing about him with a uncertain smile. But the little, clay-bespattered Italians were still sleeping, the slatternly women across the aisle were in open-mouthed oblivion, and even the crumby, crying babies were for the time stilled. Paul settled back to struggle with his impatience as best he could.

When he arrived at the Jersey City station, he hurried through his breakfast, manifestly ill at ease and keeping a sharp eye about him. After he reached the Twenty-Third Street station, he consulted a cabman, and had himself driven to a men's furnishing establishment which was just opening for the day. He spent upward of two hours there, buying with endless reconsidering and great care. His new street suit he put on in the fitting-room; the frock coat and dress clothes he had bundled into the cab with his new shirts. Then he drove to a hatter's and a shoe house. His next errand was at Tiffany's, where he selected silver-mounted brushes and a scarf-pin. He would not wait to have his silver marked, he said. Lastly, he stopped at a trunk shop on Broadway, and had his purchases packed into various travelling-bags.

It was a little after one o'clock when he drove up to the Waldorf, and, after settling with the cabman, went into the office. He registered from Washington; said his mother and father had been abroad, and that he had come down to await the arrival of their steamer. He told his story plausibly and had no trouble, since he offered to pay for them in advance, in engaging his rooms; a sleeping-room, sitting-room, and bath.

Not once, but a hundred times Paul had planned this entry into New York. He had gone over every detail of it with Charley Edwards, and in his scrapbook at home there were pages of description about New York hotels, cut from the Sunday papers.

When he was shown to his sitting-room on the eighth floor, he saw at a glance that everything was as it should be; there was but one detail in his mental picture that the place did not realize, so he rang for the bell-boy and sent him down for flowers. He moved about nervously until the boy returned, putting away his new linen and fingering it delightedly as he did so. When the flowers came, he put them hastily into water, and then tumbled into a hot bath. Presently he came out of his white bathroom, resplendent in his new silk underwear, and playing with the tassels of his red robe. The snow was whirling so fiercely outside his windows that he could scarcely see across the street; but within, the air was deliciously soft and fragrant. He put the violets and jonquils on the tabouret beside the couch, and threw himself down with a long sigh, covering himself with a Roman blanket. He was thoroughly tired; he had been in such haste, he had stood up to such a strain, covered so much ground in the last twenty-four hours, that he wanted to think how it had all come about. Lulled by the sound of the wind, the warm air, and the cool fragrance of the flowers, he sank into deep, drowsy retrospection.

It had been wonderfully simple; when they had shut him out of the theatre and concert hall, when they had taken away his bone, the whole thing was virtually determined. The rest was a mere matter of opportunity. The only thing that at all surprised him was his own courage—for he realized well enough that he had always been tormented by fear, a sort of apprehensive dread which, of late years, as the meshes of the lies he had told closed about him, had been pulling the muscles of his body tighter and tighter. Until now, he could not remember a time when he had not been dreading something. Even when he was a little boy, it was always there—behind him, or before, or on either side. There had always been the shadowed corner, the dark place into which he dared not look, but from which something seemed always to be watching him—and Paul had done things that were not pretty to watch, he knew.

But now he had a curious sense of relief, as though he had at last thrown down the gauntlet to the thing in the corner.

Yet it was but a day since he had been sulking in the traces; but yesterday afternoon that he had been sent to the bank with Denny and Carson's deposit, as usual—but this time he was instructed to leave the book to be balanced. There was above two thousand dollars in cheques, and nearly a thousand in the banknotes which he had taken from the book and quietly transferred to his pocket. At the bank he had made out a new deposit slip. His nerves had been steady enough to permit of his returning to the office, where he had finished his work and asked for a full day's holiday to-morrow, Saturday, giving a perfectly reasonable pretext. The bank book he knew, would not be returned before Monday or Tuesday, and his father would be out of town for the next week. From the time he slipped the banknotes into his pocket until he boarded the night train for New York, he had not known a moment's hesitation.

How astonishingly easy it had all been; here he was, the thing done; and this time there would be no awakening, no figure at the top of the stairs. He watched the snowflakes whirling by his window until he fell asleep.

When he awoke, it was four o'clock in the afternoon. He bounded up with a start; one of his precious days gone already! He spent nearly an hour in dressing, watching every stage of his toilet carefully in the mirror. Everything was quite perfect; he was exactly the kind of boy he had always wanted to be.

When he went downstairs, Paul took a carriage and drove up Fifth Avenue toward the Park. The snow had somewhat abated; carriages and tradesmen's wagons were hurrying soundlessly to and fro in the winter twilight; boys in woollen mufflers were shovelling off the doorsteps; the Avenue stages made fine spots of colour against the white street. Here and there on the corners whole flower gardens blooming behind glass windows, against which the snowflakes stuck and melted; violets, roses, carnations, lilies-of-the-valley—somehow vastly more lovely and alluring that they blossomed thus unnaturally in the snow. The Park itself was a wonderful stage winter-piece.

When he returned, the pause of the twilight had ceased, and the tune of the streets had changed. The snow was falling faster, lights streamed from the hotels that reared their many stories fearlessly up into the storm, defying the raging Atlantic winds. A long, black stream of carriages poured down the Avenue, intersected here and there by other streams, tending horizontally. There were a score of cabs about the entrance of his hotel, and his driver had to wait. Boys in livery were running in and out of the awning stretched across the sidewalk, up and down the red velvet carpet laid from the door to the street. Above, about, within it all, was the rumble and roar, the hurry and toss of thousands of human beings as hot for pleasure as himself, and on every side of him towered the glaring affirmation of the omnipotence of wealth.

The boy set his teeth and drew his shoulders together in a spasm of realization; the plot of all dramas, the text of all romances, the nerve-stuff of all sensations was whirling about him like the snowflakes. He burnt like a fagot in a tempest.

When Paul came down to dinner, the music of the orchestra floated up the elevator shaft to greet him. As he stepped into the thronged corridor, he sank back into one of the chairs against the wall to get his breath. The lights, the chatter, the perfumes, the bewildering medley of colour—he had, for a moment, the feeling of not being able to stand it. But only for a moment; these were his own people, he told himself. He went slowly about the corridors, through the writing-rooms, smoking-rooms, reception-rooms, as though he were exploring the chambers of an enchanted palace, built and peopled for him alone.

When he reached the dining-room he sat down at a table near a window. The flowers, the white linen, the many-coloured wine-glasses, the gay toilettes of the women, the low popping of corks, the undulating repetitions of the "Blue Danube" from the orchestra, all flooded Paul's dream with bewildering radiance. When the roseate tinge of his champagne was added—that cold, precious, bubbling stuff that creamed and foamed in his glass—Paul wondered that there were honest men in the world at all. This was what all the world was fighting for, he reflected; this was what all the struggle was about. He doubted the reality of his past. Had he ever known a place called Cordelia Street, a place where fagged-looking business men boarded the early car? Mere rivets in a machine they seemed to Paul—sickening men, with combings of children's hair always hanging to their coats, and the smell of cooking in their clothes. Cordelia Street—Ah, that belonged to another time and country! Had he not always been thus, had he not sat here night after night, from as far back as he could remember, looking pensively over just such shimmering textures, and slowly twirling the stem of a glass like this one between his thumb and middle finger? He rather thought he had.

He was not in the least abashed or lonely. He had no especial desire to meet or to know any of these people; all he demanded was the right to look on and conjecture, to watch the pageant. The mere stage properties were all he contended for. Nor was he lonely later in the evening, in his loge at the Opera. He was entirely rid of his nervous misgivings, of his forced aggressiveness, of the imperative desire to show himself different from his surroundings. He felt now that his surroundings explained him. Nobody questioned the purple; he had only to wear it passively. He had only to glance down at his dress coat to reassure himself that here it would be impossible for anyone to humiliate him.

He found it hard to leave his beautiful sitting-room to go to bed that night, and sat long watching the raging storm from his turret window. When he went to sleep, it was with the lights turned on in his bedroom; partly because of his old timidity, and partly so that, if he should wake in the night, there would be no wretched moment of doubt, no horrible suspicion of yellow wallpaper, or of Washington and Calvin above his bed.

On Sunday morning the city was practically snowbound. Paul breakfasted late, and in the afternoon he fell in with a wild San Francisco boy, a freshman at Yale, who said he had run down for a "little flyer" over Sunday. The young man offered to show Paul the night side of the town, and the two boys went off together after dinner, not returning to the hotel until seven o'clock the next morning. They had started out in the confiding warmth of a champagne friendship, but their parting in the elevator was singularly cool. The freshman pulled himself together to make his train, and Paul went to bed. He awoke at two o'clock in the afternoon, very thirsty and dizzy, and rang for ice-water, coffee, and the Pittsburgh papers.

On the part of the hotel management, Paul excited no suspicion. There was this to be said for him, that he wore his spoils with dignity and in no way made himself conspicuous. His chief greediness lay in his ears and eyes, and his excesses were not offensive ones. His dearest pleasures were the grey winter twilights in his sitting-room; his quiet enjoyment of his flowers, his clothes, his wide divan, his cigarette, and his sense of power. He could not remember a time when he had felt so at peace with himself. The mere release from the necessity of petty lying, lying every day and every day, restored his self-respect. He had never lied for pleasure, even at school; but to make himself noticed and admired, to assert his difference from other Cordelia Street boys; and he felt a good deal more manly, more honest, even, now that he had no need for boastful pretensions, now that he could, as his actor friends used to say, "dress the part."

It was characteristic that remorse did not occur to him. His golden days went by without a shadow, and he made each as perfect as he could.

On the eighth day after his arrival in New York, he found the whole affair exploited in the Pittsburgh papers, exploited with a wealth of detail which indicated that local news of a sensational nature was at a low ebb. The firm of Denny and Carson announced that the boy's father had refunded the full amount of his theft, and that they had no intention of prosecuting. The Cumberland minister had been interviewed, and expressed his hope of yet reclaiming the motherless lad, and Paul's Sabbath-School teacher declared that she would spare no effort to that end. The rumour had reached Pittsburgh that the boy had been seen in a New York hotel, and his father had gone East to find him and bring him home.

Paul had just come in to dress for dinner; he sank into a chair, weak in the knees, and clasped his head in his hands. It was to be worse than jail, even; the tepid waters of Cordelia Street were to close over him finally and forever. The grey monotony stretched before him in hopeless, unrelieved years;—Sabbath-School, Young People's Meeting, the yellow-papered room, the damp dishtowels; it all rushed back upon him with sickening vividness. He had the old feeling that the orchestra had suddenly stopped, the sinking sensation that the play was over. The sweat broke out on his face, and he sprang to his feet, looked about him with his white, conscious smile, and winked at himself in the mirror. With something of the childish belief in miracles with which he had so often gone to class, all his lessons unlearned, Paul dressed and dashed whistling down the corridor to the elevator.

He had no sooner entered the dining-room and caught the measure of the music than his remembrance was lightened by his old elastic power of claiming the moment, mounting with it, and finding it all-sufficient. The glare and glitter about him, the mere scenic accessories had again, and for the last time, their old potency. He would show himself that he was game, he would finish the thing splendidly. He doubted, more than ever, the existence of Cordelia Street, and for the first time he drank his wine recklessly. Was he not, after all, one of these fortunate beings? Was he not still himself, and in his own place? He drummed a nervous accompaniment to the music and looked about him, telling himself over and over that it had paid.

He reflected drowsily, to the swell of the violin and the chill sweetness of his wine, that he might have done it more wisely. He might have caught an outbound steamer and been well out of their clutches before now. But the other side of the world had seemed too far away and too uncertain then; he could not have waited for it; his need had been too sharp. If he had to choose over again, he would do the same thing to-morrow. He looked affectionately about the dining-room, now gilded with a soft mist. Ah, it had paid indeed!

Paul was awakened next morning by a painful throbbing in his head and feet. He had thrown himself across the bed without undressing, and had slept with his shoes on. His limbs and hands were lead-heavy, and his tongue and throat were parched. There came upon him one of those fateful attacks of clear-headedness that never occurred except when he was physically exhausted and his nerves hung loose. He lay still and closed his eyes and let the tide of realities wash over him.

His father was in New York; "stopping at some joint or other," he told himself. The memory of successive summers on the front stoop fell upon him like a weight of black water. He had not a hundred dollars left; and he knew now, more than ever, that money was everything, the wall that stood between all he loathed and all he wanted. The thing was winding itself up; he had thought of that on his first glorious day in New York, and had even provided a way to snap the thread. It lay on his dressing-table now; he had got it out last night when he came blindly up from dinner—but the shiny metal hurt his eyes, and he disliked the look of it, anyway.

He rose and moved about with a painful effort, succumbing now and again to attacks of nausea. It was the old depression exaggerated; all the world had become Cordelia Street. Yet somehow he was not afraid of anything, was absolutely calm; perhaps because he had looked into the dark corner at last, and knew. It was bad enough, what he saw there; but somehow not so bad as his long fear of it had been. He saw everything clearly now. He had a feeling that he had made the best of it, that he had lived the sort of life he was meant to live, and for half an hour he sat staring at the revolver. But he told himself that was not the way, so he went downstairs and took a cab to the ferry.

When Paul arrived at Newark, he got off the train and took another cab, directing the driver to follow the Pennsylvania tracks out of town. The snow lay heavy on the roadways and had drifted deep in the open fields. Only here and there the dead grass or dried weed stalks projected, singularly black, above it.

Once well into the country, Paul dismissed the carriage and walked, floundering along the tracks, his mind a medley of irrelevant things. He seemed to hold in his brain an actual picture of everything he had seen that morning. He remembered every feature of both his drivers, the toothless old woman from whom he had bought the red flowers in his coat, the agent from whom he had got his ticket, and all of the fellow-passengers on the ferry. His mind, unable to cope with vital matters near at hand, worked feverishly and deftly at sorting and grouping these images. They made for him a part of the ugliness of the world, of the ache in his head, and the bitter burning on his tongue. He stooped and put a handful of snow into his mouth as he walked, but that, too, seemed hot. When he reached a little hillside, where the tracks ran through a cut some twenty feet below him, he stopped and sat down.

The carnations in his coat were drooping with the cold, he noticed; their red glory over. It occurred to him that all the flowers he had seen in the show windows that first night must have gone the same way, long before this. It was only one splendid breath they had, in spite of their brave mockery at the winter outside the glass. It was a losing game in the end, it seemed, this revolt against the homilies by which the world is run. Paul took one of the blossoms carefully from his coat and scooped a little hole in the snow, where he covered it up. Then he dozed awhile, from his weak condition, seeming insensible to the cold.

The sound of an approaching train woke him and he started to his feet, remembering only his resolution, and afraid lest he should be too late. He stood watching the approaching locomotive, his teeth chattering, his lips drawn away from them in a frightened smile; once or twice he glanced nervously sidewise, as though he were being watched. When the right moment came, he jumped. As he fell, the folly of his haste occurred to him with merciless clearness, the vastness of what he had left undone. There flashed through his brain, clearer than ever before, the blue of Adriatic water, the yellow of Algerian sands.

He felt something strike his chest—his body was being thrown swiftly through the air, on and on, immeasurably far and fast, while his limbs gently relaxed. Then, because the picture-making mechanism was crushed, the disturbing visions flashed into black, and Paul dropped back into the immense design of things.

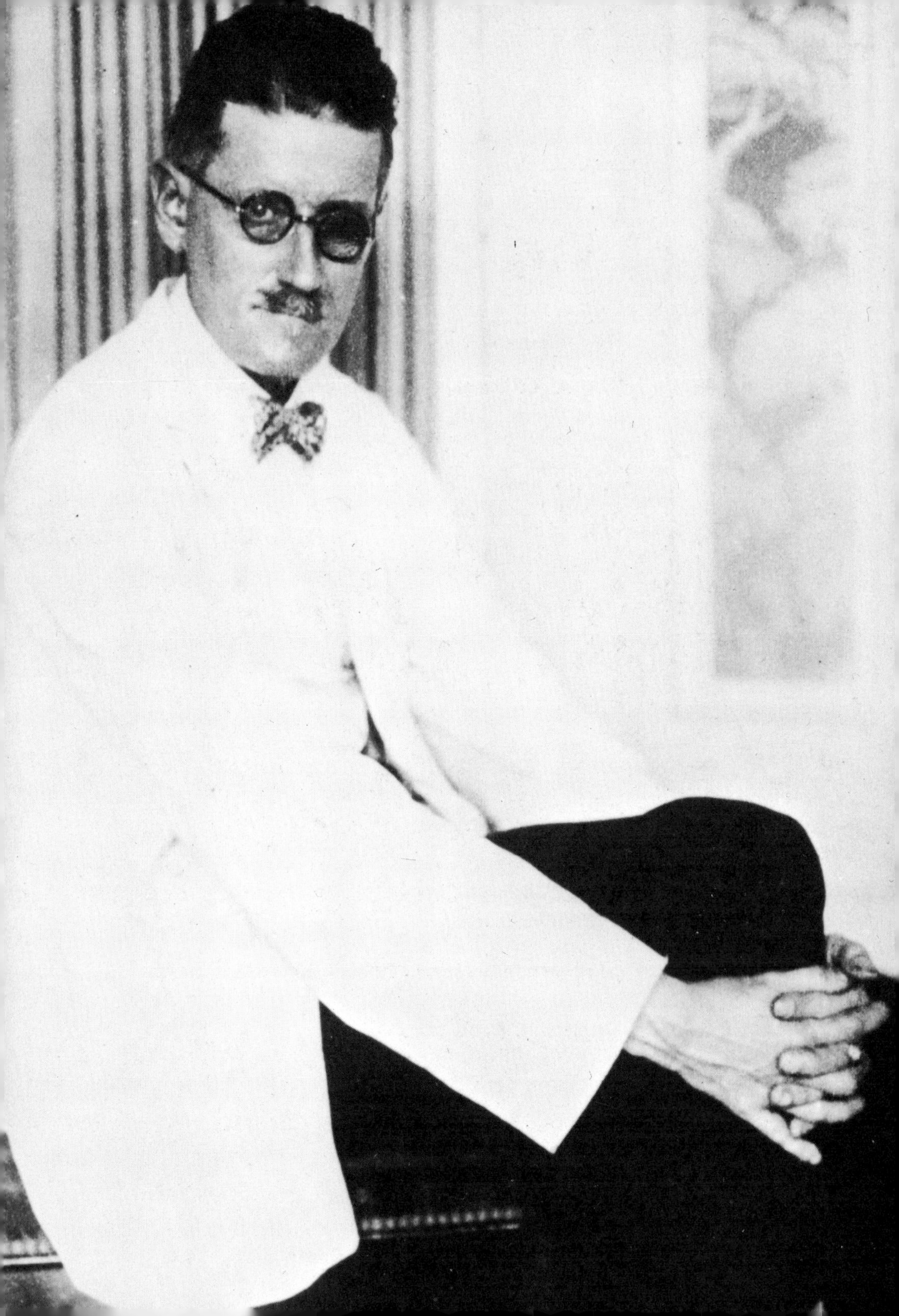

JAMES JOYCE

1882–1941

For Joyce the city of Dublin was a microcosm of the past of Western civilization: Dublin lay embalmed among classic eighteenth-century architecture; popular sentimental songs of lost loves and lost causes; the voices of Bishop Berkeley, Dean Swift, and Shelley, long dead but still present to the imagination—along with the Holy Roman Catholic Church; the hated authority of the British Empire; the ghosts of martyred national heroes; and the wishful vision of a pure Gaelic heritage.

Of course all cities have histories, but most cities also have such an active present that their history is more or less remembered only on ceremonial occasions. What Joyce observed was that the Dublin in which he was born and raised was a city with no present, no special mission in the modern world. The people he saw were endlessly engaged in making the past a substitute for their current lives. The boy in "Araby," imagining himself on a holy crusade to a fabulous Eastern land on behalf of his beloved Lady, is just acting out on an adolescent level what all his elders are doing in other ways. Gretta in "The Dead" is held in a reverie of lost love in the West country, Miss Ivors in visions of ancient Ireland revived, others in the transporting songs of the music halls and the Italian opera.

Though fascinated by this timeless microcosm, Joyce found that he could not live in it. The collection of short stories called *Dubliners* (1914) shows the city as paralyzed; and in his semiautobiographical first novel, *A Portrait of the Artist as a Young Man* (1916), Joyce presents the feeling of entrapment of the hero, Stephen Dedalus. We know by the end of the novel that Joyce's fictional double will leave Ireland. Though in *Ulysses* (1922) Stephen is back in Dublin, except for short periods Joyce himself never returned. He kept Dublin as the subject of all his work, but he himself found it necessary to remain in exile, living in France and Italy, apart from the city he portrayed with great specificity in his fiction.

From the chaste artistry of stories like the selections from *Dubliners* that follow, Joyce expanded his fiction to include more exuberant forms of Dublin life—the comic and the bawdy being especially evident (and shocking to some readers) in *Ulysses* and in his fantastically ambitious last novel, *Finnegans Wake* (1939).

Neither a wide public nor a willing publisher was immediately available for the distastefully "modern" subject matter and style of Joyce's writing. He was often in need, eventually became almost blind, and had to support his wife and children by giving English lessons and soliciting funds from friends who believed in his work. Exiled once again when the Germans overran France in 1940, Joyce made his way to Zurich, another city at the confluence of Western and Classical cultures, where he died after an operation on January 13, 1941.

More than any other modern writer, Joyce held to an ideal of the completely detached artist: an artist-god who presides over his characters without making any comment other than what can be inferred from the characters' speech and a precise arrangement of detail.

Araby

North Richmond Street, being blind, was a quiet street except at the hour when the Christian Brothers' School set the boys free. An uninhabited house of two storeys stood at the blind end, detached from its neighbours in a square ground. The other houses of the street, conscious of decent lives within them, gazed at one another with brown imperturbable faces.

The former tenant of our house, a priest, had died in the back drawing-room. Air, musty from having long been enclosed, hung in all the rooms, and the waste room behind the kitchen was littered with old useless papers. Among these I found a few paper-covered books, the pages of which were curled and damp: *The Abbot,* by Walter Scott, *The Devout Communicant* and *The Memoirs of Vidocq.* I liked the last best because its leaves were yellow. The wild garden behind the house contained a central apple-tree and a few straggling bushes under one of which I found the late tenant's rusty bicycle-pump. He had been a very charitable priest; in his will he had left all his money to institutions and the furniture of his house to his sister.

When the short days of winter came dusk fell before we had well eaten our dinners. When we met in the street the houses had grown sombre. The space of sky above us was the colour of ever-changing violet and towards it the lamps of the street lifted their feeble lanterns. The cold air stung us and we played till our bodies glowed. Our shouts echoed in the silent street. The career of our play brought us through the dark muddy lanes behind the houses where we ran the gantlet of the rough tribes from the cottages, to the back doors of the dark dripping gardens where odours arose from the ashpits, to the dark odorous stables where a coachman smoothed and combed the horse or shook music from the buckled harness. When we returned to the street light from the kitchen windows had filled the areas. If my uncle was seen turning the corner we hid in the shadow until we had seen him safely housed. Or if Mangan's sister came out on the doorstep to call her brother in to his tea we watched her from our shadow peer up and down the street. We waited to see whether she would remain or go in and, if she remained, we left our shadow and walked up to Mangan's steps resignedly. She was waiting for us, her figure defined by the light from the half-opened door. Her brother always teased her before he obeyed and I stood by the railings looking at her. Her dress swung as she moved her body and the soft rope of her hair tossed from side to side.

Every morning I lay on the floor in the front parlour watching her door. The blind was pulled down within an inch of the sash so that I could not be seen. When she came out on the doorstep my heart leaped. I ran to the hall, seized my books and followed her. I kept her brown figure always in my eye and, when we came near the point at which our ways diverged, I quickened my pace and passed her. This happened morning after morning. I had never spoken to her, except for a few casual words, and yet her name was like a summons to all my foolish blood.

Her image accompanied me even in places the most hostile to romance. On Saturday evenings when my aunt went marketing I had to go to carry some of the parcels. We walked through the flaring streets, jostled by drunken men and bargaining women, amid the curses of labourers, the shrill litanies of shop-boys who stood on guard by the barrels of pigs' cheeks, the nasal chanting of street singers, who sang a *come-all-you* about O'Donovan Rossa, or a ballad about the troubles in our native land. These noises converged in a single sensation of life for me: I imagined that I bore my chalice safely through the throng of foes. Her name sprang to my lips at moments in strange prayers and praises which I myself did not understand. My eyes were often full of tears (I could not tell why) and at times a flood from my heart seemed to pour itself out into my bosom. I thought little of the future. I did not know whether I would ever speak to her or not or, if I spoke to her, how I could tell her of my confused adoration. But my body was like a harp and her words and gestures were like fingers running upon the wires.

One evening I went into the back drawing-room in which the priest had died. It was a dark rainy evening and there was no sound in the house. Through one of the broken panes I heard the rain impinge upon the earth, the fine incessant needles of water playing in the sodden beds. Some distant lamp or lighted window gleamed below me. I was thankful that I could see so little. All my senses seemed to desire to veil themselves and, feeling that I was about to slip from them, I pressed the palms of my hands together until they trembled, murmuring: *O love! O love!* many times.

At last she spoke to me. When she addressed the first words to me I was so confused that I did not know what to answer. She asked me was I going to *Araby.* I forget whether I answered yes or no. It would be a splendid bazaar, she said; she would love to go.

—And why can't you? I asked.

While she spoke she turned a silver bracelet round and round her wrist. She could not go, she said, because there would be a retreat that week in her convent. Her brother and two other boys were fighting for their caps and I was alone at the railings. She held one of the spikes, bowing her head towards me. The light from the lamp opposite our door caught the white curve of her neck, lit up her hair that rested there and, falling, lit up the hand upon the railing. It fell over one side of her dress and caught the white border of a petticoat, just visible as she stood at ease.

—It's well for you, she said.

—If I go, I said, I will bring you something.

What innumerable follies laid waste my waking and sleeping thoughts after that evening! I wished to annihilate the tedious intervening days. I chafed against the work of school. At night in my bedroom and by day in the classroom her image came between me and the page I strove to read. The syllables of the word *Araby* were called to me through the silence in which my soul luxuriated and cast an Eastern enchantment over me. I asked for leave to go to the bazaar on Saturday night. My aunt was surprised and hoped it was not some Freemason affair. I answered few questions in class. I watched my master's face pass from amiability to sternness; he hoped I was not beginning to idle. I could not call my wandering thoughts together. I had hardly any patience with the serious work of life which, now that it stood between me and my desire, seemed to me child's play, ugly monotonous child's play.

On Saturday morning I reminded my uncle that I wished to go to the bazaar in the evening. He was fussing at the hall-stand, looking for the hat-brush, and answered me curtly:

—Yes, boy, I know.

As he was in the hall I could not go into the front parlour and lie at the window. I left the house in bad humour and walked slowly towards the school. The air was pitilessly raw and already my heart misgave me.

When I came home to dinner my uncle had not yet been home. Still it was early. I sat staring at the clock for some time and, when its ticking began to irritate me, I left the room. I mounted the staircase and gained the upper part of the house. The high cold empty gloomy rooms liberated me and I went from room to room singing. From the front window I saw my companions playing below in the street. Their cries reached me weakened and indistinct and, leaning my forehead against the cool glass, I looked over at the dark house where she lived. I may have stood there for an hour, seeing nothing but the brown-clad figure cast by my imagination, touched discreetly by the lamplight at the curved neck, at the hand upon the railings and at the border below the dress.

When I came downstairs again I found Mrs. Mercer sitting at the fire. She was an old garrulous woman, a pawnbroker's widow, who collected used stamps for some pious purpose. I had to endure the gossip of the tea-table. The meal was prolonged beyond an hour and still my uncle did not come. Mrs. Mercer stood up to go: she was sorry she couldn't wait any longer, but it was after eight o'clock and she did not like to be out late, as the night air was bad for her. When she had gone I began to walk up and down the room, clenching my fists. My aunt said:

—I'm afraid you may put off your bazaar for this night of Our Lord.

At nine o'clock I heard my uncle's latchkey in the halldoor. I heard him talking to himself and heard the hallstand rocking when it had received the weight of his overcoat. I could interpret these signs. When he was midway through his dinner I asked him to give me the money to go to the bazaar. He had forgotten.

—The people are in bed and after their first sleep now, he said.

I did not smile. My aunt said to him energetically:

—Can't you give him the money and let him go? You've kept him late enough as it is.

My uncle said he was very sorry he had forgotten. He said he believed in the old saying: *All work and no play makes Jack a dull boy.* He asked me where I was going and, when I had told him a second time he asked me did I know *The Arab's Farewell to his Steed.* When I left the kitchen he was about to recite the opening lines of the piece to my aunt.

I held a florin tightly in my hand as I strode down Buckingham Street towards the station. The sight of the streets thronged with buyers and glaring with gas recalled to me the purpose of my journey. I took my seat in a third-class carriage of a deserted train. After an intolerable delay the train moved out of the station slowly. It crept onward among ruinous houses and over the twinkling river. At Westland Row Station a crowd of people pressed to the carriage doors; but the porters moved them back, saying that it was a special train for the bazaar. I remained alone in the bare carriage. In a few minutes the train drew up beside an improvised wooden platform. I passed out on to the road and saw by the lighted dial of a clock that it was ten minutes to ten. In front of me was a large building which displayed the magical name.

I could not find any sixpenny entrance and, fearing that the bazaar would be closed, I passed in quickly through a turnstile, handing a shilling to a weary-looking man. I found myself in a big hall girdled at half its height by a gallery. Nearly all the stalls were closed and the greater part of the hall was in darkness. I recognized a silence like that which pervades a church after a service. I walked into the centre of the bazaar timidly. A few people were gathered about the stalls which were still open. Before a curtain, over which the words *Café Chantant* were written in coloured lamps, two men were counting money on a salver. I listened to the fall of the coins.

Remembering with difficulty why I had come I went over to one of the stalls and examined porcelain vases and flowered tea-sets. At the door of the stall a young lady was talking and laughing with two young gentlemen. I remarked their English accents and listened vaguely to their conversation.

—O, I never said such a thing!

—O, but you did!

—O, but I didn't!

—Didn't she say that?

—Yes. I heard her.

—O, there's a . . . fib!

Observing me the young lady came over and asked me did I wish to buy anything. The tone of her voice was not encouraging; she seemed to have spoken to me out of a sense of duty. I looked humbly at the great jars that stood like eastern guards at either side of the dark entrance to the stall and murmured:

—No, thank you.

The young lady changed the position of one of the vases and went back to the two young men. They began to talk of the same subject. Once or twice the young lady glanced at me over her shoulder.

I lingered before her stall, though I knew my stay was useless, to make my interest in her wares seem the more real. Then I turned away slowly and walked down the middle of the bazaar. I allowed the two pennies to fall against the sixpence in my pocket. I heard a voice call from one end of the gallery that the light was out. The upper part of the hall was now completely dark.

Gazing up into the darkness I saw myself as a creature driven and derided by vanity; and my eyes burned with anguish and anger.

The Dead

Lily, the caretaker's daughter, was literally run off her feet. Hardly had she brought one gentleman into the little pantry behind the office on the ground floor and helped him off with his overcoat than the wheezy hall-door bell clanged again and she had to scamper along the bare hallway to let in another guest. It was well for her she had not to attend to the ladies also. But Miss Kate and Miss Julia had thought of that and had converted the bathroom upstairs into a ladies' dressing-room. Miss Kate and Miss Julia were there, gossiping and laughing and fussing, walking after each other to the head of the stairs, peering down over the banisters and calling down to Lily to ask her who had come.

It was always a great affair, the Misses Morkan's annual dance. Everybody who knew them came to it, members of the family, old friends of the family, the members of Julia's choir, any of Kate's pupils that were grown up enough and even some of Mary Jane's pupils too. Never once had it fallen flat. For years and years it had gone off in splendid style as long as anyone could remember; ever since Kate and Julia, after the death of their brother Pat, had left the house in Stoney Batter and taken Mary Jane, their only niece, to live with them in the dark gaunt house on Usher's Island, the upper part of which they had rented from Mr. Fulham, the cornfactor on the ground floor. That was a good thirty years ago if it was a day. Mary Jane, who was then a little girl in short clothes, was now the main prop of the household for she had the organ in Haddington Road. She had been through the Academy and gave a pupils' concert every year in the upper room of the Antient Concert Rooms. Many of her pupils belonged to better-class families on the Kingstown and Dalkey line. Old as they were, her aunts also did their share. Julia, though she was quite grey, was still the leading soprano in Adam and Eve's, and Kate, being too feeble to go about much, gave music lessons to beginners on the old square piano in the back room. Lily, the caretaker's daughter, did housemaid's work for them. Though their life was modest they believed in eating well; the best of everything: diamond-bone sirloins, three-shilling tea and the best bottled stout. But Lily seldom made a mistake in the orders so that she got on well with her three mistresses. They were fussy, that was all. But the only thing they would not stand was back answers.

Of course they had good reason to be fussy on such a night. And then it was long after ten o'clock and yet there was no sign of Gabriel and his wife. Besides they were dreadfully afraid that Freddy Malins might turn up screwed. They would not wish for worlds that any of Mary Jane's pupils should see him under the influence; and when he was like that it was sometimes very hard to manage him. Freddy Malins always came late but they wondered what could be keeping Gabriel: and that was what brought them every two minutes to the banisters to ask Lily had Gabriel or Freddy come.

—O, Mr. Conroy, said Lily to Gabriel when she opened the door for him, Miss Kate and Miss Julia thought you were never coming. Good-night, Mrs. Conroy.

—I'll engage they did, said Gabriel, but they forget that my wife here takes three mortal hours to dress herself.

He stood on the mat, scraping the snow from his goloshes, while Lily led his wife to the foot of the stairs and called out:

—Miss Kate, here's Mrs. Conroy.

Kate and Julia came toddling down the dark stairs at once. Both of them kissed Gabriel's wife, said she must be perished alive and asked was Gabriel with her.

—Here I am as right as the mail, Aunt Kate! Go on up. I'll follow, called out Gabriel from the dark.

He continued scraping his feet vigorously while the three women went upstairs, laughing, to the ladies' dressing-room. A light fringe of snow lay like a cape on the shoulders of his overcoat and like toecaps on the toes of his goloshes; and, as the buttons of his overcoat slipped with a squeaking noise through the snow-stiffened frieze, a cold fragrant air from out-of-doors escaped from crevices and folds.

—Is it snowing again, Mr. Conroy? asked Lily.

She had preceded him into the pantry to help him off with his overcoat. Gabriel smiled at the three syllables she had given his surname and glanced at her. She was a slim, growing girl, pale in complexion and with hay-coloured hair. The gas in the pantry made her look still paler. Gabriel had known her when she was a child and used to sit on the lowest step nursing a rag doll.

—Yes, Lily, he answered, and I think we're in for a night of it.

He looked up at the pantry ceiling, which was shaking with the stamping and shuffling of feet on the floor above, listened for a moment to the piano and then glanced at the girl, who was folding his overcoat carefully at the end of a shelf.

—Tell me, Lily, he said in a friendly tone, do you still go to school?

—O no, sir, she answered. I'm done schooling this year and more.

—O, then, said Gabriel gaily, I suppose we'll be going to your wedding one of these fine days with your young man, eh?

The girl glanced back at him over her shoulder and said with great bitterness:

—The men that is now is only all palaver and what they can get out of you.

Gabriel coloured as if he felt he had made a mistake and, without looking at her, kicked off his goloshes and flicked actively with his muffler at his patent-leather shoes.

He was a stout tallish young man. The high colour of his cheeks pushed upwards even to his forehead where it scattered itself in a few formless patches of pale red; and on his hairless face there scintillated restlessly the polished lenses and the bright gilt rims of the glasses which screened his delicate and restless eyes. His glossy black hair was parted in the middle and brushed in a long curve behind his ears where it curled slightly beneath the groove left by his hat.

When he had flicked lustre into his shoes he stood up and pulled his waistcoat down more tightly on his plump body. Then he took a coin rapidly from his pocket.

—O Lily, he said, thrusting it into her hands, it's Christmas-time, isn't it? Just . . . here's a little. . . .

He walked rapidly towards the door.

—O no, sir! cried the girl, following him. Really, sir, I wouldn't take it.

—Christmas-time! Christmas-time! said Gabriel, almost trotting to the stairs and waving his hand to her in deprecation.

The girl, seeing that he had gained the stairs, called out after him:

—Well, thank you, sir.

He waited outside the drawing-room door until the waltz should finish, listening to the skirts that swept against it and to the shuffling of feet. He was still discomposed by the girl's bitter and sudden retort. It had cast a gloom over him which he tried to dispel by arranging his cuffs and the bows of his tie. Then he took from his waistcoat pocket a little paper and glanced at the headings he had made for his speech. He was undecided about the lines from Robert Browning for he feared they would be above the heads of his hearers. Some quotation that they could recognize from Shakespeare or from the Melodies would be better. The indelicate clacking of the men's heels and the shuffling of their soles reminded him that their grade of culture differed from his. He would only make himself ridiculous by quoting poetry to them which they could not understand. They would think that he was airing his superior education. He would fail with them just as he had failed with the girl in the pantry. He had taken up a wrong tone. His whole speech was a mistake from first to last, an utter failure.

Just then his aunts and his wife came out of the ladies' dressing-room. His aunts were two small plainly dressed old women. Aunt Julia was an inch or so the taller. Her hair, drawn low over the tops of her ears, was grey; and grey also, with darker shadows, was her large flaccid face. Though she was stout in build and stood erect her slow eyes and parted lips gave her the appearance of a woman who did not know where she was or where she was going. Aunt

Kate was more vivacious. Her face, healthier than her sister's, was all puckers and creases, like a shrivelled red apple, and her hair, braided in the same old-fashioned way, had not lost its ripe nut colour.

They both kissed Gabriel frankly. He was their favourite nephew, the son of their dead elder sister, Ellen, who had married T. J. Conroy of the Port and Docks.

—Gretta tells me you're not going to take a cab back to Monkstown tonight, Gabriel, said Aunt Kate.

—No, said Gabriel, turning to his wife, we had quite enough of that last year, hadn't we? Don't you remember, Aunt Kate, what a cold Gretta got out of it? Cab windows rattling all the way, and the east wind blowing in after we passed Merion. Very jolly it was. Gretta caught a dreadful cold.

Aunt Kate frowned severely and nodded her head at every word.

—Quite right, Gabriel, quite right, she said. You can't be too careful.

—But as for Gretta there, said Gabriel, she'd walk home in the snow if she were let.

Mrs. Conroy laughed.

—Don't mind him, Aunt Kate, she said. He's really an awful bother, what with green shades for Tom's eyes at night and making him do the dumb-bells, and forcing Eva to eat the stirabout. The poor child! And she simply hates the sight of it! . . . O, but you'll never guess what he makes me wear now!

She broke out into a peal of laughter and glanced at her husband, whose admiring and happy eyes had been wandering from her dress to her face and hair. The two aunts laughed heartily too, for Gabriel's solicitude was a standing joke with them.

—Goloshes! said Mrs. Conroy. That's the latest. Whenever it's wet underfoot I must put on my goloshes. To-night even he wanted me to put them on, but I wouldn't. The next thing he'll buy me will be a diving suit.

Gabriel laughed nervously and patted his tie reassuringly while Aunt Kate nearly doubled herself, so heartily did she enjoy the joke. The smile soon faded from Aunt Julia's face and her mirthless eyes were directed towards her nephew's face. After a pause she asked:

—And what are goloshes, Gabriel?

—Goloshes, Julia! exclaimed her sister. Goodness me, don't you know what goloshes are? You wear them over your . . . over your boots, Gretta, isn't it?

—Yes, said Mrs. Conroy. Guttapercha things. We both have a pair now. Gabriel says everyone wears them on the continent.

—O, on the continent, murmured Aunt Julia, nodding her head slowly.

Gabriel knitted his brows and said, as if he were slightly angered:

—It's nothing very wonderful but Gretta thinks it very funny because she says the word reminds her of Christy Minstrels.

—But tell me, Gabriel, said Aunt Kate, with brisk tact. Of course, you've seen about the room. Gretta was saying . . .

—O, the room is all right, replied Gabriel. I've taken one in the Gresham.

—To be sure, said Aunt Kate, by far the best thing to do. And the children, Gretta, you're not anxious about them?

—O, for one night, said Mrs. Conroy. Besides, Bessie will look after them.

—To be sure, said Aunt Kate again. What a comfort it is to have a girl like that, one you can depend on! There's that Lily, I'm sure I don't know what has come over her lately. She's not the girl she was at all.

Gabriel was about to ask his aunt some questions on this point but she broke off suddenly to gaze after her sister who had wandered down the stairs and was craning her neck over the banisters.

—Now, I ask you, she said, almost testily, where is Julia going? Julia! Julia! Where are you going?

Julia, who had gone halfway down one flight, came back and announced blandly:

—Here's Freddy.

At the same moment a clapping of hands and a final flourish of the pianist told that the waltz had ended. The drawing-room door was open from within and some couples came out. Aunt Kate drew Gabriel aside hurriedly and whispered into his ear:

—Slip down, Gabriel, like a good fellow and see if he's all right, and don't let him up if he's screwed. I'm sure he's screwed. I'm sure he is.

Gabriel went to the stairs and listened over the banisters. He could hear two persons talking in the pantry. Then he recognized Freddy Malins' laugh. He went down the stairs noisily.

—It's such a relief, said Aunt Kate to Mrs. Conroy, that Gabriel is here. I always feel easier in my mind when he's here. . . . Julia, there's Miss Daly and Miss Power will take some refreshment. Thanks for your beautiful waltz, Miss Daly. It made lovely time.

A tall wizen-faced man, with a stiff grizzled moustache and swarthy skin, who was passing out with his partner said:

—And may we have some refreshment, too, Miss Morkan?

—Julia, said Aunt Kate summarily, and here's Mr. Browne and Miss Furlong. Take them in, Julia, with Miss Daly and Miss Power.

—I'm the man for the ladies, said Mr. Browne, pursing his lips until his moustache bristled and smiling in all his wrinkles. You know, Miss Morkan, the reason they are so fond of me is—

He did not finish his sentence, but, seeing that Aunt Kate was out of earshot, at once led the three young ladies into the back room. The middle of the room was occupied by two square tables placed end to end, and on these Aunt Julia and the caretaker were straightening and smoothing a large cloth.

On the sideboard were arrayed dishes and plates, and glasses and bundles of knives and forks and spoons. The top of the closed square piano served also as a sideboard for viands and sweets. At a smaller sideboard in one corner two young men were standing, drinking hop-bitters.

Mr. Browne led his charges thither and invited them all, in jest, to some ladies' punch, hot, strong and sweet. As they said they never took anything strong he opened three bottles of lemonade for them. Then he asked one of the young men to move aside, and, taking hold of the decanter, filled out for himself a goodly measure of whisky. The young men eyed him respectfully while he took a trial sip.

—God help me, he said, smiling, it's the doctor's orders.

His wizened face broke into a broader smile, and the three young ladies laughed in musical echo to his pleasantry, swaying their bodies to and fro, with nervous jerks of their shoulders. The boldest said:

—O, now, Mr. Browne, I'm sure the doctor never ordered anything of the kind.

Mr. Browne took another sip of his whisky and said, with sidling mimicry:

—Well, you see, I'm like the famous Mrs. Cassidy, who is reported to have said: *Now Mary Grimes, if I don't take it, make me take it, for I feel I want it.*

His hot face had leaned forward a little too confidentially and he had assumed a very low Dublin accent so that the young ladies, with one instinct, received his speech in silence. Miss Furlong, who was one of Mary Jane's pupils, asked Miss Daly what was the name of the pretty waltz she had played; and Mr. Browne, seeing that he was ignored, turned promptly to the two young men who were more appreciative.

A red-faced young woman, dressed in pansy, came into the room, excitedly clapping her hands and crying:

—Quadrilles! Quadrilles!

Close on her heels came Aunt Kate, crying:

—Two gentlemen and three ladies, Mary Jane!

—O, here's Mr. Bergin and Mr. Kerrigan, said Mary Jane. Mr. Kerrigan, will you take Miss Power? Miss Furlong, may I get you a partner, Mr. Bergin. O, that'll just do now.

—Three ladies, Mary Jane, said Aunt Kate.

The two young gentlemen asked the ladies if they might have the pleasure, and Mary Jane turned to Miss Daly.

—O, Miss Daly, you're really awfully good, after playing for the last two dances, but really we're so short of ladies to-night.

—I don't mind in the least, Miss Morkan.

—But I've a nice partner for you, Mr. Bartell D'Arcy, the tenor. I'll get him to sing later on. All Dublin is raving about him.

—Lovely voice, lovely voice! said Aunt Kate.

As the piano had twice begun the prelude to the first figure Mary Jane led her recruits quickly from the room. They had hardly gone when Aunt Julia wandered slowly into the room, looking behind her at something.

—What is the matter, Julia? asked Aunt Kate anxiously. Who is it?

Julia, who was carrying in a column of table-napkins, turned to her sister and said, simply, as if the question had surprised her:

—It's only Freddy, Kate, and Gabriel with him.

In fact right behind her Gabriel could be seen piloting Freddy Malins across the landing. The latter, a young man of about forty, was of Gabriel's size and build, with very round shoulders. His face was fleshy and pallid, touched with colour only at the thick hanging lobes of his ears and at the wide wings of his nose. He had coarse features, a blunt nose, a convex and receding brow, tumid and protruded lips. His heavy-lidded eyes and the disorder of his scanty hair made him look sleepy. He was laughing heartily in a high key at a story which he had been telling Gabriel on the stairs and at the same time rubbing the knuckles of his fist backwards and forwards into his left eye.

—Good-evening, Freddy, said Aunt Julia.

Freddy Malins bade the Misses Morkan good-evening in what seemed an offhand fashion by reason of the habitual catch in his voice and then, seeing that Mr. Browne was grinning at him from the sideboard, crossed the room on rather shaky legs and began to repeat in an undertone the story he had just told to Gabriel.

—He's not so bad, is he? said Aunt Kate to Gabriel.

Gabriel's brows were dark but he raised them quickly and answered:

—O no, hardly noticeable.

—Now, isn't he a terrible fellow! she said. And his poor mother made him take the pledge on New Year's Eve. But come on, Gabriel, into the drawing-room.

Before leaving the room with Gabriel she signalled to Mr. Browne by frowning and shaking her forefinger in warning to and fro. Mr. Browne nodded in answer and, when she had gone, said to Freddy Malins:

—Now, then, Teddy, I'm going to fill you out a good glass of lemonade just to buck you up.

Freddy Malins, who was nearing the climax of his story, waved the offer aside impatiently but Mr. Browne, having first called Freddy Malins' attention to a disarray in his dress, filled out and handed him a full glass of lemonade. Freddy Malins' left hand accepted the glass mechanically, his right hand being engaged in the mechanical readjustment of his dress. Mr. Browne, whose face was once more wrinkling with mirth, poured out for himself a glass of whisky while Freddy Malins exploded, before he had well reached the climax of his story, in a kink of high-pitched bronchitic laughter and, setting down his untasted and overflowing glass, began to rub the knuckles of his left fist backwards and forwards into his left eye, repeating words of his phrase as well as his fit of laughter would allow him.

. . .

Gabriel could not listen while Mary Jane was playing her Academy piece, full of runs and difficult passages, to the hushed drawing-room. He liked music but the piece she was playing had no melody for him and he doubted whether it had any melody for the other listeners, though they had begged Mary Jane to play something. Four young men, who had come from the refreshment-room to stand in the doorway at the sound of the piano, had gone away quietly in couples after a few minutes. The only persons who seemed to follow the music were Mary Jane herself, her hands racing along the key-board or lifted from it at the pauses like those of a priestess in momentary imprecation, and Aunt Kate standing at her elbow to turn the page.

Gabriel's eyes, irritated by the floor, which glittered with beeswax under the heavy chandelier, wandered to the wall above the piano. A picture of the balcony scene in *Romeo and Juliet* hung there and beside it was a picture of the two murdered princes in the Tower which Aunt Julia had worked in red, blue and brown wools when she was a girl. Probably in the school they had gone to as girls that kind of work had been taught, for one year his mother had worked for him as a birthday present a waistcoat of purple tabinet, with little foxes' heads upon it, lined with brown satin and having round mulberry buttons. It was strange that his mother had had no musical talent though Aunt Kate used to call her the brains carrier of the Morkan family. Both she and Julia had always seemed a little proud of their serious and matronly sister. Her photograph stood before the pierglass. She held an open book on her knees and was pointing out something in it to Constantine who, dressed in a man-o'-war suit, lay at her feet. It was she who had chosen the names for her sons for she was very sensible of the dignity of family life. Thanks to her, Constantine was now senior curate in Balbriggan and, thanks to her, Gabriel himself had taken his degree in the Royal University. A shadow passed over his face as he remembered her sullen opposition to his marriage. Some slighting phrases she had used still rankled in his memory; she had once spoken of Gretta as being country cute and that was not true of Gretta at all. It was Gretta who had nursed her during all her last long illness in their house at Monkstown.

He knew that Mary Jane must be near the end of her piece for she was playing again the opening melody with runs of scales after every bar and while he waited for the end the resentment died down in his heart. The piece ended with a trill of octaves in treble and a final deep octave in the bass. Great applause greeted Mary Jane as, blushing and rolling up her music nervously, she escaped from the room. The most vigorous clapping came from the four young men in the doorway who had gone away to the refreshment-room at the beginning of the piece but had come back when the piano had stopped.

Lancers were arranged. Gabriel found himself partnered with Miss Ivors. She was a frank-mannered talkative young lady, with a freckled face and prominent brown eyes. She did not wear a low-cut bodice and the large brooch which was fixed in the front of her collar bore on it an Irish device.

When they had taken their places she said abruptly:

—I have a crow to pluck with you.

—With me? said Gabriel.

She nodded her head gravely.

—What is it? asked Gabriel, smiling at her solemn manner.

—Who is G. C.? answered Miss Ivors, turning her eyes upon him.

Gabriel coloured and was about to knit his brows, as if he did not understand, when she said bluntly:

—O, innocent Amy! I have found out that you write for *The Daily Express*. Now, aren't you ashamed of yourself?

—Why should I be ashamed of myself? asked Gabriel, blinking his eyes and trying to smile.

—Well, I'm ashamed of you, said Miss Ivors frankly. To say you'd write for a rag like that. I didn't think you were a West Briton.

A look of perplexity appeared on Gabriel's face. It was true that he wrote a literary column every Wednesday in *The Daily Express*, for which he was paid fifteen shillings. But that did not make him a West Briton surely. The books he received for review were almost more welcome than the paltry cheque. He loved to feel the covers and turn over the pages of newly printed books. Nearly every day when his teaching in the college was ended he used to wander down the quays to the second-hand booksellers, to Hickey's on Bachelor's Walk, to Webbs' or Massey's on Aston's Quay, or to O'Clohissey's in the by-street. He did not know how to meet her charge. He wanted to say that literature was above politics. But they were friends of many years' standing and their careers had been parallel, first at the University and then as teachers: he could not risk a grandiose phrase with her. He continued blinking his eyes and trying to smile and murmured lamely that he saw nothing political in writing reviews of books.

When their turn to cross had come he was still perplexed and inattentive. Miss Ivors promptly took his hand in a warm grasp and said in a soft friendly tone:

—Of course, I was only joking. Come, we cross now.

When they were together again she spoke of the University question and Gabriel felt more at ease. A friend of hers had shown her his review of

Browning's poems. That was how she had found out the secret: but she liked the review immensely. Then she said suddenly:

—O, Mr. Conroy, will you come for an excursion to the Aran Isles this summer? We're going to stay there a whole month. It will be splendid out in the Atlantic. You ought to come. Mr. Clancy is coming, and Mr. Kilkelly and Kathleen Kearney. It would be splendid for Gretta too if she'd come. She's from Connacht, isn't she?

—Her people are, said Gabriel shortly.

—But you will come, won't you? said Miss Ivors, laying her warm hand eagerly on his arm.

—The fact is, said Gabriel, I have already arranged to go—

—Go where? asked Miss Ivors.

—Well, you know, every year I go for a cycling tour with some fellows and so—

—But where? asked Miss Ivors.

—Well, we usually go to France or Belgium or perhaps Germany, said Gabriel awkwardly.

—And why do you go to France or Belgium, said Miss Ivors, instead of visiting your own land?

—Well, said Gabriel, it's partly to keep in touch with the languages and partly for a change.

—And haven't you your own language to keep in touch with—Irish? asked Miss Ivors.

—Well, said Gabriel, if it comes to that, you know, Irish is not my language.

Their neighbours had turned to listen to the cross-examination. Gabriel glanced right and left nervously and tried to keep his good humour under the ordeal which was making a blush invade his forehead.

—And haven't you your own land to visit, continued Miss Ivors, that you know nothing of, your own people, and your own country?

—O, to tell you the truth, retorted Gabriel suddenly, I'm sick of my own country, sick of it!

—Why? asked Miss Ivors.

Gabriel did not answer for his retort had heated him.

—Why? repeated Miss Ivors.

They had to go visiting together and, as he had not answered her, Miss Ivors said warmly:

—Of course, you've no answer.

Gabriel tried to cover his agitation by taking part in the dance with great energy. He avoided her eyes for he had seen a sour expression on her face. But when they met in the long chain he was surprised to feel his hand firmly pressed. She looked at him from under her brows for a moment quizzically until he smiled. Then, just as the chain was about to start again, she stood on tiptoe and whispered into his ear:

—West Briton!

When the lancers were over Gabriel went away to a remote corner of the room where Freddy Malins' mother was sitting. She was a stout feeble old woman with white hair. Her voice had a catch in it like her son's and she stuttered slightly. She had been told that Freddy had come and that he was nearly all right. Gabriel asked her whether she had had a good crossing. She lived with her married daughter in Glasgow and came to Dublin on a visit once a year. She answered placidly that she had had a beautiful crossing and that the captain had been most attentive to her. She spoke also of the beautiful house her daughter kept in Glasgow, and of all the nice friends they had there. While her tongue rambled on Gabriel tried to banish from his mind all memory of the unpleasant incident with Miss Ivors. Of course the girl or woman, or whatever she was, was an enthusiast but there was a time for all things. Perhaps he ought not to have answered her like that. But she had no right to call him a West Briton before people, even in joke. She had tried to make him ridiculous before people, heckling him and staring at him with her rabbit's eyes.

He saw his wife making her way towards him through the waltzing couples. When she reached him she said into his ear:

—Gabriel, Aunt Kate wants to know won't you carve the goose as usual. Miss Daly will carve the ham and I'll do the pudding.

—All right, said Gabriel.

—She's sending in the younger ones first as soon as this waltz is over so that we'll have the table to ourselves.

—Were you dancing? asked Gabriel.

—Of course I was. Didn't you see me? What words had you with Molly Ivors?

—No words. Why? Did she say so?

—Something like that. I'm trying to get Mr. D'Arcy to sing. He's full of conceit, I think.

—There were no words, said Gabriel moodily, only she wanted me to go for a trip to the west of Ireland and I said I wouldn't.

His wife clasped her hands excitedly and gave a little jump.

—O, do go, Gabriel, she cried. I'd love to see Galway again.

—You can go if you like, said Gabriel coldly.

She looked at him for a moment, then turned to Mrs. Malins and said:

—There's a nice husband for you, Mrs. Malins.

While she was threading her way back across the room Mrs. Malins, without adverting to the interruption, went on to tell Gabriel what beautiful places there were in Scotland and beautiful scenery. Her son-in-law brought them every year to the lakes and they used to go fishing. Her son-in-law was a splendid fisher. One day he caught a fish, a beautiful big big fish, and the man in the hotel boiled it for their dinner.

Gabriel hardly heard what she said. Now that supper was coming near he began to think again about his speech and about the quotation. When he saw Freddy Malins coming across the room to visit his mother Gabriel left the chair free for him and retired into the embrasure of the window. The room had already cleared and from the back room came the clatter of plates and knives. Those who still remained in the drawing-room seemed tired of dancing and were conversing quietly in little groups. Gabriel's warm trembling fingers tapped the cold pane of the window. How cool it must be outside! How pleasant it would be to walk out alone, first along by the river and then through the park! The snow would be lying on the branches of the trees and forming a bright cap on the top of the Wellington Monument. How much more pleasant it would be there than at the supper-table.

He ran over the headings of his speech: Irish hospitality, sad memories, the Three Graces, Paris, the quotation from Browning. He repeated to himself a phrase he had written in his review: *One feels that one is listening to a thought-tormented music.* Miss Ivors had praised the review. Was she sincere? Had she really any life of her own behind all her propagandism? There had never been ill-feeling between them until that night. It unnerved him to think that she would be at the supper-table; looking up at him while he spoke with her critical quizzing eyes. Perhaps she would not be sorry to see him fail in his speech. An idea came into his mind and gave him courage. He would say, alluding to Aunt Kate and Aunt Julia: *Ladies and Gentlemen, the generation which is now on the wane among us may have had its faults but for my part I think it had certain qualities of hospitality, of humors, of humanity, which the new and very serious and hypereducated generation that is growing up around us seems to me to lack.* Very good: that was one for Miss Ivors. What did he care that his aunts were only two ignorant old women?

A murmur in the room attracted his attention. Mr. Browne was advancing from the door, gallantly escorting Aunt Julia, who leaned upon his arm, smiling and hanging her head. An irregular musketry of applause escorted her also as far as the piano and then, as Mary Jane seated herself on the stool, and Aunt Julia, no longer smiling, half turned so as to pitch her voice fairly into the room, gradually ceased. Gabriel recognized the prelude. It was that of an old song of Aunt Julia's—*Arrayed for the Bridal.* Her voice, strong and clear in tone, attacked with great spirit the runs which embellish the air and though she sang very rapidly she did not miss even the smallest of the grace notes. To follow the voice, without looking at the singer's face, was to feel and share the excitement of swift and secure flight. Gabriel applauded loudly with all the others at the close of the song and loud applause was borne from the invisible supper-table. It sounded so genuine that a little colour struggled into Aunt

Julia's face as she bent to replace in the music-stand the old leather-bound song-book that had her initials on the cover. Freddy Malins, who had listened with his head perched sideways to hear her better, was still applauding when everyone else had ceased and talking animatedly to his mother who nodded her head gravely and slowly in acquiescence. At last, when he could clap no more, he stood up suddenly and hurried across the room to Aunt Julia whose hand he seized and held in both his hands, shaking it when words failed him or the catch in his voice proved too much for him.

—I was just telling my mother, he said, I never heard you sing so well, never. No, I never heard your voice so good as it is to-night. Now! Would you believe that now? That's the truth. Upon my word and honour that's the truth. I never heard your voice sound so fresh and so . . . so clear and fresh, never.

Aunt Julia smiled broadly and murmured something about compliments as she released her hand from his grasp. Mr. Browne extended his open hand towards her and said to those who were near him in the manner of a showman introducing a prodigy to an audience:

—Miss Julia Morkan, my lastest discovery!

He was laughing very heartily at this himself when Freddy Malins turned to him and said:

—Well, Browne, if you're serious you might make a worse discovery. All I can say is I never heard her sing half so well as long as I am coming here. And that's the honest truth.

—Neither did I, said Mr. Browne. I think her voice has greatly improved.

Aunt Julia shrugged her shoulders with meek pride:

—Thirty years ago I hadn't a bad voice as voices go.

—I often told Julia, said Aunt Kate emphatically, that she was simply thrown away in that choir. But she never would be said by me.

She turned away as if to appeal to the good sense of the others against a refractory child while Aunt Julia gazed in front of her, a vague smile of reminiscence playing on her face.

—No, continued Aunt Kate, she wouldn't be said or led by anyone, slaving there in that choir night and day, night and day. Six o'clock on Christmas morning! And all for what?

—Well, isn't it for the honour of God, Aunt Kate? asked Mary Jane, twisting round on the piano-stool and smiling.

Aunt Kate turned fiercely on her niece and said:

—I know all about the honour of God, Mary Jane, but I think it's not at all honourable for the pope to turn out the women out of the choirs that have slaved there all their lives and put little whipper-snappers of boys over their heads. I suppose it is for the good of the Church if the pope does it. But it's not just, Mary Jane, and it's not right.

She had worked herself into a passion and would have continued in defence of her sister for it was a sore subject with her but Mary Jane, seeing that all the dancers had come back, intervened pacifically:

—Now, Aunt Kate, you're giving scandal to Mr. Browne who is of the other persuasion.

Aunt Kate turned to Mr. Browne, who was grinning at this allusion to his religion, and said hastily:

—O, I don't question the pope's being right. I'm only a stupid old woman and I wouldn't presume to do such a thing. But there's such a thing as common everyday politeness and gratitude. And if I were in Julia's place I'd tell that Father Healy straight up to his face . . .

—And besides, Aunt Kate, said Mary Jane, we really are all hungry and when we are hungry we all are very quarrelsome.

—And when we are thirsty we are also quarrelsome, added Mr. Browne.

—So that we had better go to supper, said Mary Jane, and finish the discussion afterwards.

On the landing outside the drawing-room Gabriel found his wife and Mary Jane trying to persuade Miss Ivors to stay for supper. But Miss Ivors, who had put on her hat and was buttoning her cloak, would not stay. She did not feel in the least hungry and she had already overstayed her time.

—But only for ten minutes, Molly, said Mrs. Conroy. That won't delay you.

—To take a pick itself, said Mary Jane, after all your dancing.

—I really couldn't, said Miss Ivors.

—I am afraid you didn't enjoy yourself at all, said Mary Jane hopelessly.

—Ever so much, I assure you, said Miss Ivors, but you must really let me run off now.

—But how can you get home? asked Mrs. Conroy.

—O, it's only two steps up the quay.

Gabriel hesitated a moment and said:

—If you will allow me, Miss Ivors, I'll see you home if you really are obliged to go.

—I won't hear of it, she cried. For goodness sake go in to your suppers and don't mind me. I'm quite well able to take care of myself.

—Well, you're the comical girl, Molly, said Mrs. Conroy frankly.

—*Beannacht libh,* cried Miss Ivors, with a laugh, as she ran down the staircase.

Mary Jane gazed after her, a moody puzzled expression on her face, while Mrs. Conroy leaned over the banisters to listen for the hall-door. Gabriel asked himself was he the cause of her abrupt departure. But she did not seem to be in ill humour: she had gone away laughing. He stared blankly down the staircase.

At that moment Aunt Kate come toddling out of the supper-room, almost wringing her hands in despair.

—Where is Gabriel? she cried. Where on earth is Gabriel? There's everyone waiting in there, stage to let, and nobody to carve the goose!

—Here I am, Aunt Kate! cried Gabriel, with sudden animation, ready to carve a flock of geese, if necessary.

A fat brown goose lay at one end of the table and at the other end, on a bed of creased paper strewn with sprigs of parsley, lay a great ham, stripped of its outer skin and peppered over with crust crumbs, a neat paper frill round its shin and beside this was a round of spiced beef. Between these rival ends ran parallel lines of side-dishes: two little minsters of jelly, red and yellow; a shallow dish full of blocks of blancmange and red jam, a large green leaf-shaped dish with a stalk-shaped handle, on which lay bunches of purple raisins and peeled almonds, a companion dish on which lay a solid rectangle of Smyrna figs, a dish of custard topped with grated nutmeg, a small bowl full of chocolates and sweets wrapped in gold and silver papers and a glass vase in which stood some tall celery stalks. In the centre of the table there stood, as sentries to a fruit stand which upheld a pyramid of oranges and American apples, two squat old fashioned decanters of cut glass, one containing port and the other dark sherry. On the closed square piano a pudding in a huge yellow dish lay in waiting and behind it were three squads of bottles of stout and ale and minerals, drawn up according to the colours of their uniforms, the first two black, with brown and red labels, the third and smallest squad white, with transverse green sashes.

Gabriel took his seat boldly at the head of the table and, having looked to the edge of the carver, plunged his fork firmly into the goose. He felt quite at ease now for he was an expert carver and liked nothing better than to find himself at the head of a well-laden table.

—Miss Furlong, what shall I send you? he asked. A wing or a slice of the breast?

—Just a small slice of the breast.

—Miss Higgins, what for you?

—O, anything at all, Mr. Conroy.

While Gabriel and Miss Daly exchanged plates of goose and plates of ham and spiced beef Lily went from guest to guest with a dish of hot floury potatoes wrapped in a white napkin. This was Mary Jane's idea and she had also suggested apple sauce for the goose but Aunt Kate had said that plain roast goose without apple sauce had always been good enough for her and she hoped she might never eat worse. Mary Jane waited on her pupils and saw that they got the best slices and Aunt Kate and Aunt Julia opened and carried across from the piano bottles of stout and ale for the gentlemen and bottles of minerals for the ladies. There was a great deal of confusion and laughter and noise, the noise of orders and counter-orders, of knives and forks, of corks and glass-stoppers. Gabriel began to carve second helpings as soon as he finished the first round without serving himself. Everyone protested loudly so that he compromised by taking a long draught of stout for he had found the carving hot work. Mary Jane settled down quietly to her supper but Aunt Kate and Aunt Julia were still toddling round the table, walking on each other's heels, getting in each other's way and giving each other unheeded orders. Mr. Browne begged each of them to sit down and eat their suppers and so did Gabriel but they said there was time enough so that, at last, Freddy Malins stood up and, capturing Aunt Kate, plumped her down on her chair amid general laughter.

When everyone had been well served Gabriel said, smiling:

—Now, if anyone wants a little more of what vulgar people call stuffing let him or her speak.

A chorus of voices invited him to begin his own supper and Lily came forward with three potatoes which she had reserved for him.

—Very well, said Gabriel amiably, as he took another preparatory draught, kindly forget my existence, ladies and gentlemen, for a few minutes.

He set to his supper and took no part in the conversation with which the table covered Lily's removal of the plates. The subject of talk was the opera company which was then at the Theatre Royal. Mr. Bartell D'Arcy, the tenor, a dark-complexioned young man with a smart moustache, praised very highly the leading contralto of the company but Miss Furlong thought she had a rather vulgar style of production. Freddy Malins said there was a negro chieftain singing in the second part of the Gaiety pantomime who had one of the finest tenor voices he had ever heard.

—Have you heard him? he asked Mr. Bartell D'Arcy across the table.

—No, answered Mr. Bartell D'Arcy carelessly.

—Because, Freddy Malins explained, now I'd be curious to hear your opinion of him. I think he has a grand voice.

—It takes Teddy to find out the really good things, said Mr. Browne familiarly to the table.

—And why couldn't he have a voice too? asked Freddy Malins sharply. Is it because he's only a black?

Nobody answered this question and Mary Jane led the table back to the legitimate opera. One of her pupils had given her a pass for *Mignon.* Of course it was very fine, she said, but it made her think of poor Georgina Burns. Mr. Browne could go back farther still, to the old Italian companies that used to come to Dublin—Tietjens, Ilma de Murzka, Campanini, the great Trebelli, Giuglini, Ravelli, Aramburo. Those were the days, he said, when there was something like singing to be heard in Dublin. He told too of how the top gallery of the old Royal used to be packed night after night, of how one night an Italian tenor had sung five encores to *Let Me Like a Soldier Fall,* introducing a high C every time, and of how the gallery boys would sometimes in their enthusiasm unyoke the horses from the carriage of some great *prima donna* and pull her themselves through the streets to her hotel. Why did they never play the grand old operas now, he asked, *Dinorah, Lucrezia Borgia?* Because they could not get the voices to sing them: that was why.

—O, well, said Mr. Bartell D'Arcy, I presume there are as good singers today as there were then.

—Where are they? asked Mr. Browne defiantly.

—In London, Paris, Milan, said Mr. Bartell D'Arcy warmly. I suppose Caruso, for example, is quite good, if not better than any of the men you have mentioned.

—Maybe so, said Mr. Browne. But I tell you I doubt it strongly.

—O, I'd give anything to hear Caruso sing, said Mary Jane.

—For me, said Aunt Kate, who had been picking a bone, there was only one tenor. To please me, I mean. But I suppose none of you ever heard of him.

—Who was he, Miss Morkan? asked Mr. Bartell D'Arcy politely.

—His name, said Aunt Kate, was Parkinson. I heard him when he was in his prime and I think he had then the purest tenor voice that was ever put into a man's throat.

—Strange, said Mr. Bartell D'Arcy. I never even heard of him.

—Yes, yes, Miss Morkan is right, said Mr. Browne. I remember hearing of old Parkinson but he's too far back for me.

—A beautiful pure sweet mellow English tenor, said Aunt Kate with enthusiasm.

Gabriel having finished, the huge pudding was transferred to the table. The clatter of forks and spoons began again. Gabriel's wife served out spoonfuls of the pudding and passed the plates down the table. Midway down they were held up by Mary Jane, who replenished them with raspberry or orange jelly or with blancmange and jam. The pudding was of Aunt Julia's making and she received praises for it from all quarters. She herself said that it was not quite brown enough.

—Well, I hope, Miss Morkan, said Mr. Browne, that I'm brown enough for you because, you know, I'm all brown.

All the gentlemen, except Gabriel, ate some of the pudding out of compliment to Aunt Julia. As Gabriel never ate sweets the celery had been left for him. Freddy Malins also took a stalk of celery and ate it with his pudding. He had been told that celery was a capital thing for the blood and he was just then under doctor's care. Mrs. Malins, who had been silent all through the supper, said that her son was going down to Mount Melleray in a week or so. The table then spoke of Mount Melleray, how bracing the air was down there, how hospitable the monks were and how they never asked for a penny-piece from their guests.

—And do you mean to say, asked Mr. Browne incredulously, that a chap can go down there and put up there as if it were a hotel and live on the fat of the land and then come away without paying a farthing?

—O, most people give some donation to the monastery when they leave, said Mary Jane.

—I wish we had an institution like that in our Church, said Mr. Browne candidly.

He was astonished to hear that the monks never spoke, got up at two in the morning and slept in their coffins. He asked what they did it for.

—That's the rule of the order, said Aunt Kate firmly.

—Yes, but why? asked Mr. Browne.

Aunt Kate repeated that it was the rule, that was all. Mr. Browne still seemed not to understand. Freddy Malins explained to him, as best he could, that the monks were trying to make up for the sins committed by all the sinners in the outside world. The explanation was not very clear for Mr. Browne grinned and said:

—I like that idea very much but wouldn't a comfortable spring bed do them as well as a coffin?

—The coffin, said Mary Jane, is to remind them of their last end.

As the subject had grown lugubrious it was buried in a silence of the table during which Mrs. Malins could be heard saying to her neighbour in an indistinct undertone:

—They are very good men, the monks, very pious men.

The raisins and almonds and figs and apples and oranges and chocolates and sweets were now passed about the table and Aunt Julia invited all the guests to have either port or sherry. At first Mr. Bartell D'Arcy refused to take either but one of his neighbours nudged him and whispered something to him upon which he allowed his glass to be filled. Gradually as the last glasses were being filled the conversation ceased. A pause followed, broken only by the noise of the wine and by unsettlings of chairs. The Misses Morkan, all three, looked down at the tablecloth. Some one coughed once or twice and then a few gentlemen patted the table gently as a signal for silence. The silence came and Gabriel pushed back his chair and stood up.

The patting at once grew louder in encouragement and then ceased altogether. Gabriel leaned his ten trembling fingers on the tablecloth and smiled nervously at the company. Meeting a row of upturned faces he raised his eyes to the chandelier. The piano was playing a waltz tune and he could hear the skirts sweeping against the drawing-room door. People, perhaps, were standing in the snow on the quay outside, gazing up at the lighted windows and listening to the waltz music. The air was pure there. In the distance lay the park where the trees were weighted with snow. The Wellington Monument wore a gleaming cap of snow that flashed westward over the white field of Fifteen Acres.

He began:

—Ladies and Gentlemen.

—It has fallen to my lot this evening, as in years past, to perform a very pleasing task but a task for which I am afraid my poor powers as a speaker are all too inadequate.

—No, no! said Mr. Browne.

—But however that may be, I can only ask you to-night to take the will for the deed and to lend me your attention for a few moments while I endeavour to express to you in words what my feelings are on this occasion.

—Ladies and Gentlemen. It is not the first time that we have gathered together under this hospitable roof, around this hospitable board. It is not the first time that we have been the recipients—or perhaps, I had better say, the victims—of the hospitality of certain good ladies.

He made a circle in the air with his arm and paused. Everyone laughed or smiled at Aunt Kate and Aunt Julia and Mary Jane who all turned crimson with pleasure. Gabriel went on more boldly:

—I feel more strongly with every recurring year that our country has no tradition which does it so much honour and which it should guard so jealously as that of its hospitality. It is a tradition that is unique as far as my modern experience goes (and I have visited not a few places abroad) among the modern nations. Some would say, perhaps, that with us it is rather a failing than anything to be boasted of. But granted even that, it is, to my mind, a princely failing, and one that I trust will long be cultivated among us. Of one thing, at least, I am sure. As long as this one roof shelters the good ladies aforesaid—and I wish from my heart it may do for so many and many a long year to come—the tradition of genuine warm-hearted courteous Irish hospitality, which our forefathers have handed down to us and which we in turn must hand down to our descendants, is still alive among us.

A hearty murmur of assent ran round the table. It shot through Gabriel's mind that Miss Ivors was not there and that she had gone away discourteously: and he said with confidence in himself:

—Ladies and Gentlemen.

—A new generation is growing up in our midst, a generation actuated by new ideas and new principles. It is serious and enthusiastic for these new ideas and its enthusiasm, even when it is misdirected, is, I believe, in the main sincere. But we are living in a sceptical and, if I may use the phrase, a thought-tormented age: and sometimes I fear that this new generation, educated or hypereducated as it is, will lack those qualities of humanity, of hospitality, of kindly humour which belonged to an older day. Listening tonight to the names of all those great singers of the past it seemed to me, I must confess, that we were living in a less spacious age. Those days might, without exaggeration, be called spacious days: and if they are gone beyond recall let us hope, at least, that in gatherings such as this we shall still speak of them with pride and affection, still cherish in our hearts the memory of those dead and gone great ones whose fame the world will not willingly let die.

—Hear, hear! said Mr. Browne loudly.

—But yet, continued Gabriel, his voice falling into a softer inflection, there are always in gatherings such as this sadder thoughts that will recur to our minds: thoughts of the past, of youth, of changes, of absent faces that we miss here to-night. Our path through life is strewn with many such sad memories: and were we to brood upon them always we could not find the heart to go on bravely with our work among the living. We have all of us living duties and living affections which claim, and rightly claim, our strenuous endeavours.

—Therefore, I will not linger on the past. I will not let any gloomy moralizing intrude upon us here to-night. Here we are gathered together for a brief moment from the bustle and rush of our everyday routine. We are met here as friends, in the spirit of good-fellowship, as colleagues, also to a certain extent, in the true spirit of *camaraderie,* and as the guests of—what shall I call them?—the Three Graces of the Dublin musical world.

The table burst into applause and laughter at this sally. Aunt Julia vainly asked each of her neighbours in turn to tell her what Gabriel had said.

—He says we are the Three Graces, Aunt Julia, said Mary Jane.

Aunt Julia did not understand but she looked up, smiling, at Gabriel, who continued in the same vein:

—Ladies and Gentlemen.

—I will not attempt to play to-night the part that Paris played on another occasion. I will not attempt to choose between them. The task would be an invidious one and one beyond my poor powers. For when I view them in turn, whether it be our chief hostess herself, whose good heart, whose too good heart, has become a byword with all who know her, or her sister, who seems to be gifted with perennial youth and whose singing must have been a surprise and a revelation to us all to-night, or, last but not least, when I consider our youngest hostess, talented, cheerful, hard-working and the best of nieces, I confess, Ladies and Gentlemen, that I do not know to which of them I should award the prize.

Gabriel glanced down at his aunts and, seeing the large smile on Aunt Julia's face and the tears which had risen to Aunt Kate's eyes, hastened to his close. He raised his glass of port gallantly, while every member of the company fingered a glass expectantly, and said loudly:

—Let us toast them all three together. Let us drink to their health, wealth, long life, happiness and prosperity and may they long continue to hold the proud and self-won position which they hold in their profession and the position of honour and affection which they hold in our hearts.

All the guests stood up, glass in hand, and, turning towards the three seated ladies sang in unison, with Mr. Browne as leader:

For they are jolly gay fellows,
For they are jolly gay fellows,
Which nobody can deny.

Aunt Kate was making frank use of her handkerchief and even Aunt Julia seemed moved. Freddy Malins beat time with his pudding-fork and the singers turned towards one another, as if in melodious conference, while they sang, with emphasis:

Unless he tells a lie,
Unless he tells a lie.

Then, turning once more towards their hostesses, they sang:

For they are jolly gay fellows,
For they are jolly gay fellows,
For they are jolly gay fellows,
Which nobody can deny.

The acclamation which followed was taken up beyond the door of the supper-room by many of the other guests and renewed time after time, Freddy Malins acting as officer with his fork on high.

. . .

The piercing morning air came into the hall where they were standing so that Aunt Kate said:

—Close the door, somebody. Mrs. Malins will get her death of cold.

—Browne is out there, Aunt Kate, said Mary Jane.

—Browne is everywhere, said Aunt Kate, lowering her voice.

Mary Jane laughed at her tone.

—Really, she said archly, he is very attentive.

—He has been laid on here like the gas, said Aunt Kate in the same tone, all during the Christmas.

She laughed herself this time good-humoredly and then added quickly:

—But tell him to come in, Mary Jane, and close the door. I hope to goodness he didn't hear me.

At that moment the hall-door was opened and Mr. Browne came in from the doorstep, laughing as if his heart would break. He was dressed in a long green overcoat with mock astrakhan cuffs and collar and wore on his head an oval fur cap. He pointed down the snow-covered quay from where the sound of shrill prolonged whistling was borne in.

—Teddy will have all the cabs in Dublin out, he said.

Gabriel advanced from the little pantry behind the office, struggling into his overcoat and, looking round the hall, said:

—Gretta not down yet?

—She's getting on her things, Gabriel, said Aunt Kate.

—Who's playing up there? asked Gabriel.

—Nobody. They're all gone.

—O no, Aunt Kate, said Mary Jane. Bartell D'Arcy and Miss O'Callaghan aren't gone yet.

—Someone is strumming at the piano, anyhow, said Gabriel.

Mary Jane glanced at Gabriel and Mr. Browne and said with a shiver:

—It makes me feel cold to look at you two gentlemen muffled up like that. I wouldn't like to face your journey home at this hour.

—I'd like nothing better this minute, said Mr. Browne stoutly, than a rattling fine walk in the country or a fast drive with a good spanking goer between the shafts.

—We used to have a very good horse and trap at home, said Aunt Julia sadly.

—The never-to-be-forgotten Johnny, said Mary Jane, laughing.

Aunt Kate and Gabriel laughed too.

—Why, what was wonderful about Johnny? asked Mr. Browne.

—The late lamented Patrick Morkan, our grandfather, that is, explained Gabriel, commonly known in his later years as the old gentleman, was a glue-boiler.

—O, now, Gabriel, said Aunt Kate, laughing, he had a starch mill.

—Well, glue or starch, said Gabriel, the old gentleman had a horse by the name of Johnny. And Johnny used to work in the old gentleman's mill, walking round and round in order to drive the mill. That was all very well; but now comes the tragic part about Johnny. One fine day the old gentleman thought he'd like to drive out with the quality to a military review in the park.

—The Lord have mercy on his soul, said Aunt Kate compassionately.

—Amen, said Gabriel. So the old gentleman, as I said, harnessed Johnny and put on his very best tall hat and his very best stock collar and drove out in grand style from his ancestral mansion somewhere near Back Lane, I think.

Every one laughed, even Mrs. Malins, at Gabriel's manner and Aunt Kate said:

—O now, Gabriel, he didn't live in Back Lane, really. Only the mill was there.

—Out from the mansion of his forefathers, continued Gabriel, he drove with Johnny. And everything went on beautifully until Johnny came in sight of King Billy's statue: and whether he fell in love with the horse King Billy sits on or whether he thought he was back again in the mill, anyhow he began to walk around the statue.

Gabriel paced in a circle round the hall in his goloshes amid the laughter of the others.

—Round and round he went, said Gabriel, and the old gentleman, who was a very pompous old gentleman, was highly indignant. *Go on, sir! What do you mean, sir? Johnny! Johnny! Most extraordinary conduct! Can't understand the horse!*

The peals of laughter which followed Gabriel's imitation of the incident were interrupted by a resounding knock at the hall-door. Mary Jane ran to open it and let in Freddy Malins. Freddy Malins, with his hat well back on his head and his shoulders humped with cold, was puffing and steaming after his exertions.

—I could only get one cab, he said.

—O, we'll find another along the quay, said Gabriel.

—Yes, said Aunt Kate. Better not keep Mrs. Malins standing in the draught.

Mrs. Malins was helped down the front steps by her son and Mr. Browne and, after many manoeuvers, hoisted into the cab. Freddy Malins clambered in after her and spent a long time settling her on the seat, Mr. Browne helping him with advice. At last she was settled comfortably and Freddy Malins invited Mr. Browne into the cab. There was a good deal of confused talk, and then Mr. Browne got into the cab. The cabman settled his rug over his knees, and bent down for the address. The confusion grew greater and the cabman was directed differently by Freddy Malins and Mr. Browne, each of whom had his head out through a window of the cab. The difficulty was to know where to drop Mr. Browne along the route and Aunt Kate, Aunt Julia and Mary Jane helped the discussion from the doorstep with cross-directions and contradictions and abundance of laughter. As for Freddy Malins he was speechless with laughter. He popped his head in and out of the window every moment, to the great danger of his hat, and told his mother how the discussion was progressing till at last Mr. Browne shouted to the bewildered cabman above the din of everybody's laughter:

—Do you know Trinity College?

—Yes, sir, said the cabman.

—Well, drive bang up against Trinity College gates, said Mr. Browne, and then we'll tell you where to go. You understand now?

—Yes, sir, said the cabman.

—Make like a bird for Trinity College.

—Right, sir, cried the cabman.

The horse was whipped up and the cab rattled off along the quay amid a chorus of laughter and adieus.

Gabriel had not gone to the door with the others. He was in a dark part of the hall gazing up the staircase. A woman was standing near the top of the first flight, in the shadow also. He could not see her face but he could see the terracotta and salmonpink panels of her skirt which the shadow made appear black and white. It was his wife. She was leaning on the banisters, listening to something. Gabriel was surprised at her stillness and strained his ear to listen also. But he could hear little save the noise of laughter and dispute on the front steps, a few chords struck on the piano and a few notes of a man's voice singing.

He stood still in the gloom of the hall, trying to catch the air that the voice was singing and gazing up at his wife. There was grace and mystery in her attitude as if she were a symbol of something. He asked himself what is a woman standing on the stairs in the shadow, listening to distant music, a symbol of. If he were a painter he would paint her in that attitude. Her blue felt hat would show off the bronze of her hair against the darkness and the dark panels of her skirt would show off the light ones. *Distant Music* he would call the picture if he were a painter.

The hall-door was closed; and Aunt Kate, Aunt Julia and Mary Jane came down the hall, still laughing.

—Well, isn't Freddy terrible? said Mary Jane. He's really terrible.

Gabriel said nothing but pointed up the stairs towards where his wife was standing. Now that the hall-door was closed the voice and the piano could be heard more clearly. Gabriel held up his hand for them to be silent. The song seemed to be in the old Irish tonality and the singer seemed uncertain both of his words and of his voice. The voice, made plaintive by distance and by the singer's hoarseness, faintly illuminated the cadence of the air with words expressing grief:

O, the rain falls on my heavy locks
And the dew wets my skin,
My babe lies cold . . .

—O, exclaimed Mary Jane. It's Bartell D'Arcy singing and he wouldn't sing all the night. O, I'll get him to sing a song before he goes.

—O, do, Mary Jane, said Aunt Kate.

Mary Jane brushed past the others and ran to the staircase but before she reached it the singing stopped and the piano was closed abruptly.

—O, what a pity! she cried. Is he coming down, Gretta?

Gabriel heard his wife answer yes and saw her come down towards them. A few steps behind her were Mr. Bartell D'Arcy and Miss O'Callaghan.

—O, Mr. D'Arcy, cried Mary Jane, it's downright mean of you to break off like that when we were all in raptures listening to you.

—I have been at him all the evening, said Miss O'Callaghan, and Mrs. Conroy too and he told us he had a dreadful cold and couldn't sing.

—O, Mr. D'Arcy, said Aunt Kate, now that was a great fib to tell.

—Can't you see that I'm as hoarse as a crow? said Mr. D'Arcy roughly.

He went into the pantry hastily and put on his overcoat. The others, taken aback by his rude speech, could find nothing to say. Aunt Kate wrinkled her brows and made signs to the others to drop the subject. Mr. D'Arcy stood swathing his neck carefully and frowning.

—It's the weather, said Aunt Julia, after a pause.

—Yes, everybody has colds, said Aunt Kate readily, everybody.

—They say, said Mary Jane, we haven't had snow like it for thirty years; and I read this morning in the newspapers that the snow is general all over Ireland.

—I love the look of snow, said Aunt Julia sadly.

—So do I, said Miss O'Callaghan. I think Christmas is never really Christmas unless we have snow on the ground.

—But poor Mr. D'Arcy doesn't like the snow, said Aunt Kate, smiling.

Mr. D'Arcy came from the pantry, fully swathed and buttoned, and in a repentant tone told them the history of his cold. Everyone gave him advice and said it was a great pity and urged him to be very careful of his throat in the night air. Gabriel watched his wife who did not join in the conversation. She was standing right under the dusty fanlight and the flame of the gas lit up the rich bronze of her hair which he had seen her drying at the fire a few days before. She was in the same attitude and seemed unaware of the talk about her. At last she turned towards them and Gabriel saw that there was a colour on her cheeks and that her eyes were shining. A sudden tide of joy went leaping out of his heart.

—Mr. D'Arcy, she said, what is the name of that song you were singing?

—It's called *The Lass of Aughrim,* said Mr. D'Arcy, but I couldn't remember it properly. Why? Do you know it?

—*The Lass of Aughrim,* she repeated. I couldn't think of the name.

—It's a very nice air, said Mary Jane. I'm sorry you were not in voice to-night.

—Now, Mary Jane, said Aunt Kate, don't annoy Mr. D'Arcy. I won't have him annoyed.

Seeing that all were ready to start she shepherded them to the door where good-night was said:

—Well, good-night, Aunt Kate, and thanks for the pleasant evening.

—Good-night, Gabriel. Good-night, Gretta!

—Good-night, Aunt Kate, and thanks ever so much. Good-night, Aunt Julia.

—O, good-night, Gretta, I didn't see you.

—Good-night, Mr. D'Arcy. Good-night, Miss O'Callaghan.

—Good-night, Miss Morkan.

—Good-night, again.

—Good-night, all. Safe home.

—Good-night. Good-night.

The morning was still dark. A dull yellow light brooded over the houses and the river; and the sky seemed to be descending. It was slushy underfoot; and only streaks and patches of snow lay on the roofs, on the parapets of the quay and on the area railings. The lamps were still burning redly in the murky air and, across the river, the palace of the Four Courts stood out menacingly against the heavy sky.

She was walking on before him with Mr. Bartell D'Arcy, her shoes in a brown parcel tucked under one arm and her hands holding her skirt up from the slush. She had no longer any grace of attitude but Gabriel's eyes were still bright with happiness. The blood went bounding along his veins; and the thoughts went rioting through his brain, proud, joyful, tender, valorous.

She was walking on before him so lightly and so erect that he longed to run after her noiselessly, catch her by the shoulders and say something foolish and affectionate into her ear. She seemed to him so frail that he longed to defend her against something and then to be alone with her. Moments of their secret life together burst like stars upon his memory. A heliotrope envelope was lying beside his breakfast-cup and he was caressing it with his hand. Birds were twittering in the ivy and the sunny web of the curtain was shimmering along the floor: he could not eat for happiness. They were standing on the crowded platform and he was placing a ticket inside the warm palm of her glove. He was standing with her in the cold, looking through a grated window at a man making bottles in a roaring furnace. It was very cold. Her face, fragrant in the cold air, was quite close to his; and suddenly she called out to the man at the furnace:

—Is the fire hot, sir?

But the man could not hear her with the noise of the furnace. It was just as well. He might have answered rudely.

A wave of yet more tender joy escaped from his heart and went coursing in warm flood along his arteries. Like the tender fires of stars moments of their life together, that no one knew of or would ever know of, broke upon and illumined his memory. He longed to recall to her those moments, to make her forget the years of their dull existence together and remember only their moments of ecstasy. For the years, he felt, had not quenched his soul or hers.

Their children, his writing, her household cares had not quenched all their souls' tender fire. In one letter that he had written to her then he had said: *Why is it that words like these seem to me so dull and cold? Is it because there is no word tender enough to be your name?*

Like distant music these words that he had written years before were borne towards him from the past. He longed to be alone with her. When the others had gone away, when he and she were in their room in the hotel, then they would be alone together. He would call her softly:

—Gretta!

Perhaps she would not hear at once: she would be undressing. Then something in his voice would strike her. She would turn and look at him. . . .

At the corner of Winetavern Street they met a cab. He was glad of its rattling noise as it saved him from conversation. She was looking out of the window and seemed tired. The others spoke only a few words, pointing out some building or street. The horse galloped along wearily under the murky morning sky, dragging his old rattling box after his heels, and Gabriel was again in a cab with her, galloping to catch the boat, galloping to their honeymoon.

As the cab drove across O'Connell Bridge Miss O'Callaghan said:

—They say you never cross O'Connell Bridge without seeing a white horse.

—I see a white man this time, said Gabriel.

—Where? asked Mr. Bartell D'Arcy.

Gabriel pointed to the statue on which lay patches of snow. Then he nodded familiarly to it and waved his hand.

—Good-night, Dan, he said gaily.

When the cab drew up before the hotel Gabriel jumped out and, in spite of Mr. Bartell D'Arcy's protest, paid the driver. He gave the man a shilling over his fare. The man saluted and said:

—A prosperous New Year to you, sir.

—The same to you, said Gabriel cordially.

She leaned for a moment on his arm in getting out of the cab and while standing at the curbstone, bidding the others good-night. She leaned lightly on his arm, as lightly as when she had danced with him a few hours before. He had felt proud and happy then, happy that she was his, proud of her grace and wifely carriage. But now, after the kindling again of so many memories, the first touch of her body, musical and strange and perfumed, sent through him a keen pang of lust. Under the cover of silence he pressed her arm closely to his side; and, as they stood at the hotel door, he felt that they had escaped from their lives and duties, escaped from home and friends and run away together with wild and radiant hearts to a new adventure.

An old man was dozing in a great hooded chair in the hall. He lit a candle in the office and went before them to the stairs. They followed him in silence, their feet falling in soft thuds on the thickly carpeted stairs. She mounted the stairs behind the porter, her head bowed in the ascent, her frail shoulders curved as with a burden, her skirt girt tightly about her. He could have flung his arms about her hips and held her still for his arms were trembling with desire to seize her and only the stress of his nails against the palms of his hands held the wild impulse of his body in check. The porter halted on the stairs to settle his guttering candle. They halted too on the steps below him. In the silence Gabriel could hear the falling of the molten wax into the tray and the thumping of his own heart against his ribs.

The porter led them along a corridor and opened a door. Then he set his unstable candle down on a toilet-table and asked at what hour they were to be called in the morning.

—Eight, said Gabriel.

The porter pointed to the tap of the electric-light and began a muttered apology but Gabriel cut him short.

—We don't want any light. We have enough light from the street. And I say, he added, pointing to the candle, you might remove that handsome article, like a good man.

The porter took up his candle again, but slowly for he was surprised by such a novel idea. Then he mumbled good-night and went out. Gabriel shot the lock to.

A ghostly light from the street lamp lay in a long shaft from one window to the door. Gabriel threw his overcoat and hat on a couch and crossed the room towards the window. He looked down into the street in order that his emotion might calm a little. Then he turned and leaned against a chest of drawers with his back to the light. She had taken off her hat and cloak and was standing before a large swinging mirror, unhooking her waist. Gabriel paused for a few moments, watching her, and then said:

—Gretta!

She turned away from the mirror slowly and walked along the shaft of light towards him. Her face looked so serious and weary that the words would not pass Gabriel's lips. No, it was not the moment yet.

—You look tired, he said.

—I am a little, she answered.

—You don't feel ill or weak?

—No, tired: that's all.

She went on to the window and stood there, looking out. Gabriel waited again and then, fearing that diffidence was about to conquer him, he said abruptly:

—By the way, Gretta!

—What is it?

—You know that poor fellow Malins? he said quickly.

—Yes. What about him?

—Well, poor fellow, he's a decent sort of chap after all, continued Gabriel in a false voice. He gave me back that sovereign I lent him and I didn't expect it really. It's a pity he wouldn't keep away from that Browne, because he's not a bad fellow at heart.

He was trembling now with annoyance. Why did she seem so abstracted? He did not know how he could begin. Was she annoyed, too, about something? If she would only turn to him or come to him of her own accord! To take her as she was would be brutal. No, he must see some ardour in her eyes first. He longed to be master of her strange mood.

—When did you lend him the pound? she asked, after a pause.

Gabriel strove to restrain himself from breaking out into brutal language about the sottish Malins and his pound. He longed to cry to her from his soul, to crush her body against his, to overmaster her. But he said:

—O, at Christmas, when he opened that little Christmas-card shop in Henry Street.

He was in such a fever of rage and desire that he did not hear her come from the window. She stood before him for an instant, looking at him strangely. Then, suddenly raising herself on tiptoe and resting her hands lightly on his shoulders, she kissed him.

—You are a very generous person, Gabriel, she said.

Gabriel, trembling with delight at her sudden kiss and at the quaintness of her phrase, put his hands on her hair and began smoothing it back, scarcely touching it with his fingers. The washing had made it fine and brilliant. His heart was brimming over with happiness. Just when he was wishing for it she had come to him of her own accord. Perhaps her thoughts had been running with his. Perhaps she had felt the impetuous desire that was in him and then the yielding mood had come upon her. Now that she had fallen to him so easily he wondered why he had been so diffident.

He stood, holding her head between his hands. Then, slipping one arm swiftly about her body and drawing her towards him, he said softly:

—Gretta dear, what are you thinking about?

She did not answer nor yield wholly to his arm. He said again softly:

—Tell me what it is, Gretta. I think I know what is the matter. Do I know?

She did not answer at once. Then she had an outburst of tears:

—O, I am thinking about that song, *The Lass of Aughrim.*

She broke loose from him and ran to the bed and, throwing her arms across the bed-rail, hid her face. Gabriel stood stock-still for a moment in astonishment and then followed her. As he passed the way of the cheval-glass he caught sight of himself in full length, his broad, well-filled shirtfront, the face whose expression always puzzled him when he saw it in a mirror and his glimmering gilt-rimmed eyeglasses. He halted a few paces from her and said:

—What about the song? Why does that make you cry?

She raised her head from her arms and dried her eyes with the back of her hand like a child. A kinder note than he intended went into his voice.

—Why, Gretta? he asked.

—I am thinking about a person long ago who used to sing that song.

—And who was the person long ago? asked Gabriel, smiling.

—It was a person I used to know in Galway when I was living with my grandmother, she said.

The smile passed away from Gabriel's face. A dull anger began to gather again at the back of his mind and the dull fires of his lust began to glow angrily in his veins.

—Someone you were in love with? he asked ironically.

—It was a young boy I used to know, she answered, named Michael Furey. He used to sing that song, *The Lass of Aughrim*. He was very delicate.

Gabriel was silent. He did not wish her to think that he was interested in this delicate boy.

—I can see him so plainly, she said after a moment. Such big eyes he had: big dark eyes! And such an expression in them—an expression!

—O, then, you were in love with him? said Gabriel.

—I used to go out walking with him, she said, when I was in Galway.

A thought flew across Gabriel's mind.

—Perhaps that was why you wanted to go to Galway with that Ivors girl? he said coldly.

She looked at him and asked in surprise:

—What for?

Her eyes made Gabriel feel awkward. He shrugged his shoulders and said:

—How do I know? To see him perhaps.

She looked away from him along the shaft of light towards the window in silence.

—He is dead, she said at length. He died when he was only seventeen. Isn't it a terrible thing to die so young as that?

—What was he? asked Gabriel still ironically.

—He was in the gasworks, she said.

Gabriel felt humiliated by the failure of his irony and by the evocation of this figure from the dead, a boy in the gasworks. While he had been full of memories of their secret life together, full of tenderness and joy and desire, she had been comparing him in her mind with another. A shameful consciousness of his own person assailed him. He saw himself as a ludicrous figure, acting as a pennyboy for his aunts, a nervous well-meaning sentimentalist, orating to vulgarians and idealizing his own clownish lusts, the pitiable fatuous fellow he had caught a glimpse of in the mirror. Instinctively he turned his back more to the light lest she might see the shame that burned upon his forehead.

He tried to keep up his tone of cold interrogation but his voice when he spoke was humble and indifferent.

—I suppose you were in love with this Michael Furey, Gretta, he said.

—I was great with him at that time, she said.

Her voice was veiled and sad. Gabriel, feeling now how vain it would be to try to lead her whither he had purposed, caressed one of her hands and said, also sadly:

—And what did he die of so young, Gretta? Consumption, was it?

—I think he died for me, she answered.

A vague terror seized Gabriel at this answer as if, at that hour when he had hoped to triumph, some impalpable and vindictive being was coming against him, gathering forces against him in its vague world. But he shook himself free of it with an effort of reason and continued to caress her hand. He did not question her again for he felt that she would tell him of herself. Her hand was warm and moist: it did not respond to his touch but he continued to caress it just as he had caressed her first letter to him that spring morning.

—It was in the winter, she said, about the beginning of the winter when I was going to leave my grandmother's house and come up here to the convent. And he was ill at the time in his lodgings in Galway and wouldn't be let out and his people in Oughterard were written to. He was in decline, they said, or something like that. I never knew rightly.

She paused for a moment and sighed.

—Poor fellow, she said. He was very fond of me and he was such a gentle boy. We used to go out together, walking, you know, Gabriel, like the way they do in the country. He was going to study singing only for his health. He had a very good voice, poor Michael Furey.

—Well; and then? asked Gabriel.

—And then when it came to the time for me to leave Galway and come up to the convent he was much worse and I wouldn't be let see him so I wrote a letter saying I was going up to Dublin and would be back in the summer and hoping he would be better then.

She paused for a moment to get her voice under control and went on:

—Then the night before I left I was in my grandmother's house in Nuns' Island, packing up, and I heard gravel thrown up against the window. The window was so wet I couldn't see so I ran downstairs as I was and slipped out the back into the garden and there was the poor fellow at the end of the garden, shivering.

—And did you not tell him to go back? asked Gabriel.

—I implored of him to go home at once and told him he would get his death in the rain. But he said he did not want to live. I can see his eyes as well as well! He was standing at the end of the wall where there was a tree.

—And did he go home? asked Gabriel.

—Yes, he went home. And when I was only a week in the convent he died and he was buried in Oughterard where his people came from. O, on the day I heard that, that he was dead!

She stopped, choking with sobs, and overcome by emotion, flung herself face downward on the bed, sobbing in the quilt. Gabriel held her hand for a moment longer, irresolutely, and then, shy of intruding on her grief, let it fall gently and walked quietly to the window.

She was fast asleep.

Gabriel, leaning on his elbow, looked for a few moments unresentfully on her tangled hair and half-open mouth, listening to her deep-drawn breath. So she had had that romance in her life: a man had died for her sake. It hardly pained him now to think how poor a part he, her husband, had played in her life. He watched her while she slept as though he and she had never lived together as man and wife. His curious eyes rested long upon her face and on her hair: and, as he thought of what she must have been then, in that time of her first girlish beauty, a strange friendly pity for her entered his soul. He did not like to say even to himself that her face was no longer beautiful but he knew that it was no longer the face for which Michael Furey had braved death.

Perhaps she had not told him all the story. His eyes moved to the chair over which she had thrown some of her clothes. A petticoat string dangled to the floor. One boot stood up-right, its limp upper fallen down: the fellow of it lay upon its side. He wondered at his riot of emotions of an hour before. From what had it proceeded? From his aunt's supper, from his own foolish speech, from the wine and dancing, the merry-making when saying good-night in the hall, the pleasure of the walk along the river in the snow. Poor Aunt Julia! She, too, would soon be a shade with the shade of Patrick Morkan and his horse. He had caught that haggard look upon her face for a moment when she was singing *Arrayed for the Bridal.* Soon, perhaps, he would be sitting in that same drawing-room, dressed in black, his silk hat on his knees. The blinds would be drawn down and Aunt Kate would be sitting beside him, crying and blowing her nose and telling him how Julia had died. He would cast about in his mind for some words that might console her, and would find only lame and useless ones. Yes, yes: that would happen very soon.

The air of the room chilled his shoulders. He stretched himself cautiously along under the sheets and lay down beside his wife. One by one they were all becoming shades. Better pass boldly into that other world, in the full glory of some passion, than fade and wither dismally with age. He thought of how she who lay beside him had locked in her heart for so many years that image of her lover's eyes when he had told her that he did not wish to live.

Generous tears filled Gabriel's eyes. He had never felt like that himself towards any woman but he knew that such a feeling must be love. The tears gathered more thickly in his eyes and in the partial darkness he imagined he saw the form of a young man standing under a dripping tree. Other forms were near. His soul had approached that region where dwell the vast hosts of the dead. He was conscious of, but could not apprehend, their wayward and flickering existence. His own identity was fading out into a grey impalpable world: the solid world itself which these dead had one time reared and lived in was dissolving and dwindling.

A few light taps upon the pane made him turn to the window. It had begun to snow again. He watched sleepily the flakes, silver and dark, falling obliquely against the lamplight. The time had come for him to set out on his journey westward. Yes, the newspapers were right: snow was general all over Ireland. It was falling on every part of the dark central plain, on the treeless hills, falling softly upon the Bog of Allen and, farther westward, softly falling into the dark mutinous Shannon waves. It was falling, too, upon every part of the lonely churchyard on the hill where Michael Furey lay buried. It lay thickly drifted on the crooked crosses and headstones, on the spears of the little gate, on the barren thorns. His soul swooned slowly as he heard the snow falling faintly through the universe and faintly falling, like the descent of their last end, upon all the living and the dead.

FRANZ KAFKA

1883–1924

At the time of Kafka's birth, Prague epitomized the conflicts left behind by centuries of European political, religious, and class struggle. Conquered and devastated by innumerable invaders, Prague by 1883 was under the forcible rule of the Austro-Hungarian Monarchy. The violent unrest that pervaded the city during Kafka's childhood is perhaps best symbolized by the assassination at Sarajevo in 1914 of the heir-apparent to the Monarchy, Archduke Ferdinand —the event that sparked off World War I. Kafka was not politically very active, and his family seems to have had a tolerable relation with the Austrian officials, but his deep sensitivity to the cruelty and arbitrariness of absolute political power exercised by a bureaucratic government appears in much of his work, especially in his best-known novels, *The Trial* and *The Castle.*

Kafka was born into a prosperous Jewish family that was particularly closely knit because of their awareness of the religious hatreds that swirled around them. Kafka's two elder brothers died in childhood, leaving Franz the focus of all his father's intense concern for the family's future. However much his father may have loved him, Kafka could not stand the pressure, and the love-hate relationship that developed between them and is incorporated into Kafka's fiction is surely the most intense in modern literature.

After studying law Kafka worked as a minor official in a quasi-government insurance company, but all his energy was directed toward beginning to write and toward experimenting with mysticism. He was fascinated by the intense, morbid states of mind that produced in him surrealistic vision and revelation. Mysticism was popular at the time, and he was much encouraged in his experimentation by a group of friends who shared his interests. After meeting Kafka, Rudolf Steiner, the well-known spiritualist-philosopher, declared him a genuine clairvoyant. Physiologically, too, Kafka was disposed to experience extreme states of consciousness by the tuberculosis from which he suffered and eventually died. Reality for Kafka was always phantasmagoric, never firmly located in the "ordinary" apprehension of physical objects. His studies in mysticism, as well as his medical vulnerability to manic depression, helped to confirm for him the validity of the unique world that he portrays in his fiction.

This world is often more a parable of man's journey through life than a realistic portrayal of a sequence of events. Though always serious, his fiction contains a special kind of humor that acknowledges amusement as a valid response to the absurdity of the way circumstances thwart or reshape even the most elaborate and sensible human designs.

Predictably, Kafka's intense inner world affected his personal relationships. For five years, from 1912 through 1917, he was deeply in love with a woman referred to in the letters that survive only as "F. B.," but it was a tempestuous affair that, to his despair, she finally terminated. In the last year of his life he found more tranquil happiness with a woman who stayed by him until his death.

Kafka published almost none of his writing during his lifetime, and just before his death instructed his friend Max Brod to burn his manuscripts. Fortunately for us, Brod disregarded the instructions and oversaw the publication of his friend's work.

The Metamorphosis

I

As Gregor Samsa awoke one morning from uneasy dreams he found himself transformed in his bed into a gigantic insect. He was lying on his hard, as it were armor-plated, back and when he lifted his head a little he could see his dome-like brown belly divided into stiff arched segments on top of which the bed quilt could hardly keep in position and was about to slide off completely. His numerous legs, which were pitifully thin compared to the rest of his bulk, waved helplessly before his eyes.

What has happened to me? he thought. It was no dream. His room, a regular human bedroom, only rather too small, lay quiet between the four familiar walls. Above the table on which a collection of cloth samples was unpacked and spread out—Samsa was a commercial traveler—hung the picture which he had recently cut out of an illustrated magazine and put into a pretty gilt frame. It showed a lady, with a fur cap on and a fur stole, sitting upright and holding out to the spectator a huge fur muff into which the whole of her forearm had vanished!

Gregor's eyes turned next to the window, and the overcast sky—one could hear rain drops beating on the window gutter—made him quite melancholy. What about sleeping a little longer and forgetting all this nonsense, he thought, but it could not be done, for he was accustomed to sleep on his right side and in his present condition he could not turn himself over. However violently he forced himself towards his right side he always rolled on to his back again. He tried it at least a hundred times, shutting his eyes to keep from seeing his struggling legs, and only desisted when he began to feel in his side a faint dull ache he had never experienced before.

Oh God, he thought, what an exhausting job I've picked on! Traveling about day in, day out. It's much more irritating work than doing the actual business in the office, and on top of that there's the trouble of constant traveling, of worrying about train connections, the bad and irregular meals, casual acquaintances that are always new and never become intimate friends. The devil take it all! He felt a slight itching up on his belly; slowly pushed himself on his back nearer to the top of the bed so that he could lift his head more easily; identified the itching place which was surrounded by many small white spots the nature of which he could not understand and made to touch it with a leg, but drew the leg back immediately, for the contact made a cold shiver run through him.

He slid down again into his former position. This getting up early, he thought, makes one quite stupid. A man needs his sleep. Other commercials live like harem women. For instance, when I come back to the hotel of a morning to write up the orders I've got, these others are only sitting down to breakfast. Let me just try that with my chief; I'd be sacked on the spot. Anyhow, that might be quite a good thing for me, who can tell? If I didn't have to hold my hand because of my parents I'd have given notice long ago, I'd have gone to the chief and told him exactly what I think of him. That would knock him endways from his desk! It's a queer way of doing, too, this sitting on high at a desk and talking down to employees, especially when they have to come quite near because the chief is hard of hearing. Well, there's still hope; once I've saved enough money to pay back my parents' debts to him—that should take another five or six years—I'll do it without fail. I'll cut myself completely loose then. For the moment, though, I'd better get up, since my train goes at five.

He looked at the alarm clock ticking on the chest. Heavenly Father! he thought. It was half-past six o'clock and the hands were quietly moving on, it was even past the half-hour, it was getting on toward a quarter to seven. Had the alarm clock not gone off? From the bed one could see that it had been properly set for four o'clock; of course it must have gone off. Yes, but was it possible to sleep quietly through that ear-splitting noise? Well, he had not slept quietly, yet apparently all the more soundly for that. But what was he to do now? The next train went at seven o'clock; to catch that he would need to hurry like mad and his samples weren't even packed up, and he himself wasn't feeling particularly fresh and active. And even if he did catch the train he wouldn't avoid a row with the chief, since the firm's porter would have been waiting for the five o'clock train and would have long since reported his failure to turn up. The porter was a creature of the chief's, spineless and stupid. Well, supposing he were to say he was sick? But that would be most unpleasant and would look suspicious, since during his five years' employment he had not been ill once. The chief himself would be sure to come with the sick-insurance doctor, would reproach his parents with their son's laziness and would cut all excuses short by referring to the insurance doctor, who of course regarded all mankind as perfectly healthy malingerers. And would he be so far wrong on this occasion? Gregor really felt quite well, apart from a drowsiness that was utterly superfluous after such a long sleep, and he was even unusually hungry.

As all this was running through his mind at top speed without his being able to decide to leave his bed—the alarm clock had just struck a quarter to seven—there came a cautious tap at the door behind the head of his bed. "Gregor," said a voice—it was his mother's—"it's a quarter to seven. Hadn't you a train to catch?" That gentle voice! Gregor had a shock as he heard his own voice answering hers, unmistakably his own voice, it was true, but with a persistent horrible twittering squeak behind it like an undertone, that left the words in their clear shape only for the first moment and then rose up reverberating round them to destroy their sense, so that one could not be sure one had heard them rightly. Gregor wanted to answer at length and explain everything, but in the circumstances he confined himself to saying: "Yes, yes, thank you, Mother, I'm getting up now." The wooden door between them must have kept the change in his voice from being noticeable outside, for his mother contented herself with this statement and shuffled away. Yet this brief exchange of words had made the other members of the family aware that Gregor was still in the house, as they had not expected, and at one of the side doors his father was already knocking, gently, yet with his fist. "Gregor, Gregor," he called, "what's the matter with you?" And after a little while he called again in a deeper voice: "Gregor! Gregor!" At the other side door his sister was saying in a low, plaintive tone: "Gregor? Aren't you well? Are you needing anything?" He answered them both at once: "I'm just ready," and did his best to make his voice sound as normal as possible by enunciating the words very clearly and leaving long pauses between them. So his father went back to his breakfast, but his sister whispered: "Gregor, open the door, do." However, he was not thinking of opening the door, and felt thankful for the prudent habit he had acquired in traveling of locking all doors during the night, even at home.

His immediate intention was to get up quietly without being disturbed, to put on his clothes and above all eat his breakfast, and only then to consider what else was to be done, since in bed, he was well aware, his meditations would come to no sensible conclusion. He remembered that often enough in bed he had felt small aches and pains, probably caused by awkward postures, which had proved purely imaginary once he got up, and he looked forward eagerly to seeing this morning's delusions gradually fall away. That the change in his voice was nothing but the precursor of a severe chill, a standing ailment of commercial travelers, he had not the least possible doubt.

To get rid of the quilt was quite easy; he had only to inflate himself a little and it fell off by itself. But the next move was difficult, especially because he was so uncommonly broad. He would have needed arms and hands to hoist himself up; instead he had only the numerous little legs which never stopped waving in all directions and which he could not control in the least. When he tried to bend one of them it was the first to stretch itself straight; and did he succeed at last in making it do what he wanted, all the other legs meanwhile waved the more wildly in a high degree of unpleasant agitation. "But what's the use of lying idle in bed," said Gregor to himself.

He thought that he might get out of bed with the lower part of his body first, but this lower part, which he had not yet seen and of which he could form no clear conception, proved too difficult to move; it shifted so slowly; and when finally, almost wild with annoyance, he gathered his forces together and thrust out recklessly, he had miscalculated the direction and bumped heavily against the lower end of the bed, and the stinging pain he felt informed him that precisely this lower part of his body was at the moment probably the most sensitive.

So he tried to get the top part of himself out first, and cautiously moved his head towards the edge of the bed. That proved easy enough, and despite its breadth and mass the bulk of his body at last slowly followed the movement of his head. Still, when he finally got his head free over the edge of the bed he felt too scared to go on advancing, for after all if he let himself fall in this way it would take a miracle to keep his head from being injured. And at all costs he must not lose consciousness now, precisely now; he would rather stay in bed.

But when after a repetition of the same efforts he lay in his former position again, sighing, and watched his little legs struggling against each other more wildly than ever, if that were possible, and saw no way of bringing any order into this arbitrary confusion, he told himself again that it was impossible to stay in bed and that the most sensible course was to risk everything for the smallest hope of getting away from it. At the same time he did not forget meanwhile to remind himself that cool reflection, the coolest possible, was much better than desperate resolves. In such moments he focused his eyes as sharply as possible on the window, but, unfortunately, the prospect of the morning fog, which muffled even the other side of the narrow street, brought him little encouragement and comfort. "Seven o'clock already," he said to himself when the alarm clock chimed again, "seven o'clock already and still such a thick fog." And for a little while he lay quiet, breathing lightly, as if perhaps expecting such complete repose to restore all things to their real and normal condition.

But then he said to himself: "Before it strikes a quarter past seven I must be quite out of this bed, without fail. Anyhow, by that time someone will have come from the office to ask for me, since it opens before seven." And he set himself to rocking his whole body at once in a regular rhythm, with the idea of swinging it out of the bed. If he tipped himself out in that way he could keep his head from injury by lifting it at an acute angle when he fell. His back seemed to be hard and was not likely to suffer from a fall on the carpet. His biggest worry was the loud crash he would not be able to help making, which would probably cause anxiety, if not terror, behind all the doors. Still, he must take the risk.

When he was already half out of the bed—the new method was more a game than an effort, for he needed only to hitch himself across by rocking to and fro—it struck him how simple it would be if he could get help. Two strong people—he thought of his father and the servant girl—would be amply sufficient; they would only have to thrust their arms under his convex back, lever him out of the bed, bend down with their burden and then be patient enough to let him turn himself right over on to the floor, where it was to be hoped his legs would then find their proper function. Well, ignoring the fact that the doors were all locked, ought he really to call for help? In spite of his misery he could not suppress a smile at the very idea of it.

He had got so far that he could barely keep his equilibrium when he rocked himself strongly, and he would have to nerve himself very soon for the final decision since in five minutes' time it would be a quarter past seven—when the front door bell rang. "That's someone from the office," he said to himself, and grew almost rigid, while his little legs only jigged about all the faster. For a moment everything stayed quiet. "They're not going to open the door," said Gregor to himself, catching at some kind of irrational hope. But then of course the servant girl went as usual to the door with her heavy tread and opened it. Gregor needed only to hear the first good morning of the visitor to know immediately who it was—the chief clerk himself. What a fate, to be condemned to work for a firm where the smallest omission at once gave rise to the gravest suspicion! Were all employees in a body nothing but scoundrels, was there not among them one single loyal devoted man who, had he wasted only an hour or so of the firm's time in a morning, was so tormented by conscience as to be driven out of his mind and actually incapable of leaving his bed? Wouldn't it really have been sufficient to send an apprentice to inquire—if any inquiry were necessary at all—did the chief clerk himself have to come and thus indicate to the entire family, an innocent family, that this suspicious circumstance could be investigated by no one less versed in affairs than himself? And more through the agitation caused by these reflections than through any act of will Gregor swung himself out of bed with all his strength. There was a loud thump, but it was not really a crash. His fall was broken to some extent by the carpet, his back, too, was less stiff than he thought, and so there was merely a dull thud, not so very startling. Only he had not lifted his head carefully enough and had hit it; he turned it and rubbed it on the carpet in pain and irritation.

"That was something falling down in there," said the chief clerk in the next room to the left. Gregor tried to suppose to himself that something like what had happened to him today might some day happen to the chief clerk; one really could not deny that it was possible. But as if in brusque reply to this supposition the chief clerk took a couple of firm steps in the next-door room and his patent leather boots creaked. From the right-hand room his sister was whispering to inform him of the situation: "Gregor, the chief clerk's here." "I know," muttered Gregor to himself; but he didn't dare to make his voice loud enough for his sister to hear it.

"Gregor," said his father now from the left-hand room, "the chief clerk has come and wants to know why you didn't catch the early train. We don't know what to say to him. Besides, he wants to talk to you in person. So open the door, please. He will be good enough to excuse the untidiness of your room." "Good morning, Mr. Samsa," the chief clerk was calling amiably meanwhile. "He's not well," said his mother to the visitor, while his father was still speaking through the door, "he's not well, sir, believe me. What else would make him miss a train! The boy thinks about nothing but his work. It makes me almost cross the way he never goes out in the evenings; he's been here the last eight days and has stayed at home every single evening. He just sits there quietly at the table reading a newspaper or looking through railway timetables. The only amusement he gets is doing fretwork. For instance, he spent two or three evenings cutting out a little picture frame; you would be surprised to see how pretty it is; it's hanging in his room; you'll see it in a minute when Gregor opens the door. I must say I'm glad you've come, sir; we should never have got him to unlock the door by ourselves; he's so obstinate; and I'm sure he's unwell, though he wouldn't have it to be so this morning." "I'm just coming," said Gregor slowly and carefully, not moving an inch for fear of losing one word of the conversation. "I can't think of any other explanation, madam," said the chief clerk, "I hope it's nothing serious. Although on the other hand I must say that we men of business—fortunately or unfortunately—very often simply have to ignore any slight indisposition, since business must be attended to." "Well, can the chief clerk come in now?" asked Gregor's father impatiently, again knocking on the door. "No," said Gregor. In the left-hand room a painful silence followed this refusal, in the right-hand room his sister began to sob.

Why didn't his sister join the others? She was probably newly out of bed and hadn't even begun to put on her clothes yet. Well, why was she crying? Because he wouldn't get up and let the chief clerk in, because he was in danger of losing his job, and because the chief would begin dunning his parents again for the old debts? Surely these were things one didn't need to worry about for the present. Gregor was still at home and not in the least thinking of deserting the family. At the moment, true, he was lying on the carpet and no one who knew the condition he was in could seriously expect him to admit the chief clerk. But for such a small discourtesy, which could plausibly be explained away somehow later on, Gregor could hardly be dismissed on the spot. And it seemed to Gregor that it would be much more sensible to leave him in peace for the present than to trouble him with tears and entreaties. Still, of course, their uncertainty bewildered them all and excused their behavior.

"Mr. Samsa," the chief clerk called now in a louder voice, "what's the matter with you? Here you are, barricading yourself in your room, giving only 'yes' and 'no' for answers, causing your parents a lot of unnecessary trouble and neglecting—I mention this only in passing—neglecting your business duties in an incredible fashion. I am speaking here in the name of your parents and of your chief, and I beg you quite seriously to give me an immediate and precise explanation. You amaze me, you amaze me. I thought you were a quiet, dependable person, and now all at once you seem bent on making a disgraceful exhibition of yourself. The chief did hint to me early this morning a possible explanation for your disappearance—with reference to the cash payments that were entrusted to you recently—but I almost pledged my solemn word of honor that this could not be so. But now that I see how incredibly obstinate you are, I no longer have the slightest desire to take your part at all. And your position in the firm is not so unassailable. I came with the intention of telling you all this in private, but since you are wasting my time so needlessly I don't see why your parents shouldn't hear it too. For some time past your work has been most unsatisfactory; this is not the season of the year for a business boom, of course, we admit that, but a season of the year for doing no business at all, that does not exist, Mr. Samsa, must not exist."

"But, sir," cried Gregor, beside himself and in his agitation forgetting everything else, "I'm just going to open the door this very minute. A slight illness, an attack of giddiness, has kept me from getting up. I'm still lying in bed. But I feel all right again. I'm getting out of bed now. Just give me a moment or two longer! I'm not quite so well as I thought. But I'm all right, really. How a thing like that can suddenly strike one down! Only last night I was quite well, my parents can tell you, or rather I did have a slight presentiment. I must have showed some sign of it. Why didn't I report it at the office! But one always thinks that an indisposition can be got over without staying in the house. Oh sir, do spare my parents! All that you're reproaching me with now has no foundation; no one has ever said a word to me about it. Perhaps you haven't looked at the last orders I sent in. Anyhow, I can still catch the eight o'clock train, I'm much the better for my few hours' rest. Don't let me detain you here, sir; I'll be attending to business very soon, and do be good enough to tell the chief so and to make my excuses to him!"

And while all this was tumbling out pell-mell and Gregor hardly knew what he was saying, he had reached the chest quite easily, perhaps because of the practice he had had in bed, and was now trying to lever himself upright by means of it. He meant actually to open the door, actually to show himself and speak to the chief clerk; he was eager to find out what the others, after all their insistence, would say at the sight of him. If they were horrified then the responsibility was no longer his and he could stay quiet. But if they took it calmly, then he had no reason either to be upset, and could really get to the station for the eight o'clock train if he hurried. At first he slipped down a few times from the polished surface of the chest, but at length with a last heave he stood upright; he paid no more attention to the pains in the lower part of his body, however they smarted. Then he let himself fall against the back of a near-by chair, and clung with his little legs to the edges of it. That brought him into control of himself again and he stopped speaking, for now he could listen to what the chief clerk was saying.

"Did you understand a word of it?" the chief clerk was asking; "surely he can't be trying to make fools of us?" "Oh dear," cried his mother, in tears, "perhaps he's terribly ill and we're tormenting him. Grete! Grete!" she called out then. "Yes Mother?" called his sister from the other side. They were calling to each other across Gregor's room. "You must go this minute for the doctor. Gregor is ill. Go for the doctor, quick. Did you hear how he was speaking?" "That was no human voice," said the chief clerk in a voice noticeably low beside the shrillness of the mother's. "Anna! Anna!" his father was calling through the hall to the kitchen, clapping his hands, "get a locksmith at once!" And the two girls were already running through the hall with a swish of skirts —how could his sister have got dressed so quickly?—and were tearing the front door open. There was no sound of its closing again; they had evidently left it open, as one does in houses where some great misfortune has happened.

But Gregor was now much calmer. The words he uttered were no longer understandable, apparently, although they seemed clear enough to him, even clearer than before, perhaps because his ear had grown accustomed to the sound of them. Yet at any rate people now believed that something was wrong with him, and were ready to help him. The positive certainty with which these first measures had been taken comforted him. He felt himself drawn once more into the human circle and hoped for great and remarkable results from both the doctor and the locksmith, without really distinguishing precisely between them. To make his voice as clear as possible for the decisive conversation that was now imminent he coughed a little, as quietly as he could, of course, since this noise too might not sound like a human cough for all he was able to judge. In the next room meanwhile there was complete silence. Perhaps his parents were sitting at the table with the chief clerk, whispering, perhaps they were all leaning against the door and listening.

Slowly Gregor pushed the chair towards the door, then let go of it, caught hold of the door for support—the soles at the end of his little legs were somewhat sticky—and rested against it for a moment after his efforts. Then he set himself to turning the key in the lock with his mouth. It seemed, unhappily, that he hadn't really any teeth—what could he grip the key with?—but on the other hand his jaws were certainly very strong; with their help he did manage to set the key in motion, heedless of the fact that he was undoubtedly damaging them somewhere, since a brown fluid issued from his mouth, flowed over the key and dripped on the floor. "Just listen to that," said the chief clerk next door; "he's turning the key." That was a great encouragement to him, his father and mother too: "Go on, Gregor," they should have called out, "keep going, hold on to that key!" And in the belief that they were all following his efforts intently, he clenched his jaws recklessly on the key with all the force at his command. As the turning of the key progressed he circled round the lock, holding on now only with his mouth, pushing on the key, as required, or pulling it down again with all the weight of his body. The louder click of the finally yielding lock literally quickened Gregor. With a deep breath of relief he said to himself: "So I didn't need the locksmith," and laid his head on the handle to open the door wide.

Since he had to pull the door towards him, he was still invisible when it was really wide open. He had to edge himself slowly round the near half of the double door, and to do it very carefully if he was not to fall plump upon his back just on the threshold. He was still carrying out this difficult manoeuvre, with no time to observe anything else, when he heard the chief clerk utter a loud "Oh!"—it sounded like a gust of wind—and now he could see the man, standing as he was nearest to the door, clapping one hand before his open mouth and slowly backing away as if driven by some invisible steady pressure. His mother—in spite of the chief clerk's being there her hair was still undone and sticking up in all directions—first clasped her hands and looked at his father, then took two steps towards Gregor and fell on the floor among her outspread skirts, her face quite hidden on her breast. His father knotted his fist with a fierce expression on his face as if he meant to knock Gregor back into his room, then looked uncertainly round the living room, covered his eyes with his hands and wept till his great chest heaved.

Gregor did not go now into the living room, but leaned against the inside of the firmly shut wing of the door, so that only half his body was visible and his head above it bending sideways to look at the others. The light had meanwhile strengthened; on the other side of the street one could see clearly a section of the endlessly long, dark gray building opposite—it was a hospital—abruptly punctuated by its row of regular windows; the rain was still falling, but only in large singly discernible and literally singly splashing drops. The breakfast dishes were set out on the table lavishly, for breakfast was the most important meal of the day to Gregor's father, who lingered it out for hours over various newspapers. Right opposite Gregor on the wall hung a photograph of himself on military service, as a lieutenant, hand on sword, a carefree smile on his face, inviting one to respect his uniform and military bearing. The door leading to the hall was open, and one could see that the front door stood open too, showing the landing beyond and the beginning of the stairs going down.

"Well," said Gregor, knowing perfectly that he was the only one who had retained any composure, "I'll put my clothes on at once, pack up my samples and start off. Will you only let me go? You see, sir, I'm not obstinate, and I'm willing to work; traveling is a hard life, but I couldn't live without it. Where are you going, sir? To the office? Yes? Will you give a true account of all this? One can be temporarily incapacitated, but that's just the moment for remembering former services and bearing in mind that later on, when the incapacity has been got over, one will certainly work with all the more industry and concentration. I'm loyally bound to serve the chief, you know that very well. Besides, I have to provide for my parents and my sister. I'm in great difficulties, but I'll get out of them again. Don't make things any worse for me than they are. Stand up for me in the firm. Travelers are not popular there, I know.

People think they earn sacks of money and just have a good time. A prejudice there's no particular reason for revising. But you, sir, have a more comprehensive view of affairs than the rest of the staff, yes, let me tell you in confidence, a more comprehensive view than the chief himself, who, being the owner, lets his judgment easily be swayed against one of his employees. And you know very well that the traveler, who is never seen in the office almost the whole year round, can so easily fall a victim to gossip and ill luck and unfounded complaints, which he mostly knows nothing about, except when he comes back exhausted from his rounds, and only then suffers in person from their evil consequences, which he can no longer trace back to the original causes. Sir, sir, don't go away without a word to me to show that you think me in the right at least to some extent!"

But at Gregor's very first words the chief clerk had already backed away and only stared at him with parted lips over one twitching shoulder. And while Gregor was speaking he did not stand still one moment but stole away towards the door, without taking his eyes off Gregor, yet only an inch at a time, as if obeying some secret injunction to leave the room. He was already at the hall, and the suddenness with which he took his last step out of the living room would have made one believe he had burned the sole of his foot. Once in the hall he stretched his right arm before him towards the staircase, as if some supernatural power were waiting there to deliver him.

Gregor perceived that the chief clerk must on no account be allowed to go away in this frame of mind if his position in the firm were not to be endangered to the utmost. His parents did not understand this so well; they had convinced themselves in the course of years that Gregor was settled for life in this firm, and besides they were so preoccupied with their immediate troubles that all foresight had forsaken them. Yet Gregor had this foresight. The chief clerk must be detained, soothed, persuaded and finally won over; the whole future of Gregor and his family depended on it! If only his sister had been there! She was intelligent; she had begun to cry while Gregor was still lying quietly on his back. And no doubt the chief clerk, so partial to ladies, would have been guided by her; she would have shut the door of the flat and in the hall talked him out of his horror. But she was not there, and Gregor would have to handle the situation himself. And without remembering that he was still unaware what powers of movement he possessed, without even remembering that his words in all possibility, indeed in all likelihood, would again be unintelligible, he let go the wing of the door, pushed himself through the opening, started to walk towards the chief clerk, who was already ridiculously clinging with both hands to the railing on the landing; but immediately, as he was feeling for a support, he fell down with a little cry upon all his numerous legs. Hardly was he down when he experienced for the first time this morning a sense of physical comfort; his legs had firm ground under them; they were completely obedient, as he noted with joy; they even strove to carry him forward in whatever direction he chose; and he was inclined to believe that a final relief from all his sufferings was at hand. But in the same moment as he found himself on the floor, rocking with suppressed eagerness to move, not far from his mother, indeed just in front of her, she, who had seemed so completely crushed, sprang all at once to her feet, her arms and fingers outspread, cried: "Help, for God's sake, help!" bent her head down as if to see Gregor better, yet on the contrary kept backing senselessly away; had quite forgotten that the laden table stood behind her; sat upon it hastily, as if in absence of mind, when she bumped into it; and seemed altogether unaware that the big coffee pot beside her was upset and pouring coffee in a flood over the carpet.

"Mother, Mother," said Gregor in a low voice, and looked up at her. The chief clerk, for the moment, had quite slipped from his mind; instead, he could not resist snapping his jaws together at the sight of the streaming coffee. That made his mother scream again, she fled from the table and fell into the arms of his father, who hastened to catch her. But Gregor had now no time to spare for his parents; the chief clerk was already on the stairs; with his chin on the banisters he was taking one last backward look. Gregor made a spring, to be as sure as possible of overtaking him; the chief clerk must have divined his intention, for he leaped down several steps and vanished; he was still yelling "Ugh!" and it echoed through the whole staircase.

Unfortunately, the flight of the chief clerk seemed completely to upset Gregor's father, who had remained relatively calm until now, for instead of running after the man himself, or at least not hindering Gregor in his pursuit, he seized in his right hand the walking stick which the chief clerk had left behind on a chair, together with a hat and greatcoat, snatched in his left hand a large newspaper from the table and began stamping his feet and flourishing the stick and the newspaper to drive Gregor back into his room. No entreaty of Gregor's availed, indeed no entreaty was even understood; however humbly he bent his head his father only stamped on the floor the more loudly. Behind his father his mother had torn open a window, despite the cold weather, and was leaning far out of it with her face in her hands. A strong draught set in from the street to the staircase, the window curtains blew in, the newspapers on the table fluttered, stray pages whisked over the floor. Pitilessly Gregor's father drove him back, hissing and crying "Shoo!" like a savage. But Gregor was quite unpracticed in walking backwards, it really was a slow business. If he only had a chance to turn round he could get back to his room at once, but he was afraid of exasperating his father by the slowness of such a rotation and at any moment the stick in his father's hand might hit him a fatal blow on the back or on the head. In the end, however, nothing else was left for him to do since to his horror he observed that in moving backwards he could not even control the direction he took; and so, keeping an anxious eye on his father all the time over his shoulder, he began to turn round as quickly as he could, which was in reality very slowly. Perhaps his father noted his good intentions, for he did not interfere except every now and then to help him in the manoeuvre from a distance with the point of the stick. If only he would have stopped making that unbearable hissing noise! It made Gregor quite lose his head. He had turned almost completely round when the hissing noise so distracted him that he even turned a little the wrong way again. But when at last his head was fortunately right in front of the doorway, it appeared that his body was too broad simply to get through the opening. His father, of course, in his present mood was far from thinking of such a thing as opening the other half of the door, to let Gregor have enough space. He had merely the fixed idea of driving Gregor back into his room as quickly as possible. He would never have suffered Gregor to make the circumstantial preparations for standing up on end and perhaps slipping his way through the door. Maybe he was now making more noise than ever to urge Gregor forward, as if no obstacle impeded him; to Gregor, anyhow, the noise in his rear sounded no longer like the voice of one single father; this was really no joke, and Gregor thrust himself—come what might—into the doorway. One side of his body rose up, he was tilted at an angle in the doorway, his flank was quite bruised, horrid blotches stained the white door, soon he was stuck fast and, left to himself, could not have moved at all, his legs on one side fluttered trembling in the air, those on the other were crushed painfully to the floor—when from behind his father gave him a strong push which was literally a deliverance and he flew far into the room, bleeding freely. The door was slammed behind him with the stick, and then at last there was silence.

II

Not until it was twilight did Gregor awake out of a deep sleep, more like a swoon than a sleep. He would certainly have waked up of his own accord not much later, for he felt himself sufficiently rested and well-slept, but it seemed to him as if a fleeting step and a cautious shutting of the door leading into the hall had aroused him. The electric lights in the street cast a pale sheen here and there on the ceiling and the upper surfaces of the furniture, but down below, where he lay, it was dark. Slowly, awkwardly, trying out his feelers, which he now first learned to appreciate, he pushed his way to the door to see what had been happening there. His left side felt like one single long, unpleasantly tense scar, and he had actually to limp on his two rows of legs. One little leg, moreover, had been severely damaged in the course of that morning's events—it was almost a miracle that only one had been damaged—and trailed uselessly behind him.

He had reached the door before he discovered what had really drawn him to it: the smell of food. For there stood a basin filled with fresh milk in which floated little sops of white bread. He could almost have laughed with joy, since he was now still hungrier than in the morning, and he dipped his head almost over the eyes straight into the milk. But soon in disappointment he withdrew it again; not only did he find it difficult to feed because of his tender left side —and he could only feed with the palpitating collaboration of his whole body —he did not like the milk either, although milk had been his favorite drink and that was certainly why his sister had set it there for him, indeed it was almost with repulsion that he turned away from the basin and crawled back to the middle of the room.

He could see through the crack of the door that the gas was turned on in the living room, but while usually at this time his father made a habit of reading the afternoon newspaper in a loud voice to his mother and occasionally to his sister as well, not a sound was now to be heard. Well, perhaps his father had recently given up this habit of reading aloud, which his sister had mentioned so often in conversation and in her letters. But there was the same silence all around, although the flat was certainly not empty of occupants. "What a quiet life our family has been leading," said Gregor to himself, and as he sat there motionless staring into the darkness he felt great pride in the fact that he had been able to provide such a life for his parents and sister in such a fine flat. But what if all the quiet, the comfort, the contentment were now to end in horror? To keep himself from being lost in such thoughts Gregor took refuge in movement and crawled up and down the room.

Once during the long evening one of the side doors was opened a little and quickly shut again, later the other side door too; someone had apparently wanted to come in and then thought better of it. Gregor now stationed himself immediately before the living room door, determined to persuade any hesitating visitor to come in or at least to discover who it might be; but the door was not opened again and he waited in vain. In the early morning, when the doors were locked, they had all wanted to come in, now that he had opened one door and the other had apparently been opened during the day, no one came in and even the keys were on the other side of the doors.

It was late at night before the gas went out in the living room, and Gregor could easily tell that his parents and his sister had all stayed awake until then, for he could clearly hear the three of them stealing away on tiptoe. No one was likely to visit him, not until the morning, that was certain; so he had plenty of time to meditate at his leisure on how he was to arrange his life afresh. But the lofty, empty room in which he had to lie flat on the floor filled him with an apprehension he could not account for, since it had been his very own room for the past five years—and with a half-unconscious action, not without a slight feeling of shame, he scuttled under the sofa, where he felt comfortable at once, although his back was a little cramped and he could not lift his head up, and his only regret was that his body was too broad to get the whole of it under the sofa.

He stayed there all night, spending the time partly in a light slumber, from which his hunger kept waking him up with a start, and partly in worrying and sketching vague hopes, which all led to the same conclusion, that he must lie low for the present and, by exercising patience and the utmost consideration, help the family to bear the inconvenience he was bound to cause them in his present condition.

Very early in the morning, it was still almost night, Gregor had the chance to test the strength of his new resolutions, for his sister, nearly fully dressed, opened the door from the hall and peered in. She did not see him at once, yet when she caught sight of him under the sofa—well, he had to be somewhere, he couldn't have flown away, could he?—she was so startled that without being able to help it she slammed the door shut again. But as if regretting her behavior she opened the door again immediately and came in on tiptoe, as if she were visiting an invalid or even a stranger. Gregor had pushed his head forward to the very edge of the sofa and watched her. Would she notice that he had left the milk standing, and not for lack of hunger, and would she bring in some other kind of food more to his taste? If she did not do it of her own accord, he would rather starve than draw her attention to the fact, although he felt a wild impulse to dart out from under the sofa, throw himself at her feet and beg her for something to eat. But his sister at once noticed, with surprise, that the basin was still full, except for a little milk that had been spilt all around it, she lifted it immediately, not with her bare hands, true, but with a cloth and carried it away. Gregor was wildly curious to know what she would bring instead, and made various speculations about it. Yet what she actually did next, in the goodness of her heart, he could never have guessed at. To find out what he liked she brought him a whole selection of food, all set out on an old newspaper. There were old, half-decayed vegetables, bones from last night's supper covered with a white sauce that had thickened; some raisins and almonds; a piece of cheese that Gregor would have called uneatable two days ago; a dry roll of bread, a buttered roll, and a roll both buttered and salted. Besides all that, she set down again the same basin, into which she had poured some water, and which was apparently to be reserved for his exclusive use. And with fine tact, knowing that Gregor would not eat in her presence, she withdrew quickly and even turned the key, to let him understand that he could take his ease as much as he liked. Gregor's legs all whizzed towards the food. His wounds must have healed completely, moreover, for he felt no disability, which amazed him and made him reflect how more than a month ago he had cut one finger a little with a knife and had still suffered pain from the wound only the day before yesterday. Am I less sensitive now? he thought, and sucked greedily at the cheese, which above all the other edibles attracted him at once and strongly. One after another and with tears of satisfaction in his eyes he quickly devoured the cheese, the vegetables and the sauce; the fresh food, on the other hand, had no charms for him, he could not even stand the smell of it and actually dragged away to some little distance the things he could eat. He had long finished his meal and was only lying lazily on the same spot when his sister turned the key slowly as a sign for him to retreat. That roused him at once, although he was nearly asleep, and he hurried under the sofa again. But it took considerable self-control for him to stay under the sofa, even for the short time his sister was in the room, since the large meal had swollen his body somewhat and he was so cramped he could hardly breathe. Slight attacks of breathlessness afflicted him and his eyes were starting a little out of his head as he watched his unsuspecting sister sweeping together with a broom not only the remains of what he had eaten but even the things he had not touched, as if these were now of no use to anyone, and hastily shoveling it all into a bucket, which she covered with a wooden lid and carried away. Hardly had she turned her back when Gregor came from under the sofa and stretched and puffed himself out.

In this manner Gregor was fed, once in the early morning while his parents and the servant girl were still asleep, and a second time after they had all had their midday dinner, for then his parents took a short nap and the servant girl could be sent out on some errand or other by his sister. Not that they would have wanted him to starve, of course, but perhaps they could not have borne to know more about his feeding than from hearsay, perhaps too his sister wanted to spare them such little anxieties wherever possible, since they had quite enough to bear as it was.

Under what pretext the doctor and the locksmith had been got rid of on that first morning Gregor could not discover, for since what he said was not understood by the others it never struck any of them, not even his sister, that he could understand what they said, and so whenever his sister came into his room he had to content himself with hearing her utter only a sigh now and then and an occasional appeal to the saints. Later on, when she had got a little used to the situation—of course she could never get completely used to it—she sometimes threw out a remark which was kindly meant or could be so interpreted. "Well, he liked his dinner today," she would say when Gregor had made a good clearance of his food; and when he had not eaten, which gradually happened more and more often, she would say almost sadly: "Everything's been left standing again."

But although Gregor could get no news directly, he overheard a lot from the neighboring rooms, and as soon as voices were audible, he would run to the door of the room concerned and press his whole body against it. In the first few days especially there was no conversation that did not refer to him somehow, even if only indirectly. For two whole days there were family consultations at every mealtime about what should be done; but also between meals the same subject was discussed, for there were always at least two members of the family at home, since no one wanted to be alone in the flat and to leave it quite empty was unthinkable. And on the very first of these days the household cook —it was not quite clear what and how much she knew of the situation—went down on her knees to his mother and begged leave to go, and when she departed, a quarter of an hour later, gave thanks for her dismissal with tears in her eyes as if for the greatest benefit that could have been conferred on her, and without any prompting swore a solemn oath that she would never say a single word to anyone about what had happened.

Now Gregor's sister had to cook too, helping her mother; true, the cooking did not amount to much, for they ate scarcely anything. Gregor was always hearing one of the family vainly urging another to eat and getting no answer but: "Thanks, I've had all I want," or something similar. Perhaps they drank nothing either. Time and again his sister kept asking his father if he wouldn't like some beer and offered kindly to go and fetch it herself, and when he made no answer suggested that she could ask the concierge to fetch it, so that he need feel no sense of obligation, but then a round "No" came from his father and no more was said about it.

In the course of that very first day Gregor's father explained the family's financial position and prospects to both his mother and his sister. Now and then he rose from the table to get some voucher or memorandum out of the small safe he had rescued from the collapse of his business five years earlier. One could hear him opening the complicated lock and rustling papers out and shutting it again. This statement made by his father was the first cheerful information Gregor had heard since his imprisonment. He had been of the opinion that nothing at all was left over from his father's business, at least his father had never said anything to the contrary, and of course he had not asked him directly. At that time Gregor's sole desire was to do his utmost to help the family to forget as soon as possible the catastrophe which had overwhelmed the business and thrown them all into a state of complete despair. And so he had set to work with unusual ardor and almost overnight had become a commercial traveler instead of a little clerk, with of course much greater chances of earning money, and his success was immediately translated into good round coin which he could lay on the table for his amazed and happy family. These had been fine times, and they had never recurred, at least not with the same sense of glory, although later on Gregor had earned so much money that he was able to meet the expenses of the whole household and did so. They had simply got used to it, both the family and Gregor; the money was gratefully accepted and gladly given, but there was no special uprush of warm feeling. With his sister alone had he remained intimate, and it was a secret plan of his that she, who loved music, unlike himself, and could play movingly on the violin, should be sent next year to study at the Conservatorium, despite the great expense that would entail, which must be made up in some other way. During his brief visits home the Conservatorium was often mentioned in the talks he had with his sister, but always merely as a beautiful dream which could never come true, and his parents discouraged even these innocent references to it; yet Gregor had made up his mind firmly about it and meant to announce the fact with due solemnity on Christmas Day.

Such were the thoughts, completely futile in his present condition, that went through his head as he stood clinging upright to the door and listening. Sometimes out of sheer weariness he had to give up listening and let his head fall negligently against the door, but he always had to pull himself together again at once, for even the slight sound his head made was audible next door and brought all conversation to a stop. "What can he be doing now?" his father would say after a while, obviously turning towards the door, and only then would the interrupted conversation gradually be set going again.

Gregor was now informed as amply as he could wish—for his father tended to repeat himself in his explanations, partly because it was a long time since he had handled such matters and partly because his mother could not always grasp things at once—that a certain amount of investments, a very small amount it was true, had survived the wreck of their fortunes and had even increased a little because the dividends had not been touched meanwhile. And besides that, the money Gregor brought home every month—he had kept only a few dollars for himself—had never been quite used up and now amounted to a small capital sum. Behind the door Gregor nodded his head eagerly, rejoiced at this evidence of unexpected thrift and foresight. True, he could really have paid off some more of his father's debts to the chief with this extra money, and so brought much nearer the day on which he could quit his job, but doubtless it was better the way his father had arranged it.

Yet this capital was by no means sufficient to let the family live on the interest of it; for one year, perhaps, or at the most two, they could live on the principal, that was all. It was simply a sum that ought not to be touched and should be kept for a rainy day; money for living expenses would have to be earned. Now his father was still hale enough but an old man, and he had done no work for the past five years and could not be expected to do much; during these five years, the first years of leisure in his laborious though unsuccessful life, he had grown rather fat and become sluggish. And Gregor's old mother, how was she to earn a living with her asthma, which troubled her even when she walked through the flat and kept her lying on a sofa every other day panting for breath beside an open window? And was his sister to earn her bread, she who was still a child of seventeen and whose life hitherto had been so pleasant, consisting as it did in dressing herself nicely, sleeping long, helping in the housekeeping, going out to a few modest entertainments and above all playing the violin? At first whenever the need for earning money was mentioned Gregor let go his hold on the door and threw himself down on the cool leather sofa beside it, he felt so hot with shame and grief.

Often he just lay there the long nights through without sleeping at all, scrabbling for hours on the leather. Or he nerved himself to the great effort of pushing an armchair to the window, then crawled up over the window sill and, braced against the chair, leaned against the window panes, obviously in some recollection of the sense of freedom that looking out a window always used to give him. For in reality day by day things that were even a little way off were growing dimmer to his sight; the hospital across the street, which he used to execrate for being all too often before his eyes, was now quite beyond his range of vision, and if he had not known that he lived in Charlotte Street, a quiet street but still a city street, he might have believed that his window gave on a desert waste where gray sky and gray land blended indistinguishably into each other. His quick-witted sister only needed to observe twice that the armchair stood by the window; after that whenever she had tidied the room she always pushed the chair back to the same place at the window and even left the inner casements open.

If he could have spoken to her and thanked her for all she had to do for him, he could have borne her ministrations better; as it was, they oppressed him. She certainly tried to make as light as possible of whatever was disagreeable in her task, and as time went on she succeeded, of course, more and more, but time brought more enlightenment to Gregor too. The very way she came in distressed him. Hardly was she in the room when she rushed to the window, without even taking time to shut the door, careful as she was usually to shield the sight of Gregor's room from the others, and as if she were almost suffocating tore the casements open with hasty fingers, standing then in the open draught for a while even in the bitterest cold and drawing deep breaths. This noisy scurry of hers upset Gregor twice a day; he would crouch trembling under the sofa all the time, knowing quite well that she would certainly have spared him such a disturbance had she found it at all possible to stay in his presence without opening the window.

On one occasion, about a month after Gregor's metamorphosis, when there was surely no reason for her to be still startled at his appearance, she came a little earlier than usual and found him gazing out of the window, quite motionless, and thus well placed to look like a bogey. Gregor would not have been surprised had she not come in at all, for she could not immediately open the window while he was there, but not only did she retreat, she jumped back as if in alarm and banged the door shut; a stranger might well have thought that he had been lying in wait for her there meaning to bite her. Of course he hid himself under the sofa at once, but he had to wait until midday before she came again, and she seemed more ill at ease than usual. This made him realize how repulsive the sight of him still was to her, and it was bound to go on being repulsive, and what an effort it must cost her not to run away even from the sight of the small portion of his body that stuck out from under the sofa. In order to spare her that, therefore, one day he carried a sheet on his back to the sofa—it cost him four hours' labor—and arranged it there in such a way as to hide him completely, so that even if she were to bend down she could not see him. Had she considered the sheet unnecessary, she would certainly have stripped it off the sofa again, for it was clear enough that this curtaining and confining of himself was not likely to conduce to Gregor's comfort, but she left it where it was, and Gregor even fancied that he caught a thankful glance from her eye when he lifted the sheet carefully a very little with his head to see how she was taking the new arrangement.

For the first fortnight his parents could not bring themselves to the point of entering his room, and he often heard them expressing their appreciation of his sister's activities, whereas formerly they had frequently scolded her for being as they thought a somewhat useless daughter. But now, both of them often waited outside the door, his father and his mother, while his sister tidied his room, and as soon as she came out she had to tell them exactly how things were in the room, what Gregor had eaten, how he had conducted himself this time and whether there was not perhaps some slight improvement in his condition. His mother, moreover, began relatively soon to want to visit him, but his father and sister dissuaded her at first with arguments which Gregor listened to very attentively and altogether approved. Later, however, she had to be held back by main force, and when she cried out: "Do let me in to Gregor, he is my unfortunate son! Can't you understand that I must go to him?" Gregor thought that it might be well to have her come in, not every day, of course, but perhaps once a week; she understood things, after all, much better than his sister, who was only a child despite the efforts she was making and had perhaps taken on so difficult a task merely out of childish thoughtlessness.

Gregor's desire to see his mother was soon fulfilled. During the daytime he did not want to show himself at the window, out of consideration for his parents, but he could not crawl very far around the few square yards of floor space he had, nor could he bear lying quietly at rest all during the night, while he was fast losing any interest he had ever taken in food, so that for mere recreation he had formed the habit of crawling crisscross over the walls and ceiling. He especially enjoyed hanging suspended from the ceiling; it was much better than lying on the floor; one could breathe more freely; one's body swung and rocked lightly; and in the almost blissful absorption induced by this suspension it could happen to his own surprise that he let go and fell plump on the floor. Yet he now had his body much better under control than formerly, and even such a big fall did him no harm. His sister at once remarked the new distraction Gregor had found for himself—he left traces behind him of the sticky stuff on his soles wherever he crawled—and she got the idea in her head of giving him as wide a field as possible to crawl in and of removing the pieces of furniture that hindered him, above all the chest of drawers and the writing desk. But that was more than she could manage all by herself; she did not dare ask her father to help her; and as for the servant girl, a young creature of sixteen who had had the courage to stay on after the cook's departure, she could not be asked to help, for she had begged as an especial favor that she might keep the kitchen door locked and open it only on a definite summons; so there was nothing left but to apply to her mother at an hour when her father was out. And the old lady did come, with exclamations of joyful eagerness, which, however, died away at the door of Gregor's room. Gregor's sister, of course, went in first, to see that everything was in order before letting his mother enter. In great haste Gregor pulled the sheet lower as if it had been thrown accidentally over the sofa. And this time he did not peer out from under it; he renounced the pleasure of seeing his mother on this occasion and was only glad that she had come at all. "Come in, he's out of sight," said his sister, obviously leading her mother in by the hand. Gregor could now hear the two women struggling to shift the heavy old chest from its place, and his sister claiming the greater part of the labor for herself, without listening to the admonitions of her mother who feared she might overstrain herself. It took a long time. After at least a quarter of an hour's tugging his mother objected that the chest had better be left where it was, for in the first place it was too heavy and could never be got out before his father came home, and standing in the middle of the room like that it would only hamper Gregor's movements, while in the second place it was not at all certain that removing the furniture would be doing a service to Gregor. She was inclined to think to the contrary; the sight of the naked walls made her own heart heavy, and why shouldn't Gregor have the same feeling, considering that he had been used to his furniture for so long and might feel forlorn without it. "And doesn't it look," she concluded in a low voice—in fact she had been almost whispering all the time as if to avoid letting Gregor, whose exact whereabouts she did not know, hear even the tones of her voice, for she was convinced that he could not understand her words—"doesn't it look as if we were showing him, by taking away his furniture, that we have given up hope of his ever getting better and are just leaving him coldly to himself? I think it would be best to keep his room exactly as it has always been, so that when he comes back to us he will find everything unchanged and be able all the more easily to forget what has happened in between."

On hearing these words from his mother Gregor realized that the lack of all direct human speech for the past two months together with the monotony of family life must have confused his mind, otherwise he could not account for the fact that he had quite earnestly looked forward to having his room emptied of furnishing. Did he really want his warm room, so comfortably fitted with old family furniture, to be turned into a naked den in which he would certainly be able to crawl unhampered in all directions but at the price of shedding simultaneously all recollection of his human background? He had indeed been so near the brink of forgetfulness that only the voice of his mother, which he had not heard for so long, had drawn him back from it. Nothing should be taken out of his room; everything must stay as it was; he could not dispense with the good influence of the furniture on his state of mind; and even if the furniture did hamper him in his senseless crawling round and round, that was no drawback but a great advantage.

Unfortunately his sister was of the contrary opinion; she had grown accustomed, and not without reason, to consider herself an expert in Gregor's affairs as against her parents, and so her mother's advice was now enough to make her determined on the removal not only of the chest and the writing desk, which had been her first intention, but of all the furniture except the indispensable sofa. This determination was not, of course, merely the outcome of childish recalcitrance and of the self-confidence she had recently developed so unexpectedly and at such cost; she had in fact perceived that Gregor needed a lot of space to crawl about in, while on the other hand he never used the furniture at all, so far as could be seen. Another factor might have been also the enthusiastic temperament of an adolescent girl, which seeks to indulge itself on every opportunity and which now tempted Grete to exaggerate the horror of her brother's circumstances in order that she might do all the more for him. In a room where Gregor lorded it all alone over empty walls no one save herself was likely ever to set foot.

And so she was not to be moved from her resolve by her mother, who seemed moreover to be ill at ease in Gregor's room and therefore unsure of herself, was soon reduced to silence and helped her daughter as best she could to push the chest outside. Now, Gregor could do without the chest, if need be, but the writing desk he must retain. As soon as the two women had got the chest out of the room, groaning as they pushed it, Gregor stuck his head out from under the sofa to see how he might intervene as kindly and cautiously as possible. But as bad luck would have it, his mother was the first to return, leaving Grete clasping the chest in the room next door where she was trying to shift it all by herself, without of course moving it from the spot. His mother however was not accustomed to the sight of him, it might sicken her and so in alarm Gregor backed quickly to the other end of the sofa, yet could not prevent the sheet from swaying a little in front. That was enough to put her on the alert. She paused, stood still for a moment and then went back to Grete.

Although Gregor kept reassuring himself that nothing out of the way was happening, but only a few bits of furniture were being changed round, he soon had to admit that all this trotting to and fro of the two women, their little ejaculations and the scraping of furniture along the floor affected him like a vast disturbance coming from all sides at once, and however much he tucked in his head and legs and cowered to the very floor he was bound to confess that he would not be able to stand it for long. They were clearing his room out; taking away everything he loved; the chest in which he kept his fret saw and other tools was already dragged off; they were now loosening the writing desk which had almost sunk into the floor, the desk at which he had done all his homework when he was at the commercial academy, at the grammar school before that, and, yes, even at the primary school—he had no more time to waste in weighing the good intentions of the two women, whose existence he had by now almost forgotten, for they were so exhausted that they were laboring in silence and nothing could be heard but the heavy scuffling of their feet.

And so he rushed out—the women were just leaning against the writing desk in the next room to give themselves a breather—and four times changed his direction, since he really did not know what to rescue first, then on the wall opposite, which was already otherwise cleared, he was struck by the picture of the lady muffled in so much fur and quickly crawled up to it and pressed himself to the glass, which was a good surface to hold on to and comforted his hot belly. This picture at least, which was entirely hidden beneath him, was going to be removed by nobody. He turned his head towards the door of the living room so as to observe the women when they came back.

They had not allowed themselves much of a rest and were already coming; Grete had twined her arm round her mother and was almost supporting her. "Well, what shall we take now?" said Grete, looking round. Her eyes met Gregor's from the wall. She kept her composure, presumably because of her mother, bent her head down to her mother, to keep her from looking up, and said, although in a fluttering, unpremeditated voice: "Come, hadn't we better go back to the living room for a moment?" Her intentions were clear enough to Gregor, she wanted to bestow her mother in safety and then chase him down from the wall. Well, just let her try it! He clung to his picture and would not give it up. He would rather fly in Grete's face.

But Grete's words had succeeded in disquieting her mother, who took a step to one side, caught sight of the huge brown mass on the flowered wallpaper, and before she was really conscious that what she saw was Gregor screamed in a loud, hoarse voice, "Oh God, oh God!", fell with outspread arms over the sofa as if giving up, and did not move. "Gregor!" cried his sister, shaking her fist and glaring at him. This was the first time she had directly addressed him since his metamorphosis. She ran into the next room for some aromatic essence with which to rouse her mother from her fainting fit. Gregor wanted to help too—there was still time to rescue the picture—but he was stuck fast to the glass and had to tear himself loose; he then ran after his sister into the next room as if he could advise her, as he used to do; but then had to stand helplessly behind her; she meanwhile searched among various small bottles and when she turned round started in alarm at the sight of him; one bottle fell on the floor and broke; a splinter of glass cut Gregor's face and some kind of corrosive medicine splashed him; without pausing a moment longer Grete gathered up all the bottles she could carry and ran to her mother with them; she banged the door shut with her foot. Gregor was now cut off from his mother, who was perhaps nearly dying because of him; he dared not open the door for fear of frightening away his sister, who had to stay with her mother; there was nothing he could do but wait; and harassed by self-reproach and worry he began now to crawl to and fro, over everything, walls, furniture and ceiling, and finally in his despair, when the whole room seemed to be reeling round him, fell down on to the middle of the big table.

A little while elapsed, Gregor was still lying there feebly and all around was quiet; perhaps that was a good omen. Then the doorbell rang. The servant girl was of course locked in her kitchen, and Grete would have to open the door. It was his father. "What's been happening?" were his first words; Grete's face must have told him everything. Grete answered in a muffled voice, apparently hiding her head on his breast: "Mother has been fainting, but she's better now. Gregor's broken loose." "Just what I expected," said his father, "just what I've been telling you, but you women would never listen." It was clear to Gregor that his father had taken the worst interpretation of Grete's all too brief statement and was assuming that Gregor had been guilty of some violent act. Therefore Gregor must now try to propitiate his father, since he had neither time nor means for an explanation. And so he fled to the door of his own room and crouched against it, to let his father see as soon as he came in from the hall that his son had the good intention of getting back into his room immediately and that it was not necessary to drive him there, but that if only the door were opened he would disappear at once.

Yet his father was not in the mood to perceive such fine distinctions. "Ah!" he cried as soon as he appeared, in a tone which sounded at once angry and exultant. Gregor drew his head back from the door and lifted it to look at his father. Truly, this was not the father he had imagined to himself; admittedly he had been too absorbed of late in his new recreation of crawling over the ceiling to take the same interest as before in what was happening elsewhere in the flat, and he ought really to be prepared for some changes. And yet, and yet, could that be his father? The man who used to lie wearily sunk in bed whenever Gregor set out on a business journey; who welcomed him back of an evening lying in a long chair in a dressing gown; who could not really rise to his feet but only lifted his arms in greeting, and on the rare occasions when he did go out with his family, on one or two Sundays a year and on high holidays, walked between Gregor and his mother, who were slow walkers anyhow, even more slowly than they did, muffled in his old greatcoat, shuffling laboriously forward with the help of his crook-handled stick which he set down most cautiously at every step and, whenever he wanted to say anything, nearly always came to a full stop and gathered his escort around him? Now he was standing there in fine shape; dressed in a smart blue uniform with gold buttons, such as bank messengers wear; his strong double chin bulged over the stiff high collar of his jacket; from under his bushy eyebrows his black eyes darted fresh and penetrating glances; his onetime tangled white hair had been combed flat on either side of a shining and carefully exact parting. He pitched his cap, which bore a gold monogram, probably the badge of some bank, in a wide sweep across the whole room on to a sofa and with the tail-ends of his jacket thrown back, his hands in his trouser pockets, advanced with a grim visage towards Gregor. Likely enough he did not himself know what he meant to do; at any rate he lifted his feet uncommonly high, and Gregor was dumbfounded at the enormous size of his shoe soles. But Gregor could not risk standing up to him, aware as he had been from the very first day of his new life that his father believed only the severest measures suitable for dealing with him. And so he ran before his father, stopping when he stopped and scuttling forward again when his father made any kind of move. In this way they circled the room several times without anything decisive happening; indeed the whole operation did not even look like a pursuit because it was carried out so slowly. And so Gregor did not leave the floor, for he feared that his father might take as a piece of peculiar wickedness any excursion of his over the walls or the ceiling. All the same, he could not stay this course much longer, for while his father took one step he had to carry out a whole series of movements. He was already beginning to feel breathless, just as in his former life his lungs had not been very dependable. As he was staggering along, trying to concentrate his energy on running, hardly keeping his eyes open; in his dazed state never even thinking of any other escape than simply going forward; and having almost forgotten that the walls were free to him, which in this room were well provided with finely carved pieces of furniture full of knobs and crevices—suddenly something lightly flung landed close behind him and rolled before him. It was an apple; a second apple followed immediately; Gregor came to a stop in alarm; there was no point in running on, for his father was determined to bombard him. He had filled his pockets with fruit from the dish on the sideboard and was now shying apple after apple, without taking particularly good aim for the moment. The small red apples rolled about the floor as if magnetized and cannoned into each other. An apple thrown without much force grazed Gregor's back and glanced off harmlessly. But another following immediately landed right on his back and sank in; Gregor wanted to drag himself forward, as if this startling, incredible pain could be left behind him; but he felt as if nailed to the spot and flattened himself out in a complete derangement of all his senses. With his last conscious look he saw the door of his room being torn open and his mother rushing out ahead of his screaming sister, in her underbodice, for her daughter had loosened her clothing to let her breathe more freely and recover from her swoon, he saw his mother rushing towards his father, leaving one after another behind her on the floor her loosened petticoats, stumbling over her petticoats straight to his father and embracing him, in complete union with him—but here Gregor's sight began to fail—with her hands clasped round his father's neck as she begged for her son's life.

III

The serious injury done to Gregor, which disabled him for more than a month—the apple went on sticking in his body as a visible reminder, since no one ventured to remove it—seemed to have made even his father recollect that Gregor was a member of the family, despite his present unfortunate and repulsive shape, and ought not to be treated as an enemy, that, on the contrary, family duty required the suppression of disgust and the exercise of patience, nothing but patience.

And although his injury had impaired, probably for ever, his powers of movement, and for the time being it took him long, long minutes to creep across his room like an old invalid—there was no question now of crawling up the wall—yet in his own opinion he was sufficiently compensated for this worsening of his condition by the fact that towards evening the living-room door, which he used to watch intently for an hour or two beforehand, was always thrown open, so that lying in the darkness of his room, invisible to the family, he could see them all at the lamp-lit table and listen to their talk, by general consent as it were, very different from his earlier eavesdropping.

True, their intercourse lacked the lively character of former times, which he had always called to mind with a certain wistfulness in the small hotel bedrooms where he had been wont to throw himself down, tired out, on damp bedding. They were now mostly very silent. Soon after supper his father would fall asleep in his armchair; his mother and sister would admonish each other to be silent; his mother, bending low over the lamp, stitched at fine sewing for an underwear firm; his sister, who had taken a job as a salesgirl, was learning shorthand and French in the evenings on the chance of bettering herself. Sometimes his father woke up, and as if quite unaware that he had been sleeping said to his mother: "What a lot of sewing you're doing today!" and at once fell asleep again, while the two women exchanged a tired smile.

With a kind of mulishness his father persisted in keeping his uniform on even in the house; his dressing gown hung uselessly on its peg and he slept fully dressed where he sat, as if he were ready for service at any moment and even here only at the beck and call of his superior. As a result, his uniform, which was not brand-new to start with, began to look dirty, despite all the loving care of the mother and sister to keep it clean, and Gregor often spent whole evenings gazing at the many greasy spots on the garment, gleaming with gold buttons always in a high state of polish, in which the old man sat sleeping in extreme discomfort and yet quite peacefully.

As soon as the clock struck ten his mother tried to rouse his father with gentle words and to persuade him after that to get into bed, for sitting there he could not have a proper sleep and that was what he needed most, since he had to go on duty at six. But with the mulishness that had obsessed him since he became a bank messenger he always insisted on staying longer at the table, although he regularly fell asleep again and in the end only with the greatest trouble could be got out of his armchair and into his bed. However insistently Gregor's mother and sister kept urging him with gentle reminders, he would go on slowly shaking his head for a quarter of an hour, keeping his eyes shut, and refuse to get to his feet. The mother plucked at his sleeve, whispering endearments in his ear, the sister left her lessons to come to her mother's help, but Gregor's father was not to be caught. He would only sink down deeper in his chair. Not until the two women hoisted him up by the armpits did he open his eyes and look at them both, one after the other, usually with the remark: "This is a life. This is the peace and quiet of my old age." And leaning on the two of them he would heave himself up, with difficulty, as if he were a great burden to himself, suffer them to lead him as far as the door and then wave them off and go on alone, while the mother abandoned her needlework and the sister her pen in order to run after him and help him further.

Who could find time, in this overworked and tired-out family, to bother about Gregor more than was absolutely needful? The household was reduced more and more; the servant girl was turned off; a gigantic bony charwoman with white hair flying round her head came in morning and evening to do the rough work; everything else was done by Gregor's mother, as well as great piles of sewing. Even various family ornaments, which his mother and sister used to wear with pride at parties and celebrations, had to be sold, as Gregor discovered of an evening from hearing them all discuss the prices obtained. But what they lamented most was the fact that they could not leave the flat which was much too big for their present circumstances, because they could not think of any way to shift Gregor. Yet, Gregor saw well enough that consideration for him was not the main difficulty preventing the removal, for they could have easily shifted him in some suitable box with a few air holes in it; what really kept them from moving into another flat was rather their own complete hopelessness and the belief that they had been singled out for a misfortune such as had never happened to any of their relations or acquaintances. They fulfilled to the uttermost all that the world demands of poor people, the father fetched breakfast for the small clerks in the bank, the mother devoted her energy to making underwear for strangers, the sister trotted to and fro behind the counter at the behest of customers, but more than this they had not the strength to do. And the wound in Gregor's back began to nag at him afresh when his mother and sister, after getting his father into bed, came back again, left their work lying, drew close to each other and sat cheek by cheek; when his mother, pointing towards his room, said: "Shut that door now, Grete," and he was left again in darkness, while next door the women mingled their tears or perhaps sat dry-eyed staring at the table.

Gregor hardly slept at all by night or by day. He was often haunted by the idea that next time the door opened he would take the family's affairs in hand again just as he used to do; once more, after this long interval, there appeared in his thoughts the figures of the chief and the chief clerk, the commercial travelers and the apprentices, the porter who was so dull-witted, two or three friends in other firms, a chambermaid in one of the rural hotels, a sweet and fleeting memory, a cashier in a milliner's shop, whom he had wooed earnestly but too slowly—they all appeared, together with strangers or people he had quite forgotten, but instead of helping him and his family they were one and all unapproachable and he was glad when they vanished. At other times he would not be in the mood to bother about his family, he was only filled with rage at the way they were neglecting him, and although he had no clear idea of what he might care to eat he would make plans for getting into the larder to take the food that was after all his due, even if he were not hungry. His sister no longer took thought to bring him what might especially please him, but in the morning and at noon before she went to business hurriedly pushed into his room with her foot any food that was available, and in the evening cleared it out again with one sweep of the broom, heedless of whether it had been merely tasted, or—as most frequently happened—left untouched. The cleaning of his room, which she now did always in the evenings, could not have been more hastily done. Streaks of dirt stretched along the walls, here and there lay balls of dust and filth. At first Gregor used to station himself in some particularly filthy corner when his sister arrived, in order to reproach her with it, so to speak. But he could have sat there for weeks without getting her to make any improvement; she could see the dirt as well as he did, but she had simply made up her mind to leave it alone. And yet, with a touchiness that was new to her, which seemed anyhow to have infected the whole family, she jealously guarded her claim to be the sole caretaker of Gregor's room. His mother once subjected his room to a thorough cleaning, which was achieved only by means of several buckets of water—all this dampness of course upset Gregor too and he lay widespread, sulky and motionless on the sofa—but she was well punished for it. Hardly had his sister noticed the changed aspect of his room that evening than she rushed in high dudgeon into the living room and, despite the imploringly raised hands of her mother, burst into a storm of weeping, while her parents—her father had of course been startled out of his chair—looked on at first in helpless amazement; then they too began to go into action; the father reproached the mother on his right for not having left the cleaning of Gregor's room to his sister; shrieked at the sister on his left that never again was she to be allowed to clean Gregor's room; while the mother tried to pull the father into his bedroom, since he was beyond himself with agitation; the sister, shaken with sobs, then beat upon the table with her small fists; and Gregor hissed loudly with rage because not one of them thought of shutting the door to spare him such a spectacle and so much noise.

Still, even if the sister, exhausted by her daily work, had grown tired of looking after Gregor as she did formerly, there was no need for his mother's intervention or for Gregor's being neglected at all. The charwoman was there. This old widow, whose strong bony frame had enabled her to survive the worst a long life could offer, by no means recoiled from Gregor. Without being in the least curious she had once by chance opened the door of his room and at the sight of Gregor, who, taken by surprise, began to rush to and fro although no one was chasing him, merely stood there with her arms folded. From that time she never failed to open his door a little for a moment, morning and evening, to have a look at him. At first she even used to call him to her, with words which apparently she took to be friendly, such as: "Come along, then, you old dung beetle!" or "Look at the old dung beetle, then!" To such allocutions Gregor made no answer, but stayed motionless where he was, as if the door had never been opened. Instead of being allowed to disturb him so senselessly whenever the whim took her, she should rather have been ordered to clean out his room daily, that charwoman! Once, early in the morning—heavy rain was lashing on the windowpanes, perhaps a sign that spring was on the way—Gregor was so exasperated when she began addressing him again that he ran at her, as if to attack her, although slowly and feebly enough. But the charwoman instead of showing fright merely lifted high a chair that happened to be beside the door, and as she stood there with her mouth wide open it was clear that she meant to shut it only when she brought the chair down on Gregor's back. "So you're not coming any nearer?" she asked, as Gregor turned away again, and quietly put the chair back into the corner.

Gregor was now eating hardly anything. Only when he happened to pass the food laid out for him did he take a bit of something in his mouth as a pastime, kept it there for an hour at a time and usually spat it out again. At first he thought it was chagrin over the state of his room that prevented him from eating, yet he soon got used to the various changes in his room. It had become a habit in the family to push into his room things there was no room for elsewhere, and there were plenty of these now, since one of the rooms had been let to three lodgers. These serious gentlemen—all three of them with full beards, as Gregor once observed through a crack in the door—had a passion for order, not only in their own room but, since they were now members of the household, in all its arrangements, especially in the kitchen. Superfluous, not to say dirty, objects they could not bear. Besides, they had brought with them most of the furnishings they needed. For this reason many things could be dispensed with that it was no use trying to sell but that should not be thrown away either. All of them found their way into Gregor's room. The ash can likewise and the kitchen garbage can. Anything that was not needed for the moment was simply flung into Gregor's room by the charwoman, who did everything in a hurry; fortunately Gregor usually saw only the object, whatever it was, and the hand that held it. Perhaps she intended to take the things away again as time and opportunity offered, or to collect them until she could throw them all out in a heap, but in fact they just lay wherever she happened to throw them, except when Gregor pushed his way through the junk heap and shifted it somewhat, at first out of necessity, because he had not room enough to crawl, but later with increasing enjoyment, although after such excursions, being sad and weary to death, he would lie motionless for hours. And since the lodgers often ate their supper at home in the common living room, the living-room door stayed shut many an evening, yet Gregor reconciled himself to the shutting of the door, for often enough on evenings when it was opened he had disregarded it entirely and lain in the darkest corner of his room, quite unnoticed by the family. But on one occasion the charwoman left the door open a little and it stayed ajar even when the lodgers came in for supper and the lamp was lit. They set themselves at the top end of the table where formerly Gregor and his father and mother had eaten their meals, unfolded their napkins and took knife and fork in hand. At once his mother appeared in the other doorway with a dish of meat and close behind her his sister with a dish of potatoes piled high. The food steamed with a thick vapor. The lodgers bent over the food set before them as if to scrutinize it before eating it; in fact the man in the middle, who seemed to pass for an authority with the other two, cut a piece of meat as it lay on the dish, obviously to discover if it were tender or should be sent back to the kitchen. He showed satisfaction, and Gregor's mother and sister, who had been watching anxiously, breathed freely and began to smile.

The family itself took its meals in the kitchen. None the less, Gregor's father came into the living room before going into the kitchen and with one prolonged bow, cap in hand, made a round of the table. The lodgers all stood up and murmured something in their beards. When they were alone again they ate their food in almost complete silence. It seemed remarkable to Gregor that among the various noises coming in from the table he could always distinguish the sound of their masticating teeth, as if this were a sign to Gregor that one needed teeth in order to eat, and that with toothless jaws even of the finest make one could do nothing. "I'm hungry enough," said Gregor sadly to himself, "but not for that kind of food. How these lodgers are stuffing themselves, and here I am dying of starvation!"

On that very evening—during the whole of his time there Gregor could not remember ever having heard the violin—the sound of violin-playing came from the kitchen. The lodgers had already finished their supper, the one in the middle had brought out a newspaper and given the other two a page apiece, and now they were leaning back at ease and reading and smoking. When the violin began to play they pricked up their ears, got to their feet, and went on tiptoe to the hall door where they stood huddled together. Their movements must have been heard in the kitchen, for Gregor's father called out: "Is the violin-playing disturbing you, gentlemen? It can be stopped at once." "On the contrary," said the middle lodger, "could not Fräulein Samsa come and play in this room, beside us, where it is much more convenient and comfortable?" "Oh certainly," cried Gregor's father, as if he were the violin-player. The lodgers came back into the living room and waited. Presently Gregor's father arrived with the music stand, his mother carrying the music and his sister with the violin. His sister quietly made everything ready to start playing; his parents, who had never let rooms before and so had an exaggerated idea of the courtesy due to lodgers, did not venture to sit down on their own chairs; his father leaned against the door, the right hand thrust between two buttons of his livery coat, which was formally buttoned up; but his mother was offered a chair by one of the lodgers and, since she left the chair just where he had happened to put it, sat down in a corner to one side.

Gregor's sister began to play; the father and mother, from either side, intently watched the movements of her hands. Gregor, attracted by the playing, ventured to move forward a little until his head was actually inside the living room. He felt hardly any surprise at his growing lack of consideration for the others; there had been a time when he prided himself on being considerate. And yet just on this occasion he had more reason than ever to hide himself, since owing to the amount of dust which lay thick in his room and rose into the air at the slightest movement, he too was covered with dust; fluff and hair and remnants of food trailed with him, caught on his back and along his sides; his indifference to everything was much too great for him to turn on his back and scrape himself clean on the carpet, as once he had done several times a day. And in spite of his condition, no shame deterred him from advancing a little over the spotless floor of the living room.

To be sure, no one was aware of him. The family was entirely absorbed in the violin-playing; the lodgers, however, who first of all had stationed themselves, hands in pockets, much too close to the music stand so that they could all have read the music, which must have bothered his sister, had soon retreated to the window, half-whispering with downbent heads, and stayed there while his father turned an anxious eye on them. Indeed, they were making it more than obvious that they had been disappointed in their expectation of hearing good or more enjoyable violin-playing, that they had had more than enough of the performance and only out of courtesy suffered a continued disturbance of their peace. From the way they kept blowing the smoke of their cigars high in the air through nose and mouth one could divine their irritation. And yet Gregor's sister was playing so beautifully. Her face leaned sideways, intently and sadly her eyes followed the notes of music. Gregor crawled a little farther forward and lowered his head to the ground so that it might be possible for his eyes to meet hers. Was he an animal, that music had such an effect on him? He felt as if the way were opening before him to the unknown nourishment he craved. He was determined to push forward till he reached his sister, to pull at her skirt and so to let her know that she was to come into his room with her violin, for no one here appreciated her playing as he would appreciate it. He would never let her out of his room, at least, not so long as he lived; his frightful appearance would become, for the first time, useful to him; he would watch all the doors of his room at once and spit at intruders; but his sister should need no constraint, she should stay with him of her own free will; she should sit beside him on the sofa, bend down her ear to him and hear him confide that he had had the firm intention of sending her to the Conservatorium, and that, but for his mishap, last Christmas—surely Christmas was long past?—he would have announced it to everybody without allowing a single objection. After this confession his sister would be so touched that she would burst into tears, and Gregor would then raise himself to her shoulder and kiss her on the neck, which, now that she went to business, she kept free of any ribbon or collar.

"Mr. Samsa!" cried the middle lodger, to Gregor's father, and pointed, without wasting any more words, at Gregor, now working himself slowly forwards. The violin fell silent, the middle lodger first smiled to his friends with a shake of his head and then looked at Gregor again. Instead of driving Gregor out, his father seemed to think it more needful to begin by soothing down the lodgers, although they were not at all agitated and apparently found Gregor more entertaining than the violin-playing. He hurried towards them and, spreading out his arms, tried to urge them back into their own room and at the same time block their view of Gregor. They now began to be really a little angry, one could not tell whether because of the old man's behavior or because it had just dawned on them that all unwittingly they had such a neighbor as Gregor next door. They demanded explanations of his father, they waved their arms like him, tugged uneasily at their beards, and only with reluctance backed towards their room. Meanwhile Gregor's sister, who stood there as if lost when her playing was so abruptly broken off, came to life again, pulled herself together all at once after standing for a while holding violin and bow in nervelessly hanging hands and staring at her music, pushed her violin into the lap of her mother, who was still sitting in her chair fighting asthmatically for breath, and ran into the lodgers' room to which they were now being shepherded by her father rather more quickly than before. One could see the pillows and blankets flying under her accustomed fingers and being laid in order. Before the lodgers had actually reached their room she had finished making the beds and slipped out.

The old man seemed once more to be so possessed by his mulish self assertiveness that he was forgetting all the respect he should show to his lodgers. He kept driving them on and driving them on until in the very door of the bedroom the middle lodger stamped his foot loudly on the floor and so brought him to a halt. "I beg to announce," said the lodger, lifting one hand and looking also at Gregor's mother and sister, "that because of the disgusting conditions prevailing in this household and family"—here he spat on the floor with emphatic brevity—"I give you notice on the spot. Naturally I won't pay you a penny for the days I have lived here, on the contrary I shall consider bringing an action for damages against you, based on claims—believe me—that will be easily susceptible of proof." He ceased and stared straight in front of him, as if he expected something. In fact his two friends at once rushed into the breach with these words: "And we too give our notice on the spot." On that he seized the door-handle and shut the door with a slam.

Gregor's father, groping with his hands, staggered forward and fell into his chair; it looked as if he were stretching himself there for his ordinary evening nap, but the marked jerkings of his head, which was as if uncontrollable, showed that he was far from asleep. Gregor had simply stayed quiet on the spot where the lodgers had espied him. Disappointment at the failure of his plan, perhaps also the weakness arising from extreme hunger, made it impossible for him to move. He feared, with a fair degree of certainty, that at any moment the general tension would discharge itself in a combined attack upon him, and he lay waiting. He did not react even to the noise made by the violin as it fell off his mother's lap from under her trembling fingers and gave out a resonant note.

"My dear parents," said his sister, slapping her hand on the table by way of introduction, "things can't go on like this. Perhaps you don't realize that, but I do. I won't utter my brother's name in the presence of this creature, and so all I say is: we must try to get rid of it. We've tried to look after it and to put up with it as far as is humanly possible, and I don't think anyone could reproach us in the slightest."

"She is more than right," said Gregor's father to himself. His mother, who was still choking for lack of breath, began to cough hollowly into her hand with a wild look in her eyes.

His sister rushed over to her and held her forehead. His father's thoughts seemed to have lost their vagueness at Grete's words, he sat more upright, fingering his service cap that lay among the plates still lying on the table from the lodgers' supper, and from time to time looked at the still form of Gregor.

"We must try to get rid of it," his sister now said explicitly to her father, since her mother was coughing too much to hear a word, "it will be the death of both of you, I can see that coming. When one has to work as hard as we do, all of us, one can't stand this continual torment at home on top of it. At least I can't stand it any longer." And she burst into such a passion of sobbing that her tears dropped on her mother's face, where she wiped them off mechanically.

"My dear," said the old man sympathetically, and with evident understanding, "but what can we do?"

Gregor's sister merely shrugged her shoulders to indicate the feeling of helplessness that had now overmastered her during her weeping fit, in contrast to her former confidence.

"If he could understand us," said her father, half questioningly; Grete, still sobbing, vehemently waved a hand to show how unthinkable that was.

"If he could understand us," repeated the old man, shutting his eyes to consider his daughter's conviction that understanding was impossible, "then perhaps we might come to some agreement with him. But as it is—"

"He must go," cried Gregor's sister, "that's the only solution, Father. You must just try to get rid of the idea that this is Gregor. The fact that we've believed it for so long is the root of all our trouble. But how can it be Gregor? If this were Gregor, he would have realized long ago that human beings can't live with such a creature, and he'd have gone away on his own accord. Then we wouldn't have any brother, but we'd be able to go on living and keep his memory in honor. As it is, this creature persecutes us, drives away our lodgers, obviously wants the whole apartment to himself and would have us all sleep in the gutter. Just look, Father," she shrieked all at once, "he's at it again!" And in an access of panic that was quite incomprehensible to Gregor she even quitted her mother, literally thrusting the chair from her as if she would rather sacrifice her mother than stay so near to Gregor, and rushed behind her father, who also rose up, being simply upset by her agitation, and half-spread his arms out as if to protect her.

Yet Gregor had not the slightest intention of frightening anyone, far less his sister. He had only begun to turn round in order to crawl back to his room, but it was certainly a startling operation to watch, since because of his disabled condition he could not execute the difficult turning movements except by lifting his head and then bracing it against the floor over and over again. He paused and looked round. His good intentions seemed to have been recognized; the alarm had only been momentary. Now they were all watching him in melancholy silence. His mother lay in her chair, her legs stiffly outstretched and pressed together, her eyes almost closing for sheer weariness; his father and his sister were sitting beside each other, his sister's arm around the old man's neck.

Perhaps I can go on turning round now, thought Gregor, and began his labors again. He could not stop himself from panting with the effort, and had to pause now and then to take breath. Nor did anyone harass him, he was left entirely to himself. When he had completed the turn-round he began at once to crawl straight back. He was amazed at the distance separating him from his room and could not understand how in his weak state he had managed to accomplish the same journey so recently, almost without remarking it. Intent on crawling as fast as possible, he barely noticed that not a single word, not an ejaculation from his family, interfered with his progress. Only when he was already in the doorway did he turn his head round, not completely, for his neck muscles were getting stiff, but enough to see that nothing had changed behind him except that his sister had risen to her feet. His last glance fell on his mother, who was not quite overcome by sleep.

Hardly was he well inside his room when the door was hastily pushed shut, bolted and locked. The sudden noise in his rear startled him so much that his little legs gave beneath him. It was his sister who had shown such haste. She had been standing ready waiting and had made a light spring forward, Gregor had not even heard her coming, and she cried "At last!" to her parents as she turned the key in the lock.

"And what now?" said Gregor to himself, looking round in the darkness. Soon he made the discovery that he was now unable to stir a limb. This did not surprise him, rather it seemed unnatural that he should ever actually have been able to move on these feeble little legs. Otherwise he felt relatively comfortable. True, his whole body was aching, but it seemed that the pain was gradually growing less and would finally pass away. The rotting apple in his back and the inflamed area around it, all covered with soft dust, already hardly troubled him. He thought of his family with tenderness and love. The decision that he must disappear was one that he held to even more strongly than his sister, if that were possible. In this state of vacant and peaceful meditation he remained until the tower clock struck three in the morning. The first broadening of light in the world outside the window entered his consciousness once more. Then his head sank to the floor of its own accord and from his nostrils came the last faint flicker of his breath.

When the charwoman arrived early in the morning—what between her strength and her impatience she slammed all the doors so loudly, never mind how often she had been begged not to do so, that no one in the whole apartment could enjoy any quiet sleep after her arrival—she noticed nothing unusual as she took her customary peep into Gregor's room. She thought he was lying motionless on purpose, pretending to be in the sulks; she credited him with every kind of intelligence. Since she happened to have the long-handled broom in her hand she tried to tickle him up with it from the doorway. When that too produced no reaction she felt provoked and poked at him a little harder, and only when she had pushed him along the floor without meeting any resistance was her attention aroused. It did not take her long to establish the truth of the matter, and her eyes widened, she let out a whistle, yet did not waste much time over it but tore open the door of the Samsas' bedroom and yelled into the darkness at the top of her voice: "Just look at this, it's dead; it's lying here dead and done for!"

Mr. and Mrs. Samsa started up in their double bed and before they realized the nature of the charwoman's announcement had some difficulty in overcoming the shock of it. But then they got out of bed quickly, one on either side, Mr. Samsa throwing a blanket over his shoulders, Mrs. Samsa in nothing but her nightgown; in this array they entered Gregor's room. Meanwhile the door of the living room opened, too, where Grete had been sleeping since the advent of the lodgers; she was completely dressed as if she had not been to bed, which seemed to be confirmed also by the paleness of her face. "Dead?" said Mrs. Samsa, looking questioningly at the charwoman, although she could have investigated for herself, and the fact was obvious enough without investigation. "I should say so," said the charwoman, proving her words by pushing Gregor's corpse a long way to one side with her broomstick. Mrs. Samsa made a movement as if to stop her, but checked it. "Well," said Mr. Samsa, "now thanks be to God." He crossed himself, and the three women followed his example. Grete, whose eyes never left the corpse, said: "Just see how thin he was. It's such a long time since he's eaten anything. The food came out again just as it went in." Indeed, Gregor's body was completely flat and dry, as could only now be seen when it was no longer supported by the legs and nothing prevented one from looking closely at it.

"Come in beside us, Grete, for a little while," said Mrs. Samsa with a tremulous smile, and Grete, not without looking back at the corpse, followed her parents into their bedroom. The charwoman shut the door and opened the window wide. Although it was so early in the morning a certain softness was perceptible in the fresh air. After all, it was already the end of March.

The three lodgers emerged from their room and were surprised to see no breakfast; they had been forgotten. "Where's our breakfast?" said the middle lodger peevishly to the charwoman. But she put her finger to her lips and hastily, without a word, indicated by gestures that they should go into Gregor's room. They did so and stood, their hands in the pockets of their somewhat shabby coats, around Gregor's corpse in the room where it was now fully light.

At that the door of the Samsas' bedroom opened and Mr. Samsa appeared in his uniform, his wife on one arm, his daughter on the other. They all looked a little as if they had been crying; from time to time Grete hid her face on her father's arm.

"Leave my house at once!" said Mr. Samsa, and pointed to the door without disengaging himself from the women. "What do you mean by that?"

said the middle lodger, taken somewhat aback, with a feeble smile. The two others put their hands behind them and kept rubbing them together, as if in gleeful expectation of a fine set-to in which they were bound to come off the winners. "I mean just what I say," answered Mr. Samsa, and advanced in a straight line with his two companions towards the lodger. He stood his ground at first quietly, looking at the floor as if his thoughts were taking a new pattern in his head. "Then let us go, by all means," he said, and looked up at Mr. Samsa as if in a sudden access of humility he were expecting some renewed sanction for this decision. Mr. Samsa merely nodded briefly once or twice with meaning eyes. Upon that the lodger really did go with long strides into the hall; his two friends had been listening and had quite stopped rubbing their hands for some moments and now went scuttling after him as if afraid that Mr. Samsa might get into the hall before them and cut them off from their leader. In the hall they all three took their hats from the rack, their sticks from the umbrella stand, bowed in silence and quitted the apartment. With a suspiciousness which proved quite unfounded Mr. Samsa and the two women followed them out to the landing; leaning over the banister they watched the three figures slowly but surely going down the long stairs, vanishing from sight at a certain turn of the staircase on every floor and coming into view again after a moment or so; the more they dwindled, the more the Samsa family's interest in them dwindled, and when a butcher's boy met them and passed them on the stairs coming up proudly with a tray on his head, Mr. Samsa and the two women soon left the landing and as if a burden had been lifted from them went back into their apartment.

They decided to spend this day in resting and going for a stroll; they had not only deserved such a respite from work, but absolutely needed it. And so they sat down at the table and wrote three notes of excuse, Mr. Samsa to his board of management, Mrs. Samsa to her employer and Grete to the head of her firm. While they were writing, the charwoman came in to say that she was going now, since her morning's work was finished. At first they only nodded without looking up, but as she kept hovering there they eyed her irritably. "Well?" said Mr. Samsa. The charwoman stood grinning in the doorway as if she had good news to impart to the family but meant not to say a word unless properly questioned. The small ostrich feather standing upright on her hat, which had annoyed Mr. Samsa ever since she was engaged, was waving gaily in all directions. "Well, what is it then?" asked Mrs. Samsa, who obtained more respect from the charwoman than the others. "Oh," said the charwoman, giggling so amiably that she could not at once continue, "just this, you don't need to bother about how to get rid of the thing next door. It's been seen to already." Mrs. Samsa and Grete bent over their letters again, as if preoccupied; Mr. Samsa, who perceived that she was eager to begin describing it all in detail, stopped her with a decisive hand. But since she was not allowed to tell her story, she remembered the great hurry she was in, being obviously deeply huffed: "Bye, everybody," she said, whirling off violently, and departed with a frightful slamming of doors.

"She'll be given notice tonight," said Mr. Samsa, but neither from his wife nor his daughter did he get any answer, for the charwoman seemed to have shattered again the composure they had barely achieved. They rose, went to the window and stayed there, clasping each other tight. Mr. Samsa turned in his chair to look at them and quietly observed them for a little. Then he called out: "Come along, now, do. Let bygones be bygones. And you might have some consideration for me." The two of them complied at once, hastened to him, caressed him and quickly finished their letters.

Then they all three left the apartment together, which was more than they had done for months, and went by tram into the open country outside the town. The tram, in which they were the only passengers, was filled with warm sunshine. Leaning comfortably back in their seats they canvassed their prospects for the future, and it appeared on closer inspection that these were not at all bad, for the jobs they had got, which so far they had never really discussed with each other, were all three admirable and likely to lead to better things later on. The greatest immediate improvement in their condition would of course arise from moving to another house; they wanted to take a smaller and cheaper but also better situated and more easily run apartment than the one they had, which Gregor had selected. While they were thus conversing, it struck both Mr. and Mrs. Samsa, almost at the same moment, as they became aware of their daughter's increasing vivacity, that in spite of all the sorrow of recent times, which had made her cheeks pale, she had bloomed into a pretty girl with a good figure. They grew quieter and half unconsciously exchanged glances of complete agreement, having come to the conclusion that it would soon be time to find a good husband for her. And it was like a confirmation of their new dreams and excellent intentions that at the end of their journey their daughter sprang to her feet first and stretched her young body.

A Hunger Artist

During these last decades the interest in professional fasting has markedly diminished. It used to pay very well to stage such great performances under one's own management, but today that is quite impossible. We live in a different world now. At one time the whole town took a lively interest in the hunger artist; from day to day of his fast the excitement mounted; everybody wanted to see him at least once a day; there were people who bought season tickets for the last few days and sat from morning till night in front of his small barred cage; even in the nighttime there were visiting hours, when the whole effect was heightened by torch flares; on fine days the cage was set out in the open air, and then it was the children's special treat to see the hunger artist; for their elders he was often just a joke that happened to be in fashion, but the children stood open-mouthed, holding each other's hands for greater security, marveling at him as he sat there pallid in black tights, with his ribs sticking out so prominently, not even on a seat but down among straw on the ground, sometimes giving a courteous nod, answering questions with a constrained smile, or perhaps stretching an arm through the bars so that one might feel how thin it was, and then again withdrawing deep into himself, paying no attention to anyone or anything, not even to the all-important striking of the clock that was the only piece of furniture in his cage, but merely staring into vacancy with half-shut eyes, now and then taking a sip from a tiny glass of water to moisten his lips.

Besides casual onlookers there were also relays of permanent watchers selected by the public, usually butchers, strangely enough, and it was their task to watch the hunger artist day and night, three of them at a time, in case he should have some secret recourse to nourishment. This was nothing but a formality, instituted to reassure the masses, for the initiates knew well enough that during his fast the artist would never in any circumstances, not even under forcible compulsion, swallow the smallest morsel of food; the honor of his profession forbade it. Not every watcher, of course, was capable of understanding this, there were often groups of night watchers who were very lax in carrying out their duties and deliberately huddled together in a retired corner to play cards with great absorption, obviously intending to give the hunger artist the chance of a little refreshment, which they supposed he could draw from some private hoard. Nothing annoyed the artist more than such watchers; they made him miserable; they made his fast seem unendurable; sometimes he mastered his feebleness sufficiently to sing during their watch for as long as he could keep going, to show them how unjust their suspicions were. But that was of little use; they only wondered at his cleverness in being able to fill his mouth even while singing. Much more to his taste were the watchers who sat close up to the bars, who were not content with the dim night lighting of the hall but focused him in the full glare of the electric pocket torch given them by the impresario. The harsh light did not trouble him at all. In any case he could never sleep properly, and he could always drowse a little, whatever the light, at any hour, even when the hall was thronged with noisy onlookers. He was quite happy at the prospect of spending a sleepless night with such watchers; he was ready to exchange jokes with them, to tell them stories out of his nomadic life, anything at all to keep them awake and demonstrate to them again that he had no eatables in his cage and that he was fasting as not one of them could fast. But his happiest moment was when the morning came and an enormous breakfast was brought them, at his expense, on which they flung themselves with the keen appetite of healthy men after a weary night of wakefulness. Of course there were people who argued that this breakfast was an unfair attempt to bribe the watchers, but that was going rather too far, and when they were invited to take on a night's vigil without a breakfast, merely for the sake of the cause, they made themselves scarce, although they stuck stubbornly to their suspicions.

Such suspicions, anyhow, were a necessary accompaniment to the profession of fasting. No one could possibly watch the hunger artist continuously, day and night, and so no one could produce first-hand evidence that the fast had really been rigorous and continuous; only the artist himself could know that; he was therefore bound to be the sole completely satisfied spectator of his own fast. Yet for other reasons he was never satisfied; it was not perhaps mere fasting that had brought him to such skeleton thinness that many people had regretfully to keep away from his exhibitions, because the sight of him was too much for them, perhaps it was dissatisfaction with himself that had worn him down. For he alone knew, what no other initiate knew, how easy it was to fast. It was the easiest thing in the world. He made no secret of this, yet people did not believe him; at the best they set him down as modest, most of them, however, thought he was out for publicity or else was some kind of cheat who found it easy to fast because he had discovered a way of making it easy, and then had the impudence to admit the fact, more or less. He had to put up with all that, and in the course of time had got used to it, but his inner dissatisfaction always rankled, and never yet, after any term of fasting—this must be granted to his credit—had he left the cage of his own free will. The longest period of fasting was fixed by his impresario at forty days, beyond that term he was not allowed to go, not even in great cities, and there was good reason for it, too. Experience had proved that for about forty days the interest of the public could be stimulated by a steadily increasing pressure of advertisement, but after that the town began to lose interest, sympathetic support began notably to fall off; there were of course local variations as between one town and another or one country and another, but as a general rule forty days marked the limit. So on the fortieth day the flower-bedecked cage was opened, enthusiastic spectators filled the hall, a military band played, two doctors entered the cage to measure the results of the fast, which were announced through a megaphone, and finally two young ladies appeared, blissful at having been selected for the honor, to help the hunger artist down the few steps leading to a small table on which was spread a carefully chosen invalid repast. And at this very moment the artist always turned stubborn. True, he would entrust his bony arms to the outstretched helping hands of the ladies bending over him, but stand up he would not. Why stop fasting at this particular moment, after forty days of it? He had held out for a long time, an illimitably long time; why stop now, when he was in his best fasting form, or rather, not yet quite in his best fasting form? Why should he be cheated of the fame he would get for fasting longer, for being not only the record hunger artist of all time, which presumably he was already, but for beating his own record by a performance beyond human imagination, since he felt that there were no limits to his capacity for fasting? His public pretended to admire him so much, why should it have so little patience with him; if he could endure fasting longer, why shouldn't the public endure it? Besides, he was tired, he was comfortable sitting in the straw, and now he was supposed to lift himself to his full height and go down to a meal the very thought of which gave him a nausea that only the presence of the ladies kept him from betraying, and even that with an effort. And he looked up into the eyes of the ladies who were apparently so friendly and in reality so cruel, and shook his head, which felt too heavy on its strengthless neck. But then there happened yet again what always happened. The impresario came forward, without a word—for the band made speech impossible—lifted his arms in the air above the artist, as if inviting Heaven to look down upon its creature here in the straw, this suffering martyr, which indeed he was, although in quite another sense; grasped him round the emaciated waist, with exaggerated caution, so that the frail condition he was in might be appreciated; and committed him to the care of the blenching ladies, not without secretly giving him a shaking so that his legs and body tottered and swayed. The artist now submitted completely; his head lolled on his breast as if it had landed there by chance; his body was hollowed out; his legs in a spasm of self-preservation clung close to each other at the knees, yet scraped on the ground as if it were not really solid ground, as if they were only trying to find solid ground; and the whole weight of his body, a featherweight after all, relapsed onto one of the ladies, who, looking round for help and panting a little —this post of honor was not at all what she had expected it to be—first stretched her neck as far as she could to keep her face at least free from contact with the artist, then finding this impossible, and her more fortunate companion not coming to her aid but merely holding extended on her own trembling hand the little bunch of knucklebones that was the artist's, to the great delight of the spectators burst into tears and had to be replaced by an attendant who had long been stationed in readiness. Then came the food, a little of which the impresario managed to get between the artist's lips, while he sat in a kind of half-fainting trance, to the accompaniment of cheerful patter designed to distract the public's attention from the artist's condition; after that, a toast was drunk to the public, supposedly prompted by a whisper from the artist in the impresario's ear; the band confirmed it with a mighty flourish, the spectators melted away, and no one had any cause to be dissatisfied with the proceedings, no one except the hunger artist himself, he only, as always.

So he lived for many years, with small regular intervals of recuperation, in visible glory, honored by the world, yet in spite of that troubled in spirit, and all the more troubled because no one would take his trouble seriously. What comfort could he possibly need? What more could he possibly wish for? And if some good-natured person, feeling sorry for him, tried to console him by pointing out that his melancholy was probably caused by fasting, it could happen, especially when he had been fasting for some time, that he reacted with an outburst of fury and to the general alarm began to shake the bars of his cage like a wild animal. Yet the impresario had a way of punishing these outbreaks which he rather enjoyed putting into operation. He would apologize publicly for the artist's behavior, which was only to be excused, he admitted, because of the irritability caused by fasting; a condition hardly to be understood by well-fed people; then by natural transition he went on to mention the artist's equally incomprehensible boast that he could fast for much longer than he was doing; he praised the high ambition, the good will, the great self-denial undoubtedly implicit in such a statement; and then quite simply countered it by bringing out photographs, which were also on sale to the public, showing the artist on the fortieth day of a fast lying in bed almost dead from exhaustion. This perversion of the truth, familiar to the artist though it was, always unnerved him afresh and proved too much for him. What was a consequence of the premature ending of his fast was here presented as the cause of it! To fight against this lack of understanding, against a whole world of non-understanding, was impossible. Time and again in good faith he stood by the bars listening to the impresario, but as soon as the photographs appeared he always let go and sank with a groan back on to his straw, and the reassured public could once more come close and gaze at him.

A few years later when the witnesses of such scenes called them to mind, they often failed to understand themselves at all. For meanwhile the aforementioned change in public interest had set in; it seemed to happen almost overnight; there may have been profound causes for it, but who was going to bother about that; at any rate the pampered hunger artist suddenly found himself deserted one fine day by the amusement seekers, who went streaming past him to other more favored attractions. For the last time the impresario hurried him over half Europe to discover whether the old interest might still survive here and there; all in vain; everywhere, as if by secret agreement, a positive revulsion from professionl fasting was in evidence. Of course it could not really have sprung up so suddenly as all that, and many premonitory symptoms which had not been sufficiently remarked or suppressed during the rush and glitter of success now came retrospectively to mind, but it was now too late to take any countermeasures. Fasting would surely come into fashion again at some future date, yet that was no comfort for those living in the present. What, then, was the hunger artist to do? He had been applauded by thousands in his time and could hardly come down to showing himself in a street booth at village fairs, and as for adopting another profession, he was not only too old for that but too fanatically devoted to fasting. So he took leave of the impresario, his partner in an unparalleled career, and hired himself to a large circus; in order to spare his own feelings he avoided reading the conditions of his contract.

A large circus with its enormous traffic in replacing and recruiting men, animals and apparatus can always find a use for people at any time, even for a hunger artist, provided of course that he does not ask too much, and in this particular case anyhow it was not only the artist who was taken on but his famous and long-known name as well; indeed considering the peculiar nature of his performance, which was not impaired by advancing age, it could not be objected that here was an artist past his prime, no longer at the height of his professional skill, seeking a refuge in some quiet corner of a circus; on the contrary, the hunger artist averred that he could fast as well as ever, which was entirely credible; he even alleged that if he were allowed to fast as he liked, and this was at once promised him without more ado, he could astound the world by establishing a record never yet achieved, a statement which certainly provoked a smile among the other professionals, since it left out of account the change in public opinion, which the hunger artist in his zeal conveniently forgot.

He had not, however, actually lost his sense of the real situation and took it as a matter of course that he and his cage should be stationed, not in the middle of the ring as a main attraction, but outside, near the animal cages, on a site that was after all easily accessible. Large and gaily painted placards made a frame for the cage and announced what was to be seen inside it. When the public came thronging out in the intervals to see the animals, they could hardly avoid passing the hunger artist's cage and stopping there for a moment; perhaps they might even have stayed longer had not those pressing behind them in the narrow gangway, who did not understand why they should be held up on their way towards the excitements of the menagerie, made it impossible for anyone to stand gazing quietly for any length of time. And that was the reason why the hunger artist, who had of course been looking forward to these visiting hours as the main achievement of his life, began instead to shrink from them. At first he could hardly wait for the intervals; it was exhilarating to watch the crowds come streaming his way, until only too soon—not even the most obstinate self-deception, clung to almost consciously, could hold out against the fact—the conviction was borne in upon him that these people, most of them, to judge from their actions, again and again, without exception, were all on their way to the menagerie. And the first sight of them from the distance remained the best. For when they reached his cage he was at once deafened by the storm of shouting and abuse that arose from the two contending factions, which renewed themselves continuously, of those who wanted to stop and stare at him—he soon began to dislike them more than the others—not out of real interest but only out of obstinate self-assertiveness, and those who wanted to go straight on to the animals. When the first great rush was past, the stragglers came along, and these, whom nothing could have prevented from stopping to look at him as long as they had breath, raced past with long strides, hardly even glancing at him, in their haste to get to the menagerie in time. And all too rarely did it happen that he had a stroke of luck, when some father of a family fetched up before him with his children, pointed a finger at the hunger artist and explained at length what the phenomenon meant, telling stories of earlier years when he himself had watched similar but much more thrilling performances, and the children, still rather uncomprehending, since neither inside nor outside school had they been sufficiently prepared for this lesson—what did they care about fasting?—yet showed by the brightness of their intent eyes that new and better times might be coming. Perhaps, said the hunger artist to himself many a time, things would be a little better if his cage were set not quite so near the menagerie. That made it too easy for people to make their choice, to say nothing of what he suffered from the stench of the menagerie, the animals' restlessness by night, the carrying past of raw lumps of flesh for the beasts of prey, the roaring at feeding times, which depressed him continually. But he did not dare to lodge a complaint with the management; after all, he had the animals to thank for the troops of people who passed his cage, among whom there might always be one here and there to take an interest in him, and who could tell where they might seclude him if he called attention to his existence and thereby to the fact that, strictly speaking, he was only an impediment on the way to the menagerie.

A small impediment, to be sure, one that grew steadily less. People grew familiar with the strange idea that they could be expected, in times like these, to take an interest in a hunger artist, and with this familiarity the verdict went out against him. He might fast as much as he could, and he did so; but nothing could save him now, people passed him by. Just try to explain to anyone the art of fasting! Anyone who has no feeling for it cannot be made to understand it. The fine placards grew dirty and illegible, they were torn down; the little notice board telling the number of fast days achieved, which at first was changed carefully every day, had long stayed at the same figure, for after the first few weeks even this small task seemed pointless to the staff; and so the artist simply fasted on and on, as he had once dreamed of doing, and it was no trouble to him, just as he had always foretold, but no one counted the days, no one, not even the artist himself, knew what records he was already breaking, and his heart grew heavy. And when once in a time some leisurely passer-by stopped, made merry over the old figure on the board and spoke of swindling, that was in its way the stupidest lie ever invented by indifference and inborn malice, since it was not the hunger artist who was cheating; he was working honestly, but the world was cheating him of his reward.

Many more days went by, however, and that too came to an end. An overseer's eye fell on the cage one day and he asked the attendants why this perfectly good cage should be left standing there unused with dirty straw inside it; nobody knew, until one man, helped out by the notice board, remembered about the hunger artist. They poked into the straw with sticks and found him in it. "Are you still fasting?" asked the overseer. "When on earth do you mean to stop?" "Forgive me, everybody," whispered the hunger artist; only the overseer, who had his ear to the bars, understood him. "Of course," said the overseer, and tapped his forehead with a finger to let the attendants know what state the man was in, "we forgive you." "I always wanted you to admire my fasting," said the hunger artist. "We do admire it," said the overseer, affably. "But you shouldn't admire it," said the hunger artist. "Well, then we don't admire it," said the overseer, "but why shouldn't we admire it?" "Because I have to fast, I can't help it," said the hunger artist. "What a fellow you are," said the overseer; "and why can't you help it?" "Because," said the hunger artist, lifting his head a little and speaking, with his lips pursed, as if for a kiss, right into the overseer's ear, so that no syllable might be lost, "because I couldn't find the food I liked. If I had found it, believe me, I should have made no fuss and stuffed myself like you or anyone else." These were his last words, but in his dimming eyes remained the firm though no longer proud persuasion that he was still continuing to fast.

"Well, clear this out now!" said the overseer, and they buried the hunger artist, straw and all. Into the cage they put a young panther. Even the most insensitive felt it refreshing to see this wild creature leaping around the cage that had so long been dreary. The panther was all right. The food he liked was brought him without hesitation by the attendants; he seemed not even to miss his freedom; his noble body, furnished almost to the bursting point with all that it needed, seemed to carry freedom around with it too; somewhere in his jaws it seemed to lurk; and the joy of life streamed with such ardent passion from his throat that for the onlookers it was not easy to stand the shock of it. But they braced themselves, crowded round the cage, and did not want ever to move away.

D. H. LAWRENCE

1885–1930

The coal-mining industry in Lawrence's native Nottinghamshire, England, became for him a symbol of blight in the modern world. Becoming increasingly mechanized to meet the growing need for fuel in industrialized England, coal mining seemed to Lawrence not only to corrupt the earth from which it took the coal but also to insinuate a deadness into the people who lived nearby. Lawrence watched his father, a miner, succumb to the dirt and ugliness of the mine and to its dehumanizing force. Used like a machine, his father gradually lost his capacity for life: his marriage became a mockery of what had once been a vital relationship, and Lawrence's mother, a strong, long-suffering woman (rather like the main character in "Odour of Chrysanthemums") in effect turned to her son for salvation. She determined that Lawrence should be educated and escape his father's fate; and indeed he did attend the university and qualify as a biology teacher in a boys' school near London. But Mrs. Lawrence's influence on her son ran much deeper than his choice of a career; his love for her made him extraordinarily sensitive to the nuances of relationships between men and women, and especially aware of the eternal struggle between the desire to possess and be possessed and the need to be free.

As he stayed by his mother in her agonizing last stages of cancer, Lawrence felt part of himself dying too. After her death he grew dangerously ill, but he lived to confront in his writing the forces that acted so powerfully within him. Lawrence was then twenty-seven and the author of two not very remarkable novels. With a characteristic burst of exuberance he gave up school teaching, extricated himself from a stagnant affair with his childhood sweetheart, and carried away to Italy the unhappily married wife of his former professor of French, Frieda von Richthofen Weekley.

This romantic, scandalous elopement was artistically liberating for Lawrence. In six months of hard work in Italy he completed the final version of *Sons and Lovers* (1913), his first novel to show the mark of genius. More major fiction followed, and though his relationship with Frieda was more often than not turbulent, it sustained him. Eventually, they married and remained together until Lawrence died of tuberculosis at forty-five.

World War I (in which Lawrence did not serve because of his poor health) profoundly depressed him. The war seemed to him to have let loose all the inhumanity of modern industrial civilization and to have left England a spiritual wasteland. After the war Lawrence and Frieda roamed the world, seeking in the rituals of primitive peoples a means of asserting a mystical connection between man and the earth. As might be expected, their quest brought as much disappointment as success, but it did keep in the forefront of Lawrence's consciousness the special need of modern man to wrestle with the forces that insulate him from his fellow human beings, that lock him into habits and patterns of living which distort and atrophy the essential self.

Struggling against the spiritual and emotional death that afflicted the modern world, Lawrence sought to portray characters discovering a way out of their special deadness. An uninhibited acceptance of one's physical being, love that does not smother, exuberance, and a refusal to let mechanism penetrate the personality were the essential qualities to be sought. These qualities in fact constitute a kind of map of his greatest novel, *Women in Love* (1920). But always in Lawrence—perhaps because he constantly lived in awareness of his fatal disease—is the sense that the quest for life is so perilous that at any moment what has been repressed may explode into violence (as in "The Prussian Officer") or (as in Lawrence's life) one's vital energies may fail and surrender the fort to death.

The Prussian Officer

I

They had marched more than thirty kilometres since dawn, along the white, hot road where occasional thickets of trees threw a moment of shade, then out into the glare again. On either hand, the valley, wide and shallow, glittered with heat; dark green patches of rye, pale young corn, fallow and meadow and black pine woods spread in a dull, hot diagram under a glistening sky. But right in front the mountains ranged across, pale blue and very still, snow gleaming gently out of the deep atmosphere. And towards the mountains, on and on, the regiment marched between the rye fields and the meadows, between the scraggy fruit trees set regularly on either side the high road. The burnished, dark green rye threw off a suffocating heat, the mountains drew gradually nearer and more distinct. While the feet of the soldiers grew hotter, sweat ran through their hair under their helmets, and their knapsacks could burn no more in contact with their shoulders, but seemed instead to give off a cold, prickly sensation.

He walked on and on in silence, staring at the mountains ahead, that rose sheer out of the land, and stood fold behind fold, half earth, half heaven, the heaven, the barrier with slits of soft snow, in the pale, bluish peaks.

He could now walk almost without pain. At the start, he had determined not to limp. It had made him sick to take the first steps, and during the first mile or so, he had compressed his breath, and the cold drops of sweat had stood on his forehead. But he had walked it off. What were they after all but bruises! He had looked at them, as he was getting up: deep bruises on the backs of his thighs. And since he had made his first step in the morning, he had been conscious of them, till now he had a tight, hot place in his chest, with suppressing the pain, and holding himself in. There seemed no air when he breathed. But he walked almost lightly.

The Captain's hand had trembled at taking his coffee at dawn: his orderly saw it again. And he saw the fine figure of the Captain wheeling on horseback at the farm-house ahead, a handsome figure in pale blue uniform with facings of scarlet, and the metal gleaming on the black helmet and the sword-scabbard, and dark streaks of sweat coming on the silky bay horse. The orderly felt he was connected with that figure moving so suddenly on horseback: he followed it like a shadow, mute and inevitable and damned by it. And the officer was always aware of the tramp of the company behind, the march of his orderly among the men.

The Captain was a tall man of about forty, grey at the temples. He had a handsome, finely knit figure, and was one of the best horsemen in the West.

His orderly, having to rub him down, admired the amazing riding-muscles of his loins.

For the rest, the orderly scarcely noticed the officer any more than he noticed himself. It was rarely he saw his master's face: he did not look at it. The Captain had reddish-brown, stiff hair, that he wore short upon his skull. His moustache was also cut short and bristly over a full, brutal mouth. His face was rather rugged, the cheeks thin. Perhaps the man was the more handsome for the deep lines in his face, the irritable tension of his brow, which gave him the look of a man who fights with life. His fair eyebrows stood bushy over light blue eyes that were always flashing with cold fire.

He was a Prussian aristocrat, haughty and overbearing. But his mother had been a Polish Countess. Having made too many gambling debts when he was young, he had ruined his prospects in the Army, and remained an infantry captain. He had never married: his position did not allow of it, and no woman had ever moved him to it. His time he spent riding—occasionally he rode one of his own horses at the races—and at the officers' club. Now and then he took himself a mistress. But after such an event, he returned to duty with his brow still more tense, his eyes still more hostile and irritable. With the men, however, he was merely impersonal, though a devil when roused; so that, on the whole, they feared him, but had no great aversion from him. They accepted him as the inevitable.

To his orderly he was at first cold and just and indifferent: he did not fuss over trifles. So that his servant knew practically nothing about him, except just what orders he would give, and how he wanted them obeyed. That was quite simple. Then the change gradually came.

The orderly was a youth of about twenty-two, of medium height, and well built. He had strong, heavy limbs, was swarthy, with a soft, black, young moustache. There was something altogether warm and young about him. He had firmly marked eyebrows over dark, expressionless eyes, that seemed never to have thought, only to have received life direct through his senses, and acted straight from instinct.

Gradually the officer had become aware of his servant's young, vigorous, unconscious presence about him. He could not get away from the sense of the youth's person, while he was in attendance. It was like a warm flame upon the older man's tense, rigid body, that had become almost unliving, fixed. There was something so free and self-contained about him, and something in the young fellow's movement, that made the officer aware of him. And this irritated the Prussian. He did not choose to be touched into life by his servant. He might easily have changed his man, but he did not. He now very rarely looked direct at his orderly, but kept his face averted, as if to avoid seeing him. And yet as the young soldier moved unthinking about the apartment, the elder watched him, and would notice the movement of his strong young shoulders under the blue cloth, the bend of his neck. And it irritated him. To see the soldier's young, brown, shapely peasant's hand grasp the loaf or the wine-bottle sent a flash of hate or of anger through the elder man's blood. It was not that the youth was clumsy: it was rather the blind, instinctive sureness of movement of an unhampered young animal that irritated the officer to such a degree.

Once, when a bottle of wine had gone over, and the red gushed out on to the tablecloth, the officer had started up with an oath, and his eyes, bluey like fire, had held those of the confused youth for a moment. It was a shock for the young soldier. He felt something sink deeper, deeper into his soul, where nothing had ever gone before. It left him rather blank and wondering. Some of his natural completeness in himself was gone, a little uneasiness took its place. And from that time an undiscovered feeling had held between the two men.

Henceforward the orderly was afraid of really meeting his master. His subconsciousness remembered those steely blue eyes and the harsh brows, and did not intend to meet them again. So he always stared past his master, and avoided him. Also, in a little anxiety, he waited for the three months to have gone, when his time would be up. He began to feel a constraint in the Captain's presence, and the soldier even more than the officer wanted to be left alone, in his neutrality as servant.

He had served the Captain for more than a year, and knew his duty. This he performed easily, as if it were natural to him. The officer and his commands he took for granted, as he took the sun and the rain, and he served as a matter of course. It did not implicate him personally.

But now if he were going to be forced into a personal interchange with his master he would be like a wild thing caught, he felt he must get away.

But the influence of the young soldier's being had penetrated through the officer's stiffened discipline, and perturbed the man in him. He, however, was a gentleman, with long, fine hands and cultivated movements, and was not going to allow such a thing as the stirring of his innate self. He was a man of passionate temper, who had always kept himself suppressed. Occasionally there had been a duel, an outburst before the soldiers. He knew himself to be always on the point of breaking out. But he kept himself hard to the idea of the Service. Whereas the young soldier seemed to live out his warm, full nature, to give it off in his very movements, which had a certain zest, such as wild animals have in free movement. And this irritated the officer more and more.

In spite of himself, the Captain could not regain his neutrality of feeling towards his orderly. Nor could he leave the man alone. In spite of himself, he watched him, gave him sharp orders, tried to take up as much of his time as possible. Sometimes he flew into a rage with the young soldier, and bullied him. Then the orderly shut himself off, as it were out of earshot, and waited, with sullen, flushed face, for the end of the noise. The words never pierced to his intelligence, he made himself, protectively, impervious to the feelings of his master.

He had a scar on his left thumb, a deep seam going across the knuckle. The officer had long suffered from it, and wanted to do something to it. Still it was there, ugly and brutal on the young, brown hand. At last the Captain's reserve gave way. One day, as the orderly was smoothing out the tablecloth, the officer pinned down his thumb with a pencil, asking:

"How did you come by that?"

The young man winced and drew back at attention.

"A wood axe, Herr Hauptmann," he answered.

The officer waited for further explanation. None came. The orderly went about his duties. The elder man was sullenly angry. His servant avoided him. And the next day he had to use all his will-power to avoid seeing the scarred thumb. He wanted to get hold of it and—— A hot flame ran in his blood.

He knew his servant would soon be free, and would be glad. As yet, the soldier had held himself off from the elder man. The Captain grew madly irritable. He could not rest when the soldier was away, and when he was present, he glared at him with tormented eyes. He hated those fine, black brows over the unmeaning, dark eyes, he was infuriated by the free movement of the handsome limbs, which no military discipline could make stiff. And he became harsh and cruelly bullying, using contempt and satire. The young soldier only grew more mute and expressionless.

"What cattle were you bred by, that you can't keep straight eyes? Look me in the eyes when I speak to you."

And the soldier turned his dark eyes to the other's face, but there was no sight in them: he stared with the slightest possible cast, holding back his sight, perceiving the blue of his master's eyes, but receiving no look from them. And the elder man went pale, and his reddish eyebrows twitched. He gave his order, barrenly.

Once he flung a heavy military glove into the young soldier's face. Then he had the satisfaction of seeing the black eyes flare up into his own, like a blaze when straw is thrown on a fire. And he had laughed with a little tremor and a sneer.

But there were only two months more. The youth instinctively tried to keep himself intact: he tried to serve the officer as if the latter were an abstract authority and not a man. All his instinct was to avoid personal contact, even definite hate. But in spite of himself the hate grew, responsive to the officer's passion. However, he put it in the background. When he had left the Army he could dare acknowledge it. By nature he was active, and had many friends. He thought what amazing good fellows they were. But, without knowing it, he was alone. Now this solitariness was intensified. It would carry him through his term. But the officer seemed to be going irritably insane, and the youth was deeply frightened.

The soldier had a sweetheart, a girl from the mountains, independent and primitive. The two walked together, rather silently. He went with her, not to talk, but to have his arm round her, and for the physical contact. This eased him, made it easier for him to ignore the Captain; for he could rest with her held fast against his chest. And she, in some unspoken fashion, was there for him. They loved each other.

The Captain perceived it, and was mad with irritation. He kept the young man engaged all the evenings long, and took pleasure in the dark look that came on his face. Occasionally, the eyes of the two men met, those of the younger sullen and dark, doggedly unalterable, those of the elder sneering with restless contempt.

The officer tried hard not to admit the passion that had got hold of him. He would not know that his feeling for his orderly was anything but that of a man incensed by his stupid, perverse servant. So, keeping quite justified and conventional in his consciousness, he let the other thing run on. His nerves, however, were suffering. At last he slung the end of a belt in his servant's face. When he saw the youth start back, the pain-tears in his eyes and the blood on his mouth, he had felt at once a thrill of deep pleasure and of shame.

But this, he acknowledged to himself was a thing he had never done before. The fellow was too exasperating. His own nerves must be going to pieces. He went away for some days with a woman.

It was a mockery of pleasure. He simply did not want the woman. But he stayed on for his time. At the end of it, he came back in an agony of irritation, torment, and misery. He rode all the evening, then came straight in to supper. His orderly was out. The officer sat with his long, fine hands lying on the table, perfectly still, and all his blood seemed to be corroding.

At last his servant entered. He watched the strong, easy young figure, the fine eyebrows, the thick black hair. In a week's time the youth had got back his old well-being. The hands of the officer twitched and seemed to be full of mad flame. The young man stood at attention, unmoving, shut off.

The meal went in silence. But the orderly seemed eager. He made a clatter with the dishes.

"Are you in a hurry?" asked the officer, watching the intent, warm face of his servant. The other did not reply.

"Will you answer my question?" said the Captain.

"Yes, sir," replied the orderly, standing with his pile of deep Army plates. The Captain waited, looked at him, then asked again:

"Are you in a hurry?"

"Yes, sir," came the answer, that sent a flash through the listener.

"For what?"

"I was going out, sir."

"I want you this evening."

There was a moment's hesitation. The officer had a curious stiffness of countenance.

"Yes, sir," replied the servant, in his throat.

"I want you to-morrow evening also—in fact, you may consider your evenings occupied, unless I give you leave."

The mouth with the young moustache set close.

"Yes, sir," answered the orderly, loosening his lips for a moment.

He again turned to the door.

"And why have you a piece of pencil in your ear?"

The orderly hesitated, then continued on his way without answering. He set the plates in a pile outside the door, took the stump of pencil from his ear, and put it in his pocket. He had been copying a verse for his sweetheart's birthday card. He returned to finish clearing the table. The officer's eyes were dancing, he had a little, eager smile.

"Why have you a piece of pencil in your ear?" he asked.

The orderly took his hands full of dishes. His master was standing near the great green stove, a little smile on his face, his chin thrust forward. When the young soldier saw him his heart suddenly ran hot. He felt blind. Instead of answering, he turned dazedly to the door. As he was crouching to set down the dishes, he was pitched forward by a kick from behind. The pots went in a stream down the stairs, he clung to the pillar of the banisters. And as he was rising he was kicked heavily again, and again, so that he clung sickly to the post for some moments. His master had gone swiftly into the room and closed the door. The maidservant downstairs looked up the staircase and made a mocking face at the crockery disaster.

The officer's heart was plunging. He poured himself a glass of wine, part of which he spilled on the floor, and gulped the remainder, leaning against the cool, green stove. He heard his man collecting the dishes from the stairs. Pale, as if intoxicated, he waited. The servant entered again. The Captain's heart gave a pang, as of pleasure, seeing the young fellow bewildered and uncertain on his feet, with pain.

"Schöner!" he said.

The soldier was a little slower in coming to attention.

"Yes, sir!"

The youth stood before him, with pathetic young moustache, and fine eyebrows very distinct on his forehead of dark marble.

"I asked you a question."

"Yes, sir."

The officer's tone bit like acid.

"Why had you a pencil in your ear?"

Again the servant's heart ran hot, and he could not breathe. With dark, strained eyes, he looked at the officer, as if fascinated. And he stood there sturdily planted, unconscious. The withering smile came into the Captain's eyes, and he lifted his foot.

"I—I forgot it—sir," panted the soldier, his dark eyes fixed on the other man's dancing blue ones.

"What was it doing there?"

He saw the young man's breast heaving as he made an effort for words.

"I had been writing."

"Writing what?"

Again the soldier looked him up and down. The officer could hear him panting. The smile came into the blue eyes. The soldier worked his dry throat, but could not speak. Suddenly the smile lit like a flame on the officer's face, and a kick came heavily against the orderly's thigh. The youth moved a pace sideways. His face went dead, with two black, staring eyes.

"Well?" said the officer.

The orderly's mouth had gone dry, and his tongue rubbed in it as on dry brown-paper. He worked his throat. The officer raised his foot. The servant went stiff.

"Some poetry, sir," came the crackling, unrecognizable sound of his voice.

"Poetry, what poetry?" asked the Captain, with a sickly smile.

Again there was the working in the throat. The Captain's heart had suddenly gone down heavily, and he stood sick and tired.

"For my girl, sir," he heard the dry, inhuman sound.

"Oh!" he said, turning away. "Clear the table."

"Click!" went the soldier's throat; then again, "click!" and then the half-articulate:

"Yes, sir."

The young soldier was gone, looking old, and walking heavily.

The officer, left alone, held himself rigid, to prevent himself from thinking. His instinct warned him that he must not think. Deep inside him was the intense gratification of his passion, still working powerfully. Then there was a counter-action, a horrible breaking down of something inside him, a whole agony of reaction. He stood there for an hour motionless, a chaos of sensations, but rigid with a will to keep blank his consciousness, to prevent his mind grasping. And he held himself so until the worst of the stress had passed, when he began to drink, drank himself to an intoxication, till he slept obliterated. When he woke in the morning he was shaken to the base of his nature. But he had fought off the realization of what he had done. He had prevented his mind from taking it in, and suppressed it along with his instincts, and the conscious man had nothing to do with it. He felt only as after a bout of intoxication, weak, but the affair itself all dim and not to be recovered. Of the drunkenness of his passion he successfully refused remembrance. And when his orderly appeared with coffee, the officer assumed the same self he had had the morning before. He refused the event of the past night—denied it had even been—and was successful in his denial. He had not done any such thing—not he himself. Whatever there might be lay at the door of a stupid, insubordinate servant.

The orderly had gone about in a stupor all the evening. He drank some beer because he was parched, but not much, the alcohol made his feeling come back, and he could not bear it. He was dulled, as if nine-tenths of the ordinary man in him were inert. He crawled about disfigured. Still, when he thought of the kicks, he went sick, and when he thought of the threat of more kicking, in the room afterwards, his heart went hot and faint, and he panted, remembering the one that had come. He had been forced to say, "For my girl." He was much too done even to want to cry. His mouth hung slightly open, like an idiot's. He felt vacant, and wasted. So, he wandered at his work, painfully, and very slowly and clumsily, fumbling blindly with the brushes, and finding it difficult, when he sat down, to summon the energy to move again. His limbs, his jaw, were slack and nerveless. But he was very tired. He got to bed at last and slept inert, relaxed, in a sleep that was rather stupor than slumber, a dead night of stupefaction shot through with gleams of anguish.

In the morning were the manoeuvers. But he woke even before the bugle sounded. The painful ache in his chest, the dryness in his throat, the awful steady feeling of misery made his eyes come awake and dreary at once. He knew, without thinking, what had happened. And he knew that the day had come again, when he must go on with his round. The last bit of darkness was being pushed out of the room. He would have to move his inert body and go on. He was so young, and had known so little trouble, that he was bewildered. He only wished it would stay night, so that he could lie still, covered up by the darkness. And yet nothing would prevent the day from coming, nothing would save him from having to get up and saddle the Captain's horse, and make the Captain's coffee. It was there, inevitable. And then, he thought, it was impossible. Yet they would not leave him free. He must go and take the coffee to the Captain. He was too stunned to understand it. He only knew it was inevitable—inevitable, however long he lay inert.

At last, after heaving at himself, for he seemed to be a mass of inertia, he got up. But he had to force every one of his movements from behind, with his will. He felt lost, and dazed, and helpless. Then he clutched hold of the bed, the pain was so keen. And looking at his thighs, he saw the darker bruises on his swarthy flesh and he knew that, if he pressed one of his fingers on one of the bruises, he should faint. But he did not want to faint—he did not want anybody to know. No one should ever know. It was between him and the Captain. There were only the two people in the world now—himself and the Captain.

Slowly, economically, he got dressed and forced himself to walk. Everything was obscure, except just what he had his hands on. But he managed to get through his work. The very pain revived his dull senses. The worst remained yet. He took the tray and went up to the Captain's room. The officer, pale and heavy, sat at the table. The orderly, as he saluted, felt himself put out of existence. He stood still for a moment submitting to his own nullification —then he gathered himself, seemed to regain himself, and then the Captain began to grow vague, unreal, and the younger soldier's heart beat up. He clung to this situation—that the Captain did not exist—so that he himself might live. But when he saw his officer's hand tremble as he took the coffee, he felt everything falling shattered. And he went away, feeling as if he himself were coming to pieces, disintegrated. And when the Captain was there on horseback, giving orders, while he himself stood, with rifle and knapsack, sick with pain, he felt as if he must shut his eyes—as if he must shut his eyes on everything. It was only the long agony of marching with a parched throat that filled him with one single, sleep-heavy intention: to save himself.

II

He was getting used even to his parched throat. That the snowy peaks were radiant among the sky, that the whity-green glacier-river twisted through its pale shoals, in the valley below, seemed almost supernatural. But he was going mad with fever and thirst. He plodded on uncomplaining. He did not want to speak, not to anybody. There were two gulls, like flakes of water and snow, over the river. The scent of green rye soaked in sunshine came like a sickness. And the march continued, monotonously, almost like a bad sleep.

At the next farm-house, which stood low and broad near the high road, tubs of water had been put out. The soldiers clustered round to drink. They took off their helmets, and the steam mounted from their wet hair. The Captain sat on horseback, watching. He needed to see his orderly. His helmet threw a dark shadow over his light, fierce eyes, but his moustache and mouth and chin were distinct in the sunshine. The orderly must move under the presence of the figure of the horseman. It was not that he was afraid, or cowed. It was as if he was disembowelled, made empty, like an empty shell. He felt himself as nothing, a shadow creeping under the sunshine. And, thirsty as he was, he could scarcely drink, feeling the Captain near him. He would not take off his helmet to wipe his wet hair. He wanted to stay in shadow, not to be forced into consciousness. Starting, he saw the light heel of the officer prick the belly of the horse; the Captain cantered away, and he himself could relapse into vacancy.

Nothing, however, could give him back his living place in the hot, bright morning. He felt like a gap among it all. Whereas the Captain was prouder, overriding. A hot flash went through the young servant's body. The Captain was firmer and prouder with life, he himself was empty as a shadow. Again the flash went through him, dazing him out. But his heart ran a little firmer.

The company turned up the hill, to make a loop for the return. Below, from among the trees, the farmbell clanged. He saw the labourers, mowing barefoot at the thick grass, leave off their work and go downhill, their scythes hanging over their shoulders, like long, bright claws curving down behind them. They seemed like dream-people, as if they had no relation to himself. He felt as in a blackish dream: as if all the other things were there and had form, but he himself was only a consciousness, a gap that could think and perceive.

The soldiers were tramping silently up the glaring hillside. Gradually his head began to revolve, slowly, rhythmically. Sometimes it was dark before his eyes, as if he saw this world through a smoked glass, frail shadows and unreal. It gave him a pain in his head to walk.

The air was too scented, it gave no breath. All the lush green-stuff seemed to be issuing its sap, till the air was deathly, sickly with the smell of greenness. There was the perfume of clover, like pure honey and bees. Then there grew a faint acrid tang—they were near the beeches; and then a queer clattering noise, and a suffocating, hideous smell; they were passing a flock of sheep, a shepherd in a black smock, holding his crook. Why should the sheep huddle together under this fierce sun? He felt that the shepherd would not see him, though he could see the shepherd.

At last there was the halt. They stacked rifles in a conical stack, put down their kit in a scattered circle around it, and dispersed a little, sitting on a small knoll high on the hillside. The chatter began. The soldiers were steaming with heat, but were lively. He sat still, seeing the blue mountains rising upon the land, twenty kilometres away. There was a blue fold in the ranges, then out of that, at the foot, the broad, pale bed of the river, stretches of whity-green water between pinkish-grey shoals among the dark pine woods. There it was, spread out a long way off. And it seemed to come downhill, the river. There was a raft being steered, a mile away. It was a strange country. Nearer, a red-roofed, broad farm with white base and square dots of windows crouched beside the wall of beech foliage on the wood's edge. There were long strips of rye and clover and pale green corn. And just at his feet, below the knoll, was a darkish bog, where globe flowers stood breathless still on their slim stalks. And some of the pale gold bubbles were burst, and a broken fragment hung in the air. He thought he was going to sleep.

Suddenly something moved into his coloured mirage before his eyes. The Captain, a small, light-blue and scarlet figure, was trotting evenly between the strips of corn, along the level brow of the hill. And the man making flag-signals was coming on. Proud and sure moved the horseman's figure, the quick, bright thing, in which was concentrated all the light of this morning, which for the rest lay a fragile, shining shadow. Submissive, apathetic, the young soldier sat and stared. But as the horse slowed to a walk, coming up the last steep path, the great flash flared over the body and soul of the orderly. He sat waiting. The back of his head felt as if it were weighted with a heavy piece of fire. He did not want to eat. His hands trembled slightly as he moved them. Meanwhile the officer on horseback was approaching slowly and proudly. The tension grew in the orderly's soul. Then again, seeing the Captain ease himself on the saddle, the flash blazed through him.

The Captain looked at the patch of light blue and scarlet, and dark heads, scattered closely on the hillside. It pleased him. The command pleased him. And he was feeling proud. His orderly was among them in common subjection. The officer rose a little on his stirrups to look. The young soldier sat with averted, dumb face. The Captain relaxed on his seat. His slim-legged, beautiful horse, brown as a beech nut, walked proudly uphill. The Captain passed into the zone of the company's atmosphere: a hot smell of men, of sweat, of leather. He knew it very well. After a word with the lieutenant, he went a few paces higher, and sat there, a dominant figure, his sweat-marked horse swishing its tail, while he looked down on his men, on his orderly, a nonentity among the crowd.

The young soldier's heart was like fire in his chest, and he breathed with difficulty. The officer, looking downhill, saw three of the young soldiers, two pails of water between them, staggering across a sunny green field. A table had been set up under a tree, and there the slim lieutenant stood, importantly busy. Then the Captain summoned himself to an act of courage. He called his orderly.

The flame leapt into the soldier's throat as he heard the command, and he rose blindly, stifled. He saluted, standing below the officer. He did not look up. But there was the flicker in the Captain's voice.

"Go to the inn and fetch me . . ." the officer gave his commands. "Quick!" he added.

At the last word, the heart of the servant leapt with a flash, and he felt the strength come over his body. But he turned in mechanical obedience, and set off at a heavy run downhill, looking almost like a bear, his trousers bagging over his military boots. And the officer watched this blind, plunging run all the way.

But it was only the outside of the orderly's body that was obeying so humbly and mechanically. Inside had gradually accumulated a core into which all the energy of that young life was compact and concentrated. He executed his commission, and plodded quickly back uphill. There was a pain in his head, as he walked, that made him twist his features unknowingly. But hard there in the centre of his chest was himself, himself, firm, and not to be plucked to pieces.

The captain had gone up into the wood. The orderly plodded through the hot, powerfully smelling zone of the company's atmosphere. He had a curious mass of energy inside him now. The Captain was less real than himself. He approached the green entrance to the wood. There, in the half-shade, he saw the horse standing, the sunshine and the flickering shadow of leaves dancing over his brown body. There was a clearing where timber had lately been felled. Here, in the gold-green shade beside the brilliant cup of sunshine, stood two figures, blue and pink, the bits of pink showing out plainly. The Captain was talking to his lieutenant.

The orderly stood on the edge of the bright clearing, where great trunks of trees, stripped and glistening, lay stretched like naked, brown-skinned bodies. Chips of wood littered the trampled floor, like splashed light, and the bases of the felled trees stood here and there, with their raw, level tops. Beyond was the brilliant, sunlit green of a beech.

"Then I will ride forward," the orderly heard his Captain say. The lieutenant saluted and strode away. He himself went forward. A hot flash passed through his belly, as he tramped towards his officer.

The Captain watched the rather heavy figure of the young soldier stumble forward, and his veins, too, ran hot. This was to be man to man between them. He yielded before the solid, stumbling figure with bent head. The orderly stooped and put the food on a level-sawn tree-base. The Captain watched the glistening, sun-inflamed, naked hands. He wanted to speak to the young soldier, but could not. The servant propped a bottle against his thigh, pressed open the cork, and poured out the beer into the mug. He kept his head bent. The Captain accepted the mug.

"Ho!" he said, as if amiably.

The flame sprang out of the orderly's heart, nearly suffocating him.

"Yes, sir," he replied, between shut teeth.

And he heard the sound of the Captain's drinking, and he clenched his fists, such a strong torment came into his wrists. Then came the faint clang of the closing of the pot-lid. He looked up. The Captain was watching him. He glanced swiftly away. Then he saw the officer stoop and take a piece of bread from the tree-base. Again the flash of flame went through the young soldier, seeing the stiff body stoop beneath him, and his hands jerked. He looked away. He could feel the officer was nervous. The bread fell as it was being broken. The officer ate the other piece. The two men stood tense and still, the master laboriously chewing his bread, the servant staring with averted face, his fist clenched.

Then the young soldier started. The officer had pressed open the lid of the mug again. The orderly watched the lid of the mug, and the white hand that clenched the handle, as if he were fascinated. It was raised. The youth followed it with his eyes. And then he saw the thin, strong throat of the elder man moving up and down as he drank, the strong jaw working. And the instinct which had been jerking at the young man's wrists suddenly jerked free. He jumped, feeling as if it were rent in two by a strong flame.

The spur of the officer caught in a tree-root, he went down backwards with a crash, the middle of his back thudding sickeningly against a sharp-edged tree-base, the pot flying away. And in a second the orderly, with serious, earnest young face, and underlip between his teeth, had got his knee in the officer's chest and was pressing the chin backward over the farther edge of the tree-stump, pressing, with all his heart behind in a passion of relief, the tension of his wrists exquisite with relief. And with the base of his palms he shoved at the chin, with all his might. And it was pleasant, too, to have that chin, that hard jaw already slightly rough with beard, in his hands. He did not relax one hair's breadth, but, all the force of all his blood exulting in his thrust, he shoved back the head of the other man, till there was a little "cluck" and a crunching sensation. Then he felt as if his head went to vapour. Heavy convulsions shook the body of the officer, frightening and horrifying the young soldier. Yet it pleased him, too, to repress them. It pleased him to keep his hands pressing back the chin, to feel the chest of the other man yield in expiration to the weight of his strong, young knees, to feel the hard twitchings of the prostrate body jerking his own whole frame, which was pressed down on it.

But it went still. He could look into the nostrils of the other man, the eyes he could scarcely see. How curiously the mouth was pushed out, exaggerating the full lips, and the moustache bristling up from them. Then, with a start, he noticed the nostrils gradually filled with blood. The red brimmed, hesitated, ran over, and went in a thin trickle down the face to the eyes.

It shocked and distressed him. Slowly, he got up. The body twitched and sprawled there, inert. He stood and looked at in it silence. It was a pity *it* was broken. It represented more than the thing which had kicked and bullied him. He was afraid to look at the eyes. They were hideous now, only the whites showing, and the blood running to them. The face of the orderly was drawn with horror at the sight. Well, it was so. In his heart he was satisfied. He had hated the face of the Captain. It was extinguished now. There was a heavy relief in the orderly's soul. That was as it should be. But he could not bear to see the long, military body lying broken over the tree-base, the fine fingers crisped. He wanted to hide it away.

Quickly, busily, he gathered it up and pushed it under the felled tree trunks, which rested their beautiful, smooth length either end on logs. The face was horrible with blood. He covered it with the helmet. Then he pushed the limbs straight and decent, and brushed the dead leaves off the fine cloth of the uniform. So, it lay quite still in the shadow under there. A little strip of sunshine ran along the breast, from a chink between the logs. The orderly sat by it for a few moments. Here his own life also ended.

Then, through his daze, he heard the lieutenant, in a loud voice, explaining to the men outside the wood, that they were to suppose the bridge on the river below was held by the enemy. Now they were to march to the attack in such and such a manner. The lieutenant had no gift for expression. The orderly, listening from habit, got muddled. And when the lieutenant began it all again he ceased to hear.

He knew he must go. He stood up. It surprised him that the leaves were glittering in the sun, and the chips of wood reflecting white from the ground. For him a change had come over the world. But for the rest it had not—all seemed the same. Only he had left it. And he could not go back. It was his duty to return with the beer-pot and the bottle. He could not. He had left all that. The lieutenant was still hoarsely explaining. He must go, or they would overtake him. And he could not bear contact with anyone now.

He drew his fingers over his eyes, trying to find out where he was. Then he turned away. He saw the horse standing in the path. He went up to it and mounted. It hurt him to sit in the saddle. The pain of keeping his seat occupied him as they cantered through the wood. He would not have minded anything, but he could not get away from the sense of being divided from the others. The path led out of the trees. On the edge of the wood he pulled up and stood watching. There in the spacious sunshine of the valley soldiers were moving in a little swarm. Every now and then, a man harrowing on a strip of fallow shouted to his oxen, at the turn. The village and the white-towered church was small in the sunshine. And he no longer belonged to it—he sat there, beyond, like a man outside in the dark. He had gone out from everyday life into the unknown, and he could not, he even did not want to go back.

Turning from the sun-blazing valley, he rode deep into the wood. Tree-trunks, like people standing grey and still, took no notice as he went. A doe, herself a moving bit of sunshine and shadow, went running through the flecked shade. There were bright green rents in the foliage. Then it was all pine wood, dark and cool. And he was sick with pain, he had an intolerable great pulse in his head, and he was sick. He had never been ill in his life. He felt lost, quite dazed with all this.

Trying to get down from the horse, he fell, astonished at the pain and his lack of balance. The horse shifted uneasily. He jerked its bridle and sent it cantering jerkily away. It was his last connection with the rest of things.

But he only wanted to lie down and not be disturbed. Stumbling through the trees, he came on a quiet place where beeches and pine trees grew on a slope. Immediately he had lain down and closed his eyes, his consciousness went racing on without him. A big pulse of sickness beat in him as if it throbbed through the whole earth. He was burning with dry heat. But he was too busy, too tearingly active in the incoherent race of delirium to observe.

III

He came to with a start. His mouth was dry and hard, his heart beat heavily, but he had not the energy to get up. His heart beat heavily. Where was he?—the barracks—at home? There was something knocking. And, making an effort, he looked round—trees, and litter of greenery, and reddish, bright, still pieces of sunshine on the floor. He did not believe he was himself, he did not believe what he saw. Something was knocking. He made a struggle towards consciousness, but relapsed. Then he struggled again. And gradually his surroundings fell into relationship with himself. He knew, and a great pang of fear went through his heart. Somebody was knocking. He could see the heavy, black rags of a fir tree overhead. Then everything went black. Yet he did not believe he had closed his eyes. He had not. Out of the blackness sight slowly emerged again. And someone was knocking. Quickly, he saw the blood-disfigured face of his Captain, which he hated. And he held himself still with horror. Yet, deep inside him, he knew that it was so, the Captain should be dead. But the physical delirium got hold of him. Someone was knocking. He lay perfectly still, as if dead, with fear. And he went unconscious.

When he opened his eyes again, he started, seeing something creeping swiftly up a tree-trunk. It was a little bird. And the bird was whistling overhead. Tap-tap-tap—it was the small, quick bird rapping the tree-trunk with its beak, as if its head were a little round hammer. He watched it curiously. It shifted sharply, in its creeping fashion. Then, like a mouse, it slid down the bare trunk. Its swift creeping sent a flash of revulsion through him. He raised his head. It felt a great weight. Then, the little bird ran out of the shadow across a still patch of sunshine, its little head bobbing swiftly, its white legs twinkling brightly for a moment. How neat it was in its build, so compact, with pieces of white on its wings. There were several of them. They were so pretty—but they crept like swift, erratic mice, running here and there among the beech-mast.

He lay down again exhausted, and his consciousness lapsed. He had a horror of the little creeping birds. All his blood seemed to be darting and creeping in his head. And yet he could not move.

He came to with a further ache of exhaustion. There was the pain in his head, and the horrible sickness, and his inability to move. He had never been ill in his life. He did not know where he was or what he was. Probably he had got sunstroke. Or what else?—he had silenced the Captain for ever—some time ago—oh, a long time ago. There had been blood on his face, and his eyes had turned upwards. It was all right, somehow. It was peace. But now he had got beyond himself. He had never been here before. Was it life, or not life? He was by himself. They were in a big, bright place, those others, and he was outside. The town, all the country, a big bright place of light: and he was outside, here, in the darkened open beyond, where each thing existed alone. But they would all have to come out there sometime, those others. Little, and left behind him, they all were. There had been father and mother and sweetheart. What did they all matter? This was the open land.

He sat up. Something scuffled. It was a little, brown squirrel running in lovely, undulating bounds over the floor, its red tail completing the undulation of its body—and then, as it sat up, furling and unfurling. He watched it, pleased. It ran on again, friskily, enjoying itself. It flew wildly at another squirrel, and they were chasing each other, and making little scolding, chattering noises. The soldier wanted to speak to them. But only a hoarse sound came out of his throat. The squirrels burst away—they flew up the trees. And then he saw the one peeping round at him, half-way up a tree-trunk. A start of fear went through him, though, in so far as he was conscious, he was amused. It still stayed, its little, keen face staring at him half-way up the tree-trunk, its little ears pricked up, its clawey little hands clinging to the bark, its white breast reared. He started from it in panic.

Struggling to his feet, he lurched away. He went on walking, walking, looking for something—for a drink. His brain felt hot and inflamed for want of water. He stumbled on. Then he did not know anything. He went unconscious as he walked. Yet he stumbled on, his mouth open.

When, to his dumb wonder, he opened his eyes on the world again, he no longer tried to remember what it was. There was thick, golden light behind golden-green glitterings, and tall, grey-purple shafts, and darknesses further off, surrounding him, growing deeper. He was conscious of a sense of arrival. He was amid the reality, on the real, dark bottom. But there was the thirst burning in his brain. He felt lighter not so heavy. He supposed it was newness. The air was muttering with thunder. He thought he was walking wonderfully swiftly and was coming straight to relief—or was it to water?

Suddenly he stood still with fear. There was a tremendous flare of gold, immense—just a few dark trunks like bars between him and it. All the young level wheat was burnished gold glaring on its silky green. A woman, full-skirted, a black cloth on her head for head-dress, was passing like a block of shadow through the glistening, green corn, into the full glare. There was a farm, too, pale blue in shadow, and the timber black. There was a church spire, nearly fused away in the gold. The woman moved on, away from him. He had no language with which to speak to her. She was the bright, solid unreality. She would make a noise of words that would confuse him, and her eyes would look at him without seeing him. She was crossing there to the other side. He stood against a tree.

When at last he turned, looking down the long, bare grove whose flat bed was already filling dark, he saw the mountains in a wonder-light, not far away, and radiant. Behind the soft, grey ridge of the nearest range the further mountains stood golden and pale grey, the snow all radiant like pure, soft gold. So still, gleaming in the sky, fashioned pure out of the ore of the sky, they shone in their silence. He stood and looked at them, his face illuminated. And like the golden, lustrous gleaming of the snow he felt his own thirst bright in him. He stood and gazed, leaning against a tree. And then everything slid away into space.

During the night the lightning fluttered perpetually, making the whole sky white. He must have walked again. The world hung livid round him for moments, fields a level sheen of grey-green light, trees in dark bulk, and the range of clouds black across a white sky. Then the darkness fell like a shutter, and the night was whole. A faint flutter of a half-revealed world, that could not quite leap out of the darkness!—Then there again stood a sweep of pallor for the land, dark shapes looming, a range of clouds hanging overhead. The world was a ghostly shadow, thrown for a moment upon the pure darkness, which returned ever whole and complete.

And the mere delirium of sickness and fever went on inside him—his brain opening and shutting like the night—then sometimes convulsions of terror from something with great eyes that stared round a tree—then the long agony of the march, and the sun decomposing his blood—then the pang of hate for the Captain, followed by a pang of tenderness and ease. But everything was distorted, born of an ache and resolving into an ache.

In the morning he came definitely awake. Then his brain flamed with the sole horror of thirstiness! The sun was on his face, the dew was steaming from his wet clothes. Like one possessed, he got up. There, straight in front of him, blue and cool and tender, the mountains ranged across the pale edge of the morning sky. He wanted them—he wanted them alone—he wanted to leave himself and be identified with them. They did not move, they were still and soft, with white, gentle markings of snow. He stood still, mad with suffering, his hands crisping and clutching. Then he was twisting in a paroxysm on the grass.

He lay still, in a kind of dream of anguish. His thirst seemed to have separated itself from him, and to stand apart, a single demand. Then the pain he felt was another single self. Then there was the clog of his body, another separate thing. He was divided among all kinds of separate beings. There was some strange, agonized connection between them, but they were drawing further apart. Then they would all split. The sun, drilling down on him, was drilling through the bond. Then they would all fall, fall through the everlasting lapse of space. Then again, his consciousness reasserted itself. He roused on to his elbow and stared at the gleaming mountains. There they ranked, all still and wonderful between earth and heaven. He stared till his eyes went black, and the mountains, as they stood in their beauty, so clean and cool, seemed to have it, that which was lost in him.

IV

When the soldiers found him, three hours later, he was lying with his face over his arm, his black hair giving off heat under the sun. But he was still alive. Seeing the open, black mouth the young soldiers dropped him in horror.

He died in the hospital at night, without having seen again.

The doctors saw the bruises on his legs, behind, and were silent.

The bodies of the two men lay together, side by side, in the mortuary, the one white and slender, but laid rigidly at rest, the other looking as if every moment it must rouse into life again, so young and unused, from a slumber.

Odour of Chrysanthemums

I

The small locomotive engine, Number 4, came clanking, stumbling down from Selston with seven full wagons. It appeared round the corner with loud threats of speed, but the colt that it startled from among the gorse, which still flickered indistinctly in the raw afternoon, out-distanced it at a canter. A woman, walking up the railway line to Underwood, drew back into the hedge, held her basket aside, and watched the footplate of the engine advancing. The trucks thumped heavily past, one by one, with slow inevitable movement, as she stood insignificantly trapped between the jolting black wagons and the hedge; then they curved away towards the coppice where the withered oak leaves dropped noiselessly, while the birds, pulling at the scarlet hips beside the track, made off into the dusk that had already crept into the spinney. In the open, the smoke from the engine sank and cleaved to the rough grass. The fields were dreary and forsaken, and in the marshy strip that led to the whimsey, a reedy pit-pond, the fowls had already abandoned their run along the alders, to roost in the tarred fowl-house. The pit-bank loomed up beyond the pond, flames like red sores licking its ashy sides, in the afternoon's stagnant light. Just beyond rose the tapering chimneys and the clumsy black headstocks of Brinsley Colliery. The two wheels were spinning fast up against the sky, and the winding engine rapped out its little spasms. The miners were being turned up.

The engine whistled as it came into the wide bay of railway lines beside the colliery, where rows of trucks stood in harbour.

Miners, single, trailing and in groups, passed like shadows diverging home. At the edge of the ribbed level of sidings squatted a low cottage, three steps down from the cinder track. A large bony vine clutched at the house, as if to claw down the tiled roof. Round the bricked yard grew a few wintry primroses. Beyond, the long garden sloped down to a bush-covered brook course. There were some twiggy apple trees, winter-crack trees, and ragged cabbages. Beside the path hung dishevelled pink chrysanthemums, like pink cloths hung on bushes. A woman came stooping out of the felt-covered fowl-house, half-way down the garden. She closed and padlocked the door, then drew herself erect, having brushed some bits from her white apron.

She was a tall woman of imperious mien, handsome, with definite black eyebrows. Her smooth black hair was parted exactly. For a few moments she stood steadily watching the miners as they passed along the railway: then she turned towards the brook course. Her face was calm and set, her mouth was closed with disillusionment. After a moment she called:

"John!" There was no answer. She waited, and then said distinctly:

"Where are you?"

"Here!" replied a child's sulky voice from among the bushes. The woman looked piercingly through the dusk.

"Are you at that brook?" she asked sternly.

For answer the child showed himself before the raspberry-canes that rose like whips. He was a small, sturdy boy of five. He stood quite still, defiantly.

"Oh!" said the mother, conciliated. "I thought you were down at that wet brook—and you remember what I told you——"

The boy did not move or answer.

"Come, come on in," she said more gently, "it's getting dark. There's your grandfather's engine coming down the line!"

The lad advanced slowly, with resentful, taciturn movement. He was dressed in trousers and waistcoat of cloth that was too thick and hard for the size of the garments. They were evidently cut down from a man's clothes.

As they went slowly towards the house he tore at the ragged wisps of chrysanthemums and dropped the petals in handfuls along the path.

"Don't do that—it does look nasty," said his mother. He refrained, and she, suddenly pitiful, broke off a twig with three or four wan flowers and held them against her face. When mother and son reached the yard her hand hesitated, and instead of laying the flower aside, she pushed it in her apron-band. The mother and son stood at the foot of the three steps looking across the bay of lines at the passing home of the miners. The trundle of the small train was imminent. Suddenly the engine loomed past the house and came to a stop opposite the gate.

The engine-driver, a short man with round grey beard, leaned out of the cab high above the woman.

"Have you got a cup of tea?" he said in a cheery, hearty fashion.

It was her father. She went in, saying she would mash. Directly, she returned.

"I didn't come to see you on Sunday," began the little grey-bearded man.

"I didn't expect you," said his daughter.

The engine-driver winced; then, reassuming his cheery, airy manner, he said:

"Oh, have you heard then? Well, and what do you think——?"

"I think it is soon enough," she replied.

At her brief censure the little man made an impatient gesture, and said coaxingly, yet with dangerous coldness:

"Well, what's a man to do? It's no sort of life for a man of my years, to sit at my own hearth like a stranger. And if I'm going to marry again it may as well be soon as late—what does it matter to anybody?"

The woman did not reply, but turned and went into the house. The man in the engine-cab stood assertive, till she returned with a cup of tea and a piece of bread and butter on a plate. She went up the steps and stood near the footplate of the hissing engine.

"You needn't 'a' brought me bread an' butter," said her father. "But a cup of tea"—he sipped appreciatively—"it's very nice." He sipped for a moment or two, then: "I hear as Walter's got another bout on," he said.

"When hasn't he?" said the woman bitterly.

"I heerd tell of him in the 'Lord Nelson' braggin' as he was going to spend that b—— afore he went: half a sovereign that was."

"When?" asked the woman.

"A' Sat'day night—I know that's true."

"Very likely," she laughed bitterly. "He gives me twenty-three shillings."

"Aye, it's a nice thing, when a man can do nothing with his money but make a beast of himself!" said the grey-whiskered man. The woman turned her head away. Her father swallowed the last of his tea and handed her the cup.

"Aye," he sighed, wiping his mouth. "It's a settler, it is——"

He put his hand on the lever. The little engine strained and groaned, and the train rumbled towards the crossing. The woman again looked across the metals. Darkness was settling over the spaces of the railway and trucks: the miners, in grey sombre groups, were still passing home. The winding engine pulsed hurriedly, with brief pauses. Elizabeth Bates looked at the dreary flow of men, then she went indoors. Her husband did not come.

The kitchen was small and full of firelight; red coals piled glowing up the chimney mouth. All the life of the room seemed in the white, warm hearth and the steel fender reflecting the red fire. The cloth was laid for tea; cups glinted in the shadows. At the back, where the lowest stairs protruded into the room, the boy sat struggling with a knife and a piece of white wood. He was almost hidden in the shadow. It was half-past four. They had but to await the father's coming to begin tea. As the mother watched her son's sullen little struggle with the wood, she saw herself in his silence and pertinacity; she saw the father in her child's indifference to all but himself. She seemed to be occupied by her husband. He had probably gone past his home, slunk past his own door, to drink before he came in, while his dinner spoiled and wasted in waiting. She glanced at the clock, then took the potatoes to strain them in the yard. The garden and fields beyond the brook were closed in uncertain darkness. When she rose with the saucepan, leaving the drain steaming into the night behind her, she saw the yellow lamps were lit along the high road that went up the hill away beyond the space of the railway lines and the field.

Then again she watched the men trooping home, fewer now and fewer.

Indoors the fire was sinking and the room was dark red. The woman put her saucepan on the hob, and set a batter-pudding near the mouth of the oven. Then she stood unmoving. Directly, gratefully, came quick young steps to the door. Someone hung on the latch a moment, then a little girl entered and began pulling off her outdoor things, dragging a mass of curls, just ripening from gold to brown, over her eyes with her hat.

Her mother chid her coming late from school, and said she would have to keep her at home the dark winter days.

"Why, mother, it's hardly a bit dark yet. The lamp's not lighted, and my father's not home."

"No, he isn't. But it's a quarter to five! Did you see anything of him?"

The child became serious. She looked at her mother with large, wistful blue eyes.

"No, mother, I've never seen him. Why? Has he come up an' gone past, to Old Brinsley? He hasn't, mother, 'cos I never saw him."

"He'd watch that," said the mother bitterly, "he'd take care as you didn't see him. But you may depend upon it, he's seated in the 'Prince o' Wales.' He wouldn't be this late."

The girl looked at her mother piteously.

"Let's have our teas, mother, should we?" said she.

The mother called John to table. She opened the door once more and looked out across the darkness of the lines. All was deserted: she could not hear the winding-engines.

"Perhaps," she said to herself, "he's stopped to get some ripping done."

They sat down to tea. John, at the end of the table near the door, was almost lost in the darkness. Their faces were hidden from each other. The girl crouched against the fender slowly moving a thick piece of bread before the fire. The lad, his face a dusky mark on the shadow, sat watching her who was transfigured in the red glow.

"I do think it's beautiful to look in the fire," said the child.

"Do you?" said the mother. "Why?"

"It's so red, and full of little caves—and it feels so nice, and you can fair smell it."

"It'll want mending directly," replied her mother, "and then if your father comes he'll carry on and say there never is a fire when a man comes home sweating from the pit. A public-house is always warm enough."

There was silence till the boy said complainingly: "Make haste, our Annie."

"Well, I am doing! I can't make the fire do it no faster, can I?"

"She keeps wafflin' it about so's to make 'er slow," grumbled the boy.

"Don't have such an evil imagination, child," replied the mother.

Soon the room was busy in the darkness with the crisp sound of crunching. The mother ate very little. She drank her tea determinedly, and sat thinking. When she rose her anger was evident in the stern unbending of her head. She looked at the pudding in the fender, and broke out:

"It is a scandalous thing as a man can't even come home to his dinner! If it's crozzled up to a cinder I don't see why I should care. Past his very door he goes to get to a public-house, and here I sit with his dinner waiting for him——"

She went out. As she dropped piece after piece of coal on the red fire, the shadows fell on the walls, till the room was almost in total darkness.

"I canna see," grumbled John. In spite of herself, the mother laughed.

"You know the way to your mouth," she said. She set the dust-pan outside the door. When she came again like a shadow on the hearth, the lad repeated,

"I canna see."

"Good gracious!" cried the mother irritably, "you're as bad as your father if it's a bit dusk!"

Nevertheless, she took a paper spill from a sheaf on the mantelpiece and proceeded to light the lamp that hung from the ceiling in the middle of the room. As she reached up, her figure displayed itself just rounding with maternity.

"Oh, mother——!" exclaimed the girl.

"What?" said the woman, suspended in the act of putting the lampglass over the flame. The copper reflector shone handsomely on her, as she stood with uplifted arm, turning to face her daughter.

"You've got a flower in your apron!" said the child, in a little rapture at this unusual event.

"Goodness me!" exclaimed the woman, relieved. "One would think the house was afire." She replaced the glass and waited a moment before turning up the wick. A pale shadow was seen floating vaguely on the floor.

"Let me smell!" said the child, still rapturously, coming forward and putting her face to her mother's waist.

"Go along, silly!" said the mother, turning up the lamp. The light revealed their suspense so that the woman felt it almost unbearable. Annie was still bending at her waist. Irritably, the mother took the flowers out from her apron-band.

"Oh, mother—don't take them out!" Annie cried, catching her hand and trying to replace the sprig.

"Such nonsense!" said the mother, turning away. The child put the pale chrysanthemums to her lips, murmuring:

"Don't they smell beautiful!"

Her mother gave a short laugh.

"No," she said, "not to me. It was chrysanthemums when I married him, and chrysanthemums when you were born, and the first time they ever brought him home drunk, he'd got brown chrysanthemums in his buttonhole."

She looked at the children. Their eyes and their parted lips were wondering. The mother sat rocking in silence for some time. Then she looked at the clock.

"Twenty minutes to six!" In a tone of fine bitter carelessness she continued: "Eh, he'll not come now till they bring him. There he'll stick! But he needn't come rolling in here in his pit-dirt, for *I* won't wash him. He can lie on the floor—— Eh, what a fool I've been, what a fool! And this is what I came here for, to this dirty hole, rats and all, for him to slink past his very door. Twice last week—he's begun now——"

She silenced herself, and rose to clear the table.

While for an hour or more the children played, subduedly intent, fertile of imagination, united in fear of the mother's wrath, and in dread of their father's home-coming, Mrs. Bates sat in her rockingchair making a "singlet" of thick cream-coloured flannel, which gave a dull wounded sound as she tore off the grey edge. She worked at her sewing with energy, listening to the children, and her anger wearied itself, lay down to rest, opening its eyes from time to time and steadily watching, its ears raised to listen. Sometimes even her anger quailed and shrank, and the mother suspended her sewing, tracing the footsteps that thudded along the sleepers outside; she would lift her head sharply to bid the children "hush," but she recovered herself in time, and the footsteps went past the gate, and the children were not flung out of their play-world.

But at last Annie sighed, and gave in. She glanced at her wagon of slippers, and loathed the game. She turned plaintively to her mother.

"Mother!"—but she was inarticulate.

John crept out like a frog from under the sofa. His mother glanced up.

"Yes," she said, "just look at those shirt-sleeves!"

The boy held them out to survey them, saying nothing. Then somebody called in a hoarse voice away down the line, and suspense bristled in the room, till two people had gone by outside, talking.

"It is time for bed," said the mother.

"My father hasn't come," wailed Annie plaintively. But her mother was primed with courage.

"Never mind. They'll bring him when he does come—like a log." She meant there would be no scene. "And he may sleep on the floor till he wakes himself. I know he'll not go to work to-morrow after this!"

The children had their hands and faces wiped with a flannel. They were very quiet. When they had put on their night-dresses, they said their prayers, the boy mumbling. The mother looked down at them, at the brown silken bush of intertwining curls in the nape of the girl's neck, at the little black head of the lad, and her heart burst with anger at their father, who caused all three such distress. The children hid their faces in her skirts for comfort.

When Mrs. Bates came down, the room was strangely empty, with a tension of expectancy. She took up her sewing and stitched for some time without raising her head. Meantime her anger was tinged with fear.

II

The clock struck eight and she rose suddenly, dropping her sewing on her chair. She went to the stair-foot door, opened it, listening. Then she went out, locking the door behind her.

Something scuffled in the yard, and she started, though she knew it was only the rats with which the place was over-run. The night was very dark. In the great bay of railway lines, bulked with trucks, there was no trace of light, only away back she could see a few yellow lamps at the pit-top, and the red smear of the burning pit-bank on the night. She hurried along the edge of the track, then, crossing the converging lines, came to the stile by the white gates, whence she emerged on the road. Then the fear which had led her shrank. People were walking up to New Brinsley; she saw the light in the houses; twenty yards farther on were the broad windows of the "Prince of Wales," very warm and bright, and the loud voices of men could be heard distinctly. What a fool she had been to imagine that anything had happened to him! He was merely drinking over there at the "Prince of Wales." She faltered. She had never yet been to fetch him, and she never would go. So she continued her walk towards the long straggling line of houses, standing back on the highway. She entered a passage between the dwellings.

"Mr. Rigley?—Yes! Did you want him? No, he's not in at this minute."

The raw-boned woman leaned forward from her dark scullery and peered at the other, upon whom fell a dim light through the blind of the kitchen window.

"Is it Mrs. Bates?" she asked in a tone tinged with respect.

"Yes. I wondered if your Master was at home. Mine hasn't come yet."

" 'Asn't 'e! Oh Jack's been 'ome an' 'ad 'is dinner an' gone out. 'E's just gone for 'alf an hour afore bed-time. Did you call at the 'Prince of Wales'?"

"No——"

"No, you didn't like——! It's not very nice." The other woman was indulgent. There was an awkward pause. "Jack never said nothink about—about your Master," she said.

"No!—I expect he's stuck in there!"

Elizabeth Bates said this bitterly, and with recklessness. She knew that the woman across the yard was standing at her door listening, but she did not care. As she turned:

"Stop a minute! I'll just go an' ask Jack if'e knows anythink," said Mrs. Rigley.

"Oh no—I wouldn't like to put——!"

"Yes, I will, if you'll just step inside an' see as th' childer doesn't come downstairs and set themselves afire."

Elizabeth Bates, murmuring a remonstrance, stepped inside. The other woman apologised for the state of the room.

The kitchen needed apology. There were little frocks and trousers and childish undergarments on the squab and on the floor, and a litter of playthings everywhere. On the black American cloth of the table were pieces of bread and cake, crusts, slops, and a teapot with cold tea.

"Eh, ours is just as bad," said Elizabeth Bates, looking at the woman, not at the house. Mrs. Rigley put a shawl over her head and hurried out, saying:

"I shanna be a minute."

The other sat, noting with faint disapproval the general untidiness of the room. Then she fell to counting the shoes of various sizes scattered over the floor. There were twelve. She sighed and said to herself: "No wonder!"—glancing at the litter. There came the scratching of two pairs of feet on the yard, and the Rigleys entered. Elizabeth Bates rose. Rigley was a big man, with very large bones. His head looked particularly bony. Across his temple was a blue scar, caused by a wound got in the pit, a wound in which the coal-dust remained blue like tattooing.

" 'Asna 'e come whoam yit?" asked the man, without any form of greeting, but with deference and sympathy. "I couldna say wheer he is—'e's non ower theer!"—he jerked his head to signify the "Prince of Wales."

" 'E's 'appen gone up to th' 'Yew,' " said Mrs. Rigley.

There was another pause. Rigley had evidently something to get off his mind:

"Ah left 'im finishin' a stint," he began. "Loose-all 'ad bin gone about ten minutes when we com'n away, an' I shouted: 'Are ter comin', Walt?' an' 'e said: 'Go on, Ah shanna be but a'ef a minnit,' so we com'n ter th' bottom, me an' Bowers, thinkin' as 'e wor just behint, an' 'ud come up i' th' next bantle——"

He stood perplexed, as if answering a charge of deserting his mate. Elizabeth Bates, now again certain of disaster, hastened to reassure him:

"I expect 'e's gone up to th' 'Yew Tree,' as you say. It's not the first time. I've fretted myself into a fever before now. He'll come home when they carry him."

"Ay, isn't it too bad!" deplored the other woman.

"I'll just step up to Dick's an' see if 'e *is* theer," offered the man, afraid of appearing alarmed, afraid of taking liberties.

"Oh, I wouldn't think of bothering you that far," said Elizabeth Bates, with emphasis, but he knew she was glad of his offer.

As they stumbled up the entry, Elizabeth Bates heard Rigley's wife run across the yard and open her neighbor's door. At this, suddenly all the blood in her body seemed to switch away from her heart.

"Mind!" warned Rigley. "Ah've said many a time as Ah'd fill up them ruts in this entry, sumb'dy'll be breakin' their legs yit."

She recovered herself and walked quickly along with the miner.

"I don't like leaving the children in bed, and nobody in the house," she said.

"No, you dunna!" he replied courteously. They were soon at the gate of the cottage.

"Well, I shanna be many minnits. Dunna you be frettin' now, 'e'll be all right," said the butty.

"Thank you very much, Mr. Rigley," she replied.

"You're welcome!" he stammered, moving away. "I shanna be many minnits."

The house was quiet. Elizabeth Bates took off her hat and shawl, and rolled back the rug. When she had finished, she sat down. It was a few minutes past nine. She was startled by the rapid chuff of the winding-engine at the pit, and the sharp whirr of the brakes on the rope as it descended. Again she felt the painful sweep of her blood, and she put her hand to her side, saying aloud: "Good gracious!—it's only the nine o'clock deputy going down," rebuking herself.

She sat still, listening. Half an hour of this, and she was wearied out.

"What am I working myself up like this for?" she said pitiably to herself, "I s'll only be doing myself some damage."

She took out her sewing again.

At a quarter to ten there were footsteps. One person! She watched for the door to open. It was an elderly woman, in a black bonnet and a black woollen shawl—his mother. She was about sixty years old, pale, with blue eyes, and her face all wrinkled and lamentable. She shut the door and turned to her daughter-in-law peevishly.

"Eh, Lizzie, whatever shall we do, whatever shall we do!" she cried.

Elizabeth drew back a little, sharply.

"What is it, mother?" she said.

The elder woman seated herself on the sofa.

"I don't know, child, I can't tell you!"—she shook her head slowly. Elizabeth sat watching her, anxious and vexed.

"I don't know," replied the grandmother, sighing very deeply. "There's no end to my troubles, there isn't. The things I've gone through, I'm sure it's enough——!" She wept without wiping her eyes, the tears running.

"But, mother," interrupted Elizabeth, "what do you mean? What is it?"

The grandmother slowly wiped her eyes. The fountains of her tears were stopped by Elizabeth's directness. She wiped her eyes slowly.

"Poor child! Eh, you poor thing!" she moaned. "I don't know what we're going to do, I don't—and you as you are—it's a thing, it is indeed!"

Elizabeth waited.

"Is he dead?" she asked, and at the words her heart swung violently, though she felt a slight flush of shame at the ultimate extravagance of the question. Her words sufficiently frightened the old lady, almost brought her to herself.

"Don't say so, Elizabeth! We'll hope it's not as bad as that; no, may the Lord spare us that, Elizabeth. Jack Rigley came just as I was sittin' down to a glass afore going to bed, an' 'e said: ' 'Appen you'll go down th' line, Mrs. Bates. Walt's had an accident. 'Appen you'll go an' sit wi' 'er till we can get him home.' I hadn't time to ask him a word afore he was gone. An' I put my bonnet on an' come straight down, Lizzie. I thought to myself: 'Eh, that poor blessed child, if anybody should come an' tell her sudden, there's no knowin' what'll 'appen to 'er.' You mustn't let it upset you, Lizzie—or you know what to expect. How long is it, six months—or is it five, Lizzie? Ay!"—the old woman shook her head—"time slips on, it slips on! Ay!"

Elizabeth's thoughts were busy elsewhere. If he was killed—would she be able to manage on the little pension and what she could earn?—she counted up rapidly. If he was hurt—they wouldn't take him to the hospital—how tiresome he would be to nurse!—but perhaps she'd be able to get him away from the drink and his hateful ways. She would—while he was ill. The tears offered to come to her eyes at the picture. But what sentimental luxury was this she was beginning? She turned to consider the children. At any rate she was absolutely necessary for them. They were her business.

"Ay!" repeated the old woman, "it seems but a week or two since he brought me his first wages. Ay—he was a good lad, Elizabeth, he was, in his way. I don't know why he got to be such a trouble, I don't. He was a happy lad at home, only full of spirits. But there's no mistake he's been a handful of trouble, he has! I hope the Lord'll spare him to mend his ways. I hope so, I hope so. You've had a sight o' trouble with him, Elizabeth, you have indeed. But he was a jolly enough lad wi' me, he was, I can assure you. I don't know how it is. . . ."

The old woman continued to muse aloud, a monotonous irritating sound, while Elizabeth thought concentratedly, startled once, when she heard the winding-engine chuff quickly, and the brakes skirr with a shriek. Then she heard the engine more slowly, and the brakes made no sound. The old woman did not notice. Elizabeth waited in suspense. The mother-in-law talked, with lapses into silence.

"But he wasn't your son, Lizzie, an' it makes a difference. Whatever he was, I remember him when he was little, an' I learned to understand him and to make allowances. You've got to make allowances for them——"

It was half-past ten, and the old woman was saying: "But it's trouble from beginning to end; you're never too old for trouble, never too old for that——" when the gate banged back, and there were heavy feet on the steps.

"I'll go, Lizzie, let me go," cried the old woman, rising. But Elizabeth was at the door. It was a man in pit-clothes.

"They're bringin' 'im, Missis," he said. Elizabeth's heart halted a moment. Then it surged on again, almost suffocating her.

"Is he—is it bad?" she asked.

The man turned away, looking at the darkness:

"The doctor says 'e'd been dead hours. 'E saw 'im i' th' lampcabin."

The old woman, who stood just behind Elizabeth, dropped into a chair, and folded her hands, crying: "Oh, my boy, my boy!"

"Hush!" said Elizabeth, with a sharp twitch of a frown. "Be still, mother, don't waken th' children: I wouldn't have them down for anything!"

The old woman moaned softly, rocking herself. The man was drawing away. Elizabeth took a step forward.

"How was it?" she asked.

"Well, I couldn't say for sure," the man replied, very ill at ease. " 'E wor finishin' a stint an' th' butties 'ad gone, an' a lot o' stuff come down atop 'n 'im."

"And crushed him?" cried the widow, with a shudder.

"No," said the man, "it fell at th' back of 'im. 'E wor under th' face, an' it niver touched 'im. It shut 'im in. It seems 'e wor smothered."

Elizabeth shrank back. She heard the old woman behind her cry:

"What?—what did 'e say it was?"

The man replied, more loudly: " 'E wor smothered!"

Then the old woman wailed aloud, and this relieved Elizabeth.

"Oh, mother," she said, putting her hand on the old woman, "don't waken th' children, don't waken th' children."

She wept a little, unknowing, while the old mother rocked herself and moaned. Elizabeth remembered that they were bringing him home, and she must be ready. "They'll lay him in the parlour," she said to herself, standing a moment pale and perplexed.

Then she lighted a candle and went into the tiny room. The air was cold and damp, but she could not make a fire, there was no fireplace. She set down the candle and looked round. The candlelight glittered on the lustre-glasses, on the two vases that held some of the pink chrysanthemums, and on the dark mahogany. There was a cold, deathly smell of chrysanthemums in the room. Elizabeth stood looking at the flowers. She turned away, and calculated whether there would be room to lay him on the floor, between the couch and the chiffonier. She pushed the chairs aside. There would be room to lay him down and to step around him. Then she fetched the old red tablecloth, and another old cloth, spreading them down to save her bit of carpet. She shivered on leaving the parlour; so, from the dresser drawer she took a clean shirt and put it at the fire to air. All the time her mother-in-law was rocking herself in the chair and moaning.

"You'll have to move from there, mother," said Elizabeth. "They'll be bringing him in. Come in the rocker."

The old mother rose mechanically, and seated herself by the fire, continuing to lament. Elizabeth went into the pantry for another candle, and there, in the little pent-house under the naked tiles, she heard them coming. She stood still in the pantry doorway, listening. She heard them pass the end of the house, and come awkwardly down the three steps, a jumble of shuffling footsteps and muttering voices. The old woman was silent. The men were in the yard.

Then Elizabeth heard Matthews, the manager of the pit, say: "You go in first, Jim. Mind!"

The door came open, and the two women saw a collier backing into the room, holding one end of a stretcher, on which they could see the nailed pit-boots of the dead man. The two carriers halted, the man at the head stooping to the lintel of the door.

"Wheer will you have him?" asked the manager, a short, white-bearded man.

Elizabeth roused herself and came from the pantry carrying the unlighted candle.

"In the parlour," she said.

"In there, Jim!" pointed the manager, and the carriers backed round into the tiny room. The coat with which they had covered the body fell off as they awkwardly turned through the two doorways, and the women saw their man, naked to the waist, lying stripped for work. The old woman began to moan in a low voice of horror.

"Lay th' stretcher at th' side," snapped the manager, "an' put 'im on th' cloths. Mind now, mind! Look you now——!"

One of the men had knocked off a vase of chrysanthemums. He stared awkwardly, then they set down the stretcher. Elizabeth did not look at her husband. As soon as she could get in the room, she went and picked up the broken vase and the flowers.

"Wait a minute!" she said.

The three men waited in silence while she mopped up the water with a duster.

"Eh, what a job, what a job, to be sure!" the manager was saying, rubbing his brow with trouble and perplexity. "Never knew such a thing in my life, never! He'd no business to ha' been left. I never knew such a thing in my life! Fell over him clean as a whistle, an' shut him in. Not four foot of space, there wasn't—yet it scarce bruised him."

He looked down at the dead man, lying prone, half naked, all grimed with coal-dust.

" 'Sphyxiated," the doctor said. "It *is* the most terrible job I've ever known. Seems as if it was done o' purpose. Clean over him, an' shut 'im in, like a mouse-trap"—he made a sharp, descending gesture with his hand.

The colliers standing by jerked aside their heads in hopeless comment. The horror of the thing bristled upon them all.

Then they heard the girl's voice upstairs calling shrilly: "Mother, mother —who is it? Mother, who is it?"

Elizabeth hurried to the foot of the stairs and opened the door:

"Go to sleep!" she commanded sharply. "What are you shouting about? Go to sleep at once—there's nothing——"

Then she began to mount the stairs. They could hear her on the boards, and on the plaster floor of the little bedroom. They could hear her distinctly:

"What's the matter now?—what's the matter with you, silly thing?"—her voice was much agitated, with an unreal gentleness.

"I thought it was some men come," said the plaintive voice of the child. "Has he come?"

"Yes, they've brought him. There's nothing to make a fuss about. Go to sleep now, like a good child."

They could hear her voice in the bedroom, they waited whilst she covered the children under the bedclothes.

"Is he drunk?" asked the girl, timidly, faintly.

"No! No—he's not! He—he's asleep."

"Is he asleep downstairs?"

"Yes—and don't make a noise."

There was silence for a moment, then the men heard the frightened child again:

"What's that noise?"

"It's nothing, I tell you, what are you bothering for?"

The noise was the grandmother moaning. She was oblivious of everything, sitting on her chair rocking and moaning. The manager put his hand on her arm and bade her "Sh—sh!!"

The old woman opened her eyes and looked at him. She was shocked by this interruption, and seemed to wonder.

"What time is it?" The plaintive thin voice of the child, sinking back unhappily into sleep, asked this last question.

"Ten o'clock," answered the mother more softly. Then she must have bent down and kissed the children.

Matthews beckoned to the men to come away. They put on their caps and took up the stretcher. Stepping over the body, they tiptoed out of the house. None of them spoke till they were far from the wakeful children.

When Elizabeth came down she found her mother alone on the parlour floor, leaning over the dead man, the tears dropping on him.

"We must lay him out," the wife said. She put on the kettle, then returning knelt at the feet, and began to unfasten the knotted leather laces. The room was clammy and dim with only one candle, so that she had to bend her face almost to the floor. At last she got off the heavy boots and put them away.

"You must help me now," she whispered to the old woman. Together they stripped the man.

When they arose, saw him lying in the naïve dignity of death, the women stood arrested in fear and respect. For a few moments they remained still, looking down, the old mother whimpering; Elizabeth felt countermanded. She saw him, how utterly inviolable he lay in himself. She had nothing to do with him. She could not accept it. Stooping, she laid her hand on him, in claim. He was still warm, for the mine was hot where he had died. His mother had his face between her hands, and was murmuring incoherently. The old tears fell in succession as drops from wet leaves; the mother was not weeping, merely her tears flowed. Elizabeth embraced the body of her husband, with cheek and lips. She seemed to be listening, inquiring, trying to get some connection. But she could not. She was driven away. He was impregnable.

She rose, went into the kitchen, where she poured warm water into a bowl, brought soap and flannel and a soft towel.

"I must wash him," she said.

Then the old mother rose stiffly, and watched Elizabeth as she carefully washed his face, carefully brushing the big blond moustache from his mouth with the flannel. She was afraid with a bottomless fear, so she ministered to him. The old woman, jealous, said:

"Let me wipe him!"—and she kneeled on the other side drying slowly as Elizabeth washed, her big black bonnet sometimes brushing the dark head of her daughter-in-law. They worked thus in silence for a long time. They never forgot it was death, and the touch of the man's dead body gave them strange emotions, different in each of the women; a great dread possessed them both, the mother felt the lie was given to her womb, she was denied; the wife felt the utter isolation of the human soul, the child within her was a weight apart from her.

At last it was finished. He was a man of handsome body, and his face showed no traces of drink. He was blond, full-fleshed, with fine limbs. But he was dead.

"Bless him," whispered his mother, looking always at his face, and speaking out of sheer terror. "Dear lad—bless him!" She spoke in a faint, sibilant ecstasy of fear and mother love.

Elizabeth sank down again to the floor, and put her face against his neck, and trembled and shuddered. But she had to draw away again. He was dead, and her living flesh had no place against his. A great dread and weariness held her: she was so unavailing. Her life was gone like this.

"White as milk he is, clear as a twelve-month baby, bless him, the darling!" the old mother murmured to herself. "Not a mark on him, clear and clean and white, beautiful as ever a child was made," she murmured with pride. Elizabeth kept her face hidden.

"He went peaceful, Lizzie—peaceful as sleep. Isn't he beautiful, the lamb? Ay—he must ha' made his peace, Lizzie. 'Appen he made it all right, Lizzie, shut in there. He'd have time. He wouldn't look like this if he hadn't made his peace. The lamb, the dear lamb. Eh, but he had a hearty laugh. I loved to hear it. He had the heartiest laugh, Lizzie, as a lad——"

Elizabeth looked up. The man's mouth was fallen back, slightly open under the cover of the moustache. The eyes, half shut, did not show glazed in the obscurity. Life with its smoking burning gone from him, had left him apart and utterly alien to her. And she knew what a stranger he was to her. In her womb was ice of fear, because of this separate stranger with whom she had been living as one flesh. Was this what it all meant—utter, intact separateness, obscured by heat of living? In dread she turned her face away. The fact was too deadly. There had been nothing between them, and yet they had come together, exchanging their nakedness repeatedly. Each time he had taken her, they had been two isolated beings, far apart as now. He was no more responsible than she. The child was like ice in her womb. For as she looked at the dead man, her mind, cold and detached, said clearly: "Who am I? What have I been doing? I have been fighting a husband who did not exist. *He* existed all the time. What wrong have I done? What was that I have been living with? There lies the reality, this man." And her soul died in her for fear: she knew she had never seen him, he had never seen her, they had met in the dark and had fought in the dark, not knowing whom they met nor whom they fought. And now she saw, and turned silent in seeing. For she had been wrong. She had said he was something he was not; she had felt familiar with him. Whereas he was apart all the while, living as she never lived, feeling as she never felt.

In fear and shame she looked at his naked body, that she had known falsely. And he was the father of her children. Her soul was torn from her body and stood apart. She looked at his naked body and was ashamed, as if she had denied it. After all, it was itself. It seemed awful to her. She looked at his face, and she turned her own face to the wall. For his look was other than hers, his way was not her way. She had denied what he was—she saw it now. She had refused him as himself. And this had been her life, and his life. She was grateful to death, which restored the truth. And she knew she was not dead.

And all the while her heart was bursting with grief and pity for him. What had he suffered? What stretch of horror for this helpless man! She was rigid with agony. She had not been able to help him. He had been cruelly injured, this naked man, this other being, and she could make no reparation. There were the children—but the children belonged to life. This dead man had nothing to do with them. He and she were only channels through which life had flowed to issue in the children. She was a mother—but how awful she knew it now to have been a wife. And he, dead now, how awful it must have felt to be a husband. She felt that in the next world he would be a stranger to her. If they met there, in the beyond, they would only be ashamed of what had been before. But the children did not unite them. Now he was dead, she knew how eternally he was apart from her, how eternally he had nothing more to do with her. Now he had withdrawn. An anguish came over her. It was finished then: it had become hopeless between them long before he died. Yet he had been her husband. But how little!

"Have you got his shirt, 'Lizabeth?"

Elizabeth turned without answering, though she strove to weep and behave as her mother-in-law expected. But she could not. She was silenced. She went into the kitchen and returned with the garment.

"It is aired," she said, grasping the cotton shirt here and there to try. She was almost ashamed to handle him; what right had she or anyone to lay hands on him; but her touch was humble on his body. It was hard work to clothe him. He was so heavy and inert. A terrible dread gripped her all the while: that he could be so heavy and utterly inert, unresponsive, apart. The horror of the distance between them was almost too much for her—it was so infinite a gap that she must look across.

At last it was finished. They covered him with a sheet and left him lying, with his face bound. And she fastened the door of the little parlour, lest the children should see what was lying there. Then, with peace sunk heavy on her heart, she went about making tidy the kitchen. She knew she submitted to life, which was her immediate master. But from death, her ultimate master, she winced with fear and shame.

KATHERINE ANNE PORTER

b. 1890

"I was precocious, nervous, rebellious, unteachable," Porter says about herself as a child. Her description is at once honest and proud, revealing her awareness that an easier childhood might have given her—and those who loved her—less pain, and at the same time asserting her right to have grown up as she had to. In Katherine Anne Porter's fiction the cost of personal rebelliousness is a pervasive feeling of isolation that keeps her main characters disengaged from the life immediately around them, a life to which on one level they want to commit themselves.

Porter was born on a farm near San Antonio, Texas, the third of four children, into a family with a well-defined sense of its history—including among its forebears Daniel Boone, and among distant relatives O. Henry (William Sydney Porter), the popular short-story writer. Her mother died when she was two, and her grandmother took over and ruled the household with a staunch Protestant ethic of duty. When Katherine was eleven, her grandmother died, and the girl's father, perhaps hoping merely to give her a "finishing-school" education, sent her away to Roman Catholic schools. She converted to Catholicism, and carried thereafter a double sense of Protestant duty and a yearning for Catholic mystery and revelation.

Until she was twenty-five Porter read only standard literary classics (*Tristram Shandy* was one of her great favorites), no modern literature at all; and though she wrote a great deal she made no attempt to publish. "I did not choose this vocation," she said years later, "and if I had any say in the matter, I would not have chosen it." For her, the profession of writing became a kind of secular priesthood entailing years of arduous struggle with fictions within her crying out to be set down, and set down right. Her vocation stood in conflict both with the hack writing she had to do to make a bare living, and with the countries, the causes, and the people that laid other, more immediate claims on her loyalties. Between 1920 and 1931, while she was living in Mexico, her "much loved second country," she developed the art of the "perfect story" —stories like "The Grave" that portray characters trying to understand the connection between their memories and illusions from their biological and cultural heritage and the reality of the present. By then she was reading widely in modern literature and feeling many literary influences; but basically she was writing in the line of Joyce, with perhaps a more immediate debt to Katherine Mansfield, presenting the closely observed details of life as they cohere in moments of revelation. Perhaps the best-known revelation in Porter's fiction is Laura's at the end of "Flowering Judas." It brings into focus all the elements of the story: the sultry atmosphere of Mexico, the commitment (or lack of it) of the Revolution, and the strange, alien role of Laura.

In 1931 Porter won a Guggenheim Fellowship and set off from Mexico on the voyage to Germany that was to constitute the basic situation in *Ship of Fools,* her long novel that was not published till thirty-one years later. In the novel the ship is treated symbolically as the scene of an exposure of the personal and national neuroticism that had developed out of World War I and would soon produce World War II. The grimness of Berlin just before Hitler is beautifully caught in her story "The Leaning Tower" which, again characteristically, she wrote in 1931 but kept until she could get it just right, thirteen years later.

The wonder of being a woman, and the conflicting loyalties it entails, is one of Porter's most persistent themes. In "The Grave" it is explored from the point of view of the young Miranda, who is beginning to distinguish herself sexually from her brother and at the same time trying to define her relation to her family's past and to the land on which she lives. In other stories Miranda is older, lives in other countries, and tries to comprehend different relationships; but she retains always a distinctly feminine point of view.

Porter was married three times, the last time in 1938 to Albert Erskine, the editor of the *Southern Review,* in which her work had been published. They were divorced in 1942, and her lasting commitment has remained to the vocation she did not choose but to which she was inexorably called.

Flowering Judas

Braggioni sits heaped upon the edge of a straight-backed chair much too small for him, and sings to Laura in a furry, mournful voice. Laura has begun to find reasons for avoiding her own house until the latest possible moment, for Braggioni is there almost every night. No matter how late she is, he will be sitting there with a surly, waiting expression, pulling at his kinky yellow hair, thumbing the strings of his guitar, snarling a tune under his breath. Lupe the Indian maid meets Laura at the door, and says with a flicker of a glance towards the upper room, "He waits."

Laura wishes to lie down, she is tired of her hairpins and the feel of her long tight sleeves, but she says to him, "Have you a new song for me this evening?" If he says yes, she asks him to sing it. If he says no, she remembers his favorite one, and asks him to sing it again. Lupe brings her a cup of chocolate and a plate of rice, and Laura eats at the small table under the lamp, first inviting Braggioni, whose answer is always the same: "I have eaten, and besides, chocolate thickens the voice."

Laura says, "Sing, then," and Braggioni heaves himself into song. He scratches the guitar familiarly as though it were a pet animal, and sings passionately off key, taking the high notes in a prolonged painful squeal. Laura, who haunts the markets listening to the ballad singers, and stops every day to hear the blind boy playing his reed-flute in Sixteenth of September Street, listens to Braggioni with pitiless courtesy, because she dares not smile at his miserable performance. Nobody dares to smile at him. Braggioni is cruel to everyone, with a kind of specialized insolence, but he is so vain of his talents, and so sensitive to slights, it would require a cruelty and vanity greater than his own to lay a finger on the vast cureless wound of his self-esteem. It would require courage, too, for it is dangerous to offend him, and nobody has this courage.

Braggioni loves himself with such tenderness and amplitude and eternal charity that his followers—for he is a leader of men, a skilled revolutionist, and his skin has been punctured in honorable warfare—warm themselves in the reflected glow, and say to each other: "He has a real nobility, a love of humanity raised above mere personal affections." The excess of this self-love has flowed out, inconveniently for her, over Laura, who, with so many others, owes her comfortable situation and her salary to him. When he is in a very good humor, he tells her, "I am tempted to forgive you for being a *gringa. Gringita!*" and Laura, burning, imagines herself leaning forward suddenly, and with a sound backhanded slap wiping the suety smile from his face. If he notices her eyes at these moments he gives no sign.

She knows what Braggioni would offer her, and she must resist tenaciously without appearing to resist, and if she could avoid it she would not admit even to herself the slow drift of his intention. During these long evenings which have spoiled a long month for her, she sits in her deep chair with an open book on her knees, resting her eyes on the consoling rigidity of the printed page when the sight and sound of Braggioni singing threaten to identify themselves with all her remembered afflictions and to add their weight to her uneasy premonitions of the future. The gluttonous bulk of Braggioni has become a symbol of her many disillusions, for a revolutionist should be lean, animated by heroic faith, a vessel of abstract virtues. This is nonsense, she knows it now and is ashamed of it. Revolution must have leaders, and leadership is a career for energetic men. She is, her comrades tell her, full of romantic error, for what she defines as cynicism in them is merely "a developed sense of reality." She is almost too willing to say, "I am wrong, I suppose I don't really understand the principles," and afterward she makes a secret truce with herself, determined not to surrender her will to such expedient logic. But she cannot help feeling that she has been betrayed irreparably by the disunion between her way of living and her feeling of what life should be, and at times she is almost contented to rest in this sense of grievance as a private store of consolation. Sometimes she wishes to run away, but she stays. Now she longs to fly out of this room, down the narrow stairs, and into the street where the houses lean together like conspirators under a single mottled lamp, and leave Braggioni singing to himself.

Instead she looks at Braggioni, frankly and clearly, like a good child who understands the rules of behavior. Her knees cling together under sound blue serge, and her round white collar is not purposely nun-like. She wears the uniform of an idea, and has renounced vanities. She was born Roman Catholic, and in spite of her fear of being seen by someone who might make a scandal of it, she slips now and again into some crumbling little church, kneels on the chilly stone, and says a Hail Mary on the gold rosary she bought in Tehuantepec. It is no good and she ends by examining the altar with its tinsel flowers and ragged brocades, and feels tender about the battered dollshape of some male saint whose white, lace-trimmed drawers hang limply around his ankles below the hieratic dignity of his velvet robe. She has encased herself in a set of principles derived from her early training, leaving no detail of gesture or of personal taste untouched, and for this reason she will not wear lace made on machines. This is her private heresy, for in her special group the machine is sacred, and will be the salvation of the workers. She loves fine lace, and there is a tiny edge of fluted cobweb on this collar, which is one of twenty precisely alike, folded in blue tissue paper in the upper drawer of her clothes chest.

Braggioni catches her glance solidly as if he had been waiting for it, leans forward, balancing his paunch between his spread knees, and sings with tremendous emphasis, weighing his words. He has, the song relates, no father and no mother, nor even a friend to console him; lonely as a wave of the sea he comes and goes, lonely as a wave. His mouth opens round and yearns sideways, his balloon cheeks grow oily with the labor of song. He bulges marvelously in his expensive garments. Over his lavender collar, crushed upon a purple necktie, held by a diamond hoop: over his ammunition belt of tooled leather worked in silver, buckled cruelly around his gasping middle: over the tops of his glossy yellow shoes Braggioni swells with ominous ripeness, his mauve silk hose stretched taut, his ankles bound with the stout leather thongs of his shoes.

When he stretches his eyelids at Laura she notes again that his eyes are the true tawny yellow cat's eyes. He is rich, not in money, he tells her, but in power, and this power brings with it the blameless ownership of things, and the right to indulge his love of small luxuries. "I have a taste for the elegant refinements," he said once, flourishing a yellow silk handerchief before her nose. "Smell that? It is Jockey Club, imported from New York." Nonetheless he is wounded by life. He will say so presently. "It is true everything turns to dust in the hand, to gall on the tongue." He sighs and his leather belt creaks like a saddle girth. "I am disappointed in everything as it comes. Everything." He shakes his head. "You, poor thing, you will be disappointed too. You are born for it. We are more alike than you realize in some things. Wait and see. Some day you will remember what I have told you, you will know that Braggioni was your friend."

Laura feels a slow chill, a purely physical sense of danger, a warning in her blood that violence, mutilation, a shocking death, wait for her with lessening patience. She has translated this fear into something homely, immediate, and sometimes hesitates before crossing the street. "My personal fate is nothing, except as the testimony of a mental attitude," she reminds herself, quoting from some forgotten philosophic primer, and is sensible enough to add, "Anyhow, I shall not be killed by an automobile if I can help it."

"It may be true that I am as corrupt, in another way, as Braggioni," she thinks in spite of herself, "as callous, as incomplete," and if this is so, any kind of death seems preferable. Still she sits quietly, she does not run. Where could she go? Uninvited she has promised herself to this place; she can no longer imagine herself as living in another country, and there is no pleasure in remembering her life before she came here.

Precisely what is the nature of this devotion, its true motives, and what are its obligations? Laura cannot say. She spends part of her days in Xochimilco, near by, teaching Indian children to say in English, "The cat is on the mat." When she appears in the classroom they crowd about her with smiles on their wise, innocent, clay-colored faces, crying, "Good morning, titcher!" in immaculate voices, and they make of her desk a fresh garden of flowers every day.

During her leisure she goes to union meetings and listens to busy important voices quarreling over tactics, methods, internal politics. She visits the prisoners of her own political faith in their cells, where they entertain themselves with counting cockroaches, repenting of their indiscretions, composing their memoirs, writing out manifestoes and plans for their comrades who are still walking about free, hands in pockets, sniffing fresh air. Laura brings them food and cigarettes and a little money, and she brings messages disguised in equivocal phrases from the men outside who dare not set foot in the prison for fear of disappearing into the cells kept empty for them. If the prisoners confuse night and day, and complain, "Dear little Laura, time doesn't pass in this infernal hole, and I won't know when it is time to sleep unless I have a reminder," she brings them their favorite narcotics, and says in a tone that does not wound them with pity, "Tonight will really be night for you," and though her Spanish amuses them, they find her comforting, useful. If they lose patience and all faith, and curse the slowness of their friends in coming to their rescue with money and influence, they trust her not to repeat everything, and if she inquires, "Where do you think we can find money, or influence?" they are certain to answer, "Well, there is Braggioni, why doesn't he do something?"

She smuggles letters from headquarters to men hiding from firing squads in back streets in mildewed houses, where they sit in tumbled beds and talk bitterly as if all Mexico were at their heels, when Laura knows positively they might appear at the band concert in the Alameda on Sunday morning, and no one would notice them. But Braggioni says, "Let them sweat a little. The next time they may be careful. It is very restful to have them out of the way for a while." She is not afraid to knock on any door in any street after midnight, and enter in the darkness, and say to one of these men who is really in danger: "They will be looking for you—seriously—tomorrow morning after six. Here is some money from Vicente. Go to Vera Cruz and wait."

She borrows money from the Roumanian agitator to give to his bitter enemy the Polish agitator. The favor of Braggioni is their disputed territory, and Braggioni holds the balance nicely, for he can use them both. The Polish agitator talks love to her over café tables, hoping to exploit what he believes is her secret sentimental preference for him, and he gives her misinformation which he begs her to repeat as the solemn truth to certain persons. The Roumanian is more adroit. He is generous with his money in all good causes, and lies to her with an air of ingenuous candor, as if he were her good friend and confidant. She never repeats anything they may say. Braggioni never asks questions. He has other ways to discover all that he wishes to know about them.

Nobody touches her, but all praise her gray eyes, and the soft, round under lip which promises gayety, yet is always grave, nearly always firmly closed: and they cannot understand why she is in Mexico. She walks back and forth on her errands, with puzzled eyebrows, carrying her little folder of drawings and music and school papers. No dancer dances more beautifully than Laura walks, and she inspires some amusing, unexpected ardors, which cause little gossip, because nothing comes of them. A young captain who had been a soldier in Zapata's army attempted, during a horseback ride near Cuernavaca, to express his desire for her with the noble simplicity befitting a rude folk-hero: but gently, because he was gentle. This gentleness was his defeat, for when he alighted, and removed her foot from the stirrup, and essayed to draw her down into his arms, her horse, ordinarily a tame one, shied fiercely, reared and plunged away. The young hero's horse careered blindly after his stable-mate, and the hero did not return to the hotel until rather late that evening. At breakfast he came to her table in full charro dress, gray buckskin jacket and trousers with strings of silver buttons down the leg, and he was in a humorous, careless mood. "May I sit with you?" and "You are a wonderful rider. I was terrified that you might be thrown and dragged. I should never have forgiven myself. But I cannot admire you enough for your riding!"

"I learned to ride in Arizona," said Laura.

"If you will ride with me again this morning, I promise you a horse that will not shy with you," he said. But Laura remembered that she must return to Mexico City at noon.

Next morning the children made a celebration and spent their playtime writing on the blackboard, "We lov ar ticher," and with tinted chalks they drew wreaths of flowers around the words. The young hero wrote her a letter: "I am a very foolish, wasteful, impulsive man. I should have first said I love you, and then you would not have run away. But you shall see me again." Laura thought, "I must send him a box of colored crayons," but she was trying to forgive herself for having spurred her horse at the wrong moment.

A brown, shock-haired youth came and stood in her patio one night and sang like a lost soul for two hours, but Laura could think of nothing to do about it. The moonlight spread a wash of gauzy silver over the clear spaces of the garden, and the shadows were cobalt blue. The scarlet blossoms of the Judas tree were dull purple, and the names of the colors repeated themselves automatically in her mind, while she watched not the boy, but his shadow, fallen like a dark garment across the fountain rim, trailing in the water. Lupe came silently and whispered expert counsel in her ear: "If you will throw him one little flower, he will sing another song or two and go away." Laura threw the flower, and he sang a last song and went away with the flower tucked in the band of his hat. Lupe said, "He is one of the organizers of the Typographers Union, and before that he sold corridos in the Merced market, and before that, he came from Guanajuato, where I was born. I would not trust any man, but I trust least those from Guanajuato."

She did not tell Laura that he would be back again the next night, and the next, nor that he would follow her at a certain fixed distance around the Merced market, through the Zócolo, up Francisco I. Madero Avenue, and so along the Paseo de la Reforma to Chapultepec Park, and into the Philosopher's Footpath, still with that flower withering in his hat, and an indivisible attention in his eyes.

Now Laura is accustomed to him, it means nothing except that he is nineteen years old and is observing a convention with all propriety, as though it were founded on a law of nature, which in the end it might well prove to be. He is beginning to write poems which he prints on a wooden press, and he leaves them stuck like handbills in her door. She is pleasantly disturbed by the abstract, unhurried watchfulness of his black eyes which will in time turn easily towards another object. She tells herself that throwing the flower was a mistake, for she is twenty-two years old and knows better; but she refuses to regret it, and persuades herself that her negation of all external events as they occur is a sign that she is gradually perfecting herself in the stoicism she strives to cultivate against that disaster she fears, though she cannot name it.

She is not at home in the world. Every day she teaches children who remain strangers to her, though she loves their tender round hands and their charming opportunist savagery. She knocks at unfamiliar doors not knowing whether a friend or a stranger shall answer, and even if a known face emerges from the sour gloom of that unknown interior, still it is the face of a stranger. No matter what this stranger says to her, nor what her message to him, the very cells of her flesh reject knowledge and kinship in one monotonous word. No. No. No. She draws her strength from this one holy talismanic word which does not suffer her to be led into evil. Denying everything, she may walk anywhere in safety, she looks at everything without amazement.

No, repeats this firm unchanging voice of her blood; and she looks at Braggioni without amazement. He is a great man, he wishes to impress the simple girl who covers her great round breasts with thick dark cloth, and who hides long, invaluably beautiful legs under a heavy skirt. She is almost thin except for the incomprehensible fullness of her breasts, like a nursing mother's, and Braggioni, who considers himself a judge of women, speculates again on the puzzle of her notorious virginity, and takes the liberty of speech which she permits without a sign of modesty, indeed, without any sort of sign, which is disconcerting.

"You think you are so cold, *gringita!* Wait and see. You will surprise yourself some day! May I be there to advise you!" He stretches his eyelids at her, and his ill-humored cat's eyes waver in a separate glance for the two points of light marking the opposite ends of a smoothly drawn path between the swollen curve of her breasts. He is not put off by that blue serge, nor by her resolutely fixed gaze. There is all the time in the world. His cheeks are bellying with the wind of song. "O girl with the dark eyes," he sings, and reconsiders. "But yours are not dark. I can change all that. O girl with the green eyes, you have stolen my heart away!" then his mind wanders to the song, and Laura feels the weight of his attention being shifted elsewhere. Singing thus, he seems harmless, he is quite harmless, there is nothing to do but sit patiently and say "No," when the moment comes. She draws a full breath, and her mind wanders also, but not far. She dares not wander too far.

Not for nothing has Braggioni taken pains to be a good revolutionist and a professional lover of humanity. He will never die of it. He has the malice, the cleverness, the wickedness, the sharpness of wit, the hardness of heart, stipulated for loving the world profitably. *He will never die of it.* He will live to see himself kicked out from his feeding trough by other hungry world-saviors. Traditionally he must sing in spite of his life which drives him to bloodshed, he tells Laura, for his father was a Tuscany peasant who drifted to Yucatan and married a Maya woman: a woman of race, an aristocrat. They give him the love and knowledge of music, thus: and under the rip of his thumbnail, the strings of the instrument complain like exposed nerves.

Once he was called Delgadito by all the girls and married women who ran after him; he was so scrawny all his bones showed under his thin cotton clothing, and he could squeeze his emptiness to the very backbone with his two hands. He was a poet and the revolution was only a dream then; too many women loved him and sapped away his youth, and he could never find enough to eat anywhere! Now he is a leader of men, crafty men who whisper in his ear, hungry men who wait for hours outside his office for a word with him, emaciated men with wild faces who waylay him at the street gate with a timid, "Comrade, let me tell you . . ." and they blow the foul breath from their empty stomachs in his face.

He is always sympathetic. He gives them handfuls of small coins from his own pocket, he promises them work, there will be demonstrations, they must join the unions and attend the meetings, above all they must be on the watch for spies. They are closer to him than his own brothers, without them he can do nothing—until tomorrow, comrade!

Until tomorrow. "They are stupid, they are lazy, they are treacherous, they would cut my throat for nothing," he says to Laura. He has good food and abundant drink, he hires an automobile and drives in the Paseo on Sunday morning, and enjoys plenty of sleep in a soft bed beside a wife who dares not disturb him; and he sits pampering his bones in easy billows of fat, singing to Laura, who knows and thinks these things about him. When he was fifteen, he tried to drown himself because he loved a girl, his first love, and she laughed at him. "A thousand women have paid for that," and his tight little mouth turns down at the corners. Now he perfumes his hair with Jockey Club, and confides to Laura: "One woman is really as good as another for me, in the dark. I prefer them all."

His wife organizes unions among the girls in the cigarette factories, and walks in picket lines, and even speaks at meetings in the evening. But she cannot be brought to acknowledge the benefits of true liberty. "I tell her I must have my freedom, net. She does not understand my point of view." Laura has heard this many times. Braggioni scratches the guitar and meditates. "She is an instinctively virtuous woman, pure gold, no doubt of that. If she were not, I should lock her up, and she knows it."

His wife, who works so hard for the good of the factory girls, employs part of her leisure lying on the floor weeping because there are so many women in the world, and only one husband for her, and she never knows where nor when to look for him. He told her: "Unless you can learn to cry when I am not here, I must go away for good." That day he went away and took a room at the Hotel Madrid.

It is this month of separation for the sake of higher principles that has been spoiled not only for Mrs. Braggioni whose sense of reality is beyond criticism, but for Laura, who feels herself bogged in a nightmare. Tonight Laura envies Mrs. Braggioni, who is alone, and free to weep as much as she pleases about a concrete wrong. Laura has just come from a visit to the prison, and she is waiting for tomorrow with a bitter anxiety as if tomorrow may not come, but time may be caught immovably in this hour, with herself transfixed, Braggioni singing on forever, and Eugenio's body not yet discovered by the guard.

Braggioni says: "Are you going to sleep?" Almost before she can shake her head, he begins to tell her about the May-day disturbances coming on in Morelia, for the Catholics hold a festival in honor of the Blessed Virgin, and the Socialists celebrate their martyrs on that day. "There will be two independent processions, starting from either end of town, and they will march until they meet, and the rest depends . . ." He asks her to oil and load his pistols. Standing up, he unbuckles his ammunition belt, and spreads it laden across her knees. Laura sits with the shells slipping through the cleaning cloth dipped in oil, and he says again he cannot understand why she works so hard for the revolutionary idea unless she loves some man who is in it. "Are you not in love with someone?" "No," says Laura. "And no one is in love with you?" "No." "Then it is your own fault. No woman need go begging. Why, what is the matter with you? The legless beggar woman in the Alameda has a perfectly faithful lover. Did you know that?"

Laura peers down the pistol barrel and says nothing, but a long, slow faintness rises and subsides in her; Braggioni curves his swollen fingers around the throat of the guitar and softly smothers the music out of it, and when she hears him again he seems to have forgotten her, and is speaking in the hypnotic voice he uses when talking in small rooms to a listening, close-gathered crowd. Some day this world, now seemingly so composed and eternal, to the edges of every sea shall be merely a tangle of gaping trenches, of crashing walls and broken bodies. Everything must be torn from its accustomed place where it has rotted for centuries, hurled skyward and distributed, cast down again clean as rain, without separate identity. Nothing shall survive that the stiffened hands of poverty have created for the rich and no one shall be left alive except the elect spirits destined to procreate a new world cleansed of cruelty and injustice, ruled by benevolent anarchy: "Pistols are good, I love them, cannon are even better, but in the end I pin my faith to good dynamite," he concludes, and strokes the pistol lying in her hands. "Once I dreamed of destroying this city, in case it offered resistance to General Ortíz, but it fell into his hands like an overripe pear."

He is made restless by his own words, rises and stands waiting. Laura holds up the belt to him: "Put that on, and go kill somebody in Morelia, and you will be happier," she says softly. The presence of death in the room makes her bold. "Today, I found Eugenio going into a stupor. He refused to allow me to call the prison doctor. He had taken all the tablets I brought him yesterday. He said he took them because he was bored."

"He is a fool, and his death is his own business," says Braggioni, fastening his belt carefully.

"I told him if he had waited only a little while longer, you would have got him set free," says Laura. "He said he did not want to wait."

"He is a fool and we are well rid of him," says Braggioni, reaching for his hat.

He goes away. Laura knows his mood has changed, she will not see him any more for a while. He will send word when he needs her to go on errands into strange streets, to speak to the strange faces that will appear, like clay masks with the power of human speech, to mutter their thanks to Braggioni for his help. Now she is free, and she thinks, I must run while there is time. But she does not go.

Braggioni enters his own house where for a month his wife has spent many hours every night weeping and tangling her hair upon her pillow. She is weeping now, and she weeps more at the sight of him, the cause of all her sorrows. He looks about the room. Nothing is changed, the smells are good and familiar, he is well acquainted with the woman who comes toward him with no reproach except grief on her face. He says to her tenderly: "You are so good, please don't cry any more, you dear good creature." She says, "Are you tired, my angel? Sit here and I will wash your feet." She brings a bowl of water, and kneeling, unlaces his shoes, and when from her knees she raises her sad eyes under her blackened lids, he is sorry for everything, and bursts into tears. "Ah, yes, I am hungry, I am tired, let us eat something together," he says, between sobs. His wife leans her head on his arm and says, "Forgive me!" and this time he is refreshed by the solemn, endless rain of her tears.

Laura takes off her serge dress and puts on a white linen nightgown and goes to bed. She turns her head a little to one side, and lying still, reminds herself that it is time to sleep. Numbers tick in her brain like little clocks, soundless doors close of themselves around her. If you would sleep, you must not remember anything, the children will say tomorrow, good morning, my teacher, the poor prisoners who come every day bringing flowers to their jailor. 1-2-3-4-5—it is monstrous to confuse love with revolution, night with day, life with death—ah, Eugenio!

The tolling of the midnight bell is a signal, but what does it mean? Get up, Laura, and follow me: come out of your sleep, out of your bed, out of this strange house. What are you doing in this house? Without a word, without fear she rose and reached for Eugenio's hand, but he eluded her with a sharp, sly smile and drifted away. This is not all, you shall see—Murderer, he said, follow me, I will show you a new country, but it is far away and we must hurry. No, said Laura, not unless you take my hand, no; and she clung first to the stair rail, and then to the topmost branch of the Judas tree that bent down slowly and set her upon the earth, and then to the rocky ledge of a cliff, and then to the jagged wave of a sea that was not water but a desert of crumbling stone. Where are you taking me, she asked in wonder but without fear. To death, and it is a long way off, and we must hurry, said Eugenio. No, said Laura, not unless you take my hand. Then eat these flowers, poor prisoner, said Eugenio in a voice of pity, take and eat: and from the Judas tree he stripped the warm bleeding flowers, and held them to her lips. She saw that his hand was fleshless, a cluster of small white petrified branches, and his eye sockets were without light, but she ate the flowers greedily for they satisfied both hunger and thirst. Murderer! said Eugenio, and Cannibal! This is my body and my blood. Laura cried No! and at the sound of her own voice, she awoke trembling, and was afraid to sleep again.

The Grave

The grandfather, dead for more than thirty years, had been twice disturbed in his long repose by the constancy and possessiveness of his widow. She removed his bones first to Louisiana and then to Texas as if she had set out to find her own burial place, knowing well she would never return to the places she had left. In Texas she set up a small cemetery in a corner of her first farm, and as the family connection grew, and oddments of relations came over from Kentucky to settle, it contained at last about twenty graves. After the grandmother's death, part of her land was to be sold for the benefit of certain of her children, and the cemetery happened to lie in the part set aside for sale. It was necessary to take up the bodies and bury them again in the family plot in the big new public cemetery, where the grandmother had been buried. At last her husband was to lie beside her for eternity, as she had planned.

The family cemetery had been a pleasant small neglected garden of tangled rose bushes and ragged cedar trees and cypress, the simple flat stones rising out of uncropped sweet-smelling wild grass. The graves were lying open and empty one burning day when Miranda and her brother Paul, who often went together to hunt rabbits and doves, propped their twenty-two Winchester rifles carefully against the rail fence, climbed over and explored among the graves. She was nine years old and he was twelve.

They peered into the pits all shaped alike with such purposeful accuracy, and looking at each other with pleased adventurous eyes, they said in solemn tones: "These were graves!" trying by words to shape a special, suitable emotion in their minds, but they felt nothing except an agreeable thrill of wonder: they were seeing a new sight, doing something they had not done before. In them both there was also a small disappointment at the entire commonplaceness of the actual spectacle. Even if it had once contained a coffin for years upon years, when the coffin was gone a grave was just a hole in the ground. Miranda leaped into the pit that had held her grandfather's bones. Scratching around aimlessly and pleasurably as any young animal, she scooped up a lump of earth and weighed it in her palm. It had a pleasantly sweet, corrupt smell, being mixed with cedar needles and small leaves, and as the crumbs fell apart, she saw a silver dove no larger than a hazel nut, with spread wings and a neat fan-shaped tail. The breast had a deep round hollow in it. Turning it up to the fierce sunlight, she saw that the inside of the hollow was cut in little whorls. She scrambled out, over the pile of loose earth that had fallen back into one end of the grave, calling to Paul that she had found something, he must guess what . . . His head appeared smiling over the rim of another grave. He waved a closed hand at her. "I've got something too!" They ran to compare treasures, making a game of it, so many guesses each, all wrong, and a final showdown with opened palms. Paul had found a thin wide gold ring carved with intricate flowers and leaves. Miranda was smitten at sight of the ring and wished to have it. Paul seemed more impressed by the dove. They made a trade, with some little bickering. After he had got the dove in his hand, Paul said, "Don't you know what this is? This is a screw head for a *coffin!* . . . I'll bet nobody else in the world has one like this!"

Miranda glanced at it without covetousness. She had the gold ring on her thumb; it fitted perfectly. "Maybe we ought to go now," she said, "maybe one of the niggers'll see us and tell somebody." They knew the land had been sold, the cemetery was no longer theirs, and they felt like trespassers. They climbed back over the fence, slung their rifles loosely under their arms—they had been shooting at targets with various kinds of firearms since they were seven years old—and set out to look for the rabbits and doves or whatever small game might happen along. On these expeditions Miranda always followed at Paul's heels along the path, obeying instructions about handling her gun when going through fences; learning how to stand it up properly so it would not slip and fire unexpectedly; how to wait her time for a shot and not just bang away in the air without looking, spoiling shots for Paul, who really could hit things if given a chance. Now and then, in her excitement at seeing birds whizz up suddenly before her face, or a rabbit leap across her very toes, she lost her head, and almost without sighting she flung her rifle up and pulled the trigger. She hardly ever hit any sort of mark. She had no proper sense of hunting at all. Her brother would be often completely disgusted with her. "You don't care whether you get your bird or not," he said. "That's no way to hunt." Miranda could not understand his indignation. She had seen him smash his hat and yell with fury when he had missed his aim. "What I like about shooting," said Miranda, with exasperating inconsequence, "is pulling the trigger and hearing the noise."

"Then, by golly," said Paul, "whyn't you go back to the range and shoot at bulls-eyes?"

"I'd just as soon," said Miranda, "only like this, we walk around more."

"Well, you just stay behind and stop spoiling my shots," said Paul, who, when he made a kill, wanted to be certain he had made it. Miranda, who alone brought down a bird once in twenty rounds, always claimed as her own any game they got when they fired at the same moment. It was tiresome and unfair and her brother was sick of it.

"Now, the first dove we see, or the first rabbit, is mine," he told her. "And the next will be yours. Remember that and don't get smarty."

"What about snakes?" asked Miranda idly. "Can I have the first snake?"

Waving her thumb gently and watching her gold ring glitter, Miranda lost interest in shooting. She was wearing her summer roughing outfit: dark blue overalls, a light blue shirt, a hired-man's straw hat, and thick brown sandals. Her brother had the same outfit except his was a sober hickory-nut color. Ordinarily Miranda preferred her overalls to any other dress, though it was making rather a scandal in the countryside, for the year was 1903, and in the back country the law of female decorum had teeth in it. Her father had been criticized for letting his girls dress like boys and go careering around astride barebacked horses. Big sister Maria, the really independent and fearless one, in spite of her rather affected ways, rode at a dead run with only a rope knotted around her horse's nose. It was said the motherless family was running down, with the Grandmother no longer there to hold it together. It was known that she had discriminated against her son Harry in her will, and that he was in straits about money. Some of his old neighbors reflected with vicious satisfaction that now he would probably not be so stiffnecked, nor have any more high-stepping horses either. Miranda knew this, though she could not say how. She had met along the road old women of the kind who smoked corn-cob pipes, who had treated her grandmother with most sincere respect. They slanted their gummy old eyes side-ways at the granddaughter and said, "Ain't you ashamed of yoself, Missy? It's aginst the Scriptures to dress like that. Whut yo Pappy thinkin about?" Miranda, with her powerful social sense, which was like a fine set of antennae radiating from every pore of her skin, would feel ashamed because she knew well it was rude and ill-bred to shock anybody, even bad-tempered old crones, though she had faith in her father's judgment and was perfectly comfortable in the clothes. Her father had said, "They're just what you need, and they'll save your dresses for school . . ." This sounded quite simple and natural to her. She had been brought up in rigorous economy. Wastefulness was vulgar. It was also a sin. These were truths; she had heard them repeated many times and never once disputed.

Now the ring, shining with the serene purity of fine gold on her rather grubby thumb, turned her feelings against her overalls and sockless feet, toes sticking through the thick brown leather straps. She wanted to go back to the farmhouse, take a good cold bath, dust herself with plenty of Maria's violet talcum powder—provided Maria was not present to object, of course—put on the thinnest, most becoming dress she owned, with a big sash, and sit in a wicker chair under the trees . . . These things were not all she wanted, of course; she had vague stirrings of desire for luxury and a grand way of living which could not take precise form in her imagination but were founded on family legend of past wealth and leisure. These immediate comforts were what she could have, and she wanted them at once. She lagged rather far behind Paul, and once she thought of just turning back without a word and going home. She stopped, thinking that Paul would never do that to her, and so she would have to tell him. When a rabbit leaped, she let Paul have it without dispute. He killed it with one shot.

When she came up with him, he was already kneeling, examining the wound, the rabbit trailing from his hands. "Right through the head," he said complacently, as if he had aimed for it. He took out his sharp, competent bowie knife and started to skin the body. He did it very cleanly and quickly. Uncle Jimbilly knew how to prepare the skins so that Miranda always had fur coats for her dolls, for though she never cared much for her dolls she liked seeing them in fur coats. The children knelt facing each other over the dead animal. Miranda watched admiringly while her brother stripped the skin away as if he were taking off a glove. The flayed flesh emerged dark scarlet, sleek, firm; Miranda with thumb and finger felt the long fine muscles with the silvery flat strips binding them to the joints. Brother lifted the oddly bloated belly. "Look," he said, in a low amazed voice. "It was going to have young ones."

Very carefully he slit the thin flesh from the center ribs to the flanks, and a scarlet bag appeared. He slit again and pulled the bag open, and there lay a bundle of tiny rabbits, each wrapped in a thin scarlet veil. The brother pulled these off and there they were, dark gray, their sleek wet down lying in minute even ripples, like a baby's head just washed, their unbelievably small delicate ears folded close, their little blind faces almost featureless.

Miranda said, "Oh, I want to *see,*" under her breath. She looked and looked—excited but not frightened, for she was accustomed to the sight of animals killed in hunting—filled with pity and astonishment and a kind of shocked delight in the wonderful little creatures for their own sakes, they were so pretty. She touched one of them ever so carefully, "Ah, there's blood running over them," she said and began to tremble without knowing why. Yet she wanted most deeply to see and to know. Having seen, she felt at once as if she had known all along. The very memory of her former ignorance faded, she had always known just this. No one had ever told her anything outright, she had been rather unobservant of the animal life around her because she was so accustomed to animals. They seemed simply disorderly and unaccountably rude in their habits, but altogether natural and not very interesting. Her brother had spoken as if he had known about everything all along. He may have seen all this before. He had never said a word to her, but she knew now a part at least of what he knew. She understood a little of the secret formless intuitions in her own mind and body, which had been clearing up, taking form, so gradually and so steadily she had not realized that she was learning what she had to know. Paul said cautiously, as if he were talking about something forbidden: "They were just about ready to be born." His voice dropped on the last word. "I know," said Miranda, "like kittens. I know, like babies." She was quietly and terribly agitated, standing again with her rifle under her arm, looking down at the bloody heap. "I don't want the skin," she said, "I won't have it." Paul buried the young rabbits again in their mother's body, wrapped the skin around her, carried her to a clump of sage bushes, and hid her away.

He came out again at once and said to Miranda, with an eager friendliness, a confidential tone quite unusual in him, as if he were taking her into an important secret on equal terms: "Listen now. Now you listen to me, and don't ever forget. Don't you ever tell a living soul that you saw this. Don't tell a soul. Don't tell Dad because I'll get into trouble. He'll say I'm leading you into things you ought not to do. He's always saying that. So now don't go and forget and blab out something the way you're always doing . . . Now, that's a secret. Don't you tell."

Miranda never told, she did not even wish to tell anybody. She thought about the whole worrisome affair with confused unhappiness for a few days. Then it sank quietly into her mind and was heaped over by accumulated thousands of impressions, for nearly twenty years. One day she was picking her path among the puddles and crushed refuse of a market street in a strange city of a strange country, when without warning, plain and clear in its true colors as if she looked through a frame upon a scene that had not stirred nor changed since the moment it happened, the episode of that far-off day leaped from its burial place before her mind's eye. She was so reasonlessly horrified she halted suddenly staring, the scene before her eyes dimmed by the vision back of them. An Indian vendor had held up before her a tray of dyed sugar sweets, in the shapes of all kinds of small creatures: birds, baby chicks, baby rabbits, lambs, baby pigs. They were in gay colors and smelled of vanilla, maybe. . . . It was a very hot day and the smell in the market, with its piles of raw flesh and wilting flowers, was like the mingled sweetness and corruption she had smelled that other day in the empty cemetery at home: the day she had remembered always until now vaguely as the time she and her brother had found treasure in the opened graves. Instantly upon this thought the dreadful vision faded, and she saw clearly her brother, whose childhood face she had forgotten, standing again in the blazing sunshine, again twelve years old, a pleased sober smile in his eyes, turning the silver dove over and over in his hands.

F. SCOTT FITZGERALD

1896–1940

Fitzgerald was addicted to an image of a romantic life that with all his intellect he knew was impossible but that with all his being he sought. The components of this life are familiar to us—partly because Fitzgerald himself defined them so well in his fiction: money, of course, but not money that you made yourself because then you would not have been brought up with the easy negligence that he imagined rich children enjoy; beautiful women of the Southern Belle dream type who need only worshipping; football stardom at some Ivy League college; military heroism; a house on Fifth Avenue; and the kind of preeminence in a profession that headwaiters all over the world recognize. Obviously there are components of most people's daydreams here, but a kind of American historical accident packaged all these fantasies for Fitzgerald into a single ineluctable dream; and when he left his middle-class home in St. Paul, Minnesota, in September 1914 to be a freshman at Princeton, he was hooked. He died, broke, in Hollywood, then the capital of dream and illusion, twenty-six years later.

His life was a crazy, fascinating reflection of his dream. In reality he had no money until his short stories rode a brief vogue in the twenties, and he was chronically broke thereafter. The Southern Belle he married was mentally unstable and, scarcely steadied by her husband's own instability, began to have bouts of severe schizophrenia in 1929. She was hospitalized permanently in 1934. He played football at Princeton, but poorly; never saw action in the War; and had no Fifth Avenue mansion.

In his best writing, the novels *The Great Gatsby* (1925) and *Tender Is the Night* (1934), Fitzgerald confronted the conflict within himself between what he longed for and what was possible. The chief characters in these novels destroy themselves in futile attempts to make their dreams into reality, yet the most lasting impression on the reader is not of their destruction but of the poignant attractiveness of their dreams. Tougher characters, less vulnerable to romanticism, ride with them while the going is good, then desert them as their strength runs out and their dreams disintegrate. Fitzgerald's own sympathies obviously lie with his characters who fail greatly, not with those who endure.

His best short story, "Babylon Revisited," is an unusually objective portrait of a man who knows that Babylon, the fabulous, unreal Paris of the twenties, is all over. On a literal level, that illusory world of endless wealth and unlimited freedom has been destroyed by the Depression of 1929, which wiped out the Stock Market fortunes of American playboys. On a more significant level, Babylon has been destroyed because no human being has the strength to sustain it. Before the story begins, a crisis has arisen that offers the main character, Charles, a chance to save his marriage and keep custody of his daughter; but exhausted by the current of meaningless pleasure in Babylon, he fails—hooked physically on alcohol and imaginatively on the fantasy that was Babylon. As the story opens he is attempting to pick up the pieces.

Fitzgerald's feelings about his wife Zelda's schizophrenia combined guilt and resentment. That she had disintegrated seemed his fault because, having set out to create a dream life for them both, he simply had failed to produce it. Typically he had set up dramatic situations to assert his dream—big parties, family reunions, intimate confrontations—and then in painful acknowledgment of his creative impotence, got drunk. Thus he felt responsible for ruining his wife: he had failed as the artist who could have "created" her. On the other hand, he resented her for the destructive competition that she offered to his romantic image-building and the care she needed just when he was exhausted.

The guilt and resentment that Fitzgerald faced in life are compartmentalized in "Babylon Revisited." Charles' wife is dead, of physical causes. This takes the ambiguity out of Fitzgerald's feelings: the guilt is there, but now it can be redirected as acceptable resentment to Charles' wife's sister, who has, as he sees it, usurped control over his daughter. And his sister-in-law is one of the tough ones who can be looked down upon for never having even been tempted by the Babylon side of Paris, though she and her husband have lived there for years.

As the story proceeds, the issue is whether Charles' new awareness that his old life was an illusion can prevail. If it can, he can be given custody of his daughter and build some cloudy new life. But the story calls into question the likelihood that he can continue to reject the illusory Babylon. The enormous effort he has to put out to have just *one* drink every afternoon, the delight he takes in savoring the scenes of his old Babylonian life, and the nostalgia he inhales at the Ritz bar stand in balance against his determination to live an ordinary family life as an American businessman in Prague, a life which, intellectually, he knows offers the only chance of survival. Charlie's—Fitzgerald's—last question to the waiter at the Ritz is resonant of the problem of his life: "What do I owe you?"

Babylon Revisited

I

"And where's Mr. Campbell?" Charlie asked.

"Gone to Switzerland. Mr. Campbell's a pretty sick man, Mr. Wales."

"I'm sorry to hear that. And George Hardt?" Charlie inquired.

"Back in America, gone to work."

"And where is the Snow Bird?"

"He was in here last week. Anyway, his friend, Mr. Schaeffer, is in Paris."

Two familiar names from the long list of a year and a half ago. Charlie scribbled an address in his notebook and tore out the page.

"If you see Mr. Schaeffer, give him this," he said. "It's my brother-in-law's address. I haven't settled on a hotel yet."

He was not really disappointed to find Paris was so empty. But the stillness in the Ritz bar was strange and portentous. It was not an American bar any more—he felt polite in it, and not as if he owned it. It had gone back into France. He felt the stillness from the moment he got out of the taxi and saw the doorman, usually in a frenzy of activity at this hour, gossiping with a *chasseur* by the servants' entrance.

Passing through the corridor, he heard only a single, bored voice in the once-glamorous women's room. When he turned into the bar he travelled the twenty feet of green carpet with his eyes fixed straight ahead by old habit; and then, with his foot firmly on the rail, he turned and surveyed the room, encountering only a single pair of eyes that fluttered up from a newspaper in the corner. Charlie asked for the head barman, Paul, who in the latter days of the bull market had come to work in his own custom-built car—disembarking, however, with due nicety at the nearest corner. But Paul was at his country house today and Alix giving him information.

"No, no more," Charlie said, "I'm going slow these days."

Alix congratulated him: "You were going pretty strong a couple of years ago."

"I'll stick to it all right," Charlie assured him. "I've stuck to it for over a year and a half now."

"How do you find conditions in America?"

"I haven't been to America for months. I'm in business in Prague, representing a couple of concerns there. They don't know about me down there."

Alix smiled.

"Remember the night of George Hardt's bachelor dinner here?" said Charlie. "By the way, what's become of Claude Fessenden?"

Alix lowered his voice confidentially: "He's in Paris, but he doesn't come here any more. Paul doesn't allow it. He ran up a bill of thirty thousand francs, charging all his drinks and his lunches, and usually his dinner, for more than a year. And when Paul finally told him he had to pay, he gave him a bad check."

Alix shook his head sadly.

"I don't understand it, such a dandy fellow. Now he's all bloated up—" He made a plump apple of his hands.

Charlie watched a group of strident queens installing themselves in a corner.

"Nothing affects them," he thought. "Stocks rise and fall, people loaf or work, but they go on forever." The place oppressed him. He called for the dice and shook with Alix for the drink.

"Here for long, Mr. Wales?"

"I'm here for four or five days to see my little girl."

"Oh-h! You have a little girl?"

Outside, the fire-red, gas-blue, ghost-green signs shone smokily through the tranquil rain. It was late afternoon and the streets were in movement; the *bistros* gleamed. At the corner of the Boulevard des Capucines he took a taxi. The Place de la Concorde moved by in pink majesty; they crossed the logical Seine, and Charlie felt the sudden provincial quality of the Left Bank.

Charlie directed his taxi to the Avenue de l'Opéra, which was out of his way. But he wanted to see the blue hour spread over the magnificent façade, and imagine that the cab horns, playing endlessly the first few bars of *Le Plus que Lent,* were the trumpets of the Second Empire. They were closing the iron grill in front of Brentano's Book-store, and people were already at dinner behind the trim little bourgeois hedge of Duval's. He had never eaten at a really cheap restaurant in Paris. Five-course dinner, four francs fifty, eighteen cents, wine included. For some odd reason he wished that he had.

As they rolled on to the Left Bank and he felt its sudden provincialism, he thought, "I spoiled this city for myself. I didn't realize it, but the days came along one after another, and then two years were gone, and everything was gone, and I was gone."

He was thirty-five, and good to look at. The Irish mobility of his face was sobered by a deep wrinkle between his eyes. As he rang his brother-in-law's bell in the Rue Palatine, the wrinkle deepened till it pulled down his brows; he felt a cramping sensation in his belly. From behind the maid who opened the door darted a lovely little girl of nine who shrieked "Daddy!" and flew up, struggling like a fish, into his arms. She pulled his head around by one ear and set her cheek against his.

"My old pie," he said.

"Oh, daddy, daddy, daddy, daddy, dads, dads, dads!"

She drew him into the salon, where the family waited, a boy and girl his daughter's age, his sister-in-law and her husband. He greeted Marion with his voice pitched carefully to avoid either feigned enthusiasm or dislike, but her response was more frankly tepid, though she minimized her expression of unalterable distrust by directing her regard toward his child. The two men clasped hands in a friendly way and Lincoln Peters rested his for a moment on Charlie's shoulder.

The room was warm and comfortably American. The three children moved intimately about, playing through the yellow oblongs that led to other rooms; the cheer of six o'clock spoke in the eager smacks of the fire and the sounds of French activity in the kitchen. But Charlie did not relax; his heart sat up rigidly in his body and he drew confidence from his daughter, who from time to time came close to him, holding in her arms the doll he had brought.

"Really extremely well," he declared in answer to Lincoln's question. "There's a lot of business there that isn't moving at all, but we're doing even better than ever. In fact, damn well. I'm bringing my sister over from America next month to keep house for me. My income last year was bigger than it was when I had money. You see, the Czechs—"

His boasting was for a specific purpose; but after a moment, seeing a faint restiveness in Lincoln's eye, he changed the subject:

"Those are fine children of yours, well brought up, good manners."

"We think Honoria's a great little girl too."

Marion Peters came back from the kitchen. She was a tall woman with worried eyes, who had once possessed a fresh American loveliness. Charlie had never been sensitive to it and was always surprised when people spoke of how pretty she had been. From the first there had been an instinctive antipathy between them.

"Well, how do you find Honoria?" she asked.

"Wonderful. I was astonished how much she's grown in ten months. All the children are looking well."

"We haven't had a doctor for a year. How do you like being back in Paris?"

"It seems very funny to see so few Americans around."

"I'm delighted," Marion said vehemently. "Now at least you can go into a store without their assuming you're a millionaire. We've suffered like everybody, but on the whole it's a good deal pleasanter."

"But it was nice while it lasted," Charlie said. "We were a sort of royalty, almost infallible, with a sort of magic around us. In the bar this afternoon"—he stumbled, seeing his mistake—"there wasn't a man I knew."

She looked at him keenly. "I should think you'd have had enough of bars."

"I only stayed a minute. I take one drink every afternoon, and no more."

"Don't you want a cocktail before dinner?" Lincoln asked.

"I take only one drink every afternoon, and I've had that."

"I hope you keep to it," said Marion.

Her dislike was evident in the coldness with which she spoke, but Charlie only smiled; he had larger plans. Her very aggressiveness gave him an advantage, and he knew enough to wait. He wanted them to initiate the discussion of what they knew had brought him to Paris.

At dinner he couldn't decide whether Honoria was most like him or her mother. Fortunate if she didn't combine the traits of both that had brought them to disaster. A great wave of protectiveness went over him. He thought he knew what to do for her. He believed in character; he wanted to jump back a whole generation and trust in character again as the eternally valuable element. Everything else wore out.

He left soon after dinner, but not to go home. He was curious to see Paris by night with clearer and more judicious eyes than those of other days. He bought a *strapontin* for the Casino and watched Josephine Baker go through her chocolate arabesques.

After an hour he left and strolled toward Montmartre, up the Rue Pigalle into the Place Blanche. The rain had stopped and there were a few people in evening clothes disembarking from taxis in front of cabarets, and *cocottes* prowling singly or in pairs, and many Negroes. He passed a lighted door from which issued music, and stopped with the sense of familiarity; it was Bricktop's, where he had parted with so many hours and so much money. A few doors farther on he found another ancient rendezvous and incautiously put his head inside. Immediately an eager orchestra burst into sound, a pair of professional dancers leaped to their feet and a maître d'hôtel swooped toward him, crying, "Crowd just arriving, sir!" But he withdrew quickly.

"You have to be damn drunk," he thought.

Zelli's was closed, the bleak and sinister cheap hotels surrounding it were dark; up in the Rue Blanche there was more light and a local, colloquial French crowd. The Poet's Cave had disappeared, but the two great mouths of the Café of Heaven and the Café of Hell still yawned—even devoured, as he watched, the meagre contents of a tourist bus—a German, a Japanese, and an American couple who glanced at him with frightened eyes.

So much for the effort and ingenuity of Montmartre. All the catering to vice and waste was on an utterly childish scale, and he suddenly realized the meaning of the word "dissipate"—to dissipate into thin air; to make nothing out of something. In the little hours of the night every move from place to place was an enormous human jump, an increase of paying for the privilege of slower and slower motion.

He remembered thousand-franc notes given to an orchestra for playing a single number, hundred-franc notes tossed to a doorman for calling a cab.

But it hadn't been given for nothing.

It had been given, even the most wildly squandered sum, as an offering to destiny that he might not remember the things most worth remembering, the things that now he would always remember—his child taken from his control, his wife escaped to a grave in Vermont.

In the glare of a *brasserie* a woman spoke to him. He bought her some eggs and coffee, and then, eluding her encouraging stare, gave her a twenty-franc note and took a taxi to his hotel.

II

He woke upon a fine fall day—football weather. The depression of yesterday was gone and he liked the people on the streets. At noon he sat opposite Honoria at Le Grand Vatel, the only restaurant he could think of not reminiscent of champagne dinners and long luncheons that began at two and ended in a blurred and vague twilight.

"Now, how about vegetables? Oughtn't you to have some vegetables?"

"Well, yes."

"Here's *epinards* and *chou-fleur* and carrots and *haricots.*"

"I'd like *chou-fleur.*"

"Wouldn't you like to have two vegetables?"

"I usually only have one at lunch."

The waiter was pretending to be inordinately fond of children. "*Qu'elle est mignonne, la petite! Elle parle exactement comme une francaise.*"

"How about dessert? Shall we wait and see?"

The waiter disappeared. Honoria looked at her father expectantly.

"What are we going to do?"

"First, we're going to that toy store in the Rue Saint-Honoré and buy you anything you like. And then we're going to the vaudeville at the Empire."

She hesitated. "I like it about the vaudeville, but not the toy store."

"Why not?"

"Well, you brought me this doll." She had it with her. "And I've got lots of things. And we're not rich any more, are we?"

"We never were. But today you are to have anything you want."

"All right," she agreed resignedly.

When there had been her mother and a French nurse he had been inclined to be strict; now he extended himself, reached out for a new tolerance; he must be both parents to her and not shut any of her out of communication.

"I want to get to know you," he said gravely. "First let me introduce myself. My name is Charles J. Wales, of Prague."

"Oh, daddy!" her voice cracked with laughter.

"And who are you, please?" he persisted, and she accepted a rôle immediately: "Honoria Wales, Rue Palatine, Paris."

"Married or single?"

"No, not married. Single."

He indicated the doll. "But I see you have a child, madame."

Unwilling to disinherit it, she took it to her heart and thought quickly: "Yes, I've been married, but I'm not married now. My husband is dead."

He went on quickly, "And the child's name?"

"Simone. That's after my best friend at school."

"I'm very pleased that you're doing so well at school."

"I'm third this month," she boasted. "Elsie"—that was her cousin—"is only about eighteenth, and Richard is about at the bottom."

"You like Richard and Elsie, don't you?"

"Oh, yes, I like Richard quite well and I like her all right."

Cautiously and casually he asked: "And Aunt Marion and Uncle Lincoln —which do you like best?"

"Oh, Uncle Lincoln, I guess."

He was increasingly aware of her presence. As they came in, a murmur of ". . . adorable" followed them, and now the people at the next table bent all their silences upon her, staring as if she were something no more conscious than a flower.

"Why don't I live with you?" she asked suddenly. "Because mamma's dead?"

"You must stay here and learn more French. It would have been hard for daddy to take care of you so well."

"I don't really need much taking care of any more. I do everything for myself."

Going out of the restaurant, a man and a woman unexpectedly hailed him.

"Well, the old Wales!"

"Hello there, Lorraine. . . . Dunc."

Sudden ghosts out of the past: Duncan Schaeffer, a friend from college. Lorraine Quarrles, a lovely, pale blonde of thirty; one of a crowd who had helped them make months into days in the lavish times of three years ago.

"My husband couldn't come this year," she said, in answer to his question. "We're poor as hell. So he gave me two hundred a month and told me I could do my worst on that. . . . This your little girl?"

"What about coming back and sitting down?" Duncan asked.

"Can't do it." He was glad for an excuse. As always, he felt Lorraine's passionate, provocative attraction, but his own rhythm was different now.

"Well, how about dinner?" she asked.

"I'm not free. Give me your address and let me call you."

"Charlie, I believe you're sober," she said judicially. "I honestly believe he's sober, Dunc. Pinch him and see if he's sober."

Charlie indicated Honoria with his head. They both laughed.

"What's your address?" said Duncan sceptically.

He hesitated, unwilling to give the name of his hotel.

"I'm not settled yet. I'd better call you. We're going to see the vaudeville at the Empire."

"There! That's what I want to do," Lorraine said. "I want to see some clowns and acrobats and jugglers. That's just what we'll do, Dunc."

"We've got to do an errand first," said Charlie. "Perhaps we'll see you there."

"All right, you snob. . . . Good-by, beautiful little girl."

"Good-by."

Honoria bobbed politely.

Somehow, an unwelcome encounter. They liked him because he was functioning, because he was serious; they wanted to see him, because he was stronger than they were now, because they wanted to draw a certain sustenance from his strength.

At the Empire, Honoria proudly refused to sit upon her father's folded coat. She was already an individual with a code of her own, and Charlie was more and more absorbed by the desire of putting a little of himself into her before she crystallized utterly. It was hopeless to try to know her in so short a time.

Between the acts they came upon Duncan and Lorraine in the lobby where the band was playing.

"Have a drink?"

"All right, but not up at the bar. We'll take a table."

"The perfect father."

Listening abstractedly to Lorraine, Charlie watched Honoria's eyes leave their table, and he followed them wistfully about the room, wondering what they saw. He met her glance and she smiled.

"I liked that lemonade," she said.

What had she said? What had he expected? Going home in a taxi afterward, he pulled her over until her head rested against his chest.

"Darling, do you ever think about your mother?"

"Yes, sometimes," she answered vaguely.

"I don't want you to forget her. Have you got a picture of her?"

"Yes, I think so. Anyhow, Aunt Marion has. Why don't you want me to forget her?"

"She loved you very much."

"I loved her too."

They were silent for a moment.

"Daddy, I want to come and live with you," she said suddenly.

His heart leaped; he had wanted it to come like this.

"Aren't you perfectly happy?"

"Yes, but I love you better than anybody. And you love me better than anybody, don't you, now that mummy's dead?"

"Of course I do. But you won't always like me best, honey. You'll grow up and meet somebody your own age and go marry him and forget you ever had a daddy."

"Yes, that's true," she agreed tranquilly.

He didn't go in. He was coming back at nine o'clock and he wanted to keep himself fresh and new for the thing he must say then.

"When you're safe inside, just show yourself in that window."

"All right. Good-by, dads, dads, dads, dads."

He waited in the dark street until she appeared, all warm and glowing, in the window above and kissed her fingers out into the night.

III

They were waiting. Marion sat behind the coffee service in a dignified black dinner dress that just faintly suggested mourning. Lincoln was walking up and down with the animation of one who had already been talking. They were as anxious as he was to get into the question. He opened it almost immediately:

"I suppose you know what I want to see you about—why I really came to Paris."

Marion played with the black stars on her necklace and frowned.

"I'm awfully anxious to have a home," he continued. "And I'm awfully anxious to have Honoria in it. I appreciate your taking in Honoria for her mother's sake, but things have changed now"—he hesitated and then continued more forcibly—"changed radically with me, and I want to ask you to reconsider the matter. It would be silly for me to deny that about three years ago I was acting badly—"

Marion looked up at him with hard eyes.

"—but all that's over. As I told you, I haven't had more than a drink a day for over a year, and I take that drink deliberately, so that the idea of alcohol won't get too big in my imagination. You see the idea?"

"No," said Marion succinctly.

"It's a sort of stint I set myself. It keeps the matter in proportion."

"I get you," said Lincoln. "You don't want to admit it's got any attraction for you."

"Something like that. Sometimes I forget and don't take it. But I try to take it. Anyhow, I couldn't afford to drink in my position. The people I represent are more than satisfied with what I've done, and I'm bringing my sister over from Burlington to keep house for me, and I want awfully to have Honoria too. You know that even when her mother and I weren't getting along well we never let anything that happened touch Honoria. I know she's fond of me and I know I'm able to take care of her and—well, there you are. How do you feel about it?"

He knew that now he would have to take a beating. It would last an hour or two hours, and it would be difficult, but if he modulated his inevitable resentment to the chastened attitude of the reformed sinner, he might win his point in the end.

Keep your temper, he told himself. You don't want to be justified. You want Honoria.

Lincoln spoke first: "We've been talking it over ever since we got your letter last month. We're happy to have Honoria here. She's a dear little thing, and we're glad to be able to help her, but of course that isn't the question—"

Marion interrupted suddenly. "How long are you going to stay sober, Charlie?" she asked.

"Permanently, I hope."

"How can anybody count on that?"

"You know I never did drink heavily until I gave up business and came over here with nothing to do. Then Helen and I began to run around with—"

"Please leave Helen out of it. I can't bear to hear you talk about her like that."

He stared at her grimly, he had never been certain how fond of each other the sisters were in life.

"My drinking only lasted about a year and a half—from the time we came over until I—collapsed."

"It was time enough."

"It was time enough," he agreed.

"My duty is entirely to Helen," she said. "I try to think what she would have wanted me to do. Frankly, from the night you did that terrible thing you haven't really existed for me. I can't help that. She was my sister."

"Yes."

"When she was dying she asked me to look out for Honoria. If you hadn't been in a sanitarium then, it might have helped matters."

He had no answer.

"I'll never in my life be able to forget the morning when Helen knocked at my door, soaked to the skin and shivering, and said you'd locked her out."

Charlie gripped the sides of the chair. This was more difficult than he expected; he wanted to launch out into a long expostulation and explanation, but he only said: "The night I locked her out—" and she interrupted, "I don't feel up to going over that again."

After a moment's silence Lincoln said: "We're getting off the subject. You want Marion to set aside her legal guardianship and give you Honoria. I think the main point for her is whether she has confidence in you or not."

"I don't blame Marion," Charlie said slowly, "but I think she can have entire confidence in me. I had a good record up to three years ago. Of course, it's within human possibilities I might go wrong any time. But if we wait much longer I'll lose Honoria's childhood and my chance for a home." He shook his head, "I'll simply lose her, don't you see?"

"Yes, I see," said Lincoln.

"Why didn't you think of all this before?" Marion asked.

"I suppose I did, from time to time, but Helen and I were getting along badly. When I consented to the guardianship, I was flat on my back in a sanitarium and the market had cleaned me out. I knew I'd acted badly, and I thought if it would bring any peace to Helen, I'd agree to anything. But now it's different. I'm functioning, I'm behaving damn well, so far as—"

"Please don't swear at me," Marion said.

He looked at her, startled. With each remark the force of her dislike became more and more apparent. She had built up all her fear of life into one wall and faced it toward him. This trivial reproof was possibly the result of some trouble with the cook several hours before. Charlie became increasingly alarmed at leaving Honoria in this atmosphere of hostility against himself; sooner or later it would come out, in a word here, a shake of the head there, and some of that distrust would be irrevocably implanted in Honoria. But he pulled his temper down out of his face and shut it up inside him; he had won a point, for Lincoln realized the absurdity of Marion's remark and asked her lightly since when she had objected to the word "damn."

"Another thing," Charlie said: "I'm able to give her certain advantages now. I'm going to take a French governess to Prague with me. I've got a lease on a new apartment—"

He stopped, realizing that he was blundering. They couldn't be expected to accept with equanimity the fact that his income was again twice as large as their own.

"I suppose you can give her more luxuries than we can," said Marion. "When you were throwing away money we were living along watching every ten francs. . . . I suppose you'll start doing it again."

"Oh, no," he said. "I've learned. I worked hard for ten years, you know —until I got lucky in the market, like so many people. Terribly lucky. It didn't seem any use working any more, so I quit. It won't happen again."

There was a long silence. All of them felt their nerves straining, and for the first time in a year Charlie wanted a drink. He was sure now that Lincoln Peters wanted him to have his child.

Marion shuddered suddenly; part of her saw that Charlie's feet were planted on the earth now, and her own maternal feeling recognized the naturalness of his desire; but she had lived for a long time with a prejudice—a prejudice founded on a curious disbelief in her sister's happiness, and which, in the shock of one terrible night, had turned to hatred for him. It had all happened at a point in her life where the discouragement of ill health and adverse circumstances made it necessary for her to believe in tangible villainy and a tangible villain.

"I can't help what I think!" she cried out suddenly. "How much you were responsible for Helen's death, I don't know. It's something you'll have to square with your own conscience."

An electric current of agony surged through him; for a moment he was almost on his feet, an unuttered sound echoing in his throat. He hung on to himself for a moment, another moment.

"Hold on there," said Lincoln uncomfortably. "I never thought you were responsible for that."

"Helen died of heart trouble," Charlie said dully.

"Yes, heart trouble." Marion spoke as if the phrase had another meaning for her.

Then, in the flatness that followed her outburst, she saw him plainly and she knew he had somehow arrived at control over the situation. Glancing at her husband, she found no help from him, and as abruptly as if it were a matter of no importance, she threw up the sponge.

"Do what you like!" she cried, springing up from her chair. "She's your child. I'm not the person to stand in your way. I think if it were my child I'd rather see her—" She managed to check herself. "You two decide it. I can't stand this. I'm sick. I'm going to bed."

She hurried from the room; after a moment Lincoln said:

"This has been a hard day for her. You know how strongly she feels—" His voice was almost apologetic: "When a woman gets an idea in her head."

"Of course."

"It's going to be all right. I think she sees now that you—can provide for the child, and so we can't very well stand in your way or Honoria's way."

"Thank you, Lincoln."

"I'd better go along and see how she is."

"I'm going."

He was still trembling when he reached the street, but a walk down the Rue Bonaparte to the quais set him up, and as he crossed the Seine, fresh and new by the quai lamps, he felt exultant. But back in his room he couldn't sleep. The image of Helen haunted him. Helen whom he had loved so until they had senselessly begun to abuse each other's love, tear it into shreds. On that terrible February night that Marion remembered so vividly, a slow quarrel had gone on for hours. There was a scene at the Florida, and then he attempted to take her home, and then she kissed young Webb at a table; after that there was what she had hysterically said. When he arrived home alone he turned the key in the lock in wild anger. How could he know she would arrive an hour later alone, that there would be a snowstorm in which she wandered about in slippers, too confused to find a taxi? Then the aftermath, her escaping pneumonia by a miracle, and all the attendant horror. They were "reconciled," but that was the beginning of the end, and Marion, who had seen with her own eyes and who imagined it to be one of many scenes from her sister's martyrdom, never forgot.

Going over it again brought Helen nearer, and in the white, soft light that steals upon half sleep near morning he found himself talking to her again. She said that he was perfectly right about Honoria and that she wanted Honoria to be with him. She said she was glad he was being good and doing better. She said a lot of other things—very friendly things—but she was in a swing in a white dress, and swinging faster and faster all the time, so that at the end he could not hear clearly all that she said.

IV

He woke up feeling happy. The door of the world was open again. He made plans, visits, futures for Honoria and himself, but suddenly he grew sad, remembering all the plans he and Helen had made. She had not planned to die. The present was the thing—work to do and someone to love. But not to love too much, for he knew the injury that a father can do to a daughter or a mother to a son by attaching them too closely: afterward, out in the world, the child would seek in the marriage partner the same blind tenderness and, failing probably to find it, turn against love and life.

It was another bright, crisp day. He called Lincoln Peters at the bank where he worked and asked if he could count on taking Honoria when he left for Prague. Lincoln agreed that there was no reason for delay. One thing—the legal guardianship. Marion wanted to retain that a while longer. She was upset by the whole matter, and it would oil things if she felt that the situation was still in her control for another year. Charlie agreed, wanting only the tangible, visible child.

Then the question of a governess. Charlie sat in a gloomy agency and talked to a cross Béarnaise and to a buxom Breton peasant, neither of whom he could have endured. There were others whom he would see tomorrow.

He lunched with Lincoln Peters at Griffons, trying to keep down his exultation.

"There's nothing quite like your own child," Lincoln said. "But you understand how Marion feels too."

"She's forgotten how hard I worked for seven years there," Charlie said. "She just remembers one night."

"There's another thing." Lincoln hesitated. "While you and Helen were tearing around Europe throwing money away, we were just getting along. I didn't touch any of the prosperity because I never got ahead enough to carry anything but my insurance. I think Marion felt there was some kind of injustice in it—you not even working toward the end, and getting richer and richer."

"It went just as quick as it came," said Charlie.

"Yes, a lot of it stayed in the hands of *chasseurs* and saxophone players and maîtres d'hôtel—well, the big party's over now. I just said that to explain Marion's feeling about those crazy years. If you drop in about six o'clock tonight before Marion's too tired, we'll settle the details on the spot."

Back at his hotel, Charlie found a *pneumatique* that had been redirected from the Ritz bar where Charlie had left his address for the purpose of finding a certain man.

> DEAR CHARLIE: You were so strange when we saw you the other day that I wondered if I did something to offend you. If so, I'm not conscious of it. In fact, I have thought about you too much for the last year, and it's always been in the back of my mind that I might see you if I came over here. We *did* have such good times that crazy spring, like the night you and I stole the butcher's tricycle, and the time we tried to call on the president and you had the old derby rim and the wire cane. Everybody seems so old lately, but I don't feel old a bit. Couldn't we get together some time today for old time's sake? I've got a vile hangover for the moment, but will be feeling better this afternoon and will look for you about five in the sweat-shop at the Ritz.
>
> Always devotedly,
> LORRAINE.

His first feeling was one of awe that he had actually, in his mature years, stolen a tricycle and pedalled Lorraine all over the Étoile between the small hours and dawn. In retrospect it was a nightmare. Locking out Helen didn't fit in with any other act of his life, but the tricycle incident did—it was one of many. How many weeks or months of dissipation to arrive at that condition of utter irresponsibility?

He tried to picture how Lorraine had appeared to him then—very attractive; Helen was unhappy about it, though she said nothing. Yesterday, in the restaurant, Lorraine had seemed trite, blurred, worn away. He emphatically did not want to see her, and he was glad Alix had not given away his hotel address. It was a relief to think, instead, of Honoria, to think of Sundays spent with her and of saying good morning to her and of knowing she was there in his house at night, drawing her breath in the darkness.

At five he took a taxi and bought presents for all the Peters—a piquant cloth doll, a box of Roman soldiers, flowers for Marion, big linen handkerchiefs for Lincoln.

He saw, when he arrived in the apartment, that Marion had accepted the inevitable. She greeted him now as though he were a recalcitrant member of the family, rather than a menacing outsider. Honoria had been told she was going; Charlie was glad to see that her tact made her conceal her excessive happiness. Only on his lap did she whisper her delight and the question "When?" before she slipped away with the other children.

He and Marion were alone for a minute in the room, and on an impulse he spoke out boldly:

"Family quarrels are bitter things. They don't go according to any rules. They're not like aches or wounds; they're more like splits in the skin that won't heal because there's not enough material. I wish you and I could be on better terms."

"Some things are hard to forget," she answered. "It's a question of confidence." There was no answer to this and presently she asked, "When do you propose to take her?"

"As soon as I can get a governess. I hoped the day after tomorrow."

"That's impossible. I've got to get her things in shape. Not before Saturday."

He yielded. Coming back into the room, Lincoln offered him a drink.

"I'll take my daily whisky," he said.

It was warm here, it was a home, people together by a fire. The children felt very safe and important; the mother and father were serious, watchful. They had things to do for the children more important than his visit here. A spoonful of medicine was, after all, more important than the strained relations between Marion and himself. They were not dull people, but they were very much in the grip of life and circumstances. He wondered if he couldn't do something to get Lincoln out of his rut at the bank.

A long peal at the door-bell; the *bonne de toute faire* passed through and down the corridor, closely followed by the voices, which developed under the light into Duncan Schaeffer and Lorraine Quarrles.

They were gay, they were hilarious, they were roaring with laughter. For a moment Charlie was astounded; unable to understand how they ferreted out the Peters' address.

"Ah-h-h!" Duncan wagged his finger roguishly at Charlie. "Ah-h-h!"

They both slid down another cascade of laughter. Anxious and at a loss, Charlie shook hands with them quickly and presented them to Lincoln and Marion. Marion nodded, scarcely speaking. She had drawn back a step toward the fire; her little girl stood beside her, and Marion put an arm about her shoulder.

With growing annoyance at the intrusion, Charlie waited for them to explain themselves. After some concentration Duncan said:

"We came to invite you out to dinner. Lorraine and I insist that all this shishi, cagey business 'bout your address got to stop."

Charlie came closer to them, as if to force them backward down the corridor.

"Sorry, but I can't. Tell me where you'll be and I'll phone you in half an hour."

This made no impression. Lorraine sat down suddenly on the side of a chair, and focusing her eyes on Richard, cried, "Oh, what a nice little boy! Come here, little boy." Richard glanced at his mother, but did not move. With a perceptible shrug of her shoulders, Lorraine turned back to Charlie:

"Come and dine. Sure your cousins won' mine. See you so sel'om. Or solemn."

"I can't," said Charlie sharply. "You two have dinner and I'll phone you."

Her voice became suddenly unpleasant. "All right, we'll go. But I remember once when you hammered on my door at four A.M. I was enough of a good sport to give you a drink. Come on, Dunc."

Still in slow motion, with blurred, angry faces, with uncertain feet, they retired along the corridor.

"Good night," Charlie said.

"Good night!" responded Lorraine emphatically.

When he went back into the salon Marion had not moved, only now her son was standing in the circle of her other arm. Lincoln was still swinging Honoria back and forth like a pendulum from side to side.

"What an outrage!" Charlie broke out. "What an absolute outrage!"

Neither of them answered. Charlie dropped into an armchair, picked up his drink, set it down again and said:

"People I haven't seen for two years having the colossal nerve—"

He broke off. Marion had made the sound "Oh!" in one swift, furious breath, turned her body from him with a jerk and left the room.

Lincoln set down Honoria carefully.

"You children go in and start your soup," he said, and when they obeyed, he said to Charlie:

"Marion's not well and she can't stand shocks. That kind of people make her really physically sick."

"I didn't tell them to come here. They wormed your name out of somebody. They deliberately—"

"Well, it's too bad. It doesn't help matters. Excuse me a minute."

Left alone, Charlie sat tense in his chair. In the next room he could hear the children eating, talking in monosyllables, already oblivious to the scene between their elders. He heard a murmur of conversation from a farther room and then the ticking bell of a telephone receiver picked up, and in a panic he moved to the other side of the room and out of earshot.

In a minute Lincoln came back. "Look here, Charlie. I think we'd better call off dinner for tonight. Marion's in bad shape."

"Is she angry with me?"

"Sort of," he said, almost roughly. "She's not strong and—"

"You mean she's changed her mind about Honoria?"

"She's pretty bitter right now. I don't know. You phone me at the bank tomorrow."

"I wish you'd explain to her I never dreamed these people would come here. I'm just as sore as you are."

"I couldn't explain anything to her now."

Charlie got up. He took his coat and hat and started down the corridor. Then he opened the door of the dining room and said in a strange voice, "Good night, children."

Honoria rose and ran around the table to hug him.

"Good night, sweetheart," he said vaguely, and then trying to make his voice more tender, trying to conciliate something, "Good night, dear children."

V

Charlie went directly to the Ritz bar with the furious idea of finding Lorraine and Duncan, but they were not there, and he realized that in any case there was nothing he could do. He had not touched his drink at the Peters', and now he ordered a whisky-and-soda. Paul came over to say hello.

"It's a great change," he said sadly. "We do about half the business we did. So many fellows I hear about back in the States lost everything, maybe not in the first crash, but then in the second. Your friend George Hardt lost every cent, I hear. Are you back in the States?"

"No, I'm in business in Prague."

"I heard that you lost a lot in the crash."

"I did," and he added grimly, "but I lost everything I wanted in the boom."

"Selling short?"

"Something like that."

Again the memory of those days swept over him like a nightmare—the people they had met travelling; the people who couldn't add a row of figures or speak a coherent sentence. The little man Helen had consented to dance with at the ship's party, who had insulted her ten feet from the table; the women and girls carried screaming with drinks or drugs out of public places—

—The men who locked their wives out in the snow, because the snow of twenty-nine wasn't real snow. If you didn't want it to be snow, you just paid some money.

He went to the phone and called the Peters' apartment; Lincoln answered.

"I called up because this thing is on my mind. Has Marion said anything definite?"

"Marion's sick," Lincoln answered shortly. "I know this thing isn't altogether your fault, but I can't have her go to pieces about it. I'm afraid we'll have to let it slide for six months; I can't take the chance of working her up to this state again."

"I see."

"I'm sorry, Charlie."

He went back to his table. His whisky glass was empty, but he shook his head when Alix looked at it questioningly. There wasn't much he could do now except send Honoria some things; he would send her a lot of things tomorrow. He thought rather angrily that this was just money—he had given so many people money. . . .

"No, no more," he said to another waiter. "What do I owe you?"

He would come back some day; they couldn't make him pay forever. But he wanted his child, and nothing was much good now, beside that fact. He wasn't young any more, with a lot of nice thoughts and dreams to have by himself. He was absolutely sure Helen wouldn't have wanted him to be so alone.

WILLIAM FAULKNER

1897–1962

Faulkner set out to make the modern South in all its complexity the subject of his fiction. In the South's history, in its heat, its chivalric code (set side-by-side with carpetbagging trickery), its racism violently and guiltily maintained, its corruption of the land, Faulkner saw the terms of modern life. He invented a mythical county, Yoknapatawpha, Mississippi, that is a distillation of the culture he perceived. As he wrote his stories and novels about Yoknapatawpha County in the thirties and forties, the Faulkner countryside became peopled with families whose past was known, whose adventures intersected, whose imaginary land could be mapped. Faulkner never attempted to create a saga that had to be read sequentially, though obviously the more the reader knows the richer his experience.

Faulkner grew up listening to tales. His father's house was the center for relatives who enjoyed exhibiting their story-telling talents. They talked about local happenings, but especially about their family's past. And indeed there was much romance in that past. Before the Civil War Faulkner's great-grandfather had made a fortune and established himself as one of the great men in Mississippi. The Civil War helped to confirm his dedication to aristocratic values: honor, loyalty, manliness, the duty to lead. A colonel in the Confederate army, he on two occasions shot down plotters against his life. (He was finally killed, long after the war, in a duel.)

Faulkner's grandfather was president of a small railroad that *his* father had built, and later of the bank in the county-seat town of Oxford. His son, Faulkner's father, inherited a much diminished fortune. He worked on the railroad for a while and later became the secretary and business manager of the University of Mississippi. Faulkner himself spurned banking and the University, and in World War I joined the British Air Force. Upon his return he attended the University for a short time; but he had no taste for academic subjects, preferring the passionate and often high-spirited and comic life of the common people in the town.

As a young man he thought of himself as a poet, but partly under the influence of short-story writer Sherwood Anderson, whom he knew in New

Orleans in the mid-twenties, he began to combine his gift for telling a good tale, his keen ear for all kinds of speech, and his ability to sustain a mood of passionate intensity into increasingly fine fiction. In 1929 he published *The Sound and the Fury,* a novel of extraordinary virtuosity and brilliance, certainly in its story-telling technique the most original, and perhaps the best American novel of the twentieth century. During the thirties he wrote his other great novels—*As I Lay Dying* (1930), *Light in August* (1932), and *Absalom! Absalom!* (1936)—as well as many fine short stories.

In talking about his fiction, Faulkner always emphasized the backwoods quality of his part of Mississippi, not at all the rich plantation country of movie landscapes. He pointed out that his region was made up largely of settlers who had moved west from the hills of Tennessee and Kentucky, who lacked the Europeanized culture of trading centers along the river—like Natchez, and the major cities of Memphis and New Orleans. The region's only wealth was the land itself, a moderately good soil, stands of timber, and millions of acres of virgin wilderness. Its society offered few models of Old World civilization, and consequently there was a special admiration of great men, like Colonel Sartoris, who put their own distinctive stamp on the region. Faulkner's interest in heroism was stimulated by the tales he listened to, the living legend of the Civil War, and the special receptivity of his country to the hero. He read Greek tragedy avidly, and in general his taste in literature ran heavily toward the Old Testament, and toward stories of heroic overreaching like *Moby Dick,* "Heart of Darkness," *War and Peace, The Brothers Karamazov,* and Whitman's "Song of Myself." At the same time he learned to love precision and economy in language. He read *Madame Bovary* over and over again (he was fluent in French), and in addition the short stories of Chekhov and the poems of Keats.

So well does Faulkner present the tensions that exist in his Mississippi that the very atmosphere of his fiction is charged with them. In the "bloody twilight" of "Dry September" the human voice of the barber doubting that Will Mayes could have committed the crime is heard against other stupid, insistent, and finally engulfing voices of the town. Out of the speakers' various twisted and misdirected values arises an inevitable community violence, one that cannot be checked either by the barber's horror or by Will's moving expression of frightened bewilderment. Afterward the consequences linger in the suffocating air—a common guilt that cannot be denied, nor accepted either, without terrible personal distortion.

Though Faulkner himself was a white man who had necessarily to understand the black experience from the outside, he was extremely sensitive to relations between the races. In a South that seemed to him remarkable for having sold out its proclaimed values, he saw in the lives of many blacks a forging-out of the only honest terms by which one can live. And in the point of view of many southern whites, charged with the guilt of generations of slavery, he recognized a working-out of a fundamental curse on the South.

Like Hemingway, Faulkner's major work was behind him before World War II, though it was in the fifties that the two writers gained the world's recognition of their preeminence, the Nobel Prize for Literature. Faulkner's acceptance speech in 1950 is a notable assertion of human values in the postwar era.

Dry September

I

Through the bloody September twilight, aftermath of sixty-two rainless days, it had gone like a fire in dry grass—the rumor, the story, whatever it was. Something about Miss Minnie Cooper and a Negro. Attacked, insulted, frightened: none of them, gathered in the barber shop on that Saturday evening where the ceiling fan stirred, without freshening it, the vitiated air, sending back upon them, in recurrent surges of stale pomade and lotion, their own stale breath and odors, knew exactly what had happened.

"Except it wasn't Will Mayes," a barber said. He was a man of middle age; a thin, sand-colored man with a mild face, who was shaving a client. "I know Will Mayes. He's a good nigger. And I know Miss Minnie Cooper, too."

"What do you know about her?" a second barber said.

"Who is she?" the client said. "A young girl?"

"No," the barber said. "She's about forty, I reckon. She aint married. That's why I dont believe—"

"Believe, hell!" a hulking youth in a sweat-stained silk shirt said. "Wont you take a white woman's word before a nigger's?"

"I dont believe Will Mayes did it," the barber said. "I know Will Mayes."

"Maybe you know who did it, then. Maybe you already got him out of town, you damn niggerlover."

"I dont believe anybody did anything. I dont believe anything happened. I leave it to you fellows if them ladies that get old without getting married dont have notions that a man cant—"

"Then you are a hell of a white man," the client said. He moved under the cloth. The youth had sprung to his feet.

"You dont?" he said. "Do you accuse a white woman of lying?"

The barber held the razor poised above the half-risen client. He did not look around.

"It's this durn weather," another said. "It's enough to make a man do anything. Even to her."

Nobody laughed. The barber said in his mild, stubborn tone: "I aint accusing nobody of nothing. I just know and you fellows know how a woman that never—"

"You damn niggerlover!" the youth said.

"Shut up, Butch," another said. "We'll get the facts in plenty of time to act."

"Who is? Who's getting them?" the youth said. "Facts, hell! I—"

"You're a fine white man," the client said. "Aint you?" In his frothy beard he looked like a desert rat in the moving pictures. "You can tell them, Jack," he said to the youth. "If there aint any white men in this town you can count on me, even if I ain't only a drummer and a stranger."

"That's right, boys," the barber said. "Find out the truth first. I know Will Mayes."

"Well, by God!" the youth shouted. "To think that a white man in this town—"

"Shut up, Butch," the second speaker said. "We got plenty of time."

The client sat up. He looked at the speaker. "Do you claim that anything excuses a nigger attacking a white woman? Do you mean to tell me you are a white man and you'll stand for it? You better go back North where you came from. The South dont want your kind here."

"North what?" the second said. "I was born and raised in this town."

"Well, by God!" the youth said. He looked about with a strained, baffled gaze, as if he was trying to remember what it was he wanted to say or to do. He drew his sleeve across his sweating face. "Damn if I'm going to let a white woman—"

"You tell them, Jack," the drummer said. "By God, if they—"

The screen door crashed open. A man stood in the floor, his feet apart and his heavy-set body poised easily. His white shirt was open at the throat; he wore a felt hat. His hot, bold glance swept the group. His name was McLendon. He had commanded troops at the front in France and had been decorated for valor.

"Well," he said, "are you going to sit there and let a black son rape a white woman on the streets of Jefferson?"

Butch sprang up again. The silk of his shirt clung flat to his heavy shoulders. At each armpit was a dark halfmoon. "That's what I been telling them! That's what I—"

"Did it really happen?" a third said. "This aint the first man scare she ever had, like Hawkshaw says. Wasn't there something about a man on the kitchen roof, watching her undress, about a year ago?"

"What?" the client said. "What's that?" The barber had been slowly forcing him back into the chair; he arrested himself reclining, his head lifted, the barber still pressing him down.

McLendon whirled on the third speaker. "Happen? What the hell difference does it make? Are you going to let the black sons get away with it until one really does it?"

"That's what I'm telling them!" Butch shouted. He cursed, long and steady, pointless.

"Here, here," a fourth said. "Not so loud. Dont talk so loud."

"Sure," McLendon said; "no talking necessary at all. I've done my talking. Who's with me?" He poised on the balls of his feet, roving his gaze.

The barber held the drummer's face down, the razor poised. "Find out the facts first, boys. I know Willy Mayes. It wasn't him. Let's get the sheriff and do this thing right."

McLendon whirled upon him his furious, rigid face. The barber did not look away. They looked like men of different races. The other barbers had ceased also above their prone clients. "You mean to tell me," McLendon said, "that you'd take a nigger's word before a white woman's? Why, you damn niggerloving—"

The third speaker rose and grasped McLendon's arm; he too had been a soldier. "Now, now. Let's figure this thing out. Who knows anything about what really happened?"

"Figure out hell!" McLendon jerked his arm free. "All that're with me get up from there. The ones that aint—" he roved his gaze, dragging his sleeve across his face.

Three men rose. The drummer in the chair sat up. "Here," he said, jerking at the cloth about his neck; "get this rag off me. I'm with him. I dont live here, but by God, if our mothers and wives and sisters—" He smeared the cloth over his face and flung it to the floor. McLendon stood in the floor and cursed the others. Another rose and moved toward him. The remainder sat uncomfortable, not looking at one another, then one by one they rose and joined him.

The barber picked the cloth from the floor. He began to fold it neatly. "Boys, dont do that. Will Mayes never done it. I know."

"Come on," McLendon said. He whirled. From his hip pocket protruded the butt of a heavy automatic pistol. They went out. The screen door crashed behind them reverberant in the dead air.

The barber wiped the razor carefully and swiftly, and put it away, and ran to the rear, and took his hat from the wall. "I'll be back as soon as I can," he said to the other barbers. "I cant let—" He went out, running. The two other barbers followed him to the door and caught it on the rebound, leaning out and looking up the street after him. The air was flat and dead. It had a metallic taste at the base of the tongue.

"What can he do?" the first said. The second one was saying "Jees Christ, Jees Christ" under his breath. "I'd just as lief be Will Mayes as Hawk, if he gets McLendon riled."

"Jees Christ, Jees Christ," the second whispered.

"You reckon he really done it to her?" the first said.

II

She was thirty-eight or thirty-nine. She lived in a small frame house with her invalid mother and a thin, sallow, unflagging aunt, where each morning between ten and eleven she would appear on the porch in a lace-trimmed boudoir cap, to sit swinging in the porch swing until noon. After dinner she lay down for a while, until the afternoon began to cool. Then, in one of the three or four new voile dresses which she had each summer, she would go downtown to spend the afternoon in the stores with the other ladies, where they would handle the goods and haggle over the prices in cold, immediate voices, without any intention of buying.

She was of comfortable people—not the best in Jefferson, but good people enough—and she was still on the slender side of ordinary looking, with a bright, faintly haggard manner and dress. When she was young she had had a slender, nervous body and a sort of hard vivacity which had enabled her for a time to ride upon the crest of the town's social life as exemplified by the high school party and church social period of her contemporaries while still children enough to be unclass-conscious.

She was the last to realize that she was losing ground; that those among whom she had been a little brighter and louder flame than any other were beginning to learn the pleasure of snobbery—male—and retaliation—female. That was when her face began to wear that bright, haggard look. She still carried it to parties on shadowy porticoes and summer lawns, like a mask or a flag, with that bafflement of furious repudiation of truth in her eyes. One evening at a party she heard a boy and two girls, all schoolmates, talking. She never accepted another invitation.

She watched the girls with whom she had grown up as they married and got homes and children, but no man ever called on her steadily until the children of the other girls had been calling her "aunty" for several years, the while their mothers told them in bright voices about how popular Aunt Minnie had been as a girl. Then the town began to see her driving on Sunday afternoons with the cashier in the bank. He was a widower of about forty—a high-colored man, smelling always faintly of the barber shop or of whisky. He owned the first automobile in town, a red runabout; Minnie had the first motoring bonnet and veil the town ever saw. Then the town began to say: "Poor Minnie." "But she is old enough to take care of herself," others said. That was when she began to ask her old schoolmates that their children call her "cousin" instead of "aunty."

It was twelve years now since she had been relegated into adultery by public opinion, and eight years since the cashier had gone to a Memphis bank, returning for one day each Christmas, which he spent at an annual bachelors' party at a hunting club on the river. From behind their curtains the neighbors would see the party pass, and during the over-the-way Chirstmas day visiting they would tell her about him, about how well he looked, and how they heard that he was prospering in the city, watching with bright, secret eyes her haggard, bright face. Usually by that hour there would be the scent of whisky on her breath. It was supplied her by a youth, a clerk at the soda fountain: "Sure; I buy it for the old gal. I reckon she's entitled to a little fun."

Her mother kept to her room altogether now; the gaunt aunt ran the house. Against that background Minnie's bright dresses, her idle and empty days, had a quality of furious unreality. She went out in the evenings only with women now, neighbors, to the moving pictures. Each afternoon she dressed in one of the new dresses and went downtown alone, where her young "cousins" were already strolling in the late afternoons with their delicate, silken heads and thin, awkward arms and conscious hips, clinging to one another or shrieking and giggling with paired boys in the soda fountain when she passed and went on along the serried store fronts, in the doors of which the sitting and lounging men did not even follow her with their eyes any more.

III

The barber went swiftly up the street where the sparse lights, insect-swirled, glared in rigid and violent suspension in the lifeless air. The day had died in a pall of dust; above the darkened square, shrouded by the spent dust, the sky was as clear as the inside of a brass bell. Below the east was a rumor of the twice-waxed moon.

When he overtook them McLendon and three others were getting into a car parked in an alley. McLendon stooped his thick head, peering out beneath the top. "Changed your mind, did you?" he said. "Damn good thing; by God, tomorrow when this town hears about how you talked tonight—"

"Now, now," the other ex-soldier said. "Hawkshaw's all right. Come on, Hawk; jump in."

"Will Mayes never done it, boys," the barber said. "If anybody done it. Why, you all know well as I do there aint any town where they got better niggers than us. And you know how a lady will kind of think things about men when there aint any reason to, and Miss Minnie anyway—"

"Sure, sure," the soldier said. "We're just going to talk to him a little; that's all."

"Talk hell!" Butch said. "When we're through with the—"

"Shut up, for God's sake!" the soldier said. "Do you want everybody in town—"

"Tell them, by God!" McLendon said. "Tell everyone of the sons that'll let a white woman—"

"Let's go; let's go: here's the other car." The second car slid squealing out of a cloud of dust at the alley mouth. McLendon started his car and took the lead. Dust lay like fog in the street. The street lights hung nimbused as in water. They drove on out of town.

A rutted lane turned at right angles. Dust hung above it too, and above all the land. The dark bulk of the ice plant, where the Negro Mayes was night watchman, rose against the sky. "Better stop here, hadn't we?" the soldier said. McLendon did not reply. He hurled the car up and slammed to a stop, the headlights glaring on the blank wall.

"Listen here, boys," the barber said; "if he's here, dont that prove he never done it? Dont it? If it was him, he would run. Dont you see he would?" The second car came up and stopped. McLendon got down; Butch sprang down beside him. "Listen, boys," the barber said.

"Cut the lights off!" McLendon said. The breathless dark rushed down. There was no sound in it save their lungs as they sought air in the parched dust in which for two months they had lived; then the diminishing crunch of McLendon's and Butch's feet, and a moment later McLendon's voice:

"Will! . . . Will!"

Below the east the wan hemorrhage of the moon increased. It heaved above the ridge, silvering the air, the dust, so that they seemed to breathe, live, in a bowl of molten lead. There was no sound of nightbird nor insect, no sound save their breathing and a faint ticking of contracting metal about the cars. Where their bodies touched one another they seemed to sweat dryly, for no more moisture came. "Christ!" a voice said; "let's get out of here."

But they didn't move until vague noises began to grow out of the darkness ahead; then they got out and waited tensely in the breathless dark. There was another sound: a blow, a hissing expulsion of breath and McLendon cursing in undertone. They stood a moment longer, then they ran forward. They ran in a stumbling clump, as though they were fleeing something. "Kill him, kill the son," a voice whispered. McLendon flung them back.

"Not here," he said. "Get him into the car." "Kill him, kill the black son!" the voice murmured. They dragged the Negro to the car. The barber had waited beside the car. He could feel himself sweating and he knew he was going to be sick at the stomach.

"What is it, captains?" the Negro said. "I aint done nothing. 'Fore God, Mr John." Someone produced handcuffs. They worked busily about the Negro as though he were a post, quiet, intent, getting in one another's way. He submitted to the handcuffs, looking swiftly and constantly from dim face to dim face. "Who's here, captains?" he said, leaning to peer into the faces until they could feel his breath and smell his sweaty reek. He spoke a name or two. "What you all say I done, Mr John?"

McLendon jerked the car door open. "Get in!" he said.

The Negro did not move. "What you all going to do with me, Mr John? I aint done nothing. White folks, captains, I aint done nothing: I swear 'fore God." He called another name.

"Get in!" McLendon said. He struck the Negro. The others expelled their breath in a dry hissing and struck him with random blows and he whirled and cursed them, and swept his manacled hands across their faces and slashed the barber upon the mouth, and the barber struck him also. "Get him in there," McLendon said. They pushed at him. He ceased struggling and got in and sat quietly as the others took their places. He sat between the barber and the soldier, drawing his limbs in so as not to touch them, his eyes going swiftly and constantly from face to face. Butch clung to the running board. The car moved on. The barber nursed his mouth with his handkerchief.

"What's the matter, Hawk?" the soldier said.

"Nothing," the barber said. They regained the highroad and turned away from town. The second car dropped back out of the dust. They went on, gaining speed; the final fringe of houses dropped behind.

"Goddamn, he stinks!" the soldier said.

"We'll fix that," the drummer in front beside McLendon said. On the running board Butch cursed into the hot rush of air. The barber leaned suddenly forward and touched McLendon's arm.

"Let me out, John," he said.

"Jump out, niggerlover," McLendon said without turning his head. He drove swiftly. Behind them the sourceless lights of the second car glared in the dust. Presently McLendon turned into a narrow road. It was rutted with disuse. It led back to an abandoned brick kiln—a series of reddish mounds and weed- and vine-choked vats without bottom. It had been used for pasture once, until one day the owner missed one of his mules: Although he prodded carefully in the vats with a long pole, he could not even find the bottom of them.

"John," the barber said.

"Jump out, then," McLendon said, hurling the car along the ruts. Beside the barber the Negro spoke:

"Mr. Henry."

The barber sat forward. The narrow tunnel of the road rushed up and past. Their motion was like an extinct furnace blast: Cooler, but utterly dead. The car bounded from rut to rut.

"Mr. Henry," the Negro said.

The barber began to tug furiously at the door. "Look out, there!" the soldier said, but the barber had already kicked the door open and swung onto the running board. The soldier leaned across the Negro and grasped at him, but he had already jumped. The car went on without checking speed.

The impetus hurled him crashing through dust-sheathed weeds, into the ditch. Dust puffed about him, and in a thin, vicious crackling of sapless stems he lay choking and retching until the second car passed and died away. Then he rose and limped on until he reached the highroad and turned toward town, brushing at his clothes with his hands. The moon was higher, riding high and clear of the dust at last, and after a while the town began to glare beneath the dust. He went on, limping. Presently he heard cars and the glow of them grew in the dust behind him and he left the road and crouched again in the weeds until they passed. McLendon's car came last now. There were four people in it and Butch was not on the running board.

They went on; the dust swallowed them; the glare and the sound died away. The dust of them hung for a while, but soon the eternal dust absorbed it again. The barber climbed back onto the road and limped on toward town.

IV

As she dressed for supper on that Saturday evening, her own flesh felt like fever. Her hands trembled among the hooks and eyes, and her eyes had a feverish look, and her hair swirled crisp and crackling under the comb. While she was still dressing the friends called for her and sat while she donned her sheerest underthings and stockings and a new voile dress. "Do you feel strong enough to go out?" they said, their eyes bright too, with a dark glitter. "When you have had time to get over the shock, you must tell us what happened. What he said and did; everything."

In the leafed darkness, as they walked toward the square, she began to breathe deeply, something like a swimmer preparing to dive, until she ceased trembling, the four of them walking slowly because of the terrible heat and out of solicitude for her. But as they neared the square she began to tremble again, walking with her head up, her hands clenched at her sides, their voices about her murmurous, also with that feverish, glittering quality of their eyes.

They entered the square, she in the center of the group, fragile in her fresh dress. She was trembling worse. She walked slower and slower, as children eat ice cream, her head up and her eyes bright in the haggard banner of her face, passing the hotel and the coatless drummers in chairs along the curb looking around at her: "That's the one: see? The one in pink in the middle." "Is that her? What did they do with the nigger? Did they—?" "Sure. He's all right." "All right, is he?" "Sure. He went on a little trip." Then the drug store, where even the young men lounging in the doorway tipped their hats and followed with their eyes the motion of her hips and legs when she passed.

They went on, passing the lifted hats of the gentlemen, the suddenly ceased voices, deferent, protective. "Do you see?" the friends said. Their voices sounded like long, hovering sighs of hissing exultation. "There's not a Negro on the square. Not one."

They reached the picture show. It was like a miniature fairyland with its lighted lobby and colored lithographs of life caught in its terrible and beautiful mutations. Her lips began to tingle. In the dark, when the picture began, it would be all right; she could hold back the laughing so it would not waste away so fast and so soon. So she hurried on before the turning faces, the undertones of low astonishment, and they took their accustomed places where she could see the aisle against the silver glare and the young men and girls coming in two and two against it.

The lights flicked away; the screen glowed silver, and soon life began to unfold, beautiful and passionate and sad, while still the young men and girls entered, scented and sibilant in the half dark, their paired backs in silhouette delicate and sleek, their slim, quick bodies awkward, divinely young, while beyond them the silver dream accumulated inevitably on and on. She began to laugh. In trying to suppress it, it made more noise than ever; heads began to turn. Still laughing, her friends raised her and led her out, and she stood at the curb, laughing on a high, sustained note, until the taxi came up and they helped her in.

They removed the pink voile and the sheer underthings and the stockings, and put her to bed, and cracked ice for her temples, and sent for the doctor. He was hard to locate, so they ministered to her with hushed ejaculations, renewing the ice and fanning her. While the ice was fresh and cold she stopped laughing and lay still for a time, moaning only a little. But soon the laughing welled again and her voice rose screaming.

"Shhhhhhhhhhh! Shhhhhhhhhhhhhh!" they said, freshening the icepack, smoothing her hair, examining it for gray; "poor girl!" Then to one another: "Do you suppose anything really happened?" their eyes darkly aglitter, secret and passionate. "Shhhhhhhhhh! Poor girl! Poor Minnie!"

V

It was midnight when McLendon drove up to his neat new house. It was trim and fresh as a birdcage and almost as small, with its clean, green-and-white paint. He locked the car and mounted the porch and entered. His wife rose from a chair beside the reading lamp. McLendon stopped in the floor and stared at her until she looked down.

"Look at that clock," he said, lifting his arm, pointing. She stood before him, her face lowered, a magazine in her hands. Her face was pale, strained, and weary-looking. "Haven't I told you about sitting up like this, waiting to see when I come in?"

"John," she said. She laid the magazine down. Poised on the balls of his feet, he glared at her with his hot eyes, his sweating face.

"Didn't I tell you?" He went toward her. She looked up then. He caught her shoulder. She stood passive, looking at him.

"Don't, John. I couldn't sleep . . . The heat; something. Please, John. You're hurting me."

"Didn't I tell you?" He released her and half struck, half flung her across the chair, and she lay there and watched him quietly as he left the room.

He went on through the house, ripping off his shirt, and on the dark, screened porch at the rear he stood and mopped his head and shoulders with the shirt and flung it away. He took the pistol from his hip and laid it on the table beside the bed, and sat on the bed and removed his shoes, and rose and slipped his trousers off. He was sweating again already, and he stooped and hunted furiously for the shirt. At last he found it and wiped his body again, and, with his body pressed against the dusty screen, he stood panting. There was no movement, no sound, not even an insect. The dark world seemed to lie stricken beneath the cold moon and the lidless stars.

Barn Burning

The store in which the Justice of the Peace's court was sitting smelled of cheese. The boy, crouched on his nail keg at the back of the crowded room, knew he smelled cheese, and more: from where he sat he could see the ranked shelves close-packed with the solid, squat, dynamic shapes of tin cans whose labels his stomach read, not from the lettering which meant nothing to his mind but from the scarlet devils and the silver curve of fish—this, the cheese which he knew he smelled and the hermetic meat which his intestines believed he smelled coming in intermittent gusts momentary and brief between the other constant one, the smell and sense just a little of fear because mostly of despair and grief, the old fierce pull of blood. He could not see the table where the Justice sat and before which his father and his father's enemy *(our enemy* he thought in that despair; *ourn! mine and hisn both! He's my father!)* stood, but he could hear them, the two of them that is, because his father had said no word yet:

"But what proof have you, Mr. Harris?"

"I told you. The hog got into my corn. I caught it up and sent it back to him. He had no fence that would hold it. I told him so, warned him. The next time I put the hog in my pen. When he came to get it I gave him enough wire to patch up his pen. The next time I put the hog up and kept it. I rode down to his house and saw the wire I gave him still rolled on to the spool in his yard. I told him he could have the hog when he paid me a dollar pound fee. That evening a nigger came with the dollar and got the hog. He was a strange nigger. He said, 'He say to tell you wood and hay kin burn.' I said, 'What?' 'That whut he say to tell you,' the nigger said. 'Wood and hay kin burn.' That night my barn burned. I got the stock out but I lost the barn."

"Where is the nigger? Have you got him?"

"He was a strange nigger, I tell you. I don't know what became of him."

"But that's not proof. Don't you see that's not proof?"

"Get that boy up here. He knows." For a moment the boy thought too that the man meant his older brother until Harris said, "Not him. The little one. The boy," and, crouching, small for his age, small and wiry like his father, in patched and faded jeans even too small for him, with straight, uncombed, brown hair and eyes gray and wild as storm scud, he saw the men between himself and the table part and become a lane of grim faces, at the end of which he saw the Justice, a shabby, collarless, graying man in spectacles, beckoning him. He felt no floor under his bare feet; he seemed to walk beneath the palpable weight of the grim turning faces. His father, stiff in his black Sunday coat donned not for the trial but for the moving, did not even look at him.

He aims for me to lie, he thought, again with that frantic grief and despair. *And I will have to do hit.*

"What's your name, boy?" the Justice said.

"Colonel Sartoris Snopes," the boy whispered.

"Hey?" the Justice said. "Talk louder. Colonel Sartoris? I reckon anybody named for Colonel Sartoris in this country can't help but tell the truth, can they?" The boy said nothing. *Enemy! Enemy!* he thought; for a moment he could not even see, could not see that the Justice's face was kindly nor discern that his voice was troubled when he spoke to the man named Harris: "Do you want me to question this boy?" But he could hear, and during those subsequent long seconds while there was absolutely no sound in the crowded little room save that of quiet and intent breathing it was as if he had swung outward at the end of a grape vine, over a ravine, and at the top of the swing had been caught in a prolonged instant of mesmerized gravity, weightless in time.

"No!" Harris said violently, explosively. "Damnation! Send him out of here!" Now time, the fluid world, rushed beneath him again, the voices coming to him again through the smell of cheese and sealed meat, the fear and despair and the old grief of blood:

"This case is closed. I can't find against you, Snopes, but I can give you advice. Leave this country and don't come back to it."

His father spoke for the first time, his voice cold and harsh, level, without emphasis: "I aim to. I don't figure to stay in a country among people who . . ." he said something unprintable and vile, addressed to no one.

"That'll do," the Justice said. "Take your wagon and get out of this country before dark. Case dismissed."

His father turned, and he followed the stiff black coat, the wiry figure walking a little stiffly from where a Confederate provost's man's musket ball had taken him in the heel on a stolen horse thirty years ago, followed the two backs now, since his older brother had appeared from somewhere in the crowd, no taller than the father but thicker, chewing tobacco steadily, between the two lines of grim-faced men and out of the store and across the worn gallery and down the sagging steps and among the dogs and half-grown boys in the mild May dust, where as he passed a voice hissed:

"Barn burner!"

Again he could not see, whirling; there was a face in a red haze, moonlike, bigger than the full moon, the owner of it half again his size, he leaping in the red haze toward the face, feeling no blow, feeling no shock when his head struck the earth, scrabbling up and leaping again, feeling no blow this time either and tasting no blood, scrabbling up to see the other boy in full flight and himself already leaping into pursuit as his father's hand jerked him back, the harsh, cold voice speaking above him: "Go get in the wagon."

It stood in a grove of locusts and mulberries across the road. His two hulking sisters in their Sunday dresses and his mother and her sister in calico and sunbonnets were already in it, sitting on and among the sorry residue of the dozen and more movings which even the boy could remember—the battered stove, the broken beds and chairs, the clock inlaid with mother-of-pearl, which would not run, stopped at some fourteen minutes past two o'clock of a dead and forgotten day and time, which had been his mother's dowry. She was crying, though when she saw him she drew her sleeve across her face and began to descend from the wagon. "Get back," the father said.

"He's hurt. I got to get some water and wash his . . ."

"Get back in the wagon," his father said. He got in too, over the tail-gate. His father mounted to the seat where the older brother already sat and struck the gaunt mules two savage blows with the peeled willow, but without heat. It was not even sadistic; it was exactly that same quality which in later years would cause his descendants to over-run the engine before putting a motor car into motion, striking and reining back in the same movement. The wagon went on, the store with its quiet crowd of grimly watching men dropped behind; a curve in the road hid it. *Forever* he thought. *Maybe he's done satisfied now, now that he has* . . . stopping himself, not to say it aloud even to himself. His mother's hand touched his shoulder.

"Does hit hurt?" she said.

"Naw," he said. "Hit don't hurt. Lemme be."

"Can't you wipe some of the blood off before hit dries?"

"I'll wash to-night," he said. "Lemme be, I tell you."

The wagon went on. He did not know where they were going. None of them ever did or ever asked, because it was always somewhere, always a house of sorts waiting for them a day or two days or even three days away. Likely his father had already arranged to make a crop on another farm before he . . . Again he had to stop himself. He (the father) always did. There was something about his wolflike independence and even courage when the advantage was at least neutral which impressed strangers, as if they got from his latent ravening ferocity not so much a sense of dependability as a feeling that his ferocious conviction in the rightness of his own actions would be of advantage to all whose interest lay with his.

That night they camped, in a grove of oaks and beeches where a spring ran. The nights were still cool and they had a fire against it, of a rail lifted from a nearby fence and cut into lengths—a small fire, neat, niggard almost, a shrewd fire; such fires were his father's habit and custom always, even in freezing weather. Older, the boy might have remarked this and wondered why not a big one; why should not a man who had not only seen the waste and extravagance of war, but who had in his blood an inherent voracious prodigality with material not his own, have burned everything in sight? Then he might have gone a step farther and thought that that was the reason: that niggard blaze was the living fruit of nights passed during those four years in the woods hiding from all men, blue or gray, with his strings of horses (captured horses, he called them). And older still, he might have divined the true reason: that the element of fire spoke to some deep mainspring of his father's being, as the element of steel or of powder spoke to other men, as the one weapon for the preservation of integrity, else breath were not worth the breathing, and hence to be regarded with respect and used with discretion.

But he did not think this now and he had seen those same niggard blazes all his life. He merely ate his supper beside it and was already half asleep over his iron plate when his father called him, and once more he followed the stiff back, the stiff and ruthless limp, up the slope and on to the starlit road where, turning, he could see his father against the stars but without face or depth—a shape black, flat, and bloodless as though cut from tin in the iron folds of the frockcoat which had not been made for him, the voice harsh like tin and without heat like tin:

"You were fixing to tell them. You would have told him." He didn't answer. His father struck him with the flat of his hand on the side of the head, hard but without heat, exactly as he had struck the two mules at the store, exactly as he would strike either of them with any stick in order to kill a horse fly, his voice still without heat or anger: "You're getting to be a man. You got to learn. You got to learn to stick to your own blood or you ain't going to have any blood to stick to you. Do you think either of them, any man there this morning, would? Don't you know all they wanted was a chance to get at me because they knew I had them beat? Eh?" Later, twenty years later, he was to tell himself, "If I had said they wanted only truth, justice, he would have hit me again." But now he said nothing. He was not crying. He just stood there. "Answer me," his father said.

"Yes," he whispered. His father turned.

"Get on to bed. We'll be there to-morrow."

To-morrow they were there. In the early afternoon the wagon stopped before a paintless two-room house identical almost with the dozen others it had stopped before even in the boy's ten years, and again, as on the other dozen occasions, his mother and aunt got down and began to unload the wagon, although his two sisters and his father and brother had not moved.

"Likely hit ain't fitten for hawgs," one of the sisters said.

"Nevertheless, fit it will and you'll hog it and like it," his father said. "Get out of them chairs and help your Ma unload."

The two sisters got down, big, bovine, in a flutter of cheap ribbons; one of them drew from the jumbled wagon bed a battered lantern, the other a worn broom. His father handed the reins to the older son and began to climb stiffly over the wheel. "When they get unloaded, take the team to the barn and feed them." Then he said, and at first the boy thought he was still speaking to his brother: "Come with me."

"Me?" he said.

"Yes," his father said. "You."

"Abner," his mother said. His father paused and looked back—the harsh level stare beneath the shaggy, graying, irascible brows.

"I reckon I'll have a word with the man that aims to begin to-morrow owning me body and soul for the next eight months."

They went back up the road. A week ago—or before last night, that is—he would have asked where they were going, but not now. His father had struck him before last night but never before had he paused afterward to explain why; it was as if the blow and the following calm, outrageous voice still rang, repercussed, divulging nothing to him save the terrible handicap of being young, the light weight of his few years, just heavy enough to prevent his soaring free of the world as it seemed to be ordered but not heavy enough to keep him footed solid in it, to resist it and try to change the course of its events.

Presently he could see the grove of oaks and cedars and the other flowering trees and shrubs where the house would be, though not the house yet. They walked beside a fence massed with honeysuckle and Cherokee roses and came to a gate swinging open between two brick pillars, and now, beyond a sweep of drive, he saw the house for the first time and at that instant he forgot his father and the terror and despair both, and even when he remembered his father again (who had not stopped) the terror and despair did not return. Because, for all the twelve movings, they had sojourned until now in a poor country, a land of small farms and fields and houses, and he had never seen a house like this before. *Hit's big as a courthouse* he thought quietly, with a surge of peace and joy whose reason he could not have thought into words, being too young for that: *They are safe from him. People whose lives are a part of this peace and dignity are beyond his touch, he no more to them than a buzzing wasp: capable of stinging for a little moment but that's all; the spell of this peace and dignity rendering even the barns and stable and cribs which belong to it impervious to the puny flames he might contrive* . . . this, the peace and joy, ebbing for an instant as he looked again at the stiff black back, the stiff and implacable limp of the figure which was not dwarfed by the house, for the reason that it had never looked big anywhere and which now, against the serene columned backdrop, had more than ever that impervious quality of something cut ruthlessly from tin, depthless, as though, sidewise to the sun, it would cast no shadow. Watching him, the boy remarked the absolutely undeviating course which his father held and saw the stiff foot come squarely down in a pile of fresh droppings where a horse had stood in the drive and which his father could have avoided by a simple change of stride. But it ebbed only for a moment, though he could not have thought this into words either, walking on in the spell of the house, which he could even want but without envy, without sorrow, certainly never with that ravening and jealous rage which unknown to him walked in the ironlike black coat before him. *Maybe he will feel it too. Maybe it will even change him now from what maybe he couldn't help but be.*

They crossed the portico. Now he could hear his father's stiff foot as it came down on the boards with clocklike finality, a sound out of all proportion to the displacement of the body it bore and which was not dwarfed either by the white door before it, as though it had attained to a sort of vicious and ravening minimum not to be dwarfed by anything—the flat, wide, black hat, the formal coat of broadcloth which had once been black but which had now that friction-glazed greenish cast of the bodies of old house flies, the lifted sleeve which was too large, the lifted hand like a curled claw. The door opened so promptly that the boy knew the Negro must have been watching them all the time, an old man with neat grizzled hair, in a linen jacket, who stood barring the door with his body, saying, "Wipe yo foots, white man, fo you come in here. Major ain't home nohow."

"Get out of my way, nigger," his father said, without heat too, flinging the door back and the Negro also and entering, his hat still on his head. And now the boy saw the prints of the stiff foot on the doorjamb and saw them appear on the pale rug behind the machinelike deliberation of the foot which seemed to bear (or transmit) twice the weight which the body compassed. The Negro was shouting "Miss Lula! Miss Lula!" somewhere behind them, then the boy, deluged as though by a warm wave by a suave turn of carpeted stair and a pendant glitter of chandeliers and a mute gleam of gold frames, heard the swift feet and saw her too, a lady—perhaps he had never seen her like before either—in a gray, smooth gown with lace at the throat and an apron tied at the waist and the sleeves turned back, wiping cake or biscuit dough from her hands with a towel as she came up the hall, looking not at his father at all but at the tracks on the blond rug with an expression of incredulous amazement.

"I tried," the Negro cried. "I tole him to . . ."

"Will you please go away?" she said in a shaking voice. "Major de Spain is not at home. Will you please go away?"

His father had not spoken again. He did not speak again. He did not even look at her. He just stood stiff in the center of the rug, in his hat, the shaggy iron-gray brows twitching slightly above the pebble-colored eyes as he appeared to examine the house with brief deliberation. Then with the same deliberation he turned; the boy watched him pivot on the good leg and saw the stiff foot drag round the arc of the turning, leaving a final long and fading smear. His father never looked at it, he never once looked down at the rug. The Negro held the door. It closed behind them, upon the hysteric and indistinguishable woman-wail. His father stopped at the top of the steps and scraped his boot clean on the edge of it. At the gate he stopped again. He stood for a moment, planted stiffly on the stiff foot, looking back at the house. "Pretty and white, ain't it?" he said. "That's sweat. Nigger sweat. Maybe it ain't white enough yet to suit him. Maybe he wants to mix some white sweat with it."

Two hours later the boy was chopping wood behind the house within which his mother and aunt and the two sisters (the mother and aunt, not the two girls, he knew that; even at this distance and muffled by walls the flat loud voices of the two girls emanated an incorrigible idle inertia) were setting up the stove to prepare a meal, when he heard the hooves and saw the linen-clad man on a fine sorrel mare, whom he recognized even before he saw the rolled rug in front of the Negro youth following on a fat bay carriage horse—a suffused, angry face vanishing, still at full gallop, beyond the corner of the house where his father and brother were sitting in the two tilted chairs; and a moment later, almost before he could have put the axe down, he heard the hooves again and watched the sorrel mare go back out of the yard, already galloping again. Then his father began to shout one of the sisters' names, who presently emerged backward from the kitchen door dragging the rolled rug along the ground by one end while the other sister walked behind it.

"If you ain't going to tote, go on and set up the wash pot," the first said.

"You, Sarty!" the second shouted. "Set up the wash pot!" His father appeared at the door, framed against that shabbiness, as he had been against that other bland perfection, impervious to either, the mother's anxious face at his shoulder.

"Go on," the father said. "Pick it up." The two sisters stooped, broad, lethargic; stooping, they presented an incredible expanse of pale cloth and a flutter of tawdry ribbons.

"If I thought enough of a rug to have to git hit all the way from France I wouldn't keep hit where folks coming in would have to tromp on hit," the first said. They raised the rug.

"Abner," the mother said. "Let me do it."

"You go back and git dinner," his father said. "I'll tend to this."

From the woodpile through the rest of the afternoon the boy watched them, the rug spread flat in the dust beside the bubbling wash-pot, the two sisters stooping over it with that profound and lethargic reluctance, while the father stood over them in turn, implacable and grim, driving them though never raising his voice again. He could smell the harsh homemade lye they were using; he saw his mother come to the door once and look toward them with an expression not anxious now but very like despair; he saw his father turn, and he fell to with the axe and saw from the corner of his eye his father raise from the ground a flattish fragment of field stone and examine it and return to the pot, and this time his mother actually spoke: "Abner. Abner. Please don't. Please, Abner."

Then he was done too. It was dusk; the whippoorwills had already begun. He could smell coffee from the room where they would presently eat the cold food remaining from the mid-afternoon meal, though when he entered the house he realized they were having coffee again probably because there was a fire on the hearth, before which the rug now lay spread over the backs of the two chairs. The tracks of his father's foot were gone. Where they had been were now long, water-cloudy scoriations resembling the sporadic course of a lilliputian mowing machine.

It still hung there while they ate the cold food and then went to bed, scattered without order or claim up and down the two rooms, his mother in one bed, where his father would later lie, the older brother in the other, himself, the aunt, and the two sisters on pallets on the floor. But his father was not in bed yet. The last thing the boy remembered was the depthless, harsh silhouette of the hat and coat bending over the rug and it seemed to him that he had not even closed his eyes when the silhouette was standing over him, the fire almost dead behind it, the stiff foot prodding him awake. "Catch up the mule," his father said.

When he returned with the mule his father was standing in the black door, the rolled rug over his shoulder. "Ain't you going to ride?" he said.

"No. Give me your foot."

He bent his knee into his father's hand, the wiry, surprising power flowed smoothly, rising, he rising with it, on to the mule's bare back (they had owned a saddle once; the boy could remember it though not when or where) and with the same effortlessness his father swung the rug up in front of him. Now in the starlight they retraced the afternoon's path, up the dusty road rife with honeysuckle, through the gate and up the black tunnel of the drive to the lightless house, where he sat on the mule and felt the rough warp of the rug drag across his thighs and vanish.

"Don't you want me to help?" he whispered. His father did not answer and now he heard again that stiff foot striking the hollow portico with that wooden and clocklike deliberation, that outrageous overstatement of the weight it carried. The rug, hunched, not flung (the boy could tell that even in the darkness) from his father's shoulder struck the angle of wall and floor with a sound unbelievably loud, thunderous, then the foot again, unhurried and enormous; a light came on in the house and the boy sat, tense, breathing steadily and quietly and just a little fast, though the foot itself did not increase its beat at all, descending the steps now; now the boy could see him.

"Don't you want to ride now?" he whispered. "We kin both ride now," the light within the house altering now, flaring up and sinking. *He's coming down the stairs now,* he thought. He had already ridden the mule up beside the horse block; presently his father was up behind him and he doubled the reins over and slashed the mule across the neck, but before the animal could begin to trot the hard, thin arm came round him, the hard, knotted hand jerking the mule back to a walk.

In the first red rays of the sun they were in the lot, putting plow gear on the mules. This time the sorrel mare was in the lot before he heard it at all, the rider collarless and even bareheaded, trembling, speaking in a shaking voice as the woman in the house had done, his father merely looking up once before stooping again to the hame he was buckling, so that the man on the mare spoke to his stooping back:

"You must realize you have ruined that rug. Wasn't there anybody here, any of your women . . ." he ceased, shaking, the boy watching him, the older brother leaning now in the stable door, chewing, blinking slowly and steadily at nothing apparently. "It cost a hundred dollars. But you never had a hundred dollars. You never will. So I'm going to charge you twenty bushels of corn against your crop. I'll add it in your contract and when you come to the commissary you can sign it. That won't keep Mrs. de Spain quiet but maybe it will teach you to wipe your feet off before you enter her house again."

Then he was gone. The boy looked at his father, who still had not spoken or even looked up again, who was now adjusting the logger-head in the hame.

"Pap," he said. His father looked at him—the inscrutable face, the shaggy brows beneath which the gray eyes glinted coldly. Suddenly the boy went toward him, fast, stopping as suddenly. "You done the best you could!" he cried. "If he wanted hit done different why didn't he wait and tell you how? He won't git no twenty bushels! He won't git none! We'll gether hit and hide hit! I kin watch . . ."

"Did you put the cutter back in that straight stock like I told you?"

"No, sir," he said.

"Then go do it."

That was Wednesday. During the rest of that week he worked steadily, at what was within his scope and some which was beyond it, with an industry that did not need to be driven nor even commanded twice; he had this from his mother, with the difference that some at least of what he did he liked to do, such as splitting wood with the half-size axe which his mother and aunt had earned, or saved money somehow, to present him with at Christmas. In company with the two older women (and on one afternoon, even one of the sisters), he built pens for the shoat and the cow which were a part of his father's contract with the landlord, and one afternoon, his father being absent, gone somewhere on one of the mules, he went to the field.

They were running a middle buster now, his brother holding the plow straight while he handled the reins, and walking beside the straining mule, the rich black soil shearing cool and damp against his bare ankles, he thought *Maybe this is the end of it. Maybe even that twenty bushels that seems hard to have to pay for just a rug will be a cheap price for him to stop forever and always from being what he used to be;* thinking, dreaming now, so that his brother had to speak sharply to him to mind the mule: *Maybe he even won't collect the twenty bushels. Maybe it will all add up and balance and vanish—corn, rug, fire; the terror and grief, the being pulled two ways like between two teams of horses—gone, done with for ever and ever.*

Then it was Saturday; he looked up from beneath the mule he was harnessing and saw his father in the black coat and hat. "Not that," his father said. "The wagon gear." And then, two hours later, sitting in the wagon bed behind his father and brother on the seat, the wagon accomplished a final curve, and he saw the weathered paintless store with its tattered tobacco- and patent-medicine posters and the tethered wagons and saddle animals below the gallery. He mounted the gnawed steps behind his father and brother, and there again was the lane of quiet, watching faces for the three of them to walk through. He saw the man in spectacles sitting at the plank table and he did not need to be told this was a Justice of the Peace; he sent one glare of fierce, exultant, partisan defiance at the man in collar and cravat now, whom he had seen but twice before in his life, and that on a galloping horse, who now wore on his face an expression not of rage but of amazed unbelief which the boy could not have known was at the incredible circumstance of being sued by one of his own tenants, and came and stood against his father and cried at the Justice: "He ain't done it! He ain't burnt . . ."

"Go back to the wagon," his father said.

"Burnt?" the Justice said. "Do I understand this rug was burned too?"

"Does anybody here claim it was?" his father said. "Go back to the wagon." But he did not, he merely retreated to the rear of the room, crowded as that other had been, but not to sit down this time, instead, to stand pressing among the motionless bodies, listening to the voices:

"And you claim twenty bushels of corn is too high for the damage you did to the rug?"

"He brought the rug to me and said he wanted the tracks washed out of it. I washed the tracks out and took the rug back to him."

"But you didn't carry the rug back to him in the same condition it was in before you made the tracks on it."

His father did not answer, and now for perhaps half a minute there was no sound at all save that of breathing, the faint, steady suspiration of complete and intent listening.

"You decline to answer that, Mr. Snopes?" Again his father did not answer. "I'm going to find against you, Mr. Snopes. I'm going to find that you were responsible for the injury to Major de Spain's rug and hold you liable for it. But twenty bushels of corn seems a little high for a man in your circumstances to have to pay. Major de Spain claims it cost a hundred dollars. October corn will be worth about fifty cents. I figure that if Major de Spain can stand a ninety-five dollar loss on something he paid cash for, you can stand a five-dollar loss you haven't earned yet. I hold you in damages to Major de Spain to the amount of ten bushels of corn over and above your contract with him, to be paid to him out of your crop at gathering time. Court adjourned."

It had taken no time hardly, the morning was but half begun. He thought they would return home and perhaps back to the field, since they were late, far behind all other farmers. But instead his father passed on behind the wagon, merely indicating with his hand for the older brother to follow with it, and crossed the road toward the blacksmith shop opposite, pressing on after his father, overtaking him, speaking, whispering up at the harsh, calm face beneath the weathered hat: "He won't git no ten bushels neither. He won't git one. We'll . . ." until his father glanced for an instant down at him, the face absolutely calm, the grizzled eyebrows tangled above the cold eyes, the voice almost pleasant, almost gentle:

"You think so? Well, we'll wait till October anyway."

The matter of the wagon—the setting of a spoke or two and the tightening of the tires—did not take long either, the business of the tires accomplished by driving the wagon into the spring branch behind the shop and letting it stand there, the mules nuzzling into the water from time to time, and the boy on the seat with the idle reins, looking up the slope and through the sooty tunnel of the shed where the slow hammer rang and where his father sat on an upended cypress bolt, easily, either talking or listening, still sitting there when the boy brought the dripping wagon up out of the branch and halted it before the door.

"Take them on to the shade and hitch," his father said. He did so and returned. His father and the smith and a third man squatting on his heels inside the door were talking, about crops and animals; the boy, squatting too in the ammoniac dust and hoof-parings and scales of rust, heard his father tell a long and unhurried story out of the time before the birth of the older brother even when he had been a professional horsetrader. And then his father came up beside him where he stood before a tattered last year's circus poster on the other side of the store, gazing rapt and quiet at the scarlet horses, the incredible poisings and convolutions of tulle and tights and the painted leers of comedians, and said, "It's time to eat."

But not at home. Squatting beside his brother against the front wall, he watched his father emerge from the store and produce from a paper sack a segment of cheese and divide it carefully and deliberately into three with his pocket knife and produce crackers from the same sack. They all three squatted on the gallery and ate, slowly, without talking; then in the store again, they drank from a tin dipper tepid water smelling of the cedar bucket and of living beech trees. And still they did not go home. It was a horse lot this time, a tall rail fence upon and along which men stood and sat and out of which one by one horses were led, to be walked and trotted and then cantered back and forth along the road while the slow swapping and buying went on and the sun began to slant westward, they—the three of them—watching and listening, the older brother with his muddy eyes and his steady, inevitable tobacco, the father commenting now and then on certain of the animals, to no one in particular.

It was after sundown when they reached home. They ate supper by lamplight, then, sitting on the doorstep, the boy watched the night fully accomplish, listening to the whippoorwills and the frogs, when he heard his mother's voice: "Abner! No! No! Oh, God. Oh, God. Abner!" and he rose, whirled, and saw the altered light through the door where a candle stub now burned in a bottle neck on the table and his father, still in the hat and coat, at once formal and burlesque as though dressed carefully for some shabby and ceremonial violence, emptying the reservoir of the lamp back into the five-gallon kerosene can from which it had been filled, while the mother tugged at his arm until he shifted the lamp to the other hand and flung her back, not savagely or viciously, just hard, into the wall, her hands flung out against the wall for balance, her mouth open and in her face the same quality of hopeless despair as had been in her voice. Then his father saw him standing in the door.

"Go to the barn and get that can of oil we were oiling the wagon with," he said. The boy did not move. Then he could speak.

"What . . ." he cried. "What are you . . ."

"Go get that oil," his father said. "Go."

Then he was moving, running, outside the house, toward the stable: this the old habit, the old blood which he had not been permitted to choose for himself, which had been bequeathed him willy nilly and which had run for so long (and who knew where, battening on what of outrage and savagery and lust) before it came to him. *I could keep on,* he thought. *I could run on and on and never look back, never need to see his face again. Only I can't. I can't,* the rusted can in his hand now, the liquid sploshing in it as he ran back to the house and into it, into the sound of his mother's weeping in the next room, and handed the can to his father.

"Ain't you going to even send a nigger?" he cried. "At least you sent a nigger before!"

This time his father didn't strike him. The hand came even faster than the blow had, the same hand which had set the can on the table with almost excruciating care flashing from the can toward him too quick for him to follow it, gripping him by the back of his shirt and on to tiptoe before he had seen it quit the can, the face stooping at him in breathless and frozen ferocity, the cold, dead voice speaking over him to the older brother who leaned against the table, chewing with that steady, curious, sidewise motion of cows:

"Empty the can into the big one and go on. I'll catch up with you."

"Better tie him up to the bedpost," the brother said.

"Do like I told you," the father said. Then the boy was moving, his bunched shirt and the hard, bony hand between his shoulder-blades, his toes just touching the floor, across the room and into the other one, past the sisters sitting with spread heavy thighs in the two chairs over the cold hearth, and to where his mother and aunt sat side by side on the bed, the aunt's arms about his mother's shoulders.

"Hold him," the father said. The aunt made a startled movement. "Not you," the father said. "Lennie. Take hold of him. I want to see you do it." His mother took him by the wrist. "You'll hold him better than that. If he gets loose don't you know what he is going to do? He will go up yonder." He jerked his head toward the road. "Maybe I'd better tie him."

"I'll hold him," his mother whispered.

"See you do then." Then his father was gone, the stiff foot heavy and measured upon the boards, ceasing at last.

Then he began to struggle. His mother caught him in both arms, he jerking and wrenching at them. He would be stronger in the end, he knew that. But he had no time to wait for it. "Lemme go!" he cried. "I don't want to have to hit you!"

"Let him go!" the aunt said. "If you don't go, before God, I am going up there myself!"

"Don't you see I can't?" his mother cried. "Sarty! Sarty! No! No! Help me, Lizzie!"

Then he was free. His aunt grasped at him but it was too late. He whirled, running, his mother stumbled forward on to her knees behind him, crying to the nearer sister: "Catch him, Net! Catch him!" But that was too late too, the sister (the sisters were twins, born at the same time, yet either of them now gave the impression of being, encompassing as much living meat and volume and weight as any other two of the family) not yet having begun to rise from the chair, her head, face, alone merely turned, presenting to him in the flying instant an astonishing expanse of young female features untroubled by any surprise even, wearing only an expression of bovine interest. Then he was out of the room, out of the house, in the mild dust of the starlit road and the heavy rifeness of honeysuckle, the pale ribbon unspooling with terrific slowness under his running feet, reaching the gate at last and turning in, running, his heart and lungs drumming, on up the drive toward the lighted house, the lighted door. He did not knock, he burst in, sobbing for breath, incapable for the moment of speech; he saw the astonished face of the Negro in the linen jacket without knowing when the Negro had appeared.

"De Spain!" he cried, panted. "Where's . . ." then he saw the white man too emerging from a white door down the hall. "Barn!" he cried. "Barn!"

"What?" the white man said. "Barn?"

"Yes!" the boy cried. "Barn!"

"Catch him!" the white man shouted.

But it was too late this time too. The Negro grasped his shirt, but the entire sleeve, rotten with washing, carried away, and he was out that door too and in the drive again, and had actually never ceased to run even while he was screaming into the white man's face.

Behind him the white man was shouting, "My horse! Fetch my horse!" and he thought for an instant of cutting across the park and climbing the fence in the road, but he did not know the park nor how high the vine-massed fence might be and he dared not risk it. So he ran on down the drive, blood and breath roaring; presently he was in the road again though he could not see it. He could not hear either: the galloping mare was almost upon him before he heard her, and even then he held his course, as if the very urgency of his wild grief and need must in a moment more find him wings, waiting until the ultimate instant to hurl himself aside and into the weed-choked roadside ditch as the horse thundered past and on, for an instant in furious silhouette against the stars, the tranquil early summer night sky which, even before the shape of the horse and rider vanished, stained abruptly and violently upward: a long, swirling roar incredible and soundless, blotting the stars, and he springing up and into the road again, running again, knowing it was too late yet still running even after he heard the shot and, an instant later, two shots, pausing now without knowing he had ceased to run, crying "Pap! Pap!", running again before he knew he had begun to run, stumbling, tripping over something and scrabbling up again without ceasing to run, looking backward over his shoulder at the glare as he got up, running on among the invisible trees, panting, sobbing, "Father! Father!"

At midnight he was sitting on the crest of a hill. He did not know it was midnight and he did not know how far he had come. But there was no glare behind him now and he sat now, his back toward what he had called home for four days anyhow, his face toward the dark woods which he would enter when breath was strong again, small, shaking steadily in the chill darkness, hugging himself into the remainder of his thin, rotten shirt, the grief and despair now no longer terror and fear but just grief and despair. *Father. My father,* he thought. "He was brave!" he cried suddenly, aloud but not loud, no more than a whisper: "He was! He was in the war! He was in Colonel Sartoris' cav'ry!" not knowing that his father had gone to that war a private in the fine old European sense, wearing no uniform, admitting the authority of and giving fidelity to no man or army or flag, going to war as Malbrouck himself did: for booty—it meant nothing and less than nothing to him if it were enemy booty or his own.

The slow constellations wheeled on. It would be dawn and then sun-up after a while and he would be hungry. But that would be to-morrow and now he was only cold, and walking would cure that. His breathing was easier now and he decided to get up and go on, and then he found that he had been asleep because he knew it was almost dawn, the night almost over. He could tell that from the whippoorwills. They were everywhere now among the dark trees below him, constant and inflectioned and ceaseless, so that, as the instant for giving over to the day birds drew nearer and nearer, there was no interval at all between them. He got up. He was a little stiff, but walking would cure that too as it would the cold, and soon there would be the sun. He went on down the hill, toward the dark woods within which the liquid silver voices of the birds called unceasing—the rapid and urgent beating of the urgent and quiring heart of the late spring night. He did not look back.

ERNEST HEMINGWAY

1899–1961

Certainly as much as any other writer represented in this book, Hemingway lived the life he wrote about. Roughing it in the Michigan woods, driving an ambulance on the Italian front in World War I, becoming part of Paris in the twenties, hunting big game in Africa, bullfighting in Spain, reporting the Spanish Civil War, deep-sea fishing in the Caribbean—he was actively engaged in it all. In the relationship of his books to his life Hemingway is like Conrad in that what he wrote about was a real-life version of the kind of exploits found in boys' adventure stories. And like Conrad, Hemingway sought to portray the significance of exciting adventures rather than just the excitement itself. But there the similarity between the two writers ends: for Hemingway is unlike Conrad in insisting that the significance of an event can be conveyed only by a scrupulous report of "real" details—not attitudes or feelings, but facts. For Hemingway the way to express how a man felt is to describe what he did, how he did it, what he said, what happened as a result. Appeals to the reader's compassion, admiration, and awe seemed to him fakery.

There is no need for us to determine whether he or Conrad was right, for they were interested in different things: Conrad in states of perception that reveal, or distort, or possibly just miss the essence of experience; and Hemingway in experience itself so realistically reported that it conveys to the reader in the only possible way what it meant and how it felt in being lived out.

In 1961 Hemingway killed himself with a shotgun in his house in the wild and beautiful Idaho mountains. Though ill (but he had been ill many times before) and threatened by physical weakness and loss of control, he was at the time of his death at the apex of success, both monetarily and professionally: the book he had recently finished, *A Moveable Feast* (published posthumously in 1964), is a fine series of acid sketches based on his life in Paris, and is perhaps even at the level of his best novels (*The Sun Also Rises,* 1926, and *A Farewell to Arms,* 1929). But Hemingway felt that he no longer had the energy to go on creating his own self, holding back by discipline and honor the chaos that threatened to annihilate him.

It is both sad and revealing that Hemingway should die by suicide, for in his writing he sought to capture exactly those extraordinary intense moments in life when one is most aware of death. As a boy he learned from his father (who himself committed suicide) the exhilaration of surviving in the Michigan woods, and of hunting right, with respect for the hunted. Later he found equivalent moments at which one confronted death: in war, bullfighting, deep-sea fishing. The pressure of non-life, of potential chaos, is keenly felt in the stories in this book. Though we never learn what Nick's history is, he is clearly engaged in a great effort of self-reconstruction. He ritualistically insists that all the details of his journey into the woods be perfect, as if one false move would destroy the communion that is being established between him and nature. And then there is the swamp, deep and dark, where the big ones are. It fascinates Nick, but he stops short, cautiously satisfied with his reestablishment of a former self, unwilling at the moment to risk more: "In the swamp fishing was a tragic adventure. Nick did not want it." But the challenge of the swamp remains; it lingers in his mind, as his last sentence makes clear: "There were plenty of days coming when he could fish the swamp."

Norman Mailer insightfully sums up this special kind of energy in Hemingway's fiction and in his life. "It is possible," Mailer says in *Cannibals and Christians,* "that Hemingway lived every day in the style of the suicide. What a great dread is that. It is the dread that sits in the silences of his short declarative sentences. At any instant, by any failure in magic, by a mean defeat, or by a moment of cowardice, Hemingway could be thrust back again into the agonizing demands of courage."

Big Two-Hearted River: Part I

The train went on up the track out of sight, around one of the hills of burnt timber. Nick sat down on the bundle of canvas and bedding the baggage man had pitched out of the door of the baggage car. There was no town, nothing but the rails and the burned-over country. The thirteen saloons that had lined the one street of Seney had not left a trace. The foundations of the Mansion House hotel stuck up above the ground. The stone was chipped and split by the fire. It was all that was left of the town of Seney. Even the surface had been burned off the ground.

Nick looked at the burned-over stretch of hillside, where he had expected to find the scattered houses of the town and then walked down the railroad track to the bridge over the river. The river was there. It swirled against the log spiles of the bridge. Nick looked down into the clear, brown water, colored from the pebbly bottom, and watched the trout keeping themselves steady in the current with wavering fins. As he watched them they changed their positions by quick angles, only to hold steady in the fast water again. Nick watched them a long time.

He watched them holding themselves with their noses into the current, many trout in deep, fast moving water, slightly distorted as he watched far down through the glassy convex surface of the pool, its surface pushing and swelling smooth against the resistance of the log-driven piles of the bridge. At the bottom of the pool were the big trout. Nick did not see them at first. Then he saw them at the bottom of the pool, big trout looking to hold themselves on the gravel bottom in a varying mist of gravel and sand, raised in spurts by the current.

Nick looked down into the pool from the bridge. It was a hot day. A kingfisher flew up the stream. It was a long time since Nick had looked into a stream and seen trout. They were very satisfactory. As the shadow of the kingfisher moved up the stream, a big trout shot upstream in a long angle, only his shadow marking the angle, then lost his shadow as he came through the surface of the water, caught the sun, and then, as he went back into the stream under the surface, his shadow seemed to float down the stream with the current, unresisting, to his post under the bridge where he tightened facing up into the current.

Nick's heart tightened as the trout moved. He felt all the old feeling.

He turned and looked down the stream. It stretched away, pebbly-bottomed with shallows and big boulders and a deep pool as it curved away around the foot of a bluff.

Nick walked back up the ties to where his pack lay in the cinders beside the railway track. He was happy. He adjusted the pack harness around the bundle, pulling straps tight, slung the pack on his back, got his arms through the shoulder straps and took some of the pull off his shoulders by leaning his forehead against the wide band of the tumpline. Still, it was too heavy. It was much too heavy. He had his leather rod-case in his hand and leaning forward to keep the weight of the pack high on his shoulders he walked along the road that paralleled the railway track, leaving the burned town behind in the heat, and then turned off around a hill with a high, fire-scarred hill on either side onto a road that went back into the country. He walked along the road feeling the ache from the pull of the heavy pack. The road climbed steadily. It was hard work walking up-hill. His muscles ached and the day was hot, but Nick felt happy. He felt he had left everything behind, the need for thinking, the need to write, other needs. It was all back of him.

From the time he had gotten down off the train and the baggage man had thrown his pack out of the open car door things had been different. Seney was burned, the country was burned over and changed, but it did not matter. It could not all be burned. He knew that. He hiked along the road, sweating in the sun, climbing to cross the range of hills that separated the railway from the pine plains.

The road ran on, dipping occasionally, but always climbing. Nick went on up. Finally the road after going parallel to the burnt hillside reached the top. Nick leaned back against a stump and slipped out of the pack harness. Ahead of him, as far as he could see, was the pine plain. The burned country stopped off at the left with the range of hills. On ahead islands of dark pine trees rose out of the plain. Far off to the left was the line of the river. Nick followed it with his eye and caught glints of the water in the sun.

There was nothing but the pine plain ahead of him, until the far blue hills that marked the Lake Superior height of land. He could hardly see them, faint and far away in the heat-light over the plain. If he looked too steadily they were gone. But if he only half-looked they were there, the far-off hills of the height of land.

Nick sat down against the charred stump and smoked a cigarette. His pack balanced on the top of the stump, harness holding ready, a hollow molded in it from his back. Nick sat smoking, looking out over the country. He did not need to get his map out. He knew where he was from the position of the river.

As he smoked, his legs stretched out in front of him, he noticed a grasshopper walk along the ground and up onto his woolen sock. The grasshopper was black. As he had walked along the road, climbing, he had started many grasshoppers from the dust. They were all black. They were not the big grasshoppers with yellow and black or red and black wings whirring out from their black wing sheathing as they fly up. These were just ordinary hoppers, but all a sooty black in color. Nick had wondered about them as he walked, without really thinking about them. Now, as he watched the black hopper that was nibbling at the wool of his sock with its fourway lip, he realized that they had all turned black from living in the burned-over land. He realized that the fire must have come the year before, but the grasshoppers were all black now. He wondered how long they would stay that way.

Carefully he reached his hand down and took hold of the hopper by the wings. He turned him up, all his legs walking in the air, and looked at his jointed belly. Yes, it was black too, iridescent where the back and head were dusty.

"Go on, hopper," Nick said, speaking out loud for the first time. "Fly away somewhere."

He tossed the grasshopper up into the air and watched him sail away to a charcoal stump across the road.

Nick stood up. He leaned his back against the weight of his pack where it rested upright on the stump and got his arms through the shoulder straps. He stood with the pack on his back on the brow of the hill looking out across the country, toward the distant river and then struck down the hillside away from the road. Underfoot the ground was good walking. Two hundred yards down the hillside the fire line stopped. Then it was sweet fern, growing ankle high, to walk through, and clumps of jack pines; a long undulating country with frequent rises and descents, sandy underfoot and the country alive again.

Nick kept his direction by the sun. He knew where he wanted to strike the river and he kept on through the pine plain, mounting small rises to see other rises ahead of him and sometimes from the top of a rise a great solid island of pines off to his right or his left. He broke off some sprigs of the heathery sweet fern, and put them under his pack straps. The chafing crushed it and he smelled it as he walked.

He was tired and very hot, walking across the uneven, shadeless pine plain. At any time he knew he could strike the river by turning off to his left. It could not be more than a mile away. But he kept on toward the north to hit the river as far upstream as he could go in one day's walking.

For some time as he walked Nick had been in sight of one of the big islands of pine standing out above the rolling high ground he was crossing. He dipped down and then as he came slowly up to the crest of the bridge he turned and made toward the pine trees.

There was no underbrush in the island of pine trees. The trunks of the trees went straight up or slanted toward each other. The trunks were straight and brown without branches. The branches were high above. Some interlocked to make a solid shadow on the brown forest floor. Around the grove of trees was a bare space. It was brown and soft underfoot as Nick walked on it. This was the over-lapping of the pine needle floor, extending out beyond the width of the high branches. The trees had grown tall and the branches moved high, leaving in the sun this bare space they had once covered with shadow. Sharp at the edge of this extension of the forest floor commenced the sweet fern.

Nick slipped off his pack and lay down in the shade. He lay on his back and looked up into the pine trees. His neck and back and the small of his back rested as he stretched. The earth felt good against his back. He looked up at the sky, through the branches, and then shut his eyes. He opened them and looked up again. There was a wind high up in the branches. He shut his eyes again and went to sleep.

Nick woke stiff and cramped. The sun was nearly down. His pack was heavy and the straps painful as he lifted it on. He leaned over with the pack on and picked up the leather rod-case and started out from the pine trees across the sweet fern swale, toward the river. He knew it could not be more than a mile.

He came down a hillside covered with stumps into a meadow. At the edge of the meadow flowed the river. Nick was glad to get to the river. He walked upstream through the meadow. His trousers were soaked with the dew as he walked. After the hot day, the dew had come quickly and heavily. The river made no sound. It was too fast and smooth. At the edge of the meadow, before he mounted to a piece of high ground to make camp, Nick looked down the river at the trout rising. They were rising to insects come from the swamp on the other side of the stream when the sun went down. The trout jumped out of water to take them. While Nick walked through the little stretch of meadow alongside the stream, trout had jumped high out of water. Now as he looked down the river, the insects must be settling on the surface, for the trout were feeding steadily all down the stream. As far down the long stretch as he could see, the trout were rising, making circles all down the surface of the water, as though it were starting to rain.

The ground rose, wooded and sandy, to overlook the meadow, the stretch of river and the swamp. Nick dropped his pack and rod-case and looked for a level piece of ground. He was very hungry and he wanted to make his camp before he cooked. Between two jack pines, the ground was quite level. He took the ax out of the pack and chopped out two projecting roots. That leveled a piece of ground large enough to sleep on. He smoothed out the sandy soil with his hand and pulled the sweet fern bushes by their roots. His hands smelled good from the sweet fern. He smoothed the uprooted earth. He did not want anything making lumps under the blankets. When he had the ground smooth, he spread his three blankets. One he folded double, next to the ground. The other two he spread on top.

With the ax he slit off a bright slab of pine from one of the stumps and split it into pegs for the tent. He wanted them long and solid to hold in the ground. With the tent unpacked and spread on the ground, the pack, leaning against a jack pine, looked much smaller. Nick tied the rope that served the tent for a ridge-pole to the trunk of one of the pine trees and pulled the tent up off the ground with the other end of the rope and tied it to the other pine. The tent hung on the rope like a canvas blanket on a clothesline. Nick poked a pole he had cut up under the back peak of the canvas and then made it a tent by pegging out the sides. He pegged the sides out taut and drove the pegs deep, hitting them down into the ground with the flat of the ax until the rope loops were buried and the canvas was drum tight.

Across the open mouth of the tent Nick fixed cheesecloth to keep out mosquitoes. He crawled inside under the mosquito bar with various things from the pack to put at the head of the bed under the slant of the canvas. Inside the tent the light came through the brown canvas. It smelled pleasantly of canvas. Already there was something mysterious and homelike. Nick was happy as he crawled inside the tent. He had not been unhappy all day. This was different though. Now things were done. There had been this to do. Now it was done. It had been a hard trip. He was very tired. That was done. He had made his camp. He was settled. Nothing could touch him. It was a good place to camp. He was there, in the good place. He was in his home where he had made it. Now he was hungry.

He came out, crawling under the cheesecloth. It was quite dark outside. It was lighter in the tent.

Nick went over to the pack and found, with his fingers, a long nail in a paper sack of nails, in the bottom of the pack. He drove it into the pine tree, holding it close and hitting it gently with the flat of the ax. He hung the pack up on the nail. All his supplies were in the pack. They were off the ground and sheltered now.

Nick was hungry. He did not believe he had ever been hungrier. He opened and emptied a can of pork and beans and a can of spaghetti into the frying pan.

"I've got a right to eat this kind of stuff, if I'm willing to carry it," Nick said. His voice sounded strange in the darkening woods. He did not speak again.

He started a fire with some chunks of pine he got with the ax from a stump. Over the fire he stuck a wire grill, pushing the four legs down into the ground with his boot. Nick put the frying pan on the grill over the flames. He was hungrier. The beans and spaghetti warmed. Nick stirred them and mixed them together. They began to bubble, making little bubbles that rose with difficulty to the surface. There was a good smell. Nick got out a bottle of tomato catchup and cut four slices of bread. The little bubbles were coming faster now. Nick sat down beside the fire and lifted the frying pan off. He poured about half the contents out into the tin plate. It spread slowly on the plate. Nick knew it was too hot. He poured on some tomato catchup. He knew the beans and spaghetti were still too hot. He looked at the fire, then at the tent, he was not going to spoil it all by burning his tongue. For years he had never enjoyed fried bananas because he had never been able to wait for them to cool. His tongue was very sensitive. He was very hungry. Across the river in the swamp, in the almost dark, he saw a mist rising. He looked at the tent once more. All right. He took a full spoonful from the plate.

"Chrise," Nick said, "Geezus Chrise," he said happily.

He ate the whole plateful before he remembered the bread. Nick finished the second plateful with the bread, mopping the plate shiny. He had not eaten since a cup of coffee and a ham sandwich in the station restaurant at St. Ignace. It had been a very fine experience. He had been that hungry before, but had not been able to satisfy it. He could have made camp hours before if he had wanted to. There were plenty of good places to camp on the river. But this was good.

Nick tucked two big chips of pine under the grill. The fire flared up. He had forgotten to get water for the coffee. Out of the pack he got a folding canvas bucket and walked down the hill, across the edge of the meadow, to the stream. The other bank was in the white mist. The grass was wet and cold as he knelt on the bank and dipped the canvas bucket into the stream. It bellied and pulled hard in the current. The water was ice cold. Nick rinsed the bucket and carried it full up to the camp. Up away from the stream it was not so cold.

Nick drove another big nail and hung up the bucket full of water. He dipped the coffee pot half full, put some more chips under the grill onto the fire and put the pot on. He could not remember which way he made coffee. He could remember an argument about it with Hopkins, but not which side he had taken. He decided to bring it to a boil. He remembered now that was Hopkins's way. He had once argued about everything with Hopkins. While he waited for the coffee to boil, he opened a small can of apricots. He liked to open cans. He emptied the can of apricots out into a tin cup. While he watched the coffee on the fire, he drank the juice syrup of the apricots, carefully at first to keep from spilling, then meditatively, sucking the apricots down. They were better than fresh apricots.

The coffee boiled as he watched. The lid came up and coffee and grounds ran down the side of the pot. Nick took it off the grill. It was a triumph for Hopkins. He put sugar in the empty apricot cup and poured some of the coffee out to cool. It was too hot to pour and he used his hat to hold the handle of the coffee pot. He would not let it steep in the pot at all. Not the first cup. It should be straight Hopkins all the way. Hop deserved that. He was a very serious coffee drinker. He was the most serious man Nick had ever known. Not heavy, serious. That was a long time ago. Hopkins spoke without moving his lips. He had played polo. He made millions of dollars in Texas. He had borrowed carfare to go to Chicago, when the wire came that his first big well had come in. He could have wired for money. That would have been too slow.

They called Hop's girl the Blonde Venus. Hop did not mind because she was not his real girl. Hopkins said very confidently that none of them would make fun of his real girl. He was right. Hopkins went away when the telegram came. That was on the Black River. It took eight days for the telegram to reach him. Hopkins gave away his .22 caliber Colt automatic pistol to Nick. He gave his camera to Bill. It was to remember him always by. They were all going fishing again next summer. The Hop Head was rich. He would get a yacht and they would all cruise along the north shore of Lake Superior. He was excited but serious. They said good-bye and all felt bad. It broke up the trip. They never saw Hopkins again. That was a long time ago on the Black River.

Nick drank the coffee, the coffee according to Hopkins. The coffee was bitter. Nick laughed. It made a good ending to the story. His mind was starting to work. He knew he could choke it because he was tired enough. He spilled the coffee out of the pot and shook the grounds loose into the fire. He lit a cigarette and went inside the tent. He took off his shoes and trousers, sitting on the blankets, rolled the shoes up inside the trousers for a pillow and got in between the blankets.

Out through the front of the tent he watched the glow of the fire, when the night wind blew on it. It was a quiet night. The swamp was perfectly quiet. Nick stretched under the blanket comfortably. A mosquito hummed close to his ear. Nick sat up and lit a match. The mosquito was on the canvas, over his head. Nick moved the match quickly up to it. The mosquito made a satisfactory hiss in the flame. The match went out. Nick lay down again under the blanket. He turned on his side and shut his eyes. He was sleepy. He felt sleep coming. He curled up under the blanket and went to sleep.

Big Two-Hearted River: Part II

In the morning the sun was up and the tent was starting to get hot. Nick crawled out under the mosquito netting stretched across the mouth of the tent, to look at the morning. The grass was wet on his hands as he came out. He held his trousers and shoes in his hands. The sun was just up over the hill. There was the meadow, the river and the swamp. There were birch trees in the green of the swamp on the other side of the river.

The river was clear and smoothly fast in the early morning. Down about two hundred yards were three logs all the way across the stream. They made the water smooth and deep above them. As Nick watched, a mink crossed the river on the logs and went into the swamp. Nick was excited. He was excited by the early morning and the river. He was really too hurried to eat breakfast, but he knew he must. He built a little fire and put on the coffee pot.

While the water was heating in the pot he took an empty bottle and went down over the edge of the high ground to the meadow. The meadow was wet with dew and Nick wanted to catch grasshoppers for bait before the sun dried the grass. He found plenty of good grasshoppers. They were at the base of the grass stems. Sometimes they clung to a grass stem. They were cold and wet with the dew, and could not jump until the sun warmed them. Nick picked them up, taking only the medium-sized brown ones, and put them into the bottle. He turned over a log and just under the shelter of the edge were several hundred hoppers. It was a grasshopper lodging house. Nick put about fifty of the medium browns into the bottle. While he was picking up the hoppers the others warmed in the sun and commenced to hop away. They flew when they hopped. At first they made one flight and stayed stiff when they landed, as though they were dead.

Nick knew that by the time he was through with breakfast they would be as lively as ever. Without dew in the grass it would take him all day to catch a bottle full of good grasshoppers and he would have to crush many of them, slamming at them with his hat. He washed his hands at the stream. He was excited to be near it. Then he walked up to the tent. The hoppers were already jumping stiffly in the grass. In the bottle, warmed by the sun, they were jumping in a mass. Nick put in a pine stick as a cork. It plugged the mouth of the bottle enough, so the hoppers could not get out and left plenty of air passage.

He had rolled the log back and knew he could get grasshoppers there every morning.

Nick laid the bottle full of jumping grasshoppers against a pine trunk. Rapidly he mixed some buckwheat flour with water and stirred it smooth, one cup of flour, one cup of water. He put a handful of coffee in the pot and dipped a lump of grease out of a can and slid it sputtering across the hot skillet. On the smoking skillet he poured smoothly the buckwheat batter. It spread like lava, the grease spitting sharply. Around the edges the buckwheat cake began to firm, then brown, then crisp. The surface was bubbling slowly to porousness. Nick pushed under the browned under surface with a fresh pine chip. He shook the skillet sideways and the cake was loose on the surface. I won't try and flop it, he thought. He slid the chip of clean wood all the way under the cake, and flopped it over onto its face. It sputtered in the pan.

When it was cooked Nick regreased the skillet. He used all the batter. It made another big flapjack and one smaller one.

Nick ate a big flapjack and a smaller one, covered with apple butter. He put apple butter on the third cake, folded it over twice, wrapped it in oiled paper and put it in his shirt pocket. He put the apple butter jar back in the pack and cut bread for two sandwiches.

In the pack he found a big onion. He sliced it in two and peeled the silky outer skin. Then he cut one half into slices and made onion sandwiches. He wrapped them in oiled paper and buttoned them in the other pocket of his khaki shirt. He turned the skillet upside down on the grill, drank the coffee, sweetened and yellow brown with the condensed milk in it, and tidied up the camp. It was a good camp.

Nick took his fly rod out of the leather rod-case, jointed it, and shoved the rod-case back into the tent. He put on the reel and threaded the line through the guides. He had to hold it from hand to hand, as he threaded it, or it would slip back through its own weight. It was a heavy, double tapered fly line. Nick had paid eight dollars for it a long time ago. It was made heavy to lift back in the air and come forward flat and heavy and straight to make it possible to cast a fly which has no weight. Nick opened the aluminum leader box. The leaders were coiled between the damp flannel pads. Nick had wet the pads at the water cooler on the train up to St. Ignace. In the damp pads the gut leaders had softened and Nick unrolled one and tied it by a loop at the end to the heavy fly line. He fastened a hook on the end of the leader. It was a small hook; very thin and springy.

Nick took it from his hook book, sitting with the rod across his lap. He tested the knot and the spring of the rod by pulling the line taut. It was a good feeling. He was careful not to let the hook bite into his finger.

He started down to the stream, holding his rod, the bottle of grasshoppers hung from his neck by a thong tied in half hitches around the neck of the bottle. His landing net hung by a hook from his belt. Over his shoulder was a long flour sack tied at each corner into an ear. The cord went over his shoulder. The sack flapped against his legs.

Nick felt awkward and professionally happy with all his equipment hanging from him. The grasshopper bottle swung against his chest. In his shirt the breast pockets bulged against him with the lunch and his fly hook.

He stepped into the stream. It was a shock. His trousers clung tight to his legs. His shoes felt the gravel. The water was a rising cold shock.

Rushing, the current sucked against his legs. Where he stepped in, the water was over his knees. He waded with the current. The gravel slid under his shoes. He looked down at the swirl of water below each leg and tipped up the bottle to get a grasshopper.

The first grasshopper gave a jump in the neck of the bottle and went out into the water. He was sucked under in the whirl by Nick's right leg and came to the surface a little way down stream. He floated rapidly, kicking. In a quick circle, breaking the smooth surface of the water, he disappeared. A trout had taken him.

Another hopper poked his face out of the bottle. His antennae wavered. He was getting his front legs out of the bottle to jump. Nick took him by the head and held him while he threaded the slim hook under his chin, down through his thorax and into the last segments of his abdomen. The grasshopper took hold of the hook with his front feet, spitting tobacco juice on it. Nick dropped him into the water.

Holding the rod in his right hand he let out line against the pull of the grasshopper in the current. He stripped off line from the reel with his left hand and let it run free. He could see the hopper in the little waves of the current. It went out of sight.

There was a tug on the line. Nick pulled against the taut line. It was his first strike. Holding the now living rod across the current, he brought in the line with his left hand. The rod bent in jerks, the trout pumping against the current. Nick knew it was a small one. He lifted the rod straight up in the air. It bowed with the pull.

He saw the trout in the water jerking with his head and body against the shifting tangent of the line in the stream.

Nick took the line in his left hand and pulled the trout, thumping tiredly against the current, to the surface. His back was mottled the clear, water-over-gravel color, his side flashing in the sun. The rod under his right arm, Nick stooped, dipping his right hand into the current. He held the trout, never still, with his moist right hand, while he unhooked the barb from his mouth, then dropped him back into the stream.

He hung unsteadily in the current, then settled to the bottom beside a stone. Nick reached down his hand to touch him, his arm to the elbow under water. The trout was steady in the moving stream, resting on the gravel, beside a stone. As Nick's fingers touched him, touched his smooth, cool, underwater feeling he was gone, gone in a shadow across the bottom of the stream.

He's all right, Nick thought. He was only tired.

He had wet his hand before he touched the trout, so he would not disturb the delicate mucus that covered him. If a trout was touched with a dry hand, a white fungus attacked the unprotected spot. Years before when he had fished crowded streams, with fly fishermen ahead of him and behind him, Nick had again and again come on dead trout, furry with white fungus, drifted against a rock, or floating belly up in some pool. Nick did not like to fish with other men on the river. Unless they were of your party, they spoiled it.

He wallowed down the stream, above his knees in the current, through the fifty yards of shallow water above the pile of logs that crossed the stream. He did not rebait his hook and held it in his hand as he waded. He was certain he could catch small trout in the shallows, but he did not want them. There would be no big trout in the shallows this time of day.

Now the water deepened up his thighs sharply and coldly. Ahead was the smooth dammed-back flood of water above the logs. The water was smooth and dark; on the left, the lower edge of the meadow; on the right the swamp.

Nick leaned back against the current and took a hopper from the bottle. He threaded the hopper on the hook and spat on him for good luck. Then he pulled several yards of line from the reel and tossed the hopper out ahead onto the fast dark water. It floated down towards the logs, then the weight of the line pulled the bait under the surface. Nick held the rod in his right hand, letting the line run out through his fingers.

There was a long tug. Nick struck and the rod came alive and dangerous, bent double, the line tightening, coming out of water, tightening, all in a heavy, dangerous, steady pull. Nick felt the moment when the leader would break if the strain increased and let the line go.

The reel ratcheted into a mechanical shriek as the line went out in a rush. Too fast. Nick could not check it, the line rushing out, the reel note rising as the line ran out.

With the core of the reel showing, his heart feeling stopped with the excitement, leaning back against the current that mounted icily his thighs. Nick thumbed the reel hard with his left hand. It was awkward getting his thumb inside the fly reel frame.

As he put on pressure the line tightened into sudden hardness and beyond the logs a huge trout went high out of water. As he jumped, Nick lowered the tip of the rod. But he felt, as he dropped the tip to ease the strain, the moment when the strain was too great; the hardness too tight. Of course, the leader had broken. There was no mistaking the feeling when all spring left the line and it became dry and hard. Then it went slack.

His mouth dry, his heart down, Nick reeled in. He had never seen so big a trout. There was a heaviness, a power not to be held, and then the bulk of him, as he jumped. He looked as broad as a salmon.

Nick's hand was shaky. He reeled in slowly. The thrill had been too much. He felt, vaguely, a little sick, as though it would be better to sit down.

The leader had broken where the hook was tied to it. Nick took it in his hand. He thought of the trout somewhere on the bottom, holding himself steady over the gravel, far down below the light, under the logs, with the hook in his jaw. Nick knew the trout's teeth would cut through the snell of the hook. The hook would imbed itself in his jaw. He'd bet the trout was angry. Anything that size would be angry. That was a trout. He had been solidly hooked. Solid as a rock. He felt like a rock, too, before he started off. By God, he was a big one. By God, he was the biggest one I ever heard of.

Nick climbed out onto the meadow and stood, water running down his trousers and out of his shoes, his shoes squlchy. He went over and sat on the logs. He did not want to rush his sensations any.

He wriggled his toes in the water, in his shoes, and got out a cigarette from his breast pocket. He lit it and tossed the match into the fast water below the logs. A tiny trout rose at the match, as it swung around in the fast current. Nick laughed. He would finish the cigarette.

He sat on the logs, smoking, drying in the sun, the sun warm on his back, the river shallow ahead entering the woods, curving into the woods, shallows, light glittering, big water-smooth rocks, cedars along the bank and white birches, the logs warm in the sun, smooth to sit on, without bark, gray to the touch; slowly the feeling of disappointment left him. It went away slowly, the feeling of disappointment that came sharply after the thrill that made his shoulders ache. It was all right now. His rod lying out on the logs, Nick tied a new hook on the leader, pulling the gut tight until it grimped into itself in a hard knot.

He baited up, then picked up the rod and walked to the far end of the logs to get into the water, where it was not too deep. Under and beyond the logs was a deep pool. Nick walked around the shallow shelf near the swamp shore until he came out on the shallow bed of the stream.

On the left, where the meadow ended and the woods began, a great elm tree was uprooted. Gone over in a storm, it lay back into the woods, its roots clotted with dirt, grass growing in them, rising a solid bank beside the stream. The river cut to the edge of the uprooted tree. From where Nick stood he could see deep channels, like ruts, cut in the shallow bed of the stream by the flow of the current. Pebbly where he stood and pebbly and full of boulders beyond; where it curved near the tree roots, the bed of the stream was marly and between the ruts of deep water green weed fronds swung in the current.

Nick swung the rod back over his shoulder and forward, and the line, curving forward, laid the grasshopper down on one of the deep channels in the weeds. A trout struck and Nick hooked him.

Holding the rod far out toward the uprooted tree and sloshing backward in the current, Nick worked the trout, plunging, the rod bending alive, out of the danger of the weeds into the open river. Holding the rod, pumping alive against the current, Nick brought the trout in. He rushed, but always came, the spring of the rod yielding to the rushes, sometimes jerking under the water, but always bringing him in. Nick eased downstream with the rushes. The rod above his head he led the trout over the net, then lifted.

The trout hung heavy in the net, mottled trout back and silver sides in the meshes. Nick unhooked him; heavy sides, good to hold, big undershot jaw, and slipped him, heaving and big sliding, into the long sack that hung from his shoulders in the water.

Nick spread the mouth of the sack against the current and it filled, heavy with water. He held it up, the bottom in the stream, and the water poured out through the sides. Inside at the bottom was the big trout, alive in the water.

Nick moved downstream. The sack out ahead of him sunk heavy in the water, pulling from his shoulders.

It was getting hot, the sun hot on the back of his neck.

Nick had one good trout. He did not care about getting many trout. Now the stream was shallow and wide. There were trees along both banks. The trees of the left bank made short shadows on the current in the forenoon sun. Nick knew there were trout in each shadow. In the afternoon, after the sun had crossed toward the hills, the trout would be in the cool shadows on the other side of the stream.

The very biggest ones would lie up close to the bank. You could always pick them up there on the Black. When the sun was down they all moved out into the current. Just when the sun made the water blinding in the glare before it went down, you were liable to strike a big trout anywhere in the current. It was almost impossible to fish then, the surface of the water was blinding as a mirror in the sun. Of course, you could fish upstream, but in a stream like the Black, or this, you had to wallow against the current and in a deep place, the water piled up on you. It was no fun to fish upstream with this much current.

Nick moved along through the shallow stretch watching the banks for deep holes. A beech tree grew close beside the river, so that the branches hung down into the water. The stream went back in under the leaves. There were always trout in a place like that.

Nick did not care about fishing that hole. He was sure he would get hooked in the branches.

It looked deep though. He dropped the grasshopper so the current took it under water, back in under the overhanging branch. The line pulled hard and Nick struck. The trout threshed heavily, half out of water in the leaves and branches. The line was caught. Nick pulled hard and the trout was off. He reeled in and holding the hook in his hand, walked down the stream.

Ahead, close to the left bank, was a big log. Nick saw it was hollow; pointing up river the current entered it smoothly, only a little ripple spread each side of the log. The water was deepening. The top of the hollow log was gray and dry. It was partly in the shadow.

Nick took the cork out of the grasshopper bottle and a hopper clung to it. He picked him off, hooked him and tossed him out. He held the rod far out so that the hopper on the water moved into the current flowing into the hollow log. Nick lowered the rod and the hopper floated in. There was a heavy strike. Nick swung the rod against the pull. It felt as though he were hooked into the log itself, except for the live feeling.

He tried to force the fish out into the current. It came, heavily.

The line went slack and Nick thought the trout was gone. Then he saw him, very near, in the current, shaking his head, trying to get the hook out. His mouth was clamped shut. He was fighting the hook in the clear flowing current.

Looping in the line with his left hand, Nick swung the rod to make the line taut and tried to lead the trout toward the net, but he was gone, out of sight, the line pumping. Nick fought him against the current, letting him thump in the water against the spring of the rod. He shifted the rod to his left hand, worked the trout upstream, holding his weight, fighting on the rod, and then let him down into the net. He lifted him clear of the water, a heavy half circle in the net, the net dripping, unhooked him and slid him into the sack.

He spread the mouth of the sack and looked down in at the two big trout alive in the water.

Through the deepening water, Nick waded over to the hollow log. He took the sack off, over his head, the trout flopping as it came out of water, and hung it so the trout were deep in the water. Then he pulled himself up on the log and sat, the water from his trouser and boots running down into the stream. He laid his rod down, moved along to the shady end of the log and took the sandwiches out of his pocket. He dipped the sandwiches in the cold water. The current carried away the crumbs. He ate the sandwiches and dipped his hat full of water to drink, the water running out through his hat just ahead of his drinking.

It was cool in the shade, sitting on the log. He took a cigarette out and struck a match to light it. The match sunk into the gray wood, making a tiny furrow. Nick leaned over the side of the log, found a hard place and lit the match. He sat smoking and watching the river.

Ahead the river narrowed and went into a swamp. The river became smooth and deep and the swamp looked solid with cedar trees, their trunks close together, their branches solid. It would not be possible to walk through a swamp like that. The branches grew so low. You would have to keep almost level with the ground to move at all. You could not crash through the branches. That must be why the animals that lived in swamps were built the way they were, Nick thought.

He wished he had brought something to read. He felt like reading. He did not feel like going on into the swamp. He looked down the river. A big cedar slanted all the way across the stream. Beyond that the river went into the swamp.

Nick did not want to go in there now. He felt a reaction against deep wading with the water deepening up under his armpits, to hook big trout in places impossible to land them. In the swamp the banks were bare, the big cedars came together overhead, the sun did not come through, except in patches; in the fast deep water, in the half light, the fishing would be tragic. In the swamp fishing was a tragic adventure. Nick did not want it. He did not want to go down the stream any further today.

He took out his knife, opened it and stuck it in the log. Then he pulled up the sack, reached into it and brought out one of the trout. Holding him near the tail, hard to hold, alive, in his hand, he whacked him against the log. The trout quivered, rigid. Nick laid him on the log in the shade and broke the neck of the other fish the same way. He laid them side by side on the log. They were fine trout.

Nick cleaned them, slitting them from the vent to the tip of the jaw. All the insides and the gills and tongue came out in one piece. They were both males; long gray-white strips of milt, smooth and clean. All the insides clean and compact, coming out all together. Nick tossed the offal ashore for the minks to find.

He washed the trout in the stream. When he held them back up in the water they looked like live fish. Their color was not gone yet. He washed his hands and dried them on the log. Then he laid the trout on the sack spread out on the log, rolled them up in it, tied the bundle and put it in the landing net. His knife was still standing, blade stuck in the log. He cleaned it on the wood and put it in his pocket.

Nick stood up on the log, holding his rod, the landing net hanging heavy, then stepped into the water and splashed ashore. He climbed the bank and cut up into the woods, toward the high ground. He was going back to camp. He looked back. The river just showed through the trees. There were plenty of days coming when he could fish the swamp.

JORGE LUIS BORGES

b. 1899

Besides having been born in the same year, Borges shares with Nabokov a vast learning in all languages and literatures. He grew up in Buenos Aires, reading in his father's well-stocked library, continued his education in Spain and Switzerland, and then returned to Argentina to become a librarian himself. But as opposed to Nabokov's pixyish way with his erudition, Borges is deeply mystical: reality for him approaches that vertiginous simultaneity that he describes in Funes' perception of three wine glasses on a table: "Funes saw all the shoots, clusters, and grapes of the vine. He remembered the shapes of the clouds in the south at dawn on the 30th of April of 1882, and he could compare them in his recollection with the marbled grain in the design of a leather-bound book which he had seen only once."

Borges' vision of experience, in which imaginary animals from Old Norse myths exist alongside precisely observed details of contemporary Buenos Aires, probably owes a lot to the fact that after years of failing sight he went totally blind in 1957. His way of writing is like Hladik's in "The Secret Miracle": he imagines a story all at once, as in a flash of revelation rather than as a sequence of sentences, holding the story as an entity in his mind while he makes mental revisions, only then releasing it so as to speak to the ordinary world of time. This method of imagining reinforces Borges' constant subject, which is the variety of human perceptions under different conditions, in different states of mind. Thus it is as real for Borges' characters to see God in a tiny letter on a page in an atlas as it is for them to observe the shadow of a bee on a wall or feel a drop of water on their foreheads. And the connections among such perceptions may be equally surprising, since relationships are not limited to the usual cause-and-effect connections that depend on ordinary assumptions about time and space.

Borges' labyrinthine landscape of the imagination was largely unknown outside of Argentina until 1961, the year in which he shared the International Publishers' Prize with Samuel Beckett. Since then, with Borges' collaboration, several collections of his works have been translated into English, and his stature as a writer is now internationally recognized. He has made a number of public appearances in the United States and charmed audiences with his gentle, low-keyed brilliance. Politically, for many years he had difficulties in his own country: his opposition to Nazi influence in Argentina just before and during World War II put him at odds with the government, and when after the war Perón became dictator he rewarded Borges' outspoken dissent by demoting him from librarian to chicken inspector.

Funes, the Memorious

I remember him (I scarcely have the right to use this ghostly verb; only one man on earth deserved the right, and he is dead), I remember him with a dark passionflower in his hand, looking at it as no one has ever looked at such a flower, though they might look from the twilight of day until the twilight of night, for a whole life long. I remember him, his face immobile and Indian-like, and singularly *remote,* behind his cigarette. I remember (I believe) the strong delicate fingers of the plainsman who can braid leather. I remember, near those hands, a vessel in which to make maté tea, bearing the arms of the Banda Oriental; I remember, in the window of the house, a yellow rush mat, and beyond, a vague marshy landscape. I remember clearly his voice, the deliberate, resentful, nasal voice of the old eastern shore man, without the Italianate sibilants of today. I did not see him more than three times; the last time, in 1887. . . .

That all those who knew him should write something about him seems to me a very felicitous idea; my testimony may perhaps be the briefest and without doubt the poorest, and it will not be the least impartial. The deplorable fact of my being an Argentinian will hinder me from falling into a dithyramb —an obligatory form in the Uruguay, when the theme is an Uruguayan.

Littérateur, slicker, Buenos Airean: Funes did not use these insulting phrases, but I am sufficiently aware that for him I represented these unfortunate categories. Pedro Leandro Ipuche has written that Funes was a precursor of the superman, "an untamed and vernacular Zarathustra"; I do not doubt it, but one must not forget, either, that he was a countryman from the town of Fray Bentos, with certain incurable limitations.

My first recollection of Funes is quite clear, I see him at dusk, sometime in March or February of the year '84. That year, my father had taken me to spend the summer at Fray Bentos. I was on my way back from the farm at San Francisco with my cousin Bernardo Haedo. We came back singing, on horseback; and this last fact was not the only reason for my joy. After a sultry day, an enormous slate-gray storm had obscured the sky. It was driven on by a wind from the south; the trees were already tossing like madmen; and I had the apprehension (the secret hope) that the elemental downpour would catch us out in the open. We were running a kind of race with the tempest. We rode into a narrow lane which wound down between two enormously high brick footpaths. It had grown black of a sudden; I now heard rapid, almost secret steps above; I raised my eyes and saw a boy running along the narrow, cracked path as if he were running along a narrow, broken wall. I remember the loose trousers, tight at the bottom, the hemp sandals; I remember the cigarette in the hard visage, standing out against the by now limitless darkness. Bernardo unexpectedly yelled to him: "What's the time, Ireneo?" Without looking up, without stopping, Ireneo replied: "In ten minutes it will be eight o'clock, child Bernardo Juan Francisco." The voice was sharp, mocking.

I am so absent-minded that the dialogue which I have just cited would not have penetrated my attention if it had not been repeated by my cousin, who was stimulated, I think, by a certain local pride and by a desire to show himself indifferent to the other's three-sided reply.

He told me that the boy above us in the pass was a certain Ireneo Funes, renowned for a number of eccentricities, such as that of having nothing to do with people and of always knowing the time, like a watch. He added that Ireneo was the son of María Clementina Funes, an ironing woman in the town, and that his father, some people said, was an "Englishman" named O'Connor, a doctor in the salting fields, though some said the father was a horse-breaker, or scout, from the province of El Salto. Ireneo lived with his mother, at the edge of the country house of the Laurels.

In the years '85 and '86 we spent the summer in the city of Montevideo. We returned to Fray Bentos in '87. As was natural, I inquired after all my acquaintances, and finally, about "the chronometer Funes." I was told that he had been thrown by a wild horse at the San Francisco ranch, and that he had been hopelessly crippled. I remember the impression of uneasy magic which the news provoked in me: the only time I had seen him we were on horseback, coming from San Francisco, and he was in a high place; from the lips of my cousin Bernardo the affair sounded like a dream elaborated with elements out of the past. They told me that Ireneo did not move now from his cot, but remained with his eyes fixed on the backyard fig tree, or on a cobweb. At sunset he allowed himself to be brought to the window. He carried pride to the extreme of pretending that the blow which had befallen him was a good thing. . . . Twice I saw him behind the iron gate which sternly delineated his eternal imprisonment: unmoving, once, his eyes closed; unmoving also, another time, absorbed in the contemplation of a sweet-smelling sprig of lavender cotton.

At the time I had begun, not without some ostentation, the methodical study of Latin. My valise contained the *De viris illustribus* of Lhomond, the *Thesaurus* of Quicherat, Caesar's *Commentaries,* and an odd-numbered volume of the *Historia Naturalis* of Pliny, which exceeded (and still exceeds) my modest talents as a Latinist. Everything is noised around in a small town; Ireneo, at his small farm on the outskirts, was not long in learning of the arrival of these anomalous books. He sent me a flowery, ceremonious letter, in which he recalled our encounter, unfortunately brief, "on the seventh day of February of the year '84," and alluded to the glorious services which Don Gregorio Haedo, my uncle, dead the same year, "had rendered to the Two Fatherlands in the glorious campaign of Ituzaingó," and he solicited the loan of any one of the volumes, to be accompanied by a dictionary "for the better intelligence of the original text, for I do not know Latin as yet." He promised to return them in good condition, almost immediately. The letter was perfect, very nicely constructed; the orthography was of the type sponsored by Andrés Bello: *i* for *y*, *j* for *g*. At first I naturally suspected a jest. My cousins assured me it was not so, that these were the ways of Ireneo. I did not know whether to attribute to impudence, ignorance, or stupidity, the idea that the difficult Latin required no other instrument than a dictionary; in order fully to undeceive him I sent the *Gradus ad Parnassum* of Quicherat, and the Pliny.

On February 14, I received a telegram from Buenos Aires telling me to return immediately, for my father was "in no way well." God forgive me, but the prestige of being the recipient of an urgent telegram, the desire to point out to all of Fray Bentos the contradiction between the negative form of the news and the positive adverb, the temptation to dramatize my sorrow as I feigned a virile stoicism, all no doubt distracted me from the possibility of anguish. As I packed my valise, I noted that I was missing the *Gradus* and the volume of the *Historia Naturalis.* The "Saturn" was to weigh anchor on the morning of the next day; that night, after supper, I made my way to the house of Funes. Outside, I was surprised to find the night no less oppressive than the day.

Ireneo's mother received me at the modest ranch.

She told me that Ireneo was in the back room and that I should not be disturbed to find him in the dark, for he knew how to pass the dead hours without lighting the candle. I crossed the cobblestone patio, the small corridor; I came to the second patio. A great vine covered everything, so that the darkness seemed complete. Of a sudden I heard the high-pitched, mocking voice of Ireneo. The voice spoke in Latin; the voice (which came out of the obscurity) was reading, with obvious delight, a treatise or prayer or incantation. The Roman syllables resounded in the earthen patio; my suspicion made them seem undecipherable, interminable; afterward, in the enormous dialogue of that night, I learned that they made up the first paragraph of the twenty-fourth chapter of the seventh book of the *Historia Naturalis.* The subject of this chapter is memory; the last words are *ut nihil non iisdem verbis redderetur auditum.*

Without the least change in his voice, Ireneo bade me come in. He was lying on the cot, smoking. It seems to me that I did not see his face until dawn; I seem to recall the momentary glow of the cigarette. The room smelled vaguely of dampness. I sat down, and repeated the story of the telegram and my father's illness.

I come now to the most difficult point in my narrative. For the entire story has no other point (the reader might as well know it by now) than this dialogue of almost a half-century ago. I shall not attempt to reproduce his words, now irrecoverable. I prefer truthfully to make a résumé of the many things Ireneo told me. The indirect style is remote and weak; I know that I sacrifice the effectiveness of my narrative; but let my readers imagine the nebulous sentences which clouded that night.

Ireneo began by enumerating, in Latin and Spanish, the cases of prodigious memory cited in the *Historia Naturalis:* Cyrus, king of the Persians, who could call every soldier in his armies by name; Mithridates Eupator, who administered justice in the twenty-two languages of his empire; Simonides, inventor of mnemotechny; Metrodorus, who practiced the art of repeating faithfully what he heard once. With evident good faith Funes marveled that such things should be considered marvelous. He told me that previous to the rainy afternoon when the blue-tinted horse threw him, he had been—like any Christian—blind, deaf, mute, somnambulistic, memoryless. (I tried to remind him of his precise perception of time, his memory for proper names; he paid no attention to me.) For nineteen years, he said, he had lived like a person in a dream: he looked without seeing, heard without hearing, forgot everything—almost everything. On falling from the horse, he lost consciousness; when he recovered it, the present was almost intolerable it was so rich and bright; the same was true of the most ancient and most trivial memories. A little later he realized that he was crippled. This fact scarcely interested him. He reasoned (or felt) that immobility was a minimum price to pay. And now, his perception and his memory were infallible.

We, in a glance, perceive three wine glasses on the table; Funes saw all the shoots, clusters, and grapes of the vine. He remembered the shapes of the clouds in the south at dawn on the 30th of April of 1882, and he could compare them in his recollection with the marbled grain in the design of a leather-bound book which he had seen only once, and with the lines in the spray which an oar raised in the Río Negro on the eve of the battle of the Quebracho. These recollections were not simple; each visual image was linked to muscular sensations, thermal sensations, etc. He could reconstruct all his dreams, all his fancies. Two or three times he had reconstructed an entire day. He told me: *I have more memories in myself alone than all men have had since the world was a world.* And again: *My dreams are like your vigils.* And again, toward dawn: *My memory, sir, is like a garbage disposal.*

A circumference on a blackboard, a rectangular triangle, a rhomb, are forms which we can fully intuit; the same held true with Ireneo for the tempestuous mane of a stallion, a herd of cattle in a pass, the ever-changing flame or the innumerable ash, the many faces of a dead man during the course of a protracted wake. He could perceive I do not know how many stars in the sky.

These things he told me; neither then nor at any time later did they seem doubtful. In those days neither the cinema nor the phonograph yet existed;

nevertheless, it seems strange, almost incredible, that no one should have experimented on Funes. The truth is that we all live by leaving behind; no doubt we all profoundly know that we are immortal and that sooner or later every man will do all things and know everything.

The voice of Funes, out of the darkness, continued. He told me that toward 1886 he had devised a new system of enumeration and that in a very few days he had gone beyond twenty-four thousand. He had not written it down, for what he once meditated would not be erased. The first stimulus to his work, I believe, had been his discontent with the fact that "thirty-three Uruguayans" required two symbols and three words, rather than a single word and a single symbol. Later he applied his extravagant principle to the other numbers. In place of seven thousand thirteen, he would say (for example) *Maximo Perez;* in place of seven thousand fourteen, *The Train;* other numbers were *Luis Melian Lafinur, Olimar, Brimstone, Clubs, The Whale, Gas, The Caldron, Napoleon, Augustin de Vedia.* In lieu of five hundred, he would say *nine.* Each word had a particular sign, a species of mark; the last were very complicated. . . . I attempted to explain that this rhapsody of unconnected terms was precisely the contrary of a system of enumeration. I said that to say three hundred and sixty-five was to say three hundreds, six tens, five units: an analysis which does not exist in such numbers as *The Negro Timoteo* or *The Flesh Blanket.* Funes did not understand me, or did not wish to understand me.

Locke, in the seventeenth century, postulated (and rejected) an impossible idiom in which each individual object, each stone, each bird and branch had an individual name; Funes had once projected an analogous idiom, but he had renounced it as being too general, too ambiguous. In effect, Funes not only remembered every leaf on every tree of every wood, but even every one of the times he had perceived or imagined it. He determined to reduce all of his past experience to some seventy thousand recollections, which he would later define numerically. Two considerations dissuaded him: the thought that the task was interminable and the thought that it was useless. He knew that at the hour of his death he would scarcely have finished classifying even all the memories of his childhood.

The two projects I have indicated (an infinite vocabulary for the natural series of numbers, and a usable mental catalogue of all the images of memory) are lacking in sense, but they reveal a certain stammering greatness. They allow us to make out dimly, or to infer, the dizzying world of Funes. He was, let us not forget, almost incapable of general, platonic ideas. It was not only difficult for him to understand that the generic term *dog* embraced so many unlike specimens of differing sizes and different forms; he was disturbed by the fact that a dog at three-fourteen (seen in profile) should have the same name as the dog at three-fifteen (seen from the front). His own face in the mirror, his own hands, surprised him on every occasion. Swift writes that the emperor of

Lilliput could discern the movement of the minute hand; Funes could continuously make out the tranquil advances of corruption, of caries, of fatigue. He noted the progress of death, of moisture. He was the solitary and lucid spectator of a multiform world which was instantaneously and almost intolerably exact. Babylon, London, and New York have overawed the imagination of men with their ferocious splendor; no one, in those populous towers or upon those surging avenues, has felt the heat and pressure of a reality as indefatigable as that which day and night converged upon the unfortunate Ireneo in his humble South American farmhouse. It was very difficult for him to sleep. To sleep is to be abstracted from the world; Funes, on his back in his cot, in the shadows, imagined every crevice and every molding of the various houses which surrounded him. (I repeat, the least important of his recollections was more minutely precise and more lively than our perception of a physical pleasure or a physical torment.) Toward the east, in a section which was not yet cut into blocks of homes, there were some new unknown houses. Funes imagined them black, compact, made of a single obscurity; he would turn his face in this direction in order to sleep. He would also imagine himself at the bottom of the river, being rocked and annihilated by the current.

Without effort, he had learned English, French, Portuguese, Latin. I suspect, nevertheless, that he was not very capable of thought. To think is to forget a difference, to generalize, to abstract. In the overly replete world of Funes there were nothing but details, almost contiguous details.

The equivocal clarity of dawn penetrated along the earthen patio.

Then it was that I saw the face of the voice which had spoken all through the night. Ireneo was nineteen years old; he had been born in 1868; he seemed as monumental as bronze, more ancient than Egypt, anterior to the prophecies and the pyramids. It occurred to me that each one of my words (each one of my gestures) would live on in his implacable memory; I was benumbed by the fear of multiplying superfluous gestures.

Ireneo Funes died in 1889, of a pulmonary congestion.

The Secret Miracle

> And God made him die during the course of a hundred years and then He revived him and said:
> "How long have you been here?"
> "A day, or part of a day," he replied.
>
> —*The Koran,* II 261

On the night of March 14, 1939, in an apartment on the Zelternergasse in Prague, Jaromir Hladík, author of the unfinished tragedy *The Enemies,* of a *Vindication of Eternity,* and of an inquiry into the indirect Jewish sources of Jakob Boehme, dreamt a long-drawn-out chess game. The antagonists were not two individuals, but two illustrious families. The contest had begun many centuries before. No one could any longer describe the forgotten prize, but it was rumored that it was enormous and perhaps infinite. The pieces and the chessboard were set up in a secret tower. Jaromir (in his dream) was the first-born of one of the contending families. The hour for the next move, which could not be postponed, struck on all the clocks. The dreamer ran across the sands of a rainy desert—and he could not remember the chessmen or the rules of chess. At this point he awoke. The din of the rain and the clangor of the terrible clocks ceased. A measured unison, sundered by voices of command, arose from the Zelternergasse. Day had dawned, and the armored vanguards of the Third Reich were entering Prague.

On the nineteenth, the authorities received an accusation against Jaromir Hladík; on the same day, at dusk, he was arrested. He was taken to a barracks, aseptic and white, on the opposite bank of the Moldau. He was unable to refute a single one of the charges made by the Gestapo: his maternal surname was Jaroslavski, his blood was Jewish, his study of Boehme was Judaizing, his signature had helped to swell the final census of those protesting the *Anschluss.* In 1928, he had translated the *Sepher Yezirah* for the publishing house of Hermann Barsdorf; the effusive catalogue issued by this firm had exaggerated, for commercial reasons, the translator's renown; this catalogue was leafed through by Julius Rothe, one of the officials in whose hands lay Hladík's fate. The man does not exist who, outside his own specialty, is not credulous: two or three adjectives in Gothic script sufficed to convince Julius Rothe of Hladík's preeminence, and of the need for the death penalty, *pour encourager les autres.* The execution was set for the twenty-ninth of March, at nine in the morning. This delay (whose importance the reader will appreciate later) was due to a desire on the part of the authorities to act slowly and impersonally, in the manner of planets or vegetables.

Hladík's first reaction was simply one of horror. He was sure he would not have been terrified by the gallows, the block, or the knife; but to die before a firing squad was unbearable. In vain he repeated to himself that the pure and general act of dying, not the concrete circumstances, was the dreadful fact. He did not grow weary of imagining these circumstances: he absurdly tried to exhaust all the variations. He infinitely anticipated the process, from the sleepless dawn to the mysterious discharge of the rifles. Before the day set by Julius Rothe, he died hundreds of deaths, in courtyards whose shapes and angles defied geometry, shot down by changeable soldiers whose number varied and who sometimes put an end to him from close up and sometimes from far away. He faced these imaginary executions with true terror (perhaps with true courage). Each simulacrum lasted a few seconds. Once the circle was closed, Jaromir returned interminably to the tremulous eve of his death. Then he would reflect that reality does not tend to coincide with forecasts about it. With perverse logic he inferred that to foresee a circumstantial detail is to prevent its happening. Faithful to this feeble magic, he would invent, *so that they might not happen,* the most atrocious particulars. Naturally, he finished by fearing that these particulars were prophetic. During his wretched nights he strove to hold fast somehow to the fugitive substance of time. He knew that time was precipitating itself toward the dawn of the twenty-ninth. He reasoned aloud: *I am now in the night of the twenty-second. While this night lasts (and for six more nights to come) I am invulnerable, immortal.* His nights of sleep seemed to him deep, dark pools into which he might submerge. Sometimes he yearned impatiently for the firing squad's definitive volley, which would redeem him, for better or for worse, from the vain compulsion of his imagination. On the twenty-eighth, as the final sunset reverberated across the high barred windows, he was distracted from all these abject considerations by thought of his drama, *The Enemies.*

Hladík was past forty. Apart from a few friendships and many habits, the problematic practice of literature constituted his life. Like every writer, he measured the virtues of other writers by their performance, and asked that they measure him by what he conjectured or planned. All of the books he had published merely moved him to a complex repentance. His investigation of the work of Boehme, of Ibn Ezra, and of Fludd was essentially a product of mere application; his translation of the *Sepher Yezirah* was characterized by negligence, fatigue, and conjecture. He judged his *Vindication of Eternity* to be perhaps less deficient: the first volume is a history of the diverse eternities devised by man, from the immutable Being of Parmenides to the alterable past of Hinton; the second volume denies (with Francis Bradley) that all the events in the universe make up a temporal series. He argues that the number of experiences possible to man is not infinite, and that a single "repetition" suffices to demonstrate that time is a fallacy.... Unfortunately, the arguments that demonstrate this fallacy are not any less fallacious. Hladík was in the habit of running through these arguments with a certain disdainful perplexity. He had also written a series of expressionist poems; these, to the discomfiture of the author, were included in an anthology in 1924, and there was no anthology of later date which did not inherit them. Hladík was anxious to redeem himself from his equivocal and languid past with his verse drama, *The Enemies.* (He favored the verse form in the theater because it prevents the spectators from forgetting unreality, which is the necessary condition of art.)

This opus preserved the dramatic unities (time, place, and action). It transpires in Hradcany, in the library of the Baron Roemerstadt, on one of the last evenings of the nineteenth century. In the first scene of the first act, a stranger pays a visit to Roemerstadt. (A clock strikes seven, the vehemence of a setting sun glorifies the window panes, the air transmits familiar and impassioned Hungarian music.) This visit is followed by others; Roemerstadt does not know the people who come to importune him, but he has the uncomfortable impression that he has seen them before: perhaps in a dream. All the visitors fawn upon him, but it is obvious—first to the spectators of the drama, and then to the Baron himself—that they are secret enemies, sworn to ruin him. Roemerstadt manages to outwit, or evade, their complex intrigues. In the course of the dialogue, mention is made of his betrothed, Julia de Weidenau, and of a certain Jaroslav Kubin, who at one time had been her suitor. Kubin has now lost his mind and thinks he is Roemerstadt. . . . The dangers multiply. Roemerstadt, at the end of the second act, is forced to kill one of the conspirators. The third and final act begins. The incongruities gradually mount up: actors who seemed to have been discarded from the play reappear; the man who had been killed by Roemerstadt returns, for an instant. Someone notes that the time of day has not advanced: the clock strikes seven, the western sun reverberates in the high windowpanes, impassioned Hungarian music is carried on the air. The first speaker in the play reappears and repeats the words he had spoken in the first scene of the first act. Roemerstadt addresses him without the least surprise. The spectator understands that Roemerstadt is the wretched Jaroslav Kubin. The drama has never taken place: it is the circular delirium which Kubin unendingly lives and relives.

Hladík had never asked himself whether this tragicomedy of errors was preposterous or admirable, deliberate or casual. Such a plot, he intuited, was the most appropriate invention to conceal his defects and to manifest his strong points, and it embodied the possibility of redeeming (symbolically) the fundamental meaning of his life. He had already completed the first act and a scene or two of the third. The metrical nature of the work allowed him to go over it continually, rectifying the hexameters, without recourse to the manuscript. He thought of the two acts still to do, and of his coming death. In the darkness, he addressed himself to God. *If I exist at all, if I am not one of Your repetitions and errata, I exist as the author of* The Enemies. *In order to bring this drama, which may serve to justify me, to justify You, I need one more year. Grant me that year,*

You to whom belong the centuries and all time. It was the last, the most atrocious night, but ten minutes later sleep swept over him like a dark ocean and drowned him.

Toward dawn, he dreamt he had hidden himself in one of the naves of the Clementine Library. A librarian wearing dark glasses asked him: *What are you looking for?* Hladík answered: *God.* The Librarian told him: *God is in one of the letters on one of the pages of one of the 400,000 volumes of the Clementine. My fathers and the fathers of my fathers have sought after that letter. I've gone blind looking for it.* He removed his glasses, and Hladík saw that his eyes were dead. A reader came in to return an atlas. *This atlas is useless,* he said, and handed it to Hladík, who opened it at random. As if through a haze, he saw a map of India. With a sudden rush of assurance, he touched one of the tiniest letters. An ubiquitous voice said: *The time for your work has been granted.* Hladík awoke.

He remembered that the dreams of men belong to God, and that Maimonides wrote that the words of a dream are divine, when they are all separate and clear and are spoken by someone invisible. He dressed. Two soldiers entered his cell and ordered him to follow them.

From behind the door, Hladík had visualized a labyrinth of passageways, stairs, and connecting blocks. Reality was less rewarding: the party descended to an inner courtyard by a single iron stairway. Some soldiers—uniforms unbuttoned—were testing a motorcycle and disputing their conclusions. The sergeant looked at his watch: it was 8:44. They must wait until nine. Hladík, more insignificant than pitiful, sat down on a pile of firewood. He noticed that the soldiers' eyes avoided his. To make his wait easier, the sergeant offered him a cigarette. Hladík did not smoke. He accepted the cigarette out of politeness or humility. As he lit it, he saw that his hands shook. The day was clouding over. The soldiers spoke in low tones, as though he were already dead. Vainly, he strove to recall the woman of whom Julia de Weidenau was the symbol. . . .

The firing squad fell in and was brought to attention. Hladík, standing against the barracks wall, waited for the volley. Someone expressed fear the wall would be splashed with blood. The condemned man was ordered to step forward a few paces. Hladík recalled, absurdly, the preliminary maneuvers of a photographer. A heavy drop of rain grazed one of Hladík's temples and slowly rolled down his cheek. The sergeant barked the final command.

The physical universe stood still.

The rifles converged upon Hladík, but the men assigned to pull the triggers were immobile. The sergeant's arm eternalized an inconclusive gesture. Upon a courtyard flagstone a bee cast a stationary shadow. The wind had halted, as in a painted picture. Hladík began a shriek, a syllable, a twist of the hand. He realized he was paralyzed. Not a sound reached him from the stricken world.

He thought: *I'm in hell, I'm dead.*

He thought: *I've gone mad.*

He thought: *Time has come to a halt.*

Then he reflected that in that case, his thought, too, would have come to a halt. He was anxious to test this possibility: he repeated (without moving his lips) the mysterious Fourth Eclogue of Virgil. He imagined that the already remote soldiers shared his anxiety; he longed to communicate with them. He was astonished that he felt no fatigue, no vertigo from his protracted immobility. After an indeterminate length of time he fell asleep. On awakening he found the world still motionless and numb. The drop of water still clung to his cheek; the shadow of the bee still did not shift in the courtyard; the smoke from the cigarette he had thrown down did not blow away. Another "day" passed before Hladík understood.

He had asked God for an entire year in which to finish his work: His omnipotence had granted him the time. For his sake, God projected a secret miracle: German lead would kill him, at the determined hour, but in his mind a year would elapse between the command to fire and its execution. From perplexity he passed to stupor, from stupor to resignation, from resignation to sudden gratitude.

He disposed of no document but his own memory; the mastering of each hexameter as he added it, had imposed upon him a kind of fortunate discipline not imagined by those amateurs who forget their vague, ephemeral, paragraphs. He did not work for posterity, nor even for God, of whose literary preferences he possessed scant knowledge. Meticulous, unmoving, secretive, he wove his lofty invisible labyrinth in time. He worked the third act over twice. He eliminated some rather too-obvious symbols: the repeated striking of the hour, the music. There were no circumstances to constrain him. He omitted, condensed, amplified; occasionally, he chose the primitive version. He grew to love the courtyard, the barracks; one of the faces endlessly confronting him made him modify his conception of Roemerstadt's character. He discovered that the hard cacophonies which so distressed Flaubert are mere visual superstitions: debilities and annoyances of the written word, not of the sonorous, the sounding one. . . . He brought his drama to a conclusion: he lacked only a single epithet. He found it: the drop of water slid down his cheek. He began a wild cry, moved his face aside. A quadruple blast brought him down.

Jaromir Hladík died on March 29, at 9:02 in the morning.

VLADIMIR NABOKOV

1899–1977

Nabokov was born and brought up in a rich, privileged, cultured world that has no counterpart today—certainly not in Russia and not really anywhere else either. A broad country estate on which the young Nabokov studied nature and became a lepidopterist (an expert on butterflies); French and English governesses; annual luxurious pilgrimages to the French Riviera—the life of the European high bourgeoisie of a vanished era was Nabokov's. It was all destroyed by World War I and the Bolshevik Revolution. At nineteen Nabokov became a permanent exile from his country, with memories of childhood that seemed as much the stuff of fairy tales as of reality. After his exile from Russia he entered Trinity College, Cambridge, England, taking a first-class degree in modern languages in 1922, the same year in which his beloved and admired father was assassinated by two Russian monarchist gunmen. Now the head of his family, he moved to Berlin, where there was a large group of Russian émigrés from whose constant political discussion and intrigue Nabokov remained somewhat detached. In Berlin and later in Paris he supported himself in various ways—coaching tennis, teaching languages, making up chess problems for magazines—but he never deviated from his main objective of becoming a major writer. During the thirties he produced a steady stream of articles, poems, stories, and novels written mostly in Russian but also in German, French, and English. The finest is *Dar,* or in the English translation *The Gift,* written in 1938, just before he was to undergo yet another exile when Hitler overran France. Nabokov with his wife and son escaped to America, and in the next twenty years he not only became an American citizen but an American writer as well. He embraced the country—its special kind of English, its movies, highways, motels, colleges, butterflies—and the results are apparent in his two best novels (written in English): *Lolita* (1955), which at last brought him enough money so he could devote himself exclusively to writing, and *Pale Fire* (1962). After 1960 Nabokov lived most of the year in Montreux, Switzerland, retaining both his citizenship and an affectionate attachment to the United States.

The narrators of these two stories are haunted. Ghosts from the past stalk them, and in one sense they write to assert that now: New York, 1943 is real, and what happened in France or Russia years ago is just a memory. But *just* a memory? To these narrators memory, the recapturing of the past, is the supreme creative act that alone reveals the meaning of otherwise chaotic and bizarre experience. Perhaps like Nabokov himself, remembering not only his bygone youth but a different civilization, the narrators are not exempt from nostalgia. A mark of their toughness and reliability—and Nabokov's—is that their nostalgia does not consist of a longing to *return* to the past; indeed, except for certain isolated moments that stick in the memory like the frozen life of a snapshot, their past was not especially pleasant, was, in fact, always a disappointment. Thus in "First Love," nothing comes of the boy's "first love" except the beautiful memory that is this story. The tension in the stories is not between a nostalgically recollected past and the present, but between the beautiful patterns that imagination can impose on experience and the disorganized (maybe even hostile) nature of experience itself.

One of the most useful approaches to Nabokov is through identifying different kinds of time in his stories. There is always the sought-after stillness of a picture postcard: frozen time in which the narrator can arrange himself in perfect harmony with a setting that he knows will not change. Unfortunately, however, such stillness is not to be found in the real world; the tick of the clock, the turning of the earth, destroys it—carrying the boy from his first love, the newly married husband from his bride. What remains possible, though, is an apparently only second-best kind of time, a mixture of ideal and real time—memory—which also must be sought but is at least achievable in the real world. The narrator in effect asks us to join him in establishing memory against the rapidly moving time-stream without. If he and we succeed, the result is a story whose subject is the destruction of ideal time by real time (often imaged by a train moving relentlessly through a landscape of pictures merely glimpsed).

The relationships among the ideal, real, and the part-ideal, part-real times are very delicate, and if the narrator is to do what he sets out to do—create a story—he has to maintain a constructive tension among them. A difficult job, for he is never a dispassionate observer but someone who as he writes is tempted to leap into his story and to substitute his life *then* for his life *now.*

Precariousness is a condition of life in Nabokov's stories, and another way of approaching the stories is to look at what *threatens* the narrator—both in the past that he describes and in his present effort of reconstruction. The major threats are the relentless passage of time itself and the failure of memory

("I cannot recall the dog's name and this bothers me," the narrator of "First Love" says); but there are subtler threats as well. One certainly is the possibility that man's surroundings may be totally irrelevant to his personality. When the narrator of "That in Aleppo Once . . ." walks out of the railroad station to find the train with his wife on it gone, what he sees is not a correlative of his grief and panic—some indication that physical reality is in harmony with his sensibility—but the blank inhuman irrelevance of "naked indifferent rails and a lone piece of orange peel."

Another threat to Nabokov's narrators is the presence of competing story-tellers who want to make their own fiction out of events in the narrator's life. What annoys the narrator of "That in Aleppo Once . . ." as much as the loss of his wife is her maddening habit of putting him into a hundred different stories and scattering them throughout Europe. As his title indicates, the narrator wants to think of himself as a kind of deceived Othello; and it is specially galling for him to face the fact that not only may he have unknowingly played his marriage according to his wife's script, but that now this story he is telling, *his* story, has to compete with all of hers. The threat is double: to his understanding of what happened, and to his art.

Sometimes the competition with the rival story-teller is not so direct: the narrator has just a vague feeling that, despite the form that he is trying to impose on his experience, it all really happened like a myth. In short, the narrator's view of himself as a human being who has willed his actions may be illusory; he may actually have been a puppet acting out an age-old drama and failing to perceive the determining pattern behind what happened. As the narrator of "That in Aleppo Once . . ." says of a carriage ride that seems ominously beyond his control, "What was driving us was something more than a booted and buckled fool."

In general, then, the precariousness that charges Nabokov's fiction is generated by a multitude of threats to all that is superbly human: time sweeping experience before it: art turning out to be self-satisfying dreams; language to be a mere game, like chess; the world to be unresponsive to human sensibility; and Fate, not man's will, dictating our lives. These narrators, both very human, are haunted by these possibilities, and they wistfully set out to express what it feels like to live with them.

First Love

I

In the early years of this century, a travel agency on Nevski Avenue displayed a three-foot-long model of an oak-brown international sleeping car. In delicate verisimilitude it completely outranked the painted tin of my clockwork trains. Unfortunately it was not for sale. One could make out the blue upholstery inside, the embossed leather lining of the compartment walls, their polished panels, inset mirrors, tulip-shaped reading lamps, and other maddening details. Spacious windows alternated with narrower ones, single or geminate, and some of these were of frosted glass. In a few of the compartments, the beds had been made.

The then great and glamorous Nord Express (it was never the same after World War I), consisting solely of such international cars and running but twice a week, connected St. Petersburg with Paris. I would have said: directly with Paris, had passengers not been obliged to change from one train to a superficially similar one at the Russo-German frontier (Verzhbolovo-Eydtkuhnen), where the ample and lazy Russian sixty-and-a-half-inch gauge was replaced by the fifty-six-and-a-half-inch standard of Europe and coal succeeded birch logs.

In the far end of my mind I can unravel, I think, at least five such journeys to Paris, with the Riviera or Biarritz as their ultimate destination. In 1909, the year I now single out, my two small sisters had been left at home with nurses and aunts. Wearing gloves and a traveling cap, my father sat reading a book in the compartment he shared with our tutor. My brother and I were separated from them by a washroom. My mother and her maid occupied a compartment adjacent to ours. The odd one of our party, my father's valet, Osip (whom, a decade later, the pedantic Bolsheviks were to shoot, because he appropriated our bicycles instead of turning them over to the nation), had a stranger for companion.

In April of that year, Peary had reached the North Pole. In May, Chaliapin had sung in Paris. In June, bothered by rumors of new and better Zeppelins, the United States War Department had told reporters of plans for an aerial Navy. In July, Blériot had flown from Calais to Dover (with a little additional loop when he lost his bearings). It was late August now. The firs and marshes of northwestern Russia sped by, and on the following day gave way to German pine barrens and heather.

At a collapsible table, my mother and I played a card game called *durachki*. Although it was still broad daylight, our cards, a glass, and on a different plane the locks of a suitcase were reflected in the window. Through forest and field, and in sudden ravines, and among scuttling cottages, those discarnate gamblers kept steadily playing on for steadily sparkling stakes.

"*Ne budet-li, ti ved' ustal* [Haven't you had enough, aren't you tired]?" my mother would ask, and then would be lost in thought as she slowly shuffled the cards. The door of the compartment was open and I could see the corridor window, where the wires—six thin black wires—were doing their best to slant up, to ascend skywards, despite the lightning blows dealt them by one telegraph pole after another; but just as all six, in a triumphant swoop of pathetic elation, were about to reach the top of the window, a particularly vicious blow would bring them down, as low as they had ever been, and they would have to start all over again.

When, on such journeys as these, the train changed its pace to a dignified amble and all but grazed house fronts and shop signs, as we passed through some big German town, I used to feel a twofold excitement, which terminal stations could not provide. I saw a city with its toylike trams, linden trees, and brick walls enter the compartment, hobnob with the mirrors, and fill to the brim the windows on the corridor side. This informal contact between train and city was one part of the thrill. The other was putting myself in the place of some passer-by who, I imagined, was moved as I would be moved myself to see the long, romantic, auburn cars, with their intervestibular connecting curtains as black as bat wings and their metal lettering copper-bright in the low sun, unhurriedly negotiate an iron bridge across an everyday thoroughfare and then turn, with all windows suddenly ablaze, around a last block of houses.

There were drawbacks to those optical amalgamations. The wide-windowed dining car, a vista of chaste bottles of mineral water, miter-folded napkins, and dummy chocolate bars (whose wrappers—Cailler, Kohler, and so forth—enclosed nothing but wood) would be perceived at first as a cool haven beyond a consecution of reeling blue corridors; but as the meal progressed toward its fatal last course, one would keep catching the car in the act of being recklessly sheathed, lurching waiters and all, in the landscape, while the landscape itself went through a complex system of motion, the day-time moon stubbornly keeping abreast of one's plate, the distant meadows opening fanwise, the near trees sweeping up on invisible swings toward the track, a parallel rail line all at once committing suicide by anastomosis, a bank of nictitating grass rising, rising, rising, until the little witness of mixed velocities was made to disgorge his portion of *omelette aux confitures de fraises.*

It was at night, however, that the *Compagnie Internationale des Wagons-Lits et des Grands Express Europeens* lived up to the magic of its name. From my bed under my brother's bunk (Was he asleep? Was he there at all?), in the semidarkness of our compartment, I watched things, and parts of things, and shadows, and sections of shadows cautiously moving about and getting nowhere. The woodwork gently creaked and crackled. Near the door that led to the toilet, a dim garment on a peg and, higher up, the tassel of the blue, bivalved night light swung rhythmically. It was hard to correlate those halting approaches, that hooded stealth, with the headlong rush of the outside night, which I knew *was* rushing by, spark-streaked, illegible.

I would put myself to sleep by the simple act of identifying myself with the engine driver. A sense of drowsy well-being invaded my veins as soon as I had everything nicely arranged—the carefree passengers in their rooms enjoying the ride I was giving them, smoking, exchanging knowing smiles, nodding, dozing; the waiters and cooks and train guards (whom I had to place somewhere) carousing in the diner; and myself, goggled and begrimed, peering out of the engine cab at the tapering track, at the ruby or emerald point in the black distance. And then, in my sleep, I would see something totally different —a glass marble rolling under a grand piano or a toy engine lying on its side with its wheels still working gamely.

A change in the speed of the train sometimes interrupted the current of my sleep. Slow lights were stalking by; each, in passing, investigated the same chink, and then a luminous compass measured the shadows. Presently, the train stopped with a long-drawn Westinghousian sigh. Something (my brother's spectacles, as it proved next day) fell from above. It was marvelously exciting to move to the foot of one's bed, with part of the bedclothes following, in order to undo cautiously the catch of the window shade, which could be made to slide only halfway up, impeded as it was by the edge of the upper berth.

Like moons around Jupiter, pale moths revolved about a lone lamp. A dismembered newspaper stirred on a bench. Somewhere on the train one could hear muffled voices, somebody's comfortable cough. There was nothing particularly interesting in the portion of station platform before me, and still I could not tear myself away from it until it departed of its own accord.

Next morning, wet fields with misshapen willows along the radius of a ditch or a row of poplars afar, traversed by a horizontal band of milky-white mist, told one that the train was spinning through Belgium. It reached Paris at 4 P.M.; and even if the stay was only an overnight one, I had always time to purchase something—say, a little brass *Tour Eiffel,* rather roughly coated with silver paint—before we boarded at noon on the following day the Sud Express, which, on its way to Madrid, dropped us around 10 P.M. at the La Négresse station of Biarritz, a few miles from the Spanish frontier.

II

Biarritz still retained its quiddity in those days. Dusty blackberry bushes and weedy *terrains à vendre* bordered the road that led to our villa. The Carlton was still being built. Some thirty-six years had to elapse before Brigadier General Samuel McCroskey would occupy the royal suite of the Hotel du

Palais, which stands on the site of a former palace, where, in the sixties, that incredibly agile medium, Daniel Home, is said to have been caught stroking with his bare foot (in imitation of a ghost hand) the kind, trustful face of Empress Eugénie. On the promenade near the Casino, an elderly flower girl, with carbon eyebrows and a painted smile, nimbly slipped the plump torus of a carnation into the buttonhole of an intercepted stroller whose left jowl accentuated its royal fold as he glanced down sideways at the coy insertion of the flower.

Along the back line of the *plage*, various seaside chairs and stools supported the parents of straw-hatted children who were playing in front on the sand. I could be seen on my knees trying to set a found comb aflame by means of a magnifying glass. Men sported white trousers that to the eye of today would look as if they had comically shrunk in the washing; ladies wore, that particular season, light coats with silk-faced lapels, hats with big crowns and wide brims, dense embroidered white veils, frill-fronted blouses, frills at their wrists, frills on their parasols. The breeze salted one's lips. At a tremendous pace a stray golden-orange butterfly came dashing across the palpitating *plage*.

Additional movement and sound were provided by vendors hawking *cacahuètes*, sugared violets, pistachio ice cream of a heavenly green, cachou pellets, and huge convex pieces of dry, gritty, waferlike stuff that came from a red barrel. With a distinctness that no later superpositions have dimmed, I see that waffleman stomp along through deep mealy sand, with the heavy cask on his bent back. When called, he would sling it off his shoulder by a twist of its strap, bang it down on the sand in a Tower of Pisa position, wipe his face with his sleeve, and proceed to manipulate a kind of arrow-and-dial arrangement with numbers on the lid of the cask. The arrow rasped and whirred around. Luck was supposed to fix the size of a sou's worth of wafer. The bigger the piece, the more I was sorry for him.

The process of bathing took place on another part of the beach. Professional bathers, burly Basques in black bathing suits, were there to help ladies and children enjoy the terrors of the surf. Such a *baigneur* would place you with your back to the incoming wave and hold you by the hand as the rising, rotating mass of foamy, green water violently descended upon you from behind, knocking you off your feet with one mighty wallop. After a dozen of these tumbles, the *baigneur*, glistening like a seal, would lead his panting, shivering, moistly snuffling charge landward, to the flat foreshore, where an unforgettable old woman with gray hairs on her chin promptly chose a bathing robe from several hanging on a clothesline. In the security of a little cabin, one would be helped by yet another attendant to peel off one's soggy, sand-heavy bathing suit. It would plop onto the boards, and, still shivering, one would step out of it and trample on its bluish, diffuse stripes. The cabin smelt of pine. The attendant, a hunchback with beaming wrinkles, brought a basin of steaming-hot water, in which one immersed one's feet. From him I learned, and have preserved ever since in a glass cell of my memory, that "butterfly" in the Basque language is *misericoletea*—or at least it sounded so (among the seven words I have found in dictionaries the closest approach is *micheletea*).

III

On the browner and wetter part of the *plage,* that part which at low tide yielded the best mud for castles, I found myself digging, one day, side by side with a little French girl called Colette.

She would be ten in November, I had been ten in April. Attention was drawn to a jagged bit of violet mussel shell upon which she had stepped with the bare sole of her narrow long-toed foot. No, I was not English. Her greenish eyes seemed flecked with the overflow of the freckles that covered her sharp-featured face. She wore what might now be termed a playsuit, consisting of a blue jersey with rolled-up sleeves and blue knitted shorts. I had taken her at first for a boy and then had been puzzled by the bracelet on her thin wrist and the corkscrew brown curls dangling from under her sailor cap.

She spoke in birdlike bursts of rapid twitter, mixing governess English and Parisian French. Two years before, on the same *plage,* I had been much attached to the lovely, sun-tanned little daughter of a Serbian physician; but when I met Colette, I knew at once that this was the real thing. Colette seemed to me so much stranger than all my other chance playmates at Biarritz! I somehow acquired the feeling that she was less happy than I, less loved. A bruise on her delicate, downy forearm gave rise to awful conjectures. "He pinches as bad as my mummy," she said, speaking of a crab. I evolved various schemes to save her from her parents, who were "*des bourgeois de Paris*" as I heard somebody tell my mother with a slight shrug. I interpreted the disdain in my own fashion, as I knew that those people had come all the way from Paris in their blue-and-yellow limousine (a fashionable adventure in those days) but had drably sent Colette with her dog and governess by an ordinary coach train. The dog was a female fox terrier with bells on her collar and a most waggly behind. From sheer exuberance, she would lap up salt water out of Colette's toy pail. I remember the sail, the sunset, and the lighthouse pictured on that pail, but I cannot recall the dog's name, and this bothers me.

During the two months of our stay at Biarritz, my passion for Colette all but surpassed my passion for butterflies. Since my parents were not keen to meet hers, I saw her only on the beach; but I thought of her constantly. If I noticed she had been crying, I felt a surge of helpless anguish that brought tears to my own eyes. I could not destroy the mosquitoes that had left their bites on her frail neck, but I could, and did, have a successful fist fight with a red-haired boy who had been rude to her. She used to give me warm handfuls of hard candy. One day, as we were bending together over a starfish, and Colette's ringlets were tickling my ear, she suddenly turned toward me and kissed me on the cheek. So great was my emotion that all I could think of saying was, "You little monkey."

I had a gold coin that I assumed would pay for our elopement. Where did I want to take her? Spain? America? The mountains above Pau? "*Là-bas, là-bas, dans la montagne,*" as I had heard Carmen sing at the opera. One strange night, I lay awake, listening to the recurrent thud of the ocean and planning our flight. The ocean seemed to rise and grope in the darkness and then heavily fall on its face.

Of our actual getaway, I have little to report. My memory retains a glimpse of her obediently putting on rope-soled canvas shoes, on the lee side of a flapping tent, while I stuffed a folding butterfly net into a brown paper bag. The next glimpse is of our evading pursuit by entering a pitch-dark *cinema* near the Casino (which, of course, was absolutely out of bounds). There we sat, holding hands across the dog, which now and then gently jingled in Colette's lap, and were shown a jerky, drizzly, but highly exciting bullfight at St. Sebástian. My final glimpse is of myself being led along the promenade by my tutor. His long legs move with a kind of ominous briskness and I can see the muscles of his grimly set jaw working under the tight skin. My bespectacled brother, aged nine, whom he happens to hold with his other hand, keeps trotting out forward to peer at me with awed curiosity, like a little owl.

Among the trivial souvenirs acquired at Biarritz before leaving, my favorite was not the small bull of black stone and not the sonorous sea shell but something which now seems almost symbolic—a meerschaum penholder with a tiny peephole of crystal in its ornamental part. One held it quite close to one's eye, screwing up the other, and when one had got rid of the shimmer of one's own lashes, a miraculous photographic view of the bay and of the line of cliffs ending in a lighthouse could be seen inside.

And now a delightful thing happens. The process of recreating that penholder and the microcosm in its eyelet stimulates my memory to a last effort. I try again to recall the name of Colette's dog—and, sure enough, along those remote beaches, over the glossy evening sands of the past, where each footprint slowly fills up with sunset water, here it comes, here it comes, echoing and vibrating: Floss, Floss, Floss!

Colette was back in Paris by the time we stopped there for a day before continuing our homeward journey; and there, in a fawn park under a cold blue sky, I saw her (by arrangement between our mentors, I believe) for the last time. She carried a hoop and a short stick to drive it with, and everything about her was extremely proper and stylish in an autumnal, Parisian, *tenue-de-ville-pour-fillettes* way. She took from her governess and slipped into my brother's hand a farewell present, a box of sugar-coated almonds, meant, I knew, solely for me; and instantly she was off, tap-tapping her glinting hoop through light and shade, around and around a fountain choked with dead leaves near which I stood. The leaves mingle in my memory with the leather of her shoes and gloves, and there was, I remember, some detail in her attire (perhaps a ribbon on her Scottish cap, or the pattern of her stockings) that reminded me then of the rainbow spiral in a glass marble. I still seem to be holding that wisp of iridescence, not knowing exactly where to fit it, while she runs with her hoop ever faster around me and finally dissolves among the slender shadows cast on the graveled path by the interlaced arches of its low looped fence.

"That in Aleppo Once . . ."

Dear V.—Among other things, this is to tell you that at last I am here, in the country whither so many sunsets have led. One of the first persons I saw was our good old Gleb Alexandrovich Gekko gloomily crossing Columbus Avenue in quest of the *petit cafe du coin* which none of us three will ever visit again. He seemed to think that somehow or other you were betraying our national literature, and he gave me your address with a deprecatory shake of his gray head, as if you did not deserve the treat of hearing from me.

I have a story for you. Which reminds me—I mean putting it like this reminds me—of the days when we wrote our first udder-warm bubbling verse, and all things, a rose, a puddle, a lighted window, cried out to us: "I'm a rhyme!" Yes, this is a most useful universe. We play, we die: *ig-rhyme, umi rhyme.* And the sonorous souls of Russian verbs lend a meaning to the wild gesticulation of trees or to some discarded newspaper sliding and pausing, and shuffling again, with abortive flaps and apterous jerks along an endless wind-swept embankment. But just now I am not a poet. I come to you like that gushing lady in Chekhov who was dying to be described.

I married, let me see, about a month after you left France and a few weeks before the gentle Germans roared into Paris. Although I can produce documentary proofs of matrimony, I am positive now that my wife never existed. You may know her name from some other source, but that does not matter: it is the name of an illusion. Therefore, I am able to speak of her with as much detachment as I would of a character in a story (one of your stories, to be precise).

It was love at first touch rather than at first sight, for I had met her several times before without experiencing any special emotions; but one night, as I was seeing her home, something quaint she had said made me stoop with a laugh and lightly kiss her on the hair—and of course we all know of that blinding blast which is caused by merely picking up a small doll from the floor of a carefully abandoned house: the soldier involved hears nothing; for him it is but an ecstatic soundless and boundless expansion of what had been during his life a pin point of light in the dark center of his being. And really, the reason we think of death in celestial terms is that the visible firmament, especially at night (above our blacked-out Paris with the gaunt arches of its Boulevard Exelmans and the ceaseless Alpine gurgle of desolate latrines), is the most adequate and ever-present symbol of that vast silent explosion.

But I cannot discern her. She remains as nebulous as my best poem—the one you made such gruesome fun of in the *Literaturnie Zapiski.* When I want to imagine her, I have to cling mentally to a tiny brown birthmark on her downy forearm, as one concentrates upon a punctuation mark in an illegible sentence. Perhaps, had she used a greater amount of make-up or used it more constantly, I might have visualized her face today, or at least the delicate transverse furrows of dry, hot rouged lips; but I fail, I fail—although I still feel their elusive touch now and then in the blindman's buff of my senses, in that sobbing sort of dream when she and I clumsily clutch at each other through a heart-breaking mist and I cannot see the color of her eyes for the blank luster of brimming tears drowning their irises.

She was much younger than I—not as much younger as was Nathalie of the lovely bare shoulders and long earrings in relation to swarthy Pushkin; but still there was a sufficient margin for that kind of retrospective romanticism which finds pleasure in imitating the destiny of a unique genius (down to the jealousy, down to the filth, down to the stab of seeing her almond-shaped eyes turn to her blond Cassio behind her peacock-feathered fan) even if one cannot imitate his verse. She liked mine though, and would scarcely have yawned as the other was wont to do every time her hustand's poem happened to exceed the length of a sonnet. If she has remained a phantom to me, I may have been one to her: I suppose she had been solely attracted by the obscurity of my poetry; then tore a hole through its veil and saw a stranger's unlovable face.

As you know, I had been for some time planning to follow the example of your fortunate flight. She described to me an uncle of hers who lived, she said, in New York: he had taught riding at a Southern college and had wound up by marrying a wealthy American woman; they had a little daughter born deaf. She said she had lost their address long ago, but a few days later it miraculously turned up, and we wrote a dramatic letter to which we never received any reply. This did not much matter, as I had already obtained a sound affidavit from Professor Lomchenko of Chicago; but little else had been done in the way of getting the necessary papers, when the invasion began, whereas I foresaw that if we stayed on in Paris some helpful compatriot of mine would sooner or later point out to the interested party sundry passages in one of my books where I argued that, with all her many black sins, Germany was still bound to remain forever and ever the laughing stock of the world.

So we started upon our disastrous honeymoon. Crushed and jolted amid the apocalyptic exodus, waiting for unscheduled trains that were bound for unknown destinations, walking through the stale stage setting of abstract towns, living in a permanent twilight of physical exhaustion, we fled; and the farther we fled, the clearer it became that what was driving us on was something more than a booted and buckled fool with his assortment of variously propelled junk—something of which he was a mere symbol, something monstrous and impalpable, a timeless and faceless mass of immemorial horror that still keeps coming at me from behind even here, in the green vacuum of Central Park.

Oh, she bore it gamely enough—with a kind of dazed cheerfulness. Once, however, quite suddenly she started to sob in a sympathetic railway carriage. "The dog," she said, "the dog we left. I cannot forget the poor dog." The honesty of her grief shocked me, as we had never had any dog. "I know," she said, "but I tried to imagine we had actually bought that setter. And just think, he would be now whining behind a locked door." There had never been any talk of buying a setter.

I should also not like to forget a certain stretch of highroad and the sight of a family of refugees (two women, a child) whose old father, or grandfather, had died on the way. The sky was a chaos of black and flesh-colored clouds with an ugly sunburst beyond a hooded hill, and the dead man was lying on his back under a dusty plane tree. With a stick and their hands the women had tried to dig a roadside grave, but the soil was too hard; they had given it up and were sitting side by side, among the anemic poppies, a little apart from the corpse and its upturned beard. But the little boy was still scratching and scraping and tugging until he tumbled a flat stone and forgot the object of his solemn exertions as he crouched on his haunches, his thin, eloquent neck showing all its vertebrae to the headsman, and watched with surprise and delight thousands of minute brown ants seething, zigzagging, dispersing, heading for places of safety in the Gard, and the Aude, and the Drome, and the Var, and the Basses-Pyrénées—we two paused only in Pau.

Spain proved too difficult and we decided to move on to Nice. At a place called Faugères (a ten-minute stop) I squeezed out of the train to buy some food. When a couple of minutes later I came back, the train was gone, and the muddled old man responsible for the atrocious void that faced me (coal dust glittering in the heat between naked indifferent rails, and a lone piece of orange peel) brutally told me that, anyway, I had had no right to get out.

In a better world I could have had my wife located and told what to do (I had both tickets and most of the money); as it was, my nightmare struggle with the telephone proved futile, so I dismissed the whole series of diminutive voices barking at me from afar, sent two or three telegrams which are probably on their way only now, and late in the evening took the next local to Montpellier, farther than which her train would not stumble. Not finding her there, I had to choose between two alternatives: going on because she might have boarded the Marseilles train which I had just missed, or going back because she might have returned to Faugères. I forgot now what tangle of reasoning led me to Marseilles and Nice.

Beyond such routine action as forwarding false data to a few unlikely places, the police did nothing to help: one man bellowed at me for being a nuisance; another sidetracked the question by doubting the authenticity of my marriage certificate because it was stamped on what he contended to be the wrong side; a third, a fat *commissaire* with liquid brown eyes confessed that he wrote poetry in his spare time. I looked up various acquaintances among the numerous Russians domiciled or stranded in Nice. I heard those among them who chanced to have Jewish blood talk of their doomed kinsmen crammed into hell-bound trains; and my own plight, by contrast, acquired a commonplace air of irreality while I sat in some crowded café with the milky blue sea in front of me and a shell-hollow murmur behind telling and retelling the tale of massacre and misery, and the gray paradise beyond the ocean, and the ways and whims of harsh consuls.

A week after my arrival an indolent plain-clothes man called upon me and took me down a crooked and smelly street to a black-stained house with the word "hotel" almost erased by dirt and time; there, he said, my wife had been found. The girl he produced was an absolute stranger, of course; but my friend Holmes kept on trying for some time to make her and me confess we were married, while her taciturn and muscular bedfellow stood by and listened, his bare arms crossed on his striped chest.

When at length I got rid of those people and had wandered back to my neighborhood, I happened to pass by a compact queue waiting at the entrance of a food store; and there, at the very end, was my wife, straining on tiptoe to catch a glimpse of what exactly was being sold. I think the first thing she said to me was that she hoped it was oranges.

Her tale seemed a trifle hazy, but perfectly banal. She had returned to Faugères and gone straight to the Commissariat instead of making inquiries at the station, where I had left a message for her. A party of refugees suggested that she join them; she spent the night in a bicycle shop with no bicycles, on the floor, together with three elderly women who lay, she said, like three logs in a row. Next day she realized that she had not enough money to reach Nice. Eventually she borrowed some from one of the log-women. She got into the wrong train, however, and traveled to a town the name of which she could not remember. She had arrived at Nice two days ago and had found some friends at the Russian church. They had told her I was somewhere around, looking for her, and would surely turn up soon.

Some time later, as I sat on the edge of the only chair in my garret and held her by her slender young hips (she was combing her soft hair and tossing her head back with every stroke), her dim smile changed all at once into an odd quiver and she placed one hand on my shoulder, staring down at me as if I were a reflection in a pool, which she had noticed for the first time.

"I've been lying to you, dear," she said. "*Ya lgunia.* I stayed for several nights in Montpellier with a brute of a man I met on the train. I did not want it at all. He sold hair lotions."

The time, the place, the torture. Her fan, her gloves, her mask. I spent that night and many others getting it out of her bit by bit, but not getting it all. I was under the strange delusion that first I must find out every detail, reconstruct every minute, and only then decide whether I could bear it. But the limit of desired knowledge was unattainable, nor could I ever foretell the approximate point after which I might imagine myself satiated, because of course the denominator of every fraction of knowledge was potentially as infinite as the number of intervals between the fractions themselves.

Oh, the first time she had been too tired to mind, and the next had not minded because she was sure I had deserted her; and she apparently considered that such explanations ought to be a kind of consolation prize for me instead of the nonsense and agony they really were. It went on like that for eons, she breaking down every now and then, but soon rallying again, answering my unprintable questions in a breathless whisper or trying with a pitiful smile to wriggle into the semisecurity of irrelevant commentaries, and I crushing and crushing the mad molar till my jaw almost burst with pain, a flaming pain which seemed somehow preferable to the dull, humming ache of humble endurance.

And mark, in between the periods of this inquest, we were trying to get from reluctant authorities certain papers which in their turn would make it lawful to apply for a third kind which would serve as a stepping-stone towards a permit enabling the holder to apply for yet other papers which might or might not give him the means of discovering how and why it had happened. For even if I could imagine the accursed recurrent scene, I failed to link up its sharp-angled grotesque shadows with the dim limbs of my wife as she shook and rattled and dissolved in my violent grasp.

So nothing remained but to torture each other, to wait for hours on end in the Prefecture, filling forms, conferring with friends who had already probed the innermost viscera of all visas, pleading with secretaries, and filling forms again, with the result that her lusty and versatile traveling salesman became blended in a ghastly mix-up with rat-whiskered snarling officials, rotting bundles of obsolete records, the reek of violet ink, bribes slipped under gangrenous blotting paper, fat flies tickling moist necks with their rapid cold padded feet, new-laid clumsy concave photographs of your six subhuman doubles, the tragic eyes and patient politeness of petitioners born in Slutzk, Starodub, or Bobruisk, the funnels and pulleys of the Holy Inquisition, the awful smile of the bald man with the glasses, who had been told that his passport could not be found.

I confess that one evening, after a particularly abominable day, I sank down on a stone bench weeping and cursing a mock world where millions of lives were being juggled by the clammy hands of consuls and *commissaires.* I noticed she was crying too, and then I told her that nothing would really have mattered the way it mattered now, had she not gone and done what she did.

"You will think me crazy," she said with a vehemence that, for a second, almost made a real person of her, "but I didn't—I swear that I didn't. Perhaps I live several lives at once. Perhaps I wanted to test you. Perhaps this bench is a dream and we are in Saratov or on some star."

It would be tedious to niggle the different stages through which I passed before accepting finally the first version of her delay. I did not talk to her and was a good deal alone. She would glimmer and fade, and reappear with some trifle she thought I would appreciate—a handful of cherries, three precious cigarettes or the like—treating me with the unruffled mute sweetness of a nurse that trips from and to a gruff convalescent. I ceased visiting most of our mutual friends because they had lost all interest in my passport affairs and seemed to have turned vaguely inimical. I composed several poems. I drank all the wine I could get. I clasped her one day to my groaning breast, and we went for a week to Caboule and lay on the round pink pebbles of the narrow beach. Strange to say, the happier our new relations seemed, the stronger I felt an undercurrent of poignant sadness, but I kept telling myself that this was an intrinsic feature of all true bliss.

In the meantime, something had shifted in the moving pattern of our fates and at last I emerged from a dark and hot office with a couple of plump *visas de sortie* cupped in my trembling hands. Into these the U.S.A. serum was duly injected, and I dashed to Marseilles and managed to get tickets for the very next boat. I returned and tramped up the stairs. I saw a rose in a glass on the table—the sugar pink of its obvious beauty, the parasitic air bubbles clinging to its stem. Her two spare dresses were gone, her comb was gone, her checkered coat was gone, and so was the mauve hairband with a mauve bow that had been her hat. There was no note pinned to the pillow, nothing at all in the room to enlighten me, for of course the rose was merely what French rhymsters call *une cheville.*

I went to the Veretennikovs, who could tell me nothing; to the Hellmans, who refused to say anything; and to the Elagins, who were not sure whether to tell me or not. Finally the old lady—and you know what Anna Vladimirovna is like at crucial moments—asked for her rubber-tipped cane, heavily but energetically dislodged her bulk from her favorite armchair, and took me into the garden. There she informed me that, being twice my age, she had the right to say I was a bully and a cad.

You must imagine the scene: the tiny graveled garden with its blue Arabian Nights jar and solitary cypress; the cracked terrace where the old lady's father had dozed with a rug on his knees when he retired from his Novgorod governorship to spend a few last evenings in Nice; the pale-green sky; a whiff of vanilla in the deepening dusk; the crickets emitting their metallic trill pitched at two octaves above middle C; and Anna Vladimirovna, the folds of her cheeks jerkily dangling as she flung at me a motherly but quite undeserved insult.

During several preceding weeks, my dear V., every time she had visited by herself the three or four families we both knew, my ghostly wife had filled the eager ears of all those kind people with an extraordinary story. To wit: that she had madly fallen in love with a young Frenchman who could give her a turreted home and a crested name; that she had implored me for a divorce and I had refused; that in fact I had said I would rather shoot her and myself than sail to New York alone; that she had said her father in a similar case had acted like a gentleman; that I had answered I did not give a hoot for her *cocu de père.*

There were loads of other preposterous details of the kind—but they all hung together in such a remarkable fashion that no wonder the old lady made me swear I would not seek to pursue the lovers with a cocked pistol. They had gone, she said, to a château in Lozère. I inquired whether she had ever set eyes upon the man. No, but she had been shown his picture. As I was about to leave, Anna Vladimirovna, who had slightly relaxed and had even given me her five fingers to kiss, suddenly flared up again, struck the gravel with her cane, and said in her deep strong voice: "But one thing I shall never forgive you—her dog, that poor beast which you hanged with your own hands before leaving Paris."

Whether the gentleman of leisure had changed into a traveling salesman, or whether the metamorphosis had been reversed or whether again he was neither the one nor the other, but the nondescript Russian who had courted her before our marriage—all this was absolutely inessential. She had gone. That was the end. I should have been a fool had I begun the nightmare business of searching and waiting for her all over again.

On the fourth morning of a long and dismal sea voyage, I met on the deck a solemn but pleasant old doctor with whom I had played chess in Paris. He asked me whether my wife was very much incommoded by the rough seas. I answered that I had sailed alone; whereupon he looked taken aback and then said he had seen her a couple of days before going on board, namely in Marseilles, walking, rather aimlessly he thought, along the embankment. She said that I would presently join her with bag and tickets.

This is, I gather, the point of the whole story—although if you write it, you had better not make him a doctor, as that kind of thing has been overdone. It was at that moment that I suddenly knew for certain that she had never existed at all. I shall tell you another thing. When I arrived I hastened to satisfy a certain morbid curiosity: I went to the address she had given me once; it proved to be an anonymous gap between two office buildings; I looked for her uncle's name in the directory; it was not there; I made some inquiries, and Gekko, who knows everything, informed me that the man and his horsey wife existed all right, but had moved to San Francisco after their deaf little girl had died.

Viewing the past graphically, I see our mangled romance engulfed in a deep valley of mist between the crags of two matter-of-fact mountains: life had been real before, life will be real from now on, I hope. Not tomorrow, though. Perhaps after tomorrow. You, happy mortal, with your lovely family (how is Ines? how are the twins?) and your diversified work (how are the lichens?), can hardly be expected to puzzle out my misfortune in terms of human communion, but you may clarify things for me through the prism of your art.

Yet the pity of it. Curse your art, I am hideously unhappy. She keeps on walking to and fro where the brown nets are spread to dry on the hot stone slabs and the dappled light of the water plays on the side of a moored fishing boat. Somewhere, somehow, I have made some fatal mistake. There are tiny pale bits of broken fish scales glistening here and there in the brown meshes. It may all end in *Aleppo* if I am not careful. Spare me, V.: you would load your dice with an unbearable implication if you took that for a title.

RICHARD WRIGHT

1908–1960

Wright was born in the Deep South, the son of a sharecropper on a plantation in Natchez, Mississippi. After years of disastrous crop failures, his father deserted the family, and his mother, a trained grade-school teacher, had to move from place to place working as a maid.

When Wright graduated (as valedictorian) from an all-black grammar school, he had not had a single complete year of schooling in any one place. At that point, the end of his formal education, his chances of rising from the kinds of jobs he had to take—yard boy, brass polisher, porter—were infinitesimal. And to think of acquiring the learning, the training, or even the time to be a writer seemed pure fantasy. Furthermore, Wright knew at first hand what happened to "uppity" blacks in Mississippi: his uncle was murdered, a friend's brother castrated, for being less than respectful. It was at the time when he was first out of school and looking for work that the dominant theme of Wright's fiction was forged: the passionate necessity of escape from an atmosphere charged with fear to someplace, anyplace, even if there was no way to imagine what that place might be.

For Wright, the place was first Memphis, then Chicago. Chicago was hardly a paradise in the Depression, but there he managed to support himself meagerly by selling quarter-a-week insurance. He regularly sent money home to his mother, then crippled, and spent long hours reading in the public library. In his reading he was especially attracted to the naturalist school of writers, who portrayed environment and social conditions as determinants of personality. The works of naturalists such as Dreiser were a good influence on Wright because through them he learned to give his cry of rage the solid specification needed to make it available to readers. Wright learned how to portray not only the suffering individual but also the reality of the world that stifled and oppressed him.

In 1938 *Story Magazine* awarded Wright a $500 prize for his first book, a collection of stories entitled *Uncle Tom's Children.* From that time on his success as a writer was assured. He began to turn his attention from the plight of the rural southern black to that of the black exploited in the ghettos of

Chicago and New York. His great story, "The Man Who Lived Underground," is on one level an elaborate metaphor of the urban black's relation to the city. Though a member of the Communist party during the Depression, Wright saw too deeply into the individual to represent blacks as being simply victims of capitalism. In the late thirties he wrote a novel, *Lawd Today,* about the suffocating life of a black postal worker in Chicago, but he withheld publication (the novel was finally published posthumously), apparently because it developed into a far more complicated portrait than the party line demanded.

Native Son (1940) established Wright as a major literary figure. This novel made explicit a belief that had previously been powerfully implicit in his fiction: that violence is the only possible way for the black to break out of the stereotype forced on him by society. The murder in the novel forces two kinds of recognitions: for white society, the recognition that its fear and guilt about blacks cannot be quieted by oppression, without terrible consequences; for the hero, Bigger Thomas, a new awareness that he is a human being who can "will" himself into life.

After World War II, Wright became increasingly committed to these essentially existential perceptions and, dissatisfied with the mechanical explanations of Communism, he moved to France and joined the circle of French Existentialists led by Sartre. Still he remained dedicated to the cause of blacks in America. Not only was the vision of rage and violence in his fiction prophetic of many aspects of Black Power today, but Wright also worked directly for causes that are now recognized as crucial: he studied African culture and fostered an awareness of the role of African history in the black experience in America; and in *White Man, Listen* (1957) he collected a series of his lectures demanding that emerging black nations be allowed to develop their own cultures free of white colonialism.

Big Boy Leaves Home

I

Yo mama don wear no drawers . . .

Clearly, the voice rose out of the woods, and died away. Like an echo another voice caught it up:

Ah seena when she pulled em off . . .

Another, shrill, cracking, adolescent:

N she washed 'em in alcohol . . .

Then a quartet of voices, blending in harmony, floated high above the tree tops:

N she hung 'em out in the hall . . .

Laughing easily, four black boys came out of the woods into cleared pasture. They walked lollingly in bare feet, beating tangled vines and bushes with long sticks.

"Ah wished Ah knowed some mo lines t tha song."

"Me too."

"Yeah, when yuh gits t where she hangs em out in the hall yuh has t stop."

"Shucks, whut goes wid *hall?*"

"*Call.*"

"*Fall.*"

"*Wall.*"

"*Quall.*"

They threw themselves on the grass, laughing.

"Big Boy?"

"Huh?"

"Yuh know one thing?"

"Whut?"

"Yuh sho is crazy!"

"Crazy?"

"Yeah, yuh crazys a bed-bug!"

"Crazy bout whut?"

"Man, whoever hearda *quall?*"

"Yuh said yuh wanted something to go wid *hall,* didnt yuh?"

"Yeah, but whuts a *quall?*"

"Nigger, a *qualls* a *quall.*"

They laughed easily, catching and pulling long green blades of grass with their toes.

"Waal, ef a *qualls* a *quall,* whut IS a *quall?*"

"Oh, Ah know."

"Whut?"

"Tha ol song goes something like this:

Yo mama don wear no drawers,
Ah seena when she pulled em off,
N she washed em in alcohol,
N she hung em out in the hall,
N then she put em back on her QUALL!"

They laughed again. Their shoulders were flat to the earth, their knees propped up, and their faces square to the sun.

"Big Boy, yuhs CRAZY!"

"Don ax me nothin else."

"Nigger, yuhs CRAZY!"

They fell silent, smiling, drooping the lids of their eyes softly against the sunlight.

"Man, don the groun feel warm?"

"Jus lika bed."

"Jeeesus, Ah could stay here ferever."

"Me too."

"Ah kin feel tha ol sun goin all thu me."

"Feels like mah bones is warm."

In the distance a train whistled mournfully.

"There goes number fo!"

"Hittin on all six!"

"Highballin it down the line!"

"Boun fer up Noth, Lawd, boun fer up Noth!"

They began to chant, pounding bare heels in the grass.

Dis train boun fo Glory
Dis train, Oh Hallelujah
Dis train boun fo Glory
Dis train, Oh Hallelujah
Dis train boun fo Glory
Ef yuh ride no need fer fret er worry
Dis train, Oh Hallelujah
Dis train . . .

Dis train don carry no gambler
Dis train, Oh Hallelujah
Dis train don carry no gambler
Dis train, Oh Hallelujah
Dis train don carry no gambler

No fo day creeper er midnight rambler
Dis train, Oh Hallelujah
Dis train . . .

When the song ended they burst out laughing, thinking of a train bound for Glory.

"Gee, thas a good ol song!"

"Huuuuummmmmmmmman . . ."

"What?"

"Geeee whiiiiiiiz . . ."

"Whut?"

"Somebody don let win! Das whut!"

Buck, Bobo and Lester jumped up. Big Boy stayed on the ground, feigning sleep.

"Jeeesus, tha sho stinks!"

"Big Boy!"

Big Boy feigned to snore.

"Big Boy!"

Big Boy stirred as though in sleep.

"Big Boy!"

"Hunh?"

"Yuh rotten inside!"

"Rotten?"

"Lawd cant yuh smell it?"

"Smell whut?"

"Nigger, yuh mus gotta bad col!"

"Smell whut?"

"NIGGER, YUH BROKE WIN!"

Big Boy laughed and fell back on the grass, closing his eyes.

"The hen whut cackles is the hen whut laid the egg."

"We ain no hens."

"Yuh cackled, didnt yuh?"

The three moved off with noses turned up.

"C mon!"

"Where yuh-all goin?"

"T the creek fer a swim."

"Yeah, les swim."

"Naw buddy naw!" said Big Boy, slapping the air with a scornful palm.

"Aw, c mon! Don be a heel!"

"N git *lynched?* Hell naw!"

"He ain gonna see us."

"How yuh know?"

"Cause he ain."

"Yuh-all go on. Ahma stay right here," said Big Boy.

"Hell, let im stay! C mon, les go," said Buck.

The three walked off, swishing at grass and bushes with sticks. Big Boy looked lazily at their backs.

"Hey!"

Walking on, they glanced over their shoulders.

"Hey, niggers!"

"C mon!"

Big Boy grunted, picked up his stick, pulled to his feet, and stumbled off.

"Wait!"

"C mon!"

He ran, caught up with them, leaped upon their backs, bearing them to the ground.

"Quit, Big Boy!"

"Gawddam, nigger!"

"Git t hell offa me!"

Big Boy sprawled in the grass beside them, laughing and pounding his heels in the ground.

"Nigger, whut yuh think we is, hosses?"

"How come yuh awways hoppin on us?"

"Lissen, wes goona double-team on yuh one of these days n beat yo ol ass good."

Big Boy smiled.

"Sho nough?"

"Yeah, don yuh like it?"

"We gonna beat yuh sos yuh cant walk!"

"N dare yuh t do nothin erbout it!"

Big Boy bared his teeth.

"C mon! Try it now!"

The three circled around him.

"Say, Buck, yuh grab his feets!"

"N yuh git his head, Lester!"

"N Bobo, yuh berhin n grab his arms!"

Keeping more than arm's length, they circled round and round Big Boy.

"C mon!" said Big Boy, feinting at one and then the other.

Round and round they circled, but could not seem to get any closer. Big Boy stopped and braced his hands on his hips.

"Is all three of yuh-all scareda me?"

"Les git im some other time," said Bobo, grinning.

"Yeah, we kin ketch yuh when yuh ain thinkin," said Lester.

"We kin trick yuh," said Buck.

They laughed and walked together.

Big Boy belched.

"Ahm hongry," he said.

"Me too."

"Ah wished Ah hada big hot pota belly-busters!"

"Cooked wid some good ol salty ribs . . ."

"N some good ol egg cornbread . . ."

"N some buttermilk . . ."

"N some hot peach cobbler swimmin in juice . . ."

"Nigger, hush!"

They began to chant, emphasizing the rhythm by cutting at grass with sticks.

Bye n bye
Ah wanna piece of pie
Pies too sweet
Ah wanna piece of meat
Meats too red
Ah wanna piece of bread
Breads too brown
Ah wanna go t town
Towns too far
Ah wanna ketch a car
Cars too fas
Ah fall n break mah ass
Ahll understan it better bye n bye . . .

They climbed over a barbed-wire fence and entered a stretch of thick woods. Big Boy was whistling softly, his eyes half-closed.

"LES GIT IM!"

Buck, Lester, and Bobo whirled, grabbed Big Boy about the neck, arms, and legs, bearing him to the ground. He grunted and kicked wildly as he went back into weeds.

"Hol im tight!"

"Git his arms! Git his arms!"

"Set on his legs so he cant kick!"

Big Boy puffed heavily, trying to get loose.

"WE GOT YUH NOW, GAWDDAMMIT, WE GOT YUH NOW!"

"Thas a Gawddam lie!" said Big Boy. He kicked, twisted, and clutched for a hold on one and then the other.

"Say, yuh-all hep me hol his arms!" said Bobo.

"Aw, we got this bastard now!" said Lester.

"Thas a Gawddam lie!" said Big Boy again.

"Say, yuh-all hep me hol his arms!" called Bobo.

Big Boy managed to encircle the neck of Bobo with his left arm. He tightened his elbow scissors-like and hissed through his teeth:

"Yuh got me, ain yuh?"

"Hol im!"

"Les beat this bastard's ass!"

"Say hep me hol his *arms!* Hes got aholda mah *neck!*" cried Bobo.

Big Boy squeezed Bobo's neck and twisted his head to the ground.

"Yuh got me, ain yuh?"

"Quit, Big Boy, yuh chokin me; yuh hurtin mah neck!" cried Bobo.

"Turn me loose!" said Big Boy.

"Ah ain got yuh! Its the others whut got yuh!" pleaded Bobo.

"Tell them others t git t hell offa me or Ahma break yo neck," said Big Boy.

"Ssssay, yyuh-all gggit ooooffa Bbig Boy. Hhhes got me," gurgled Bobo.

"Cant yuh hol im?"

"Nnaw, hhes ggot mmah nneck . . ."

Big Boy squeezed tighter.

"N Ahma break it too less yuh tell em t git t hell offa me!"

"Ttturn mmmeee llloose," panted Bobo, tears gushing.

"Cant yuh hol im, Bobo?" asked Buck.

"Nnaw, yuh-all tturn im lloose; hhhes got mah nnneck . . ."

"Grab his neck, Bobo . . ."

"Ah cant; yugurgur . . ."

To save Bobo, Lester and Buck got up and ran to a safe distance. Big Boy released Bobo, who staggered to his feet, slobbering and trying to stretch a crick out of his neck.

"Shucks, nigger, yuh almos broke mah neck," whimpered Bobo.

"Ahm goona break yo ass nex time," said Big Boy.

"Ef Bobo coulda hel yuh we woulda had yuh," yelled Lester.

"Ah wuznt gonna let im do that," said Big Boy.

They walked together again, swishing sticks.

"Yuh see," began Big Boy, "when a ganga guys jump on yuh, all yuh gotta do is jus put the heat on one of them n make im tell the others t let up, see?"

"Gee, thas a good idee!"

"Yeah, thas a good idee!"

"But yuh almos broke mah neck, man," said Bobo.

"Ahma smart nigger," said Big Boy, thrusting out his chest.

II

They came to the swimming hole.

"Ah ain goin in," said Bobo.

"Done got scared?" asked Big Boy.

"Naw, Ah ain scared . . ."

"How come yuh ain goin in?"

"Yuh know ol man Harvey don erllow no niggers t swim in this hole."

"N jus las year he took a shot at Bob fer swimmin in here," said Lester.

"Shucks, ol man Harvey ain studyin bout us niggers," said Big Boy.

"Hes at home thinkin about his jelly-roll," said Buck.

They laughed.

"Buck, yo mins lowern a snakes belly," said Lester.

"Ol man Harveys too doggone ol t think erbout jelly-roll," said Big Boy.

"Hes dried up; all the saps done lef im," said Bobo.

"C mon, les go!" said Big Boy.

Bobo pointed.

"See tha sign over yonder?"

"Yeah."

"Whut it say?"

"NO TRESPASSIN," read Lester.

"Know whut tha mean?"

"Mean ain no dogs n niggers erllowed," said Buck.

"Waal, wes here now," said Big Boy. "Ef he ketched us even like this thered be trouble, so we just as waal go on in . . ."

"Ahm wid the nex one!"

"Ahll go ef anybody else goes!"

Big Boy looked carefully in all directions. Seeing nobody, he began jerking off his overalls.

"LAS ONE INS A OL DEAD DOG!"

"THAS YO MA!"

"THAS YO PA!"

"THAS BOTH YO MA N YO PA!"

They jerked off their clothes and threw them in a pile under a tree. Thirty seconds later they stood, black and naked, on the edge of the hole under a sloping embankment. Gingerly Big Boy touched the water with his foot.

"Man, this waters col," he said.

"Ahm gonna put mah cloes back on," said Bobo, withdrawing his foot.

Big Boy grabbed him about the waist.

"Like hell yuh is!"

"Git outta the way, nigger!" Bobo yelled.

"Thrown im in!" said Lester.

"Duck im!"

Bobo crouched, spread his legs, and braced himself against Big Boy's body. Locked in each other's arms, they tussled on the edge of the hole, neither able to throw the other.

"C mon, les me n yuh push em in."

"O.K."

Laughing, Lester and Buck gave the two locked bodies a running push. Big Boy and Bobo splashed, sending up silver spray in the sunlight. When Big Boy's head came up he yelled:

"Yuh bastard!"

"Tha wuz yo ma yuh pushed!" said Bobo, shaking his head to clear the water from his eyes.

They did a surface dive, came up and struck out across the creek. The muddy water foamed. They swam back, waded into shallow water, breathing heavily and blinking eyes.

"C mon in!"

"Man, the waters fine!"

Lester and Buck hesitated.

"Les wet em," Big Boy whispered to Bobo.

Before Lester and Buck could back away, they were dripping wet from handsful of scooped water.

"Hey, quit!"

"Gawddam, nigger! Tha waters col!"

"C mon in!" called Big Boy.

"We jus as waal go on in now," said Buck.

"Look n see ef anybodys comin."

Kneeling, they squinted among the trees.

"Ain nobody."

"C mon, les go."

They waded in slowly, pausing each few steps to catch their breath. A desperate water battle began. Closing eyes and backing away, they shunted water into one another's faces with the flat palms of hands.

"Hey, cut it out!"

"Yeah, Ahm bout drownin!"

They came together in water up to their navels, blowing and blinking. Big Boy ducked, upsetting Bobo.

"Look out, nigger!"

"Don holler so loud!"

"Yeah, they kin hear yo ol big mouth a mile erway."

"This waters too col fer me."

"Thas cause it rained yistiddy."

They swam across and back again.

"Ah wish we hada bigger place t swim in."

"The white folks got plenty swimmin pools n we ain got none."

"Ah useta swim in the ol Missippi when we lived in Vicksburg."

Big Boy put his head under the water and blew his breath. A sound came like that of a hippopotamus.

"C mon, les be hippos."

Each went to a corner of the creek and put his mouth just below the surface and blew like a hippopotamus. Tiring, they came and sat under the embankment.

"Look like Ah gotta chill."

"Me too."

"Les stay here n dry off."

"Jeeesus, Ahm col!"

They kept still in the sun, suppressing shivers. After some of the water had dried off their bodies they began to talk through clattering teeth.

"Whut would yuh do ef ol man Harveyd come erlong right now?"

"Run like hell!"

"Man, Ahd run so fas hed thinka black streaka lightnin shot pass im."

"But spose he hada gun?"

"Aw, nigger, shut up!"

They were silent. They ran their hands over wet, trembling legs, brushing water away. Then their eyes watched the sun sparkling on the restless creek.

Far away a train whistled.

"There goes number seven!"

"Heading fer up Noth!"

"Blazin it down the line!"

"Lawd, Ahm goin Noth some day."

"Me too, man."

"They say colored folks up Noth is got ekual rights."

They grew pensive. A black winged butterfly hovered at the water's edge. A bee droned. From somewhere came the sweet scent of honeysuckles. Dimly they could hear sparrows twittering in the woods. They rolled from side to side, letting sunshine dry their skins and warm their blood. They plucked blades of grass and chewed them.

"Oh!"

They looked up, their lips parting.

"Oh!"

A white woman, poised on the edge of the opposite embankment, stood directly in front of them, her hat in her hand and her hair lit by the sun.

"Its a woman!" whispered Big Boy in an underbreath. "A *white* woman!"

They stared, their hands instinctively covering their groins. Then they scrambled to their feet. The white woman backed slowly out of sight. They stood for a moment, looking at one another.

"Les git outta here!" Big Boy whispered.

"Wait till she goes erway."

"Les run, theyll ketch us here naked like this!"

"Mabbe theres a man wid her."

"C mon, les git our cloes," said Big Boy.

They waited a moment longer, listening.

"Whut t hell! Ahma git mah cloes," said Big Boy.

Grabbing at short tufts of grass, he climbed the embankment.

"Don run out there now!"

"C mon back, fool!"

Bobo hesitated. He looked at Big Boy, and then at Buck and Lester.

"Ahm goin wid Big Boy n git mah cloes," he said.

"Don run out there naked like tha, fool!" said Buck. "Yuh don know whos out there!"

Big Boy was climbing over the edge of the embankment.

"C mon," he whispered.

Bobo climbed after. Twenty-five feet away the woman stood. She had one hand over her mouth. Hanging by fingers, Buck and Lester peeped over the edge.

"C mon back; that womans scared," said Lester.

Big Boy stopped, puzzled. He looked at the woman. He looked at the bundle of clothes. Then he looked at Buck and Lester.

"C mon, les git our cloes!"

He made a step.

"Jim!" the woman screamed.

Big Boy stopped and looked around. His hands hung loosely at his sides. The woman, her eyes wide, her hand over her mouth, backed away to the tree where their clothes lay in a heap.

"Big Boy, come back n wait till shes gone!"

Bobo ran to Big Boy's side.

"Les go home! Theyll ketch us here," he urged.

Big Boy's throat felt tight.

"Lady, we wanna git our cloes," he said.

Buck and Lester climbed the embankment and stood indecisively. Big Boy ran toward the tree.

"Jim!" the woman screamed. "Jim! Jim!"

Black and naked, Big Boy stopped three feet from her.

"We wanna git our cloes," he said again, his words coming mechanically.

He made a motion.

"You go away! You go away! I tell you, you go away!"

Big Boy stopped again, afraid. Bobo ran and snatched the clothes. Buck and Lester tried to grab theirs out of his hands.

"You go away! You go away! You go away!" the woman screamed.

"Les go!" said Bobo, running toward the woods.

CRACK!

Lester grunted, stiffened, and pitched forward. His forehead struck a toe of the woman's shoes.

Bobo stopped, clutching the clothes. Buck whirled. Big Boy stared at Lester, his lips moving.

"Hes gotta gun; hes gotta gun!" yelled Buck, running wildly.

CRACK!

Buck stopped at the edge of the embankment, his head jerked backward, his body arched stiffly to one side; he toppled headlong, sending up a shower of bright spray to the sunlight. The creek bubbled.

Big Boy and Bobo backed away, their eyes fastened fearfully on a white man who was running toward them. He had a rifle and wore an army officer's uniform. He ran to the woman's side and grabbed her hand.

"You hurt, Bertha, you hurt?"

She stared at him and did not answer.

The man turned quickly. His face was red. He raised the rifle and pointed it at Bobo. Bobo ran back, holding the clothes in front of his chest.

"Don shoot me, Mistah, don shoot me . . ."

Big Boy lunged for the rifle, grabbing the barrel.

"You black sonofabitch!"

Big Boy clung desperately.

"Let go, you black bastard!"

The barrel pointed skyward.

CRACK!

The white man, taller and heavier, flung Big Boy to the ground. Bobo dropped the clothes, ran up, and jumped onto the white man's back.

"You black sonsofbitches!"

The white man released the rifle, jerked Bobo to the ground, and began to batter the naked boy with his fists. Then Big Boy swung, striking the man in the mouth with the barrel. His teeth caved in and he fell, dazed. Bobo was on his feet.

"C mon, Big Boy, les go!"

Breathing hard, the white man got up and faced Big Boy. His lips were trembling, his neck and chin wet with blood. He spoke quietly.

"Give me that gun, boy!"

Big Boy leveled the rifle and backed away.

The white man advanced.

"Boy, I say give me that gun!"

Bobo had the clothes in his arms.

"Run, Big Boy, run!"

The man came at Big Boy.

"Ahll kill yuh; Ahll kill yuh!" said Big Boy.

His fingers fumbled for the trigger.

The man stopped, blinked, spat blood. His eyes were bewildered. His face whitened. Suddenly, he lunged for the rifle, his hands outstretched.

CRACK!

He fell forward on his face.

"Jim!"

Big Boy and Bobo turned in surprise to look at the woman.

"Jim!" she screamed again, and fell weakly at the foot of the tree.

Big Boy dropped the rifle, his eyes wide. He looked around. Bobo was crying and clutching the clothes.

"Big Boy, Big Boy . . ."

Big Boy looked at the rifle, started to pick it up, but didn't. He seemed at a loss. He looked at Lester, then at the white man; his eyes followed a thin stream of blood that seeped to the ground.

"Yuh done killed him," mumbled Bobo.

"Les go home!"

Naked, they turned and ran toward the woods. When they reached the barbed-wire fence they stopped.

"Les git our cloes on," said Big Boy.

They slipped quickly into overalls. Bobo held Lester's and Buck's clothes.

"Whut we gonna do wid these?"

Big Boy stared. His hands twitched.

"Leave em."

They climbed the fence and ran through the woods. Vines and leaves switched their faces. Once Bobo tripped and fell.

"C mon!" said Big Boy.

Bobo started crying, blood streaming from his scratches.

"Ahm scared!"

"C mon! Don cry! We wanna git hom fo they ketches us!"

"Ahm scared!" said Bobo again, his eyes full of tears.

Big Boy grabbed his hand and dragged him along.

"C mon!"

III

They stopped when they got to the end of the woods. They could see the open road leading home, home to ma and pa. But they hung back, afraid. The thick shadows cast from the trees were friendly and sheltering. But the wide glare of sun stretching out over the fields was pitiless. They crouched behind an old log.

"We gotta git home," said Big Boy.

"They's gonna lynch us," said Bobo, half-questioningly.

Big Boy did not answer.

"Theys gonna lynch us," said Bobo again.

Big Boy shuddered.

"Hush!" he said. He did not want to think of it. He could not think of it; there was but one thought, and he clung to that one blindly. He had to get home, home to ma and pa.

Their heads jerked up. Their ears had caught the rhythmic jingle of a wagon. They fell to the ground and clung flat to the side of a log. Over the crest of the hill came the top of a hat. A white face. Then shoulders in a blue shirt. A wagon drawn by two horses pulled into full view.

Big Boy and Bobo held their breath, waiting. Their eyes followed the wagon till it was lost in dust around a bend in the road.

"We gotta git home," said Big Boy.

"Ahm scared," said Bobo.

"C mon! Les keep t the fields."

They ran till they came to the cornfields. Then they went slower, for last year's corn stubbles bruised their feet.

They came in sight of a brickyard.

"Wait a minute," gasped Big Boy.

They stopped.

"Ahm goin on t mah home n yuh better go on t yos."

Bobo's eyes grew round.

"Ahm scared!"

"Yuh better go on!"

"Lemme go wid yuh; they'll ketch me . . ."

"Ef yuh kin git home mabbe yo folks kin hep yuh t git erway."

Big Boy started off. Bobo grabbed him.

"Lemme go wid yuh!"

Big Boy shook free.

"Ef yuh stay here theys gonna lynch yuh!" he yelled, running.

After he had gone about twenty-five yards he turned and looked; Bobo was flying through the woods like the wind.

Big Boy slowed when he came to the railroad. He wondered if he ought to go through the streets or down the track. He decided on the tracks. He could dodge a train better than a mob.

He trotted along the ties, looking ahead and back. His cheek itched, and he felt it. His hand came away smeared with blood. He wiped it nervously on his overalls.

When he came to his back fence he heaved himself over. He landed among a flock of startled chickens. A bantam rooster tried to spur him. He slipped and fell in front of the kitchen steps, grunting heavily. The ground was slick with greasy dishwater.

Panting, he stumbled through the doorway.

"Lawd, Big Boy, whuts wrong wid yuh?"

His mother stood gaping in the middle of the floor. Big Boy flopped wordlessly onto a stool, almost toppling over. Pots simmered on the stove. The kitchen smelled of food cooking.

"Whuts the matter, Big Boy?"

Mutely, he looked at her. Then he burst into tears. She came and felt the scratches on his face.

"Whut happened t yuh, Big Boy? Somebody been botherin yuh?"

"They after me, Ma! They after me . . ."

"Who!"

"Ah . . . Ah . . . We . . ."

"Big Boy, whuts wrong wid yuh?"

"He killed Lester n Buck," he muttered simply.

"Killed!"

"Yessum."

"Lester n Buck!"

"Yessum, Ma!"

"How killed?"

"He shot em, Ma!"

"Lawd Gawd in Heaven, have mercy on us all! This is mo trouble, mo trouble," she moaned, wringing her hands.

"N Ah killed im, Ma . . ."

She stared, trying to understand.

"Whut happened, Big Boy?"

"We tried t git our cloes from the tree . . ."

"Whut tree?"

"We waz swimmin, Ma. N the white woman . . ."

"*White* woman? . . ."

"Yessum. She wuz at the swimmin hole . . ."

"Lawd have mercy! Ah knowed yuh boys waz gonna keep on til yuh got into somethin like this!"

She ran into the hall.

"Lucy!"

"Mam?"

"C mere!"

"Mam?"

"C mere, Ah say!"

"Whutcha wan, Ma? Ahm sewin."

"Chile, will yuh c mere like Ah ast yuh?"

Lucy came to the door holding an unfinished apron in her hands. When she saw Big Boy's face she looked wildly at her mother.

"Whuts the matter?"

"Wheres Pa?"

"Hes out front, Ah reckon."

"Git im, quick!"

"Whuts the matter, Ma?"

"Go git yo Pa, Ah say!"

Lucy ran out. The mother sank into a chair, holding a dish rag. Suddenly, she sat up.

"Big Boy, Ah thought yuh waz at school?"

Big Boy looked at the floor.

"How come yuh didnt go t school?"

"We went t the woods."

She sighed.

"Ah done done all Ah kin fer yuh, Big Boy. Only Gawd kin hep yuh now."

"Ma, don let em git me; don let em git me . . ."

His father came into the doorway. He stared at Big Boy, then at his wife.

"Whuts Big Boy inter now?" he asked sternly.

"Saul, Big Boys done gone n got inter trouble wid the white folks."

The old man's mouth dropped, and he looked from one to the other.

"Saul, we gotta git im erway from here."

"Open yo mouth n talk! Whut yuh been doin?" The old man gripped Big Boy's shoulders and peered at the scratches on his face.

"Me n Lester n Buck n Bobo waz out on ol man Harveys place swimmin . . ."

"Saul, its a *white* woman!"

Big Boy winced. The old man compressed his lips and stared at his wife. Lucy gaped at her brother as though she had never seen him before.

"Whut happened? Cant yuh-all talk?" the old man thundered, with a certain helplessness in his voice.

"We wuz swimmin," Big Boy began, "n then a white woman comes up t the hole. We got up right erway t git our cloes sos we could git erway, n she started screamin. Our cloes wuz right by the tree where she wuz standing, n when we started to git em she jus screamed. We tol her we wanted our cloes . . . Yuh see, Pa, she wuz standin right *by* our cloes; n when we went t git em she jus screamed . . . Bobo got the cloes, n then he shot Lester . . ."

"*Who* shot Lester?"

"The white man."

"Whut white man?"

"Ah dunno, Pa. He wuz a soljer, n he had a rifle."

"A *soljer?*

"Yessuh, Pa. A soljer."

The old man frowned.

"N then whut yuh-all do?"

"Waal, Buck said, 'Hes gotta gun!' N we started runnin. N then he shot Buck, n he fell in the swimmin hole. We didnt see im no mo . . . He wuz close on us then. He looked at the white woman n then he started to shoot Bobo. Ah grabbed the gun, n we started fightin. Bobo jumped on his back. He started beatin Bobo. Then Ah hit im wid the gun. Then he started at me n Ah shot im. Then we run . . ."

"Who seen?"

"Nobody."

"Wheres Bobo?"

"He went home."

"Anybody run after yuh-all?"

"Nawsuh."

"Yuh see anybody?"

"Nawsuh. Nobody but a white man. But he didnt see us."

"How long fo yuh-all lef the swimmin hole?"

"Little while ergo."

The old man nervously brushed his hand across his eyes and walked to the door. His lips moved, but no words came.

"Saul, whut we gonna do?"

"Lucy," began the old man, "go t Brother Sanders n tell im Ah said c mere; n go t Brother Jenkins n tell im Ah said c mere; n go t Elder Peters n tell im Ah said c mere. N don say nothin t nobody but whut Ah tol yuh. N when yuh git thu come straight back. Now go!"

Lucy dropped her apron across the back of a chair and ran down the steps. The mother bent over, crying and praying. The old man walked slowly over to Big Boy.

"Big Boy?"

Big Boy swallowed.

"Ahm talkin t yuh!"

"Yessuh."

"How come yuh didnt go t school this mawnin?"

"We went t the woods."

"Didnt yo ma send yuh t school?"

"Yessuh."

"How come yuh didnt go?"

"We went t the woods."

"Don yuh know thas wrong?"

"Yessuh."

"How come yuh go?"

Big Boy looked at his fingers, knotted them, and squirmed in his seat.

"AHM TALKIN T YUH!"

His wife straightened up and said reprovingly:

"Saul!"

The old man desisted, yanking nervously at the shoulder straps of his overalls.

"How long wuz the woman there?"

"Not long."

"Wuz she young?"

"Yessuh. Lika gal."

"Did yuh-all say anythin t her?"

"Nawsuh. We jus said we wanted our cloes."

"N whut she say?"

"Nothin, Pa. She jus backed erway t the tree n screamed."

The old man stared, his lips trying to form a question.

"Big Boy, did yuh-all bother her?"

"Nawsuh, Pa. We didn *touch* her."

"How long fo the white man come up?"

"Right erway."

"Whut he say?"

"Nothin. He jus cussed us."

Abruptly the old man left the kitchen.

"Ma, cant Ah go fo they ketches me?"

"Sauls doin whut he kin."

"Ma, Ma, Ah don wan em t ketch me . . ."

"Sauls doin whut he kin. Nobody but the good Lawd kin hep us now."

The old man came back with a shotgun and leaned it in a corner. Fascinatedly, Big Boy looked at it.

There was a knock at the front door.

"Liza, see whos there."

She went. They were silent, listening. They could hear her talking.

"Whos there?"

"Me."

"Who?"

"Me, Brother Sanders."

"C mon in. Sauls waitin fer yuh."

Sanders paused in the doorway, smiling.

"Yuh sent fer me, Brother Morrison?"

"Brother Sanders, wes in deep trouble here."

Sanders came all the way into the kitchen.

"Yeah?"

"Big Boy done gone n killed a white man."

Sanders stopped short, then came forward, his face thrust out, his mouth open. His lips moved several times before he could speak.

"A *white* man?"

"They gonna kill me; they gonna kill me!" Big Boy cried, running to the old man.

"Saul, cant we git im erway somewhere?"

"Here now, take it easy; take it easy," said Sanders, holding Big Boy's wrists.

"They gonna kill me; they gonna lynch me!"

Big Boy slipped to the floor. They lifted him to a stool. His mother held him closely, pressing his head to her bosom.

"Whut we gonna do?" asked Sanders.

"Ah done sent fer Brother Jenkins n Elder Peters."

Sanders leaned his shoulders against the wall. Then, as the full meaning of it all came to him, he exclaimed:

"Theys gonna git a mob! . . ." His voice broke off and his eyes fell on the shotgun.

Feet came pounding on the steps. They turned toward the door. Lucy ran in crying. Jenkins followed. The old man met him in the middle of the room, taking his hand.

"Wes in bad trouble here, Brother Jenkins. Big Boy's done gone n killed a white man. Yuh-alls gotta hep me . . ."

Jenkins looked hard at Big Boy.

"Elder Peters says hes comin," said Lucy.

"When all this happen?" asked Jenkins.

"Near bout a hour ergo, now," said the old man.

"Whut we gonna do?" asked Jenkins.

"Ah wanna wait till Elder Peters come," said the old man helplessly.

"But we gotta work fas ef we gonna do anythin," said Sanders. "Well git in trouble jus standin here like this."

Big Boy pulled away from his mother.

"Pa, lemme go now. Lemme go now!"

"Be still, Big Boy!"

"Where kin yuh go?"

"Ah could ketch a freight!"

"Thas *sho* death!" said Jenkins. "Theyll be watchin em all!"

"Kin yuh-all hep me wid some money?" the old man asked.

They shook their heads.

"Saul, whut kin we do? Big Boy cant stay here."

There was another knock at the door.

The old man backed stealthily to the shotgun.

"Lucy go!"

Lucy looked at him, hesitating.

"Ah better go," said Jenkins.

It was Elder Peters. He came in hurriedly.

"Good evening, everybody!"

"How yuh, Elder?"

"Good evenin."

"How yuh today?"

Peters looked around the crowded kitchen.

"Whuts the matter?"

"Elder, wes in deep trouble," began the old man. "Big Boy n some mo boys . . ."

". . . Lester n Buck n Bobo . . ."

". . . wuz over on ol man Harveys place swimmin . . ."

"N he don like us niggers *none,*" said Peters emphatically. He widened his legs and put his thumbs in the armholes of his vest.

". . . n some white woman . . ."

"Yeah?" said Peters, coming closer.

". . . comes erlong n the boys tries t git their cloes where they don lef em under a tree. Waal, she started screamin n all, see? Reckon she thought the boys wuz after her. Then a white man in a soljers suit shoots two of em . . ."

". . . Lester n Buck . . ."

"Huummm," said Peters. "Tha wuz ol man Harveys son."

"Harveys son?"

"Yuh mean the one tha wuz in the Army?"

"Yuh mean Jim?"

"Yeah," said Peters. "The papers said he wuz here fer a vacation from his regiment. N tha woman the boys saw wuz jus erbout his wife . . ."

They stared at Peters. Now that they knew what white person had been killed, their fears became definite.

"N whut else happened?"

"Big Boy shot the man . . ."

"Harveys *son?*"

"He had t, Elder. He wuz gonna shoot im ef he didnt . . ."

"Lawd!" said Peters. He looked around and put his hat back on.

"How long ergo wuz this?"

"Mighty near an hour, now, Ah reckon."

"Do the white folks know yit?"

"Don know, Elder."

"Yuh-all better git this boy outta here right now," said Peters. "Cause ef yuh don theres gonna be a lynchin . . ."

"Where kin Ah go, Elder?" Big Boy ran up to him.

They crowded around Peters. He stood with his legs wide apart, looking up at the ceiling.

"Mabbe we kin hide im in the church til he kin git erway," said Jenkins.

Peters' lips flexed.

"Naw, Brother, thall never do! Theyll git im there sho. N anyhow, ef they ketch im there itll ruin us all. We gotta git the boy outta town . . ."

Sanders went up to the old man.

"Lissen," he said in a whisper. "Mah son, Will, the one whut drives fer the Magnolia Express Company, is taking a truck o goods t Chicawgo in the mawnin. If we kin hide Big Boy somewhere till then, we kin put im on the truck . . ."

"Pa, please, lemme go wid Will when he goes in the mawnin," Big Boy begged.

The old man stared at Sanders.

"Yuh reckon thas safe?"

"Its the only thing yuh *kin* do," said Peters.

"But where we gonna hide im till then?"

"Whut time yo boy leavin out in the mawnin?"

"At six."

They were quiet, thinking. The water kettle on the stove sang.

"Pa, Ah knows where Will passes erlong wid the truck out on Bullards Road. Ah kin hide in one of them ol kilns . . ."

"Where?"

"In one of them kilns we built . . ."

"But theyll git yuh there," wailed the mother.

"But there ain no place else fer im t go."

"Theres some holes big ernough fer me t git in n stay till Will comes erlong," said Big Boy. "Please, Pa, lemme go fo they ketches me . . ."

"Let im go!"

"Please, Pa . . ."

The old man breathed heavily.

"Lucy, git his things!"

"Saul, theyll git im out there!" wailed the mother, grabbing Big Boy.

Peters pulled her away.

"Sister Morrison, ef yuh don let im go n git erway from here hes gonna be caught shos theres a Gawd in Heaven!"

Lucy came running with Big Boy's shoes and pulled them on his feet. The old man thrust a battered hat on his head. The mother went to the stove and dumped the skillet of corn pone into her apron. She wrapped it, and unbuttoning Big Boy's overalls, pushed it into his bosom.

"Heres somethin fer yuh t eat; n pray, Big Boy, cause thas all anybody kin do now . . ."

Big Boy pulled to the door, his mother clinging to him.

"Let im go, Sister Morrison!"

"Run fas, Big Boy!"

Big Boy raced across the yard, scattering the chickens. He paused at the fence and hollered back:

"Tell Bobo where Ahm hidin n tell im t c mon!"

IV

He made for the railroad, running straight toward the sunset. He held his left hand tightly over his heart, holding the hot pone of corn bread there. At times he stumbled over the ties, for his shoes were tight and hurt his feet. His throat burned from thirst; he had had no water since noon.

He veered off the track and trotted over the crest of a hill, following Bullard's Road. His feet slipped and slid in the dust. He kept his eyes straight ahead, fearing every clump of shrubbery, every tree. He wished it were night. If he could only get to the kilns without meeting anyone. Suddenly a thought came to him like a blow. He recalled hearing the old folks tell tales of blood-hounds, and fear made him run slower. None of them had thought of that. Spose blood-houns wuz put on his trail? Lawd! Spose a whole pack of em, foamin n howlin, tore im t pieces? He went limp and his feet dragged. Yeah, thas whut they wuz gonna send after im, blood-houns! N then thered be no way fer im t dodge! Why hadnt Pa let im take tha shotgun? He stopped. He oughta go back n git tha shotgun. And then when the mob came he would take some with him.

In the distance he heard the approach of a train. It jarred him back to a sharp sense of danger. He ran again, his big shoes sopping up and down in the dust. He was tired and his lungs were bursting from running. He wet his lips, wanting water. As he turned from the road across a plowed field he heard the train roaring at his heels. He ran faster, gripped in terror.

He was nearly there now. He could see the black clay on the sloping hillside. Once inside a kiln he would be safe. For a little while, at least. He thought of the shotgun again. If he only had something! Someone to talk to . . . Thas right! Bobo! Bobod be wid im. Hed almost fergot Bobo. Bobod bringa gun; he knowed he would. N tergether they could kill the whole mob. Then in the mawning theyd git inter Will's truck n go far erway, t Chicawgo . . .

He slowed to a walk, looking back and ahead. A light wind skipped over the grass. A beetle lit on his cheek and he brushed it off. Behind the dark pines hung a red sun. Two bats flapped against that sun. He shivered, for he was growing cold; the sweat on his body was drying.

He stopped at the foot of the hill, trying to choose between two patches of black kilns high above him. He went to the left, for there lay the ones he, Bobo, Lester, and Buck had dug only last week. He looked around again; the landscape was bare. He climbed the embankment and stood before a row of black pits sinking four and five feet deep into the earth. He went to the largest and peered in. He stiffened when his ears caught the sound of a whir. He ran back a few steps and poised on his toes. Six foot of snake slid out of the pit and went into coil. Big Boy looked around wildly for a stick. He ran down the slope, peering into the grass. He stumbled over a tree limb. He picked it up and tested it by striking it against the ground.

Warily, he crept back up the slope, his stick poised. When about seven feet from the snake he stopped and waved the stick. The coil grew tighter, the whir sounded louder, and a flat head reared to strike. He went to the right, and the flat head followed him, the blue-black tongue darting forth; he went to the left, and the flat head followed him there too.

He stopped, teeth clenched. He had to kill this snake. Jus had t kill im! This wuz the safest pit on the hillside. He waved the stick again, looking at the snake before, thinking of a mob behind. The flat head reared higher. With stick over shoulder, he jumped in, swinging. The stick sang through the air, catching the snake on the side of the head, sweeping him out of coil. There was a brown writhing mass. Then Big Boy was upon him, pounding blows home, one on top of the other. He fought viciously, his eyes red, his teeth bared in a snarl. He beat till the snake lay still; then he stomped it with his heel, grinding its head into the dirt.

He stopped, limp, wet. The corners of his lips were white with spittle. He spat and shuddered.

Cautiously, he went to the hole and peered. He longed for a match. He imagined whole nests of them in there waiting. He put the stick into the hole and waved it around. Stooping, he peered again. It mus be awright. He looked over the hillside, his eyes coming back to the dead snake. Then he got to his knees and backed slowly into the hole.

When inside he felt there must be snakes all about him, ready to strike. It seemed he could see and feel them there, waiting tensely in coil. In the dark he imagined long white fangs ready to sink into his neck, his side, his legs. He wanted to come out, but kept still. Shucks, he told himself, ef there wuz any snakes in here they sho woulda done bit me by now. Some of his fear left, and he relaxed.

With elbows on ground and chin on palms, he settled. The clay was cold to his knees and thighs, but his bosom was kept warm by the hot pone of corn bread. His thirst returned and he longed for a drink. He was hungry, too. But he did not want to eat the corn pone. Naw, not now. Mabbe after erwhile, after Bobo came. Then theyd both eat the corn pone.

The view from his hole was fringed by the long tufts of grass. He could see all the way to Bullard's Road, and even beyond. The wind was blowing, and in the east the first touch of dusk was rising. Every now and then a bird floated past, a spot of wheeling black printed against the sky. Big Boy sighed, shifted his weight, and chewed at a blade of grass. A wasp droned. He heard number nine, far away and mournful.

The train made him remember how they had dug these kilns on long hot summer days, how they had made boilers out of big tin cans, filled them with water, fixed stoppers for steam, cemented them in holes with wet clay, and built fires under them. He recalled how they had danced and yelled when a stopper blew out of a boiler, letting out a big spout of steam and a shrill whistle. There were times when they had the whole hillside blazing and smoking. Yeah, yuh see, Big Boy wuz Casey Jones n wuz speedin it down the gleamin rails of the Southern Pacific. Bobo had number two on the Santa Fe. Buck wuz on the Illinoy Central. Lester the Nickel Plate. Lawd, how they shelved the wood in! The boiling water would almost jar the cans loose from the clay. More and more pine-knots and dry leaves would be piled under the cans. Flames would grow so tall they would have to shield their eyes. Sweat would pour off their faces. Then, suddenly, a peg would shoot high into the air, and

Pssseeeezzzzzzzzzzzzzzzzzzz . . .

Big Boy sighed and stretched out his arm, quenching the flames and scattering the smoke. Why didnt Bobo c mon? He looked over the fields; there was nothing but dying sunlight. His mind drifted back to the kilns. He remembered the day when Buck, jealous of his winning, had tried to smash his kiln. Yeah, that ol sonofabitch! Naw, Lawd! He didnt go t say tha! Whut wuz he thinkin erbout? Cussin the dead! Yeah, po ol Buck wuz dead now. N Lester too. Yeah, it wuz awright fer Buck t smash his kiln. Sho. N he wished he hadnt socked ol Buck so hard tha day. He wuz sorry fer Buck now. N he sho wished he hadnt cussed po ol Bucks ma, neither. Tha wuz sinful! Mabbe Gawd would git im fer tha? But he didnt go t do it! Po Buck! Po Lester! Hed never treat anybody like tha ergin, never . . .

Dusk was slowly deepening. Somewhere, he could not tell exactly where, a cricket took up a fitful song. The air was growing soft and heavy. He looked over the fields, longing for Bobo . . .

He shifted his body to ease the cold damp of the ground, and thought back over the day. Yeah, hed been dam right erbout not wantin t go swimmin. N ef hed followed his right min hed neverve gon n got inter all this trouble. At first hed said naw. But shucks, somehow hed just went on wid the res. Yeah, he shoulda went on t school tha mawnin, like Ma told im to do. But, hell, who wouldnt git tireda awways drivin a guy t school! Tha wuz the big trou awways drivin a guy t school. He wouldnt be in all this trouble now ef it wuznt fer that Gawddam school! Impatiently, he took the grass out of his mouth and threw it away, demolishing the little red school house . . .

Yeah, ef they had all kept still n quiet when tha ol white woman showed-up, mabbe shedve went on off. But yuh never kin tell erbout these white folks.

Mabbe she wouldntve went. Mabbe tha white man woulda killed all of em! All *fo* of em! Yeah, yuh never kin tell erbout white folks. Then, ergin, mabbe tha white woman woulda went on off n laffed. Yeah, mabbe tha white man woulda said: *Yuh nigger bastards git t hell outta here! Yuh know Gawddam well yuh don berlong here!* N then they woulda grabbed their cloes n run like all hell . . . He blinked the white man away. Where wuz Bobo? Why didnt he hurry up n c mon?

He jerked another blade and chewed. Yeah, ef pa had only let im have tha shotgun! He could stan off a whole mob wid a shotgun. He looked at the ground as he turned a shotgun over in his hands. Then he leveled it at an advancing white man. *Boooom!* The man curled up. Another came. He reloaded quickly, and let him have what the other had got. He too curled up. Then another came. He got the same medicine. Then the whole mob swirled around him, and he blazed away, getting as many as he could. They closed in; but, by Gawd, he had done his part, hadnt he? N the newspapersd say: NIGGER KILLS DOZEN OF MOB BEFO LYNCHED! Er mabbe theyd say: TRAPPED NIGGER SLAYS TWENTY BEFO KILLED! He smiled a little. Tha wouldnt be so bad, would it? Blinking the newspaper away, he looked over the fields. Where wuz Bobo? Why didnt he hurry up n c mon?

He shifted, trying to get a crick out of his legs. Shucks, he wuz gittin tireda this. N it wuz almos dark now. Yeah, there wuz a little bittie star way over yonder in the eas. Mabbe tha white man wuznt dead? Mabbe they wuznt even looking fer im? Mabbe he could go back home now? Naw, better wait erwhile. Thad be bes. But, Lawd, ef he only had some water! He could hardly swallow, his throat was so dry. Gawddam them white folks! Thas all they wuz good fer, t run a nigger down lika rabbit! Yeah, they git yuh in a corner n then they let yuh have it. A thousan of em! He shivered, for the cold of the clay was chilling his bones. Lawd, spose they foun im here in this hole? N wid nobody t hep im? . . . But ain no use in thinking erbout tha; wait till trouble come fo yuh start fightin it. But ef tha mob came one by one hed wipe em all out. Clean up the whole bunch. He caught one by the neck and choked him long and hard, choked him till his tongue and eyes popped out. Then he jumped upon his chest and stomped him like he had stomped that snake. When he had finished with one, another came. He choked him too. Choked till he sank slowly to the ground, gasping . . .

"Hoalo!"

Big Boy snatched his fingers from the white man's neck and looked over the fields. He saw nobody. Had someone spied him? He was sure that somebody had hollered. His heart pounded. But, shucks, nobody couldnt see im here in this hole . . . But mabbe theyd seen im when he wuz comin n had laid low n wuz now closin in on im! Praps they wuz signalin fer the others? Yeah, they wuz creepin up on im! Mabbe he oughta git up n run . . . Oh! Mabbe tha wuz

Bobo? Yeah, Bobo! He oughta clim out n see ef Bobo wuz lookin fer im . . . He stiffened.

"Hoalo!"

"Hoalo!"

"Wheres yuh?"

"Over here on Bullards Road!"

"C mon over!"

"Awright!"

He heard footsteps. Then voices came again, low and far away this time.

"Seen anybody?"

"Naw. Yuh?"

"Naw."

"Yuh reckon they got erway?"

"Ah dunno. Its hard t tell."

"Gawddam them sonofabitchin niggers!"

"We oughta kill ever black bastard in this country!"

"Waal, Jim got two of em, anyhow."

"But Bertha said there wuz *fo!*"

"Where in hell they hidin?"

"She said one of em wuz named Big Boy, or something like tha."

"We went t his shack lookin fer im."

"Yeah?"

"But we didnt fin im."

"These niggers stick tergether; they don never tell on each other."

"We looked all thu the shack n couldnt fin hide ner hair of im. Then we drove the ol woman n man out n set the shack on fire . . ."

"Jeesus! Ah wished Ah coulda been there!"

"Yuh shoulda heard the ol nigger woman howl . . ."

"Hoalo!"

"C mon over!"

Big Boy eased to the edge and peeped. He saw a white man with a gun slung over his shoulder running down the slope. Wuz they gonna search the hill? Lawd, there wuz no way fer im t git erway now; he wuz caught! He shoulda knowed they'd git im here. N he didnt hava thing, notta thing t fight wid. Yeah, soon as the blood-houns came theyd fin im. Lawd, have mercy! Theyd lynch im right here on the hill . . . Theyd git im n tie im t a stake n burn im erlive! Lawd! Nobody but the good Lawd could hep im now, nobody . . .

He heard more feet running. He nestled deeper. His chest ached. Nobody but the good Lawd could hep now. They wuz crowdin all round im n when they hada big crowd theyd close in on im. Then itd be over . . . The good Lawd would have t hep im, cause nobody could hep im now, nobody . . .

And then he went numb when he remembered Bobo. Spose Bobod come now? Hed be caught sho! Both of em would be caught! They'd make Bobo tell where he wuz! Bobo oughta not try to come now. Somebody oughta tell im . . . But there wuz nobody; there wuz no way . . .

He eased slowly back to the opening. There was a large group of men. More were coming. Many had guns. Some had coils of rope slung over shoulders.

"Ah tell yuh they still here, somewhere . . .

"But we looked all over!"

"What t hell! Wouldnt do t let em git erway!"

"Naw. Ef they git erway notta woman in this town would be safe."

"Say, whuts tha yuh got?"

"Er pillar."

"Fer whut?"

"Feathers, fool!"

"Chris! Thisll be hot ef we kin ketch them niggers!"

"Ol Anderson said he wuz gonna bringa barrela tar!"

"Ah got some gasoline in mah car ef yuh need it."

Big Boy had no feelings now. He was waiting. He did not wonder if they were coming after him. He just waited. He did not wonder about Bobo. He rested his cheek against the cold clay, waiting.

A dog barked. He stiffened. It barked again. He balled himself into a knot at the bottom of the hole, waiting. Then he heard the patter of dog feet.

"Look!"

"Whuts he got?"

"Its a snake!"

"Yeah, the dogs foun a snake!"

"Gee, its a big one!"

"Shucks, Ah wish he could fin one of them sonofabitchin niggers!"

The voices sank to low murmurs. Then he heard number twelve, its bell tolling and whistle crying as it slid along the rails. He flattened himself against the clay. Someone was singing:

"*We'll hang ever nigger t a sour apple tree . . .*"

When the song ended there was hard laughter. From the other side of the hill he heard the dog barking furiously. He listened. There was more than one dog now. There were many and they were barking their throats out.

"Hush, Ah hear them dogs!"

"When theys barkin like tha theys foun somethin!"

"Here they come over the hill!"

"WE GOT IM! WE GOT IM!"

There came a roar. Tha mus be Bobo; tha mus be Bobo . . . In spite of his fear, Big Boy looked. The road, and half of the hillside across the road, were covered with men. A few were on the top of the hill, stenciled against the sky. He could see dark forms moving up the slopes. They were yelling.

"By Gawd, we got im!"

"C mon!"

"Where is he?"

"Theyre bringin im over the hill!"

"Ah got a rope fer im!"

"Say, somebody go n git the others!"

"Where is he? Cant we see im, Mister?"

"They say Berthas comin, too."

"Jack! Jack! Don leave me! Ah wanna see im!"

"Theyre bringin im over the hill, sweetheart!"

"AH WANNA BE THE FIRS T PUT A ROPE ON THA BLACK BASTARDS NECK!"

"Les start the fire!"

"Heat the tar!"

"Ah got some chains t chain im."

"Bring im over this way!"

"Chris, Ah wished Ah hada drink . . ."

Big Boy saw men moving over the hill. Among them was a long dark spot. Tha mus be Bobo; tha mus be Bobo theys carryin . . . They'll git im here. He oughta git up n run. He clamped his teeth and ran his hand across his forehead, bringing it away wet. He tried to swallow, but could not; his throat was dry.

They had started the song again:

"*We'll hang ever nigger t a sour apple tree . . .*"

There were women singing now. Their voices made the song round and full. Song waves rolled over the top of pine trees. The sky sagged low, heavy with clouds. Wind was rising. Sometimes cricket cries cut surprisingly across the mob song. A dog had gone to the utmost top of the hill. At each lull of the song his howl floated full into the night.

Big Boy shrank when he saw the first tall flame light the hillside. Would they see im here? Then he remembered you could not see into the dark if you were standing in the light. As flames leaped higher he saw two men rolling a barrel up the slope.

"Say, gimme a han here, will yuh?"

"Awright, heave!"

"C mon! Straight up! Git t the other end!"

"Ah got the feathers here in this pillar!"

"BRING SOME MO WOOD!"

Big Boy could see the barrel surrounded by flames. The mob fell back, forming a dark circle. Theyd fin im here! He had a wild impulse to climb out and fly across the hills. But his legs would not move. He stared hard, trying to find Bobo. His eyes played over a long dark spot near the fire. Fanned by wind, flames leaped higher. He jumped. That dark spot had moved. Lawd, thas Bobo; thas Bobo . . .

He smelt the scent of tar, faint at first, then stronger. The wind brought it full into his face, then blew it away. His eyes burned and he rubbed them with his knuckles. He sneezed.

"LES GIT SOURVINEERS!"

He saw the mob close in around the fire. Their faces were hard and sharp in the light of the flames. More men and women were coming over the hill. The long dark spot was smudged out.

"Everybody git back!"

"Look! Hes gotta finger!"

"C MON! GIT THE GALS BACK FROM THE FIRE!"

"Hes got one of his ears, see?"

"Whuts the matter!"

"A woman fell out! Fainted, Ah reckon . . ."

The stench of tar permeated the hillside. The sky was black and the wind was blowing hard.

"HURRY UP N BURN THE NIGGER FO IT RAINS!"

Big Boy saw the mob fall back, leaving a small knot of men about the fire. Then, for the first time, he had a full glimpse of Bobo. A black body flashed in the light. Bobo was struggling, twisting; they were binding his arms and legs.

When he saw them tilt the barrel he stiffened. A scream quivered. He knew the tar was on Bobo. The mob fell back. He saw a tar-drenched body glistening and turning.

"THE BASTARDS GOT IT!"

There was a sudden quiet. Then he shrank violently as the wind carried, like a flurry of snow, a widening spiral of white feathers into the night. The flames leaped tall as the trees. The scream came again. Big Boy trembled and looked. The mob was running down the slopes, leaving the fire clear. Then he saw a writhing white mass cradled in yellow flame, and heard screams, one on top of the other, each shriller and shorter than the last. The mob was quiet now, standing still, looking up the slopes at the writhing white mass gradually growing black, growing black in a cradle of yellow flame.

"PO ON MO GAS!"

"Gimme a lif, will yuh!"

Two men were struggling, carrying between them a heavy can. They set it down, tilted it, leaving it so that the gas would trickle down to the hollowed earth around the fire.

Big Boy slid back into the hole, his face buried in clay. He had no feelings now, no fears. He was numb, empty, as though all blood had been drawn from him. Then his muscles flexed taut when he heard a faint patter. A tiny stream of cold water seeped to his knees, making him push back to a drier spot. He looked up; rain was beating in the grass.

"Its rainin!"

"C mon, les git t town!"

". . . don worry, when the fire git thu wid im hell be gone . . ."

"Wait, Charles! Don leave me; its slippery here . . ."

"Ahll take some of yuh ladies back in mah car . . ."

Big Boy heard the dogs barking again, this time closer. Running feet pounded past. Cold water chilled his ankles. He could hear raindrops steadily hissing.

Now a dog was barking at the mouth of the hole, barking furiously, sensing a presence there. He balled himself into a knot and clung to the bottom, his knees and shins buried in water. The bark came louder. He heard paws scraping and felt the hot scent of dog breath on his face. Green eyes glowed and drew nearer as the barking, muffled by the closeness of the hole, beat upon his eardrums. Backing till his shoulders pressed against the clay, he held his breath. He pushed out his hands, his fingers stiff. The dog yawped louder, advancing, his bark rising sharp and thin. Big Boy rose to his knees, his hands before him. Then he flattened out still more against the bottom, breathing lungsful of hot dog scent, breathing it slowly, hard, but evenly. The dog came closer, bringing hotter dog scent. Big Boy could go back no more. His knees were slipping and slopping in the water. He braced himself, ready. Then, he never exactly knew how—he never knew whether he had lunged or the dog had lunged—they were together, rolling in the water. The green eyes were beneath him, between his legs. Dognails bit into his arms. His knees slipped backward and he landed full on the dog; the dog's breath left in a heavy gasp. Instinctively, he fumbled for the throat as he felt the dog twisting between his knees. The dog snarled, long and low, as though gathering strength. Big Boy's hands traveled swiftly over the dog's back, groping for the throat. He felt dognails again and saw green eyes, but his fingers had found the throat. He choked, feeling his fingers sink; he choked, throwing back his head and stiffening his arms. He felt the dog's body heave, felt dognails digging into his loins. With strength flowing from fear, he closed his fingers, pushing his full weight on the dog's throat. The dog heaved again, and lay still . . . Big Boy heard the sound of his own breathing filling the hole, and heard shouts and footsteps above him going past.

For a long, long time he held the dog, held it long after the last footstep had died out, long after the rain had stopped.

V

Morning found him still on his knees in a puddle of rainwater, staring at the stiff body of a dog. As the air brightened he came to himself slowly. He held still for a long time, as though waking from a dream, as though trying to remember.

The chug of a truck came over the hill. He tried to crawl to the opening. His knees were stiff and a thousand needle-like pains shot from the bottom of his feet to the calves of his legs. Giddiness made his eyes blur. He pulled up and looked. Through brackish light he saw Will's truck standing some twenty-five yards away, the engine running. Will stood on the runningboard, looking over the slopes of the hill.

Big Boy scuffled out, falling weakly in the wet grass. He tried to call to Will, but his dry throat would make no sound. He tried again.

"Will!"

Will heard, answering:

"Big Boy, c mon!"

He tried to run, and fell. Will came, meeting him in the tall grass.

"C mon," Will said, catching his arm.

They struggled to the truck.

"Hurry up!" said Will, pushing him onto the runningboard.

Will pushed back a square trapdoor which swung above the back of the driver's seat. Big Boy pulled through, landing with a thud on the bottom. On hands and knees he looked around in the semi-darkness.

"Wheres Bobo?"

Big Boy stared.

"Wheres Bobo?"

"They got im."

"When?"

"Las night."

"The mob?"

Big Boy pointed in the direction of a charred sapling on the slope of the opposite hill. Will looked. The trapdoor fell. The engine purred, the gears whined, and the truck lurched forward over the muddy road, sending Big Boy on his side.

For a while he lay as he had fallen, on his side, too weak to move. As he felt the truck swing around a curve he straightened up and rested his back against a stack of wooden boxes. Slowly, he began to make out objects in the darkness. Through two long cracks fell thin blades of daylight. The floor was of smooth steel, and cold to his thighs. Splinters and bits of sawdust danced with the rumble of the truck. Each time they swung around a curve he was pulled over the floor; he grabbed at corners of boxes to steady himself. Once he heard the crow of a rooster. It made him think of home, of ma and pa. He thought he remembered hearing somewhere that the house had burned, but could not remember where . . . It all seemed unreal now.

He was tired. He dozed, swaying with the lurch. Then he jumped awake. The truck was running smoothly, on gravel. Far away he heard two short blasts from the Buckeye Lumber Mill. Unconsciously, the thought sang through his mind: Its six erclock . . .

The trapdoor swung in. Will spoke through a corner of his mouth.

"How yuh comin?"

"Awright."

"How they git Bobo?"

"He wuz coming over the hill."

"Whut they do?"

"They burnt im . . . Will, Ah wan some water; mah throats like fire . . ."

"Well git some when we pass a fillin station."

Big Boy leaned back and dozed. He jerked awake when the truck stopped. He heard Will get out. He wanted to peep through the trapdoor, but was afraid. For a moment, the wild fear he had known in the hole came back. Spose theyd search n fin im? He quieted when he heard Will's footstep on the runningboard. The trapdoor pushed in. Will's hat came through, dripping.

"Take it, quick!"

Big Boy grabbed, spilling water into his face. The truck lurched. He drank. Hard cold lumps of brick rolled into his hot stomach. A dull pain made him bend over. His intestines seemed to be drawing into a tight knot. After a bit it eased, and he sat up, breathing softly.

The truck swerved. He blinked his eyes. The blades of daylight had turned brightly golden. The sun had risen.

The truck sped over the asphalt miles, sped northward, jolting him, shaking out of his bosom the crumbs of corn bread, making them dance with the splinters and sawdust in the golden blades of sunshine.

He turned on his side and slept.

The Man Who Lived Underground

I've got to hide, he told himself. His chest heaved as he waited, crouching in a dark corner of the vestibule. He was tired of running and dodging. Either he had to find a place to hide, or he had to surrender. A police car swished by through the rain, its siren rising sharply. They're looking for me all over . . . He crept to the door and squinted through the fogged plate glass. He stiffened as the siren rose and died in the distance. Yes, he had to hide, but where? He gritted his teeth. Then a sudden movement in the street caught his attention. A throng of tiny columns of water snaked into the air from the perforations of a manhole cover. The columns stopped abruptly, as though the perforations had become clogged; a gray spout of sewer water jutted up from underground and lifted the circular metal cover, juggled it for a moment, then let it fall with a clang.

He hatched a tentative plan: he would wait until the siren sounded far off, then he would go out. He smoked and waited, tense. At last the siren gave him his signal; it wailed, dying, going away from him. He stepped to the sidewalk, then paused and looked curiously at the open manhole, half expecting the cover to leap up again. He went to the center of the street and stooped and peered into the hole, but could see nothing. Water rustled in the black depths.

He started with terror; the siren sounded so near that he had the idea that he had been dreaming and had awakened to find the car upon him. He dropped instinctively to his knees and his hands grasped the rim of the manhole. The siren seemed to hoot directly above him and with a wild gasp of exertion he snatched the cover far enough off to admit his body. He swung his legs over the opening and lowered himself into watery darkness. He hung for an eternal moment to the rim by his finger tips, then he felt rough metal prongs and at once he knew that sewer workmen used these ridges to lower themselves into manholes. Fist over fist, he let his body sink until he could feel no more prongs. He swayed in dank space; the siren seemed to howl at the very rim of the manhole. He dropped and was washed violently into an ocean of warm, leaping water. His head was battered against a wall and he wondered if this were death. Frenziedly his fingers clawed and sank into a crevice. He steadied himself and measured the strength of the current with his own muscular tension. He stood slowly in water that dashed past his knees with fearful velocity.

He heard a prolonged scream of brakes and the siren broke off. Oh, God! They had found him! Looming above his head in the rain a white face hovered over the hole. "How did this damn thing get off?" he heard a policeman ask. He saw the steel cover move slowly until the hole looked like a quarter moon turned black. "Give me a hand here," someone called. The cover clanged into place, muffling the sights and sounds of the upper world. Knee-deep in the pulsing current, he breathed with aching chest, filling his lungs with the hot stench of yeasty rot.

From the perforations of the manhole cover, delicate lances of hazy violet sifted down and wove a mottled pattern upon the surface of the streaking current. His lips parted as a car swept past along the wet pavement overhead, its heavy rumble soon dying out, like the hum of a plane speeding through a dense cloud. He had never thought that cars could sound like that; everything seemed strange and unreal under here. He stood in darkness for a long time, knee-deep in rustling water, musing.

The odor of rot had become so general that he no longer smelled it. He got his cigarettes, but discovered that his matches were wet. He searched and found a dry folder in the pocket of his shirt and managed to strike one; it flared weirdly in the wet gloom, glowing greenishly, turning red, orange, then yellow. He lit a crumpled cigarette; then, by the flickering light of the match, he looked for support so that he would not have to keep his muscles flexed against the pouring water. His pupils narrowed and he saw to either side of him two steaming walls that rose and curved inward some six feet above his head to form a dripping, mouse-colored dome. The bottom of the sewer was a sloping V-trough. To the left, the sewer vanished in ashen fog. To the right was a steep down-curve into which water plunged.

He saw now that had he not regained his feet in time, he would have been swept to death, or had he entered any other manhole he would have probably drowned. Above the rush of the current he heard sharper juttings of water; tiny streams were spewing into the sewer from smaller conduits. The match died; he struck another and saw a mass of debris sweep past him and clog the throat of the down-curve. At once the water began rising rapidly. Could he climb out before he drowned? A long hiss sounded and the debris was sucked from sight; the current lowered. He understood now what had made the water toss the manhole cover; the down-curve had become temporarily obstructed and the perforations had become clogged.

He was in danger; he might slide into a down-curve; he might wander with a lighted match into a pocket of gas and blow himself up; or he might contract some horrible disease . . . Though he wanted to leave, an irrational impulse held him rooted. To the left, the convex ceiling swooped to a height of less than five feet. With cigarette slanting from pursed lips, he waded with taut muscles, his feet sloshing over the slimy bottom, his shoes sinking into spongy slop, the slate-colored water cracking in creamy foam against his knees. Pressing his flat left palm against the lowered ceiling, he struck another match and saw a metal pole nestling in a niche of the wall. Yes, some sewer workman had left it. He reached for it, then jerked his head away as a whisper of scurrying life whisked past and was still. He held the match close and saw a huge rat, wet with slime, blinking beady eyes and baring tiny fangs. The light blinded the rat and the frizzled head moved aimlessly. He grabbed the pole and let it fly against the rat's soft body; there was shrill piping and the grizzly body splashed into the dun-colored water and was snatched out of sight, spinning in the scuttling stream.

He swallowed and pushed on, following the curve of the misty cavern, sounding the water with the pole. By the faint light of another manhole cover he saw, amid loose wet brick, a hole with walls of damp earth leading into blackness. Gingerly he poked the pole into it; it was hollow and went beyond the length of the pole. He shoved the pole before him, hoisted himself upward, got to his hands and knees, and crawled. After a few yards he paused, struck to wonderment by the silence; it seemed that he had traveled a million miles away from the world. As he inched forward again he could sense the bottom of the dirt tunnel becoming dry and lowering slightly. Slowly he rose and to his astonishment he stood erect. He could not hear the rustling of the water now and he felt confoundingly alone, yet lured by the darkness and silence.

He crept a long way, then stopped, curious, afraid. He put his right foot forward and it dangled in space; he drew back in fear. He thrust the pole outward and it swung in emptiness. He trembled, imagining the earth crumbling and burying him alive. He scratched a match and saw that the dirt floor sheered away steeply and widened into a sort of cave some five feet below him. An old sewer, he muttered. He cocked his head, hearing a feathery cadence which he could not identify. The match ceased to burn.

Using the pole as a kind of ladder, he slid down and stood in darkness. The air was a little fresher and he could still hear vague noises. Where was he? He felt suddenly that someone was standing near him and he turned sharply, but there was only darkness. He poked cautiously and felt a brick wall; he followed it and the strange sounds grew louder. He ought to get out of here. This was crazy. He could not remain here for any length of time; there was no food and no place to sleep. But the faint sounds tantalized him; they were strange but familiar. Was it a motor? A baby crying? Music? A siren? He groped on, and the sounds came so clearly that he could feel the pinch and timbre of human voices. Yes, singing! That was it! He listened with open mouth. It was a church service. Enchanted, he groped toward the waves of melody.

Jesus, take me to your home above
And fold me in the bosom of Thy love . . .

The singing was on the other side of the brick wall. Excited, he wanted to watch the service without being seen. Whose church was it? He knew most of the churches in this area above ground, but the singing sounded too strange and detached for him to guess. He looked to the left, to the right, down to the black dirt, then upward and was startled to see a bright sliver of light slicing the darkness like the blade of a razor. He struck one of his two remaining matches and saw rusty pipes running along an old concrete ceiling. Photographically he located the exact position of the pipes in his mind. The match flame sank and he sprang upward; his hands clutched a pipe. He swung his legs and tossed his body onto the bed of pipes and they creaked, swaying up and down; he thought that the tier was about to crash, but nothing happened. He edged to the crevice and saw a segment of black men and women, dressed in white robes, singing, holding tattered songbooks in their black palms. His first impulse was to laugh, but he checked himself.

What was he doing? He was crushed with a sense of guilt. Would God strike him dead for that? The singing swept on and he shook his head, disagreeing in spite of himself. They oughtn't to do that, he thought. But he could think of no reason *why* they should not do it. Just singing with the air of the sewer blowing in on them . . . He felt that he was gazing upon something abysmally obscene, yet he would not bring himself to leave.

After a long time he grew numb and dropped to the dirt. Pain throbbed in his legs and a deeper pain, induced by the sight of those black people groveling and begging for something they could never get, churned in him. A vague conviction made him feel that those people should stand unrepentant and yield no quarter in singing and praying, yet *he* had run away from the police, had pleaded with them to believe in *his* innocence. He shook his head, bewildered.

How long had he been down here? He did not know. This was a new kind of living for him; the intensity of feelings he had experienced when looking at the church people sing made him certain that he had been down here a long time, but his mind told him that the time must have been short. In this darkness the only notion he had of time was when a match flared and measured time by its fleeting light. He groped back through the hole toward the sewer and the waves of song subsided and finally he could not hear them at all. He came to where the earth hole ended and he heard the noise of the current and time lived again for him, measuring the moments by the wash of the water.

The rain must have slackened, for the flow of water had lessened and came only to his ankles. Ought he to go up into the streets and take his chances on hiding somewhere else? But they would surely catch him. The mere thought of dodging and running again from the police made him tense. No, he would stay and plot how to elude them. But what could he do down here? He walked forward into the sewer and came to another manhole cover; he stood beneath it, debating. Fine pencils of gold spilled suddenly from the little circles in the manhole cover and trembled on the surface of the current. Yes, street lamps . . . It must be night . . .

He went forward for about a quarter of an hour, wading aimlessly, poking the pole carefully before him. Then he stopped, his eyes fixed and intent. What's that? A strangely familiar image attracted and repelled him. Lit by the yellow stems from another manhole cover was a tiny nude body of a baby snagged by debris and half-submerged in water. Thinking that the baby was alive, he moved impulsively to save it, but his roused feelings told him that it was dead, cold, nothing, the same nothingness he had felt while watching the men and women singing in the church. Water blossomed about the tiny legs, the tiny arms, the tiny head, and rushed onward. The eyes were closed, as though in sleep; the fists were clenched, as though in protest; and the mouth gaped black in a soundless cry.

He straightened and drew in his breath, feeling that he had been staring for all eternity at the ripples of veined water skimming impersonally over the shriveled limbs. He felt as condemned as when the policemen had accused him. Involuntarily he lifted his hand to brush the vision away, but his arm fell listlessly to his side. Then he acted; he closed his eyes and reached forward slowly with the soggy shoe of his right foot and shoved the dead baby from where it had been lodged. He kept his eyes closed, seeing the little body twisting in the current as it floated from sight. He opened his eyes, shivered, placed his knuckles in the sockets, hearing the water speed in the somber shadows.

He tramped on, sensing at times a sudden quickening in the current as he passed some conduit whose waters were swelling the stream that slid by his feet. A few minutes later he was standing under another manhole cover, listening to the faint rumble of noises above ground. Streetcars and trucks, he mused. He looked down and saw a stagnant pool of gray-green sludge; at intervals a balloon pocket rose from the scum, glistening a bluish-purple, and burst. Then another. He turned, shook his head, and tramped back to the dirt cave by the church, his lips quivering.

Back in the cave, he sat and leaned his back against a dirt wall. His body was trembling slightly. Finally his senses quieted and he slept. When he awakened he felt stiff and cold. He had to leave this foul place, but leaving meant facing those policemen who had wrongly accused him. No, he could not go back aboveground. He remembered the beating they had given him and how he had signed his name to a confession, a confession which he had not even read. He had been too tired when they had shouted at him, demanding that he sign his name; he had signed it to end his pain.

He stood and groped about in the darkness. The church singing had stopped. How long had he slept? He did not know. But he felt refreshed and hungry. He doubled his fist nervously, realizing that he could not make a decision. As he walked about he stumbled over an old rusty iron pipe. He picked it up and felt a jagged edge. Yes, there was a brick wall and he could dig into it. What would he find? Smiling, he groped to the brick wall, sat, and began digging idly into damp cement. I can't make any noise, he cautioned himself. As time passed he grew thirsty, but there was no water. He had to kill time or go aboveground. The cement came out of the wall easily; he extracted four bricks and felt a soft draft blowing into his face. He stopped, afraid. What was beyond? He waited a long time and nothing happened; then he began digging again, soundlessly, slowly; he enlarged the hole and crawled through into a dark room and collided with another wall. He felt his way to the right; the wall ended and his fingers toyed in space, like the antennae of an insect.

He fumbled on and his feet struck something hollow, like wood. What's this? He felt with his fingers. Steps . . . He stooped and pulled off his shoes and mounted the stairs and saw a yellow chink of light shining and heard a low voice speaking. He placed his eye to a keyhole and saw the nude waxen figure of a man stretched out upon a white table. The voice, low-pitched and vibrant, mumbled indistinguishable words, neither rising nor falling. He craned his neck and squinted to see the man who was talking, but he could not locate him. Above the naked figure was suspended a huge glass container filled with a blood-red liquid from which a white rubber tube dangled. He crouched closer to the door and saw the tip end of a black object lined with pink satin. A coffin, he breathed. This is an undertaker's establishment . . . A fine-spun lace of ice covered his body and he shuddered. A throaty chuckle sounded in the depths of the yellow room.

He turned to leave. Three steps down it occurred to him that a light switch should be nearby; he felt along the wall, found an electric button, pressed it, and a blinding glare smote his pupils so hard that he was sightless, defenseless. His pupils contracted and he wrinkled his nostrils at a peculiar odor. At once he knew that he had been dimly aware of this odor in the darkness, but the light had brought it sharply to his attention. Some kind of stuff they use to embalm, he thought. He went down the steps and saw piles of lumber, coffins, and a long workbench. In one corner was a tool chest. Yes, he could use tools, could tunnel through walls with them. He lifted the lid of the chest and saw nails, a hammer, a crowbar, a screwdriver, a light bulb, and a long length of electric wire. Good! He would lug these back to his cave.

He was about to hoist the chest to his shoulders when he discovered a door behind the furnace. Where did it lead? He tried to open it and found it securely bolted. Using the crowbar so as to make no sound, he pried the door open; it swung on creaking hinges, outward. Fresh air came to his face and he caught the faint roar of faraway sound. Easy now, he told himself. He widened the door and a lump of coal rattled toward him. A coalbin . . . Evidently the door led into another basement. The roaring noise was louder now, but he could not identify it. Where was he? He groped slowly over the coal pile, then ranged in darkness over a gritty floor. The roaring noise seemed to come from above him, then below. His fingers followed a wall until he touched a wooden ridge. A door, he breathed.

The noise died to a low pitch; he felt his skin prickle. It seemed that he was playing a game with an unseen person whose intelligence outstripped his. He put his ear to the flat surface of the door. Yes, voices . . . Was this a prize fight stadium? The sound of the voices came near and sharp, but he could not tell if they were joyous or despairing. He twisted the knob until he heard a soft click and felt the springy weight of the door swinging toward him. He was afraid to open it, yet captured by curiosity and wonder. He jerked the door wide and saw on the far side of the basement a furnace glowing red. Ten feet away was still another door, half ajar. He crossed and peered through the door into an empty, high-ceilinged corridor that terminated in a dark complex of shadow. The belling voices rolled about him and his eagerness mounted. He stepped into the corridor and the voices swelled louder. He crept on and came to a narrow stairway leading circularly upward; there was no question but that he was going to ascend those stairs.

Mounting the spiraled staircase, he heard the voices roll in a steady wave, then leap to crescendo, only to die away, but always remaining audible. Ahead of him glowed red letters: E-X-I-T. At the top of the steps he paused in front of a black curtain that fluttered uncertainly. He parted the folds and looked into a convex depth that gleamed with clusters of shimmering lights. Sprawled below him was a stretch of human faces, tilted upward, chanting, whistling, screaming, laughing. Dangling before the faces, high upon a screen of silver, were jerking shadows. A movie, he said with slow laughter breaking from his lips.

He stood in a box in the reserved section of a movie house and the impulse he had had to tell the people in the church to stop their singing seized him. These people were laughing at their lives, he thought with amazement. They were shouting and yelling at the animated shadows of themselves. His compassion fired his imagination and he stepped out of the box, walked out upon thin air, walked on down to the audience; and, hovering in the air just above them, he stretched out his hand to touch them . . . His tension snapped and he found himself back in the box, looking down into the sea of faces. No; it could not be done; he could not awaken them. He sighed. Yes, these people were children, sleeping in their living, awake in their dying.

He turned away, parted the black curtain, and looked out. He saw no one. He started down the white stone steps and when he reached the bottom he saw a man in trim blue uniform coming toward him. So used had he become to being underground that he thought that he could walk past the man, as though he were a ghost. But the man stopped. And he stopped.

"Looking for the men's room, sir?" the man asked, and, without waiting for an answer, he turned and pointed. "This way, sir. The first door to your right."

He watched the man turn and walk up the steps and go out of sight. Then he laughed. What a funny fellow! He went back to the basement and stood in the red darkness, watching the glowing embers in the furnace. He went to the sink and turned the faucet and the water flowed in a smooth silent stream that looked like a spout of blood. He brushed the mad image from his mind and began to wash his hands leisurely, looking about for the usual bar of soap. He found one and rubbed it in his palms until a rich lather bloomed in his cupped fingers, like a scarlet sponge. He scrubbed and rinsed his hands meticulously, then hunted for a towel; there was none. He shut off the water, pulled off his shirt, dried his hands on it; when he put it on again he was grateful for the cool dampness that came to his skin.

Yes, he was thirsty; he turned on the faucet again, bowled his fingers and when the water bubbled over the brim of his cupped palms, he drank in long, slow swallows. His bladder grew tight; he shut off the water, faced the wall, bent his head, and watched a red stream strike the floor. His nostrils wrinkled against acrid wisps of vapor; though he had tramped in the waters of the sewer, he stepped back from the wall so that his shoes, wet with sewer slime, would not touch his urine.

He heard footsteps and crawled quickly into the coalbin. Lumps rattled noisily. The footsteps came into the basement and stopped. Who was it? Had someone heard him and come down to investigate? He waited, crouching, sweating. For a long time there was silence, then he heard the clang of metal and a brighter glow lit the room. Somebody's tending the furnace, he thought. Footsteps came closer and he stiffened. Looming before him was a white face lined with coal dust, the face of an old man with watery blue eyes. Highlights spotted his gaunt cheekbones, and he held a huge shovel. There was a screechy scrape of metal against stone, and the old man lifted a shovelful of coal and went from sight.

The room dimmed momentarily, then a yellow glare came as coal flared at the furnace door. Six times the old man came to the bin and went to the furnace with shovels of coal, but not once did he lift his eyes. Finally he dropped the shovel, mopped his face with a dirty handkerchief, and sighed: "Wheeew!" He turned slowly and trudged out of the basement, his footsteps dying away.

He stood, and lumps of coal clattered down the pile. He stepped from the bin and was startled to see the shadowy outline of an electric bulb hanging above his head. Why had not the old man turned it on? Oh, yes . . . He understood. The old man had worked here for so long that he had no need for light; he had learned a way of seeing in his dark world, like those sightless worms that inch along underground by a sense of touch.

His eyes fell upon a lunch pail and he was afraid to hope that it was full.

He picked it up; it was heavy. He opened it. *Sandwiches!* He looked guiltily around; he was alone. He searched farther and found a folder of matches and a half-empty tin of tobacco; he put them eagerly into his pocket and clicked off the light. With the lunch pail under his arm, he went through the door, groped over the pile of coal, and stood again in the lighted basement of the undertaking establishment. I've got to get those tools, he told himself. And turn off that light. He tiptoed back up the steps and switched off the light; the invisible voice still droned on behind the door. He crept down and, seeing with his fingers, opened the lunch pail and tore off a piece of paper bag and brought out the tin and spilled grains of tobacco into the makeshift concave. He rolled it and wet it with spittle, then inserted one end into his mouth and lit it: he sucked smoke that bit his lungs. The nicotine reached his brain, went out along his arms to his finger tips, down to his stomach, and over all the tired nerves of his body.

He carted the tools to the hole he had made in the wall. Would the noise of the falling chest betray him? But he would have to take a chance; he had to have those tools. He lifted the chest and shoved it; it hit the dirt on the other side of the wall with a loud clatter. He waited, listening; nothing happened. Head first, he slithered through and stood in the cave. He grinned, filled with a cunning idea. Yes, he would now go back into the basement of the undertaking establishment and crouch behind the coal pile and dig another hole. Sure! Fumbling, he opened the tool chest and extracted a crowbar, a screwdriver, and a hammer; he fastened them securely about his person.

With another lumpish cigarette in his flexed lips, he crawled back through the hole and over the coal pile and sat, facing the brick wall. He jabbed with the crowbar and the cement sheered away; quicker than he thought, a brick came loose. He worked an hour; the other bricks did not come easily. He sighed, weak from effort. I ought to rest a little, he thought. I'm hungry. He felt his way back to the cave and stumbled along the wall till he came to the tool chest. He sat upon it, opened the lunch pail, and took out two thick sandwiches. He smelled them. Pork chops . . . His mouth watered. He closed his eyes and devoured a sandwich, savoring the smooth rye bread and juicy meat. He ate rapidly, gulping down lumpy mouthfuls that made him long for water. He ate the other sandwich and found an apple and gobbled that up too, sucking the core till the last trace of flavor was drained from it. Then, like a dog, he ground the meat bones with his teeth, enjoying the salty, tangy marrow. He finished and stretched out full length on the ground and went to sleep. . . .

. . . His body was washed by cold water that gradually turned warm and he was buoyed upon a stream and swept out to sea where waves rolled gently and suddenly he found himself walking upon the water how strange and delightful to walk upon the water and he came upon a nude woman holding a nude baby in her arms and the woman was sinking into the water holding the baby above her head and screaming *help* and he ran over the water to the woman and he reached her just before she went down and he took the baby from her hands and stood watching the breaking bubbles where the woman sank and he called *lady* and still no answer yes dive down there and rescue that woman but he could not take this baby with him and he stooped and laid the baby tenderly upon the surface of the water expecting it to sink but it floated and he leaped into the water and held his breath and strained his eyes to see through the gloomy volume of water but there was no woman and he opened his mouth and called *lady* and the water bubbled and his chest ached and his arms were tired but he could not see the woman and he called again *lady lady* and his feet touched sand at the bottom of the sea and his chest felt as though it would burst and he bent his knees and propelled himself upward and water rushed past him and his head bobbed out and he breathed deeply and looked around where was the baby the baby was gone and he rushed over the water looking for the baby calling *where is it* and the empty sky and sea threw back his voice *where is it* and he began to doubt that he could stand upon the water and then he was sinking and as he struggled the water rushed him downward spinning dizzily and he opened his mouth to call for help and water surged into his lungs and he choked . . .

He groaned and leaped erect in the dark, his eyes wide. The images of terror that thronged his brain would not let him sleep. He rose, made sure that the tools were hitched to his belt, and groped his way to the coal pile and found the rectangular gap from which he had taken the bricks. He took out the crowbar and hacked. Then dread paralyzed him. How long had he slept? Was it day or night now? He had to be careful. Someone might hear him if it were day. He hewed softly for hours at the cement, working silently. Faintly quivering in the air above him was the dim sound of yelling voices. Crazy people, he muttered. They're still there in that movie . . .

Having rested, he found the digging much easier. He soon had a dozen bricks out. His spirits rose. He took out another brick and his fingers fluttered in space. Good! What lay ahead of him? Another basement? He made the hole larger, climbed through, walked over an uneven floor and felt a metal surface. He lighted a match and saw that he was standing behind a furnace in a basement; before him, on the far side of the room, was a door. He crossed and opened it; it was full of odds and ends. Daylight spilled from a window above his head.

Then he was aware of a soft, continuous tapping. What was it? A clock? No, it was louder than a clock and more irregular. He placed an old empty box beneath the window, stood upon it, and looked into an areaway. He eased the window up and crawled through; the sound of the tapping came clearly now. He glanced about; he was alone. Then he looked upward at a series of window ledges. The tapping identified itself. That's a typewriter, he said to himself. It seemed to be coming from just above. He grasped the ridges of a rain pipe and lifted himself upward; through a half-inch opening of window he saw a doorknob about three feet away. No, it was not a doorknob; it was a small circular disk made of stainless steel with many fine markings upon it. He held his breath; an eerie white hand, seemingly detached from its arm, touched the metal knob and whirled it, first to the left, then to the right. It's a safe! . . . Suddenly he could see the dial no more; a huge metal door swung slowly toward him and he was looking into a safe filled with green wads of paper money, rows of coins wrapped in brown paper, and glass jars and boxes of various sizes. His heart quickened. Good Lord! The white hand went in and out of the safe, taking wads of bills and cylinders of coins. The hand vanished and he heard the muffled click of the big door as it closed. Only the steel dial was visible now. The typewriter still tapped in his ears, but he could not see it. He blinked, wondering if what he had seen was real. There was more money in that safe than he had seen in all his life.

As he clung to the rain pipe, a daring idea came to him and he pulled the screwdriver from his belt. If the white hand twirled that dial again, he would be able to see how far to left and right it spun and he would have the combination! His blood tingled. I can scratch the numbers right here, he thought. Holding the pipe with one hand, he made the sharp edge of the screwdriver bite into the brick wall. Yes, he could do it. Now, he was set. Now, he had a reason for staying here in the underground. He waited for a long time, but the white hand did not return. Goddamn! Had he been more alert, he could have counted the twirls and he would have had the combination. He got down and stood in the areaway, sunk in reflection.

How could he get into that room? He climbed back into the basement and saw wooden steps leading upward. Was that the room where the safe stood? Fearing that the dial was now being twirled, he clambered through the window, hoisted himself up the rain pipe, and peered; he saw only the naked gleam of the steel dial. He got down and doubled his fists. Well, he would explore the basement. He returned to the basement room and mounted the steps to the door and squinted through the keyhole; all was dark, but the tapping was still somewhere near, still faint and directionless. He pushed the door in; along one wall of a room was a table piled with radios and electrical equipment. A radio shop, he muttered.

Well, he could rig up a radio in his cave. He found a sack, slid the radio into it, and slung it across his back. Closing the door, he went down the steps and stood again in the basement, disappointed. He had not solved the problem of the steel dial and he was irked. He set the radio on the floor and again hoisted himself through the window and up the rain pipe and squinted; the metal door was swinging shut. Goddamn! He's worked the combination again. If I had been patient, I'd have had it! How could he get into that room? He *had* to get into it. He could jimmy the window, but it would be much better if he could get in without any traces. To the right of him, he calculated, should be the basement of the building that held the safe; therefore, if he dug a hole right *here,* he ought to reach his goal.

He began a quiet scraping; it was hard work, for the bricks were not damp. He eventually got one out and lowered it softly to the floor. He had to be careful; perhaps people were beyond this wall. He extracted a second layer of brick and found still another. He gritted his teeth, ready to quit. I'll dig one more, he resolved. When the next brick came out he felt air blowing into his face. He waited to be challenged, but nothing happened.

He enlarged the hole and pulled himself through and stood in quiet darkness. He scratched a match to flame and saw steps; he mounted and peered through a keyhole: Darkness . . . He strained to hear the typewriter, but there was only silence. Maybe the office had closed? He twisted the knob and swung the door in; a frigid blast made him shiver. In the shadows before him were halves and quarters of hogs and lambs and steers hanging from metal hooks on the low ceiling, red meat encased in folds of cold white fat. Fronting him was frost-coated glass from behind which came indistinguishable sounds. The odor of fresh raw meat sickened him and he backed away. A meat market, he whispered.

He ducked his head, suddenly blinded by light. He narrowed his eyes; the red-white rows of meat were drenched in yellow glare. A man wearing a crimson spotted jacket came in and took down a bloody meat cleaver. He eased the door to, holding it ajar just enough to watch the man, hoping that the darkness in which he stood would keep him from being seen. The man took down a hunk of steer and placed it upon a bloody wooden block and bent forward and whacked with the cleaver. The man's face was hard, square, grim; a jet of mustache smudged his upper lip and a glistening cowlick of hair fell over his left eye. Each time he lifted the cleaver and brought it down upon the meat, he let out a short, deep-chested grunt. After he had cut the meat, he wiped blood off the wooden block with a sticky wad of gunny sack and hung the cleaver upon a hook. His face was proud as he placed the chunk of meat in the crook of his elbow and left.

The door slammed and the light went off; once more he stood in shadow. His tension ebbed. From behind the frosted glass he heard the man's voice: "Forty-eight cents a pound, ma'am." He shuddered, feeling that there was something he had to do. But what? He stared fixedly at the cleaver, then he sneezed and was terrified for fear that the man had heard him. But the door did not open. He took down the cleaver and examined the sharp edge smeared with cold blood. Behind the ice-coated glass a cash register rang with a vibrating, musical tinkle.

Absent-mindedly holding the meat cleaver, he rubbed the glass with his thumb and cleared a spot that enabled him to see into the front of the store. The shop was empty, save for the man who was now putting on his hat and coat. Beyond the front window a wan sun shone in the streets; people passed and now and then a fragment of laughter or the whir of a speeding auto came to him. He peered closer and saw on the right counter of the shop a mosquito netting covering pears, grapes, lemons, oranges, bananas, peaches, and plums. His stomach contracted.

The man clicked out the light and he gritted his teeth, muttering, Don't lock the icebox door . . The man went through the door of the shop and locked it from the outside. Thank God! Now, he would eat some more! He waited, trembling. The sun died and its rays lingered on in the sky, turning the streets to dusk. He opened the door and stepped inside the shop. In reverse letters across the front window was: NICK'S FRUITS AND MEATS. He laughed, picked up a soft ripe yellow pear and bit into it; juice squirted; his mouth ached as his saliva glands reacted to the acid of the fruit. He ate three pears, gobbled six bananas, and made away with several oranges, taking a bite out of their tops and holding them to his lips and squeezing them as he hungrily sucked the juice.

He found a faucet, turned it on, laid the cleaver aside, pursed his lips under the stream until his stomach felt about to burst. He straightened and belched, feeling satisfied for the first time since he had been underground. He sat upon the floor, rolled and lit a cigarette, his bloodshot eyes squinting against the film of drifting smoke. He watched a patch of sky turn red, then purple; night fell and he lit another cigarette, brooding. Some part of him was trying to remember the world he had left, and another part of him did not want to remember it. Sprawling before him in his mind was his wife, Mrs. Wooten for whom he worked, the three policemen who had picked him up . . . He possessed them now more completely than he had ever possessed them when he had lived aboveground. How this had come about he could not say, but he had no desire to go back to them. He laughed, crushed the cigarette, and stood up.

He went to the front door and gazed out. Emotionally he hovered between the world aboveground and the world underground. He longed to go out, but sober judgment urged him to remain here. Then impulsively he pried the lock loose with one swift twist of the crowbar; the door swung outward. Through the twilight he saw a white man and a white woman coming toward him. He held himself tense, waiting for them to pass; but they came directly to the door and confronted him.

"I want to buy a pound of grapes," the woman said.

Terrified, he stepped back into the store. The white man stood to one side and the woman entered.

"Give me a pound of dark ones," the woman said.

The white man came slowly forward, blinking his eyes.

"Where's Nick?" the man asked.

"Were you just closing?" the woman asked.

"Yes, ma'am," he mumbled. For a second he did not breathe, then he mumbled again: "Yes, ma'am."

"I'm sorry," the woman said.

The street lamps came on, lighting the store somewhat. Ought he run? But that would raise an alarm. He moved slowly, dreamily, to a counter and lifted up a bunch of grapes and showed them to the woman.

"Fine," the woman said. "But isn't that more than a pound?"

He did not answer. The man was staring at him intently.

"Put them in a bag for me," the woman said, fumbling with her purse.

"Yes, ma'am."

He saw a pile of paper bags under a narrow ledge; he opened one and put the grapes in.

"Thanks," the woman said, taking the bag and placing a dime in his dark palm.

"Where's Nick?" the man asked again. "At supper?"

"Sir? Yes, sir," he breathed.

They left the store and he stood trembling in the doorway. When they were out of sight, he burst out laughing and crying. A trolley car rolled noisily past and he controlled himself quickly. He flung the dime to the pavement with a gesture of contempt and stepped into the warm night air. A few shy stars trembled above him. The look of things was beautiful, yet he felt a lurking threat. He went to an unattended newsstand and looked at a stack of papers. He saw a headline: HUNT NEGRO FOR MURDER.

He felt that someone had slipped up on him from behind and was stripping off his clothes; he looked about wildly, went quickly back into the store, picked up the meat cleaver where he had left it near the sink, then made his way through the icebox to the basement. He stood for a long time, breathing heavily. They know I didn't do anything, he muttered. But how could he prove it? He had signed a confession. Though innocent, he felt guilty, condemned. He struck a match and held it near the steel blade, fascinated and repelled by the dried blotches of blood. Then his fingers gripped the handle of the cleaver with all the strength of his body, he wanted to fling the cleaver from him, but he could not. The match flame wavered and fled; he struggled through the hole and put the cleaver in the sack with the radio. He was determined to keep it, for what purpose he did not know.

He was about to leave when he remembered the safe. Where was it? He wanted to give up, but felt that he ought to make one more try. Opposite the last hole he had dug, he tunneled again, plying the crowbar. Once he was so exhausted that he lay on the concrete floor and panted. Finally he made another hole. He wriggled through and his nostrils filled with the fresh smell of coal. He struck a match; yes, the usual steps led upward. He tiptoed to a door and eased it open. A fair-haired white girl stood in front of a steel cabinet, her blue eyes wide upon him. She turned chalky and gave a high-pitched scream. He bounded down the steps and raced to his hole and clambered through, replacing the bricks with nervous haste. He paused, hearing loud voices.

"What's the matter, Alice?"

"A man . . ."

"What man? Where?"

"A man was at that door . . ."

"Oh, nonsense!"

"He was looking at me through the door!"

"Aw, you're dreaming."

"I *did* see a man!"

The girl was crying now.

"There's nobody here."

Another man's voice sounded.

"What is it, Bob?"

"Alice says she saw a man in here, in that door!"

"Let's take a look."

He waited, poised for flight. Footsteps descended the stairs.

"There's nobody down here."

"The window's locked."

"And there's no door."

"You ought to fire that dame."

"Oh, I don't know. Women are that way."

"She's too hysterical."

The men laughed. Footsteps sounded again on the stairs. A door slammed. He sighed, relieved that he had escaped. But he had not done what he had set out to do; his glimpse of the room had been too brief to determine if the safe was there. He had to know. Boldly he groped through the hole once more; he reached the steps and pulled off his shoes and tip-toed up and peered through the keyhole. His head accidentally touched the door and it swung silently in a fraction of an inch; he saw the girl bent over the cabinet, her back to him. Beyond her was the safe. He crept down the steps, thinking exultingly: I found it!

Now he had to get the combination. Even if the window in the areaway was locked and bolted, he could gain entrance when the office closed. He scoured through the holes he had dug and stood again in the basement where he had left the radio and the cleaver. Again he crawled out of the window and lifted himself up the rain pipe and peered. The steel dial showed lonely and bright, reflecting the yellow glow of an unseen light. Resigned to a long wait, he sat and leaned against the wall. From far off came the faint sounds of life aboveground; once he looked with a baffled expression at the dark sky. Frequently he rose and climbed the pipe to see the white hand spin the dial, but nothing happened. He bit his lip with impatience. It was not the money that was luring him, but the mere fact that he could get it with impunity. Was the hand now twirling the dial? He rose and looked, but the white hand was not in sight.

Perhaps it would be better to watch continuously? Yes; he clung to the pipe and watched the dial until his eyes thickened with tears. Exhausted, he stood again in the areaway. He heard a door being shut and he clawed up the pipe and looked. He jerked tense as a vague figure passed in front of him. He stared unblinkingly, hugging the pipe with one hand and holding the screwdriver with the other, ready to etch the combination upon the wall. His ears caught: *Dong . . . Dong . . . Dong . . . Dong . . . Dong . . . Dong . . . Dong . . .* Seven o'clock, he whispered. Maybe they were closing now? What kind of a store would be open as late as this? he wondered. Did anyone live in the rear? Was there a night watchman? Perhaps the safe was *already* locked for the night! Goddamn! While he had been eating in that shop, they had locked up everything . . . Then, just as he was about to give up, the white hand touched the dial and turned it once to the right and stopped at six. With quivering fingers, he etched 1—R—6 upon the brick wall with the tip of the screwdriver. The hand twirled the dial twice to the left and stopped at two, and he engraved 2—L—2 upon the wall. The dial was spun four times to the right and stopped at six again; he wrote 4—R—6. The dial rotated three times to the left and was centered straight up and down; he wrote 3—L—0. The door swung open and again he saw the piles of green money and the rows of wrapped coins. I got it, he said grimly.

Then he was stone still, astonished. There were two hands now. A right hand lifted a wad of green bills and deftly slipped it up the sleeve of a left arm. The hands trembled; again the right hand slipped a packet of bills up the left sleeve. He's stealing, he said to himself. He grew indignant, as if the money belonged to him. Though *he* had planned to steal the money, he despised and pitied the man. He felt that his stealing the money and the man's stealing were two entirely different things. He wanted to steal the money merely for the sensation involved in getting it, and he had no intention whatever of spending a penny of it; but he knew that the man who was now stealing it was going to spend it, perhaps for pleasure. The huge steel door closed with a soft click.

Though angry, he was somewhat satisfied. The office would close soon. I'll clean the place out, he mused. He imagined the entire office staff cringing with fear; the police would question everyone for a crime they had not committed, just as they had questioned him. And they would have no idea of how the money had been stolen until they discovered the holes he had tunneled in the walls of the basements. He lowered himself and laughed mischievously, with the abandoned glee of an adolescent.

He flattened himself against the wall as the window above him closed with rasping sound. He looked; somebody was bolting the window securely with a metal screen. That won't help you, he snickered to himself. He clung to the rain pipe until the yellow light in the office went out. He went back into the basement, picked up the sack containing the radio and cleaver, and crawled through the two holes he had dug and groped his way into the basement of the building that held the safe. He moved in slow motion, breathing softly. Be careful now, he told himself. There might be a night watchman ... In his memory was the combination written in bold white characters as upon a blackboard. Eel-like he squeezed through the last hole and crept up the steps and put his hand on the knob and pushed the door in about three inches. Then his courage ebbed; his imagination wove dangers for him.

Perhaps the night watchman was waiting in there, ready to shoot. He dangled his cap on a forefinger and poked it past the jamb of the door. If anyone fired, they would hit his cap; but nothing happened. He widened the door, holding the crowbar high above his head, ready to beat off an assailant. He stood like that for five minutes; the rumble of a streetcar brought him to himself. He entered the room. Moonlight floated in from a side window. He confronted the safe, then checked himself. Better take a look around first ... He stepped about and found a closed door. Was the night watchman in there? He opened it and saw a washbowl, a faucet, and a commode. To the left was still another door that opened into a huge dark room that seemed empty; on the far side of that room he made out the shadow of still another door. Nobody's here, he told himself.

He turned back to the safe and fingered the dial; it spun with ease. He laughed and twirled it just for fun. Get to work, he told himself. He turned the dial to the figures he saw on the blackboard of his memory; it was so easy that he felt that the safe had not been locked at all. The heavy door eased loose and he caught hold of the handle and pulled hard, but the door swung open with a slow momentum of its own. Breathless, he gaped at wads of green bills, rows of wrapped coins, curious glass jars full of white pellets, and many oblong green metal boxes. He glanced guiltily over his shoulders; it seemed impossible that someone should not call to him to stop.

They'll be surprised in the morning, he thought. He opened the top of the sack and lifted a wad of compactly tied bills; the money was crisp and new. He admired the smooth, cleancut edges. The fellows in Washington sure know how to make this stuff, he mused. He rubbed the money with his fingers, as though expecting it to reveal hidden qualities. He lifted the wad to his nose and smelled the fresh odor of ink. Just like any other paper, he mumbled. He dropped the wad into the sack and picked up another. Holding the bag, he thought and laughed.

There was in him no sense of possessiveness; he was intrigued with the form and color of the money, with the manifold reactions which he knew that men aboveground held toward it. The sack was one-third full when it occurred to him to examine the denominations of the bills; without realizing it, he had put many wads of one-dollar bills into the sack. Aw, nuts, he said in disgust. Take the big ones . . . He dumped the one-dollar bills onto the floor and swept all the hundred-dollar bills he could find into the sack, then he raked in rolls of coins with crooked fingers.

He walked to a desk upon which sat a typewriter, the same machine which the blond girl had used. He was fascinated by it; never in his life had he used one of them. It was a queer instrument of business; something beyond the rim of his life. Whenever he had been in an office where a girl was typing, he had almost always spoken in whispers. Remembering vaguely what he had seen others do, he inserted a sheet of paper into the machine; it went in lopsided and he did not know how to straighten it. Spelling in a soft diffident voice, he pecked out his name on the keys: *freddaniels.* He looked at it and laughed. He would learn to type correctly one of these days.

Yes, he would take the typewriter too. He lifted the machine and placed it atop the bulk of money in the sack. He did not feel that he was stealing, for the cleaver, the radio, the money, and the typewriter were all on the same level of value, all meant the same thing to him. They were the serious toys of the men who lived in the dead world of sunshine and rain he had left, the world that had condemned him, branded him guilty.

But what kind of a place is this? He wondered. What was in that dark room to his rear? He felt for his matches and found that he had only one left. He leaned the sack against the safe and groped forward into the room, encountering smooth, metallic objects that felt like machines. Baffled, he touched a wall and tried vainly to locate an electric switch. Well, he *had* to strike his last match. He knelt and struck it, cupping the flame near the floor with his palms. The place seemed to be a factory, with benches and tables. There were bulbs with green shades spaced about the tables; he turned on a light and twisted it low so that the glare was limited. He saw a half-filled packet of cigarettes and appropriated it. There were stools at the benches and he concluded that men worked here at some trade. He wandered and found a few half-used folders of matches. If only he could find more cigarettes! But there were none.

But what kind of a place was this? On a bench he saw a pad of paper captioned: PEER'S—MANUFACTURING JEWELERS. His lips formed an "O," then he snapped off the light and ran back to the safe and lifted one of the glass jars and stared at the tiny white pellets. Gingerly he picked up one and found that it was wrapped in tissue paper. He peeled the paper and saw a glittering stone that looked like glass, glinting white and blue sparks. Diamonds, he breathed.

Roughly he tore the paper from the pellets and soon his palm quivered with precious fire. Trembling, he took all four glass jars from the safe and put them into the sack. He grabbed one of the metal boxes, shook it, and heard a tinny rattle. He pried off the lid with the screwdriver. Rings! Hundreds of them . . . Were they worth anything? He scooped up a handful and jets of fire shot fitfully from the stones. These are diamonds, too, he said. He pried open another box. Watches! A chorus of soft, metallic ticking filled his ears. For a moment he could not move, then he dumped all the boxes into the sack.

He shut the safe door, then stood looking around, anxious not to overlook anything. Oh! He had seen a door in the room where the machines were. What was in there? More valuables? He re-entered the room, crossed the floor, and stood undecided before the door. He finally caught hold of the knob and pushed the door in; the room beyond was dark. He advanced cautiously inside and ran his fingers along the wall for the usual switch, then he was stark still. *Something had moved in the room!* What was it? Ought he to creep out, taking the rings and diamonds and money? Why risk what he already had? He waited and the ensuing silence gave him confidence to explore further. Dare he strike a match? Would not a match flame make him a good target? He tensed again as he heard a faint sigh; he was now convinced that there was something alive near him, something that lived and breathed. On tiptoe he felt slowly along the wall, hoping that he would not collide with anything. Luck was with him; he found the light switch.

No; don't turn the light on . . . Then suddenly he realized that he did not know in what direction the door was. Goddamn! He had to turn the light on or strike a match. He fingered the switch for a long time, then thought of an idea. He knelt upon the floor, reached his arm up to the switch and flicked the button, hoping that if anyone shot, the bullet would go above his head. The moment the light came on he narrowed his eyes to see quickly. He sucked in his breath and his body gave a violent twitch and was still. In front of him, so close that it made him want to bound up and scream, was a human face.

He was afraid to move lest he touch the man. If the man had opened his eyes at that moment, there was no telling what he might have done. The man —long and rawboned—was stretched out on his back upon a little cot, sleeping in his clothes, his head cushioned by a dirty pillow; his face, clouded by a dark stubble of beard, looked straight up to the ceiling. The man sighed, and he grew tense to defend himself; the man mumbled and turned his face away from the light. I've got to turn off that light, he thought. Just as he was about to rise, he saw a gun and cartridge belt on the floor at the man's side. Yes, he would take the gun and cartridge belt, not to use them, but just to keep them, as one takes a memento from a country fair. He picked them up and was about to click off the light when his eyes fell upon a photograph perched upon a chair near the man's head; it was the picture of a woman, smiling, shown against a background of open fields; at the woman's side were two young children, a boy and a girl. He smiled indulgently; he could send a bullet into that man's brain and time would be over for him . . .

He clicked off the light and crept silently back into the room where the safe stood; he fastened the cartridge belt about him and adjusted the holster at his right hip. He strutted about the room on tiptoe, lolling his head nonchalantly, then paused, abruptly pulled the gun, and pointed it with grim face toward an imaginary foe. "Boom!" he whispered fiercely. Then he bent forward with silent laughter. That's just like they do it in the movies, he said.

He contemplated his loot for a long time, then got a towel from the washroom and tied the sack securely. When he looked up he was momentarily frightened by his shadow looming on the wall before him. He lifted the sack, dragged it down the basement steps, lugged it across the basement, gasping for breath. After he had struggled through the hole, he clumsily replaced the bricks, then tussled with the sack until he got it to the cave. He stood in the dark, wet with sweat, brooding about the diamonds, the rings, the watches, the money; he remembered the singing in the church, the people yelling in the movie, the dead baby, the nude man stretched out upon the white table . . . He saw these items hovering before his eyes and felt that some dim meaning linked them together, that some magical relationship made them kin. He stared with vacant eyes, convinced that all of these images, with their tongueless reality, were striving to tell him something . . .

Later, seeing with his fingers, he untied the sack and set each item neatly upon the dirt floor. Exploring, he took the bulb, the socket, and the wire out of the tool chest; he was elated to find a double socket at one end of the wire. He crammed the stuff into his pockets and hoisted himself upon the rusty pipes and squinted into the church; it was dim and empty. Somewhere in this wall were live electric wires; but where? He lowered himself, groped and tapped the wall with the butt of the screwdriver; listening vainly for hollow sounds. I'll just take a chance and dig, he said.

For an hour he tried to dislodge a brick, and when he struck a match, he found that he had dug a depth of only an inch! No use in digging here, he sighed. By the flickering light of a match, he looked upward, then lowered his eyes, only to glance up again, startled. Directly above his head, beyond the pipes, was a wealth of electric wiring. I'll be damned, he snickered.

He got an old dull knife from the chest and, seeing again with his fingers, separated the two strands of wire and cut away the insulation. Twice he received a slight shock. He scraped the wiring clean and managed to join the two twin ends, then screwed in the bulb. The sudden illumination blinded him and he shut his lids to kill the pain in his eyeballs. I've got that much done, he thought jubilantly.

He placed the bulb on the dirt floor and the light cast a blatant glare on the bleak clay walls. Next he plugged one end of the wire that dangled from the radio into the light socket and bent down and switched on the button; almost at once there was the harsh sound of static, but no words or music. Why won't it work? he wondered. Had he damaged the mechanism in any way? Maybe it needed grounding? Yes . . . he rummaged in the tool chest and found another length of wire, fastened it to the ground of the radio, and then tied the opposite end to a pipe. Rising and growing distinct, a slow strain of music entranced him with its measured sound. He sat upon the chest, deliriously happy.

Later he searched again in the chest and found a half-gallon can of glue; he opened it and smelled a sharp odor. Then he recalled that he had not even looked at the money. He took a wad of green bills and weighed it in his palm, then broke the seal and held one of the bills up to the light and studied it closely. *The United States of America will pay to the bearer on demand one hundred dollars,* he read in slow speech; then: *This note is legal tender for all debts, public and private. . . .* He broke into a musing laugh, feeling that he was reading of the doings of people who lived on some far-off planet. He turned the bill over and saw on the other side of it a delicately beautiful building gleaming with paint and set amidst green grass. He had no desire whatever to count the money; it was what it stood for—the various currents of life swirling aboveground—that captivated him. Next he opened the rolls of coins and let them slide from their paper wrappings to the ground; the bright, new gleaming pennies and nickles and dimes piled high at his feet, a glowing mound of shimmering copper and silver. He sifted them through his fingers, listening to their tinkle as they struck the conical heap.

Oh, yes! He had forgotten. He would now write his name on the typewriter. He inserted a piece of paper and poised his fingers to write. But what was his name? He stared, trying to remember. He stood and glared about the dirt cave, his name on the tip of his lips. But it would not come to him. Why was he here? Yes, he had been running away from the police. But why? His mind was blank. He bit his lips and sat again, feeling a vague terror. But why worry? He laughed, then pecked slowly: *itwasalonghotday.* He was determined to type the sentence without making any mistakes. How did one make capital letters? He experimented and luckily discovered how to lock the machine for capital letters and then shift it back to lower case. Next he discovered how to make spaces, then he wrote neatly and correctly: *It was a long hot day.* Just why he selected that sentence he did not know; it was merely the ritual of performing the thing that appealed to him. He took the sheet out of the machine and looked around with stiff neck and hard eyes and spoke to an imaginary person.

"Yes, I'll have the contracts ready tomorrow."

He laughed. That's just the way they talk, he said. He grew weary of the game and pushed the machine aside. His eyes fell upon the can of glue, and a mischievous idea bloomed in him, filling him with nervous eagerness. He leaped up and opened the can of glue, then broke the seals on all the wads of money. I'm going to have some wallpaper, he said with a luxurious, physical laugh that made him bend at the knees. He took the towel with which he had tied the sack and balled it into a swab and dipped it into the can of glue and dabbed glue onto the wall; then he pasted one green bill by the side of another. He stepped back and cocked his head. Jesus! That's funny . . . He slapped his thighs and guffawed. He had triumphed over the world aboveground! He was free! If only people could see this! He wanted to run from this cave and yell his discovery to the world.

He swabbed all the dirt walls of the cave and pasted them with green bills; when he had finished the walls blazed with a yellow-green fire. Yes, this room would be his hide-out; between him and the world that had branded him guilty would stand this mocking symbol. He had not stolen the money; he had simply picked it up, just as a man would pick up firewood in a forest. And that was how the world aboveground now seemed to him, a wild forest filled with death.

The walls of money finally palled on him and he looked about for new interests to feed his emotions. The cleaver! He drove a nail into the wall and hung the bloody cleaver upon it. Still another idea welled up. He pried open the metal boxes and lined them side by side on the dirt floor. He grinned at the gold and fire. From one box he lifted up a fistful of ticking gold watches and dangled them by their gleaming chains. He stared with an idle smile, then began to wind them up; he did not attempt to set them at any given hour, for there was no time for him now. He took a fistful of nails and drove them into the papered walls and hung the watches upon them, letting them swing down by their glittering chains, trembling and ticking busily against the backdrop of green with the lemon sheen of the electric light shining upon the metal watch casings, converting the golden disks into blobs of liquid yellow. Hardly had he hung up the last watch than the idea extended itself; he took more nails from the chest and drove them into the green paper and took the boxes of rings and went from nail to nail and hung up the golden bands. The blue and white sparks from the stones filled the cave with brittle laughter, as though enjoying his hilarious secret. People certainly can do some funny things, he said to himself.

He sat upon the tool chest, alternately laughing and shaking his head soberly. Hours later he became conscious of the gun sagging at his hip and he pulled it from the holster. He had seen men fire guns in movies, but somehow his life had never led him into contact with firearms. A desire to feel the sensation others felt in firing came over him. But someone might hear . . . Well, what if they did? They would not know where the shot had come from. Not in their wildest notions would they think that it had come from under the streets! He tightened his fingers on the trigger; there was a deafening report and it seemed that the entire underground had caved in upon his eardrums; and in the same instant there flashed an orange-blue spurt of flame that died quickly but lingered on as a vivid after-image. He smelled the acrid stench of burnt powder filling his lungs and he dropped the gun abruptly.

The intensity of his feelings died and he hung the gun and cartridge belt upon the wall. Next he lifted the jars of diamonds and turned them bottom upward, dumping the white pellets upon the ground. One by one he picked them up and peeled the tissue paper from them and piled them in a neat heap. He wiped his sweaty hands on his trousers, lit a cigarette, and commenced playing another game. He imagined that he was a rich man who lived aboveground in the obscene sunshine and he was strolling through a park of a summer morning, smiling, nodding to his neighbors, sucking an after-breakfast cigar. Many times he crossed the floor of the cave, avoiding the diamonds with his feet, yet subtly gauging his footsteps so that his shoes, wet with sewer slime, would strike the diamonds at some undetermined moment. After twenty minutes of sauntering, his right foot smashed into the heap and diamonds lay scattered in all directions, glinting with a million tiny chuckles of icy laughter. Oh, shucks, he mumbled in mock regret, intrigued by the damage he had wrought. He continued walking, ignoring the brittle fire. He felt that he had a glorious victory locked in his heart.

He stooped and flung the diamonds more evenly over the floor and they showered rich sparks, collaborating with him. He went over the floor and trampled the stones just deeply enough for them to be faintly visible, as though they were set deliberately in the prongs of a thousand rings. A ghostly light bathed the cave. He sat on the chest and frowned. Maybe *any*thing's right, he mumbled. Yes, if the world as men had made it was right, then anything else was right, any act a man took to satisfy himself, murder, theft, torture.

He straightened with a start. What was happening to him? He was drawn to these crazy thoughts, yet they made him feel vaguely guilty. He would stretch out upon the ground, then get up; he would want to crawl again through the holes he had dug, but would restrain himself; he would think of going again up into the streets, but fear would hold him still. He stood in the middle of the cave, surrounded by green walls and a laughing floor, trembling. He was going to do something, but what? Yes, he was afraid of himself, afraid of doing some nameless thing.

To control himself, he turned on the radio. A melancholy piece of music rose. Brooding over the diamonds on the floor was like looking up into a sky full of restless stars; then the illusion turned into its opposite: he was high up in the air looking down at the twinkling lights of a sprawling city. The music ended and a man recited news events. In the same attitude in which he had contemplated the city, so now, as he heard the cultivated tone, he looked down upon land and sea as men fought, as cities were razed, as planes scattered death upon open towns, as long lines of trenches wavered and broke. He heard the names of generals and the names of mountains and the names of countries and the names and numbers of divisions that were in action on different battle fronts. He saw black smoke billowing from the stacks of warships as they neared each other over wastes of water and he heard their huge thunder as red-hot shells screamed across the surface of night seas. He saw hundreds of planes wheeling and droning in the sky and heard the clatter of machine guns as they fought each other and he saw planes falling in plumes of smoke and blaze of fire. He saw steel tanks rumbling across fields of ripe wheat to meet other tanks and there was a loud clang of steel as numberless tanks collided. He saw troops with fixed bayonets charging in waves against other troops who held fixed bayonets and men groaned as steel ripped into their bodies and they went down to die . . . The voice of the radio faded and he was staring at the diamonds on the floor at his feet.

He shut off the radio, fighting an irrational compulsion to act. He walked aimlessly about the cave, touching the walls with his finger tips. Suddenly he stood still. *What was the matter with him?* Yes, he knew . . . It was these walls; these crazy walls were filling him with a wild urge to climb out into the dark sunshine aboveground. Quickly he doused the light to banish the shouting walls, then sat again upon the tool chest. Yes, he was trapped. His muscles were flexed taut and sweat ran down his face. He knew now that he could not stay here and he could not go out. He lit a cigarette with shaking fingers; the match flame revealed the green-papered walls with militant distinctness; the purple on the gun barrel glinted like a threat; the meat cleaver brooded with its eloquent splotches of blood; the mound of silver and copper smoldered angrily; the diamonds winked at him from the floor; and the gold watches ticked and trembled, crowning time the king of consciousness, defining the limits of living . . . The match blaze died and he bolted from where he stood and collided brutally with the nails upon the walls. The spell was broken. He shuddered, feeling that, in spite of his fear, sooner or later he would go up into that dead sunshine and somehow say something to somebody about all this.

He sat again upon the tool chest. Fatigue weighed upon his forehead and eyes. Minutes passed and he relaxed. He dozed, but his imagination was alert. He saw himself rising, wading again in the sweeping water of the sewer; he came to a manhole and climbed out and was amazed to discover that he had hoisted himself into a room filled with armed policemen who were watching him intently. He jumped awake in the dark; he had not moved. He sighed, closed his eyes, and slept again; this time his imagination designed a scheme of protection for him. His dreaming made him feel that he was standing in a room watching over his own nude body lying stiff and cold upon a white table. At the far end of the room he saw a crowd of people huddled in a corner, afraid of his body. Though lying dead upon the table he was standing in some mysterious way at his side, warding off the people, guarding his body, and laughing to himself as he observed the situation. They're scared of me, he thought.

He awakened with a start, leaped to his feet, and stood in the center of the black cave. It was a full minute before he moved again. He hovered between sleeping and waking, unprotected, a prey of wild fears. He could neither see nor hear. One part of him was asleep; his blood coursed slowly and his flesh was numb. On the other hand he was roused to a strange, high pitch of tension. He lifted his fingers to his face, as though about to weep. Gradually his hands lowered and he struck a match, looking about, expecting to see a door through which he could walk to safety; but there was no door, only the green walls and the moving floor. The match flame died and it was dark again.

Five minutes later he was still standing when the thought came to him that he had been asleep. Yes . . . But he was not yet fully awake; he was still queerly blind and deaf. How long had he slept? Where was he? Then suddenly he recalled the green-papered walls of the cave and in the same instant he heard loud singing coming from the church beyond the wall. Yes, they woke me up, he muttered. He hoisted himself and lay atop the bed of pipes and brought his face to the narrow slit. Men and women stood here and there between pews. A song ended and a young black girl tossed back her head and closed her eyes and broke plaintively into another hymn:

Glad, glad, glad, oh, so glad
I got Jesus in my soul . . .

Those few words were all she sang, but what her words did not say, her emotions said as she repeated the lines, varying the mood and tempo, making her tone express meanings which her conscious mind did not know. Another woman melted her voice with the girl's, and then an old man's voice merged with that of the two women. Soon the entire congregation was singing:

Glad, glad, glad, oh, so glad
I got Jesus in my soul . . .

They're wrong, he whispered in the lyric darkness. He felt that their search for a happiness they could never find made them feel that they had committed some dreadful offense which they could not remember or understand. He was now in possession of the feeling that had gripped him when he had first come into the underground. It came to him in a series of questions: Why was this sense of guilt so seemingly innate, so easy to come by, to think, to feel, so verily physical? It seemed that when one felt this guilt one was retracing in one's feelings a faint pattern designed long before; it seemed that one was always trying to remember a gigantic shock that had left a haunting impression upon one's body which one could not forget or shake off, but which had been forgotten by the conscious mind, creating in one's life a state of eternal anxiety.

He had to tear himself away from this; he got down from the pipes. His nerves were so taut that he seemed to feel his brain pushing through his skull. He felt that he had to do something, but he could not figure out what it was. Yet he knew that if he stood here until he made up his mind, he would never move. He crawled through the hole he had made in the brick wall and the exertion afforded him respite from tension. When he entered the basement of the radio store, he stopped in fear, hearing loud voices.

"Come on, boy! Tell us what you did with the radio!"

"Mister, I didn't steal the radio! I swear!"

He heard a dull thumping sound and he imagined a boy being struck violently.

"Please, mister!"

"Did you take it to a pawn shop?"

"No, sir! I didn't steal the radio! I got a radio at home," the boy's voice pleaded hysterically. "Go to my home and look!"

There came to his ears the sound of another blow. It was so funny that he had to clap his hand over his mouth to keep from laughing out loud. They're beating some poor boy, he whispered to himself, shaking his head. He felt a sort of distant pity for the boy and wondered if he ought to bring back the radio and leave it in the basement. No. Perhaps it was a good thing that they were beating the boy; perhaps the beating would bring to the boy's attention, for the first time in his life, the secret of his existence, the guilt that he could never get rid of.

Smiling, he scampered over a coal pile and stood again in the basement of the building where he had stolen the money and jewelry. He lifted himself into the areaway, climbed the rain pipe, and squinted through a two-inch opening of window. The guilty familiarity of what he saw made his muscles tighten. Framed before him in a bright tableau of daylight was the night watchman sitting upon the edge of a chair, stripped to the waist, his head sagging forward, his eyes red and puffy. The watchman's face and shoulders were stippled with red and black welts. Back of the watchman stood the safe, the steel door wide open showing the empty vault. Yes, they think he did it, he mused.

Footsteps sounded in the room and a man in a blue suit passed in front of him, then another, then still another. Policemen, he breathed. Yes, they were trying to make the watchman confess, just as they had once made him confess to a crime he had not done. He stared into the room, trying to recall something. Oh . . . Those were the same policemen who had beaten him, had made him sign that paper when he had been too tired and sick to care. Now, they were doing the same thing to the watchman. His heart pounded as he saw one of the policemen shake a finger into the watchman's face.

"Why don't you admit it's an inside job, Thompson?" the policeman said.

"I've told you all I know," the watchman mumbled through swollen lips.

"But nobody was here but you!" the policeman shouted.

"I was sleeping," the watchman said. "It was wrong, but I was sleeping, all that night!"

"Stop telling us that lie!"

"It's the truth!"

"When did you get the combination?"

"I don't know how to open the safe," the watchman said.

He clung to the rain pipe, tense; he wanted to laugh, but he controlled himself. He felt a great sense of power; yes, he could go back to the cave, rip the money off the walls, pick up the diamonds and rings, and bring them here and write a note, telling them where to look for their foolish toys. No . . . What good would that do? It was not worth the effort. The watchman was guilty; although he was not guilty of the crime of which he had been accused, he was guilty, had always been guilty. The only thing that worried him was that the man who had been really stealing was not being accused. But he consoled himself; they'll catch him sometime during his life.

He saw one of the policemen slap the watchman across the mouth.

"Come clean, you bastard!"

"I've told you all I know," the watchman mumbled like a child.

One of the police went to the rear of the watchman's chair and jerked it from under him; the watchman pitched forward upon his face.

"Get up!" a policeman said.

Trembling, the watchman pulled himself up and sat limply again in the chair.

"Now, are you going to talk?"

"I've told you all I know," the watchman gasped.

"Where did you hide the stuff?"

"I didn't take it!"

"Thompson, your brains are in your feet," one of the policemen said. "We're going to string you up and get them back into your skull."

He watched the policemen clamp handcuffs on the watchman's wrists and ankles; then they lifted the watchman and swung him upside-down and hoisted his feet to the edge of a door. The watchman hung, head down, his eyes bulging. They're crazy, he whispered to himself as he clung to the ridges of the pipe.

"You going to talk?" a policeman shouted into the watchman's ear.

He heard the watchman groan.

"We'll let you hang there till you talk, see?"

He saw the watchman close his eyes.

"Let's take 'im down. He passed out," a policeman said.

He grinned as he watched them take the body down and dump it carelessly upon the floor. The policeman took off the handcuffs.

"Let 'im come to. Let's get a smoke," a policeman said.

The three policemen left the scope of his vision. A door slammed. He had an impulse to yell to the watchman that he could escape through the hole in the basement and live with him in the cave. But he wouldn't understand, he told himself. After a moment he saw the watchman rise and stand, swaying from weakness. He stumbled across the room to a desk, opened a drawer, and took out a gun. He's going to kill himself, he thought, intent, eager, detached, yearning to see the end of the man's actions. As the watchman stared vaguely about he lifted the gun to his temple; he stood like that for some minutes, biting his lips until a line of blood etched its way down a corner of his chin. No, he oughtn't do that, he said to himself in a mood of pity.

"Don't!" he half whispered and half yelled.

The watchman looked wildly about; he had heard him. But it did not help; there was a loud report and the watchman's head jerked violently and he fell like a log and lay prone, the gun clattering over the floor.

The three policemen came running into the room with drawn guns. One of the policemen knelt and rolled the watchman's body over and stared at a ragged, scarlet hole in the temple.

"Our hunch was right," the kneeling policeman said. "He was guilty, all right."

"Well, this ends the case," another policeman said.

"He knew he was licked," the third one said with grim satisfaction.

He eased down the rain pipe, crawled back through the holes he had made, and went back into his cave. A fever burned in his bones. He had to act, yet he was afraid. His eyes stared in the darkness as though propped open by invisible hands, as though they had become lidless. His muscles were rigid and he stood for what seemed to him a thousand years.

When he moved again his actions were informed with precision, his muscular system reinforced from a reservoir of energy. He crawled through the hole of earth, dropped into the gray sewer current, and sloshed ahead. When his right foot went forward at a street intersection, he fell backward and shot down into water. In a spasm of terror his right hand grabbed the concrete ledge of a down-curve and he felt the streaking water tugging violently at his body. The current reached his neck and for a moment he was still. He knew if he moved clumsily he would be sucked under. He held onto the ledge with both hands and slowly pulled himself up. He sighed, standing once more in the sweeping water, thankful that he had missed death.

He waded on through sludge, moving with care, until he came to a web of light sifting down from a manhole cover. He saw steel hooks running up the side of the sewer wall; he caught hold and lifted himself and put his shoulder to the cover and moved it an inch. A crash of sound came to him as he looked into a hot glare of sunshine through which blurred shapes moved. Fear scalded him and he dropped back into the pallid current and stood paralyzed in the shadows. A heavy car rumbled past overhead, jarring the pavement, warning him to stay in his world of dark light, knocking the cover back into place with an imperious clang.

He did not know how much fear he felt, for fear claimed him completely; yet it was not a fear of the police or of people, but a cold dread at the thought of the actions he knew he would perform if he went out into that cruel sunshine. His mind said no; his body said yes; and his mind could not understand his feelings. A low whine broke from him and he was in the act of uncoiling. He climbed upward and heard the faint honking of auto horns. Like a frantic cat clutching a rag, he clung to the steel prongs and heaved his shoulder against the cover and pushed it off halfway. For a split second his eyes were drowned in the terror of yellow light and he was in deeper darkness than he had ever known in the underground.

Partly out of the hole, he blinked, regaining enough sight to make out meaningful forms. An odd thing was happening: No one was rushing forward to challenge him. He had imagined the moment of his emergence as a desperate tussle with men who wanted to cart him off to be killed; instead, life froze about him as the traffic stopped. He pushed the cover aside, stood, swaying in a world so fragile that he expected it to collapse and drop him into some deep void. But nobody seemed to pay him heed. The cars were now swerving to shun him and the gaping hole.

"Why in hell don't you put up a red light, dummy?" a raucous voice yelled.

He understood; they thought that he was a sewer workman. He walked toward the sidewalk, weaving unsteadily through the moving traffic.

"Look where you're going, nigger!"

"That's right! Stay there and get killed!"

"You blind, you bastard?"

"Go home and sleep your drunk off!"

A policeman stood at the curb, looking in the opposite direction. When he passed the policeman, he feared that he would be grabbed, but nothing happened. Where was he? Was this real? He wanted to look about to get his bearings, but felt that something awful would happen to him if he did. He wandered into a spacious doorway of a store that sold men's clothing and saw his reflection in a long mirror: his cheekbones protruded from a hairy black face; his greasy cap was perched askew upon his head and his eyes were red and glassy. His shirt and trousers were caked with mud and hung loosely. His hands were gummed with a black stickiness. He threw back his head and laughed so loudly that passers-by stopped and stared.

He ambled on down the sidewalk, not having the merest notion of where he was going. Yet, sleeping within him, was the drive to go somewhere and say something to somebody. Half an hour later his ears caught the sound of spirited singing.

The Lamb, the Lamb, the Lamb
I hear thy voice a-calling
The Lamb, the Lamb, the Lamb
I feel thy grace a-falling

A church! He exclaimed. He broke into a run and came to brick steps leading downward to a subbasement. This is it! The church into which he had peered. Yes, he was going in and tell them. What? He did not know; but once face to face with them, he would think of what to say. Must be Sunday, he mused. He ran down the steps and jerked the door open; the church was crowded and a deluge of song swept over him.

The Lamb, the Lamb, the Lamb
Tell me again your story
The Lamb, the Lamb, the Lamb
Flood my soul with your glory

He stared at the singing faces with a trembling smile.

"Say!" he shouted.

Many turned to look at him, but the song rolled on. His arm was jerked violently.

"I'm sorry, Brother, but you can't do that in here," a man said.

"But, mister!"

"You can't act rowdy in God's house," the man said.

"He's filthy," another man said.

"But I want to tell 'em," he said loudly.

"He stinks," someone muttered.

The song had stopped, but at once another one began.

Oh, wondrous sight upon the cross
Vision sweet and divine
Oh, wondrous sight upon the cross
Full of such love sublime

He attempted to twist away, but other hands grabbed him and rushed him into the doorway.

"Let me alone!" he screamed, struggling.

"Get out!"

"He's drunk," somebody said. "He ought to be ashamed!"

"He acts crazy!"

He felt that he was failing and he grew frantic.

"But, mister, let me tell—"

"Get away from this door, or I'll call the police!"

He stared, his trembling smile fading in a sense of wonderment.

"The police," he repeated vacantly.

"Now, get!"

He was pushed toward the brick steps and the door banged shut. The waves of song came.

Oh, wondrous sight, wondrous sight
Lift my heavy heart above
Oh, wondrous sight, wondrous sight
Fill my weary soul with love

He was smiling again now. Yes, the police ... That was it! Why had he not thought of it before? The idea had been deep down in him, and only now did it assume supreme importance. He looked up and saw a street sign: COURT STREET—HARTSDALE AVENUE. He turned and walked northward, his mind filled with the image of the police station. Yes, that was where they had beaten him, accused him, and had made him sign a confession of his guilt. He would go there and clear up everything, make a statement. What statement? He did not know. He was the statement, and since it was all so clear to him, surely he would be able to make it clear to others.

He came to the corner of Hartsdale Avenue and turned westward. Yeah, there's the station ... A policeman came down the steps and walked past him without a glance. He mounted the stone steps and went through the door, paused; he was in a hallway where several policemen were standing, talking, smoking. One turned to him.

"What do you want, boy?"

He looked at the policeman and laughed.

"What in hell are you laughing about?" the policeman asked.

He stopped laughing and stared. His whole being was full of what he wanted to say to them, but he could not say it.

"Are you looking for the Desk Sergeant?"

"Yes, sir," he said quickly; then: "Oh, no, sir."

"Well, make up your mind, now."

Four policemen grouped themselves around him.

"I'm looking for the men," he said.

"What men?"

Peculiarly, at that moment he could not remember the names of the policemen; he recalled their beating him, the confession he had signed, and how he had run away from them. He saw the cave next to the church, the money on the walls, the guns, the rings, the cleaver, the watches, and the diamonds on the floor.

"They brought me here," he began.

"When?"

His mind flew back over the blur of the time lived in the underground blackness. He had no idea of how much time had elapsed, but the intensity of what had happened to him told him that it could not have transpired in a short space of time, yet his mind told him that time must have been brief.

"It was a long time ago." He spoke like a child relating a dimly remembered dream. "It was a long time," he repeated, following the promptings of his emotions. "They beat me . . . I was scared . . . I ran away."

A policeman raised a finger to his temple and made a derisive circle.

"Nuts," the policeman said.

"Do you know what place this is, boy?"

"Yes, sir. The police station," he answered sturdily, almost proudly.

"Well, who do you want to see?"

"The men," he said again, feeling that surely they knew the men. "You know the men," he said in a hurt tone.

"What's your name?"

He opened his lips to answer and no words came. He had forgotten. But what did it matter if he had? It was not important.

"Where do you live?"

Where did he live? It had been so long ago since he had lived up here in this strange world that he felt it was foolish even to try to remember. Then for a moment the old mood that had dominated him in the underground surged back. He leaned forward and spoke eagerly.

"They said I killed the woman."

"What woman?" a policeman asked.

"And I signed a paper that said I was guilty," he went on, ignoring their questions. "Then I ran off . . ."

"Did you run off from an institution?"

"No, sir," he said, blinking and shaking his head. "I came from under the ground. I pushed off the manhole cover and climbed out . . ."

"All right, now," a policeman said, placing an arm about his shoulder. "We'll send you to the psycho and you'll be taken care of."

"Maybe he's a Fifth Columnist!" a policeman shouted.

There was laughter and, despite his anxiety, he joined in. But the laughter lasted so long that it irked him.

"I got to find those men," he protested mildly.

"Say, boy, what have you been drinking?"

"Water," he said. "I got some water in a basement."

"Were the men you ran away from dressed in white, boy?"

"No, sir," he said brightly. "They were men like you."

An elderly policeman caught hold of his arm.

"Try and think hard. Where did they pick you up?"

He knitted his brows in an effort to remember, but he was blank inside. The policeman stood before him demanding logical answers and he could no longer think with his mind; he thought with his feelings and no words came.

"I was guilty," he said. "Oh, no sir. I wasn't then, I mean, mister!"

"Aw, talk sense. Now, where did they pick you up?"

He felt challenged and his mind began reconstructing events in reverse; his feelings ranged back over the long hours and he saw the cave, the sewer, the bloody room where it was said that a woman had been killed.

"Oh, yes, sir," he said, smiling. "I was coming from Mrs. Wooten's."

"Who is she?"

"I work for her."

"Where does she live?"

"Next door to Mrs. Peabody, the woman who was killed."

The policemen were very quiet now, looking at him intently.

"What do you know about Mrs. Peabody's death, boy?"

"Nothing, sir. But they said I killed her. But it doesn't make any difference. I'm guilty!"

"What are you talking about, boy?"

His smile faded and he was possessed with memories of the underground; he saw the cave next to the church and his lips moved to speak. But how could he say it? The distance between what he felt and what these men meant was vast. Something told him, as he stood there looking into their faces, that he would never be able to tell them, that they would never believe him even if he told them.

"All the people I saw was guilty," he began slowly.

"Aw, nuts," a policeman muttered.

"Say," another policeman said, "that Peabody woman was killed over on Winewood. That's Number Ten's beat."

"Where's Number Ten?" a policeman asked.

"Upstairs in the swing room," someone answered.

"Take this boy up, Sam," a policeman ordered.

"O.K. Come along, boy."

An elderly policeman caught hold of his arm and led him up a flight of wooden stairs, down a long hall, and to a door.

"Squad Ten!" the policeman called through the door.

"What?" a gruff voice answered.

"Someone to see you!"

"About what?"

The old policeman pushed the door in and then shoved him into the room.

He stared, his lips open, his heart barely beating. Before him were the three policemen who had picked him up and had beaten him to extract the confession. They were seated about a small table, playing cards. The air was blue with smoke and sunshine poured through a high window, lighting up fantastic smoke shapes. He saw one of the policemen look up; the policeman's face was tired and a cigarette dropped limply from one corner of his mouth and both of his fat, puffy eyes were squinting and his hands gripped his cards.

"Lawson!" the man exclaimed.

The moment the man's name sounded he remembered the names of all of them: Lawson, Murphy, and Johnson. How simple it was. He waited, smiling, wondering how they would react when they knew that he had come back.

"Looking for me?" the man who had been called Lawson mumbled, sorting his cards. "For what?"

So far only Murphy, the red-headed one, had recognized him.

"Don't you-all remember me?" he blurted, running to the table.

All three of the policemen were looking at him now. Lawson, who seemed the leader, jumped to his feet.

"Where in hell have you been?"

"Do you know 'im, Lawson?" the old policeman asked.

"Huh?" Lawson frowned. "Oh, yes. I'll handle 'im." The old policeman left the room and Lawson crossed to the door and turned the key in the lock. "Come here, boy," he ordered in a cold tone.

He did not move; he looked from face to face. Yes, he would tell them about his cave.

"He looks batty to me," Johnson said, the one who had not spoken before.

"Why in hell did you come back here?" Lawson said.

"I—I just didn't want to run away no more," he said. "I'm all right, now." He paused; the men's attitude puzzled him.

"You've been hiding, huh?" Lawson asked in a tone that denoted that he had not heard his previous words. "You told us you were sick, and when we left you in the room, you jumped out of the window and ran away."

Panic filled him. Yes, they were indifferent to what he would say! They were waiting for him to speak and they would laugh at him. He had to rescue himself from this bog; he had to force the reality of himself upon them.

"Mister, I took a sackful of money and pasted it on the walls . . ." he began.

"I'll be damned," Lawson said.

"Listen," said Murphy, "let me tell you something for your own good. We don't want you, see? You're free, free as air. Now go home and forget it. It was all a mistake. We caught the guy who did the Peabody job. He wasn't colored at all. He was an Eyetalian."

"Shut up!" Lawson yelled. "Have you no sense!"

"But I want to tell 'im," Murphy said.

"We can't let this crazy fool go," Lawson exploded. "He acts nuts, but this may be a stunt . . ."

"I was down in the basement," he began in a childlike tone, as though repeating a lesson learned by heart; "and I went into a movie . . ." His voice failed. He was getting ahead of his story. First, he ought to tell them about the singing in the church, but what words could he use? He looked at them appealingly. "I went into a shop and took a sackful of money and diamonds and watches and rings . . . I didn't steal 'em, I'll give 'em all back. I just took 'em to play with . . ." He paused, stunned by their disbelieving eyes.

Lawson lit a cigarette and looked at him coldly.

"What did you do with the money?" he asked in a quiet, waiting voice.

"I pasted the hundred-dollar bills on the walls."

"What walls?" Lawson asked.

"The walls of the dirt room," he said, smiling, "the room next to the church. I hung up the rings and the watches and I stamped the diamonds into the dirt . . ." He saw that they were not understanding what he was saying. He grew frantic to make them believe, his voice tumbled on eagerly. "I saw a dead baby and a dead man . . ."

"Aw, you're nuts," Lawson snarled, shoving him into a chair.

"But mister . . ."

"Johnson, where's the paper he signed?" Lawson asked.

"What paper?"

"The confession, fool!"

Johnson pulled out his billfold and extracted a crumpled piece of paper. "Yes, sir, mister," he said, stretching forth his hand. "That's the paper I signed . . ."

Lawson slapped him and he would have toppled had his chair not struck a wall behind him. Lawson scratched a match and held the paper over the flame; the confession burned down to Lawson's fingertips.

He stared, thunderstruck; the sun of the underground was fleeting and the terrible darkness of the day stood before him. They did not believe him, but he *had* to make them believe him!

"But mister . . ."

"It's going to be all right, boy," Lawson said with a quiet, soothing laugh.

"I've burned your confession, see? You didn't sign anything." Lawson came close to him with the black ashes cupped in his palm. "You don't remember a thing about this, do you?"

"Don't you-all be scared of me," he pleaded, sensing their uneasiness. "I'll sign another paper, if you want me to. I'll show you the cave."

"What's your game, boy?" Lawson asked suddenly.

"What are you trying to find out?" Johnson asked.

"Who sent you here?" Murphy demanded.

"Nobody sent me, mister," he said. "I just want to show you the room . . ."

"Aw, he's plumb bats," Murphy said. "Let's ship 'im to the psycho."

"No," Lawson said. "He's playing a game and I wish to God I knew what it was."

There flashed through his mind a definite way to make them believe him; he rose from the chair with nervous excitement.

"Mister, I saw the night watchman blow his brains out because you accused him of stealing," he told them. "But he didn't steal the money and diamonds. I took 'em."

Tigerishly Lawson grabbed his collar and lifted him bodily.

"*Who told you about that?*"

"Don't get excited, Lawson," Johnson said. "He read about it in the papers."

Lawson flung him away.

"He couldn't have," Lawson said, pulling papers from his pocket. "I haven't turned in the reports yet."

"Then how *did* he find out?" Murphy asked.

"Let's get out of here," Lawson said with quick resolution. "Listen, boy, we're going to take you to a nice, quiet place, see?

"Yes, sir," he said. "And I'll show you the underground."

"Goddamn," Lawson muttered, fastening the gun at his hip. He narrowed his eyes at Johnson and Murphy. "Listen," he spoke just above a whisper, "say nothing about this, you hear?"

"O.K.," Johnson said.

"Sure," Murphy said.

Lawson unlocked the door and Johnson and Murphy led him down the stairs. The hallway was crowded with policemen.

"What have you got there, Lawson?"

"What did he do, Lawson?"

"He's psycho, ain't he, Lawson?"

Lawson did not answer; Johnson and Murphy led him to the car parked at the curb, pushed him into the back seat. Lawson got behind the steering wheel and the car rolled forward.

"What's up, Lawson?" Murphy asked.

"Listen," Lawson began slowly, "we tell the papers that he spilled about the Peabody job, then he escapes. The Wop is caught and we tell the papers that we steered them wrong to trap the real guy, see? Now this dope shows up and acts nuts. If we let him go, he'll squeal that we framed him, see?"

"I'm all right, mister," he said, feeling Murphy's and Johnson's arms locked rigidly into his. "I'm guilty . . . I'll show you everything in the underground. I laughed and laughed . . ."

"Shut that fool up!" Lawson ordered.

Johnson tapped him across the head with a blackjack and he fell back against the seat cushion, dazed.

"Yes, sir," he mumbled. "I'm all right."

The car sped along Hartsdale Avenue, then swung onto Pine Street and rolled to State Street, then turned south. It slowed to a stop, turned in the middle of a block, and headed north again.

"You're going around in circles, Lawson," Murphy said.

Lawson did not answer; he was hunched over the steering wheel. Finally he pulled the car to a stop at a curb.

"Say, boy, tell us the truth," Lawson asked quietly. "Where did you hide?"

"I didn't hide, mister."

The three policemen were staring at him now; he felt that for the first time they were willing to understand him.

"Then what happened?"

"Mister, when I looked through all of those holes and saw how people were living, I loved 'em . . ."

"Cut out that crazy talk!" Lawson snapped. "Who sent you back here?"

"Nobody, mister."

"Maybe he's talking straight," Johnson ventured.

"All right," Lawson said. "Nobody hid you. Now, tell us *where* you hid."

"I went underground . . ."

"What goddamn underground do you keep talking about?"

"I just went . . ." He paused and looked into the street, then pointed to a manhole cover. "I went down in there and stayed."

"In the *sewer?*"

"Yes, sir."

The policemen burst into a sudden laugh and ended quickly. Lawson swung the car around and drove to Woodside Avenue; he brought the car to a stop in front of a tall apartment building.

"What're we going to do, Lawson?" Murphy asked.

"I'm taking him up to my place," Lawson said. "We've got to wait until night. There's nothing we can do now."

They took him out of the car and led him into a vestibule.

"Take the steps," Lawson muttered.

They led him up four flights of stairs and into the living room of a small apartment. Johnson and Murphy let go of his arms and he stood uncertainly in the middle of the room.

"Now, listen, boy," Lawson began, "forget those wild lies you've been telling us. Where did you hide?"

"I just went underground, like I told you."

The room rocked with laughter. Lawson went to a cabinet and got a bottle of whisky; he placed glasses for Johnson and Murphy. The three of them drank.

He felt that he could not explain himself to them. He tried to muster all the sprawling images that floated in him; the images stood out sharply in his mind, but he could not make them have the meaning for others that they had for him. He felt so helpless that he began to cry.

"He's nuts, all right," Johnson said. "All nuts cry like that."

Murphy crossed the room and slapped him.

"Stop that raving!"

A sense of excitement flooded him; he ran to Murphy and grabbed his arm.

"Let me show you the cave," he said. "Come on, and you'll see!"

Before he knew it a sharp blow had clipped him on the chin; darkness covered his eyes. He dimly felt himself being lifted and laid out on the sofa. He heard low voices and struggled to rise, but hard hands held him down. His brain was clearing now. He pulled to a sitting posture and stared with glazed eyes. It had grown dark. How long had he been out?

"Say, boy," Lawson said soothingly, "will you show us the underground?"

His eyes shone and his heart swelled with gratitude. Lawson believed him! He rose, glad; he grabbed Lawson's arm, making the policeman spill whisky from the glass to his shirt.

"Take it easy, goddammit," Lawson said.

"Yes, sir."

"O.K. We'll take you down. But you'd better be telling us the truth, you hear?"

He clapped his hands in wild joy.

"I'll show you everything!"

He had triumphed at last! He would now do what he had felt was compelling him all along. At last he would be free of his burden.

"Take 'im down," Lawson ordered.

They led him down to the vestibule; when he reached the sidewalk he saw that it was night and a fine rain was falling.

"It's just like when I went down," he told them.

"What?" Lawson asked.

"The rain," he said, sweeping his arm in a wide arc. "It was raining when I went down. The rain made the water rise and lift the cover off."

"Cut it out," Lawson snapped.

They did not believe him now, but they would. A mood of high selflessness throbbed in him. He could barely contain his rising spirits. They would see what he had seen; they would feel what he had felt. He would lead them through all the holes he had dug and . . . He wanted to make a hymn, prance about in physical ecstasy, throw his arm about the policemen in fellowship.

"Get into the car," Lawson ordered.

He climbed in and Johnson and Murphy sat at either side of him; Lawson slid behind the steering wheel and started the motor.

"Now, tell us where to go," Lawson said.

"It's right around the corner from where the lady was killed," he said.

The car rolled slowly and he closed his eyes, remembering the song he had heard in the church, the song that had wrought him to such a high pitch of terror and pity. He sang softly, lolling his head:

Glad, glad, glad, oh, so glad
I got Jesus in my soul . . .

"Mister," he said, stopping his song, "you ought to see how funny the rings look on the wall." He giggled. "I fired a pistol, too. Just once, to see how it felt."

"What do you suppose he's suffering from?" Johnson asked.

"Delusions of grandeur, maybe," Murphy said.

"Maybe it's because he lives in a white man's world," Lawson said.

"Say, boy, what did you eat down there?" Murphy asked, prodding Johnson anticipatorily with his elbow.

"Pears, oranges, bananas, and pork chops," he said.

The car filled with laughter.

"You didn't eat any watermelon?" Lawson asked, smiling.

"No, sir," he answered calmly. "I didn't see any."

The three policemen roared harder and louder.

"Boy, you're sure some case," Murphy said, shaking his head in wonder. The car pulled to a curb.

"All right, boy," Lawson said. "Tell us where to go."

He peered through the rain and saw where he had gone down. The streets, save for a few dim lamps glowing softly through the rain, were dark and empty.

"Right there, mister," he said, pointing.

"Come on; let's take a look," Lawson said.

"Well, suppose he did hide down there," Johnson said, "what is that supposed to prove?"

"I don't believe he hid down there," Murphy said.

"It won't hurt to look," Lawson said. "Leave things to me."

Lawson got out of the car and looked up and down the street.

He was eager to show them the cave now. If he could show them what he had seen, then they would feel what he had felt and they in turn would show it to others and those others would feel as they had felt, and soon everybody would be governed by the same impulse of pity.

"Take 'im out," Lawson ordered.

Johnson and Murphy opened the door and pushed him out; he stood trembling in the rain, smiling. Again Lawson looked up and down the street; no one was in sight. The rain came down hard, slanting like black wires across the wind-swept air.

"All right," Lawson said. "Show us."

He walked to the center of the street, stopped and inserted a finger in one of the tiny holes of the cover and tugged, but he was too weak to budge it.

"Did you really go down in there, boy?" Lawson asked; there was a doubt in his voice.

"Yes, sir. Just a minute. I'll show you."

"Help 'im get that damn thing off," Lawson said.

Johnson stepped forward and lifted the cover; it clanged against the wet pavement. The hole gaped round and black.

"I went down in there," he announced with pride.

Lawson gazed at him for a long time without speaking, then he reached his right hand to his holster and drew his gun.

"Mister, I got a gun just like that down there," he said, laughing and looking into Lawson's face. "I fired it once then hung it on the wall. I'll show you."

"Show us how you went down," Lawson said quietly.

"I'll go down first, mister, and then you-all can come after me, hear?" he spoke like a little boy playing a game.

"Sure, sure," Lawson said soothingly. "Go ahead. We'll come."

He looked brightly at the policemen; he was bursting with happiness. He bent down and placed his hands on the rim of the hole and sat on the edge, his feet dangling into watery darkness. He heard the familiar drone of the gray current. He lowered his body and hung for a moment by his fingers, then he went downward on the steel prongs, hand over hand, until he reached the last rung. He dropped and his feet hit the water and he felt the stiff current trying to suck him away. He balanced himself quickly and looked back upward at the policemen.

"Come on, you-all!" he yelled, casting his voice above the rustling at his feet.

The vague forms that towered above him in the rain did not move. He laughed, feeling that they doubted him. But, once they saw the things he had done, they would never doubt again.

"Come on! The cave isn't far!" he yelled. "But be careful when your feet hit the water, because the current's pretty rough down here!"

Lawson still held the gun. Murphy and Johnson looked at Lawson quizzically.

"What are we going to do, Lawson?" Murphy asked.

"Come on, you-all!" he begged in a shout.

He saw Lawson raise the gun and point it directly at him. Lawson's face twitched, as though he were hesitating.

Then there was a thunderous report and a streak of fire ripped through his chest. He was hurled into the water, flat on his back. He looked in amazement at the blurred white faces looming above him. They shot me, he said to himself. The water flowed past him, blossoming in foam about his arms, his legs, and his head. His jaw sagged and his mouth gaped soundless. A vast pain gripped his head and gradually squeezed out consciousness. As from a great distance he heard hollow voices.

"What did you shoot him for, Lawson?"

"I had to."

"Why?"

"You've got to shoot his kind. They'd wreck things."

As though in a deep dream, he heard a metallic clank; they had replaced the manhole cover, shutting out forever the sound of wind and rain. From overhead came the muffled roar of a powerful motor and the swish of a speeding car. He felt the strong tide pushing him slowly into the middle of the sewer, turning him about. For a split second there hovered before his eyes the glittering cave, the shouting walls, and the laughing floor . . . Then his mouth was full of thick, bitter water. The current spun him around. He sighed and closed his eyes, a whirling object rushing alone in the darkness, veering, tossing, lost in the heart of the earth.

EUDORA WELTY

b. 1909

Eudora Welty is one of the major figures in the southern literary renaissance of the twenties and thirties. This surge of productivity among southern writers was not a cohesive movement: most of the writers involved worked alone and were influenced more from outside than from within the South; and Faulkner, the greatest of them all, was notably reticent in literary society, much preferring the company of his fellow farmers in Lafayette County. But individually, southern writers, with their varied understandings of the South, have dominated the major fiction of the United States in the twentieth century, as New England writers dominated the nineteenth century. In addition to Faulkner and Welty, their number includes Katherine Anne Porter, Richard Wright, Ralph Ellison, Carson McCullers, Flannery O'Connor, Robert Penn Warren, Lillian Hellman, and the poets John Crowe Ransom and Allen Tate.

Welty was born the daughter of a bank president in the state capital of Jackson, Mississippi, 150 miles south of Faulkner country. After studying at Mississippi College for Women for two years, she spent the last two years of college at the University of Wisconsin, taking a B.A. there in 1929. For the next three years (years that contained the Stock Market Crash and the start of the Depression) she lived in New York and studied advertising at Columbia. She returned to Jackson in 1932 determined to be a writer.

In a biographical account of Jane Austen, Welty raises a question that has obvious relevance to her own career. "Perennial objectors," she remarks, "like to ask how Jane Austen, a spinster who lived all her life in her father's rectory and in later family houses in Bath, Southampton, and Chawton, whose notion of going elsewhere was an excursion to Lyme Regis, could have had any way of knowing very much about life." Welty's answer to these perennial objectors is also a validation of a latter-day writer's nearly lifetime residence in Jackson, Mississippi: "Jane Austen was *born* knowing a great deal—for one thing, that the interesting situations of life can, and notably do, take place at home."

Welty struck her distinctive note of compassion and humor in the first stories she published in the *Southern Review* beginning in 1936. She is deeply engaged in the simple struggle for survival of the poor in Mississippi, and at the same time—most notably in "Why I Live at the P.O."—she is a master of a comedy that proceeds out of affection rather than contempt. She has earned critical acclaim for her many novels and collections of short stories, and in 1973 received the Pulitzer Prize for her novel *The Optimist's Daughter.*

Welty characteristically writes about the lonely individual who has sacrificed too many human dimensions to get along. The travelling salesman is sensitive: to the weather, to the relationships with the dirt farmer and his wife. All his reactions come irrationally, suddenly, and (because the salesman is not in his usual, conventional state of mind) surprisingly. He is a man who has lost his standard way of coping, and what is revealed to him is the poverty of his usual reactions. He finds himself falling back on a salesman's patter to shut out the reality that he has denied, and faced with the reality he has refused all his life his heart can no longer stand it.

Welty is a very good literary critic, and a fine collection of hers in this genre is *The Eye of the Story: Selected Essays and Reviews* (Random House, 1978).

Why I Live at the P.O.

I was getting along fine with Mama, Papa-Daddy and Uncle Rondo until my sister Stella-Rondo just separated from her husband and came back home again. Mr. Whitaker! Of course I went with Mr. Whitaker first, when he first appeared here in China Grove, taking "Pose Yourself" photos, and Stella-Rondo broke us up. Told him I was one-sided. Bigger on one side than the other, which is a deliberate, calculated falsehood: I'm the same. Stella-Rondo is exactly twelve months to the day younger than I am and for that reason she's spoiled.

She's always had anything in the world she wanted and then she'd throw it away. Papa-Daddy gave her this gorgeous Add-a-Pearl necklace when she was eight years old and she threw it away playing baseball when she was nine, with only two pearls.

So as soon as she got married and moved away from home the first thing she did was separate! From Mr. Whitaker! This photographer with the popeyes she said she trusted. Came home from one of those towns up in Illinois and to our complete surprise brought this child of two.

Mama said she like to made her drop dead for a second. "Here you had this marvelous blonde child and never so much as wrote your mother a word about it," says Mama. "I'm thoroughly ashamed of you." But of course she wasn't.

Stella-Rondo just calmly takes off this *hat,* I wish you could see it. She says, "Why, Mama, Shirley-T.'s adopted, I can prove it."

"How?" says Mama, but all I says was, "H'm!" There I was over the hot stove, trying to stretch two chickens over five people and a completely unexpected child into the bargain, without one moment's notice.

"What do you mean—'H'm!'?" says Stella-Rondo, and Mama says, "I heard that, Sister."

I said that oh, I didn't mean a thing, only that whoever Shirley-T. was, she was the spit-image of Papa-Daddy if he'd cut off his beard, which of course he'd never do in the world. Papa-Daddy's Mama's papa and sulks.

Stella-Rondo got furious! She said, "Sister, I don't need to tell you you got a lot of nerve and always did have and I'll thank you to make no future reference to my adopted child whatsoever."

"Very well," I said. "Very well, very well. Of course I noticed at once she looks like Mr. Whitaker's side too. That frown. She looks like a cross between Mr. Whitaker and Papa-Daddy."

"Well, all I can say is she isn't."

"She looks exactly like Shirley Temple to me," says Mama, but Shirley-T. just ran away from her.

So the first thing Stella-Rondo did at the table was turn Papa-Daddy against me.

"Papa-Daddy," she says. He was trying to cut up his meat. "Papa-Daddy!" I was taken completely by surprise. Papa-Daddy is about a million years old and's got this long-long beard. "Papa-Daddy, Sister says she fails to understand why you don't cut off your beard."

So Papa-Daddy l-a-y-s down his knife and fork! He's real rich. Mama says he is, he says he isn't. So he says, "Have I heard correctly? You don't understand why I don't cut off my beard?"

"Why," I says, "Papa-Daddy, of course I understand, I did not say any such of a thing, the idea!"

He says, "Hussy!"

I says, "Papa-Daddy, you know I wouldn't any more want you to cut off your beard than the man in the moon. It was the farthest thing from my mind! Stella-Rondo sat there and made that up while she was eating breast of chicken."

But he says, "So the postmistress fails to understand why I don't cut off my beard. Which job I got you through my influence with the government. 'Bird's nest'—is that what you call it?"

Not that it isn't the next to smallest P.O. in the entire state of Mississippi.

I says, "Oh, Papa-Daddy," I says, "I didn't say any such of a thing, I never dreamed it was a bird's nest, I have always been grateful though this is the next to smallest P.O. in the state of Mississippi, and I do not enjoy being referred to as a hussy by my own grandfather."

But Stella-Rondo says, "Yes, you did say it too. Anybody in the world could of heard you, that had ears."

"Stop right there," says Mama, looking at *me.*

So I pulled my napkin straight back through the napkin ring and left the table.

As soon as I was out of the room Mama says, "Call her back, or she'll starve to death," but Papa-Daddy says, "This is the beard I started growing on the Coast when I was fifteen years old." He would of gone on till nightfall if Shirley-T. hadn't lost the Milky Way she ate in Cairo.

So Papa-Daddy says, "I am going out and lie in the hammock, and you can all sit here and remember my words: I'll never cut off my beard as long as I live, even one inch, and I don't appreciate it in you at all." Passed right by me in the hall and went straight out and got in the hammock.

It would be a holiday. It wasn't five minutes before Uncle Rondo suddenly appeared in the hall in one of Stella-Rondo's flesh-colored kimonos, all cut on the bias, like something Mr. Whitaker probably thought was gorgeous.

"Uncle Rondo!" I says. "I didn't know who that was! Where are you going?"

"Sister," he says, "get out of my way, I'm poisoned."

"If you're poisoned stay away from Papa-Daddy," I says. "Keep out of the hammock. Papa-Daddy will certainly beat you on the head if you come within forty miles of him. He thinks I deliberately said he ought to cut off his beard after he got me the P.O., and I've told him and told him and told him, and he acts like he just don't hear me. Papa-Daddy must of gone stone deaf."

"He picked a fine day to do it then," says Uncle Rondo, and before you could say "Jack Robinson" flew out in the yard.

What he'd really done, he'd drunk another bottle of that prescription. He does it every single Fourth of July as sure as shooting, and it's horribly expensive. Then he falls over in the hammock and snores. So he insisted on zigzagging right on out to the hammock, looking like a half-wit.

Papa-Daddy woke up with this horrible yell and right there without moving an inch he tried to turn Uncle Rondo against me. I heard every word he said. Oh, he told Uncle Rondo I didn't learn to read till I was eight years old and he didn't see how in the world I ever got the mail put up at the P.O., much less read it all, and he said if Uncle Rondo could only fathom the lengths he had gone to to get me that job! And he said on the other hand he thought Stella-Rondo had a brilliant mind and deserved credit for getting out of town. All the time he was just lying there swinging as pretty as you please and looping out his beard, and poor Uncle Rondo was *pleading* with him to slow down the hammock, it was making him as dizzy as a witch to watch it. But that's what Papa-Daddy likes about a hammock. So Uncle Rondo was too dizzy to get turned against me for the time being. He's Mama's only brother and is a good case of a one-track mind. Ask anybody. A certified pharmacist.

Just then I heard Stella-Rondo raising the upstairs window. While she was married she got this peculiar idea that it's cooler with the windows shut and locked. So she has to raise the window before she can make a soul hear her outdoors.

So she raises the window and says, "*Oh!*" You would have thought she was mortally wounded.

Uncle Rondo and Papa-Daddy didn't even look up, but kept right on with what they were doing. I had to laugh.

I flew up the stairs and threw the door open! I says, "What in the world's the matter, Stella-Rondo? You mortally wounded?"

"No," she says, "I am not mortally wounded but I wish you would do me the favor of looking out that window there and telling me what you see."

So I shade my eyes and look out the window.

"I see the front yard," I says.

"Don't you see any human beings?" she says.

"I see Uncle Rondo trying to run Papa-Daddy out of the hammock," I says. "Nothing more. Naturally, it's so suffocating-hot in the house, with all the windows shut and locked, everybody who cares to stay in their right mind will have to go out and get in the hammock before the Fourth of July is over."

"Don't you notice anything different about Uncle Rondo?" asks Stella-Rondo.

"Why, no, except he's got on some terrible-looking flesh-colored contraption I wouldn't be found dead in, is all I can see," I says.

"Never mind, you won't be found dead in it, because it happens to be part of my trousseau, and Mr. Whitaker took several dozen photographs of me in it," says Stella-Rondo. "What on earth could Uncle Rondo *mean* by wearing part of my trousseau out in the broad open daylight without saying so much as 'Kiss my foot,' *knowing* I only got home this morning after my separation and hung my negligee up on the bathroom door, just as nervous as I could be?"

"I'm sure I don't know, and what do you expect me to do about it?" I says. "Jump out the window?"

"No, I expect nothing of the kind. I simply declare that Uncle Rondo looks like a fool in it, that's all," she says. "It makes me sick to my stomach."

"Well, he looks as good as he can," I says. "As good as anybody in reason could." I stood up for Uncle Rondo, please remember. And I said to Stella-Rondo, "I think I would do well not to criticize so freely if I were you and came home with a two-year-old child I had never said a word about, and no explanation whatever about my separation."

"I asked you the instant I entered this house not to refer one more time to my adopted child, and you gave me your word of honor you would not," was all Stella-Rondo would say, and started pulling out every one of her eyebrows with some cheap Kress tweezers.

So I merely slammed the door behind me and went down and made some green-tomato pickle. Somebody had to do it. Of course Mama had turned both the niggers loose; she always said no earthly power could hold one anyway on the Fourth of July, so she wouldn't even try. It turned out that Jaypan fell in the lake and came within a very narrow limit of drowning.

So Mama trots in. Lifts up the lid and says, "H'm! Not very good for your Uncle Rondo in his precarious condition, I must say. Or poor little adopted Shirley-T. Shame on you!"

That made me tired. I says, "Well, Stella-Rondo had better thank her lucky stars it was her instead of me came trotting in with that very peculiar-looking child. Now if it had been me that trotted in from Illinois and brought a peculiar-looking child of two, I shudder to think of the reception I'd of got, much less controlled the diet of an entire family."

"But you must remember, Sister, that you were never married to Mr. Whitaker in the first place and didn't go up to Illinois to live," says Mama, shaking a spoon in my face. "If you had I would of been just as overjoyed to see you and your little adopted girl as I was to see Stella-Rondo, when you wound up with your separation and came on back home."

"You would not," I says.

"Don't contradict me, I would," says Mama.

But I said she couldn't convince me though she talked till she was blue in the face. Then I said, "Besides, you know as well as I do that that child is not adopted."

"She most certainly is adopted," says Mama, stiff as a poker.

I says, "Why, Mama, Stella-Rondo had her just as sure as anything in this world, and just too stuck up to admit it."

"Why, Sister," said Mama. "Here I thought we were going to have a pleasant Fourth of July, and you start right out not believing a word your own baby sister tells you!"

"Just like Cousin Annie Flo. Went to her grave denying the facts of life," I remind Mama.

"I told you if you ever mentioned Annie Flo's name I'd slap your face," says Mama, and slaps my face.

"All right, you wait and see," I says.

"I," says Mama, "*I* prefer to take my children's word for anything when it's humanly possible." You ought to see Mama, she weighs two hundred pounds and has real tiny feet.

Just then something perfectly horrible occurred to me.

"Mama," I says, "can that child talk?" I simply had to whisper! "Mama, I wonder if that child can be—you know—in any way? Do you realize," I says, "that she hasn't spoken one single, solitary word to a human being up to the minute? This is the way she looks," I says, and I looked like this.

Well, Mama and I just stood there and stared at each other. It was horrible!

"I remember well that Joe Whitaker frequently drank like a fish," says Mama. "I believed to my soul he drank *chemicals.*" And without another word she marches to the foot of the stairs and calls Stella-Rondo.

"Stella-Rondo? O-o-o-o-o! Stella-Rondo!"

"What?" says Stella-Rondo from upstairs. Not even the grace to get up off the bed.

"Can that child of yours talk?" asks Mama.

Stella-Rondo says, "Can she what?"

"Talk! Talk!" says Mama. "Burdyburdyburdyburdy!"

So Stella-Rondo yells back, "Who says she can't talk?"

"Sister says so," says Mama.

"You didn't have to tell me, I know whose word of honor don't mean a thing in this house," says Stella-Rondo.

And in a minute the loudest Yankee voice I ever heard in my life yells out, "OE'm Pop-OE the Sailor-r-r-r Ma-a-an!" and then somebody jumps up and down in the upstairs hall. In another second the house would of fallen down.

"Not only talks, she can tap-dance!" calls Stella-Rondo. "Which is more than some people I won't name can do."

"Why, the little precious darling thing!" Mama says, so surprised. "Just as smart as she can be!" Starts talking baby talk right there. Then she turns on me. "Sister, you ought to be thoroughly ashamed! Run upstairs this instant and apologize to Stella-Rondo and Shirley-T."

"Apologize for what?" I says. "I merely wondered if the child was normal, that's all. Now that she's proved she is, why, I have nothing further to say."

But Mama just turned on her heel and flew out, furious. She ran right upstairs and hugged the baby. She believed it was adopted. Stella-Rondo hadn't done a thing but turn her against me from upstairs while I stood there helpless over the hot stove. So that made Mama, Papa-Daddy and the baby all on Stella-Rondo's side.

Next, Uncle Rondo.

I must say that Uncle Rondo has been marvelous to me at various times in the past and I was completely unprepared to be made to jump out of my skin, the way it turned out. Once Stella-Rondo did something perfectly horrible to him—broke a chain letter from Flanders Field—and he took the radio back he had given her and gave it to me. Stella-Rondo was furious! For six months we all had to call her Stella instead of Stella-Rondo, or she wouldn't answer. I always thought Uncle Rondo had all the brains of the entire family. Another time he sent me to Mammoth Cave, with all expenses paid.

But this would be the day he was drinking that prescription, the Fourth of July.

So at supper Stella-Rondo speaks up and says she thinks Uncle Rondo ought to try to eat a little something. So finally Uncle Rondo said he would try a little cold biscuits and ketchup, but that was all. So *she* brought it to him.

"Do you think it wise to disport with ketchup in Stella-Rondo's flesh-colored kimono?" I says. Trying to be considerate! If Stella-Rondo couldn't watch out for her trousseau, somebody had to.

"Any objections?" asks Uncle Rondo, just about to pour out all the ketchup.

"Don't mind what she says, Uncle Rondo," says Stella-Rondo. "Sister has been devoting this solid afternoon to sneering out my bedroom window at the way you look."

"What's that?" says Uncle Rondo. Uncle Rondo has got the most terrible temper in the world. Anything is liable to make him tear the house down if it comes at the wrong time.

So Stella-Rondo says, "Sister says, 'Uncle Rondo certainly does look like a fool in that pink kimono!' "

Do you remember who it was really said that?

Uncle Rondo spills out all the ketchup and jumps out of his chair and tears off the kimono and throws it down on the dirty floor and puts his foot on it. It had to be sent all the way to Jackson to the cleaners and re-pleated.

"So that's your opinion of your Uncle Rondo, is it?" he says. "I look like a fool, do I? Well, that's the last straw. A whole day in this house with nothing to do, and then to hear you come out with a remark like that behind my back!"

"I didn't say any such of a thing, Uncle Rondo," I says, "and I'm not saying who did, either. Why, I think you look all right. Just try to take care of yourself and not talk and eat at the same time," I says. "I think you better go lie down."

"Lie down my foot," says Uncle Rondo. I ought to of known by that he was fixing to do something perfectly horrible.

So he didn't do anything that night in the precarious state he was in—just played Casino with Mama and Stella-Rondo and Shirley-T. and gave Shirley-T. a nickel with a head on both sides. It tickled her nearly to death, and she called him "Papa." But at 6:30 A.M. the next morning he threw a whole five-cent package of some unsold one-inch firecrackers from the store as hard as he could into my bedroom and they every one went off. Not one bad one in the string. Anybody else, there'd be one that wouldn't go off.

Well, I'm just terribly susceptible to noise of any kind, the doctor has always told me I was the most sensitive person he had ever seen in his whole life, and I was simply prostrated. I couldn't eat! People tell me they heard it as far as the cemetery, and old Aunt Jep Patterson, that had been holding her own so good, thought it was Judgment Day and she was going to meet her whole family. It's usually so quiet here.

And I'll tell you it didn't take me any longer than a minute to make up my mind what to do. There I was with the whole entire house on Stella-Rondo's side and turned against me. If I have anything at all I have pride.

So I just decided I'd go straight down to the P.O. There's plenty of room there in the back, I says to myself.

Well! I made no bones about letting the family catch on to what I was up to. I didn't try to conceal it.

The first thing they knew, I marched in where they were all playing Old Maid and pulled the electric oscillating fan out by the plug, and everything got real hot. Next I snatched the pillow I'd done the needlepoint on right off the davenport from behind Papa-Daddy. He went "Ugh!" I beat Stella-Rondo up the stairs and finally found my charm bracelet in her bureau drawer under a picture of Nelson Eddy.

"So that's the way the land lies," says Uncle Rondo. There he was, piecing on the ham. "Well, Sister, I'll be glad to donate my army cot if you got any place to set it up, providing you'll leave right this minute and let me get some peace." Uncle Rondo was in France.

"Thank you kindly for the cot and 'peace' is hardly the word I would select if I had to resort to firecrackers at 6:30 A.M. in a young girl's bedroom," I says back to him. "And as to where I intend to go, you seem to forget my position as postmistress of China Grove, Mississippi," I says. "I've always got the P.O."

Well, that made them all sit up and take notice.

I went out front and started digging up some four-o'clocks to plant around the P.O.

"Ah-ah-ah!" says Mama, raising the window. "Those happen to be my four-o'clocks. Everything planted in that star is mine. I've never known you to make anything grow in your life."

"Very well," I says. "But I take the fern. Even you, Mama, can't stand there and deny that I'm the one watered that fern. And I happen to know where I can send in a box top and get a packet of one thousand mixed seeds, no two the same kind, free."

"Oh, where?" Mama wants to know.

But I says, "Too late. You 'tend to your house, and I'll 'tend to mine. You hear things like that all the time if you know how to listen to the radio. Perfectly marvelous offers. Get anything you want free."

So I hope to tell you I marched in and got that radio, and they could of all bit a nail in two, especially Stella-Rondo, that it used to belong to, and she well knew she couldn't get it back, I'd sue for it like a shot. And I very politely took the sewing-machine motor I helped pay the most on to give Mama for Christmas back in 1929, and a good big calendar, with the first-aid remedies on it. The thermometer and the Hawaiian ukulele certainly were rightfully mine, and I stood on the step-ladder and got all my watermelon-rind preserves and every fruit and vegetable I'd put up, every jar. Then I began to pull the tacks out of the bluebird wall vases on the archway to the dining room.

"Who told you you could have those, Miss Priss?" says Mama, fanning as hard as she could.

"I bought 'em and I'll keep track of 'em," I says. "I'll tack 'em up one on each side of the post-office window, and you can see 'em when you come to ask me for your mail, if you're so dead to see 'em."

"Not I! I'll never darken the door to that post office again if I live to be a hundred," Mama says. "Ungrateful child! After all the money we spent on you at the Normal."

"Me either," says Stella-Rondo. "You can just let my mail lie there and *rot,* for all I care. I'll never come and relieve you of a single, solitary piece."

"I should worry," I says. "And who you think's going to sit down and write you all those big fat letters and postcards, by the way? Mr. Whitaker? Just because he was the only man ever dropped down in China Grove and you got him—unfairly—is he going to sit down and write you a lengthy correspondence after you come home giving no rhyme nor reason whatsoever for your separation and no explanation for the presence of that child? I may not have your brilliant mind, but I fail to see it."

So Mama says, "Sister, I've told you a thousand times that Stella-Rondo simply got homesick, and this child is far too big to be hers," and she says, "Now, why don't you all just sit down and play Casino?"

Then Shirley-T. sticks out her tongue at me in this perfectly horrible way. She has no more manners than the man in the moon. I told her she was going to cross her eyes like that some day and they'd stick.

"It's too late to stop me now," I says. "You should have tried that yesterday. I'm going to the P.O. and the only way you can possibly see me is to visit me there."

So Papa-Daddy says, "You'll never catch me setting foot in that post office, even if I should take a notion into my head to write a letter some place." He says, "I won't have you reachin' out of that little old window with a pair of shears and cuttin' off any beard of mine. I'm too smart for you!"

"We all are," says Stella-Rondo.

But I said, "If you're so smart, where's Mr. Whitaker?"

So then Uncle Rondo says, "I'll thank you from now on to stop reading all the orders I get on postcards and telling everybody in China Grove what you think is the matter with them," but I says, "I draw my own conclusions and will continue in the future to draw them." I says, "If people want to write their inmost secrets on penny postcards, there's nothing in the wide world you can do about it, Uncle Rondo."

"And if you think we'll ever *write* another postcard you're sadly mistaken," says Mama.

"Cutting off your nose to spite your face then," I says. "But if you're all determined to have no more to do with the U.S. mail, think of this: What will Stella-Rondo do now, if she wants to tell Mr. Whitaker to come after her?"

"Wah!" says Stella-Rondo. I knew she'd cry. She had a conniption fit right there in the kitchen.

"It will be interesting to see how long she holds out," I says. "And now —I am leaving."

"Good-bye," says Uncle Rondo.

"Oh, I declare," says Mama, "to think that a family of mine should quarrel on the Fourth of July, or the day after, over Stella-Rondo leaving old Mr. Whitaker and having the sweetest little adopted child! It looks like we'd all be glad!"

"Wah!" says Stella-Rondo, and has a fresh conniption fit.

"*He* left *her*—you mark my words," I says. "That's Mr. Whitaker. I know Mr. Whitaker. After all, I knew him first. I said from the beginning he'd up and leave her. I foretold every single thing that's happened."

"Where did he go?" asks Mama.

"Probably to the North Pole, if he knows what's good for him," I says.

But Stella-Rondo just bawled and wouldn't say another word. She flew to her room and slammed the door.

"Now look what you've gone and done, Sister," says Mama. "You go apologize."

"I haven't got time, I'm leaving," I says.

"Well, what are you waiting around for?" asks Uncle Rondo.

So I just picked up the kitchen clock and marched off, without saying "Kiss my foot" or anything, and never did tell Stella-Rondo good-bye.

There was a nigger girl going along on a little wagon right in front.

"Nigger girl," I says, "come help me haul these things down the hill, I'm going to live in the post office."

Took her nine trips in her express wagon. Uncle Rondo came out on the porch and threw her a nickel.

And that's the last I've laid eyes on any of my family or my family laid eyes on me for five solid days and nights. Stella-Rondo may be telling the most horrible tales in the world about Mr. Whitaker, but I haven't heard them. As I tell everybody, I draw my own conclusions.

But oh, I like it here. It's ideal, as I've been saying. You see, I've got everything cater-cornered, the way I like it. Hear the radio? All the war news. Radio, sewing machine, book ends, ironing board and that great big piano lamp —peace, that's what I like. Butter-bean vines planted all along the front where the strings are.

Of course, there's not much mail. My family are naturally the main people in China Grove, and if they prefer to vanish from the face of the earth, for all the mail they get or the mail they write, why, I'm not going to open my mouth. Some of the folks here in town are taking up for me and some turned against me. I know which is which. There are always people who will quit buying stamps just to get on the right side of Papa-Daddy.

But here I am, and here I'll stay. I want the world to know I'm happy.

And if Stella-Rondo should come to me this minute, on bended knees, and *attempt* to explain the incidents of her life with Mr. Whitaker, I'd simply put my fingers in both my ears and refuse to listen.

Death of a Travelling Salesman

R. J. Bowman, who for fourteen years had travelled for a shoe company through Mississippi, drove his Ford along a rutted dirt path. It was a long day! The time did not seem to clear the noon hurdle and settle into soft afternoon. The sun, keeping its strength here even in winter, stayed at the top of the sky, and every time Bowman stuck his head out of the dusty car to stare up the road, it seemed to reach a long arm down and push against the top of his head, right through his hat—like the practical joke of an old drummer, long on the road. It made him feel all the more angry and helpless. He was feverish, and he was not quite sure of the way.

This was his first day back on the road after a long siege of influenza. He had had very high fever, and dreams, and had become weakened and pale, enough to tell the difference in the mirror, and he could not think clearly . . . All afternoon, in the midst of his anger, and for no reason, he had thought of his dead grandmother. She had been a comfortable soul. Once more Bowman wished he could fall into the big feather bed that had been in her room . . . Then he forgot her again.

This desolate hill country! And he seemed to be going the wrong way—it was as if he were going back, far back. There was not a house in sight. . . . There was no use wishing he were back in bed, though. By paying the hotel doctor his bill he had proved his recovery. He had not even been sorry when the pretty trained nurse said good-bye. He did not like illness, he distrusted it, as he distrusted the road without signposts. It angered him. He had given the nurse a really expensive bracelet, just because she was packing up her bag and leaving.

But now—what if in fourteen years on the road he had never been ill before and never had an accident? His record was broken, and he had even begun almost to question it . . . He had gradually put up at better hotels, in the bigger towns, but weren't they all, eternally, stuffy in summer and draughty in winter? Women? He could only remember little rooms within little rooms, like a nest of Chinese paper boxes, and if he thought of one woman he saw the worn loneliness that the furniture of that room seemed built of. And he himself—he was a man who always wore rather wide-brimmed black hats, and in the wavy hotel mirrors had looked something like a bull-fighter, as he paused for that inevitable instant on the landing, walking downstairs to supper . . . He leaned out of the car again, and once more the sun pushed at his head.

Bowman had wanted to reach Beulah by dark, to go to bed and sleep off his fatigue. As he remembered, Beulah was fifty miles away from the last town, on a gravelled road. This was only a cow trail. How had he ever come to such a place? One hand wiped the sweat from his face, and he drove on.

He had made the Beulah trip before. But he had never seen this hill or this petering-out path before—or that cloud, he thought shyly, looking up and then down quickly—any more than he had seen this day before. Why did he not admit he was simply lost and had been for miles? . . . He was not in the habit of asking the way of strangers, and these people never knew where the very roads they lived on went to; but then he had not even been close enough to anyone to call out. People standing in the fields now and then, or on top of the haystacks, had been too far away, looking like leaning sticks or weeds, turning a little at the solitary rattle of his car across their countryside, watching the pale sobered winter dust where it chunked out behind like big squashes down the road. The stares of these distant people had followed him solidly like a wall, impenetrable, behind which they turned back after he had passed.

The cloud floated there to one side like the bolster on his grandmother's bed. It went over a cabin on the edge of a hill, where two bare chinaberry trees clutched at the sky. He drove through a heap of dead oak leaves, his wheels stirring their weightless sides to make a silvery melancholy whistle as the car passed through their bed. No car had been along this way ahead of him. Then he saw that he was on the edge of a ravine that fell away, a red erosion, and that this was indeed the road's end.

He pulled the brake. But it did not hold, though he put all his strength into it. The car, tipped toward the edge, rolled a little. Without doubt, it was going over the bank.

He got out quietly, as though some mischief had been done him and he had his dignity to remember. He lifted his bag and sample case out, set them down, and stood back and watched the car roll over the edge. He heard something—not the crash he was listening for, but a slow un-uproarious crackle. Rather distastefully he went to look over, and he saw that his car had fallen into a tangle of immense grape vines as thick as his arm, which caught it and held it, rocked it like a grotesque child in a dark cradle, and then, as he watched, concerned somehow that he was not still inside it, released it gently to the ground.

He sighed.

Where am I? he wondered with a shock. Why didn't I do something? All his anger seemed to have drifted away from him. There was the house, back on the hill. He took a bag in each hand and with almost childlike willingness went toward it. But his breathing came with difficulty, and he had to stop to rest.

It was a shotgun house, two rooms and an open passage between, perched on the hill. The whole cabin slanted a little under the heavy heaped-up vine that covered the roof, light and green, as though forgotten from summer. A woman stood in the passage.

He stopped still. Then all of a sudden his heart began to behave strangely.

Like a rocket set off, it began to leap and expand into uneven patterns of beats which showered into his brain, and he could not think. But in scattering and falling it made no noise. It shot up with great power, almost elation, and fell gently, like acrobats into nets. It began to pound profoundly, then waited irresponsibly, hitting in some sort of inward mockery first at his ribs, then against his eyes, then under his shoulder blades, and against the roof of his mouth when he tried to say, "Good afternoon, madam." But he could not hear his heart—it was as quiet as ashes falling. This was rather comforting; still, it was shocking to Bowman to feel his heart beating at all.

Stockstill in his confusion, he dropped his bags, which seemed to drift in slow bulks gracefully through the air and to cushion themselves on the grey prostrate grass near the doorstep.

As for the woman standing there, he saw at once that she was old. Since she could not possibly hear his heart, he ignored the pounding and now looked at her carefully, and yet in his distraction dreamily, with his mouth open.

She had been cleaning the lamp, and held it, half blackened, half clear, in front of her. He saw her with the dark passage behind her. She was a big woman with a weather-beaten but unwrinkled face; her lips were held tightly together, and her eyes looked with a curious dulled brightness into his. He looked at her shoes, which were like bundles. If it were summer she would be barefoot . . . Bowman, who automatically judged a woman's age on sight, set her age at fifty. She wore a formless garment of some grey coarse material, rough-dried from a washing, from which her arms appeared pink and unexpectedly round. When she never said a word, and sustained her quiet pose of holding the lamp, he was convinced of the strength in her body.

"Good afternoon, madam," he said.

She stared on, whether at him or at the air around him he could not tell, but after a moment she lowered her eyes to show that she would listen to whatever he had to say.

"I wonder if you would be interested—" He tried once more. "An accident—my car . . ."

Her voice emerged low and remote, like a sound across a lake. "Sonny he ain't here."

"Sonny?"

"Sonny ain't here now."

Her son—a fellow able to bring my car up, he decided in blurred relief. He pointed down the hill. "My car's in the bottom of the ditch. I'll need help."

"Sonny ain't here, but he'll be here."

She was becoming clearer to him and her voice stronger, and Bowman saw that she was stupid.

He was hardly surprised at the deepening postponement and tedium of his journey. He took a breath, and heard his voice speaking over the silent blows of his heart. "I was sick. I am not strong yet . . . May I come in?"

He stooped and laid his big black hat over the handle on his bag. It was a humble motion, almost a bow, that instantly struck him as absurd and betraying of all his weakness. He looked up at the woman, the wind blowing his hair. He might have continued for a long time in this unfamiliar attitude; he had never been a patient man, but when he was sick he had learned to sink submissively into the pillows, to wait for his medicine. He waited on the woman.

Then she, looking at him with blue eyes, turned and held open the door, and after a moment Bowman, as if convinced in his action, stood erect and followed her in.

Inside, the darkness of the house touched him like a professional hand, the doctor's. The woman set the half-cleaned lamp on a table in the centre of the room and pointed, also like a professional person, a guide, to a chair with a yellow cowhide seat. She herself crouched on the hearth, drawing her knees up under the shapeless dress.

At first he felt hopefully secure. His heart was quieter. The room was enclosed in the gloom of yellow pine boards. He could see the other room, with the foot of an iron bed showing, across the passage. The bed had been made up with a red-and-yellow pieced quilt that looked like a map or a picture, a little like his grandmother's girlhood painting of Rome burning.

He had ached for coolness, but in this room it was cold. He stared at the hearth with dead coals lying on it and iron pots in the corners. The hearth and smoked chimney were of the stone he had seen ribbing the hills, mostly slate. Why is there no fire? he wondered.

And it was so still. The silence of the fields seemed to enter and move familiarly through the house. The wind used the open hall. He felt that he was in a mysterious, quiet, cool danger. It was necessary to do what? . . . To talk.

"I have a nice line of women's low-priced shoes . . ." he said.

But the woman answered, "Sonny'll be here. He's strong. Sonny'll move your car."

"Where is he now?"

"Farms for Mr. Redmond."

Mr. Redmond. Mr. Redmond. That was someone he would never have to encounter, and he was glad. Somehow the name did not appeal to him . . . In a flare of touchiness and anxiety, Bowman wished to avoid even mention of unknown men and their unknown farms.

"Do you two live here alone?" He was surprised to hear his old voice, chatty, confidential, inflected for selling shoes, asking a question like that—a thing he did not even want to know.

"Yes. We are alone."

He was surprised at the way she answered. She had taken a long time to say that. She had nodded her head in a deep way too. Had she wished to affect him with some sort of premonition? he wondered unhappily. Or was it only that she would not help him, after all, by talking with him? For he was not strong enough to receive the impact of unfamiliar things without a little talk to break their fall. He had lived a month in which nothing had happened except in his head and his body—an almost inaudible life of heartbeats and dreams that came back, a life of fever and privacy, a delicate life which had left him weak to the point of—what? Of begging. The pulse in his palm leapt like a trout in a brook.

He wondered over and over why the woman did not go ahead with cleaning the lamp. What prompted her to stay there across the room, silently bestowing her presence upon him? He saw that with her it was not a time for doing little tasks. Her face was grave; she was feeling how right she was. Perhaps it was only politeness. In docility he held his eyes stiffly wide; they fixed themselves on the woman's clasped hands as though she held the cord they were strung on.

Then, "Sonny's coming," she said.

He himself had not heard anything, but there came a man passing the window and then plunging in at the door, with two hounds beside him. Sonny was a big enough man, with his belt slung low about his hips. He looked at least thirty. He had a hot, red face that was yet full of silence. He wore muddy blue pants and an old military coat stained and patched. World War? Bowman wondered. Great God, it was a Confederate coat. On the back of his light hair he had a wide filthy black hat which seemed to insult Bowman's own. He pushed down the dogs from his chest. He was strong with dignity and heaviness in his way of moving . . . There was the resemblance to his mother.

They stood side by side . . . He must account again for his presence here.

"Sonny, this man, he had his car to run off over the prec'pice an' wants to know if you will git it out for him," the woman said after a few minutes.

Bowman could not even state his case.

Sonny's eyes lay upon him.

He knew he should offer explanations and show money—at least appear either penitent or authoritative. But all he could do was to shrug slightly.

Sonny brushed by him going to the window, followed by the eager dogs, and looked out. There was effort even in the way he was looking, as if he could throw his sight out like a rope. Without turning Bowman felt that his own eyes could have seen nothing: it was too far.

"Got me a mule out there an' got me a block an' tackle," said Sonny meaningfully. "I *could* catch me my mule an' git me my ropes, an' before long I'd git your car out the ravine."

He looked completely round the room, as if in meditation, his eyes roving in their own distance. Then he pressed his lips firmly and yet shyly together, and with the dogs ahead of him this time, he lowered his head and strode out.

The hard earth sounded, cupping to his powerful way of walking—almost a stagger.

Mischievously, at the suggestion of those sounds, Bowman's heart leapt again. It seemed to walk about inside him.

"Sonny's goin' to do it," the woman said. She said it again, singing it almost, like a song. She was sitting in her place by the hearth.

Without looking out, he heard some shouts and the dogs barking and the pounding of hoofs in short runs on the hill. In a few minutes Sonny passed under the window with a rope, and there was a brown mule with quivering, shining, purple-looking ears. The mule actually looked in the window. Under his eyelashes it turned target-like eyes into his. Bowman averted his head and saw the woman looking serenely back at the mule, with only satisfaction in her face.

She sang a little more, under her breath. It occurred to him, and it seemed quite marvellous, that she was not really talking to him, but rather following the thing that came about with words that were unconscious and part of her looking.

So he said nothing, and this time when he did not reply he felt a curious and strong emotion, not fear, rise up in him.

This time, when his heart leapt, something—his soul—seemed to leap too, like a little colt invited out of a pen. He stared at the woman while the frantic nimbleness of his feeling made his head sway. He could not move; there was nothing he could do, unless perhaps he might embrace this woman who sat there growing old and shapeless before him.

But he wanted to leap up, to say to her, I have been sick and I found out then, only then, how lonely I am. Is it too late? My heart puts up a struggle inside me, and you may have heard it, protesting against emptiness . . . It should be full, he would rush on to tell her, thinking of his heart now as a deep lake, it should be holding love like other hearts. It should be flooded with love. There would be a warm spring day . . . Come and stand in my heart, whoever you are, and a whole river would cover your feet and rise higher and take your knees in whirlpools, and draw you down to itself, your whole body, your heart too.

But he moved a trembling hand across his eyes, and looked at the placid crouching woman across the room. She was still as a statue. He felt ashamed and exhausted by the thought that he might, in one more moment, have tried by simple words and embraces to communicate some strange thing—something which seemed always to have just escaped him . . .

Sunlight touched the farthest pot on the hearth. It was late afternoon. This time to-morrow he would be somewhere on a good gravelled road, driving his car past things that happened to people, quicker than their happening. Seeing ahead to the next day, he was glad, and knew that this was no time to embrace an old woman. He could feel in his pounding temples the readying of his blood for motion and for hurrying away.

"Sonny's hitched up your car by now," said the woman. "He'll git it out the ravine right shortly."

"Fine!" he cried with his customary enthusiasm.

Yet it seemed a long time that they waited. It began to get dark. Bowman was cramped in his chair. Any man should know enough to get up and walk around while he waited. There was something like guilt in such stillness and silence.

But instead of getting up, he listened . . . His breathing restrained, his eyes powerless in the growing dark, he listened uneasily for a warning sound, forgetting in wariness what it would be. Before long he heard something—soft, continuous, insinuating.

"What's the noise?" he asked, his voice jumping into the dark. Then wildly he was afraid it would be his heart beating so plainly in the quiet room, and she would tell him so.

"You might hear the stream," she said grudgingly.

Her voice was closer. She was standing by the table. He wondered why she did not light the lamp. She stood there in the dark and did not light it.

Bowman would never speak to her now, for the time was past. I'll sleep in the dark, he thought, in his bewilderment pitying himself.

Heavily she moved on to the window. Her arm, vaguely white, rose straight from her full side and she pointed out into the darkness.

"That white speck's Sonny," she said, talking to herself.

He turned unwillingly and peered over her shoulder; he hesitated to rise and stand beside her. His eyes searched the dusky air. The white speck floated smoothly toward her finger, like a leaf on a river, growing whiter in the dark. It was as if she had shown him something secret, part of her life, but had offered no explanation. He looked away. He was moved almost to tears, feeling for no reason that she had made a silent declaration equivalent to his own. His hand waited upon his chest.

Then a step shook the house, and Sonny was in the room. Bowman felt how the woman left him there and went to the other man's side.

"I done got your car out, mister," said Sonny's voice in the dark. "She's settin' a-waitin' in the road, turned to go back where she come from."

"Fine!" said Bowman, projecting his own voice to loudness. "I'm surely much obliged—I could never have done it myself—I was sick . . ."

"I could do it easy," said Sonny.

Bowman could feel them both waiting in the dark, and he could hear the dogs panting out in the yard, waiting to bark when he should go. He felt strangely helpless and resentful. Now that he could go, he longed to stay. From what was he being deprived? His chest was rudely shaken by the violence of his heart. These people cherished something here that he could not see, they withheld some ancient promise of food and warmth and light. Between them they had a conspiracy. He thought of the way she had moved away from him and gone to Sonny, she had flowed toward him. He was shaking with cold, he was tired, and it was not fair. Humbly and yet angrily he stuck his hand into his pocket.

"Of course I'm going to pay you for everything—"

"We don't take money for such," said Sonny's voice belligerently.

"I want to pay. But do something more . . . Let me stay—to-night . . ." He took another step toward them. If only they could see him, they would know his sincerity, his real need! His voice went on, "I'm not very strong yet, I'm not able to walk far, even back to my car, maybe, I don't know—I don't know exactly where I am—"

He stopped. He felt as if he might burst into tears. What would they think of him!

Sonny came over and put his hands on him. Bowman felt them pass (they were professional too) across his chest, over his hips. He could feel Sonny's eyes upon him in the dark.

"You ain't no revenuer come sneakin' here, mister, ain't got no gun?"

To this end of nowhere! And yet *he* had come. He made a grave answer. "No."

"You can stay."

"Sonny," said the woman, "You'll have to borry some fire."

"I'll go git it from Redmond's," said Sonny.

"What!" Bowman strained to hear their words to each other.

"Our fire, it's out, and Sonny's got to borry some, because it's dark an' cold," she said.

"But matches—I have matches—"

"We don't have no need for 'em," she said proudly. "Sonny's goin' after his own fire."

"I'm goin' to Redmond's," said Sonny with an air of importance, and he went out.

After they had waited a while, Bowman looked out the window and saw a light moving over the hill. It spread itself out like a little fan. It zigzagged along the field, darting and swift, not like Sonny at all . . . Soon enough, Sonny staggered in, holding a burning stick behind him in tongs, fire flowing in his wake, blazing light into the corners of the room.

"We'll make a fire now," the woman said, taking the brand.

When that was done she lit the lamp. It showed its dark and light. The whole room turned golden-yellow like some sort of flower, and the walls smelled of it and seemed to tremble with the quiet rushing of the fire and the waving of the burning lampwick in its funnel of light.

The woman moved among the iron pots. With the tongs she dropped hot coals on top of the iron lids. They made a set of soft vibrations, like the sound of a bell far away.

She looked up and over at Bowman, but he could not answer. He was trembling . . .

"Have a drink, mister?" Sonny asked. He had brought in a chair from the other room and sat astride it with his folded arms across the back. Now we are all visible, to one another, Bowman thought, and cried, "Yes sir, you bet, thanks!"

"Come after me and do just what I do," said Sonny.

It was another excursion into the dark. They went through the hall, out to the back of the house, past a shed and a hooded well. They came to a wilderness of thicket.

"Down on your knees," said Sonny.

"What?" Sweat broke out on his forehead.

He understood when Sonny began to crawl through a sort of tunnel that the bushes made over the ground. He followed, startled in spite of himself when a twig or a thorn touched him gently without making a sound, clinging to him and finally letting him go.

Sonny stopped crawling and, crouched on his knees, began to dig with both his hands into the dirt. Bowman shyly struck matches and made a light. In a few minutes Sonny pulled up a jug. He poured out some of the whisky into a bottle from his coat pocket, and buried the jug again. "You never know who's liable to knock at your door," he said, and laughed. "Start back," he said, almost formally. "Ain't no need for us to drink outdoors, like hogs."

At the table by the fire, sitting opposite each other in their chairs, Sonny and Bowman took drinks out of the bottle, passing it across. The dogs slept; one of them was having a dream.

"This is good," said Bowman. "That is what I needed." It was just as though he were drinking the fire off the hearth.

"He makes it," said the woman with quiet pride.

She was pushing the coals off the pots, and the smells of corn bread and coffee circled the room. She set everything on the table before the men, with a bone-handled knife stuck into one of the potatoes, splitting out its golden fiber. Then she stood for a minute looking at them, tall and full above them where they sat. She leaned a little toward them.

"You-all can eat now," she said, and suddenly smiled.

Bowman had just happened to be looking at her. He set his cup back on the table in unbelieving protest. A pain pressed at his eyes. He saw that she was not an old woman. She was young, still young. He could think of no number of years for her. She was the same age as Sonny, and she belonged to him. She stood with the deep dark corner of the room behind her, the shifting yellow light scattering over her head and her grey formless dress, trembling over her tall body when it bent over them in its sudden communication. She was young. Her teeth were shining and her eyes glowed. She turned and walked slowly and heavily out of the room, and he heard her sit down on the cot and then lie down. The pattern on the quilt moved.

"She goin' to have a baby," said Sonny, popping a bite into his mouth.

Bowman could not speak. He was shocked with knowing what was really in this house. A marriage, a fruitful marriage. That simple thing. Anyone could have had that.

Somehow he felt unable to be indignant or protest, although some sort of joke had certainly been played upon him. There was nothing remote or mysterious here—only something private. The only secret was the ancient communication between two people. But the memory of the woman's waiting silently by the cold hearth, of the man's stubborn journey a mile away to get fire, and how they finally brought out their food and drink and filled the room proudly with all they had to show, was suddenly too clear and too enormous within him for response . . .

"You ain't as hungry as you look," said Sonny.

The woman came out of the bedroom as soon as the men had finished, and ate her supper while her husband stared peacefully into the fire.

Then they put the dogs out, with the food that was left.

"I think I'd better sleep here by the fire, on the floor," said Bowman.

He felt that he had been cheated, and that he could afford now to be generous. Ill though he was, he was not going to ask them for their bed. He was through with asking favors in this house, now that he understood what was there.

"Sure, mister."

But he had not known yet how slowly he understood. They had not meant to give him their bed. After a little interval they both rose and looking at him gravely went into the other room.

He lay stretched by the fire until it grew low and dying. He watched every tongue of blaze lick out and vanish. "There will be special reduced prices on all footwear during the month of January," he found himself repeating quietly, and then he lay with his lips tight shut.

How many noises the night had! He heard the stream running, the fire dying, and he was sure now that he heard his heart beating, too, the sound it made under his ribs. He heard breathing, round and deep, of the man and his wife in the room across the passage. And that was all. But emotion swelled patiently within him, and he wished that the child were his.

He must get back to where he had been before. He stood weakly before the red coals, and put on his overcoat. It felt too heavy on his shoulders. As he started out he looked and saw that the woman had never got through with cleaning the lamp. On some impulse he put all the money from his billfold under its fluted glass base, almost ostentatiously.

Ashamed, shrugging a little, and then shivering, he took his bags and went out. The cold of the air seemed to lift him bodily. The moon was in the sky.

On the slope he began to run, he could not help it. Just as he reached the road, where his car seemed to sit in the moonlight like a boat, his heart began to give off tremendous explosions like a rifle, bang bang bang.

He sank in fright on to the road, his bags falling about him. He felt as if all this had happened before. He covered his heart with both hands to keep anyone from hearing the noise it made.

But nobody heard it.

TILLIE OLSEN

b. 1913

Born in Nebraska, Olsen experienced the poverty of the working class in both mining towns and farming villages in the West. She writes very feelingly about those experiences in her novel *Yonnondio,* published in 1974 but written years before while the events were fresh in her mind. Her stories explore loyalties between men and women, and what role the past plays in current relationships.

She has lived in the Bay area of California for years, mostly raising her children, but known to the readers of that region as a precise artist with a great gift for the realistic short story. Her collection of short stories *Tell Me a Riddle* considerably increased the number of her admirers. The title story of that volume (printed here) won the O. Henry Prize for the best short story of 1961.

More recently she has been able to resume a full-time writing career, often in combination with directing creative writing workshops at leading American universities. Her new book *Silences* (Delacorte-Seymour Lawrence, 1978) is a study of how in the past numerous writers have been forced by a variety of pressures to cease writing. Like everything she does, this book is highly original—passionate in argument, and scholarly in its range of historical and biographical reference.

Tell Me a Riddle

1

For forty-seven years they had been married. How deep back the stubborn, gnarled roots of the quarrel reached, no one could say—but only now, when tending to the needs of others no longer shackled them together, the roots swelled up visible, split the earth between them, and the tearing shook even to the children, long since grown.

Why now, why now? wailed Hannah.

As if when we grew up weren't enough, said Paul.

Poor Ma. Poor Dad. It hurts so for both of them, said Vivi. They never had very much; at least in old age they should be happy.

Knock their heads together, insisted Sammy; tell 'em: you're too old for this kind of thing; no reason not to get along now.

Lennie wrote to Clara: They've lived over so much together; what could possibly tear them apart?

Something tangible enough.

Arthritic hands, and such work as he got, occasional. Poverty all his life, and there was little breath left for running. He could not, could not turn away from this desire: to have the troubling of responsibility, the fretting with money, over and done with; to be free, to be *care*free where success was not measured by accumulation, and there was use for the vitality still in him.

There was a way. They could sell the house, and with the money join his lodge's Haven, cooperative for the aged. Happy communal life, and was he not already an official; had he not helped organize it, raise funds, served as a trustee?

But she—would not consider it.

"What do we need all this for?" he would ask loudly, for her hearing aid was turned down and the vacuum was shrilling. "Five rooms" (pushing the sofa so she could get into the corner) "furniture" (smoothing down the rug) "floors and surfaces to make work. Tell me, why do we need it?" And he was glad he could ask in a scream.

"Because I'm use't."

"Because you're use't. This is a reason, Mrs. Word Miser? Used to can get unused!"

"Enough unused I have to get used to already. . . . Not enough words?" turning off the vacuum a moment to hear herself answer. "Because soon enough we'll need only a little closet, no windows, no furniture, nothing to make work, but for worms. Because now I want room. . . . Screech and blow like you're doing, you'll need that closet even sooner. . . . Ha, again!" for the vacuum bag wailed, puffed half up, hung stubbornly limp. "This time fix it so it stays; quick before the phone rings and you get too important-busy."

But while he struggled with the motor, it seethed in him. Why fix it? Why have to bother? And if it can't be fixed, have to wring the mind with how to pay the repair? At the Haven they come in with their own machines to clean your room or your cottage; you fish, or play cards, or make jokes in the sun, not with knotty fingers fight to mend vacuums.

Over the dishes, coaxingly: "For once in your life, to be free, to have everything done for you, like a queen."

"I never liked queens."

"No dishes, no garbage, no towel to sop, no worry what to buy, what to eat."

"And what else would I do with my empty hands? Better to eat at my own table when I want, and to cook and eat how I want."

"In the cottages they buy what you ask, and cook it how you like. *You* are the one who always used to say: better mankind born without mouths and stomachs than always to worry for money to buy, to shop, to fix, to cook, to wash, to clean."

"How cleverly you hid that you heard. I said it then because eighteen hours a day I ran. And you never scraped a carrot or knew a dish towel sops. Now—for you and me—who cares? A herring out of a jar is enough. But when *I* want, and nobody to bother." And she turned off her ear button, so she would not have to hear.

But as *he* had no peace, juggling and rejuggling the money to figure: how will I pay for this now?; prying out the storm windows (there they take care of this); jolting in the streetcar on errands (there I would not have to ride to take care of this or that); fending the patronizing relatives just back from Florida (at the Haven it matters what one is, not what one can afford), he gave *her* no peace.

"Look! In their bulletin. A reading circle. Twice a week it meets."

"Haumm," her answer of not listening.

"A reading circle. Chekhov they read that you like, and Peretz. Cultured people at the Haven that you would enjoy."

"Enjoy!" She tasted the word. "Now, when it pleases you, you find a reading circle for me. And forty years ago when the children were morsels and there was a Circle, did you stay home with them once so I could go? Even once? You trained me well. I do not need others to enjoy. Others!" Her voice trembled. "Because *you* want to be there with others. Already it makes me sick to think of you always around others. Clown, grimacer, floormat, yesman, entertainer, whatever they want of you."

And now it was he who turned on the television loud so he need not hear.

Old scar tissue ruptured and the wounds festered anew. Chekhov indeed. She thought without softness of that young wife, who in the deep night hours while she nursed the current baby, and perhaps held another in her lap, would try to stay awake for the only time there was to read. She would feel again the weather of the outside on his cheek when, coming late from a meeting, he would find her so, and stimulated and ardent, sniffing her skin, coax: "I'll put the baby to bed, and you—put the book away, don't read, don't read."

That had been the most beguiling of all the "don't read, put your book away" her life had been. Chekhov indeed!

"Money?" She shrugged him off. "Could we get poorer than once we were? And in America, who starves?"

But as still he pressed:

"Let me alone about money. Was there ever enough? Seven little ones—for every penny I had to ask—and sometimes, remember, there was nothing. But always *I* had to manage. Now *you* manage. Rub your nose in it good."

But from those years she had had to manage, old humiliations and terrors rose up, lived again, and forced her to relive them. The children's needings; that grocer's face or this merchant's wife she had had to beg credit from when credit was a disgrace; the scenery of the long blocks walked around when she could not pay; school coming, and the desperate going over the old to see what could yet be remade; the soups of meat bones begged "for-the-dog" one winter. . . .

Enough. Now they had no children. Let *him* wrack his head for how they would live. She would not exchange her solitude for anything. *Never again to be forced to move to the rhythms of others.*

For in this solitude she had won to a reconciled peace.

Tranquillity from having the empty house no longer an enemy, for it stayed clean—not as in the days when it was her family, the life in it, that had seemed the enemy: tracking, smudging, littering, dirtying, engaging her in endless defeating battle—and on whom her endless defeat had been spewed.

The few old books, memorized from rereading; the pictures to ponder (the magnifying glass superimposed on her heavy eyeglasses). Or if she wishes, when he is gone, the phonograph, that if she turns up very loud and strains, she can hear: the ordered sounds and the struggling.

Out in the garden, growing things to nurture. Birds to be kept out of the pear tree, and when the pears are heavy and ripe, the old fury of work, for all must be canned, nothing wasted.

And her one social duty (for she will not go to luncheons or meetings) the boxes of old clothes left with her, as with a life-practised eye for finding what is still wearable within the worn (again the magnifying glass superimposed on the heavy glasses) she scans and sorts—this for rag or rummage, that for mending and cleaning, and this for sending away.

Being able at last to live within, and not move to the rhythms of others, as life had forced her to: denying; removing; isolating; taking the children one by one; then deafening, half-blinding—and at last, presenting her solitude.

And in it she had won to a reconciled peace.

Now he was violating it with his constant campaigning: *Sell the house and move to the Haven.* (You sit, you sit—there too you could sit like a stone.) He was making of her a battleground where old grievances tore. (Turn on your ear button—I am talking.) And stubbornly she resisted—so that from wheedling, reasoning manipulation, it was bitterness he now started with.

And it came to where every happening lashed up a quarrel.

"I will sell the house anyway," he flung at her one night. "I am putting it up for sale. There will be a way to make you sign."

The television blared, as always it did on the evenings he stayed home, and as always it reached her only as noise. She did not know if the tumult was in her or outside. Snap! she turned the sound off. "Shadows," she whispered to him, pointing to the screen, "look, it is only shadows." And in a scream: "Did you say that you will sell the house? Look at me, not at that. I am no shadow. You cannot sell without me."

"Leave on the television. I am watching."

"Like Paulie, like Jenny, a four-year-old. Staring at shadows. *You cannot sell the house.*"

"I will. We are going to the Haven. There you would not hear the television when you do not want it. I could sit in the social room and watch. You could lock yourself up to smell your unpleasantness in a room by yourself—for who would want to come near you?"

"No, no selling." A whisper now.

"The television is shadows. Mrs. Enlightened! Mrs. Cultured! A world comes into your house—and it is shadows. People you would never meet in a thousand lifetimes. Wonders. When you were four years old, yes, like Paulie, like Jenny, did you know of Indian dances, alligators, how they use bamboo in Malaya? No, you scratched in your dirt with the chickens and thought Olshana was the world. Yes, Mrs. Unpleasant, I will sell the house, for there better can we be rid of each other than here."

She did not know if the tumult was outside, or in her. Always a ravening inside, a pull to the bed, to lie down, to succumb.

"Have you thought maybe Ma should let a doctor have a look at her?" asked their son Paul after Sunday dinner, regarding his mother crumpled on the couch, instead of, as was her custom, busying herself in Nancy's kitchen.

"Why not the President too?"

"Seriously, Dad. This is the third Sunday she's lain down like that after dinner. Is she that way at home?"

"A regular love affair with the bed. Every time I start to talk to her."

Good protective reaction, observed Nancy to herself. The workings of hos-til-ity.

"Nancy could take her. I just don't like how she looks. Let's have Nancy arrange an appointment."

"You think she'll go?" regarding his wife gloomily. "All right, we have to have doctor bills, we have to have doctor bills." Loudly: "Something hurts you?"

She startled, looked to his lips. He repeated: "Mrs. Take It Easy, something hurts?"

"Nothing. . . . Only you."

"A woman of honey. That's why you're lying down?"

"Soon I'll get up to do the dishes, Nancy."

"Leave them, Mother, I like it better this way."

"Mrs. Take It Easy, Paul says you should start ballet. You should go to see a doctor and ask: how soon can you start ballet?"

"A doctor?" she begged. "Ballet?"

"We were talking, Ma," explained Paul, "you don't seem any too well. It would be a good idea for you to see a doctor for a checkup."

"I get up now to do the kitchen. Doctors are bills and foolishness, my son. I need no doctors."

"At the Haven," he could not resist pointing out, "a doctor is *not* bills. He lives beside you. You start to sneeze, he is there before you open up a Kleenex. You can be sick there for free, all you want."

"Diarrhea of the mouth, is there a doctor to make you dumb?"

"Ma. Promise me you'll go. Nancy will arrange it."

"It's all of a piece when you think of it," said Nancy, "the way she attacks my kitchen, scrubbing under every cup hook, doing the inside of the oven so I can't enjoy Sunday dinner, knowing that half-blind or not, she's going to find every speck of dirt. . . ."

"Don't, Nancy, I've told you—it's the only way she knows to be useful. What did the *doctor* say?"

"A real fatherly lecture. Sixty-nine is young these days. Go out, enjoy life, find interests. Get a new hearing aid, this one is antiquated. Old age is sickness only if one makes it so. Geriatrics, Inc."

"So there was nothing physical."

"Of course there was. How can you live to yourself like she does without there being? Evidence of a kidney disorder, and her blood count is low. He gave her a diet, and she's to come back for follow-up and lab work. . . . But he was clear enough: Number One prescription—start living like a human being. . . . When I think of your dad, who could really play the invalid with that arthritis of his, as active as a teenager, and twice as much fun. . . ."

"You didn't tell me the doctor says your sickness is in you, how you live." He pushed his advantage. "Life and enjoyments you need better than medicine. And this diet, how can you keep it? To weigh each morsel and scrape away each bit of fat, to make this soup, that pudding. There, at the Haven, they have a dietician, they would do it for you."

She is silent.

"You would feel better there, I know it," he says gently. "There there is life and enjoyments all around."

"What is the matter, Mr. Importantbusy, you have no card game or meeting you can go to?"—turning her face to the pillow.

For a while he cut his meetings and going out, fussed over her diet, tried to wheedle her into leaving the house, brought in visitors:

> "I should come to a fashion tea. I should sit and look at pretty babies in clothes I cannot buy. This is pleasure"
>
> "Always you are better than everyone else. The doctor said you should go out. Mrs. Brem comes to you with goodness and you turn her away."
>
> "Because *you* asked her to, she asked me."
>
> "They won't come back. People you need, the doctor said. Your own cousins I asked; they were willing to come and make peace as if nothing had happened. . . ."
>
> "No more crushers of people, pushers, hypocrites, around me. No more in *my* house. You go to them if you like."
>
> "Kind he is to visit. And you, like ice."
>
> "A babbler. All my life around babblers. Enough!"

"She's even worse, Dad? Then let her stew a while," advised Nancy. "You can't let it destroy you; it's a psychological thing, maybe too far gone for any of us to help."

So he let her stew. More and more she lay silent in bed, and sometimes did not even get up to make the meals. No longer was the tongue-lashing inevitable if he left the coffee cup where it did not belong, or forgot to take out the garbage or mislaid the broom. The birds grew bold that summer and for once pocked the pears, undisturbed.

A bellyful of bitterness and every day the same quarrel in a new way and a different old grievance the quarrel forced her to enter and relive. And the new torment: I am not really sick, the doctor said it, then why do I feel so sick?

One night she asked him: "You have a meeting tonight? Do not go. Stay . . . with me."

He had planned to watch "This Is Your Life," but half sick himself from the heavy heat, and sickening therefore the more after the brooks and woods of the Haven, with satisfaction he grated:

"Hah, Mrs. Live Alone And Like It wants company all of a sudden. It doesn't seem so good the time of solitary when she was a girl exile in Siberia. 'Do not go. Stay with me.' A new song for Mrs. Free As A Bird. Yes, I am going out, and while I am gone chew this aloneness good, and think how you keep us both from where if you want people, you do not need to be alone."

"Go, go. All your life you have gone without me."

After him she sobbed curses he had not heard in years, old-country curses from their childhood: Grow, oh shall you grow like an onion, with your head in the ground. Like the hide of a drum shall you be, beaten in life, beaten in death. Oh shall you be like a chandelier, to hang, and to burn. . . .

She was not in their bed when he came back. She lay on the cot on the sun porch. All week she did not speak or come near him; nor did he try to make peace or care for her.

He slept badly, so used to her next to him. After all the years, old harmonies and dependencies deep in their bodies; she curled to him, or he coiled to her, each warmed, warming, turning as the other turned, the nights a long embrace.

It was not the empty bed or the storm that woke him, but a faint singing. *She* was singing. Shaking off the drops of rain, the lightning riving her lifted face, he saw her so; the cot covers on the floor.

"This is a private concert?" he asked. "Come in, you are wet."

"I can breathe now," she answered; "my lungs are rich." Though indeed the sound was hardly a breath.

"Come in, come in." Loosing the bamboo shades. "Look how wet you are." Half helping, half carrying her, still faint-breathing her song.

A Russian love song of fifty years ago.

He had found a buyer, but before he told her, he called together those children who were close enough to come. Paul, of course, Sammy from New Jersey, Hannah from Connecticut, Vivi from Ohio.

With a kindling of energy for her beloved visitors, she arrayed the house, cooked and baked. She was not prepared for the solemn after-dinner conclave, they too probing in and tearing. Her frightened eyes watched from mouth to mouth as each spoke.

His stories were eloquent and funny of her refusal to go back to the doctor; of the scorned invitations; of her stubborn silence or the bile "like a Niagara"; of her contrariness: "If I clean it's no good how I cleaned; if I don't clean, I'm still a master who thinks he has a slave."

(Vinegar he poured on me all his life; I am well marinated; how can I be honey now?)

Deftly he marched in the rightness for moving to the Haven; their money from social security free for visiting the children, not sucked into daily needs and into the house; the activities in the Haven for him; but mostly the Haven for *her:* her health, her need of care, distraction, amusement, friends who shared her interests.

"This does offer an outlet for Dad," said Paul; "he's always been an active person. And economic peace of mind isn't to be sneezed at, either. I could use a little of that myself."

But when they asked: "And you, Ma, how do you feel about it?" could only whisper:

"For him it is good. It is not for me. I can no longer live between people."

"You lived all your life *for* people," Vivi cried.

"Not with." Suffering doubly for the unhappiness on her children's faces.

"You have to find some compromise," Sammy insisted. "Maybe sell the house and buy a trailer. After forty-seven years there's surely some way you can find to live in peace."

"There is no help, my children. Different things we need."

"Then live alone!" He could control himself no longer. "I have a buyer for the house. Half the money for you, half for me. Either alone or with me to the Haven. You think I can live any longer as we are doing now?"

"Ma doesn't have to make a decision this minute, however you feel, Dad," Paul said quickly, "and you wouldn't want her to. Let's let it lay a few months, and then talk some more."

"I think I can work it out to take Mother home with me for a while," Hannah said. "You both look terrible, but especially you, Mother. I'm going to ask Phil to have a look at you."

"Sure," cracked Sammy. "What's the use of a doctor husband if you can't get free service out of him once in a while for the family? And absence might make the heart . . . you know."

"There was something after all," Paul told Nancy in a colorless voice. "That was Hannah's Phil calling. Her gall bladder. . . . Surgery."

"Her *gall* bladder. If that isn't classic. 'Bitter as gall'—talk of psychosom——"

He stepped closer, put his hand over her mouth, and said in the same colorless, plodding voice, "We have to get Dad. They operated at once. The cancer was everywhere, surrounding the liver, everywhere. They did what they could . . . at best she has a year. Dad . . . we have to tell him."

2

Honest in his weakness when they told him, and that she was not to know. "I'm not an actor. She'll know right away by how I am. Oh that poor woman. I am old too, it will break me into pieces. Oh that poor woman. She will spit on me: 'So my sickness was how I live.' Oh Paulie, how she will be, that poor woman. Only she should not suffer. . . . I can't stand sickness, Paulie, I can't go with you."

But went. And play-acted.

"A grand opening and you did not even wait for me. . . . A good thing Hannah took you with her."

"Fashion teas I needed. They cut out what tore in me; just in my throat something hurts yet. . . . Look! so many flowers, like a funeral. Vivi called, did Hannah tell you? And Lennie from San Francisco, and Clara; and Sammy is coming." Her gnome's face pressed happily into the flowers.

> It is impossible to predict in these cases, but once over the immediate effects of the operation, she should have several months of comparative well-being.
>
> *The money, where will come the money?*
>
> Travel with her, Dad. Don't take her home to the old associations. The other children will want to see her.
>
> *The money, where will I wring the money?*
>
> Whatever happens, she is not to know. No, you can't ask her to sign papers to sell the house; nothing to upset her. Borrow instead, then after. . . .
>
> *I had wanted to leave you each a few dollars to make life easier, as other fathers do. There will be nothing left now. (Failure! you and your "business is exploitation." Why didn't you make it when it could be made?—Is that what you're thinking, Sammy?)*
>
> Sure she's unreasonable, Dad—but you have to stay with her; if there's to be any happiness in what's left of her life, it depends on you.
>
> *Prop me up, children, think of me, too. Shuffled, chained with her, bitter woman. No Haven, and the little money going. . . . How happy she looks, poor creature.*

The look of excitement. The straining to hear everything (the new hearing aid turned full). Why are you so happy, dying woman?

How the petals are, fold on fold, and the gladioli color. The autumn air. —

Stranger grandsons, tall above the little gnome grandmother, the little spry grandfather. Paul in a frenzy of picture-taking before going.

She, wandering the great house. Feeling the books; laughing at the maple shoemaker's bench of a hundred years ago used as a table. The ear turned to music.

"Let us go home. See how good I walk now." "One step from the hospital," he answers, "and she wants to fly. Wait till Doctor Phil says."

"Look—the birds too are flying home. Very good Phil is and will not show it, but he is sick of sickness by the time he comes home."

"Mrs. Telepathy, to read minds," he answers; "read mine what it says: when the trunks of medicines become a suitcase, then we will go."

The grandboys, they do not know what to say to us. . . . Hannah, she runs around here, there, when is there time for herself?

Let us go home. Let us go home.

Musing; gentleness—*but for the incidents of the rabbi in the hospital, and of the candles of benediction.*

Of the rabbi in the hospital:

Now tell me what happened, Mother.

From the sleep I awoke, Hannah's Phil, and he stands there like a devil in a dream and calls me by name. I cannot hear. I think he prays. Go away, please, I tell him, I am not a believer. Still he stands, while my heart knocks with fright.

You scared *him*, Mother. He thought you were delirious.

Who sent him? Why did he come to me?

It is a custom. The men of God come to visit those of their religion they might help. The hospital makes up the list for them—race, religion —and you are on the Jewish list.

Not for rabbis. At once go and make them change. Tell them to write: Race, human: Religion, none.

And of the candles of benediction:

Look how you have upset yourself, Mrs. Excited Over Nothing. Pleasant memories you should leave.

Go in, go back to Hannah and the lights. Two weeks I saw candles and said nothing. But she asked me.

So what was so terrible? She forgets you never did, she asks you to light the Friday candles and say the benediction like Phil's mother when she visits. If the candles give her pleasure, why shouldn't she have the pleasure?

Not for pleasure she does it. For emptiness. Because his family does. Because all around her do.

That is not a good reason too? But you did not hear her. For heritage, she told you. For the boys, from the past they should have tradition.

Superstition! From our ancestors, savages, afraid of the dark, of themselves: mumbo words and magic lights to scare away ghosts.

She told you: how it started does not take away the goodness. For centuries, peace in the house it means.

Swindler! does she look back on the dark centuries? Candles bought instead of bread and stuck into a potato for a candlestick? Religion that stifled and said: in Paradise, woman, you will be the footstool of your husband, and in life—poor chosen Jew—ground under, despised, trembling in cellars. And cremated. And cremated.

This is religion's fault? You think you are still an orator of the 1905 revolution? Where are the pills for quieting? Which are they?

Heritage. How have we come from our savage past, how no longer to be savages—this to teach. To look back and learn what humanizes—this to teach. To smash all ghettos that divide us—not to go back, not to go back—this to teach. Learned books in the house, will humankind live or die, and she gives to her boys—superstition.

Hannah that is so good to you. Take your pill, Mrs. Excited For Nothing, swallow.

Heritage! But when did I have time to teach? Of Hannah I asked only hands to help.

Swallow.

Otherwise—musing; gentleness.

Not to travel. To go home.

The children want to see you. We have to show them you are as thorny a flower as ever.

Not to travel.

Vivi wants you should see her new baby. She sent the tickets—airplane tickets—a Mrs. Roosevelt she wants to make of you. To Vivi's we have to go.

A new baby. How many warm, seductive babies. She holds him stiffly, *away* from her, so that he wails. And a long shudder begins, and the sweat beads on her forehead.

"Hush, shush," croons the grandfather, lifting him back. "You should forgive your grandmamma, little prince, she has never held a baby before, only seen them in glass cases. Hush, shush."

"You're tired, Ma," says Vivi. "The travel and the noisy dinner. I'll take you to lie down."

(A long travel from, to, what the feel of a baby evokes.)

In the airplane, cunningly designed to encase from motion (no wind, no feel of flight), she had sat severely and still, her face turned to the sky through which they cleaved and left no scar.

So this was how it looked, the determining, the crucial sky, and this was how man moved through it, remote above the dwindled earth, the concealed human life. Vulnerable life, that could scar.

There was a steerage ship of memory that shook across a great, circular sea: clustered, ill human beings: and through the thick-stained air, tiny fretting waters in a window round like the airplane's—sun round, moon round. (The round thatched roofs of Olshana.) Eye round—like the smaller window that framed distance the solitary year of exile when only her eyes could travel, and no voice spoke. And the polar winds hurled themselves across snows trackless and endless and white—like the clouds which had closed together below and hidden the earth.

Now they put a baby in her lap. Do not ask me, she would have liked to beg. Enough the worn face of Vivi, the remembered grandchildren. I cannot, cannot. . . .

Cannot, what? Unnatural grandmother, not able to make herself embrace a baby.

She lay there in the bed of the two little girls, her new hearing aid turned full, listening to the sound of the children going to sleep, the baby's fretful crying and hushing, the clatter of dishes being washed and put away. They thought she slept. Still she rode on.

It was not that she had not loved her babies, her children. The love—the passion of tending—had risen with the need like a torrent; and like a torrent drowned and immolated all else. But when the need was done—oh the power that was lost in the painful damming back and drying up of what still surged, but had nowhere to go. Only the thin pulsing left that could not quiet, suffering over lives one felt, but could no longer hold nor help.

On that torrent she had borne them to their own lives, and the riverbed was desert long years now. Not there would she dwell, a memoried wraith. Surely that was not all, surely there was more. Still the springs, the springs were in her seeking. Somewhere an older power that beat for life. Somewhere coherence, transport, meaning. If they would but leave her in the air now stilled of clamor, in the reconciled solitude, to journey on.

And they put a baby in her lap. Immediacy to embrace, and the breath of *that* past: warm flesh like this that had claims and nuzzled away all else and with lovely mouths devoured; hot-living like an animal—intensely and now; the turning maze; the long drunkenness; the drowning into needing and being needed. Severely she looked back—and the shudder seized her again, and the sweat. Not that way. Not there, not now could she, not yet. . . .

And all that visit, she could not touch the baby.

"Daddy, is it the . . . sickness she's like that?" asked Vivi. "I was so glad to be having the baby—for her. I told Tim, it'll give her more happiness than anything, being around a baby again. And she hasn't played with him once."

He was not listening. "Aahh little seed of life, little charmer," he crooned, "Hollywood should see you. A heart of ice you would melt. Kick, kick. The future you'll have for a ball. In 2050 still kick. Kick for your grandaddy then."

Attentive with the older children; sat through their performances (command performance; we command you to be the audience); helped Ann sort autumn leaves to find the best for a school program; listened gravely to Richard tell about his rock collection, while her lips mutely formed the words to remember: *igneous, sedimentary, metamorphic;* looked for missing socks, books, and bus tickets; watched the children whoop after their grandfather who knew how to tickle, chuck, lift, toss, do tricks, tell secrets, make jokes, match riddle for riddle. (Tell me a riddle, Grammy. I know no riddles, child.) Scrubbed sills and woodwork and furniture in every room; folded the laundry; straightened drawers: emptied the heaped baskets waiting for ironing (while he or Vivi or Tim nagged: You're supposed to rest here, you've been sick) but to none tended or gave food—and could not touch the baby.

After a week she said: "Let us go home. Today call about the tickets."

"You have important business, Mrs. Inahurry? The President waits to consult with you?" He shouted, for the fear of the future raced in him. "The clothes are still warm from the suitcase, your children cannot show enough how glad they are to see you, and you want home. There is plenty of time for home. We cannot be with the children at home."

"Blind to around you as always: the little ones sleep four in a room because we take their bed. We are two more people in a house with a new baby, and no help."

"Vivi is happy so. The children should have their grandparents a while, she told to me. I should have my mommy and daddy. . . ."

"Babbler and blind. Do you look at her so tired? How she starts to talk and she cries? I am not strong enough yet to help. Let us go home."

(To reconciled solitude.)

For it seemed to her the crowded noisy house was listening to her, listening for *her. She could feel it like a great ear pressed under her heart. And everything knocked: quick constant raps: let me in, let me in.*

How was it that soft reaching tendrils also became blows that knocked?

C'mon, Grandma, I want to show you. . . .

Tell me a riddle, Grandma. *(I know no riddles.)*

Look, Grammy, he's so dumb he can't even find his hands. (Dody and the baby on a blanket over the fermenting autumn mould.)

I made them—for you (Ann) (Flat paper dolls with aprons that lifted on scalloped skirts that lifted on flowered pants; hair of yarn and great ringed questioning eyes.)

Watch me, Grandma. (Richard snaking up the tree, hanging exultant, free, with one hand at the top. Below Dody hunching over in pretend-cooking.) *(Climb too, Dody, climb and look.)*

Be my nap bed, Grammy. (The "No!" too late.) Morty's abandoned heaviness, while his fingers ladder up and down her hearing-aid cord to his drowsy chant: eentsiebeentsiespider. *(Children trust.)*

It's to start off your own rock collection, Grandma. That's a trilobite fossil, 200 million years old (millions of years on a boy's mouth) and that one's obsidian, black glass.

Knocked and knocked.

Mother, I *told* you the teacher said we had to bring it back all filled out this morning. Didn't you even ask Daddy? Then tell *me* which plan and I'll check it: evacuate or stay in the city or wait for you to come and take me away. (Seeing the look of straining to hear.) It's for Disaster, Grandma. *(Children trust.)*

Vivi in the maze of the long, the lovely drunkenness. The old old noises: baby sounds; screaming of a mother flayed to exasperation; children quarreling; children playing; singing; laughter.

And Vivi's tears and memories, spilling so fast, half the words not understood.

She had started remembering out loud deliberately, so her mother would know the past was cherished, still lived in her.

Nursing the baby: My friends marvel, and I tell them, oh it's easy to be such a cow. I remember how beautiful my mother seemed nursing my brother, and the milk just flows. . . . Was that Davy? It must have been Davy. . . .

Lowering a hem: How did you ever . . . when I think how you made everything we wore . . . Tim, just think, seven kids and Mommy sewed everything . . . do I remember you sang while you sewed? That white dress with the red apples on the skirt you fixed over for me, was it Hannah's or Clara's before it was mine?

Washing sweaters: Ma, I'll never forget, one of those days so nice you washed clothes outside; one of the first spring days it must have been. The bubbles just danced while you scrubbed, and we chased after, and you stopped to show us how to blow our own bubbles with green onion stalks . . . you always. . . .

"Strong onion, to still make you cry after so many years," her father said, to turn the tears into laughter.

While Richard bent over his homework: Where is it now, do we still have it, the Book of the Martyrs? It always seemed so, well—exalted, when you'd put it on the round table and we'd all look at it together; there was even a halo from the lamp. The lamp with the beaded fringe you could move up and down; they're in style again, pulley lamps like that, but without the fringe. You know the book I'm talking about, Daddy, the Book of the Martyrs, the first picture was a bust of Spartacus? Socrates? I wish there was something like that for the children, Mommy, to give them what you. . . . (And the tears splashed again.)

(What I intended and did not? Stop it, daughter, stop it, leave that time. And he, the hyprocrite, sitting there with tears in his eyes—it was nothing to you then, nothing.)

. . . The time you came to school and I almost died of shame because of your accent and because I knew you knew I was ashamed; how could I? . . . Sammy's harmonica and you danced to it once, yes you did, you and Davy squealing in your arms. . . . That time you bundled us up and walked us down to the railway station to stay the night 'cause it was heated and we didn't have any coal, that winter of the strike, you didn't think I remembered that, did you, Mommy? . . . How you'd call us out to see the sunsets. . . .

Day after day, the spilling memories. Worse now, questions, too. Even the grandchildren: Grandma, in the olden days, when you were little. . . .

It was the afternoons that saved.

While they thought she napped, she would leave the mosaic on the wall (of children's drawings, maps, calendars, pictures, Ann's cardboard dolls with their great ringed questioning eyes) and hunch in the girls' cupboard, on the low shelf where the shoes stood, and the girls' dresses covered.

For that while she would painfully sheathe against the listening house, the tendrils and noises that knocked, and Vivi's spilling memories. Sometimes it helped to braid and unbraid the sashes that dangled, or to trace the pattern on the hoop slips.

Today she had jacks and children under jet trails to forget. Last night, Ann and Dody silhouetted in the window against a sunset of flaming man-made clouds of jet trail, their jacks ball accenting the peaceful noise of dinner being made. Had she told them, yes she had told them of how they played jacks in her village though there was no ball, no jacks. Six stones, round and flat, toss them out, the seventh on the back of the hand, toss, catch and swoop up as many as possible, toss again. . . .

Of stones (repeating Richard) there are three kinds: earth's fire jetting; rock of layered centuries; crucibled new out of the old (*igneous, sedimentary, metamorphic*). But there was that other—frozen to black glass, never to transform or hold the fossil memory . . . (let not my seed fall on stone). There was an ancient man who fought to heights a great rock that crashed back down eternally—eternal labor, freedom, labor . . . (stone will perish, but the word remain). And you, David, who with a stone slew, screaming: Lord, take my heart of stone and give me flesh.

Who was screaming? Why was she back in the common room of the prison, the sun motes dancing in the shafts of light, and the informer being brought in, a prisoner now, like themselves. And Lisa leaping, yes, Lisa, the gentle and tender, biting at the betrayer's jugular. Screaming and screaming.

No, it is the children screaming. Another of Paul and Sammy's terrible fights?

In Vivi's house. Severely: you are in Vivi's house.

Blows, screams, a call: "Grandma!" For her? Oh please not for her. Hide, hunch behind the dresses deeper. But a trembling little body hurls itself beside her—surprised, smothered laughter, arms surround her neck, tears rub dry on her cheek, and words too soft to understand whisper into her ear (Is this where you hide too, Grammy? It's my secret place, we have a secret now).

And the sweat beads, and the long shudder seizes.

It seemed the great ear pressed inside now, and the knocking. "We have to go home," she told him, "I grow ill here."

"It's your own fault, Mrs. Bodybusy, you do not rest, you do too much." He raged, but the fear was in his eyes. "It was a serious operation, they told you to take care. . . . All right, we will go to where you can rest."

But where? Not home to death, not yet. He had thought to Lennie's, to Clara's; beautiful visits with each of the children. She would have to rest first, be stronger. If they could but go to Florida—it glittered before him, the never-realized promise of Florida, California: of course. (The money, the money, dwindling!) Los Angeles first for sun and rest, then to Lennie's in San Francisco.

He told her the next day. "You saw what Nancy wrote: snow and wind back home, a terrible winter. And look at you—all bones and a swollen belly. I called Phil: he said: 'A prescription, Los Angeles sun and rest.' "

She watched the words on his lips. "You have sold the house," she cried, "that is why we do not go home. That is why you talk no more of the Haven, why there is money for travel. After the children you will drag me to the Haven."

"The Haven! Who thinks of the Haven any more? Tell her, Vivi, tell Mrs. Suspicious: a prescription, sun and rest, to make you healthy. . . . And how could I sell the house without *you?*"

At the place of farewells and greetings, of winds of coming and winds of going, they say their good-byes.

They look back at her with the eyes of others before them: Richard with her own blue blaze; Ann with the nordic eyes of Tim; Morty's dreaming brown of a great-grandmother he will never know; Dody with the laughing eyes of him who had been her springtide love (who stands beside her now); Vivi's, all tears.

The baby's eyes are closed in sleep.

Good-bye, my children.

3

It is to the back of the great city he brought her, to the dwelling places of the cast-off old. Bounded by two lines of amusement piers to the north and to the south, and between a long straight paving rimmed with black benches facing the sand—sands so wide the ocean is only a far fluting.

In the brief vacation season, some of the boarded stores fronting the sands open, and families, young people and children, may be seen. A little tasselled tram shuttles between the piers, and the lights of roller coasters prink and tweak over those who come to have sensation made in them.

The rest of the year it is abandoned to the old, all else boarded up and still; seemingly empty, except the occasional days and hours when the sun, like a tide, sucks them out of the low rooming houses, casts them onto the benches and sandy rim of the walk—and sweeps them into decaying enclosures once again.

A few newer apartments glint among the low bleached squares. It is in one of these Lennie's Jeannie has arranged their rooms. "Only a few miles north and south people pay hundreds of dollars a month for just this gorgeous air, Grandaddy, just this ocean closeness."

She had been ill on the plane, lay ill for days in the unfamiliar room. Several times the doctor came by—left medicine she would not take. Several times Jeannie drove in the twenty miles from work, still in her Visiting Nurse uniform, the lightness and brightness of her like a healing.

"Who can believe it is winter?" he asked one morning. "Beautiful it is outside like an ad. Come, Mrs. Invalid, come to taste it. You are well enough to sit in here, you are well enough to sit outside. The doctor said it too."

But the benches were encrusted with people, and the sands at the sidewalk's edge. Besides, she had seen the far ruffle of the sea: "there take me," and though she leaned against him, it was she who led.

Plodding and plodding, sitting often to rest, he grumbling. Patting the sand so warm. Once she scooped up a handful, cradling it close to her better eye; peered, and flung it back. And as they came almost to the brink and she could see the glistening wet, she sat down, pulled off her shoes and stockings, left him and began to run. "You'll catch cold," he screamed, but the sand in his shoes weighed him down—he who had always been the agile one—and already the white spray creamed her feet.

He pulled her back, took a handkerchief to wipe off the wet and the sand. "Oh no," she said, "the sun will dry," seized the square and smoothed it flat, dropped on it a mound of sand, knotted the kerchief corners and tied it to a bag—"to look at with the strong glass" (for the first time in years explaining an action of hers)—and lay down with the bag against her cheek, looking toward the shore that nurtured life as it first crawled toward consciousness the millions of years ago.

He took her one Sunday in the evil-smelling bus, past flat miles of blister houses, to the home of relatives. Oh what is this? she cried as the light began to smoke and the houses to dim and recede. Smog, he said, everyone knows but you. . . . Outside he kept his arms about her, but she walked with hands pushing the heavy air as if to open it, whispered: who has done this? sat down suddenly to vomit at the curb and for a long while refused to rise.

One's age as seen on the altered face of those known in youth. Is this they he has come to visit? This Max and Rose, smooth and pleasant, introducing them to polite children, disinterested grandchildren, "the whole family, once a month on Sundays. And why not? We have the room, the help, the food."

Talk of cars, of houses, of success: this son that, that daughter this. And *your* children? Hastily skimped over, the intermarriages, the obscure work—"my doctor son-in-law, Phil"—all he has to offer. She silent in a corner. (Carsick like a baby, he explains.) Years since he has taken her to visit anyone but the children, and old apprehensions prickle: "no incidents," he silently begs, "no incidents." He itched to tell them. "A very sick woman," significantly, indicating her with his eyes, "a very sick woman." Their restricted faces did not react. "Have you thought maybe she'd do better at Palm Springs?" Rose asked. "Or at least a nicer section of the beach, nicer people, a pool." Not to have to say "money" he said instead: "would she have sand to look at through a magnifying glass?" and went on, detail after detail, the old habit betraying of parading the queerness of her for laughter.

After dinner—the others into the living room in men- or women-clusters, or into the den to watch TV—the four of them alone. She sat close to him, and did not speak. Jokes, stories, people they had known, beginning of reminiscence, Russia fifty-sixty years ago. Strange words across the Duncan Phyfe table: *hunger; secret meetings; human rights; spies; betrayals; prison; escape*—interrupted by one of the grandchildren: "Commercial's on; any Coke left? Gee, you're missing a real hair-raiser." And then a granddaughter (Max proudly: "look at her, an American queen") drove them home on her way back to U.C.L.A. No incident—except that there had been no incidents.

The first few mornings she had taken with her the magnifying glass, but he would sit only on the benches, so she rested at the foot, where slatted bench shadows fell, and unless she turned her hearing aid down, other voices invaded.

Now on the days when the sun shone and she felt well enough, he took her on the tram to where the benches ranged in oblongs, some with tables for checkers or cards. Again the blanket on the sand in the striped shadows, but she no longer brought the magnifying glass. He played cards, and she lay in the sun and looked towards the waters; or they walked—two blocks down to the scaling hotel, two blocks back—past chili-hamburger stands, open-doored bars, next-to-new and perpetual rummage sale stores.

Once, out of the aimless walkers, slow and shuffling like themselves, someone ran unevenly towards them, embraced, kissed, wept: "dear friends, old friends." A friend of *hers*, not his: Mrs. Mays who had lived next door to them in Denver when the children were small.

Thirty years are compressed into a dozen sentences; and the present, not even in three. All is told: the children scattered; the husband dead; she lives in a room two blocks up from the sing hall—and points to the domed auditorium jutting before the pier. The leg? phlebitis; the heavy breathing? that, one does not ask. She, too, comes to the benches each day to sit. And tomorrow, tomorrow, are they going to the community sing? Of course he would have heard of it, everybody goes—the big doings they wait for all week. They have never been? She will come to them for dinner tomorrow and they will all go together.

So it is that she sits in the wind of the singing, among the thousand various faces of age.

She had turned off her hearing aid at once they came into the auditorium—as she would have wished to turn off sight.

One by one they streamed by and imprinted on her—and though the savage zest of their singing came voicelessly soft and distant, the faces still roared—the faces densened the air—chorded into

children-chants, mother-croons, singing of the chained
love serenades, Beethoven storms, mad Lucia's scream
drunken joy-songs, keens for the dead, work-singing

> *while from floor to balcony to dome a bare-footed sore-covered little girl threaded the sound-thronged tumult, danced her ecstasy of grimace to flutes that scratched at a cross-roads village wedding*

Yes, faces became sound, and the sound became faces; and faces and sound became weight—pushed, pressed

"Air"—her hands claw his.

"Whenever I enjoy myself. . . ." Then he saw the gray sweat on her face. "Here. Up. Help me, Mrs. Mays," and they support her out to where she can gulp the air in sob after sob.

"A doctor, we should get for her a doctor."

"Tch, it's nothing," says Ellen Mays, "I get it all the time. You've missed the tram; come to my place. Fix your hearing aid, honey . . . close . . . tea. My view. See, she *wants* to come. Steady now, that's how." Adding mysteriously: "Remember your advice, easy to keep your head above water, empty things float. Float."

The singing a fading march for them, tall woman with a swollen leg, weaving little man, and the swollen thinness they help between.

The stench in the hall: mildew? decay? "We sit and rest then climb. My gorgeous view. We help each other and here we are."

The stench along into the slab of room. A washstand for a sink, a box with oilcloth tacked around for a cupboard, a three-burner gas plate. Artificial flowers, colorless with dust. Everywhere pictures foaming: wedding, baby, party, vacation, graduation, family pictures. From the narrow couch under a slit of window, sure enough the view: lurching rooftops and a scallop of ocean heaving, preening, twitching under the moon.

"While the water heats. Excuse me . . . down the hall." Ellen Mays has gone.

"You'll live?" he asks mechanically, sat down to feel his fright; tried to pull her alongside.

She pushed him away. "For air," she said; stood clinging to the dresser. Then, in a terrible voice:

After a lifetime of room. Of many rooms.

Shhh.

You remember how she lived. Eight children. And now one room like a coffin.

She pays rent!

Shrinking the life of her into one room like a coffin Rooms and rooms like this I lie on the quilt and hear them talk

Please, Mrs. Orator-without-Breath.

Once you went for coffee   I walked   I saw   A Balzac   a Chekhov to write it   Rummage   Alone   On scraps

Better old here than in the old country!

On scraps   Yet they sang like   like   Wondrous!   *Humankind one has to believe*   So strong   for what?   To rot   not grow?

Your poor lungs beg you. They sob between each word.

Singing.   Unused   the life in them.   She   in this poor room   with her pictures   Max   You   The children   Everywhere   unused the life   And who has meaning?   Century after century   still all in us   not   to grow?

Coffins, rummage, plants: sick woman. Oh lay down. We will get for you the doctor.

"And when will it end. Oh, *the end.*" *That* nightmare thought, and this time she writhed, crumpled against him, seized his hand (for a moment again the weight, the soft distant roaring of humanity) and on the strangled-for breath, begged: "Man . . . we'll destroy ourselves?"

And looking for answer—in the helpless pity and fear for her (for *her*) that distorted his face—she understood the last months, and knew that she was dying.

4

"Let us go home," she said after several days.

"You are in training for a cross-country run? That is why you do not even walk across the room? Here, like a prescription Phil said, till you are stronger from the operation. You want to break doctor's orders?"

She saw the fiction was necessary to him, was silent; then: "At home I will get better. If the doctor here says?"

"And winter? And the visits to Lennie and to Clara? All right," for he saw the tears in her eyes, "I will write Phil, and talk to the doctor."

Days passed. He reported nothing. Jeannie came and took her out for air, past the boarded concessions, the hooded and tented amusement rides, to the end of the pier. They watched the spent waves feeding the new, the gulls in the clouded sky; even up where they sat, the wind-blown sand stung.

She did not ask to go down the crooked steps to the sea.

Back in her bed, while he was gone to the store, she said: "Jeannie, this doctor, he is not one I can ask questions. Ask him for me, can I go home?"

Jeannie looked at her, said quickly: "Of course, poor Granny. You want your own things around you, don't you? I'll call him tonight. . . . Look, I've something to show you," and from her purse unwrapped a large cookie, intricately shaped like a little girl. "Look at the curls—can you hear me well, Granny?—and the darling eyelashes. I just came from a house where they were baking them."

"The dimples, there in the knees," she marveled, holding it to the better light, turning, studying, "like art. Each singly they cut, or a mold?"

"Singly," said Jeannie, "and if it is a child only the mother can make them. Oh Granny, it's the likeness of a real little girl who died yesterday—Rosita. She was three years old. *Pan del Muerto,* the Bread of the Dead. It was the custom in the part of Mexico they came from."

Still she turned and inspected. "Look, the hollow in the throat, the little cross necklace. . . . I think for the mother it is a good thing to be busy with such bread. You know the family?"

Jeannie nodded. "On my rounds. I nursed. . . . Oh Granny, it is like a party; they play songs she liked to dance to. The coffin is lined with pink velvet and she wears a white dress. There are candles. . . ."

"In the house?" Surprised, "They keep her in the house?"

"Yes," said Jeannie, "and it is against the health law. I think she is . . . prepared there. The father said it will be sad to bury her in this country; in Oaxaca they have a feast night with candles each year; everyone picnics on the graves of those they loved until dawn."

"Yes, Jeannie, the living must comfort themselves." And closed her eyes.

"You want to sleep, Granny?"

"Yes, tired from the pleasure of you. I may keep the Rosita? There stand it, on the dresser, where I can see; something of my own around me."

In the kitchenette, helping her grandfather unpack the groceries, Jeannie said in her light voice:

"I'm resigning my job, Grandaddy."

"Ah, the lucky young man. Which one is he?"

"Too late. You're spoken for." She made a pyramid of cans, unstacked, and built again.

"Something is wrong with the job?"

"With me. I can't be"—she searched for the word—"what they call professional enough. I let myself feel things. And tomorrow I have to report a family. . . ." The cans clicked again. "It's not that, either. I just don't know what I want to do, maybe go back to school, maybe go to art school. I thought if you went to San Francisco I'd come along and talk it over with Momma and Daddy. But I don't see how you can go. She wants to go home. She asked me to ask the doctor."

The doctor told her himself. "Next week you may travel, when you are a little stronger." But next week there was the fever of an infection, and by the time that was over, she could not leave the bed—a rented hospital bed that stood beside the double bed he slept in alone now.

Outwardly the days repeated themselves. Every other afternoon and evening he went out to his newfound cronies, to talk and play cards. Twice a week, Mrs. Mays came. And the rest of the time, Jeannie was there.

By the sickbed stood Jeannie's FM radio. Often into the room the shapes of music came. She would lie curled on her side, her knees drawn up, intense in listening (Jeannie sketched her so, coiled, convoluted like an ear), then thresh her hand out and abruptly snap the radio mute—still to lie in her attitude of listening, concealing tears.

Once Jeannie brought in a young Marine to visit, a friend from high-school days she had found wandering near the empty pier. Because Jeannie asked him to, gravely, without self-consciousness, he sat himself cross-legged on the floor and performed for them a dance of his native Samoa.

Long after they left, a tiny thrumming sound could be heard where, in her bed, she strove to repeat the beckon, flight, surrender of his hands, the fluttering footbeats, and his low plaintive calls.

Hannah and Phil sent flowers. To deepen her pleasure, he placed one in her hair. "Like a girl," he said, and brought the hand mirror so she could see. She looked at the pulsing red flower, the yellow skull face; a desolate, excited laugh shuddered from her, and she pushed the mirror away—but let the flower burn.

The week Lennie and Helen came, the fever returned. With it the excited laugh, and incessant words. She, who in her life had spoken but seldom and then only when necessary (never having learned the easy, social uses of words), now in dying, spoke incessantly.

In a half-whisper: "Like Lisa she is, your Jeannie. Have I told you of Lisa who taught me to read? Of the highborn she was, but noble in herself. I was sixteen; they beat me; my father beat me so I would not go to her. It was forbidden, she was a Tolstoyan. At night, past dogs that howled, terrible dogs, my son, in the snows of winter to the road, I to ride in her carriage like a lady, to books. To her, life was holy, knowledge was holy, and she taught me to read. They hung her. Everything that happens one must try to understand why. She killed one who betrayed many. Because of betrayal, betrayed all she lived and believed. In one minute she killed, before my eyes (there is so much blood in a human being, my son), in prison with me. All that happens, one must try to understand.

"The name?" Her lips would work. "The name that was their pole star; the doors of the death houses fixed to open on it; I read of it my year of penal servitude. Thuban!" very excited, "Thuban, in ancient Egypt the pole star. Can you see, look out to see it, Jeannie, if it swings around *our* pole star that seems to *us* not to move.

"Yes, Jeannie, at your age my mother and grandmother had already buried children . . . yes, Jeannie, it is more than oceans between Olshana and you . . .

yes, Jeannie, they danced, and for all the bodies they had they might as well be chickens, and indeed, they scratched and flapped their arms and hopped.

"And Andrei Yefimitch, who for twenty years had never known of it and never wanted to know, said as if he wanted to cry: but why my dear friend this malicious laughter?" Telling to herself half-memorized phrases from her few books. "Pain I answer with tears and cries, baseness with indignation, meanness with repulsion . . . for life may be hated or wearied of, but never despised."

Delirious: "Tell me, my neighbor, Mrs. Mays, the pictures never lived, but what of the flowers? Tell them who ask: no rabbis, no ministers, no priests, no speeches, no ceremonies: ah, false—let the living comfort themselves. Tell Sammy's boy, he who flies, tell him to go to Stuttgart and see where Davy has no grave. And what? . . . And what? where millions have no graves—save air."

In delirium or not, wanting the radio on; not seeming to listen, the words still jetting, wanting the music on. Once, silencing it abruptly as of old, she began to cry, unconcealed tears this time. "You have pain, Granny?" Jeannie asked.

"The music," she said, "still it is there and we do not hear; knocks, and our poor human ears too weak. What else, what else we do not hear?"

Once she knocked his hand aside as he gave her a pill, swept the bottles from her bedside table: "no pills, let me feel what I feel," and laughed as on his hands and knees he groped to pick them up.

Nighttimes her hand reached across the bed to hold his.

A constant retching began. Her breath was too faint for sustained speech now, but still the lips moved:

When no longer necessary to injure others
Pick pick pick Blind chicken
As a human being responsibility

"David!" imperious, "Basin!" and she would vomit, rinse her mouth, the wasted throat working to swallow, and begin the chant again.

She will be better off in the hospital now, the doctor said.

He sent the telegrams to the children, was packing her suitcase, when her hoarse voice startled. She had roused, was pulling herself to sitting.

"Where now?" she asked. "Where now do you drag me?"

"You do not even have to have a baby to go this time," he soothed, looking for the brush to pack. "Remember, after Davy you told me—worthy to have a baby for the pleasure of the hospital?"

"Where now? Not home yet?" Her voice mourned. "Where *is* my home?"

He rose to ease her back. "The doctor, the hospital," he started to explain, but deftly, like a snake, she had slithered out of bed and stood swaying, propped behind the night table.

"Coward," she hissed, "runner."

"You stand," he said senselessly.

"To take me there and run. Afraid of a little vomit."

He reached her as she fell. She struggled against him, half slipped from his arms, pulled herself up again.

"Weakling," she taunted, "to leave me there and run. Betrayer. All your life you have run."

He sobbed, telling Jeannie. "A Marilyn Monroe to run for her virtue. Fifty-nine pounds she weighs, the doctor said, and she beats at me like a Dempsey. Betrayer, she cries, and I running like a dog when she calls; day and night, running to her, her vomit, the bed pan . . ."

"She needs you, Grandaddy," said Jeannie. "Isn't that what they call love? I'll see if she sleeps, and if she does, poor worn-out darling, we'll have a party, you and I: I brought us rum babas."

They did not move her. By her bed now stood the tall hooked pillar that held the solutions—blood and dextrose—to feed her veins. Jeannie moved down the hall to take over the sickroom, her face so radiant, her grandfather asked her once: "you are in love?" (Shameful the joy, the pure overwhelming joy from being with her grandmother; the peace, the serenity that breathed.) "My darling escape," she answered incoherently, "my darling Granny"—as if that explained.

Now one by one the children came, those that were able. Hannah, Paul, Sammy. Too late to ask: and what did you learn with your living, Mother, and what do we need to know?

Clara, the eldest, clenched:

> *Pay me back, Mother, pay me back for all you took from me. Those others you crowded into your heart. The hands I needed to be for you, the heaviness, the responsibility.*
>
> *Is this she? Noises the dying make, the crablike hands crawling over the covers. The ethereal singing.*
>
> *She hears that music, that singing from childhood; forgotten sound—not heard since, since. . . . And the hardness breaks like a cry: Where did we lose each other, first mother, singing mother?*
>
> *Annulled: the quarrels, the gibing, the harshness between; the fall into silence and the withdrawal.*
>
> *I do not know you, Mother. Mother, I never knew you.*

Lennie, suffering not alone for her who was dying, but for that in her which never lived (for that which in him might never live). From him too, unspoken words: *good-bye Mother who taught me to mother myself.*

Not Vivi, who must stay with her children; not Davy, but he is already here, having to die again with *her* this time, for the living take their dead with them when they die.

Light she grew, like a bird, and, like a bird, sound bubbled in her throat while the body fluttered in agony. Night and day, asleep or awake (though indeed there was no difference now) the songs and the phrases leaping.

And he, who had once dreaded a long dying (from fear of himself, from horror of the dwindling money) now desired her quick death profoundly, for *her* sake. He no longer went out, except when Jeannie forced him; no longer laughed, except when, in the bright kitchenette, Jeannie coaxed his laughter (and she, who seemed to hear nothing else, would laugh too, conspiratorial wisps of laughter).

Light, like a bird, the fluttering body, the little claw hands, the beaked shadow on her face; and the throat, bubbling, straining.

He tried not to listen, as he tried not to look on the face in which only the forehead remained familiar, but trapped with her the long nights in that little room, the sounds worked themselves into his consciousness, with their punctuation of death swallows, whimpers, gurglings.

Even in reality (swallow) life's lack of it

Slaveships deathtrains clubs eeenough

The bell summon what enables

78,000 in one minute (whisper of a scream) *78,000 human beings we'll destroy ourselves?*

"Aah, Mrs. Miserable," he said, as if she could hear, "all your life working, and now in bed you lie, servants to tend, you do not even need to call to be tended, and still you work. Such hard work it is to die? Such hard work?"

The body threshed, her hand clung in his. A melody, ghost-thin, hovered on her lips, and like a guilty ghost, the vision of her bent in listening to it, silencing the record instantly he was near. Now, heedless of his presence, she floated the melody on and on.

"Hid it from me," he complained, "how many times you listened to remember it so?" And tried to think when she had first played it, or first begun to silence her few records when he came near—but could reconstruct nothing. There was only this room with its tall hooked pillar and its swarm of sounds.

No man one except through others

Strong with the not yet in the now

Dogma dead war dead one country

"It helps, Mrs. Philosopher, words from books? It helps?" And it seemed to him that for seventy years she had hidden a tape recorder, infinitely microscopic, within her, that it had coiled infinite mile on mile, trapping every song, every melody, every word read, heard, and spoken—and that maliciously she was playing back only what said nothing of him, of the children, of their intimate life together.

"Left us indeed, Mrs. Babbler," he reproached, "you who called others babbler and cunningly saved your words. A lifetime you tended and loved, and now not a word of us, for us. Left us indeed? Left me."

And he took out his solitaire deck, shuffled the cards loudly, slapped them down.

Lift high banner of reason (tatter of an orator's voice) *justice freedom light*

Humankind life worthy capacities

Seeks (blur of shudder) *belong human being*

"Words, words," he accused, "and what human beings did *you* seek around you, Mrs. Live Alone, and what humankind think worthy?"

Though even as he spoke, he remembered she had not always been isolated, had not always wanted to be alone (as he knew there had been a voice before this gossamer one; before the hoarse voice that broke from silence to lash, make incidents, shame him—a girl's voice of eloquence that spoke their holiest dreams). But again he could reconstruct, image, nothing of what had been before, or when, or how, it had changed.

Ace, queen, jack. The pillar shadow fell, so, in two tracks; in the mirror depths glistened a moonlike blob, the empty solution bottle. And it worked in him: *of reason and justice and freedom . . . Dogma dead:* he remembered the full quotation, laughed bitterly. "Hah, good you do not know what you say; good Victor Hugo died and did not see it, his twentieth century."

Deuce, ten, five. Dauntlessly she began a song of their youth of belief:

These things shall be, a loftier race
than e'er the world hath known shall rise
with flame of freedom in their souls
and light of knowledge in their eyes

King, four jack. "In the twentieth century, hah!"

They shall be gentle, brave and strong
to spill no drop of blood, but dare
all
on earth and fire and sea and air

"To spill no drop of blood, hah! So, cadaver, and you too, cadaver Hugo, 'in the twentieth century ignorance will be dead, dogma will be dead, war will be dead, and for all mankind one country—of fulfilment?' Hah!"

And every life (long strangling cough) *shall be a song*

The cards fell from his fingers. Without warning, the bereavement and betrayal he had sheltered—compounded through the years—hidden even from himself—revealed itself,

uncoiled,
released,
sprung

and with it the monstrous shapes of what had actually happened in the century.

A ravening hunger or thirst seized him. He groped into the kitchenette, switched on all three lights, piled a tray—"you have finished your night snack, Mrs. Cadaver, now I will have mine." And he was shocked at the tears that splashed on the tray.

"Salt tears. For free. I forgot to shake on salt?"

Whispered: "Lost, how much I lost."

Escaped to the grandchildren whose childhoods were childish, who had never hungered, who lived unravaged by disease in warm houses of many rooms, had all the school for which they cared, could walk on any street, stood a head taller than their grandparents, towered above—beautiful skins, straight backs, clear straightforward eyes. "Yes, you in Olshana," he said to the town of sixty years ago, "they would be nobility to you."

And was this not the dream then, come true in ways undreamed? he asked.

And are there no other children in the world? he answered, as if in her harsh voice.

And the flame of freedom, the light of knowledge?
And the drop, to spill no drop of blood?

And he thought that at six Jeannie would get up and it would be his turn to go to her room and sleep, that he could press the buzzer and she would come now; that in the afternoon Ellen Mays was coming, and this time they would play cards and he could marvel at how rouge can stand half an inch on the cheek; that in the evening the doctor would come, and he could beg him to be merciful, to stop the feeding solutions, to let her die.

To let her die, and with her their youth of belief out of which her bright, betrayed words foamed; stained words, that on her working lips came stainless.

Hours yet before Jeannie's turn. He could press the buzzer and wake her to come now; he could take a pill, and with it sleep; he could pour more brandy into his milk glass, though what he had poured was not yet touched.

Instead he went back, checked her pulse, gently tended with his knotty fingers as Jeannie had taught.

She was whimpering; her hand crawled across the covers for his. Compassionately he enfolded it, and with his free hand gathered up the cards again. Still was there thirst or hunger ravening in him.

That world of their youth—dark, ignorant, terrible with hate and disease—how was it that living in it, in the midst of corruption, filth, treachery, degradation, they had not mistrusted man nor themselves; had believed so beautifully, so . . . falsely?

"Aaah, children," he said out loud, "how we believed, how we belonged." And he yearned to package for each of the children, the grandchildren, for everyone, *that joyous certainty, that sense of mattering, of moving and being moved, of being one and indivisible with the great of the past, with all that freed, ennobled man.* Package it, stand on corners, in front of stadiums and on crowded beaches, knock on doors, give it as a fabled gift.

"And why not in cereal boxes, in soap packages?" he mocked himself. "Aah. You have taken my senses, cadaver."

Words foamed, died unsounded. Her body writhed; she made kissing motions with her mouth. (Her lips moving as she read, poring over the Book of the Martyrs, the magnifying glass superimposed over the heavy eyeglasses.) *Still she believed?* "Eva!" he whispered. "Still you believed? You lived by it? These Things Shall Be?"

"One pound soup meat," she answered distinctly, "one soup bone."

"My ears heard you. Ellen Mays was witness: 'Humankind . . . one has to believe.' " Imploringly: "Eva!"

"Bread, day-old." She was mumbling. "Please, in a wooden box . . . for kindling. The thread, hah, the thread breaks. Cheap thread"—and a gurgling, enormously loud, began in her throat.

"I ask for stone; she gives me bread—day-old." He pulled his hand away, shouted: "Who wanted questions? Everything you have to wake?" Then dully, "Ah, let me help you turn, poor creature."

Words jumbled, cleared. In a voice of crowded terror:

"Paul, Sammy, don't fight.

"Hannah, have I ten hands?

"How can I give it, Clara, how can I give it if I don't have?"

"You lie," he said sturdily, "there was joy too." Bitterly: "Ah how cheap you speak of us at the last."

As if to rebuke him, as if her voice had no relationship with her flailing body, she sang clearly, beautifully, a school song the children had taught her when they were little; begged:

"Not look my hair where they cut. . . ."

(The crown of braids shorn.) And instantly he left the mute old woman poring over the Book of the Martyrs; went past the mother treading at the sewing machine, singing with the children; past the girl in her wrinkled prison dress, hiding her hair with scarred hands, lifting to him her awkward, shamed, imploring eyes of love; and took her in his arms, dear, personal, fleshed, in all the heavy passion he had loved to rouse from her.

"Eva!"

Her little claw hand beat the covers. How much, how much can a man stand? He took up the cards, put them down, circled the beds, walked to the dresser, opened, shut drawers, brushed his hair, moved his hand bit by bit over the mirror to see what of the reflection he could blot out with each move, and felt that at any moment he would die of what was unendurable. Went to press the buzzer to wake Jeannie, looked down, saw on Jeannie's sketch pad the hospital bed, with *her;* the double bed alongside, with him; the tall pillar feeding into her veins, and their hands, his and hers, clasped, feeding each other. And as if he had been instructed he went to his bed, lay down, holding the sketch (as if it could shield against the monstrous shapes of loss, of betrayal, of death) and with his free hand took hers back into his.

So Jeannie found them in the morning.

That last day the agony was perpetual. Time after time it lifted her almost off the bed, so they had to fight to hold her down. He could not endure and left the room; wept as if there never would be tears enough.

Jeannie came to comfort him. In her light voice she said: Grandaddy, Grandaddy don't cry. She is not there, she promised me. On the last day, she said she would go back to when she first heard music, a little girl on the road of the village where she was born. She promised me. It is a wedding and they dance, while the flutes so joyous and vibrant tremble in the air. Leave her there, Grandaddy, it is all right. She promised me. Come back, come back and help her poor body to die.

For two of that generation
Seevya and Genya
Infinite, dauntless, incorruptible

Death deepens the wonder

I Stand Here Ironing

I stand here ironing, and what you asked me moves tormented back and forth with the iron.

"I wish you would manage the time to come in and talk with me about your daughter. I'm sure you can help me understand her. She's a youngster who needs help and whom I'm deeply interested in helping."

"Who needs help." Even if I came, what good would it do? You think because I am her mother I have a key, or that in some way you could use me as a key? She has lived for nineteen years. There is all that life that has happened outside of me, beyond me.

And when is there time to remember, to sift, to weigh, to estimate, to total? I will start and there will be an interruption and I will have to gather it all together again. Or I will become engulfed with all I did or did not do, with what should have been and what cannot be helped.

She was a beautiful baby. The first and only one of our five that was beautiful at birth. You do not guess how new and uneasy her tenancy in her now-loveliness. You did not know her all those years she was thought homely, or see her poring over her baby pictures, making me tell her over and over how beautiful she had been—and would be, I would tell her—and was now, to the seeing eye. But the seeing eyes were few or non-existent. Including mine.

I nursed her. They feel that's important nowadays. I nursed all the children, but with her, with all the fierce rigidity of first motherhood, I did like the books then said. Though her cries battered me to trembling and my breasts ached with swollenness, I waited till the clock decreed.

Why do I put that first? I do not even know if it matters, or if it explains anything.

She was a beautiful baby. She blew shining bubbles of sound. She loved motion, loved light, loved color and music and textures. She would lie on the floor in her blue overalls patting the surface so hard in ecstasy her hands and feet would blur. She was a miracle to me, but when she was eight months old I had to leave her daytimes with the woman downstairs to whom she was no miracle at all, for I worked or looked for work and for Emily's father, who "could no longer endure" (he wrote in his good-bye note) "sharing want with us."

I was nineteen. It was the pre-relief, pre-WPA world of the depression. I would start running as soon as I got off the streetcar, running up the stairs, the place smelling sour, and awake or asleep to startle awake, when she saw me she would break into a clogged weeping that could not be comforted, a weeping I can hear yet.

After a while I found a job hashing at night so I could be with her days, and it was better. But it came to where I had to bring her to his family and leave her.

It took a long time to raise the money for her fare back. Then she got chicken pox and I had to wait longer. When she finally came, I hardly knew her, walking quick and nervous like her father, looking like her father, thin, and dressed in a shoddy red that yellowed her skin and glared at the pockmarks. All the baby loveliness gone.

She was two. Old enough for nursery school they said, and I did not know then what I know now—the fatigue of the long day, and the lacerations of group life in the kinds of nurseries that are only parking places for children.

Except that it would have made no difference if I had known. It was the only place there was. It was the only way we could be together, the only way I could hold a job.

And even without knowing, I knew. I knew the teacher that was evil because all these years it has curdled into my memory, the little boy hunched in the corner, her rasp, "why aren't you outside, because Alvin hits you? that's no reason, go out, scaredy." I knew Emily hated it even if she did not clutch and implore "don't go Mommy" like the other children, mornings.

She always had a reason why we should stay home. Momma, you look sick, Momma. I feel sick, Momma, the teachers aren't there today, they're sick. Momma, we can't go, there was a fire there last night. Momma, it's a holiday today, no school, they told me.

But never a direct protest, never rebellion. I think of our others in their three-, four-year-oldness—the explosions, the tempers, the denunciations, the demands—and I feel suddenly ill. I put the iron down. What in me demanded that goodness in her? And what was the cost, the cost to her of such goodness?

The old man living in the back once said in his gentle way: "You should smile at Emily more when you look at her." What *was* in my face when I looked at her? I loved her. There were all the acts of love.

It was only with the others I remembered what he said, and it was the face of joy, and not of care or tightness or worry I turned to them—too late for Emily. She does not smile easily, let alone almost always as her brothers and sisters do. Her face is closed and sombre, but when she wants, how fluid. You must have seen it in her pantomimes, you spoke of her rare gift for comedy on the stage that rouses a laughter out of the audience so dear they applaud and applaud and do not want to let her go.

Where does it come from, that comedy? There was none of it in her when she came back to me that second time, after I had had to send her away again. She had a new daddy now to learn to love, and I think perhaps it was a better time.

Except when we left her alone nights, telling ourselves she was old enough.

"Can't you go some other time, Mommy, like tomorrow?" she would ask. "Will it be just a little while you'll be gone? Do you promise?"

The time we came back, the front door open, the clock on the floor in the hall. She rigid awake. "It wasn't just a little while. I didn't cry. Three times I called you, just three times, and then I ran downstairs to open the door so you could come faster. The clock talked loud. I threw it away, it scared me what it talked."

She said the clock talked loud again that night I went to the hospital to have Susan. She was delirious with the fever that comes before red measles, but she was fully conscious all the week I was gone and the week after we were home when she could not come near the new baby or me.

She did not get well. She stayed skeleton thin, not wanting to eat, and night after night she had nightmares. She would call for me, and I would rouse from exhaustion to sleepily call back: "You're all right, darling, go to sleep, it's just a dream," and if she still called, in a sterner voice, "now go to sleep, Emily, there's nothing to hurt you." Twice, only twice, when I had to get up for Susan anyhow, I went in to sit with her.

Now when it is too late (as if she would let me hold and comfort her like I do the others) I get up and go to her at once at her moan or restless stirring. "Are you awake, Emily? Can I get you something?" And the answer is always the same: "No, I'm all right, go back to sleep, Mother."

They persuaded me at the clinic to send her away to a convalescent home in the country where "she can have the kind of food and care you can't manage for her, and you'll be free to concentrate on the new baby." They still send children to that place. I see pictures on the society page of sleek young women planning affairs to raise money for it, or dancing at the affairs, or decorating Easter eggs or filling Christmas stockings for the children.

They never have a picture of the children so I do not know if the girls still wear those gigantic red bows and the ravaged looks on the every other Sunday when parents can come to visit "unless otherwise notified"—as we were notified the first six weeks.

Oh it is a handsome place, green lawns and tall trees and fluted flower beds. High up on the balconies of each cottage the children stand, the girls in their red bows and white dresses, the boys in white suits and giant red ties. The parents stand below shrieking up to be heard and the children shriek down to be heard, and between them the invisible wall "Not To Be Contaminated by Parental Germs or Physical Affection."

There was a tiny girl who always stood hand in hand with Emily. Her parents never came. One visit she was gone. "They moved her to Rose College," Emily shouted in explanation. "They don't like you to love anybody here."

She wrote once a week, the labored writing of a seven-year-old. "I am fine.

How is the baby. If I write my leter nicly I will have a star. Love." There never was a star. We wrote every other day, letters she could never hold or keep but only hear read—once. "We simply do not have room for children to keep any personal possessions," they patiently explained when we pieced one Sunday's shrieking together to plead how much it would mean to Emily, who loved so to keep things, to be allowed to keep her letters and cards.

Each visit she looked frailer. "She isn't eating," they told us.

(They had runny eggs for breakfast or mush with lumps, Emily said later, I'd hold it in my mouth and not swallow. Nothing ever tasted good, just when they had chicken.)

It took us eight months to get her released home, and only the fact that she gained back so little of her seven lost pounds convinced the social worker.

I used to try to hold and love her after she came back, but her body would stay stiff, and after a while she'd push away. She ate little. Food sickened her, and I think much of life too. Oh she had physical lightness and brightness, twinkling by on skates, bouncing like a ball up and down up and down over the jump rope, skimming over the hill; but these were momentary.

She fretted about her appearance, thin and dark and foreign-looking at a time when every little girl was supposed to look or thought she should look a chubby blonde replica of Shirley Temple. The doorbell sometimes rang for her, but no one seemed to come and play in the house or be a best friend. Maybe because we moved so much.

There was a boy she loved painfully through two school semesters. Months later she told me how she had taken pennies from my purse to buy him candy. "Licorice was his favorite and I brought him some every day, but he still liked Jennifer better'n me. Why, Mommy?" The kind of question for which there is no answer.

School was a worry to her. She was not glib or quick in a world where glibness and quickness were easily confused with ability to learn. To her overworked and exasperated teachers she was an overconscientious "slow learner" who kept trying to catch up and was absent entirely too often.

I let her be absent, though sometimes the illness was imaginary. How different from my now-strictness about attendance with the others. I wasn't working. We had a new baby, I was home anyhow. Sometimes, after Susan grew old enough, I would keep her home from school, too, to have them all together.

Mostly Emily had asthma, and her breathing, harsh and labored, would fill the house with a curiously tranquil sound. I would bring the two old dresser mirrors and her boxes of collections to her bed. She would select beads and single earrings, bottle tops and shells, dried flowers and pebbles, old postcards and scraps, all sorts of oddments; then she and Susan would play Kingdom, setting up landscapes and furniture, peopling them with action.

Those were the only times of peaceful companionship between her and Susan. I have edged away from it, that poisonous feeling between them, that terrible balancing of hurts and needs I had to do between the two, and did so badly, those earlier years.

Oh there are conflicts between the others too, each one human, needing, demanding, hurting, taking—but only between Emily and Susan, no, Emily toward Susan that corroding resentment. It seems so obvious on the surface, yet it is not obvious. Susan, the second child, Susan, golden- and curly-haired and chubby, quick and articulate and assured, everything in appearance and manner Emily was not; Susan, not able to resist Emily's precious things, losing or sometimes clumsily breaking them; Susan telling jokes and riddles to company for applause while Emily sat silent (to say to me later: that was *my* riddle, Mother, I told it to Susan); Susan, who for all the five years' difference in age was just a year behind Emily in developing physically.

I am glad for that slow physical development that widened the difference between her and her contemporaries, though she suffered over it. She was too vulnerable for that terrible world of youthful competition, of preening and parading, of constant measuring of yourself against every other, of envy, "If I had that copper hair," "If I had that skin. . . ." She tormented herself enough about not looking like the others, there was enough of the unsureness, the having to be conscious of words before you speak, the constant caring—what are they thinking of me? without having it all magnified by the merciless physical drives.

Ronnie is calling. He is wet and I change him. It is rare there is such a cry now. That time of motherhood is almost behind me when the ear is not one's own but must always be racked and listening for the child cry, the child call. We sit for a while and I hold him, looking out over the city spread in charcoal with its soft aisles of light. "*Shoogily,*" he breathes and curls closer. I carry him back to bed, asleep. *Shoogily.* A funny word, a family word, inherited from Emily, invented by her to say: *comfort.*

In this and other ways she leaves her seal, I say aloud. And startle at my saying it. What do I mean? What did I start to gather together, to try and make coherent? I was at the terrible, growing years. War years. I do not remember them well. I was working, there were four smaller ones now, there was not time for her. She had to help be a mother, and housekeeper, and shopper. She had to set her seal. Mornings of crisis and near hysteria trying to get lunches packed, hair combed, coats and shoes found, everyone to school or Child Care on time, the baby ready for transportation. And always the paper scribbled on by a smaller one, the book looked at by Susan then mislaid, the homework not done. Running out to that huge school where she was one, she was lost, she was a drop; suffering over the unpreparedness, stammering and unsure in her classes.

There was so little time left at night after the kids were bedded down. She would struggle over books, always eating (it was in those years she developed her enormous appetite that is legendary in our family) and I would be ironing, or preparing food for the next day, or writing V-mail to Bill, or tending the baby. Sometimes, to make me laugh, or out of her despair, she would imitate happenings or types at school.

I think I said once: "Why don't you do something like this in the school amateur show?" One morning she phoned me at work, hardly understandable through the weeping: "Mother, I did it. I won, I won; they gave me first prize; they clapped and clapped and wouldn't let me go."

Now suddenly she was Somebody, and as imprisoned in her difference as she had been in anonymity.

She began to be asked to perform at other high schools, even in colleges, then at city and statewide affairs. The first one we went to, I only recognized her that first moment when thin, shy, she almost drowned herself into the curtains. Then: Was this Emily? The control, the command, the convulsing and deadly clowning, the spell, then the roaring, stamping audience, unwilling to let this rare and precious laughter out of their lives.

Afterwards: You ought to do something about her with a gift like that —but without money or knowing how, what does one do? We have left it all to her, and the gift has as often eddied inside, clogged and clotted, as been used and growing.

She is coming. She runs up the stairs two at a time with her light graceful step, and I know she is happy tonight. Whatever it was that occasioned your call did not happen today.

"Aren't you ever going to finish the ironing, Mother? Whistler painted his mother in a rocker. I'd have to paint mine standing over an ironing board." This is one of her communicative nights and she tells me everything and nothing as she fixes herself a plate of food out of the icebox.

She is so lovely. Why did you want me to come in at all? Why were you concerned? She will find her way.

She starts up the stairs to bed. "Don't get me up with the rest in the morning." "But I thought you were having midterms." "Oh, those," she comes back in, kisses me, and says quite lightly, "in a couple of years when we'll all be atom-dead they won't matter a bit."

She has said it before. She *believes* it. But because I have been dredging the past, and all that compounds a human being is so heavy and meaningful in me, I cannot endure it tonight.

I will never total it all. I will never come in to say: She was a child seldom smiled at. Her father left me before she was a year old. I had to work her first six years when there was work, or I sent her home and to his relatives. There were years she had care she hated. She was dark and thin and foreign-looking in a world where the prestige went to blondness and curly hair and dimples, she was slow where glibness was prized. She was a child of anxious, not proud, love. We were poor and could not afford for her the soil of easy growth. I was a young mother, I was a distracted mother. There were the other children pushing up, demanding. Her younger sister seemed all that she was not. There were years she did not want me to touch her. She kept too much in herself, her life was such she had to keep too much in herself. My wisdom came too late. She has much to her and probably little will come of it. She is a child of her age, of depression, of war, of fear.

Let her be. So all that is in her will not bloom—but in how many does it? There is still enough left to live by. Only help her to know—help make it so there is cause for her to know—that she is more than this dress on the ironing board, helpless before the iron.

RALPH ELLISON

b. 1914

Born in Oklahoma City—in 1914 a rigidly segregationist frontier city, with crisscrossing ties to the Old South, the commercial East, and the new West—Ellison grew up sorting his own identity out of an especially rich mix of materials. For reasons that he never learned, his father (who died when he was three) named him Ralph Waldo after the great New England sage, so that as a boy he was constantly embarrassed by the painful comedy of being a small child with a big name. At first, he thought people were confusing him with the Emersons who lived next door. As he grew older, Ellison's curiosity about his own name and identity encouraged him to explore the variety of names, languages, and personal styles in Oklahoma City: those of fire-and-brimstone preachers, bootleggers, pimps, roustabouts, con-men, Indians who had made their lives in the black community, and blacks who had made theirs with the Indians. Young Ellison worked in a drugstore where, he says, "I heard stories of searching for buried treasure and of headless horsemen . . ., of Jesse James, of Negro outlaws and black United States marshals, of slaves who became chiefs of Indian tribes and of the exploits of Negro cowboys."

During his boyhood, while Ellison was developing the sensibility of a writer, his conscious efforts were devoted to becoming a musician. He studied composition and played both in the school orchestra and in local jazz bands, and when he went off to college at Tuskegee Institute in Alabama it was to study to be a composer of classical symphonies. The next summer he went to New York to find work. In New York, Ellison's life took a new direction: he failed to find a job, but instead fell under the influence of Richard Wright. He had already begun to read widely—T. S. Eliot's *The Waste Land* was the first major influence on him—and Wright encouraged him to try writing himself. His identity as a writer, perhaps foreordained by his having been named after the most famous writer of the last century, began to emerge. Ellison never went back to Tuskegee. He stayed on in New York writing a little and supporting himself as best he could through the Depression. In 1952 *Invisible Man,* his only novel so far, brought him great acclaim, and continues to hold its place as one of the classic American novels written since World War II. "Battle

Royal,'' printed here, is the first chapter of *Invisible Man;* Ellison has also published it as a short story.

Since 1952 Ellison has been writing short critical pieces (many collected in *Shadow and Act,* 1964), teaching at various universities, and working on a long-awaited second novel, which has become legendary before its time. Some rumors predict that it will be as long as three volumes.

Ellison is currently Distinguished Professor of English at New York University.

Battle Royal

It goes a long way back, some twenty years. All my life I had been looking for something, and everywhere I turned someone tried to tell me what it was. I accepted their answers too, though they were often in contradiction and even self-contradictory. I was naïve. I was looking for myself and asking everyone except myself questions which I, and only I, could answer. It took me a long time and much painful boomeranging of my expectations to achieve a realization everyone else appears to have been born with: That I am nobody but myself. But first I had to discover that I am an invisible man!

And yet I am no freak of nature, nor of history. I was in the cards, other things having been equal (or unequal) eighty-five years ago. I am not ashamed of my grandparents for having been slaves. I am only ashamed of myself for having at one time been ashamed. About eighty-five years ago they were told that they were free, united with others of our country in everything pertaining to the common good, and, in everything social, separate like the fingers of the hand. And they believed it. They exulted in it. They stayed in their place, worked hard, and brought up my father to do the same. But my grandfather is the one. He was an odd old guy, my grandfather, and I am told I take after him. It was he who caused the trouble. On his deathbed he called my father to him and said, "Son, after I'm gone I want you to keep up the good fight. I never told you, but our life is a war and I have been a traitor all my born days, a spy in the enemy's country ever since I give up my gun back in the Reconstruction. Live with your head in the lion's mouth. I want you to overcome 'em with yeses, undermine 'em with grins, agree 'em to death and destruction, let 'em swoller you till they vomit or bust wide open." They thought the old man had gone out of his mind. He had been the meekest of men. The younger children were rushed from the room, the shades drawn and the flame of the lamp turned so low that it sputtered on the wick like the old man's breathing. "Learn it to the younguns," he whispered fiercely; then he died.

But my folks were more alarmed over his last words than over his dying. It was as though he had not died at all, his words caused so much anxiety. I was warned emphatically to forget what he had said and, indeed, this is the first time it has been mentioned outside the family circle. It had a tremendous effect upon me, however. I could never be sure of what he meant. Grandfather had been a quiet old man who never made any trouble, yet on his deathbed he had called himself a traitor and a spy, and he had spoken of his meekness as a dangerous activity. It became a constant puzzle which lay unanswered in the back of my mind. And whenever things went well for me I remembered my grandfather and felt guilty and uncomfortable. It was as though I was carrying out his advice in spite of myself. And to make it worse, everyone loved me for it. I was praised by the most lily-white men of the town. I was considered an example of desirable conduct—just as my grandfather had been. And what puzzled me was that the old man had defined it as *treachery.* When I was praised for my conduct I felt a guilt that in some way I was doing something that was really against the wishes of the white folks, that if they had understood they would have desired me to act just the opposite, that I should have been sulky and mean, and that that really would have been what they wanted, even though they were fooled and thought they wanted me to act as I did. It made me afraid that some day they would look upon me as a traitor and I would be lost. Still I was more afraid to act any other way because they didn't like that at all. The old man's words were like a curse. On my graduation day I delivered an oration in which I showed that humility was the secret, indeed, the very essence of progress. (Not that I believed this—how could I, remembering my grandfather?—I only believed that it worked.) It was a great success. Everyone praised me and I was invited to give the speech at a gathering of the town's leading white citizens. It was a triumph for our whole community.

It was the main ballroom of the leading hotel. When I got there I discovered that it was on the occasion of a smoker, and I was told that since I was to be there anyway I might as well take part in the battle royal to be fought by some of my schoolmates as part of the entertainment. The battle royal came first.

All of the town's big shots were there in their tuxedoes, wolfing down the buffet foods, drinking beer and whiskey and smoking black cigars. It was a large room with a high ceiling. Chairs were arranged in neat rows around three sides of a portable boxing ring. The fourth side was clear, revealing a gleaming space of polished floor. I had some misgivings over the battle royal, by the way. Not from a distaste for fighting, but because I didn't care too much for the other fellows who were to take part. They were tough guys who seemed to have no grandfather's curse worrying their minds. No one could mistake their toughness. And besides, I suspected that fighting a battle royal might detract from the dignity of my speech. In those pre-invisible days I visualized myself as a potential Booker T. Washington. But the other fellows didn't care too much for me either, and there were nine of them. I felt superior to them in my way, and I didn't like the manner in which we were all crowded together into the servants' elevator. Nor did they like my being there. In fact, as the warmly lighted floors flashed past the elevator we had words over the fact that I, by taking part in the fight, had knocked one of their friends out of a night's work.

We were led out of the elevator through a rococo hall into an anteroom and told to get into our fighting togs. Each of us was issued a pair of boxing gloves and ushered out into the big mirrored hall, which we entered looking cautiously about us and whispering, lest we might accidentally be heard above the noise of the room. It was foggy with cigar smoke. And already the whiskey was taking effect. I was shocked to see some of the most important men of the town quite tipsy. They were all there—bankers, lawyers, judges, doctors, fire chiefs, teachers, merchants. Even one of the more fashionable pastors. Something we could not see was going on up front. A clarinet was vibrating sensuously and the men were standing up and moving eagerly forward. We were a small tight group, clustered together, our bare upper bodies touching and shining with anticipatory sweat; while up front the big shots were becoming increasingly excited over something we still could not see. Suddenly I heard the school superintendent, who had told me to come, yell, "Bring up the shines, gentlemen! Bring up the little shines!"

We were rushed up to the front of the ballroom, where it smelled even more strongly of tobacco and whiskey. Then we were pushed into place. I almost wet my pants. A sea of faces, some hostile, some amused, ringed around us, and in the center, facing us, stood a magnificent blonde—stark naked. There was dead silence. I felt a blast of cold air chill me. I tried to back away, but they were behind me and around me. Some of the boys stood with lowered heads, trembling. I felt a wave of irrational guilt and fear. My teeth chattered, my skin turned to goose flesh, my knees knocked. Yet I was strongly attracted and looked in spite of myself. Had the price of looking been blindness, I would have looked. The hair was yellow like that of a circus kewpie doll, the face heavily powdered and rouged, as though to form an abstract mask, the eyes hollow and smeared a cool blue, the color of a baboon's butt. I felt a desire to spit upon her as my eyes brushed slowly over her body. Her breasts were firm and round as the domes of East Indian temples, and I stood so close as to see the fine skin texture and beads of pearly perspiration glistening like dew around the pink and erected buds of her nipples. I wanted at one and the same time to run from the room, to sink through the floor, or go to her and cover her from my eyes and the eyes of the others with my body; to feel the soft thigh, to caress her and destroy her, to love her and murder her, to hide from her, and yet to stroke where below the small American flag tattooed upon her belly her thighs formed a capital V. I had a notion that of all in the room she saw only me with her impersonal eyes.

And then she began to dance, a slow sensuous movement; the smoke of a hundred cigars clinging to her like the thinnest of veils. She seemed like a fair bird-girl girdled in veils calling to me from the angry surface of some gray and threatening sea. I was transported. Then I became aware of the clarinet playing and the big shots yelling at us. Some threatened us if we looked and others if we did not. On my right I saw one boy faint. And now a man grabbed a silver pitcher from a table and stepped close as he dashed ice water upon him and stood him up and forced two of us to support him as his head hung and moans issued from his thick bluish lips. Another boy began to plead to go home. He was the largest of the group, wearing dark red fighting trunks much too small to conceal the erection which projected from him as though in answer to the insinuating low-registered moaning of the clarinet. He tried to hide himself with his boxing gloves.

And all the while the blonde continued dancing, smiling faintly at the big shots who watched her with fascination, and faintly smiling at our fear. I noticed a certain merchant who followed her hungrily, his lips loose and drooling. He was a large man who wore diamond studs in a shirtfront which swelled with the ample paunch underneath, and each time the blonde swayed her undulating hips he ran his hand through the thin hair of his bald head and, with his arms upheld, his posture clumsy like that of an intoxicated panda, wound his belly in a slow and obscene grind. This creature was completely hypnotized. The music had quickened. As the dancer flung herself about with a detached expression on her face, the men began reaching out to touch her. I could see their beefy fingers sink into the soft flesh. Some of the others tried to stop them and she began to move around the floor in graceful circles, as they gave chase, slipping and sliding over the polished floor. It was mad. Chairs went crashing, drinks were spilt, as they ran laughing and howling after her. They caught her just as she reached the door, raised her from the floor, and tossed her as college boys are tossed at a hazing, and above her red, fixed-smiling lips I saw the terror and disgust in her eyes, almost like my own terror and that which I saw in some of the other boys. As I watched, they tossed her twice and her soft breasts seemed to flatten against the air and her legs flung wildly as she spun. Some of the more sober ones helped her to escape. And I started off the floor, heading for the anteroom with the rest of the boys.

Some were still crying and in hysteria. But as we tried to leave we were stopped and ordered to get into the ring. There was nothing to do but what we were told. All ten of us climbed under the ropes and allowed ourselves to be blindfolded with broad bands of white cloth. One of the men seemed to feel a bit sympathetic and tried to cheer us up as we stood with our backs against the ropes. Some of us tried to grin. "See that boy over there?" one of the men said. "I want you to run across at the bell and give it to him right in the belly. If you don't get him, I'm going to get you. I don't like his looks." Each of us was told the same. The blindfolds were put on. Yet even then I had been going over my speech. In my mind each word was as bright as flame. I felt the cloth pressed into place, and frowned so that it would be loosened when I relaxed.

But now I felt a sudden fit of blind terror. I was unused to darkness. It was as though I had suddenly found myself in a dark room filled with poisonous cottonmouths. I could hear the bleary voices yelling insistently for the battle royal to begin.

"Get going in there!"

"Let me at that big nigger!"

I strained to pick up the school superintendent's voice, as though to squeeze some security out of that slightly more familiar sound.

"Let me at those black sonsabitches!" someone yelled.

"No, Jackson, no!" another voice yelled. "Here, somebody, help me hold Jack."

"I want to get at that ginger-colored nigger. Tear him limb from limb," the first voice yelled.

I stood against the ropes trembling. For in those days I was what they called ginger-colored, and he sounded as though he might crunch me between his teeth like a crisp ginger cookie.

Quite a struggle was going on. Chairs were being kicked about and I could hear voices grunting as with a terrific effort. I wanted to see, to see more desperately than ever before. But the blindfold was as tight as a thick skin-puckering scab and when I raised my gloved hands to push the layers of white aside a voice yelled, "Oh, no you don't, black bastard! Leave that alone!"

"Ring the bell before Jackson kills him a coon!" someone boomed in the sudden silence. And I heard the bell clang and the sound of feet scuffling forward.

A glove smacked against my head. I pivoted, striking out stiffly as someone went past, and felt the jar ripple along the length of my arm to my shoulder. Then it seemed as though all nine of the boys had turned upon me at once. Blows pounded me from all sides while I struck out as best I could. So many blows landed upon me that I wondered if I were not the only blindfolded fighter in the ring, or if the man called Jackson hadn't succeeded in getting me after all.

Blindfolded, I could no longer control my motions. I had no dignity. I stumbled about like a baby or a drunken man. The smoke had become thicker and with each new blow it seemed to sear and further restrict my lungs. My saliva became like hot bitter glue. A glove connected with my head, filling my mouth with warm blood. It was everywhere. I could not tell if the moisture I felt upon my body was sweat or blood. A blow landed hard against the nape of my neck. I felt myself going over, my head hitting the floor. Streaks of blue light filled the black world behind the blindfold. I lay prone, pretending that I was knocked out, but felt myself seized by hands and yanked to my feet. "Get going, black boy! Mix it up!" My arms were like lead, my head smarting from blows. I managed to feel my way to the ropes and held on, trying to catch my breath. A glove landed in my mid-section and I went over again, feeling as though the smoke had become a knife jabbed into my guts. Pushed this way and that by the legs milling around me I finally pulled erect and discovered that I could see the black, sweat-washed forms weaving in the smoky-blue atmosphere like drunken dancers weaving to the rapid drum-like thuds of blows.

Everyone fought hysterically. It was complete anarchy. Everybody fought everybody else. No group fought together for long. Two, three, four, fought one, then turned to fight each other, were themselves attacked. Blows landed below the belt and in the kidney, with the gloves open as well as closed, and with my eye partly opened now there was not so much terror. I moved carefully, avoiding blows, although not too many to attract attention, fighting from group to group. The boys groped about like blind, cautious crabs crouching to protect their mid-sections, their heads pulled in short against their shoulders, their arms stretched nervously before them, with their fists testing the smoke-filled air like the knobbed feelers of hypersensitive snails. In one corner I glimpsed a boy violently punching the air and heard him scream in pain as he smashed his hand against a ring post. For a second I saw him bent over holding his hand, then going down as a blow caught his unprotected head. I played one group against the other, slipping in and throwing a punch then stepping out of range while pushing the others into the melee to take the blows blindly aimed at me. The smoke was agonizing and there were no rounds, no bells at three minute intervals to relieve our exhaustion. The room spun round me, a swirl of lights, smoke, sweating bodies surrounded by tense white faces. I bled from both nose and mouth, the blood spattering upon my chest.

The men kept yelling, "Slug him, black boy! Knock his guts out!"

"Uppercut him! Kill him! Kill that big boy!"

Taking a fake fall, I saw a boy going down heavily beside me as though we were felled by a single blow, saw a sneaker-clad foot shoot into his groin as the two who had knocked him down stumbled upon him. I rolled out of range, feeling a twinge of nausea.

The harder we fought the more threatening the men became. And yet, I had begun to worry about my speech again. How would it go? Would they recognize my ability? What would they give me?

I was fighting automatically when suddenly I noticed that one after another of the boys was leaving the ring. I was surprised, filled with panic; as though I had been left alone with an unknown danger. Then I understood. The boys had arranged it among themselves. It was the custom for the two men left in the ring to slug it out for the winner's prize. I discovered this too late. When the bell sounded two men in tuxedoes leaped into the ring and removed the blindfold. I found myself facing Tatlock, the biggest of the gang. I felt sick at my stomach. Hardly had the bell stopped ringing in my ears than it clanged again and I saw him moving swiftly toward me. Thinking of nothing else to do I hit him smash on the nose. He kept coming, bringing the rank sharp violence of stale sweat. His face was a black blank of a face, only his eyes alive —with hate of me and aglow with a feverish terror from what had happened to us all. I became anxious. I wanted to deliver my speech and he came at me as though he meant to beat it out of me. I smashed him again and again, taking his blows as they came. Then on a sudden impulse I struck him lightly and as we clinched, I whispered, "Fake like I knocked you out, you can have the prize."

"I'll break your behind," he whispered hoarsely.

"For *them?*"

"For *me,* sonofabitch!"

They were yelling for us to break it up and Tatlock spun me half around with a blow, and as a joggled camera sweeps in a reeling scene, I saw the howling red faces crouching tense beneath the cloud of bluegray smoke. For a moment the world wavered, unraveled, flowed, then my head cleared and Tatlock bounced before me. That fluttering shadow before my eyes was his jabbing left hand. Then falling forward, my head against his damp shoulder, I whispered,

"I'll make it five dollars more."

"Go to hell!"

But his muscles relaxed a trifle beneath my pressure and I breathed, "Seven?"

"Give it to your ma," he said, ripping me beneath the heart.

And while I still held him I butted him and moved away. I felt myself bombarded with punches. I fought back with hopeless desperation. I wanted to deliver my speech more than anything else in the world, because I felt that only these men could judge truly my ability, and now this stupid clown was ruining my chances. I began fighting carefully now, moving in to punch him and out again with my greater speed. A lucky blow to his chin and I had him going too—until I heard a loud voice yell, "I got my money on the big boy."

Hearing this, I almost dropped my guard. I was confused: Should I try to win against the voice out there? Would not this go against my speech, and was not this a moment for humility, for nonresistance? A blow to my head as I danced about sent my right eye popping like a jack-in-the-box and settled my dilemma. The room went red as I fell. It was a dream fall, my body languid and fastidious as to where to land, until the floor became impatient and smashed up to meet me. A moment later I came to. An hypnotic voice said FIVE emphatically. And I lay there, hazily watching a dark red spot of my own blood shaping itself into a butterfly, glistening and soaking into the soiled gray world of the canvas.

When the voice drawled TEN I was lifted up and dragged to a chair. I sat dazed. My eye pained and swelled with each throb of my pounding heart and I wondered if now I would be allowed to speak. I was wringing wet, my mouth still bleeding. We were grouped along the wall now. The other boys ignored me as they congratulated Tatlock and speculated as to how much they would be paid. One boy whimpered over his smashed hand. Looking up front, I saw attendants in white jackets rolling the portable ring away and placing a small square rug in the vacant space surrounded by chairs. Perhaps, I thought, I will stand on the rug to deliver my speech.

Then the M.C. called to us, "Come on up here boys and get your money."

We ran forward to where the men laughed and talked in their chairs, waiting. Everyone seemed friendly now.

"There it is on the rug," the man said. I saw the rug covered with coins of all dimensions and a few crumpled bills. But what excited me, scattered here and there, were the gold pieces.

"Boys, it's all yours," the man said. "You get all you grab."

"That's right, Sambo," a blond man said, winking at me confidentially.

I trembled with excitement, forgetting my pain. I would get the gold and the bills, I thought. I would use both hands. I would throw my body against the boys nearest me to block them from the gold.

"Get down around the rug now," the man commanded, "and don't anyone touch it until I give the signal."

"This ought to be good," I heard.

As told, we got around the square rug on our knees. Slowly the man raised his freckled hand as we followed it upward with our eyes.

I heard, "These niggers look like they're about to pray!"

Then, "Ready," the man said. "Go!"

I lunged for a yellow coin lying on the blue design of the carpet, touching it and sending a surprised shriek to join those rising around me. I tried frantically to remove my hand but could not let go. A hot, violent force tore through my body, shaking me like a wet rat. The rug was electrified. The hair bristled up on my head as I shook myself free. My muscles jumped, my nerves jangled, writhed. But I saw that this was not stopping the other boys. Laughing in fear and embarrassment, some were holding back and scooping up the coins knocked off by the painful contortions of the others. The men roared above us as we struggled.

"Pick it up, goddammit, pick it up!" someone called like a bass-voiced parrot. "Go on, get it!"

I crawled rapidly around the floor, picking up the coins, trying to avoid the coppers and to get greenbacks and the gold. Ignoring the shock by laughing, as I brushed the coins off quickly, I discovered that I could contain the electricity—a contradiction, but it works. Then the men began to push us onto the rug. Laughing embarrassedly, we struggled out of their hands and kept after the coins. We were all wet and slippery and hard to hold. Suddenly I saw a boy lifted into the air, glistening with sweat like a circus seal, and dropped, his back landing flush upon the charged rug, heard him yell and saw him literally dance upon his back, his elbows beating a frenzied tattoo upon the floor, his muscles twitching like the flesh of a horse stung by many flies. When he finally rolled off, his face was gray and no one stopped him when he ran from the floor amid booming laughter.

"Get the money," the M.C. called. "That's good hard American cash!"

And we snatched and grabbed, snatched and grabbed. I was careful not to come too close to the rug now, and when I felt the hot whiskey breath descend upon me like a cloud of foul air I reached out and grabbed the leg of a chair. It was occupied and I held on desperately.

"Leggo, nigger! Leggo!"

The huge face wavered down to mine as he tried to push me free. But my body was slippery and he was too drunk. It was Mr. Colcord, who owned a chain of movie houses and "entertainment palaces." Each time he grabbed me I slipped out of his hands. It became a real struggle. I feared the rug more than I did the drunk, so I held on, surprising myself for a moment by trying to topple *him* upon the rug. It was such an enormous idea that I found myself actually carrying it out. I tried not to be obvious, yet when I grabbed his leg, trying to tumble him out of the chair, he raised up roaring with laughter, and, looking at me with soberness dead in the eye, kicked me viciously in the chest. The chair leg flew out of my hand and I felt myself going and rolled. It was as though I had rolled through a bed of hot coals. It seemed a whole century would pass before I would roll free, a century in which I was seared through the deepest levels of my body to the fearful breath within me and the breath seared and heated to the point of explosion. It'll all be over in a flash, I thought as I rolled clear. It'll all be over in a flash.

But not yet, the men on the other side were waiting, red faces swollen as though from apoplexy as they bent forward in their chairs. Seeing their fingers coming toward me I rolled away as a fumbled football rolls off the receiver's fingertips, back into the coals. That time I luckily sent the rug sliding out of place and heard the coins ringing against the floor and the boys scuffling to pick them up and the M.C. calling, "All right, boys, that's all. Go get dressed and get your money."

I was limp as a dish rag. My back felt as though it had been beaten with wires.

When we had dressed the M.C. came in and gave us each five dollars, except Tatlock, who got ten for being last in the ring. Then he told us to leave. I was not to get a chance to deliver my speech, I thought. I was going out into the dim alley in despair when I was stopped and told to go back. I returned to the ballroom, where the men were pushing back their chairs and gathering in groups to talk.

The M.C. knocked on a table for quiet. "Gentlemen," he said, "we almost forgot an important part of the program. A most serious part, gentlemen. This boy was brought here to deliver a speech which he made at his graduation yesterday . . ."

"Bravo!"

"I'm told that he is the smartest boy we've got out there in Greenwood. I'm told that he knows more big words than a pocket-sized dictionary."

Much applause and laughter.

"So now, gentlemen, I want you to give him your attention."

There was still laughter as I faced them, my mouth dry, my eye throbbing. I began slowly, but evidently my throat was tense, because they began shouting, "Louder! Louder!"

"We of the younger generation extol the wisdom of that great leader and educator," I shouted, "who first spoke these flaming words of wisdom: 'A ship lost at sea for many days suddenly sighted a friendly vessel. From the mast of the unfortunate vessel was seen a signal: "Water, water; we die of thirst!" The answer from the friendly vessel came back: "Cast down your bucket where you are." The captain of the distressed vessel, at last heeding the injunction, cast down his bucket, and it came up full of fresh sparkling water from the mouth of the Amazon River.' And like him I say, and in his words, 'To those of my race who depend upon bettering their condition in a foreign land, or who underestimate the importance of cultivating friendly relations with the Southern white man, who is his next-door neighbor, I would say: "Cast down your bucket where you are"—cast it down in making friends in every manly way of the people of all races by whom we are surrounded . . .' "

I spoke automatically and with such fervor that I did not realize that the men were still talking and laughing until my dry mouth, filling up with blood from the cut, almost strangled me. I coughed, wanting to stop and go to one of the tall brass, sand-filled spittoons to relieve myself, but a few of the men, especially the superintendent, were listening and I was afraid. So I gulped it down, blood, saliva and all, and continued. (What powers of endurance I had during those days! What enthusiasm! What a belief in the rightness of things!) I spoke even louder in spite of the pain. But still they talked and still they laughed, as though deaf with cotton in dirty ears. So I spoke with greater emotional emphasis. I closed my ears and swallowed blood until I was nauseated. The speech seemed a hundred times as long as before, but I could not leave out a single word. All had to be said, each memorized nuance considered, rendered. Nor was that all. Whenever I uttered a word of three or more syllables a group of voices would yell for me to repeat it. I used the phrase "social responsibility" and they yelled:

"What's that word you say, boy?"

"Social responsibility," I said.

"What?"

"Social . . ."

"Louder."

". . . responsibility."

"More!"

"Respon—"

"Repeat!"

"—sibility."

The room filled with the uproar of laughter until, no doubt, distracted by having to gulp down my blood, I made a mistake and yelled a phrase I had often seen denounced in newspaper editorials, heard debated in private.

"Social . . ."

"What?" they yelled.

". . . equality—"

The laughter hung smokelike in the sudden stillness. I opened my eyes, puzzled. Sounds of displeasure filled the room. The M.C. rushed forward. They shouted hostile phrases at me. But I did not understand.

A small dry mustached man in the front row blared out, "Say that slowly, son!"

"What sir?"

"What you just said!"

"Social responsibility, sir," I said.

"You weren't being smart, were you, boy?" he said, not unkindly.

"No, sir!"

"You sure that about 'equality' was a mistake?"

"Oh, yes, sir," I said. "I was swallowing blood."

"Well, you had better speak more slowly so we can understand. We mean to do right by you, but you've got to know your place at all times. All right, now, go on with your speech."

I was afraid. I wanted to leave but I wanted also to speak and I was afraid they'd snatch me down.

"Thank you, sir," I said, beginning where I had left off, and having them ignore me as before.

Yet when I finished there was a thunderous applause. I was surprised to see the superintendent come forth with a package wrapped in white tissue paper, and, gesturing for quiet, address the men.

"Gentlemen, you see that I did not overpraise this boy. He makes a good speech and some day he'll lead his people in the proper paths. And I don't have to tell you that that is important in these days and times. This is a good, smart boy, and so to encourage him in the right direction, in the name of the Board of Education I wish to present him a prize in the form of this . . ."

He paused, removing the tissue paper and revealing a gleaming calfskin brief case.

". . . in the form of this first-class article from Shad Whitmore's shop."

"Boy," he said, addressing me, "take this prize and keep it well. Consider it a badge of office. Prize it. Keep developing as you are and some day it will be filled with important papers that will help shape the destiny of your people."

I was so moved that I could hardly express my thanks. A rope of bloody saliva forming a shape like an undiscovered continent drooled upon the leather and I wiped it quickly away. I felt an importance that I had never dreamed.

"Open it and see what's inside," I was told.

My fingers a-tremble, I complied, smelling the fresh leather and finding an official-looking document inside. It was a scholarship to the state college for Negroes. My eyes filled with tears and I ran awkwardly off the floor.

I was overjoyed; I did not even mind when I discovered that the gold pieces I had scrambled for were brass pocket tokens advertising a certain make of automobile.

When I reached home everyone was excited. Next day the neighbors came to congratulate me. I even felt safe from grandfather, whose deathbed curse usually spoiled my triumphs. I stood beneath his photograph with my brief case in hand and smiled triumphantly into his stolid black peasant's face. It was a face that fascinated me. The eyes seemed to follow everywhere I went.

That night I dreamed I was at a circus with him and that he refused to laugh at the clowns no matter what they did. Then later he told me to open my brief case and read what was inside and I did, finding an official envelope stamped with the state seal; and inside the envelope I found another and another, endlessly, and I thought I would fall of weariness. "Them's years," he said. "Now open that one." And I did and in it I found an engraved document containing a short message in letters of gold. "Read it," my grandfather said. "Out loud."

"To Whom It May Concern," I intoned. "Keep This Nigger-Boy Running."

I awoke with the old man's laughter ringing in my ears.

(It was a dream I was to remember and dream again for many years after. But at that time I had no insight into its meaning. First I had to attend college.)

Flying Home

When Todd came to, he saw two faces suspended above him in a sun so hot and blinding that he could not tell if they were black or white. He stirred, feeling a pain that burned as though his whole body had been laid open to the sun which glared into his eyes. For a moment an old fear of being touched by white hands seized him. Then the very sharpness of the pain began slowly to clear his head. Sounds came to him dimly. He done come to. Who are they? he thought. Naw he ain't, I coulda sworn he was white. Then he heard clearly:

"You hurt bad?"

Something within him uncoiled. It was a Negro sound.

"He's still out," he heard.

"Give 'im time. . . . Say, son, you hurt bad?"

Was he? There was that awful pain. He lay rigid, hearing their breathing and trying to weave a meaning between them and his being stretched painfully upon the ground. He watched them warily, his mind traveling back over a painful distance. Jagged scenes, swiftly unfolding as in a movie trailer, reeled through his mind, and he saw himself piloting a tailspinning plane and landing and landing and falling from the cockpit and trying to stand. Then, as in a great silence, he remembered the sound of crunching bone, and now, looking up into the anxious faces of an old Negro man and a boy from where he lay in the same field, the memory sickened him and he wanted to remember no more.

"How you feel, son?"

Todd hesitated, as though to answer would be to admit an inacceptable weakness. Then, "It's my ankle," he said.

"Which one?"

"The left."

With a sense of remoteness he watched the old man bend and remove his boot, feeling the pressure ease.

"That any better?"

"A lot. Thank you."

He had the sensation of discussing someone else, that his concern was with some far more important thing, which for some reason escaped him.

"You done broke it bad," the old man said. "We have to get you to a doctor."

He felt that he had been thrown into a tailspin. He looked at his watch; how long had he been here? He knew there was but one important thing in the world, to get the plane back to the field before his officers were displeased.

"Help me up," he said. "Into the ship."

"But it's broke too bad. . . ."

"Give me your arm!"

"But, son . . ."

Clutching the old man's arm he pulled himself up, keeping his left leg clear, thinking, "I'd never make him understand," as the leather-smooth face came parallel with his own.

"Now, let's see."

He pushed the old man back, hearing a bird's insistent shrill. He swayed giddily. Blackness washed over him, like infinity.

"You best sit down."

"No, I'm O.K."

"But, son. You jus' gonna make it worse. . . ."

It was a fact that everything in him cried out to deny, even against the flaming pain in his ankle. He would have to try again.

"You mess with that ankle they have to cut your foot off," he heard.

Holding his breath, he started up again. It pained so badly that he had to bite his lips to keep from crying out and he allowed them to help him down with a pang of despair.

"It's best you take it easy. We gon' git you a doctor."

Of all the luck, he thought. Of all the rotten luck, now I have done it. The fumes of high-octane gasoline clung in the heat, taunting him.

"We kin ride him into town on old Ned," the boy said.

Ned? He turned, seeing the boy point toward an ox team browsing where the buried blade of a plow marked the end of a furrow. Thoughts of himself riding an ox through the town, past streets full of white faces, down the concrete runways of the airfield made swift images of humiliation in his mind. With a pang he remembered his girl's last letter. "Todd," she had written, "I don't need the papers to tell me you had the intelligence to fly. And I have always known you to be as brave as anyone else. The papers annoy me. Don't you be contented to prove over and over again that you're brave or skillful just because you're black, Todd. I think they keep beating that dead horse because they don't want to say why you boys are not yet fighting. I'm really disappointed, Todd. Anyone with brains can learn to fly, but then what? What about using it, and who will you use it for? I wish, dear, you'd write about this. I sometimes think they're playing a trick on us. It's very humiliating. . . ." He wiped cold sweat from his face, thinking, What does she know of humiliation? She's never been down South. Now the humiliation would come. When you must have them judge you, knowing that they never accept your mistakes as your own, but hold it against your whole race—that was humiliation. Yes, and humiliation was when you could never be simply yourself, when you were always a part of this old black ignorant man. Sure, he's all right. Nice and kind and helpful. But he's not you. Well, there's one humiliation I can spare myself.

"No," he said, "I have orders not to leave the ship. . . ."

"Aw," the old man said. Then turning to the boy, "Teddy, then you better hustle down to Mister Graves and get him to come. . . ."

"No, wait!" he protested before he was fully aware. Graves might be white. "Just have him get word to the field, please. They'll take care of the rest."

He saw the boy leave, running.

"How far does he have to go?"

"Might' nigh a mile."

He rested back, looking at the dusty face of his watch. But now they know something has happened, he thought. In the ship there was a perfectly good radio, but it was useless. The old fellow would never operate it. That buzzard knocked me back a hundred years, he thought. Irony danced within him like the gnats circling the old man's head. With all I've learned I'm dependent upon this "peasant's" sense of time and space. His leg throbbed. In the plane, instead of time being measured by the rhythms of pain and a kid's legs, the instruments would have told him at a glance. Twisting upon his elbows he saw where dust had powdered the plane's fuselage, feeling the lump form in his throat that was always there when he thought of flight. It's crouched there, he thought, like the abandoned shell of a locust. I'm naked without it. Not a machine, a suit of clothes you wear. And with a sudden embarrassment and wonder he whispered, "It's the only dignity I have. . . ."

He saw the old man watching, his torn overalls clinging limply to him in the heat. He felt a sharp need to tell the old man what he felt. But that would be meaningless. If I tried to explain why I need to fly back, he'd think I was simply afraid of white officers. But it's more than fear . . . a sense of anguish clung to him like the veil of sweat that hugged his face. He watched the old man, hearing him humming snatches of a tune as he admired the plane. He felt a furtive sense of resentment. Such old men often came to the field to watch the pilots with childish eyes. At first it had made him proud; they had been a meaningful part of a new experience. But soon he realized they did not understand his accomplishments and they came to shame and embarrass him, like the distasteful praise of an idiot. A part of the meaning of flying had gone then, and he had not been able to regain it. If I were a prizefighter I would be more human, he thought. Not a monkey doing tricks, but a man. They were pleased simply that he was a Negro who could fly, and that was not enough. He felt cut off from them by age, by understanding, by sensibility, by technology and by his need to measure himself against the mirror of other men's appreciation. Somehow he felt betrayed, as he had when as a child he grew to discover that his father was dead. Now for him any real appreciation lay with his white officers; and with them he could never be sure. Between ignorant black men and condescending whites, his course of flight seemed mapped by the nature of things away from all needed and natural landmarks. Under some sealed orders, couched in ever more technical and mysterious terms, his path curved swiftly away from both the shame the old man symbolized and the cloudy terrain of white men's regard. Flying blind, he knew but one point of landing and there he would receive his wings. After that the enemy would appreciate his skill and he would assume his deepest meaning, he thought sadly, neither from those who condescended nor from those who praised without understanding, but from the enemy who would recognize his manhood and skill in terms of hate. . . .

He sighed, seeing the oxen making queer, prehistoric shadows against the dry brown earth.

"You just take it easy, son," the old man soothed. "That boy won't take long. Crazy as he is about airplanes."

"I can wait," he said.

"What kinda airplane you call this here'n?"

"An Advanced Trainer," he said, seeing the old man smile. His fingers were like gnarled dark wood against the metal as he touched the low-slung wing.

" 'Bout how fast can she fly?"

"Over two hundred an hour."

"Lawd! That's so fast I bet it don't seem like you moving!"

Holding himself rigid, Todd opened his flying suit. The shade had gone and he lay in a ball of fire.

"You mind if I take a look inside? I was always curious to see. . . ."

"Help yourself. Just don't touch anything."

He heard him climb upon the metal wing, grunting. Now the questions would start. Well, so you don't have to think to answer. . . .

He saw the old man looking over into the cockpit, his eyes bright as a child's.

"You must have to know a lot to work all these here things."

He was silent, seeing him step down and kneel beside him.

"Son, how come you want to fly way up there in the air?"

Because it's the most meaningful act in the world . . . because it makes me less like you, he thought.

But he said: "Because I like it, I guess. It's as good a way to fight and die as I know."

"Yeah? I guess you right," the old man said. "But how long you think before they gonna let you all fight?"

He tensed. This was the question all Negroes asked, put with the same timid hopefulness and longing that always opened a greater void within him than that he had felt beneath the plane the first time he had flown. He felt light-headed. It came to him suddenly that there was something sinister about the conversation, that he was flying unwillingly into unsafe and uncharted regions. If he could only be insulting and tell this old man who was trying to help him to shut up!

"I bet you one thing . . ."

"Yes?"

"That you was plenty scared coming down."

He did not answer. Like a dog on a trail the old man seemed to smell out his fears and he felt anger bubble within him.

"You sho' scared me. When I seen you coming down in that thing with it a-rollin' and a-jumpin' like a pitchin' hoss, I thought sho' you was a goner. I almost had me a stroke!"

He saw the old man grinning, "Ever'thin's been happening round here this morning, come to think of it."

"Like what?" he asked.

"Well, first thing I know, here come two white fellers looking for Mister Rudolph, that's Mister Graves's cousin. That got me worked up right away. . . ."

"Why?"

"Why? 'Cause he done broke outta the crazy house, that's why. He liable to kill somebody," he said. "They oughta have him by now though. Then here you come. First I think it's one of them white boys. Then doggone if you don't fall outta there. Lawd, I'd done heard about you boys but I haven't never seen one o' you-all. Cain't tell you how it felt to see somebody what look like me in a airplane!"

The old man talked on, the sound streaming around Todd's thoughts like air flowing over the fuselage of a flying plane. You were a fool, he thought, remembering how before the spin the sun had blazed bright against the bill-board signs beyond the town, and how a boy's blue kite had bloomed beneath him, tugging gently in the wind like a strange, odd-shaped flower. He had once flown such kites himself and tried to find the boy at the end of the invisible cord. But he had been flying too high and too fast. He had climbed steeply away in exultation. Too steeply, he thought. And one of the first rules you learn is that if the angle of thrust is too steep the plane goes into a spin. And then, instead of pulling out of it and going into a dive you let a buzzard panic you. A lousy buzzard!

"Son, what made all that blood on the glass?"

"A buzzard," he said, remembering how the blood and feathers had sprayed back against the hatch. It had been as though he had flown into a storm of blood and blackness.

"Well, I declare! They's lots of 'em around here. They after dead things. Don't eat nothing what's alive."

"A little bit more and he would have made a meal out of me," Todd said grimly.

"They bad luck all right. Teddy's got a name for 'em, calls 'em jimcrows," the old man laughed.

"It's a damned good name."

"They the damnedest birds. Once I seen a hoss all stretched out like he was sick, you know. So I hollers, 'Gid up from there, suh!' Just to make sho! An' doggone, son, if I don't see two ole jimcrows come flying right up outa that hoss's insides! Yessuh! The sun was shinin' on 'em and they couldn't a been no greasier if they'd been eating barbecue."

Todd thought he would vomit, his stomach quivered.

"You made that up," he said.

"Nawsuh! Saw him just like I see you."

"Well, I'm glad it was you."

"You see lots a funny things down here, son."

"No, I'll let you see them," he said.

"By the way, the white folks round here don't like to see you boys up there in the sky. They ever bother you?"

"No."

"Well, they'd like to."

"Someone always wants to bother someone else," Todd said. "How do you know?"

"I just know."

"Well," he said defensively, "no one has bothered us."

Blood pounded in his ears as he looked away into space. He tensed, seeing a black spot in the sky, and strained to confirm what he could not clearly see.

"What does that look like to you?" he asked excitedly.

"Just another bad luck, son."

Then he saw the movement of wings with disappointment. It was gliding smoothly down, wings outspread, tail feathers gripping the air, down swiftly —gone behind the green screen of trees. It was like a bird he had imagined there, only the sloping branches of the pines remained, sharp against the pale stretch of sky. He lay barely breathing and stared at the point where it had disappeared, caught in a spell of loathing and admiration. Why did they make them so disgusting and yet teach them to fly so well? It's like when I was up in heaven, he heard, starting.

The old man was chuckling, rubbing his stubbled chin.

"What did you say?"

"Sho', I died and went to heaven . . . maybe by time I tell you about it they be done come after you."

"I hope so," he said wearily.

"You boys ever sit around and swap lies?"

"Not often. Is this going to be one?"

"Well, I ain't so sho', on account of it took place when I was dead." The old man paused, "That wasn't no lie 'bout the buzzards, though."

"All right," he said.

"Sho' you want to hear 'bout heaven?"

"Please," he answered, resting his head upon his arm.

"Well, I went to heaven and right away started to sproutin' me some wings. Six good ones, they was. Just like them the white angels had. I couldn't hardly believe it. I was so glad that I went off on some clouds by myself and tried 'em out. You know, 'cause I didn't want to make a fool outta myself the first thing. . . ."

It's an old tale, Todd thought. Told me years ago. Had forgotten. But at least it will keep him from talking about buzzards.

He closed his eyes, listening.

". . . First thing I done was to git up on a low cloud and jump off. And doggone, boy, if them wings didn't work! First I tried the right; then I tried the left; then I tried 'em both together. Then Lawd, I started to move on out among the folks. I let 'em see me. . . ."

He saw the old man gesturing flight with his arms, his face full of mock pride as he indicated an imaginary crowd, thinking, It'll be in the newspapers, as he heard, ". . . so I went and found me some colored angels—somehow I didn't believe I was an angel till I seen a real black one, ha, yes! Then I was sho'—but they tole me I better come down 'cause us colored folks had to wear a special kin' a harness when we flew. That was how come they wasn't flyin'. Oh yes, an' you had to be extra strong for a black man even, to fly with one of them harnesses. . . ."

This is a new turn, Todd thought, what's he driving at?

"So I said to myself, I ain't gonna be bothered with no harness! Oh naw! 'Cause if God let you sprout wings you oughta have sense enough not to let nobody make you wear something what gits in the way of flyin'. So I starts to flyin'. Heck, son," he chuckled, his eyes twinkling, "you know I had to let eve'ybody know that old Jefferson could fly good as anybody else. And I could too, fly smooth as a bird! I could even loop-the-loop—only I had to make sho' to keep my long white robe down roun' my ankles. . . ."

Todd felt uneasy. He wanted to laugh at the joke, but his body refused, as of an independent will. He felt as he had as a child when after he had chewed a sugar-coated pill which his mother had given him, she had laughed at his efforts to remove the terrible taste.

". . . Well," he heard, "I was doing all right 'til I got to speeding. Found out I could fan up a right strong breeze, I could fly so fast. I could do all kin'sa stunts too. I started flying up to the stars and divin' down and zooming roun' the moon. Man, I like to scare the devil outa some ole white angels. I was raisin' hell. Not that I meant any harm, son. But I was just feeling good. It was so good to know I was free at last. I accidentally knocked the tips offa some stars and they tell me I caused a storm and a coupla lynchings down here in Macon County—though I swear I believe them boys what said that was making up lies on me. . . ."

He's mocking me, Todd thought angrily. He thinks it's a joke. Grinning down at me . . . His throat was dry. He looked at his watch; why the hell didn't they come? Since they had to, why? One day I was flying down one of them heavenly streets. You got yourself into it, Todd thought. Like Jonah in the whale.

"Justa throwin' feathers in everybody's face. An' old Saint Peter called me in. Said, 'Jefferson, tell me two things, what you doin' flyin' without a harness; an' how come you flyin' so fast?' So I tole him I was flyin' without a harness 'cause it got in my way, but I couldn'ta been flyin' so fast, 'cause I wasn't usin' but one wing. Saint Peter said, 'You wasn't flyin' with but one wing?' 'Yessuh,' I says, scared-like. So he says, 'Well, since you got sucha extra fine pair of wings you can leave off yo' harness awhile. But from now on none of that there one-wing flyin', 'cause you gittin' up too damn much speed!' "

And with one mouth full of bad teeth you're making too damned much talk, thought Todd. Why don't I send him after the boy? His body ached from the hard ground and seeking to shift his position he twisted his ankle and hated himself for crying out.

"It gittin' worse?"

"I . . . I twisted it," he groaned.

"Try not to think about it, son. That's what I do."

He bit his lip, fighting pain with counter-pain as the voice resumed its rhythmical droning. Jefferson seemed caught in his own creation.

". . . After all that trouble I just floated roun' heaven in slow motion. But I forgot, like colored folks will do, and got to flyin' with one wing again. This time I was restin' my old broken arm and got to flyin' fast enough to shame the devil. I was comin' so fast, Lawd, I got myself called befo' ole Saint Peter again. He said, 'Jeff, didn't I warn you 'bout that speedin'?' 'Yessuh,' I says, 'but it was an accident.' He looked at me sad-like and shook his head and I knowed I was gone. He said, 'Jeff, you and that speedin' is a danger to the heavenly community. If I was to let you keep on flyin', heaven wouldn't be nothin' but uproar. Jeff, you got to go!' Son, I argued and pleaded with that old white man, but it didn't do a bit of good. They rushed me straight to them pearly gates and gimme a parachute and a map of the state of Alabama . . ."

Todd heard him laughing so that he could hardly speak, making a screen between them upon which his humiliation glowed like fire.

"Maybe you'd better stop awhile," he said, his voice unreal.

"Ain't much more," Jefferson laughed. "When they gimme the parachute old Saint Peter ask me if I wanted to say a few words before I went. I felt so bad I couldn't hardly look at him, specially with all them white angels standin' around. Then somebody laughed and made me mad. So I tole him, 'Well, you done took my wings. And you puttin' me out. You got charge of things so's I can't do nothin' about it. But you got to admit just this: While I was up here I was the flyinest sonofabitch what ever hit heaven!' "

At the burst of laughter Todd felt such an intense humiliation that only great violence would wash it away. The laughter which shook the old man like a boiling purge set up vibrations of guilt within him which not even the intricate machinery of the plane would have been adequate to transform and he heard himself screaming, "Why do you laugh at me this way?"

He hated himself at that moment, but he had lost control. He saw Jefferson's mouth fall open, "What—?"

"Answer me!"

His blood pounded as though it would surely burst his temples and he tried to reach the old man and fell, screaming, "Can I help it because they won't let us actually fly? Maybe we are a bunch of buzzards feeding on a dead horse, but we can hope to be eagles, can't we? Can't we?"

He fell back, exhausted, his ankle pounding. The saliva was like straw in his mouth. If he had the strength he would strangle this old man. This grinning, gray-headed clown who made him feel as he felt when watched by the white officers at the field. And yet this old man had neither power, prestige, rank nor technique. Nothing that could rid him of this terrible feeling. He watched him, seeing his face struggle to express a turmoil of feeling.

"What you mean, son? What you talking 'bout . . . ?"

"Go away. Go tell your tales to the white folks."

"But I didn't mean nothing like that. . . . I . . . I wasn't tryin' to hurt your feelings. . . ."

"Please. Get the hell away from me!"

"But I didn't, son. I didn't mean all them things a-tall."

Todd shook as with a chill, searching Jefferson's face for a trace of the mockery he had seen there. But now the face was somber and tired and old. He was confused. He could not be sure that there had ever been laughter there, that Jefferson had ever really laughed in his whole life. He saw Jefferson reach out to touch him and shrank away, wondering if anything except the pain, now causing his vision to waver, was real. Perhaps he had imagined it all.

"Don't let it get you down, son," the voice said pensively.

He heard Jefferson sigh wearily, as though he felt more than he could say. His anger ebbed, leaving only the pain.

"I'm sorry," he mumbled.

"You just wore out with pain, was all. . . ."

He saw him through a blur, smiling. And for a second he felt the embarrassed silence of understanding flutter between them.

"What you was doin' flyin' over this section, son? Wasn't you scared they might shoot you for a cow?"

Todd tensed. Was he being laughed at again? But before he could decide, the pain shook him and a part of him was lying calmly behind the screen of pain that had fallen between them, recalling the first time he had ever seen a plane. It was as though an endless series of hangars had been shaken ajar in the air base of his memory and from each, like a young wasp emerging from its cell, arose the memory of a plane.

The first time I ever saw a plane I was very small and planes were new in the world. I was four-and-a-half and the only plane that I had ever seen was a model suspended from the ceiling of the automobile exhibit at the State Fair. But I did not know that it was only a model. I did not know how large a real plane was, nor how expensive. To me it was a fascinating toy, complete in itself, which my mother said could only be owned by rich little white boys. I stood rigid with admiration, my head straining backwards as I watched the gray little plane describing arcs above the gleaming tops of the automobiles. And I vowed that, rich or poor, someday I would own such a toy. My mother had to drag me out of the exhibit and not even the merry-go-round, the Ferris wheel, or the racing horses could hold my attention for the rest of the Fair. I was too busy imitating the tiny drone of the plane with my lips, and imitating with my hands the motion, swift and circling, that it made in flight.

After that I no longer used the pieces of lumber that lay about our back yard to construct wagons and autos . . . now it was used for airplanes. I built biplanes, using pieces of board for wings, a small box for the fuselage, another piece of wood for the rudder. The trip to the Fair had brought something new into my small world. I asked my mother repeatedly when the Fair would come back again. I'd lie in the grass and watch the sky, and each fighting bird became a soaring plane. I would have been good a year just to have seen a plane again. I became a nuisance to everyone with my questions about airplanes. But planes were new to the old folks, too, and there was little that they could tell me. Only my uncle knew some of the answers. And better still, he could carve propellers from pieces of wood that would whirl rapidly in the wind, wobbling noisily upon oiled nails.

I wanted a plane more than I'd wanted anything; more than I wanted the red wagon with rubber tires, more than the train that ran on a track with its train of cars. I asked my mother over and over again:

"Mamma?"

"What do you want, boy?" she'd say.

"Mamma, will you get mad if I ask you?" I'd say.

"What do you want now? I ain't got time to be answering a lot of fool questions. What you want?"

"Mamma, when you gonna get me one . . . ?" I'd ask.

"Get you one what?" she'd say.

"You know, Mamma; what I been asking you. . . ."

"Boy," she'd say, "if you don't want a spanking you better come on an' tell me what you talking about so I can get on with my work."

"Aw, Mamma, you know. . . ."

"What I just tell you?" she'd say.

"I mean when you gonna buy me a airplane."

"AIRPLANE! Boy, is you crazy? How many times I have to tell you to stop that foolishness. I done told you them things cost too much. I bet I'm gon' wham the living daylight out of you if you don't quit worrying me 'bout them things!"

But this did not stop me, and a few days later I'd try all over again.

Then one day a strange thing happened. It was spring and for some reason I had been hot and irritable all morning. It was a beautiful spring. I could feel it as I played barefoot in the backyard. Blossoms hung from the thorny black locust trees like clusters of fragrant white grapes. Butterflies flickered in the sunlight above the short new dew-wet grass. I had gone in the house for bread and butter and coming out I heard a steady unfamiliar drone. It was unlike anything I had ever heard before. I tried to place the sound. It was no use. It was a sensation like that I had when searching for my father's watch, heard ticking unseen in a room. It made me feel as though I had forgotten to perform some task that my mother had ordered . . . then I located it, overhead. In the sky, flying quite low and about a hundred yards off was a plane! It came so slowly that it seemed barely to move. My mouth hung wide; my bread and butter fell into the dirt. I wanted to jump up and down and cheer. And when the idea struck I trembled with excitement: "Some little white boy's plane's done flew away and all I got to do is stretch out my hands and it'll be mine!" It was a little plane like that at the Fair, flying no higher than the eaves of our roof. Seeing it come steadily forward I felt the world grow warm with promise. I opened the screen and climbed over it and clung there, waiting. I would catch the plane as it came over and swing down fast and run into the house before anyone could see me. Then no one could come to claim the plane. It droned nearer. Then when it hung like a silver cross in the blue directly above me I stretched out my hand and grabbed. It was like sticking my finger through a soap bubble. The plane flew on, as though I had simply blown my breath after it. I grabbed again, frantically, trying to catch the tail. My fingers clutched the air and disappointment surged tight and hard in my throat. Giving one last desperate grasp, I strained forward. My fingers ripped from the screen. I was falling. The ground burst hard against me. I drummed the earth with my heels and when my breath returned, I lay there bawling.

My mother rushed through the door.

"What's the matter, chile! What on earth is wrong with you?"

"It's gone! It's gone!"

"What gone?"

"The airplane . . ."

"Airplane?"

"Yessum, jus' like the one at the Fair. . . . I . . . I tried to stop it an' it kep' right on going. . . ."

"When, boy?"

"Just now," I cried, through my tears.

"Where it go, boy, what way?"

"Yonder, there . . ."

She scanned the sky, her arms akimbo and her checkered apron flapping in the wind as I pointed to the fading plane. Finally she looked down at me, slowly shaking her head.

"It's gone! It's gone!" I cried.

"Boy, is you a fool?" she said. "Don't you see that there's a real airplane 'stead of one of them toy ones?"

"Real . . . ?" I forgot to cry. "Real?"

"Yass, real. Don't you know that thing you reaching for is bigger'n a auto? You here trying to reach for it and I bet it's flying 'bout two hundred miles higher'n this roof." She was disgusted with me. "You come on in this house before somebody else sees what a fool you done turned out to be. You must think these here lil ole arms of you'n is mighty long. . . ."

I was carried into the house and undressed for bed and the doctor was called. I cried bitterly, as much from the disappointment of finding the plane so far beyond my reach as from the pain.

When the doctor came I heard my mother telling him about the plane and asking if anything was wrong with my mind. He explained that I had had a fever for several hours. But I was kept in bed for a week and I constantly saw the plane in my sleep, flying just beyond my fingertips, sailing so slowly that it seemed barely to move. And each time I'd reach out to grab it I'd miss and through each dream I'd hear my grandma warning:

Young man, young man,
Yo' arms too short
To box with God. . . .

"Hey, son!"

At first he did not know where he was and looked at the old man pointing, with blurred eyes.

"Ain't that one of you-all's airplanes coming after you?"

As his vision cleared he saw a small black shape above a distant field, soaring through waves of heat. But he could not be sure and with the pain he feared that somehow a horrible recurring fantasy of being split in twain by the whirling blades of a propeller had come true.

"You think he sees us?" he heard.

"See? I hope so."

"He's coming like a bat outa hell!"

Straining, he heard the faint sound of a motor and hoped it would soon be over.

"How you feeling?"

"Like a nightmare," he said.

"Hey, he's done curved back the other way!"

"Maybe he saw us," he said. "Maybe he's gone to send out the ambulance and ground crew." And, he thought with despair, maybe he didn't even see us.

"Where did you send the boy?"

"Down to Mister Graves," Jefferson said. "Man what owns this land."

"Do you think he phoned?"

Jefferson looked at him quickly.

"Aw sho'. Dabney Graves is got a bad name on accounta them killings but he'll call though. . . ."

"What killings?"

"Them five fellers . . . ain't you heard?" he asked with surprise.

"No."

"Everybody knows 'bout Dabney Graves, especially the colored. He done killed enough of us."

Todd had the sensation of being caught in a white neighborhood after dark.

"What did they do?" he asked.

"Thought they was men," Jefferson said. "An' some he owed money, like he do me. . . ."

"But why do you stay here?"

"You black, son."

"I know, but . . ."

"You have to come by the white folks, too."

He turned away from Jefferson's eyes, at once consoled and accused. And I'll have to come by them soon, he thought with despair. Closing his eyes, he heard Jefferson's voice as the sun burned blood-red upon his lips.

"I got nowhere to go," Jefferson said, "an' they'd come after me if I did. But Dabney Graves is a funny fellow. He's all the time making jokes. He can be mean as hell, then he's liable to turn right around and back the colored against the white folks. I seen him do it. But me, I hates him for that more'n anything else. 'Cause just as soon as he gits tired helping a man he don't care what happens to him. He just leaves him stone cold. And then the other white folks is double hard on anybody he done helped. For him it's just a joke. He don't give a hilla beans for nobody—but hisself. . . ."

Todd listened to the thread of detachment in the old man's voice. It was as though he held his words arm's length before him to avoid their destructive meaning.

"He'd just as soon do you a favor and then turn right around and have you strung up. Me, I stays outa his way 'cause down here that's what you gotta do."

If my ankle would only ease for a while, he thought. The closer I spin toward the earth the blacker I become, flashed through his mind. Sweat ran into his eyes and he was sure that he would never see the plane if his head continued whirling. He tried to see Jefferson, what it was that Jefferson held in his hand? It was a little black man, another Jefferson! A little black Jefferson that shook with fits of belly-laughter while the other Jefferson looked on with detachment. Then Jefferson looked up from the thing in his hand and turned to speak, but Todd was far away, searching the sky for a plane in a hot dry land on a day and age he had long forgotten. He was going mysteriously with his mother through empty streets where black faces peered from behind drawn shades and someone was rapping at a window and he was looking back to see a hand and a frightened face frantically beckoning from a cracked door and his mother was looking down the empty perspective of the street and shaking her head and hurrying him along and at first it was only a flash he saw and a motor was droning as through the sun-glare he saw it gleaming silver as it circled and he was seeing a burst like a puff of white smoke and hearing his mother yell, Come along, boy, I got no time for them fool airplanes, I got no time, and he saw it a second time, the plane flying high, and the burst appeared suddenly and fell slowly, billowing out and sparkling like fireworks and he was watching and being hurried along as the air filled with a flurry of white pinwheeling cards that caught in the wind and scattered over the rooftops and into the gutters and a woman was running and snatching a card and reading it and screaming and he darted into the shower, grabbing as in winter he grabbed for snowflakes and bounding away at his mother's, Come on here, boy! Come on, I say! and he was watching as she took the card away, seeing her face grow puzzled and turning taut as her voice quavered, "Niggers Stay From The Polls," and died to a moan of terror as he saw the eyeless sockets of a white hood staring at him from the card and above he saw the plane spiraling gracefully, agleam in the sun like a fiery sword. And seeing it soar he was caught, transfixed between a terrible horror and a horrible fascination.

The sun was not so high now, and Jefferson was calling and gradually he saw three figures moving across the curving roll of the field.

"Look like some doctors, all dressed in white," said Jefferson.

They're coming at last, Todd thought. And he felt such a release of tension within him that he thought he would faint. But no sooner did he close his eyes than he was seized and he was struggling with three white men who were forcing his arms into some kind of coat. It was too much for him, his arms were pinned to his sides and as the pain blazed in his eyes, he realized that it was a straitjacket. What filthy joke was this?

"That oughta hold him, Mister Graves," he heard.

His total energies seemed focused in his eyes as he searched their faces. That was Graves; the other two wore hospital uniforms. He was poised between two poles of fear and hate as he heard the one called Graves saying, "He looks kinda purty in that there suit, boys. I'm glad you dropped by."

"This boy ain't crazy, Mister Graves," one of the others said. "He needs a doctor, not us. Don't see how you led us way out here anyway. It might be a joke to you, but your Cousin Rudolph liable to kill somebody. White folks or niggers, don't make no difference. . . ."

Todd saw the man turn red with anger. Graves looked down upon him, chuckling.

"This nigguh belongs in a straitjacket, too, boys. I knowed that the minit Jeff's kid said something 'bout a nigguh flyer. You all know you cain't let the nigguh git up that high without his going crazy. The nigguh brain ain't built right for high altitudes. . . ."

Todd watched the drawling red face, feeling that all the unnamed horror and obscenities that he had ever imagined stood materialized before him.

"Let's git outta here," one of the attendants said.

Todd saw the other reach toward him, realizing for the first time that he lay upon a stretcher as he yelled.

"Don't put your hands on me!"

They drew back, surprised.

"What's that you say, nigguh?" asked Graves.

He did not answer and thought that Graves's foot was aimed at his head. It landed on his chest and he could hardly breathe. He coughed helplessly, seeing Graves's lips stretch taut over his yellow teeth, and tried to shift his head. It was as though a half-dead fly was dragging slowly across his face and a bomb seemed to burst within him. Blasts of hot, hysterical laughter tore from his chest, causing his eyes to pop and he felt that the veins in his neck would surely burst. And then a part of him stood behind it all, watching the surprise in Graves's red face and his own hysteria. He thought he would never stop, he would laugh himself to death. It rang in his ears like Jefferson's laughter and he looked for him, centering his eyes desperately upon his face, as though somehow he had become his sole salvation in an insane world of outrage and humiliation. It brought a certain relief. He was suddenly aware that although his body was still contorted it was an echo that no longer rang in his ears. He heard Jefferson's voice with gratitude.

"Mister Graves, the Army done tole him not to leave his airplane."

"Nigguh, Army or no, you gittin' off my land! That airplane can stay 'cause it was paid for by taxpayers' money. But you gittin' off. An' dead or alive, it don't make no difference to me."

Todd was beyond it now, lost in a world of anguish.

"Jeff," Graves said, "you and Teddy come and grab holt. I want you to take this here black eagle over to that nigguh airfield and leave him."

Jefferson and the boy approached him silently. He looked away, realizing and doubting at once that only they could release him from his overpowering sense of isolation.

They bent for the stretcher. One of the attendants moved toward Teddy.

"Think you can manage it, boy?"

"I think I can, suh," Teddy said.

"Well, you better go behind then, and let yo' pa go ahead so's to keep that leg elevated."

He saw the white men walking ahead as Jefferson and the boy carried him along in silence. Then they were pausing and he felt a hand wiping his face; then he was moving again. And it was as though he had been lifted out of his isolation, back into the world of men. A new current of communication flowed between the man and boy and himself. They moved him gently. Far away he heard a mockingbird liquidly calling. He raised his eyes, seeing a buzzard poised unmoving in space. For a moment the whole afternoon seemed suspended and he waited for the horror to seize him again. Then like a song within his head he heard the boy's soft humming and saw the dark bird glide into the sun and glow like a bird of flaming gold.

BERNARD MALAMUD

b. 1914

Malamud catches the essence of the streets of his native Brooklyn—the voices, accents, turns of phrase, that reveal people's ethnic identity and, at the same time, their special individuality. When Malamud was a boy his parents worked long hours and he was allowed to roam the streets, dreaming and observing. What he saw and heard appears constantly in his fiction. It is the background against which his characters play out their lives; and the sensibility through which the reader perceives this background is often that of a boy —a good, kind, somewhat lonely boy who watches adults at various sorts of joy, nastiness, and violence.

One of Malamud's finest talents is his ability to portray the relationships that developed in the big-city ghettos between the Jews, who were gradually moving out during the twenties and thirties, and the blacks who were moving up from the South to take their place in the Jews' old tenement houses. In "Black Is My Favorite Color" Nat Lime's sweet but uncomprehending attempt to love blacks more than he loves whites exposes a wide range of emotion, from the comic insistence of Charity Sweetness on eating her hard-boiled eggs in the toilet to the deeply felt cry of Ornita rejecting Nat: "I got troubles of my own." To this Brooklyn of racial intermixing, Malamud brought a compassionate Yiddish sense of humor—a conviction that do what you will the absurd will happen to you—and a tragic feel for human suffering, the literary prototype of which he found in Dostoyevsky. The blacks he portrays are, of course, seen from a Jewish point of view, and it is this fact that constitutes the central irony in "Angel Levine." He treats both blacks and Jews with sympathy but with a comic irony that reveals a deep relationship between them.

Malamud began writing in high school, went to City College in New York, graduating in 1936, and, after doing various jobs to support himself during the Depression, earned an M.A. in English from Columbia in 1942. He taught English in Oregon (a fictionalized version of his experience there is *A New Life,* 1961), and more recently at Bennington. With the publication of *The Assistant* in 1957, his reputation as a writer was assured. His short stories are collected in *The Magic Barrel* (1958), which won the National Book Award, *Idiots First* (1963) and *Rembrandt's Hat* (1973). *The Fixer* (1966) won the National Book Award and the Pulitzer Prize. His novel *The Tenants* (1971) is an extended treatment of black-Jewish relationships.

Black Is My Favorite Color

Charity Sweetness sits in the toilet eating her two hard-boiled eggs while I'm having my ham sandwich and coffee in the kitchen. That's how it goes only don't get the idea of ghettoes. If there's a ghetto I'm the one that's in it. She's my cleaning woman from Father Divine and comes in once a week to my small three-room apartment on my day off from the liquor store. "Peace," she says to me, "Father reached on down and took me right up in Heaven." She's a small person with a flat body, frizzy hair, and a quiet face that the light shines out of, and Mama had such eyes before she died. The first time Charity Sweetness came in to clean, a little more than a year and a half, I made the mistake to ask her to sit down at the kitchen table with me and eat her lunch. I was still feeling not so hot after Ornita left but I'm the kind of a man—Nat Lime, forty-four, a bachelor with a daily growing bald spot on the back of my head, and I could lose frankly fifteen pounds—who enjoys company so long as he has it. So she cooked up her two hardboiled eggs and sat down and took a small bite out of one of them. But after a minute she stopped chewing and she got up and carried the eggs in a cup in the bathroom, and since then she eats there. I said to her more than once, "Okay, Charity Sweetness, so have it your way, eat the eggs in the kitchen by yourself and I'll eat when you're done," but she smiles absentmindedly, and eats in the toilet. It's my fate with colored people.

Although black is still my favorite color you wouldn't know it from my luck except in short quantities even though I do all right in the liquor store business in Harlem, on Eighth Avenue between 110th and 111th. I speak with respect. A large part of my life I've had dealings with Negro people, most on a business basis but sometimes for friendly reasons with genuine feeling on both sides. I'm drawn to them. At this time of my life I should have one or two good colored friends but the fault isn't necessarily mine. If they knew what was in my heart towards them, but how can you tell that to anybody nowadays? I've tried more than once but the language of the heart either is a dead language or else nobody understands it the way you speak it. Very few. What I'm saying is, personally for me there's only one human color and that's the color of blood. I like a black person if not because he's black, then because I'm white. It comes to the same thing. If I wasn't white my first choice would be black. I'm satisfied to be white because I have no other choice. Anyway, I got an eye for color. I appreciate. Who wants everybody to be the same? Maybe it's like some kind of talent. Nat Lime might be a liquor dealer in Harlem, but once in the jungle in New Guinea in the Second War, I got the idea when I shot at a running Jap and missed him, that I had some kind of a talent, though maybe it's the kind where you have a marvelous idea now and then but in the end what do they come to? After all, it's a strange world.

Where Charity Sweetness eats her eggs makes me think about Buster Wilson when we were both boys in the Williamsburg section of Brooklyn. There was this long block of run-down dirty frame houses in the middle of a not-so-hot white neighborhood full of pushcarts. The Negro houses looked to me like they had been born and died there, dead not long after the beginning of the world. I lived on the next street. My father was a cutter with arthritis in both hands, big red knuckles and swollen fingers so he didn't cut, and my mother was the one who went to work. She sold paper bags from a second-hand pushcart in Ellery Street. We didn't starve but nobody ate chicken unless we were sick or the chicken was. This was my first acquaintance with a lot of black people and I used to poke around on their poor block. I think I thought, brother, if there can be like this, what can't there be? I mean I caught an early idea what life was about. Anyway I met Buster Wilson there. He used to play marbles by himself. I sat on the curb across the street, watching him shoot one marble lefty and the other one righty. The hand that won picked up the marbles. It wasn't so much of a game but he didn't ask me to come over. My idea was to be friendly, only he never encouraged, he discouraged. Why did I pick him out for a friend? Maybe because I had no others then, we were new in the neighborhood, from Manhattan. Also I liked his type. Buster did everything alone. He was a skinny kid and his brothers' clothes hung on him like worn-out potato sacks. He was a beanpole boy, about twelve, and I was then ten. His arms and legs were burnt out matchsticks. He always wore a brown wool sweater, one arm half unraveled, the other went down to the wrist. His long and narrow head had a white part cut straight in the short woolly hair, maybe with a ruler there, by his father, a barber but too drunk to stay a barber. In those days though I had little myself I was old enough to know who was better off, and the whole block of colored houses made me feel bad in the daylight. But I went there as much as I could because the street was full of life. In the night it looked different, it's hard to tell a cripple in the dark. Sometimes I was afraid to walk by the houses when they were dark and quiet. I was afraid there were people looking at me that I couldn't see. I liked it better when they had parties at night and everybody had a good time. The musicians played their banjos and saxophones and the houses shook with the music and laughing. The young girls, with the pretty dresses and ribbons in their hair, caught me in my throat when I saw them through the windows.

But with the parties came drinking and fights. Sundays were bad days after the Saturday night parties. I remember once that Buster's father, also long and loose, always wearing a dirty gray Homburg hat, chased another black man in the street with a half-inch chisel. The other one, maybe five feet high, lost his shoe and when they wrestled on the ground he was already bleeding through his suit, a thick red blood smearing the sidewalk. I was frightened by the blood and wanted to pour it back in the man who was bleeding from the chisel. On another time Buster's father was playing in a crap game with two big bouncy red dice, in the back of an alley between two middle houses. Then about six men started fist-fighting there, and they ran out of the alley and hit each other in the street. The neighbors, including children, came out and watched, everybody afraid but nobody moving to do anything. I saw the same thing near my store in Harlem, years later, a big crowd watching two men in the street, their breaths hanging in the air on a winter night, murdering each other with switch knives, but nobody moved to call a cop. I didn't either. Anyway, I was just a young kid but I still remember how the cops drove up in a police paddy wagon and broke up the fight by hitting everybody they could hit with big nightsticks. This was in the days before LaGuardia. Most of the fighters were knocked out cold, only one or two got away. Buster's father started to run back in his house but a cop ran after him and cracked him on his Homburg hat with a club, right on the front porch. Then the Negro men were lifted up by the cops, one at the arms and the other at the feet, and they heaved them in the paddy wagon. Buster's father hit the back of the wagon and fell, with his nose spouting very red blood, on top of three other men. I personally couldn't stand it, I was scared of the human race so I ran home, but I remember Buster watching without any expression in his eyes. I stole an extra fifteen cents from my mother's pocketbook and I ran back and asked Buster if he wanted to go to the movies. I would pay. He said yes. This was the first time he talked to me.

So we went more than once to the movies. But we never got to be friends. Maybe because it was a one-way proposition—from me to him. Which includes my invitations to go with me, my (poor mother's) movie money, Hershey chocolate bars, watermelon slices, even my best Nick Carter and Merriwell books that I spent hours picking up in the junk shops, and that he never gave me back. Once he let me go in his house to get a match so we could smoke some butts we found, but it smelled so heavy, so impossible, I died till I got out of there. What I saw in the way of furniture I won't mention—the best was falling apart in pieces. Maybe we went to the movies all together five or six matinees that spring and in the summertime, but when the shows were over he usually walked home by himself.

"Why don't you wait for me, Buster?" I said. "We're both going in the same direction."

But he was walking ahead and didn't hear me. Anyway he didn't answer.

One day when I wasn't expecting it he hit me in the teeth. I felt like crying but not because of the pain. I spit blood and said, "What did you hit me for? What did I do to you?"

"Because you a Jew bastard. Take your Jew movies and your Jew candy and shove them up your Jew ass."

And he ran away.

I thought to myself how was I to know he didn't like the movies. When I was a man I thought, you can't force it.

Years later, in the prime of my life, I met Mrs. Ornita Harris. She was standing by herself under an open umbrella at the bus stop, crosstown 110th, and I picked up her green glove that she had dropped on the wet sidewalk. It was in the end of November. Before I could ask her was it hers, she grabbed the glove out of my hand, closed her umbrella, and stepped in the bus. I got on right after her.

I was annoyed so I said, "If you'll pardon me, Miss, there's no law that you have to say thanks, but at least don't make a criminal out of me."

"Well, I'm sorry," she said, "but I don't like white men trying to do me favors."

I tipped my hat and that was that. In ten minutes I got off the bus but she was already gone.

Who expected to see her again but I did. She came into my store about a week later for a bottle of scotch.

"I would offer you a discount," I told her, "but I know you don't like a certain kind of a favor and I'm not looking for a slap in the face."

Then she recognized me and got a little embarrassed.

"I'm sorry I misunderstood you that day."

"So mistakes happen."

The result was she took the discount. I gave her a dollar off.

She used to come in about every two weeks for a fifth of Haig and Haig. Sometimes I waited on her, sometimes my helpers, Jimmy or Mason, also colored, but I said to give the discount. They both looked at me but I had nothing to be ashamed. In the spring when she came in we used to talk once in a while. She was a slim woman, dark but not the most dark, about thirty years I would say, also well built, with a combination nice legs and a good-size bosom that I like. Her face was pretty, with big eyes and high cheek bones, but lips a little thick and nose a little broad. Sometimes she didn't feel like talking, she paid for the bottle, less discount, and walked out. Her eyes were tired and she didn't look to me like a happy woman.

I found out her husband was once a window cleaner on the big buildings, but one day his safety belt broke and he fell fifteen stories. After the funeral she got a job as a manicurist in a Times Square barber shop. I told her I was a bachelor and lived with my mother in a small three-room apartment on West Eighty-third near Broadway. My mother had cancer, and Ornita said she was very sorry.

One night in July we went out together. How that happened I'm still not so sure. I guess I asked her and she didn't say no. Where do you go out with a Negro woman? We went to the Village. We had a good dinner and walked in Washington Square Park. It was a hot night. Nobody was surprised when they saw us, nobody looked at us like we were against the law. If they looked maybe they saw my new lightweight suit that I bought yesterday and my shiny bald spot when we walked under a lamp, also how pretty she was for a man of my type. We went in a movie on West Eighth Street. I didn't want to go in but she said she had heard about the picture. We went in like strangers and we came out like strangers. I wondered what was in her mind and I thought to myself, whatever is in there it's not a certain white man that I know. All night long we went together like we were chained. After the movie she wouldn't let me take her back to Harlem. When I put her in a taxi she asked me, "Why did we bother?"

For the steak, I wanted to say. Instead I said, "You're worth the bother."

"Thanks anyway."

Kiddo, I thought to myself after the taxi left, you just found out what's what, now the best thing is forget her.

It's easy to say. In August we went out the second time. That was the night she wore a purple dress and I thought to myself, my God, what colors. Who paints that picture paints a masterpiece. Everybody looked at us but I had pleasure. That night when she took off her dress it was in a furnished room I had the sense to rent a few days before. With my sick mother, I couldn't ask her to come to my apartment, and she didn't want me to go home with her where she lived with her brother's family on West 115th near Lenox Avenue. Under her purple dress she wore a black slip, and when she took that off she had white underwear. When she took off the white underwear she was black again. But I know where the next white was, if you want to call it white. And that was the night I think I fell in love with her, the first time in my life though I have liked one or two nice girls I used to go with when I was a boy. It was a serious proposition. I'm the kind of a man when I think of love I'm thinking of marriage. I guess that's why I am a bachelor.

That same week I had a holdup in my place, two big men—both black—with revolvers. One got excited when I rang open the cash register so he could take the money and he hit me over the ear with his gun. I stayed in the hospital a couple of weeks. Otherwise I was insured. Ornita came to see me. She sat on a chair without talking much. Finally I saw she was uncomfortable so I suggested she ought to go home.

"I'm sorry it happened," she said.

"Don't talk like it's your fault."

When I got out of the hospital my mother was dead. She was a wonderful person. My father died when I was thirteen and all by herself she kept the family alive and together. I sat shive for a week and remembered how she sold paper bags on her pushcart. I remembered her life and what she tried to teach me. Nathan, she said, if you ever forget you are a Jew a goy will remind you. Mama, I said, rest in peace on this subject. But if I do something you don't like, remember, on earth it's harder than where you are. Then when my week of mourning was finished, one night I said, "Ornita, let's get married. We're both honest people and if you love me like I love you it won't be such a bad time. If you don't like New York I'll sell out here and we'll move someplace else. Maybe to San Francisco where nobody knows us. I was there for a week in the Second War and I saw white and colored living together."

"Nat," she answered me, "I like you but I'd be afraid. My husband woulda killed me."

"Your husband is dead."

"Not in my memory."

"In that case I'll wait."

"Do you know what it'd be like—I mean the life we could expect?"

"Ornita," I said, "I'm the kind of a man, if he picks his own way of life he's satisfied."

"What about children? Were you looking forward to half-Jewish polka dots?"

"I was looking forward to children."

"I can't," she said.

Can't is can't. I saw she was afraid and the best thing was not to push. Sometimes when we met she was so nervous that whatever we did she couldn't enjoy it. At the same time I still thought I had a chance. We were together more and more. I got rid of my furnished room and she came to my apartment—I gave away Mama's bed and bought a new one. She stayed with me all day on Sundays. When she wasn't so nervous she was affectionate, and if I know what love is, I had it. We went out a couple of times a week, the same way—usually I met her in Times Square and sent her home in a taxi, but I talked more about marriage and she talked less against it. One night she told me she was still trying to convince herself but she was almost convinced. I took an inventory of my liquor stock so I could put the store up for sale.

Ornita knew what I was doing. One day she quit her job, the next day she took it back. She also went away a week to visit her sister in Philadelphia for a little rest. She came back tired but said maybe. Maybe is maybe so I'll wait. The way she said it was closer to yes. That was the winter two years ago. When she was in Philadelphia I called up a friend of mine from the Army, now CPA, and told him I would appreciate an invitation for an evening. He knew why. His wife said yes right away. When Ornita came back we went there. The wife made a fine dinner. It wasn't a bad time and they told us to come again. Ornita had a few drinks. She looked relaxed, wonderful. Later, because of a twenty-four hour taxi strike I had to take her home on the subway. When we got to the 116th Street station she told me to stay on the train, and she would walk the couple of blocks to her house. I didn't like a woman walking alone on the streets at that time of the night. She said she never had any trouble but I insisted nothing doing. I said I would walk to her stoop with her and when she went upstairs I would go back to the subway.

On the way there, on 115th in the middle of the block before Lenox, we were stopped by three men—maybe they were boys. One had a black hat with a half-inch brim, one a green cloth hat, and the third wore a black leather cap. The green hat was wearing a short coat and the other two had long ones. It was under a street light but the leather cap snapped a six-inch switchblade open in the light.

"What you doin' with this white son of a bitch?" he said to Ornita.

"I'm minding my own business," she answered him, "and I wish you would too."

"Boys," I said, "we're all brothers. I'm a reliable merchant in the neighborhood. This young lady is my dear friend. We don't want any trouble. Please let us pass."

"You talk like a Jew landlord," said the green hat. "Fifty a week for a single room."

"No charge fo' the rats," said the half-inch brim.

"Believe me, I'm no landlord. My store is 'Nathan's Liquors' between Hundred Tenth and Eleventh. I also have two colored clerks, Mason and Jimmy, and they will tell you I pay good wages as well as I give discounts to certain customers."

"Shut your mouth, Jewboy," said the leather cap, and he moved the knife back and forth in front of my coat button. "No more black pussy for you."

"Speak with respect about this lady, please."

I got slapped on my mouth.

"That ain't no lady," said the long face in the half-inch brim, "that's black pussy. She deserve to have evvy bit of her hair shaved off. How you like to have evvy bit of your hair shave off, black pussy?"

"Please leave me and this gentleman alone or I'm gonna scream long and loud. That's my house three doors down."

They slapped her. I never heard such a scream. Like her husband was falling fifteen stories.

I hit the one that slapped her and the next I knew I was lying in the gutter with a pain in my head. I thought, goodbye, Nat, they'll stab me for sure, but all they did was take my wallet and run in three different directions.

Ornita walked back with me to the subway and she wouldn't let me go home with her again.

"Just get home safely."

She looked terrible. Her face was gray and I still remembered her scream. It was a terrible winter night, very cold February, and it took me an hour and ten minutes to get home. I felt bad for leaving her but what could I do?

We had a date downtown the next night but she didn't show up, the first time.

In the morning I called her place of business.

"For God's sake, Ornita, if we got married and moved away we wouldn't have that kind of trouble that we had. We wouldn't come in that neighborhood any more."

"Yes, we would. I have family there and don't want to move anyplace else. The truth of it is I can't marry you, Nat. I got troubles enough of my own."

"I coulda sworn you love me."

"Maybe I do but I can't marry you."

"For God's sake, why?"

"I got enough trouble of my own."

I went that night in a cab to her brother's house to see her. He was a quiet man with a thin mustache. "She gone," he said, "left for a long visit to some close relatives in the South. She said to tell you she appreciate your intentions but didn't think it will work out."

"Thank you kindly," I said.

Don't ask me how I got home.

Once on Eighth Avenue, a couple of blocks from my store, I saw a blind man with a white cane tapping on the sidewalk. I figured we were going in the same direction so I took his arm.

"I can tell you're white," he said.

A heavy colored woman with a full shopping bag rushed after us.

"Never mind," she said, "I know where he live."

She pushed me with her shoulder and I hurt my leg on the fire hydrant.

That's how it is. I give my heart and they kick me in my teeth.

"Charity Sweetness—you hear me?—come out of that goddamn toilet!"

The Magic Barrel

Not long ago there lived in uptown New York, in a small, almost meager room, though crowded with books, Leo Finkle, a rabbinical student in the Yeshivah University. Finkle, after six years of study, was to be ordained in June and had been advised by an acquaintance that he might find it easier to win himself a congregation if he were married. Since he had no present prospects of marriage, after two tormented days of turning it over in his mind, he called Pinye Salzman, a marriage broker whose two-line advertisement he had read in the *Forward*.

The matchmaker appeared one night out of the dark fourth-floor hallway of the graystone rooming house where Finkle lived, grasping a black, strapped portfolio that had been worn thin with use. Salzman, who had been long in the business, was of slight but dignified build, wearing an old hat, and an overcoat too short and tight for him. He smelled frankly of fish, which he loved to eat, and although he was missing a few teeth, his presence was not displeasing, because of an amiable manner curiously contrasted with mournful eyes. His voice, his lips, his wisp of beard, his bony fingers were animated, but give him a moment of repose and his mild blue eyes revealed a depth of sadness, a characteristic that put Leo a little at ease although the situation, for him, was inherently tense.

He at once informed Salzman why he had asked him to come, explaining that his home was in Cleveland, and that but for his parents, who had married comparatively late in life, he was alone in the world. He had for six years devoted himself almost entirely to his studies, as a result of which, understandably, he had found himself without time for a social life and the company of young women. Therefore he thought it the better part of trial and error—of embarrassing fumbling—to call in an experienced person to advise him on these matters. He remarked in passing that the function of the marriage broker was ancient and honorable, highly approved in the Jewish community, because it made practical the necessary without hindering joy. Moreover, his own parents had been brought together by a matchmaker. They had made, if not a financially profitable marriage—since neither had possessed any worldly goods to speak of—at least a successful one in the sense of their everlasting devotion to each other. Salzman listened in embarrassed surprise, sensing a sort of apology. Later, however, he experienced a glow of pride in his work, an emotion that had left him years ago, and he heartily approved of Finkle.

The two went to their business. Leo had led Salzman to the only clear place in the room, a table near a window that overlooked the lamp-lit city. He seated himself at the matchmaker's side but facing him, attempting by an act of will to suppress the unpleasant tickle in his throat. Salzman eagerly unstrapped his portfolio and removed a loose rubber band from a thin packet of much-handled cards. As he flipped through them, a gesture and sound that physically hurt Leo, the student pretended not to see and gazed steadfastly out the window. Although it was still February, winter was on its last legs, signs of which he had for the first time in years begun to notice. He now observed the round white moon, moving high in the sky through a cloud menagerie, and watched with half-open mouth as it penetrated a huge hen, and dropped out of her like an egg laying itself. Salzman, though pretending through eyeglasses he had just slipped on, to be engaged in scanning the writing on the cards, stole occasional glances at the young man's distinguished face, noting with pleasure the long, severe scholar's nose, brown eyes heavy with learning, sensitive yet ascetic lips, and a certain, almost hollow quality of the dark cheeks. He gazed around at shelves upon shelves of books and let out a soft, contented sigh.

When Leo's eyes fell upon the cards, he counted six spread out in Salzman's hand.

"So few?" he asked in disappointment.

"You wouldn't believe me how much cards I got in my office," Salzman replied. "The drawers are already filled to the top, so I keep them now in a barrel, but is every girl good for a new rabbi?"

Leo blushed at this, regretting all he had revealed of himself in a curriculum vitae he had sent to Salzman. He had thought it best to acquaint him with his strict standards and specifications, but in having done so, felt he had told the marriage broker more than was absolutely necessary.

He hesitantly inquired, "Do you keep photographs of your clients on file?"

"First comes family, amount of dowry, also what kind promises," Salzman replied, unbuttoning his tight coat and settling himself in the chair. "After comes pictures, rabbi."

"Call me Mr. Finkle. I'm not yet a rabbi."

Salzman said he would, but instead called him doctor, which he changed to rabbi when Leo was not listening too attentively.

Salzman adjusted his horn-rimmed spectacles, gently cleared his throat and read in an eager voice the contents of the top card:

"Sophie P. Twenty four years. Widow one year. No children. Educated high school and two years college. Father promises eight thousand dollars. Has wonderful wholesale business. Also real estate. On the mother's side comes teachers, also one actor. Well known on Second Avenue."

Leo gazed up in surprise. "Did you say a widow?"

"A widow don't mean spoiled, rabbi. She lived with her husband maybe four months. He was a sick boy she made a mistake to marry him."

"Marrying a widow has never entered my mind."

"This is because you have no experience. A widow, especially if she is young and healthy like this girl, is a wonderful person to marry. She will be thankful to you the rest of her life. Believe me, if I was looking now for a bride, I would marry a widow."

Leo reflected, then shook his head.

Salzman hunched his shoulders in an almost imperceptible gesture of disappointment. He placed the card down on the wooden table and began to read another:

"Lily H. High school teacher. Regular. Not a substitute. Has savings and new Dodge car. Lived in Paris one year. Father is successful dentist thirty-five years. Interested in professional man. Well Americanized family. Wonderful opportunity."

"I knew her personally," said Salzman. "I wish you could see this girl. She is a doll. Also very intelligent. All day you could talk to her about books and theyater and what not. She also knows current events."

"I don't believe you mentioned her age?"

"Her age?" Salzman said, raising his brows. "Her age is thirty-two years."

Leo said after a while, "I'm afraid that seems a little too old."

Salzman let out a laugh. "So how old are you, rabbi?"

"Twenty-seven."

"So what is the difference, tell me, between twenty-seven and thirty-two? My own wife is seven years older than me. So what did I suffer?—nothing. If Rothschild's a daughter wants to marry you, would you say on account her age, no?"

"Yes," Leo said dryly.

Salzman shook off the no in the yes. "Five years don't mean a thing. I give you my word that when you will live with her for one week you will forget her age. What does it mean five years—that she lived more and knows more than somebody who is younger? On this girl, God bless her, years are not wasted. Each one that it comes makes better the bargain."

"What subject does she teach in high school?"

"Languages. If you heard the way she speaks French, you will think it is music. I am in the business twenty-five years, and I recommend her with my whole heart. Believe me, I know what I'm talking, rabbi."

"What's on the next card?" Leo said abruptly.

Salzman reluctantly turned up the third card:

"Ruth K. Nineteen years. Honor student. Father offers thirteen thousand cash to the right bridegroom. He is a medical doctor. Stomach specialist with marvelous practice. Brother in law owns own garment business. Particular people."

Salzman looked as if he had read his trump card.

"Did you say nineteen?" Leo asked with interest.

"On the dot."

"Is she attractive?" He blushed. "Pretty?"

Salzman kissed his finger tips. "A little doll. On this I give you my word. Let me call the father tonight and you will see what means pretty."

But Leo was troubled. "You're sure she's that young?"

"This I am positive. The father will show you the birth certificate."

"Are you positive there isn't something wrong with her?" Leo insisted.

"Who says there is wrong?"

"I don't understand why an American girl her age should go to a marriage broker."

A smile spread over Salzman's face.

"So for the same reason you went, she comes."

Leo flushed. "I am pressed for time."

Salzman, realizing he had been tactless, quickly explained. "The father came, not her. He wants she should have the best, so he looks around himself. When we will locate the right boy he will introduce him and encourage. This makes a better marriage than if a young girl without experience takes for herself. I don't have to tell you this."

"But don't you think this young girl believes in love?" Leo spoke uneasily.

Salzman was about to guffaw but caught himself and said soberly, "Love comes with the right person, not before."

Leo parted dry lips but did not speak. Noticing that Salzman had snatched a glance at the next card, he cleverly asked, "How is her health?"

"Perfect," Salzman said, breathing with difficulty. "Of course, she is a little lame on her right foot from an auto accident that it happened to her when she was twelve years, but nobody notices on account she is so brilliant and also beautiful."

Leo got up heavily and went to the window. He felt curiously bitter and upbraided himself for having called in the marriage broker. Finally, he shook his head.

"Why not?" Salzman persisted, the pitch of his voice rising.

"Because I detest stomach specialists."

"So what do you care what is his business? After you marry her do you need him? Who says he must come every Friday night in your house?"

Ashamed of the way the talk was going, Leo dismissed Salzman, who went home with heavy, melancholy eyes.

Though he had felt only relief at the marriage broker's departure, Leo was in low spirits the next day. He explained it as arising from Salzman's failure to produce a suitable bride for him. He did not care for his type of clientele. But when Leo found himself hesitating whether to seek out another matchmaker, one more polished than Pinye, he wondered if it could be—his protestations to the contrary, and although he honored his father and mother—that he did not, in essence, care for the matchmaking institution? This thought he quickly put out of mind yet found himself still upset. All day he ran around in the woods—missed an important appointment, forgot to give out his laundry, walked out of a Broadway cafeteria without paying and had to run back with the ticket in his hand; had even not recognized his landlady in the street when she passed with a friend and courteously called out, "A good evening to you, Doctor Finkle." By nightfall, however, he had regained sufficient calm to sink his nose into a book and there found peace from his thoughts.

Almost at once there came a knock on the door. Before Leo could say enter, Salzman, commercial cupid, was standing in the room. His face was gray and meager, his expression hungry, and he looked as if he would expire on his feet. Yet the marriage broker managed, by some trick of the muscles, to display a broad smile.

"So good evening. I am invited?"

Leo nodded, disturbed to see him again, yet unwilling to ask the man to leave.

Beaming still, Salzman laid his portfolio on the table. "Rabbi, I got for you tonight good news."

"I've asked you not to call me rabbi. I'm still a student."

"Your worries are finished. I have for you a first-class bride."

"Leave me in peace concerning this subject." Leo pretended lack of interest.

"The world will dance at your wedding."

"Please, Mr. Salzman, no more."

"But first must come back my strength," Salzman said weakly. He fumbled with the portfolio straps and took out of the leather case an oily paper bag, from which he extracted a hard, seeded roll and a small, smoked white fish. With a quick motion of his hand he stripped the fish out of its skin and began ravenously to chew. "All day in a rush," he muttered.

Leo watched him eat.

"A sliced tomato you have maybe?" Salzman hesitantly inquired.

"No."

The marriage broker shut his eyes and ate. When he had finished he carefully cleaned up the crumbs and rolled up the remains of the fish, in the paper bag. His spectacled eyes roamed the room until he discovered, amid some piles of books, a one-burner gas stove. Lifting his hat he humbly asked, "A glass tea you got, rabbi?"

Conscience-stricken, Leo rose and brewed the tea. He served it with a chunk of lemon and two cubes of lump sugar, delighting Salzman.

After he had drunk his tea, Salzman's strength and good spirits were restored.

"So tell me, rabbi," he said amiably, "you considered some more the three clients I mentioned yesterday?"

"There was no need to consider."

"Why not?"

"None of them suits me."

"What then suits you?"

Leo let it pass because he could give only a confused answer.

Without waiting for a reply, Salzman asked, "You remember this girl I talked to you—the high school teacher?"

"Age thirty-two?"

But, surprisingly, Salzman's face lit in a smile. "Age twenty-nine."

Leo shot him a look. "Reduced from thirty-two?"

"A mistake," Salzman avowed. "I talked today with the dentist. He took me to his safety deposit box and showed me the birth certificate. She was twenty-nine years last August. They made her a party in the mountains where she went for her vacation. When her father spoke to me the first time I forgot to write the age and I told you thirty-two, but now I remember this was a different client, a widow."

"The same one you told me about? I thought she was twenty-four?"

"A different. Am I responsible that the world is filled with widows?"

"No, but I'm not interested in them, nor for that matter, in school teachers."

Salzman pulled his clasped hands to his breast. Looking at the ceiling he devoutly exclaimed, "Yiddishe kinder, what can I say to somebody that he is not interested in high school teachers? So what then you are interested?"

Leo flushed but controlled himself.

"In what else will you be interested," Salzman went on, "if you not interested in this fine girl that she speaks four languages and has personally in the bank ten thousand dollars? Also her father guarantees further twelve thousand. Also she has a new car, wonderful clothes, talks on all subjects, and she will give you a first-class home and children. How near do we come in our life to paradise?"

"If she's so wonderful, why wasn't she married ten years ago?"

"Why?" said Salzman with a heavy laugh. "—Why? Because she is *partikiler.* This is why. She wants the *best.*"

Leo was silent, amused at how he had entangled himself. But Salzman had aroused his interest in Lily H., and he began seriously to consider calling on her. When the marriage broker observed how intently Leo's mind was at work on the facts he had supplied, he felt certain they would soon come to an agreement.

Late Saturday afternoon, conscious of Salzman, Leo Finkle walked with Lily Hirschorn along Riverside Drive. He walked briskly and erectly, wearing with distinction the black fedora he had that morning taken with trepidation out of the dusty hat box on his closet shelf, and the heavy black Saturday coat he had thoroughly whisked clean. Leo also owned a walking stick, a present from a distant relative, but quickly put temptation aside and did not use it. Lily, petite and not unpretty, had on something signifying the approach of spring. She was au courant, animatedly, with all sorts of subjects, and he weighed her words and found her surprisingly sound—score another for Salzman, whom he uneasily sensed to be somewhere around, hiding perhaps high in a tree along the street, flashing the lady signals with a pocket mirror; or perhaps a cloven-hoofed Pan, piping nuptial ditties as he danced his invisible way before them, strewing wild buds on the walk and purple grapes in their path, symbolizing fruit of a union, though there was of course still none.

Lily startled Leo by remarking, "I was thinking of Mr. Salzman, a curious figure, wouldn't you say?"

Not certain what to answer, he nodded.

She bravely went on, blushing, "I for one am grateful for his introducing us. Aren't you?"

He courteously replied, "I am."

"I mean," she said with a little laugh—and it was all in good taste, or at least gave the effect of being not in bad—"do you mind that we came together so?"

He was not displeased with her honesty, recognizing that she meant to set the relationship aright, and understanding that it took a certain amount of experience in life, and courage, to want to do it quite that way. One had to have some sort of past to make that kind of beginning.

He said that he did not mind. Salzman's function was traditional and honorable—valuable for what it might achieve, which, he pointed out, was frequently nothing.

Lily agreed with a sigh. They walked on for a while and she said after a long silence, again with a nervous laugh, "Would you mind if I asked you something a little bit personal? Frankly I find the subject fascinating." Although Leo shrugged, she went on half embarrassedly, "How was it that you came to your calling? I mean was it a sudden passionate inspiration?"

Leo, after a time, slowly replied, "I was always interested in the Law."

"You saw revealed in it the presence of the Highest?"

He nodded and changed the subject. "I understand that you spent a little time in Paris, Miss Hirschorn?"

"Oh, did Mr. Salzman tell you, Rabbi Finkle?" Leo winced but she went on, "It was ages ago and almost forgotten. I remember I had to return for my sister's wedding."

And Lily would not be put off. "When," she asked in a trembly voice, "did you become enamored of God?"

He stared at her. Then it came to him that she was talking not about Leo Finkle, but of a total stranger, some mystical figure, perhaps even passionate prophet that Salzman had dreamed up for her—no relation to the living or dead. Leo trembled with rage and weakness. The trickster had obviously sold her a bill of goods, just as he had him, who'd expected to become acquainted with a young lady of twenty-nine, only to behold, the moment he laid eyes upon her strained and anxious face, a woman past thirty-five and aging rapidly. Only his self control had kept him this long in her presence.

"I am not," he said gravely, "a talented religious person," and in seeking words to go on, found himself possessed by shame and fear. "I think," he said in a strained manner, "that I came to God not because I loved Him, but because I did not."

This confession he spoke harshly because its unexpectedness shook him.

Lily wilted. Leo saw a profusion of loaves of bread go flying like ducks high over his head, not unlike the winged loaves by which he had counted himself to sleep last night. Mercifully, then, it snowed, which he would not put past Salzman's machinations.

He was infuriated with the marriage broker and swore he would throw him out of the room the minute he reappeared. But Salzman did not come that night, and when Leo's anger had subsided, an unaccountable despair grew in its place. At first he thought this was caused by his disappointment in Lily, but before long it became evident that he had involved himself with Salzman without a true knowledge of his own intent. He gradually realized—with an emptiness that seized him with six hands—that he had called in the broker to find him a bride because he was incapable of doing it himself. This terrifying insight he had derived as a result of his meeting and conversation with Lily Hirschorn. Her probing questions had somehow irritated him into revealing—to himself more than her—the true nature of his relationship to God, and from that it had come upon him, with shocking force, that apart from his parents, he had never loved anyone. Or perhaps it went the other way, that he did not love God so well as he might, because he had not loved man. It seemed to Leo that his whole life stood starkly revealed and he saw himself for the first time as he truly was—unloved and loveless. This bitter but somehow not fully unexpected revelation brought him to a point of panic, controlled only by extraordinary effort. He covered his face with his hands and cried.

The week that followed was the worst of his life. He did not eat and lost weight. His beard darkened and grew ragged. He stopped attending seminars and almost never opened a book. He seriously considered leaving the Yeshivah, although he was deeply troubled at the thought of the loss of all his years of study—saw them like pages torn from a book, strewn over the city—and at the devastating effect of this decision upon his parents. But he had lived without knowledge of himself, and never in the Five Books and all the Commentaries

—mea culpa—had the truth been revealed to him. He did not know where to turn, and in all this desolating loneliness there was no *to whom,* although he often thought of Lily but not once could bring himself to go downstairs and make the call. He became touchy and irritable, especially with his landlady, who asked him all manner of personal questions; on the other hand, sensing his own disagreeableness, he waylaid her on the stairs and apologized abjectly, until mortified, she ran from him. Out of this, however, he drew the consolation that he was a Jew and that a Jew suffered. But gradually, as the long and terrible week drew to a close, he regained his composure and some idea of purpose in life: to go on as planned. Although he was imperfect, the ideal was not. As for his quest of a bride, the thought of continuing afflicted him with anxiety and heartburn, yet perhaps with this new knowledge of himself he would be more successful than in the past. Perhaps love would now come to him and a bride to that love. And for this sanctified seeking who needed a Salzman?

The marriage broker, a skeleton with haunted eyes, returned that very night. He looked, withal, the picture of frustrated expectancy—as if he had steadfastly waited the week at Miss Lily Hirschorn's side for a telephone call that never came.

Casually coughing, Salzman came immediately to the point: "So how did you like her?"

Leo's anger rose and he could not refrain from chiding the matchmaker: "Why did you lie to me, Salzman?"

Salzman's pale face went dead white, the world had snowed on him.

"Did you not state that she was twenty-nine?" Leo insisted.

"I give you my word—"

"She was thirty-five, if a day. *At least* thirty-five."

"Of this don't be too sure. Her father told me—"

"Never mind. The worst of it was that you lied to her."

"How did I lie to her, tell me?

"You told her things about me that weren't true. You made me out to be more, consequently less than I am. She had in mind a totally different person, a sort of semimystical Wonder Rabbi."

"All I said, you was a religious man."

"I can imagine."

Salzman sighed. "This is my weakness that I have," he confessed. "My wife says to me I shouldn't be a salesman, but when I have two fine people that they would be wonderful to be married, I am so happy that I talk too much." He smiled wanly. "This is why Salzman is a poor man."

Leo's anger left him. "Well, Salzman, I'm afraid that's all."

The marriage broker fastened hungry eyes on him.

"You don't want any more a bride?"

"I do," said Leo, "but I have decided to seek her in a different way. I am no longer interested in an arranged marriage. To be frank, I now admit the necessity of premarital love. That is, I want to be in love with the one I marry."

"Love?" said Salzman, astounded. After a moment he remarked, "For us, our love is our life, not for the ladies. In the ghetto they—"

"I know, I know," said Leo. "I've thought of it often. Love, I have said to myself, should be a by-product of living and worship rather than its own end. Yet for myself I find it necessary to establish the level of my need and fulfill it."

Salzman shrugged but answered, "Listen, rabbi, if you want love, this I can find for you also. I have such beautiful clients that you will love them the minute your eyes will see them."

Leo smiled unhappily. "I'm afraid you don't understand."

But Salzman hastily unstrapped his portfolio and withdrew a manila packet from it.

"Pictures," he said, quickly laying the envelope on the table.

Leo called after him to take the pictures away, but as if on the wings of the wind, Salzman had disappeared.

March came. Leo had returned to his regular routine. Although he felt not quite himself yet—lacked energy—he was making plans for a more active social life. Of course it would cost something, but he was an expert in cutting corners; and when there were no corners left he would make circles rounder. All the while Salzman's pictures had lain on the table, gathering dust. Occasionally as Leo sat studying, or enjoying a cup of tea, his eyes fell on the manila envelope, but he never opened it.

The days went by and no social life to speak of developed with a member of the opposite sex—it was difficult, given the circumstances of his situation. One morning Leo toiled up the stairs to his room and stared out of the window at the city. Although the day was bright his view of it was dark. For some time he watched the people in the street below hurrying along and then turned with a heavy heart to his little room. On the table was the packet. With a sudden relentless gesture he tore it open. For a half-hour he stood by the table in a state of excitement, examining the photographs of the ladies Salzman had included. Finally, with a deep sigh he put them down. There were six, of varying degrees of attractiveness, but look at them long enough and they all became Lily Hirschorn: all past their prime, all starved behind bright smiles, not a true personality in the lot. Life, despite their frantic yoohooings, had passed them by; they were pictures in a brief case that stank of fish. After a while, however, as Leo attempted to return the photographs into the envelope, he found in it another, a snapshot of the type taken by a machine for a quarter. He gazed at it a moment and let out a cry.

Her face deeply moved him. Why, he could at first not say. It gave him the impression of youth—spring flowers, yet age—a sense of having been used to the bone, wasted; this came from the eyes, which were hauntingly familiar, yet absolutely strange. He had a vivid impression that he had met her before, but try as he might he could not place her although he could almost recall her name, as if he had read it in her own handwriting. No, this couldn't be: he would have remembered her. It was not, he affirmed, that she had an extraordinary beauty—no, though her face was attractive enough; it was that *something* about her moved him. Feature for feature, even some of the ladies of the photographs could do better; but she leaped forth to his heart—had *lived,* or wanted to—more than just wanted, perhaps regretted how she had lived—had somehow deeply suffered: it could be seen in the depths of those reluctant eyes, and from the way the light enclosed and shone from her, and within her, opening realms of possibility: this was her own. Her he desired. His head ached and eyes narrowed with the intensity of his gazing, then as if an obscure fog had blown up in the mind, he experienced fear of her and was aware that he had received an impression, somehow, of evil. He shuddered, saying softly, it is thus with us all. Leo brewed some tea in a small pot and sat sipping it without sugar, to calm himself. But before he had finished drinking, again with excitement he examined the face and found it good: good for Leo Finkle. Only such a one could understand him and help him seek whatever he was seeking. She might, perhaps, love him. How she had happened to be among the discards in Salzman's barrel he could never guess, but he knew he must urgently go find her.

Leo rushed downstairs, grabbed up the Bronx telephone book, and searched for Salzman's home address. He was not listed, nor was his office. Neither was he in the Manhattan book. But Leo remembered having written down the address on a slip of paper after he had read Salzman's advertisement in the "personals" column of the *Forward.* He ran up to his room and tore through his papers, without luck. It was exasperating. Just when he needed the matchmaker he was nowhere to be found. Fortunately Leo remembered to look in his wallet. There on a card he found his name written and a Bronx address. No phone number was listed, the reason—Leo now recalled—he had originally communicated with Salzman by letter. He got on his coat, put a hat on over his skull cap and hurried to the subway station. All the way to the far end of the Bronx he sat on the edge of his seat. He was more than once tempted to take out the picture and see if the girl's face was as he remembered it, but he refrained, allowing the snapshot to remain in his inside coat pocket, content to have her so close. When the train pulled into the station he was waiting at the door and bolted out. He quickly located the street Salzman had advertised.

The building he sought was less than a block from the subway, but it was not an office building, nor even a loft, nor a store in which one could rent office space. It was a very old tenement house. Leo found Salzman's name in pencil on a soiled tag under the bell and climbed three dark flights to his apartment. When he knocked, the door was opened by a thin, asthmatic, gray-haired woman, in felt slippers.

"Yes?" she said, expecting nothing. She listened without listening. He could have sworn he had seen her, too, before but knew it was an illusion.

"Salzman—does he live here? Pinye Salzman," he said, "the matchmaker?"

She stared at him a long minute. "Of course."

He felt embarrassed. "Is he in?"

"No." Her mouth, though left open, offered nothing more.

"The matter is urgent. Can you tell me where his office is?"

"In the air." She pointed upward.

"You mean he has no office?" Leo asked.

"In his socks."

He peered into the apartment. It was sunless and dingy, one large room divided by a half-open curtain, beyond which he could see a sagging metal bed. The near side of a room was crowded with rickety chairs, old bureaus, a three-legged table, racks of cooking utensils, and all the apparatus of a kitchen. But there was no sign of Salzman or his magic barrel, probably also a figment of the imagination. An odor of frying fish made Leo weak to the knees.

"Where is he?" he insisted. "I've got to see your husband."

At length she answered, "So who knows where he is? Every time he thinks a new thought he runs to a different place. Go home, he will find you."

"Tell him Leo Finkle."

She gave no sign she had heard.

He walked downstairs, depressed.

But Salzman, breathless, stood waiting at his door.

Leo was astounded and overjoyed. "How did you get here before me?"

"I rushed."

"Come inside."

They entered. Leo fixed tea, and a sardine sandwich for Salzman. As they were drinking he reached behind him for the packet of pictures and handed them to the marriage broker.

Salzman put down his glass and said expectantly, "You found somebody you like?"

"Not among these."

The marriage broker turned away.

"Here is the one I want." Leo held forth the snapshot.

Salzman slipped on his glasses and took the picture into his trembling hand. He turned ghastly and let out a groan.

"What's the matter?" cried Leo.

"Excuse me. Was an accident this picture. She isn't for you."

Salzman frantically shoved the manila packet into his portfolio. He thrust the snapshot into his pocket and fled down the stairs.

Leo, after momentary paralysis, gave chase and cornered the marriage broker in the vestibule. The landlady made hysterical outcries but neither of them listened.

"Give me back the picture, Salzman."

"No." The pain in his eyes was terrible.

"Tell me who she is then."

"This I can't tell you. Excuse me."

He made to depart, but Leo, forgetting himself, seized the matchmaker by his tight coat and shook him frenziedly.

"Please," sighed Salzman. "*Please.*"

Leo ashamedly let him go. "Tell me who she is," he begged. "It's very important for me to know."

"She is not for you. She is a wild one—wild, without shame. This is not a bride for a rabbi."

"What do you mean wild?"

"Like an animal. Like a dog. For her to be poor was a sin. This is why to me she is dead now."

"In God's name, what do you mean?"

"Her I can't introduce to you," Salzman cried.

"Why are you so excited?"

"Why, he asks," Salzman said, bursting into tears. "This is my baby, my Stella, she should burn in hell."

Leo hurried up to bed and hid under the covers. Under the covers he thought his life through. Although he soon fell asleep he could not sleep her out of his mind. He woke, beating his breast. Though he prayed to be rid of her, his prayers went unanswered. Through days of torment he endlessly struggled not to love her; fearing success, he escaped it. He then concluded to convert her to goodness, himself to God. The idea alternately nauseated and exalted him.

He perhaps did not know that he had come to a final decision until he encountered Salzman in a Broadway cafeteria. He was sitting alone at a rear table, sucking the bony remains of a fish. The marriage broker appeared haggard, and transparent to the point of vanishing.

Salzman looked up at first without recognizing him. Leo had grown a pointed beard and his eyes were weighted with wisdom.

"Salzman," he said, "love has at last come to my heart."

"Who can love from a picture?" mocked the marriage broker.

"It is not impossible."

"If you can love her, then you can love anybody. Let me show you some new clients that they just sent me their photographs. One is a little doll."

"Just her I want," Leo murmured.

"Don't be a fool, doctor. Don't bother with her."

"Put me in touch with her, Salzman," Leo said humbly. "Perhaps I can be of service."

Salzman had stopped eating and Leo understood with emotion that it was now arranged.

Leaving the cafeteria, he was, however, afflicted by a tormenting suspicion that Salzman had planned it all to happen this way.

Leo was informed by letter that she would meet him on a certain corner, and she was there one spring night, waiting under a street lamp. He appeared, carrying a small bouquet of violets and rosebuds. Stella stood by the lamp post, smoking. She wore white with red shoes, which fitted his expectations, although in a troubled moment he had imagined the dress red, and only the shoes white. She waited uneasily and shyly. From afar he saw that her eyes—clearly her father's—were filled with desperate innocence. He pictured, in her, his own redemption. Violins and lit candles revolved in the sky. Leo ran forward with flowers outthrust.

Around the corner, Salzman, leaning against a wall, chanted prayers for the dead.

DORIS LESSING

b. 1919

Lessing is a writer who seeks to portray in the twentieth century the kind of large-scale fictional representation of contemporary life and thought that she admires Tolstoy and Balzac and Stendahl for having achieved in the nineteenth. Her five-volume novel, *Children of Violence,* published over a seventeen-year period beginning in 1952, testifies to her ambition to catch the essence of an era on a scale as ample as that of *War and Peace.* Her best-known novel, *The Golden Notebook* (1962), is a massive work with a unique structure (different aspects of the protagonist's personality are recorded in different-colored notebooks). It tries to encompass feelings about living at this moment in history, to get them down, and if possible to refine them in the central, golden notebook.

Lessing's background offers rich opportunity for the exercise of her historical sensibility. Her father, an Englishman who had been seriously wounded in World War I, elected to escape a stifling job in a bank to make his living in the British colonies. She was born, then, in Persia, in the shadow of the war. She moved to Southern Rhodesia when her father bought a farm there (she later came to realize that this family farm had in effect been stolen from the Africans by the British government). Some of her most moving fiction deals with her girlhood in the strange and beautiful African countryside, surrounded by black people in total subservience to the white settlers but with their own fascinating ancient culture. A lonely girl, largely self-educated, she was English by heritage but remote from life in England, a stranger–ruler in Africa. The mechanized barbarism of World War II appalled her, and perhaps in reaction she fell in with a group of Communists who for a time convinced her that the party had a program that would ensure a more humane and less racist world. She became a Communist in 1942 ("emotionally if not organizationally," she says) and after the war spent some time in Moscow. Then in the mid-fifties, disillusioned by the murder and brutality in Russia under Stalin, she came to realize that her allegiance to the party had been born of a vain hope of both helping to create a good world *and* achieving personal freedom through political doctrine. She abandoned party membership, seeing it as a surrender not very different from a surrender to the "colonial small-town atmosphere" from which she had fled.

Having confronted other major crises of the individual and society in the twentieth century, Lessing now is inevitably thought of in connection with the Women's Movement. The themes of her fiction—the struggle of a woman to lead her own life apart from social stereotypes, to think and act in a way that matters historically—are so clearly relevant that she has been enthusiastically embraced by the movement. With a characteristically long view of cultural trends, she has remained aloof, rejecting active participation but accepting the broadly humanistic role that she is credited with.

While admiring the epic ambitions of Doris Lessing, most readers find her most effective on a more intimate scale, in her many stories and parts of novels that portray relations between men and women. There she acknowledges the primacy of the inner consciousness rather than the external political world. Since *The Golden Notebook* she has moved from a portrayal of the failure of political movements to a consideration of the source of political failure within the individual. To some extent influenced by the psychiatrist R. D. Laing, she writes about the problem of maintaining a "creative schizophrenia" against the repressive forces of society that work to regularize people into "sane" and therefore manipulable citizens. Her novel *Briefing for a Descent into Hell* (1971) presents a Cambridge professor who, having lost all awareness of his conventional identity through an attack of amnesia, discovers a more vital self in his "madness," but then is literally shocked and drugged by traditional medical treatment back to his old dead identity.

Doris Lessing lives quietly in London, where she moved with her son after her second marriage dissolved in 1949 (she is officially prohibited from returning to Southern Rhodesia because of her views on race). Her two marriages, she says, have had no permanent effect on her, though she remains fascinated by the subject of women who are, like the chief character in "He," defined almost exclusively by their roles as wives.

He

"Goodness! You gave me a start, Mary. . . ."

Mary Brooke was quietly knitting beside the stove. "Thought I'd drop in," she said.

Annie Blake pulled off her hat, and flopped a net of bread and vegetables on the table; at the same time her eyes were anxiously inspecting her kitchen: there was an unwashed dish in the sink, a cloth over a chair. "Everything's in such a mess," she said irritably.

Mary Brooke, eyes fixed on her knitting, said: "Eh, sit down. It's clean as can be."

After a hesitation Annie flopped herself into the chair, and shut her eyes. "Those stairs. . . ." she panted. Then: "Like a cuppa tea, Mary?"

Mary quickly pushed her knitting away, and said: "You sit still. I'll do it." She heaved up her large tired body, filled a kettle from the tap, and set it on the flame. Then, following her friend's anxious glance, she hung the dishcloth where it belonged and shut the door. The kitchen was so clean and neat it could have gone on exhibition. She sat down, reached for her knitting and knitted without looking at it, contemplating the wall across the room. "He was carrying on like anything last night," she observed.

Annie's drooping lids flew open, her light body straightened. "Yes?" she murmured casually. Her face was tense.

"What can you expect with that type? She doesn't get the beds made before dinner-time. There's dirt everywhere. He was giving it to her proper. Dirty slut, he called her."

"She won't do for him what I did, that's certain," said Annie bitterly.

"Shouting and banging until nearly morning—we all heard it." She counted purl, plain, purl, and added: "Don't last long, do it? Six months he's been with her now?"

"He never lifted his hand to me, *that's* certain," said Annie victoriously.

"That's right love. Two purl. One plain."

"Nasty temper he's got. I'd be up summer and winter at four, cleaning those offices till ten, then cleaning for Mrs. Lynd till dinner-time. Then if he got home and found his dinner not ready, he'd start, shout and carry-on—well, I'd say, if you can't wait five minutes, get home and cook it yourself, I'd say. I bring in as much money as you do, don't I? But he never lifted a finger. Bone lazy. Men are all the same."

Mary gave her friend a swift searching glance, then murmured: "Eh, you can't tell *me*. . . ."

"I'd have the kids and the cleaning and the cooking, and working all day—sometimes when he was unemployed I'd bring in all the money . . . and he wouldn't even put the kettle on for me. Women's work, he said."

"Two purl, plain." But Mary's kindly face seemed to suggest that she was waiting to say something else. "We all know what it is," she agreed at last, patiently.

Annie rose lightly, pulled the shrieking kettle off the flame and reached for the teapot. Seen from the back she looked twenty, slim and erect. When she turned with the steaming pot, she caught a glimpse of herself—she set down the pot, and went to the mirror. She stood touching her face anxiously. "Look at me!" She pushed a long sagging curl into position, then shrugged: "Well, who's to care what I look like anyway?"

She began setting out the cups. She had a thin face, sharpened by worry, small sharp blue eyes. As she sat down, she nervously felt her hair. "I must get the curlers on to my hair," she muttered.

"Heard from the boys?"

Annie's hand fell and clenched itself on the table. "Not a word from Charlie for months. They don't think . . . he'll turn up one fine day and expect his place laid, if I know my Charlie. Tommy's after a job in Manchester, Mrs. Thomas said. But I had a nice letter from Dick. . . ." Her face softened; her eyes were soft and reminiscent. "He wrote about his father. He should respect him, I said, no matter what he's done. It's not his place to criticize his father, I said."

"You're lucky in your boys, Annie."

"They're good workers, no one can say they aren't. And they've never done anything they shouldn't. They don't take after their dad, *that's* certain."

At this, Mary's eyes showed a certain tired irony. "Eh, Annie—but we all do things we shouldn't." This gaining no response from the bitter Annie, she added cautiously: "I saw him this morning in the street."

Annie's cup clattered down into the saucer. "Was he alone?"

"No. But he took me aside—he said I could give you a message if I was passing this way—he might be dropping in this evening instead of tomorrow with your money, he said. Thursday *she* goes to her mother's—I suppose he thinks while the cat's away. . . ."

Annie had risen, in a panic. She made herself sit down again, and stirred her tea. The spoon tinkled in the cup with the quivering of her hand. "He's regular with the money, anyway," she said heavily. "I didn't have to take him into court. He offered. And I suppose he needn't, now the boys are out keeping themselves."

"He still feels for you, Annie. . . ." Mary was leaning forward, speaking in a direct appeal. "He does, really."

"He never felt for anyone but himself," snapped Annie. "Never."

Mary let a sigh escape her. "Oh well. . . ." she murmured. "Well, I'll be getting along to do the supper." She stuffed her knitting into her carry-all, and said consolingly: "You're lucky. No one to get after you if you feel like sitting a bit. No one to worry about but yourself. . . ."

"Oh don't think I'm wasting any tears over *him*. I'm taking it easy for the first time in my life. You slave your life out for your man and your kids. Then off they go, with not so much as a thank-you. Now I can please myself."

"I wouldn't mind being in your place," said Mary loyally. At the door she remarked, apparently at random: "Your floor's so clean you could eat off it."

The moment Mary was gone, Annie rushed into her apron, and began sweeping. She got down to her knees to polish the floor, and then took off her dress and washed herself at the sink. She combed her dragging wisps of pale hair; and did each one up neatly with a pin till her face was surrounded by a ring of little sausages. She put back her dress and sat down at the table. Not a moment too soon. The door opened, and Rob Blake stood there.

He was a thin, rather stooping man, with an air of apology. He said politely: "You busy, Annie?"

"Sit down," she commanded sharply. He stopped loosely in the doorway for a moment, then came forward, minding his feet. Even so she winced as she saw the dusty marks on the gleaming linoleum. "Take it easy," he said with friendly sarcasm. "You can put up with my dust once a week, can't you?"

She smiled stiffly, her blue eyes fastened anxiously on him, while he pulled out a chair and sat down. "Well, Annie?"

To this conciliatory opening she did not respond. After a moment she remarked: "I heard from Dick. He's thinking of getting married."

"Getting married now? That puts us on the shelf, don't it?"

"*You*'re not on any shelf that I can see," she snapped.

"Now—Annie . . ." he deprecated, with an appealing smile. She showed no signs of softening. Seeing her implacable face, his smile faded, and he took an envelope from his pocket and pushed it over.

"Thanks," she said, hardly glancing at it. Then that terrible bitterness came crowding up, and he heard the words: "If you can spare it from *her*."

He let that one pass; he looked steadily at his wife, as if seeking a way past that armour of anger. He watched her, passing the tip of his tongue nervously over his lips.

"Some women know how to keep themselves free from kids and responsibilities. They just do this and that, and take up with anyone they please. None of the dirty work for *them*."

He gave a sigh, and was on the point of getting up, when she demanded: "Like a cuppa tea?"

"I wouldn't mind." He let himself sink back again.

While she worked at the stove, her back to him, he was looking around the kitchen: his face had a look of tired, disappointed irony. An ageing man, but there was a dogged set to his shoulders. Trying to find the right words, he remarked: "Not so much work for you now, Annie."

But she did not answer. She returned with the two cups, and put the sugar into his for him. This wifely gesture encouraged him. "Annie," he began, "Annie—can't we talk this over . . ." He was stirring the tea clumsily, not looking at it, leaning forward. The cup knocked over. "Oh look what you've done," she cried out, "just look at the mess." She snatched up a cloth and wiped the table.

"It's only a drop of tea, Annie," he protested at last, shrinking a little aside from her furious energy.

"Only a drop of tea—I can polish and clean half the day, and then in a minute the place is like a pig-sty."

His face darkened with remembered irritation.

"Yes, I've heard," she went on accusingly, "she lets the beds lie until dinner, and the place isn't cleaned from one week to the next."

"At least she cares more for me than she does for a clean floor," he shouted. Now they looked at each other with hatred.

At this delicate moment there came a shout: "Rob. Rob!"

She laughed angrily. "She's got you where she wants you—waits and spies on you and now she comes after you."

"Rob! You there, Rob?" It was a loud, confident, female voice.

"She sounds just what she is, a proper . . ."

"Shut up," he interrupted. He was breathing heavily. "You keep that tongue of yours quiet, now."

Her eyes were full of tears, but the blue shone through bright and vengeful. "Rob, Rob—and off you trot like a little dog."

He got up from the table heavily, as a loud knock came at the door.

Annie's mouth quivered at the insult of it. And *his* first instinct was to stand by her—she could see that. He looked apologetically at her, then went to the door, opened it an inch and said in a low furious voice: "Don't you do that now. Do you hear me!" He shut the door, leaned against it, facing Annie. "Annie," he said again, in an awkward appeal. "Annie . . ."

But she sat at her table, hands folded in a trembling knot before her, her face tight and closed against him.

"Oh all right!" he said at last despairingly, angry. "You've always got to be in the right about everything, haven't you? That's all that matters to you, if you're in the right. Bloody plaster saint, you are." He went out quickly.

She sat quite still, listening until it was quiet. Then she drew a deep breath, and put her two fists to her cheeks, as if trying to keep them still. She was sitting thus when Mary Brooke came in. "You let him go?" she said incredulously.

"And good riddance, too."

Mary shrugged. Then she suggested bravely: "You shouldn't be so hard on him, Annie—give him a chance."

"I'd see him dead first," said Annie through shaking lips. Then: "I'm forty-five, and I might as well be on the dust-heap." And then, after a pause, in a remote, cold voice: "We've been together twenty-five years. Three kids. And then he goes off with that . . . with that . . ."

"You're well rid of him, and that's a fact," agreed Mary swiftly.

"Yes I am, and I know it . . ." Annie was swaying from side to side in her chair. Her face was stony, but the tears were trickling steadily down, following a path worn from nose to chin. They rolled off and splashed on to her white collar.

"Annie," implored her friend. "Annie . . ."

Annie's face quivered, and Mary was across the room and had her in her arms. "That's right, love, that's right, that's right, love," she crooned.

"I don't know what gets into me," wept Annie, her voice coming muffled from Mary's large shoulder. "I can't keep my wicked tongue still. He's fed up and sick of that—cow, and I drive him away. I can't help it. I don't know what gets into me."

"There now, love, there now, love." The big fat comfortable woman was rocking the frail Annie like a baby. "Take it easy, love. He'll be back, you'll see."

"You think he will?" asked Annie, lifting her face up to see if her friend was lying to comfort her.

"Would you like me to go and see if I can fetch him back for you now?"

In spite of her longing, Annie hesitated. "Do you think it'll be all right?" she said doubtfully.

"I'll go, and slip in a word when *she's* not around."

"Will you do that, Mary?"

Mary got up, patting at her crumpled dress. "You wait here, love," she said imploringly. She went to the door and said as she went out: "Take it easy, now, Annie. Give him a chance."

"I go running after him to ask him back?" Annie's pride spoke out of her in a wail.

"Do you want him back or don't you?" demanded Mary, patient to the last, although there was a hint of exasperation now. Annie did not say anything, so Mary went running out.

Annie sat still, watching the door tensely. But vague rebellious angry thoughts were running through her head: "If I want to keep him, I can't ever say what I think, I can't ever say what's true—I'm nothing to him but a convenience, but if I say so he'll just up and off . . ."

But that was not the whole truth; she remembered the affection in his face, and for a moment the bitterness died. Then she remembered her long hard life, the endless work, work, work—she remembered, all at once, as if she were feeling it now, her aching back when the children were small; she could see him lying on the bed reading the newspaper when she could hardly drag herself. . . . "It's all very well," she cried out to herself, "it's not right, it just isn't right. . . ." A terrible feeling of injustice was gripping her; and it was just this feeling she must push down, keep under, if she wanted him. For she knew finally, and this was stronger than anything else, that without him there would be no meaning in her life at all.

To Room Nineteen

This is a story, I suppose, about a failure in intelligence: the Rawlings' marriage was grounded in intelligence.

They were older when they married than most of their married friends: in their well-seasoned late twenties. Both had had a number of affairs, sweet rather than bitter; and when they fell in love—for they did fall in love—had known each other for some time. They joked that they had saved each other "for the real thing." That they had waited so long (but not too long) for this real thing was to them a proof of their sensible discrimination. A good many of their friends had married young, and now (they felt) probably regretted lost opportunities; while others, still unmarried, seemed to them arid, self-doubting, and likely to make desperate or romantic marriages.

Not only they, but others, felt they were well-matched: their friends' delight was an additional proof of their happiness. They had played the same rôles, male and female, in this group or set, if such a wide, loosely connected, constantly changing constellation of people could be called a set. They had both become, by virtue of their moderation, their humour, and their abstinence from painful experience, people to whom others came for advice. They could be, and were, relied on. It was one of those cases of a man and a woman linking themselves whom no one else had ever thought of linking, probably because of their similarities. But then everyone exclaimed: Of course! How right! How was it we never thought of it before!

And so they married among general rejoicing, and because of their foresight and their sense for what was probable, nothing was a surprise to them.

Both had well-paid jobs. Matthew was a sub-editor on a large London newspaper, and Susan worked in an advertising firm. He was not the stuff of which editors or publicized journalists are made, but he was much more than "a sub-editor," being one of the essential background people who in fact steady, inspire and make possible the people in the limelight. He was content with this position. Susan had a talent for commercial drawing. She was humorous about the advertisements she was responsible for, but she did not feel strongly about them one way or the other.

Both, before they married, had had pleasant flats, but they felt it unwise to base a marriage on either flat, because it might seem like a submission of personality on the part of the one whose flat it was not. They moved into a new flat in South Kensington on the clear understanding that when their marriage had settled down (a process they knew would not take long, and was in fact more a humorous concession to popular wisdom than what was due to themselves) they would buy a house and start a family.

And this is what happened. They lived in their charming flat for two years, giving parties and going to them, being a popular young married couple, and then Susan became pregnant, she gave up her job, and they bought a house in Richmond. It was typical of this couple that they had a son first, then a daughter, then twins, son and daughter. Everything right, appropriate, and what everyone would wish for, if they could choose. But people did feel these two had chosen; this balanced and sensible family was no more than what was due to them because of their infallible sense for *choosing* right.

And so they lived with their four children in their gardened house in Richmond and were happy. They had everything they had wanted and had planned for.

And yet ...

Well, even this was expected, that there must be a certain flatness ...

Yes, yes, of course, it was natural they sometimes felt like this. Like what?

Their life seemed to be like a snake biting its tail. Matthew's job for the sake of Susan, children, house, and garden—which caravanserai needed a well-paid job to maintain it. And Susan's practical intelligence for the sake of Matthew, the children, the house and the garden—which unit would have collapsed in a week without her.

But there was no point about which either could say: "For the sake of *this* is all the rest." Children? But children can't be a centre of life and a reason for being. They can be a thousand things that are delightful, interesting, satisfying, but they can't be a well-spring to live from. Or they shouldn't be. Susan and Matthew knew that well enough.

Matthew's job? Ridiculous. It was an interesting job, but scarcely a reason for living. Matthew took pride in doing it well; but he could hardly be expected to be proud of the newspaper: the newspaper he read, *his* newspaper, was not the one he worked for.

Their love for each other? Well, that was nearest it. If this wasn't a centre, what was? Yes, it was around this point, their love, that the whole extraordinary structure revolved. For extraordinary it certainly was. Both Susan and Matthew had moments of thinking so, of looking in secret disbelief at this thing they had created: marriage, four children, big house, garden, charwomen, friends, cars ... and this *thing,* this entity, all of it had come into existence, been blown into being out of nowhere, because Susan loved Matthew and Matthew loved Susan. Extraordinary. So that was the central point, the well-spring.

And if one felt that it simply was not strong enough, important enough, to support it all, well whose fault was that? Certainly neither Susan's nor Matthew's. It was in the nature of things. And they sensibly blamed neither themselves nor each other.

On the contrary, they used their intelligence to preserve what they had created from a painful and explosive world: they looked around them, and took lessons. All around them, marriages collapsing, or breaking, or rubbing along (even worse, they felt). They must not make the same mistakes, they must not.

They had avoided the pitfall so many of their friends had fallen into—of buying a house in the country *for the sake of the children;* so that the husband became a week-end husband, a week-end father, and the wife always careful not to ask what went on in the town-flat which they called (in joke) a bachelor flat. No, Matthew was a full-time husband, a full-time father, and at nights, in the big married bed in the big married bedroom (which had an attractive view of the river) they lay beside each other talking and he told her about his day, and what he had done, and who he had met; and she told him about her day (not as interesting, but that was not her fault) for both knew of the hidden resentments and deprivations of the woman who has lived her own life and, above all, has earned her own living, and is now dependent on a husband for outside interests and money.

Nor did Susan make the mistake of taking a job for the sake of her independence, which she might very well have done, since her old firm, missing her qualities of humour, balance, and sense, invited her often to go back. Children needed their mother to a certain age, that both parents knew and agreed on; and when these four healthy wisely-brought up children were of the right age, Susan would work again, because she knew, and so did he, what happened to women of fifty at the height of their energy and ability, with grown-up children who no longer needed their full devotion.

So here was this couple, testing their marriage, looking after it, treating it like a small boat full of helpless people in a very stormy sea. Well, of course, so it was . . . The storms of the world were bad, but not too close—which is not to say they were selfishly felt, Susan and Matthew were both well-informed and responsible people. And the inner storms and quicksands were understood and charted. So everything was all right. Everything was in order. Yes, things were under control.

So what did it matter if they felt dry, flat. People like themselves, fed on a hundred books (psychological, anthropological, sociological) could scarcely be unprepared for the dry, controlled wistfulness which is the distinguishing mark of the intelligent marriage. Two people, endowed with education, with discrimination, with judgement, linked together voluntarily from their will to be happy together and to be of use to others—one sees them everywhere, one knows them, one even is that thing oneself: sadness because so much is after all so little. These two, unsurprised, turned towards each other with even more courtesy and gentle love: this was life, that two people, no matter how carefully chosen, could not be everything to each other. In fact, even to say so, to think in such a way, was banal, they were ashamed to do it.

It was banal, too, when one night Matthew came home late and confessed he had been to a party, taken a girl home and slept with her. Susan forgave him, of course. Except that forgiveness is hardly the word. Understanding, yes. But if you understand something, you don't forgive it, you are the thing itself: forgiveness is for what you *don't* understand. Nor had he *confessed*—what sort of a word is that?

The whole thing was not important. After all, years ago they had joked: of course I'm not going to be faithful to you, no one can be faithful to one other person for a whole lifetime. (And there was the word *faithful*—stupid, all these words, stupid, belonging to a savage old world.) But the incident left both of them irritable. Strange, but they were both bad-tempered, annoyed. There was something unassimilable about it.

Making love splendidly after he had come home that night, both had felt that the idea that Myra Jenkins, a pretty girl met at a party, could be even relevant, was ridiculous. They had loved each other for over a decade, would love each other for years more. Who, then, was Myra Jenkins?

Except, thought Susan, unaccountably bad-tempered, she was (is?) the first. In ten years. So either the ten years' fidelity was not important, or she isn't. (No, no, there is something wrong with this way of thinking, there must be.) But, if she isn't important, presumably it wasn't important either when Matthew and I first went to bed with each other that afternoon whose delight even now (like a very long shadow at sundown) lays a soft, wand-like finger over us. (Why did I say sundown?) Well, if what we felt that afternoon was not important, nothing is important, because if it hadn't been for what we felt, we wouldn't be Mr and Mrs Rawlings with four children, etc., etc. The whole thing is *absurd*—for him to have come home and told me was absurd. For him not to have told me was absurd. For me to care, or for that matter not to care is absurd . . . and who is Myra Jenkins? Why no one at all.

There was only one thing to do, and of course these sensible people did it: they put the thing behind them, and consciously, knowing what they were doing, moved forward into a different phase of their marriage, giving thanks for past good fortune as they did so.

For it was inevitable that the handsome, blonde, attractive, manly man, Matthew Rawlings, should be at times tempted (oh, what a word!) by the attractive girls at parties she could not attend because of the four children; and that sometimes he would succumb (a word even more repulsive if possible) and that she, a good-looking woman in the big well-tended garden at Richmond would sometimes be pierced as by an arrow from the sky with bitterness. Except that bitterness was not in order, it was out of court. Did the casual girls touch the marriage? They did not. Rather it was they who knew defeat because of the handsome Matthew Rawlings's marriage body and soul to Susan Rawlings.

In that case why did Susan feel (though luckily not for longer than a few seconds at a time) as if life had become a desert, and that nothing mattered, and that her children were not her own?

Meanwhile, her intelligence continued to assert that all was well. What if her Matthew did have an occasional sweet afternoon, the odd affair? For she knew quite well, except in her moments of aridity, that they were very happy, that the affairs were not important.

Perhaps that was the trouble? It was in the nature of things that the adventures and delights could no longer be hers, because of the four children and the big house that needed so much attention. But perhaps she was secretly wishing, and even knowing that she did, that the wildness and the beauty could be his. But he was married to her. She was married to him. They were married inextricably. And therefore the gods could not strike him with the real magic, not really. Well, was it Susan's fault that after he came home from an adventure he looked harassed rather than fulfilled? (In fact, that was how she knew he had been *unfaithful,* because of his sullen air, and his glances at her, similar to hers at him: what is it that I share with this person that shields all delight from me?) But none of it was anybody's fault. (But what, did they feel, ought to be somebody's fault?) Nobody's fault, nothing to be at fault, no one to blame, no one to offer or to take it . . . and nothing wrong, either, except that Matthew never was really struck, as he wanted to be, by joy; and that Susan was more and more often threatened by emptiness. (It was usually in the garden that she was invaded by this feeling: she was coming to avoid the garden, unless the children or Matthew were with her.) There was no need to use the dramatic words, unfaithful, forgive, and the rest: intelligence forbade them. Intelligence barred, too, quarrelling, sulking, anger, silences of withdrawal, accusations and tears. Above all, intelligence forbids tears.

A high price has to be paid for the happy marriage with the four healthy children in the large white gardened house.

And they were paying it, willingly, knowing what they were doing. When they lay side by side, or breast to breast in the big civilized bedroom overlooking the wild sullied river, they laughed, often, for no particular reason; but they knew it was really because of these two small people, Susan and Matthew, supporting such an edifice on their intelligent love. The laugh comforted them; it saved them both, though from what, they did not know.

They were now both forty-ish. The older children, boy and girl, were ten and eight, at school. The twins, six, were still at home. Susan did not have nurses or girls to help her: childhood is short; and she did not regret the hard work. Often enough she was bored, since small children can be boring; she was often very tired; but she regretted nothing. In another decade, she would turn herself back into being a woman with a life of her own.

Soon the twins would go to school, and they would be away from home from nine until four. These hours, so Susan saw it, would be the preparation for her own slow emancipation away from the rôle of hub-of-the-family into woman-with-her-own-life. She was already planning for the hours of freedom when all the children would be "off her hands." That was the phrase used by Matthew and by Susan and by their friends, for the moment when the youngest child went off to school. "They'll be off your hands, darling Susan, and you'll have time to yourself." So said Matthew, the intelligent husband, who had often enough commended and consoled Susan, standing by her in spirit during the years when her soul was not her own, as she said, but her children's.

What it amounted to was that Susan saw herself as she had been at twenty-eight, unmarried; and then again somewhere about fifty, blossoming from the root of what she had been twenty years before. As if the essential Susan was in abeyance, as if she were in cold storage. Matthew said something like this to Susan one night: and she agreed that it was true—and she did feel something like that. What, then, was this essential Susan? She did not know. Put like that it sounded ridiculous, and she did not really feel it. Anyway, they had a long discussion about the whole thing before going off to sleep in each other's arms.

So the twins went off to their school, two bright affectionate children who had no problems about it, since their older brother and sister had trodden this path so successfully before them. And now Susan was going to be alone in the big house, every day of the school-term, except for the daily woman who came in to clean.

It was now, for the first time in this marriage, that something happened which neither of them had foreseen.

This is what happened. She returned, at nine-thirty, from taking the twins to the school by car, looking forward to seven blissful hours of freedom. On the first morning she was simply restless, worrying about the twins "naturally enough" since this was their first day away at school. She was hardly able to contain herself until they came back. Which they did happily, excited by the world of school, looking forward to the next day. And the next day Susan took them, dropped them, came back, and found herself reluctant to enter her big and beautiful home because it was as if something was waiting for her there that she did not wish to confront. Sensibly, however, she parked the car in the garage, entered the house, spoke to Mrs Parkes the daily woman about her duties, and went up to her bedroom. She was possessed by a fever which drove her out again, downstairs, into the kitchen, where Mrs Parkes was making cake and did not need her, and into the garden. There she sat on a bench and tried to calm herself, looking at trees, at a brown glimpse of the river. But she was filled with tension, like a panic: as if an enemy was in the garden with her. She spoke to herself severely, thus: All this is quite natural. First, I spent twelve years of my adult life working, *living my own life.* Then I married, and from the moment I became pregnant for the first time I signed myself over, so to speak, to other people. To the children. Not for one moment in twelve years have I been alone, had time to myself. So now I have to learn to be myself again. That's all.

And she went indoors to help Mrs Parkes cook and clean, and found some sewing to do for the children. She kept herself occupied every day. At the end of the first term she understood she felt two contrary emotions. First: secret astonishment and dismay that during those weeks when the house was empty of children she had, in fact, been more occupied (had been careful to keep herself occupied) than ever she had been when the children were around her needing her continual attention. Second: that now she knew the house would be full of them, and for five weeks, she resented the fact she would never be alone. She was already looking back at those hours of sewing, cooking (but by herself) as at a lost freedom which would not be hers for five long weeks. And the two months of term which would succeed the five weeks stretched alluringly open to her—freedom. But what freedom?—when, in fact, she had been so careful *not* to be free of small duties during the last weeks? She looked at herself, Susan Rawlings, sitting in a big chair by the window in the bedroom, sewing shirts or dresses, which she might just as well have bought. She saw herself making cakes for hours at a time in the big family kitchen: yet usually she bought cakes. What she saw was a woman alone, that was true, but she had not felt alone. For instance, Mrs Parkes was always somewhere in the house. And she did not like being in the garden at all, because of the closeness there of the enemy—irritation, restlessness, emptiness, whatever it was, that keeping her hands occupied made less dangerous for some reason.

Susan did not tell Matthew of these thoughts. They were not sensible. She did not recognize herself in them. What should she say to her dear friend and husband Matthew: "When I go into the garden, that is, if the children are not there, I feel as if there is an enemy there waiting to invade me." "What enemy, Susan darling?" "Well, I don't know, really . . ." "Perhaps you should see a doctor?"

No, clearly this conversation should not take place. The holidays began and Susan welcomed them. Four children, lively, energetic, intelligent, demanding: she was never, not for a moment of her day, alone. If she were in a room, they would be in the next room, or waiting for her to do something for them; or it would soon be time for lunch or tea, or to take one of them to the dentist. Something to do: five weeks of it, thank goodness.

On the fourth day of these so welcome holidays, she found she was storming with anger at the twins, two shrinking beautiful children who (and this is what checked her) stood hand in hand looking at her with sheer dismayed disbelief. This was their calm mother, shouting at them. And for what? They had come to her with some game, some bit of nonsense. They looked at each other, moved closer for support, and went off hand in hand, leaving Susan holding on to the window-sill of the living-room, breathing deep, feeling sick.

She went to lie down, telling the older children she had a headache. She heard the boy Harry telling the little ones: "It's all right, mother's got a headache." She heard that *it's all right* with pain.

That night she said to her husband: "Today I shouted at the twins, quite unfairly." She sounded miserable, and he said gently: "Well, what of it?"

"It's more of an adjustment than I thought, their going to school."

"But, Susie, Susie darling . . ." For she was crouched weeping on the bed. He comforted her: "Susan, what is all this about? You shouted at them? What of it? If you shouted at them fifty times a day it wouldn't be more than the little devils deserve." But she wouldn't laugh. She wept. Soon he comforted her with his body. She became calm. Calm, she wondered what was wrong with her, and why she should mind so much that she might, just once, have behaved unjustly with the children. What did it matter? They had forgotten it all long ago: mother had a headache and everything was all right.

It was a long time later that Susan understood that that night, when she had wept and Matthew had driven the misery out of her with his big solid body, was the last time, in their married life, that they had been, to use their mutual language—with each other. And even that was a lie, because she had not told him of her real fears at all.

The five weeks passed, and Susan was in control of herself, and good and kind, and she looked forward to the holidays with a mixture of fear and longing. She did not know what to expect. She took the twins off to school (the elder children took themselves to school) and she returned to the house determined to face the enemy wherever he was, in the house, or the garden or —where?

She was again restless, she was possessed by restlessness. She cooked and sewed and worked as before, day after day, while Mrs Parkes remonstrated: Mrs Rawlings, what's the need for it? I can do that, it's what you pay me for.

And it was so irrational, that she checked herself. She would put the car in the garage, go up to her bedroom, and sit, hands in her lap, forcing herself to be quiet. She listened to Mrs Parkes moving around the house. She looked out into the garden and saw the branches shake the trees. She sat defeating the enemy, restlessness. Emptiness. She ought to be thinking about her life, about herself. But she did not. Or perhaps she could not. As soon as she forced her mind to think about Susan (for what else did she want to be alone for?) it skipped off to thoughts of butter or school clothes. Or it thought of Mrs Parkes. She realized that she sat listening for the movements of the cleaning woman, following her every turn, bend, thought. She followed her in her mind from kitchen to bathroom, from table to oven, and it was as if the duster, the cleaning cloth, the saucepan, were in her own hand. She would hear herself saying: "No, not like that, don't put that there. . . . Yet she did not give a damn what Mrs Parkes did, or if she did it at all. Yet she could not prevent herself from being conscious of her every minute. Yes, this was what was wrong with her: she needed, when she was alone, to be really alone, with no one near. She could not endure the knowledge that in ten minutes or in half an hour Mrs Parkes would call up the stairs: Mrs Rawlings, there's no silver polish, Madam, we're out of flour.

So she left the house and went to sit in the garden where she was screened from the house by trees. She waited for the demon to appear and claim her, but he did not.

She was keeping him off, because she had not, after all, come to an end of arranging herself.

She was planning how to be somewhere where Mrs Parkes would not come after her with a cup of tea, or a demand to be allowed to telephone (always irritating since Susan did not care who she telephoned or how often) or just a nice talk about something. Yes, she needed a place, or a state of affairs where it would not be necessary to keep reminding herself: In ten minutes I must telephone Matthew about . . . and at half past three I must leave early for the children because the car needs cleaning. And at ten o'clock tomorrow I must remember——She was possessed with resentment that the seven hours of freedom in every day (during weekdays in the school-term) were not free, that never, not for one second, ever, was she free from the pressure of time, from having to remember this or that. She could never forget herself; never really let herself go into forgetfulness.

Resentment. It was poisoning her. (She looked at this emotion and thought it was absurd.) Yet she felt it. She was a prisoner . . . (She looked at this thought, too, and it was no good telling herself it was a ridiculous one.) She must tell Matthew—but what? She was filled with emotions that were utterly ridiculous, that she despised, yet that nevertheless she was feeling so strongly she could not shake them off.

The school holidays came round, and this time they were for nearly two months, and she behaved with a conscious controlled decency that nearly drove her crazy. She would lock herself in the bathroom, and sit on the edge of the bath, breathing deep, trying to let go into some kind of calm. Or she went up into the spare room, usually empty, where no one would expect her to be. She heard the children calling Mother, Mother, and kept silent, feeling guilty. Or she went to the very end of the garden, by herself, and looked at the slow-moving brown river; she looked at the river and closed her eyes and breathed slow and deep, taking it into her being, into her veins.

Then she returned to the family, wife and mother, smiling and responsible, feeling as if the pressure of these people—four lively children and her husband, were a painful pressure on the surface of her skin, a hand pressing on her brain. She did not once break down into irritation during these holidays, but it was like living out a prison sentence, and when the children went back to school, she sat on a white stone seat near the flowing river, and she thought: It is not even a year since the twins went to school, since *they were off my hands* (what on earth did I think I meant when I used that stupid phrase?) and yet I'm a different person. I'm simply not myself. I don't understand it.

Yet she had to understand it. For she knew that this structure—big white house, on which the mortgage still cost four hundred a year, a husband, so good and kind and insightful, four children, all doing so nicely, and the garden where she sat, and Mrs Parkes the cleaning woman—all this depended on her, and yet she could not understand why, or even what it was she contributed to it.

She said to Matthew in their bedroom: "I think there must be something wrong with me."

And he said: "Surely not, Susan? You look marvellous—you're as lovely as ever."

She looked at the handsome blond man, with his clear, intelligent, blue-eyed face, and thought: Why is it I can't tell him? Why not? And she said: "I need to be alone more than I am."

At which he swung his slow blue gaze at her, and she saw what she had been dreading: Incredulity. Disbelief. And fear. An incredulous blue stare from a stranger who was her husband, as close to her as her own breath.

He said: "But the children are at school and off your hands."

She said to herself: I've got to force myself to say: Yes, but do you realize that I never feel free? There's never a moment I can say to myself: "There's nothing I have to remind myself about, nothing I have to do in half an hour, or an hour, or two hours. . . ."

But she said: "I don't feel well."

He said: "Perhaps you need a holiday."

She said, appalled: "But not without you, surely?" For she could not imagine herself going off without him. Yet that was what he meant. Seeing her face, he laughed, and opened his arms, and she went into them, thinking: Yes, yes, but why can't I say it? And what is it I have to say?

She tried to tell him, about never being free. And he listened and said: "But, Susan, what sort of freedom can you possibly want—short of being dead! Am I ever free? I go to the office, and I have to be there at ten—all right, half past ten, sometimes. And I have to do this or that, don't I? Then I've got to come home at a certain time—I don't mean it, you know I don't—but if I'm not going to be back home at six I'll telephone you. When can I ever say to myself: I have nothing to be responsible for in the next six hours?"

Susan, hearing this, was remorseful. Because it was true. The good marriage, the house, the children, depended just as much on his voluntary bondage as it did on hers. But why did he not feel bound? Why didn't he chafe and become restless? No, there was something really wrong with her and this proved it.

And that word *bondage*—why had she used it? She had never felt marriage, or the children, as bondage. Neither had he, or surely they wouldn't be together lying in each other's arms content after twelve years of marriage.

No, her state (whatever it was) was irrelevant, nothing to do with her real good life with her family. She had to accept the fact that, after all, she was an irrational person and to live with it. Some people had to live with crippled arms, or stammers, or being deaf. She would have to live knowing she was subject to a state of mind she could not own.

Nevertheless, as a result of this conversation with her husband, there was a new régime next holidays.

The spare room at the top of the house now had a cardboard sign saying: Private! Do not Disturb! on it. (This sign had been drawn in coloured chalks by the children, after a discussion between the parents in which it was decided this was psychologically the right thing.) The family and Mrs Parkes knew this was "Mother's Room" and that she was entitled to her privacy. Many serious conversations took place between Matthew and the children about not taking mother for granted. Susan overheard the first, between father and Harry, the older boy, and was surprised at her irritation over it. Surely she could have a room somewhere in that big house and retire into it without such a fuss being made? Without it being so solemnly discussed? Why couldn't she simply have announced: "I'm going to fit out the little top room for myself, and when I'm in it I'm not to be disturbed for anything short of fire"? Just that, and finished; instead of long, earnest discussions. When she heard Harry and Matthew explaining it to the twins with Mrs Parkes coming in: "Yes, well a family sometimes gets on top of a woman . . ." she had to go right away to the bottom of the garden until the devils of exasperation had finished their dance in her blood.

But now there was a room, and she could go there when she liked, she used it seldom: she felt even more caged there than in her bedroom. One day she had gone up there after a lunch for ten children she had cooked and served because Mrs Parkes was not there, and had sat alone for a while looking into the garden. She saw the children stream out from the kitchen and stand looking up at the window where she sat behind the curtains. They were all—her children and their friends—discussing Mother's Room. A few minutes later, the chase of children in some game came pounding up the stairs, but ended as abruptly as if they had fallen over a ravine, so sudden was the silence. They had remembered she was there, and had gone silent in a great gale of Hush! Shhhhhh, Quiet, you'll disturb her. . . . And they went tiptoeing downstairs like criminal conspirators. When she came down to make tea for them, they all apologized. The twins put their arms around her, from front and back, making a human cage of loving limbs, and promised it would never occur again. "We forgot, Mummy, we forgot all about it!"

What it amounted to was that Mother's Room, and her need for privacy had become a valuable lesson in respect for other people's rights. Quite soon Susan was going up to the room only because it was a lesson it was a pity to drop. Then she took sewing up there, and the children and Mrs Parkes came in and out: It had become another family room.

She sighed, and smiled, and resigned herself—she made jokes at her own expense with Matthew over the room. That is, she did from the self she liked, she respected. But at the same time, something inside her howled with impatience, with rage.... And she was frightened. One day she found herself kneeling by her bed and praying: "Dear God, keep it away from me, keep him away from me." She meant, the devil, for she now thought of it, not caring if she were irrational, as some sort of demon. She imagined him, or it, as a youngish man, or perhaps a middle-aged man pretending to be young. Or a man young-looking from immaturity? At any rate, she saw the young-looking face which, when she drew closer, had dry lines about mouth and eyes. He was thinnish, meagre in build. And he had a reddish complexion, and ginger hair. That was he—a gingery, energetic man, and he wore a reddish hairy jacket, unpleasant to the touch.

Well, one day she saw him. She was standing at the bottom of the garden, watching the river ebb past, when she raised her eyes and saw this person, or being, sitting on the white stone bench. He was looking at her, and grinning. In his hand was a long crooked stick, which he had picked off the ground, or broken off the tree above him. He was absent-mindedly, out of an absent-minded or freakish impulse of spite, using the stick to stir around in the coils of a blindworm or a grass-snake (or some kind of snake-life creature: it was whitish and unhealthy to look at, unpleasant). The snake was twisting about, flinging its coils from side to side in a kind of dance of protest against the teasing prodding stick.

Susan looked at him thinking: Who is the stranger? What is he doing in our garden? Then she recognized the man around whom her terrors had crystallized. As she did so, he vanished. She made herself walk over to the bench. A shadow from a branch lay across thin emerald grass, moving jerkily over its roughness, and she could see why she had taken it for a snake, lashing and twisting. She went back to the house thinking: Right then, so I've seen him with my own eyes, so I'm not crazy after all—there *is* a danger because I've seen him. He is lurking in the garden and sometimes even in the house, and he wants *to get into me and to take me over*.

She dreamed of having a room or a place, anywhere, where she could go and sit, by herself, no one knowing where she was.

Once, near Victoria, she found herself outside a newsagent that had Rooms to Let advertised. She decided to rent a room, telling no one. Sometimes she could take the train in to Richmond and sit alone in it for an hour or two.

Yet how could she? A room would cost three or four pounds a week, and she earned no money, and how could she explain to Matthew that she needed such a sum. What for? It did not occur to her that she was taking it for granted she wasn't going to tell him about the room.

Well, it was out of the question, having a room; yet she knew she must.

One day, when a school-term was well-established, and none of the children had measles or other ailments, and everything seemed in order, she did the shopping early, explained to Mrs Parkes she was meeting an old school-friend, took the train to Victoria, searched until she found a small quiet hotel, and asked for a room for the day. They did not let rooms by the day, the manageress said, looking doubtful, since Susan so obviously was not the kind of woman who needed a room for unrespectable reasons. Susan made a long explanation about not being well, being unable to shop without frequest rests for lying down. At last she was allowed to rent the room provided she paid a full night's price for it. She was taken up by the manageress and a maid, both concerned over the state of her health . . . which must be pretty bad if, living at Richmond (she had signed her name and address in the register) she needed a shelter at Victoria.

The room was ordinary and anonymous, and was just what Susan needed. She put a shilling in the gas fire, and sat, eyes shut, in a dingy armchair with her back to a dingy window. She was alone. She was alone. She was alone. She could feel pressures lifting off her. First the sounds of traffic came very loud; then they seemed to vanish; she might even have slept a little. A knock on the door: it was Miss Townsend the manageress, bringing her a cup of tea with her own hands, so concerned was she over Susan's long silence and possible illness.

Miss Townsend was a lonely woman of fifty, running this hotel with all the rectitude expected of her, and she sensed in Susan the possibility of understanding companionship. She stayed to talk. Susan found herself in the middle of a fantastic story about her illness, which got more and more improbable as she tried to make it tally with the large house at Richmond, well-off husband, and four children. Suppose she said instead: Miss Townsend, I'm here in your hotel because I need to be alone for a few hours, above all *alone and with no one knowing where I am.* She said it mentally, and saw, mentally, the look that would inevitably come on Miss Townsend's elderly maiden's face. "Miss Townsend, my four children and my husband are driving me insane, do you understand that? Yes, I can see from the gleam of hysteria in your eyes that comes from loneliness controlled but only just contained that I've got everything in the world you've ever longed for. Well, Miss Townsend, I don't want any of it. You can have it, Miss Townsend. I wish I was absolutely alone in the world, like you. Miss Townsend, I'm besieged by seven devils, Miss Townsend, Miss Townsend, let me stay here in your hotel where the devils can't get me . . ." Instead of saying all this, she described her anaemia, agreed to try Miss Townsend's remedy for it, which was raw liver, minced, between wholemeal bread, and said yes, perhaps it would be better if she stayed at home and let a friend do shopping for her. She paid her bill and left the hotel, defeated.

At home Mrs Parkes said she didn't really like it, no, not really, when Mrs Rawlings was away from nine in the morning until five. The teacher had telephoned from school to say Joan's teeth were paining her, and she hadn't known what to say; and what was she to make for the children's tea, Mrs Rawlings hadn't said.

All this was nonsense, of course. Mrs Parkes's complaint was that Susan had withdrawn herself spiritually, leaving the burden of the big house on her.

Susan looked back at her day of "freedom" which had resulted in her becoming a friend to the lonely Miss Townsend, and in Mrs Parkes's remonstrances. Yet she remembered the short blissful hour of being alone, really alone. She was determined to arrange her life, no matter what it cost, so that she could have that solitude more often. An absolute solitude, where no one knew her or cared about her.

But how? She thought of saying to her old employer: I want you to back me up in a story with Matthew that I am doing part-time work for you. The truth is that . . . but she would have to tell him a lie too, and which lie? She could not say: I want to sit by myself three or four times a week in a rented room. And, besides, he knew Matthew, and she could not really ask him to tell lies on her behalf, apart from his being bound to think it meant a lover.

Suppose she really took a part-time job, which she could get through fast and efficiently, leaving time for herself. What job? Addressing envelopes? Canvassing?

And there was Mrs Parkes, working widow, who knew exactly what she was prepared to give to the house, who knew by instinct when her mistress withdrew in spirit from her responsibilities. Mrs Parkes was one of the servers of this world, but she needed someone to serve. She had to have Mrs Rawlings, her madam, at the top of the house or in the garden, so that she could come and get support from her: "Yes, the bread's not what it was when I was a girl, yes, Harry's got a wonderful appetite, I wonder where he puts it all, yes it's lucky the twins are so much of a size, they can wear each other's shoes, that's a saving in these hard times, yes, the cherry jam from Switzerland is not a patch on the jam from Poland, and three times the price . . ." And so on. That sort of talk Mrs Parkes must have, every day, or she would leave, not knowing herself why she left.

Susan Rawlings, thinking these thoughts, found that she was prowling through the great thicketed garden like a wild cat: she was walking up the stairs, down the stairs, through the rooms, into the garden, along the brown running river, back, up through the house, down again . . . it was a wonder Mrs

Parkes did not think it strange. But, on the contrary, Mrs Rawlings could do what she liked, she could stand on her head if she wanted, provided she was *there*. Susan Rawlings prowled and muttered through her house, hating Mrs Parkes, hating poor Miss Townsend, dreaming of her hour of solitude in the dingy respectability of Miss Townsend's hotel bedroom, and she knew quite well she was mad. Yes, she was mad!

She said to Matthew that she must have a holiday. Matthew agreed with her. This was not as things had been once—how they had talked in each other's arms in the marriage bed. He had, she knew, diagnosed her finally as *unreasonable*. She had become someone outside himself that he had to manage. They were living side by side in this house like two tolerably friendly strangers.

Having told Mrs Parkes, or rather, asked for her permission, she went off on a walking holiday in Wales. She chose the remotest place she knew of. Every morning the children telephoned her before they went off to school, to encourage and support her, just as they had over Mother's Room. Every evening she telephoned them, spoke to each child in turn, and then to Matthew. Mrs Parkes, given permission to telephone for instructions or advice, did so every day at lunchtime. When, as happened three times, Mrs Rawlings was out on the mountainside, Mrs Parkes asked that she should ring back at such-and-such a time, for she would not be happy in what she was doing without Mrs Rawlings's blessing.

Susan prowled over wild country with the telephone wire holding her to her duty like a leash. The next time she must telephone, or wait to be telephoned, nailed her to her cross. The mountains themselves seemed trammelled by her unfreedom. Everywhere on the mountains, where she met no one at all, from breakfast-time to dusk, excepting sheep, or a shepherd, she came face to face with her own craziness which might attack her in the broadest valleys, so that they seemed too small; or on a mountain-top from which she could see a hundred other mountains and valleys, so that they seemed too low, too small, with the sky pressing down too close. She would stand gazing at a hill-side brilliant with ferns and bracken, jewelled with running water, and see nothing but her devil, who lifted inhuman eyes at her from where he leaned negligently on a rock, switching at his ugly yellow boots with a leafy twig.

She returned to her home and family, with the Welsh emptiness at the back of her mind like a promise of freedom.

She told her husband she wanted to have an *au pair* girl.

They were in their bedroom, it was late at night, the children slept. He sat, shirted and slippered, in a chair by the window, looking out. She sat brushing her hair and watching him in the mirror. A time-hallowed scene in the connubial bedroom. He said nothing, while she heard the arguments coming into his mind, only to be rejected because every one was *reasonable*. "It seems strange to get one now, after all, the children are at school most of the day. Surely the time for you to have help was when you were stuck with them day and night. Why don't you ask Mrs Parkes to cook for you, she's even offered to—I can understand if you are tired of cooking for six people. But you know that an *au pair* girl means all kinds of problems, it's not like having an ordinary char in during the day. . . ."

Finally he said carefully: "Are you thinking of going back to work?"

"No," she said, "no, not really." She made herself sound vague, rather stupid. She went on brushing her black hair and peering at herself so as to be oblivious of the short, uneasy glances her Matthew kept giving her. "Do you think we can't afford it," she went on vaguely, not at all the old efficient Susan who knew exactly what they could afford.

"It's not that," he said, looking out of the window at dark trees, so as not to look at her. Meanwhile, she examined a round, candid, pleasant face with clear dark brows and clear grey eyes. A sensible face. She brushed thick healthy black hair and thought: Yet that's the reflection of a mad woman. How very strange! Much more to the point if what looked back at me was the gingery green-eyed demon with his dry meagre smile . . . why wasn't Matthew agreeing? After all, what else could he do? She was breaking her part of the bargain and there was no way of forcing her to keep it: that her spirit, her soul, should live in this house, so that the people in it could grow like plants in water, and Mrs Parkes remain content in their service. In return for this, he would be a good loving husband, and responsible towards the children. Well, nothing like this had been true of either of them for a long time. He did his duty, perfunctorily; she did not even pretend to do hers. And he had become like other husbands, with his real life in his work and the people he met there, and very likely a serious affair. All this was her fault.

At last he drew heavy curtains, blotting out the trees, and turned to force her attention: "Susan, are you really sure we need a girl?" But she would not meet his appeal at all: she was running the brush over her hair again and again, lifting fine black clouds in a small hiss of electricity. She was peering in and smiling as if she were amused at the clinging hissing hair that followed the brush.

"Yes, I think it would be a good idea on the whole," she said, with the cunning of a madwoman evading the real point.

In the mirror she could see her Matthew lying on his back, his hands behind his head, staring upwards, his face sad and hard. She felt her heart (the old heart of Susan Rawlings) soften and call out to him. But she set it to be indifferent.

He said: "Susan, the children?" It was an appeal that *almost* reached her. He opened his arms, lifting them from where they had lain by his sides, palms up, empty. She had only to run across and fling herself into them, on to his hard, warm chest, and melt into herself, into Susan. But she could not. She would not see his lifted arms. She said vaguely: "Well, surely it'll be even better for them? We'll get a French or a German girl and they'll learn the language."

In the dark she lay beside him, feeling frozen, a stranger. She felt as if Susan had been spirited away. She disliked very much this woman who lay here, cold and indifferent beside a suffering man, but she could not change her.

Next morning she set about getting a girl, and very soon came Sophie Traub from Hamburg, a girl of twenty, laughing, healthy, blue-eyed, intending to learn English. Indeed, she already spoke a good deal. In return for a room —"Mother's Room"—and her food, she undertook to do some light cooking, and to be with the children when Mrs Rawlings asked. She was an intelligent girl and understood perfectly what was needed. Susan said: "I go off sometimes, for the morning or for the day—well, sometimes the children run home from school, or they ring up, or a teacher rings up. I should be here, really. And there's the daily woman . . ." And Sophie laughed her deep fruity fräulein's laugh, showed her fine white teeth and her dimples, and said: "You want some person to play mistress of the house sometimes, not so?"

"Yes, that is just so," said Susan, a bit dry, despite herself, thinking in secret fear how easy it was, how much nearer to the end she was than she thought. Healthy Fräulein Traub's instant understanding of their position proved this to be true.

The *au pair* girl, because of her own common sense, or (as Susan said to herself with her new inward shudder) because she had been *chosen* so well by Susan, was a success with everyone, the children liking her, Mrs Parkes forgetting almost at once that she was German, and Matthew finding her "nice to have around the house." For he was now taking things as they came, from the surface of life, withdrawn both as a husband and a father from the household.

One day Susan saw how Sophie and Mrs Parkes were talking and laughing in the kitchen, and she announced that she would be away until tea-time. She knew exactly where to go and what she must look for. She took the District Line to South Kensington, changed to the Circle, got off at Paddington, and walked around looking at the smaller hotels until she was satisfied with one which had "Fred's Hotel" painted on window-panes that needed cleaning. The façade was a faded shiny yellow, like unhealthy skin. A door at the end of a passage said she must knock; she did, and Fred appeared. He was not at all attractive, not in any way, being fattish, and run-down, and wearing a tasteless striped suit. He had small sharp eyes in a white creased face, and was quite prepared to let Mrs Jones (she chose the farcical name deliberately, staring him out) have a room three days a week from ten until six. Provided, of course, that she paid in advance each time she came? Susan produced fifteen shillings (no price had been set by him) and held it out, still fixing him with a bold unblinking challenge she had not known until then she could use at will. Looking at her still, he took up a ten shilling note from her palm between thumb and forefinger, fingered it; then shuffled up two half-crowns, held out his own palm with these bits of money displayed thereon, and let his gaze lower broodingly at them. They were standing in the passage, a red-shaded light above, bare boards beneath, and a strong smell of floor polish rising about them. He shot his gaze up at her over the still-extended palm, and smiled as if to say: What do you take me for? "I shan't," said Susan, "be using this room for the purposes of making money." He still waited. She added another five shillings, at which he nodded and said: "You pay, and I ask no questions." "Good," said Susan. He now went past her to the stairs, and there waited a moment: the light from the street door being in her eyes, she lost sight of him momentarily. Then she saw a sober-suited, white-faced, white-balding little man trotting up the stairs like a waiter, and she went after him. They proceeded in utter silence up the stairs of this house where no questions were asked—"Fred's Hotel," which could afford the freedom for its visitors that poor Miss Townsend's hotel could not. The room was hideous. It had a single window, with thin green brocade curtains, a three-quarter bed that had a cheap green satin bedspread on it, a fireplace with a gas-fire and a shilling meter by it, a chest of drawers, and a green wicker armchair.

"Thank you," said Susan, knowing that Fred (if this was Fred, and not George, or Herbert or Charlie) was looking at her, not so much with curiosity, an emotion he would not own to, for professional reasons, but with a philosophical sense of what was appropriate. Having taken her money and shown her up and agreed to everything, he was clearly disapproving of her for coming here. She did not belong here at all, so his look said. (But she knew, already, how very much she did belong: the room had been waiting for her to join it.) "Would you have me called at five o'clock, please?" and he nodded and went downstairs.

It was twelve in the morning. She was free. She sat in the armchair, she simply sat, she closed her eyes and sat and let herself be alone. She was alone and no one knew where she was. When a knock came on the door she was annoyed, and prepared to show it: but it was Fred himself, it was five o'clock and he was calling her as ordered. He flicked his sharp little eyes over the room —bed, first. It was undisturbed. She might never have been in the room at all. She thanked him, said she would be returning the day after tomorrow, and left. She was back home in time to cook supper, to put the children to bed, to cook a second supper for her husband and herself later. And to welcome Sophie back from the pictures where she had gone with a friend. All these things she did cheerfully, willingly. But she was thinking all the time of the hotel room, she was longing for it with her whole being.

Three times a week. She arrived promptly at ten, looked Fred in the eyes, gave him twenty shillings, followed him up the stairs, went into the room, and shut the door on him with gentle firmness. For Fred, disapproving of her being here at all, was quite ready to let friendship, or at least acquaintanceship, follow his disapproval, if only she would let him. But he was content to go off on her dismissing nod, with the twenty shillings in his hand.

She sat in the armchair and shut her eyes.

What did she *do* in the room? Why, nothing at all. From the chair, when it had rested her, she went to the window, stretching her arms, smiling, treasuring her anonymity, to look out. She was no longer Susan Rawlings, mother of four, wife of Matthew, employer of Mrs Parkes and of Sophie Traub, with these and those relations with friends, schoolteachers, tradesmen. She no longer was mistress of the big white house and garden, owning clothes suitable for this and that activity or occasion. She was Mrs Jones and she was alone, and she had no past and no future. Here I am, she thought, after all these years of being married and having children and playing those rôles of responsibility—and I'm just the same. Yet there have been times I thought that nothing existed of me except the rôles that went with being Mrs Matthew Rawlings. Yes, here I am, and if I never saw any of my family again, here I would still be—how very strange that is! And she leaned on the sill, and looked into the street, loving the men and women who passed, because she did not know them. She looked at the downtrodden buildings over the street, and at the sky, wet and dingy, or sometimes blue, and she felt she had never seen buildings or sky before. And then she went back to the chair, empty, her mind a blank. Sometimes she talked aloud, saying nothing—an exclamation, meaningless, followed by a comment about the floral pattern on the thin rug, or a stain on the green satin coverlet. For the most part, she wool-gathered—what word is there for it?—brooded, wandered, simply went dark, feeling emptiness run deliciously through her veins like the movement of her blood.

This room had become more her own than the house she lived in. One morning she found Fred taking her a flight higher than usual. She stopped, refusing to go up, and demanded her usual room, number 19. "Well, you'll have to wait half an hour, then," he said. Willingly she descended to the dark disinfectant-smelling hall, and sat waiting until the two, man and woman, came down the stairs, giving her swift indifferent glances before they hurried out into the street, separating at the door. She went up to the room, *her* room, which they had just vacated. It was no less hers, though the windows were set wide open, and a maid was straightening the bed as she came in.

After these days of solitude, it was both easy to play her part as mother and wife, and difficult—because it was so easy: she felt an imposter. She felt as if her shell moved here, with her family, answering to Mummy, Mother, Susan, Mrs Rawlings. She was surprised no one saw through her, that she wasn't turned out of doors, as a fake. On the contrary, it seemed the children loved her more; Matthew and she "got on" pleasantly, and Mrs Parkes was happy in her work under (for the most part, it must be confessed) Sophie Traub. At night she lay beside her husband, and they made love again, apparently just as they used to, when they were really married. But she, Susan, or the being who answered so readily and improbably to the name of Susan, was not there: she was in Fred's Hotel, in Paddington, waiting for the easing hours of solitude to begin.

Soon she made a new arrangement with Fred and with Sophie. It was for five days a week. As for the money, five pounds, she simply asked Matthew for it. She saw that she was not even frightened he might ask what for: he would give it to her, she knew that, and yet it was terrifying it could be so, for this close couple, these partners, had once known the destination of every shilling they must spend. He agreed to give her five pounds a week. She asked for just so much, not a penny more. He sounded indifferent about it. It was as if he were paying her, she thought: *paying her off*—yes, that was it. Terror came back for a moment, when she understood this, but she stilled it: things had gone too far for that. Now, every week on Sunday nights, he gave her five pounds, turning away from her before their eyes could meet on the transaction. As for Sophie Traub, she was to be somewhere in or near the house until six at night, after which she was free. She was not to cook, or to clean, she was simply to be there. So she gardened or sewed, and asked friends in, being a human being who was bound to have a lot of friends. If the children were sick, she nursed them. If teachers telephoned, she answered them sensibly. For the five daytimes in the school week, she was altogether the mistress of the house.

One night in the bedroom, Matthew asked: "Susan, I don't want to interfere, don't think that, please, but are you sure you are well?"

She was brushing her hair at the mirror. She made two more strokes on either side of her head, before she replied: "Yes, dear, I am sure I am well."

He was again lying on his back, his big blond head on his hands, his elbows angled up and part-concealing his face. He said: "Then, Susan, I have to ask you this question, though you must understand, I'm not putting any sort of pressure on you . . ." (Susan heard the word pressure with dismay, because this was inevitable, of course she could not go on like this) ". . . are things going to go on like this?"

"Well," she said, going vague and bright and idiotic again, so as to escape, "Well, I don't see why not."

He was jerking his elbows up and down, in annoyance or in pain, and, looking at him, she saw he had got thin, even gaunt; and restless angry movements were not what she remembered of him. He said: "Do you want a divorce, is that it?"

At this, Susan only with the greatest difficulty stopped herself from laughing: she could hear the bright bubbling laughter she *would* have emitted, had she let herself. He could only mean one thing: she had a lover, and that was why she spent her days in London, as lost to him as if she had vanished to another continent.

Then the small panic set in again: she understood that he hoped she did have a lover, he was begging her to say so, because otherwise it would be too terrifying.

She thought this out, as she brushed her hair, watching the fine black stuff fly up to make its little clouds of electricity, hiss, hiss, hiss: behind her head, across the room, was a blue wall. She realized she was absorbed in watching the black hair making shapes against the blue. She should be answering him. "Do *you* want a divorce, Matthew?"

He said: "That surely isn't the point, is it?"

"You brought it up, I didn't," she said, brightly, suppressing meaningless tinkling laughter.

Next day she asked Fred: "Have inquiries been made for me?"

He hesitated, and she said: "I've been coming here a year now. I've made no trouble, and you've been paid every day. I have a right to be told."

"As a matter of fact, Mrs Jones, a man did come asking."

"A man from a detective agency?"

"Well, he could have been, couldn't he?"

"I was asking you . . . well, what did you tell him?"

"I told him a Mrs Jones came every weekday from ten until five or six and stayed in No. 19 by herself."

"Describing me?"

"Well, Mrs Jones, I had no alternative, put yourself in my place."

"By rights I should deduct what that man gave you for the information."

He raised shocked eyes: she was not the sort of person to make jokes like this! Then he chose to laugh: a pinkish wet slit appeared across his white crinkled face: his eyes positively begged her to laugh, otherwise he might lose some money. She remained grave, looking at him.

He stopped laughing and said: "You want to go up now?"—returning to the familiarity, the comradeship, of the country where no questions are asked, on which (and he knew it) she depended completely.

She went up to sit in her wicker-chair. But it was not the same. Her husband had searched her out. (The world had searched her out.) The pressures were on her. She was here with his connivance. He might walk in at any moment, here, into Room 19. She imagined the report from the detective agency: "A woman calling herself Mrs Jones, fitting the description of your wife (etc., etc., etc.) stays alone all day in Room No. 19. She insists on this room, waits for it if it is engaged. As far as the proprietor knows, she receives no visitors there, male or female." A report something on these lines, Matthew must have received.

Well, of course he was right: things couldn't go on like this. He had put an end to it all simply by sending the detective after her.

She tried to shrink herself back into the shelter of the room, a snail pecked out of its shell and trying to squirm back. But the peace of the room had gone. She was trying consciously to revive it, trying to let go into the dark creative trance (or whatever it was) that she had found there. It was no use, yet she craved for it, she was as ill as a suddenly deprived addict.

Several times she returned to the room, to look for herself there, but instead she found the unnamed spirit of restlessness, a prickling fevered hunger for movement, an irritable self-consciousness that made her brain feel as if it had coloured lights going on and off inside it. Instead of the soft dark that had been the room's air, were now waiting for her demons that made her dash blindly about, muttering words of hate; she was impelling herself from point to point like a moth dashing itself against a window-pane, sliding to the bottom, fluttering off on broken wings, then crashing into the invisible barrier again. And again and again. Soon she was exhausted, and she told Fred that for a while she would not be needing the room, she was going on holiday. Home she went, to the big white house by the river. The middle of a weekday, and she felt guilty at returning to her own home when not expected. She stood unseen, looking in at the kitchen window. Mrs Parkes, wearing a discarded floral overall of Susan's, was stooping to slide something into the oven. Sophie, arms folded, was leaning her back against a cupboard and laughing at some joke made by a girl not seen before by Susan—a dark foreign girl, Sophie's visitor. In an armchair Molly, one of the twins, lay curled, sucking her thumb and watching the grown-ups. She must have some sickness, to be kept from school. The child's listless face, the dark circles under her eyes, hurt Susan: Molly was looking at the three grownups working and talking in exactly the same way Susan looked at the four through the kitchen window: she was remote, shut off from them.

But then, just as Susan imagined herself going in, picking up the little girl, and sitting in an armchair with her, stroking her probably heated forehead, Sophie did just that: she had been standing on one leg, the other knee flexed, its foot set against the wall. Now she let her foot in its ribbon-tied red shoe slide down the wall, stood solid on two feet, clapping her hands before and behind her, and sang a couple of lines in German, so that the child lifted her heavy eyes at her and began to smile. Then she walked, or rather skipped over to the child, swung her up, and let her fall into her lap at the same moment she sat herself. She said "Hopla! Hopla! Molly . . ." and began stroking the dark untidy young head that Molly laid on her shoulder for comfort.

Well. . . . Susan blinked the tears of farewell out of her eyes, and went quietly up the house to her bedroom. There she sat looking at the river through the trees. She felt at peace, but in a way that was new to her. She had no desire to move, to talk, to do anything at all. The devils that had haunted the house, the garden, were not there; but she knew it was because her soul was in Room 19 in "Fred's Hotel"; she was not really here at all. It was a sensation that should have been frightening: to sit at her own bedroom window, listening to Sophie's rich young voice sing German nursery songs to her child, listening to Mrs Parkes clatter and move below, and to know that all this had nothing to do with her: she was already out of it.

Later, she made herself go down and say she was home: it was unfair to be here unannounced. She took lunch with Mrs Parkes, Sophie, Sophie's Italian friend Maria, and her daughter Molly, and felt like a visitor.

A few days later, at bedtime, Matthew said: "Here's your five pounds," and pushed them over at her. Yet he must have known she had not been leaving the house at all.

She shook her head, gave it back to him, and said, in explanation, not in accusation: "As soon as you knew where I was, there was no point."

He nodded, not looking at her. He was turned away from her: thinking, she knew, how best to handle this wife who terrified him.

He said: "I wasn't trying to . . . it's just that I was worried."

"Yes, I know."

"I must confess that I was beginning to wonder . . ."

"You thought I had a lover?"

"Yes, I am afraid I did."

She knew that he wished she had. She sat wondering how to say: "For a year now I've been spending all my days in a very sordid hotel room. It's the place where I'm happy. In fact, without it I don't exist." She heard herself saying this, and understood how terrified he was that she might. So instead she said: "Well, perhaps you're not far wrong."

Probably Matthew would think the hotel proprietor lied: he would want to think so.

"Well," he said, and she could hear his voice spring up, so to speak, with relief: "in that case I must confess I've got a bit of an affair on myself."

She said, detached and interested: "Really? Who is she?" and saw Matthew's startled look because of this reaction.

"It's Phil. Phil Hunt."

She had known Phil Hunt well in the old unmarried days. She was thinking: No, she won't do, she's too neurotic and difficult. She's never been happy yet. Sophie's much better: Well, Matthew will see that himself, sensible as he is.

This line of thought went on in silence, while she said aloud: "It's no point telling you about mine, because you don't know him."

Quick, quick, invent, she thought. Remember how you invented all that nonsense for Miss Townsend.

She began slowly, careful not to contradict herself: "His name is Michael . . ." (*Michael what?*) ". . . Michael Plant." (What a silly name!) "He's rather like you—in looks, I mean." And, indeed, she could imagine herself being touched by no one but Matthew himself. "He's a publisher." (Really? Why?) "He's got a wife already and two children."

She brought out this fantasy, proud of herself.

Matthew said: "Are you two thinking of marrying?"

She said, before she could stop herself: "Good God, *no!*"

She realized, if Matthew wanted to marry Phil Hunt, that this was too emphatic, but apparently it was all right for his voice sounded relieved as he said: "It is a bit impossible to imagine oneself married to anyone else, isn't it?" With which he pulled her to him, so that her head lay on his shoulder. She turned her face into the dark of his flesh, and listened to the blood pounding through her ears saying: I am alone, I am alone, I am alone.

In the morning Susan lay in bed while he dressed.

He had been thinking things out in the night, because now he said: "Susan, why don't we make a foursome?"

Of course, she said to herself, of course he would be bound to say that. If one is sensible, if one is reasonable, if one never allows oneself a base thought or an envious emotion, naturally one says: Let's make a foursome!

"Why not?" she said.

"We could all meet for lunch. I mean, it's ridiculous, you sneaking off to filthy hotels, and me staying late at the office, and all the lies everyone has to tell."

What on earth did I say his name was?—she panicked, then said: "I think it's a good idea, but Michael is away at the moment. When he comes back though—and I'm sure you two would like each other."

"He's away, is he?—so that's why you've been . . ." Her husband put his hand to the knot of his tie in a gesture of male coquetry she would not before have associated with him; and he bent to kiss her cheek with the expression that goes with the words: Oh, you naughty little puss! And she felt its answering look, naughty and coy, come on to her face.

Inside she was dissolving in horror at them both, at how far they had both sunk from honesty of emotion.

So now she was saddled with a lover, and he had a mistress! How ordinary, how reassuring, how jolly! And now they would make a foursome of it, and go about to theatres and restaurants. After all, the Rawlings could well afford that sort of thing, and presumably the publisher Michael Plant could afford to do himself and his mistress quite well. No there was nothing to stop the four of them developing the most intricate relationship of civilized tolerance, all enveloped in a charming afterglow of autumnal passion. Perhaps they would all go off on holidays together? She had known people who did. Or perhaps

Matthew would draw the line there? Why should he, though, if he was capable of talking about "foursomes" at all?

She lay in the empty bedroom, listening to the car drive off with Matthew in it, off to work. Then she heard the children clattering off to school to the accompaniment of Sophie's cheerfully ringing voice. She slid down into the hollow of the bed, for shelter against her own irrelevance. And she stretched out her hand to the hollow where her husband's body had lain, but found no comfort there: he was not her husband. She curled herself up in a small tight ball under the clothes: she could stay here all day, all week, indeed, all her life.

But in a few days she must produce Michael Plant, and—but how? She must presumably find some agreeable man prepared to impersonate a publisher called Michael Plant. And in return for which she would—what? Well, for one thing they would make love. The idea made her want to cry with sheer exhaustion. Oh no, she had finished with all that—the proof of it was that the words "make love," or even imagining it, trying hard to revive no more than the pleasures of sensuality, let alone affection, or love, made her want to run away and hide from the sheer effort of the thing. . . . Good Lord, why make love at all? Why make love with anyone? Or if you are going to make love, what does it matter who with? Why shouldn't she simply walk into the street, pick up a man and have a roaring sexual affair with him. Why not? Or even with "Fred"? What difference did it make.

But she had let herself in for it—an interminable stretch of time with a lover, called Michael, as part of a gallant civilized foursome. Well she could not, and she would not.

She got up, dressed, went down to find Mrs Parkes, and asked her for the loan of a pound, since Matthew, she said, had forgotten to leave her money. She exchanged with Mrs Parkes variations on the theme that husbands are all the same, they don't think, and without saying a word to Sophie, whose voice could be heard upstairs from the telephone, walked to the Underground, travelled to South Kensington, changed to the Inner Circle, got out at Paddington, and walked to Fred's Hotel. There she told Fred that she wasn't going on holiday after all, she needed the room. She would have to wait an hour, Fred said. She went to a busy tearoom-cum-restaurant around the corner, and sat watching the people flow in and out the door that kept swinging open and shut, watched them mingle and merge and separate, felt her being flow into them, into their movement. When the hour was up she left a half-crown for her pot of tea, and left the place without looking back at it, just as she had left her house, the big, beautiful white house, without another look, but silently dedicating it to Sophie. She returned to Fred, received the key of No. 19, now free, and ascended the grimy stairs slowly, letting floor after floor fall away below her, keeping her eyes lifted, so that floor after floor descended jerkily to her level of vision, and fell away out of sight.

No. 19 was the same. She saw everything with an acute, narrow, checking glance: the cheap shine of the satin spread, which had been replaced carelessly after the two bodies had finished their convulsions under it, a trace of powder on the glass that topped the chest of drawers; an intense green shade in a fold of the curtain. She stood at the window, looking down, watching people pass and pass and pass until her mind went dark from the constant movement. Then she sat in the wicker-chair, letting herself go slack. But she had to be careful, because she did not want, today, to be surprised by Fred's knock at five o'clock.

The demons were not here. They had gone forever, because she was buying her freedom from them. She was slipping already into the dark fructifying dream that seemed to caress her inwardly, like the movement of her blood . . . but she had to think about Matthew first. Should she write a letter for the coroner? But what should she say? She would like to leave him with the look on his face she had seen this morning—banal, admittedly, but at least confidently healthy. Well, that was impossible, one did not look like that with a wife dead from suicide. But how to leave him believing she was dying because of a man—because of the fascinating publisher Michael Plant? Oh, how ridiculous! How absurd! How humiliating! But she decided not to trouble about it, simply not to think about the living. If he wanted to believe she had a lover, he would believe it. And he *did* want to believe it. Even when he found out that there was no publisher in London called Michael Plant, he would think: Oh, poor Susan, she was afraid to give me his real name.

And what did it matter whether he married Phil Hunt or Sophie? Though it ought to be Sophie, who was already the mother of those children . . . and what hypocrisy to sit here worrying about the children, when she was going to leave them because she had not got the energy to stay.

She had about four hours. She spent them delightfully, darkly, sweetly, letting herself slide gently, gently, to the edge of the river. Then, with hardly a break in her consciousness, she got up, pushed the thin rug against the door, made sure the windows were tight shut, put two shillings in the meter, and turned on the gas. For the first time since she had been in the room she lay on the hard bed that smelled stale, that smelled of sweat and sex.

She lay on her back on the green satin cover, but her legs were chilly. She got up, found a blanket folded in the bottom of the chest of drawers, and carefully covered her legs with it. She was quite content lying there, listening to the faint soft hiss of the gas that poured into the room, into her lungs, into her brain, as she drifted off into the dark river.

GRACE PALEY

b. 1922

Paley has been known in New York City circles for years for her perfect stories. She currently teaches at Sarah Lawrence, but is not only a City native and resident but also inspires the loyalty of all discriminating creative writers in the area surrounding it. Her book of short stories *Enormous Changes at the Last Minute* (1974) confirmed the reputation that she already had among her fellow writers, and spread it throughout America.

As one can see from her story reprinted here, "A Conversation with My Father," she writes an open-ended story, giving her characters the freedom to develop as they please. Her father, a physician devoted to the distinguished tradition of Tolstoy and Turgenyev, prefers the closed short-story form that "settles" the fate of one's characters—either by death or marriage, or by a similar estopment of their fictional energy. For Paley, life goes on after the treatment of the character stops, and in the reader's imagination all eventualities are possible, conditioned of course by the likelihoods, the psychological probabilities, that have been established by the story. Her subjects are not objects to be picked up with pincers but full human beings with the power to escape the confines of her art.

Paley always writes with the assumption that her characters *can* make enormous changes at the last minute. Anything can happen in her world—quite the opposite of, say, that of Barthelme, who portrays people struggling with their environment only finally to sink back into it. With the will to change their lives, these characters typically find that they are constricted by details of their everyday lives so that their response to the extraordinary is finally to see it as irrelevant. Troubling, but the extraordinary gradually becomes another, different and levitated world which one comes to take for granted. Paley's assumption gives her characters great amplitude to act; they are not predestined (as in classical drama, for example) to follow a certain course. Thus her stories have a constant element of surprise: we can't guess what her characters will do next because they are free to do anything.

Paley has raised two children, and was a very active member of the Peace Movement in the 1960s.

A Conversation with My Father

My father is eighty-six years old and in bed. His heart, that bloody motor, is equally old and will not do certain jobs any more. It still floods his head with brainy light. But it won't let his legs carry the weight of his body around the house. Despite my metaphors, this muscle failure is not due to his old heart, he says, but to a potassium shortage. Sitting on one pillow, leaning on three, he offers last-minute advice and makes a request.

"I would like you to write a simple story just once more," he says, "the kind de Maupassant wrote, or Chekhov, the kind you used to write. Just recognizable people and then write down what happened to them next."

I say, "Yes, why not? That's possible." I want to please him, though I don't remember writing that way. I *would* like to try to tell such a story, if he means the kind that begins: "There was a woman . . ." followed by plot, the absolute line between two points which I've always despised. Not for literary reasons, but because it takes all hope away. Everyone, real or invented, deserves the open destiny of life.

Finally I thought of a story that had been happening for a couple of years right across the street. I wrote it down, then read it aloud. "Pa," I said, "how about this? Do you mean something like this?"

> Once in my time there was a woman and she had a son. They lived nicely, in a small apartment in Manhattan. This boy at about fifteen became a junkie, which is not unusual in our neighborhood. In order to maintain her close friendship with him, she became a junkie too. She said it was part of the youth culture, with which she felt very much at home. After a while, for a number of reasons, the boy gave it all up and left the city and his mother in disgust. Hopeless and alone, she grieved. We all visit her.

"O.K., Pa, that's it," I said, "an unadorned and miserable tale."

"But that's not what I mean," my father said. "You misunderstood me on purpose. You know there's a lot more to it. You know that. You left everything out. Turgenev wouldn't do that. Chekhov wouldn't do that. There are in fact Russian writers you never heard of, you don't have an inkling of, as good as anyone, who can write a plain ordinary story, who would not leave out what you have left out. I object not to facts but to people sitting in trees talking senselessly, voices from who knows where . . ."

"Forget that one, Pa, what have I left out now? In this one?"

"Her looks, for instance."

"Oh. Quite handsome, I think. Yes."

"Her hair?"

"Dark, with heavy braids, as though she were a girl or a foreigner."

"What were her parents like, her stock? That she became such a person. It's interesting, you know."

"From out of town. Professional people. The first to be divorced in their county. How's that? Enough?" I asked.

"With you, it's all a joke," he said. "What about the boy's father? Why didn't you mention him? Who was he? Or was the boy born out of wedlock?"

"Yes," I said. "He was born out of wedlock."

"For Godsakes, doesn't anyone in your stories get married? Doesn't anyone have the time to run down to City Hall before they jump into bed?"

"No," I said. "In real life, yes. But in my stories, no."

"Why do you answer me like that?"

"Oh, Pa, this is a simple story about a smart woman who came to N.Y.C. full of interest love trust excitement very up to date, and about her son, what a hard time she had in this world. Married or not, it's of small consequence."

"It is of great consequence," he said.

"O.K.," I said.

"O.K. O.K. yourself," he said, "but listen. I believe you that she's good-looking, but I don't think she was so smart."

"That's true," I said. "Actually that's the trouble with stories. People start out fantastic. You think they're extraordinary, but it turns out as the work goes along, they're just average with a good education. Sometimes the other way around, the person's a kind of dumb innocent, but he outwits you and you can't even think of an ending good enough."

"What do you do then?" he asked. He had been a doctor for a couple of decades and then an artist for a couple of decades and he's still interested in details, craft, technique.

"Well, you just have to let the story lie around till some agreement can be reached between you and the stubborn hero."

"Aren't you talking silly, now?" he asked. "Start again," he said. "It so happens I'm not going out this evening. Tell the story again. See what you can do this time."

"O.K.," I said. "But it's not a five-minute job." Second attempt:

> Once, across the street from us, there was a fine handsome woman, our neighbor. She had a son whom she loved because she'd known him since birth (in helpless chubby infancy, and in the wrestling, hugging ages, seven to ten, as well as earlier and later). This boy, when he fell into the fist of adolescence, became a junkie. He was not a hopeless one. He was in fact hopeful, an ideologue and successful converter. With his busy brilliance, he wrote persuasive articles for his high-school newspaper. Seeking a wider audience,

using important connections, he drummed into Lower Manhattan newsstand distribution a periodical called *Oh! Golden Horse!*

In order to keep him from feeling guilty (because guilt is the stony heart of nine tenths of all clinically diagnosed cancers in America today, she said), and because she had always believed in giving bad habits room at home where one could keep an eye on them, she too became a junkie. Her kitchen was famous for a while —a center for intellectual addicts who knew what they were doing. A few felt artistic like Coleridge and others were scientific and revolutionary like Leary. Although she was often high herself, certain good mothering reflexes remained, and she saw to it that there was lots of orange juice around and honey and milk and vitamin pills. However, she never cooked anything but chili, and that no more than once a week. She explained, when we talked to her, seriously, with neighborly concern, that it was her part in the youth culture and she would rather be with the young, it was an honor, than with her own generation.

One week, while nodding through an Antonioni film, this boy was severely jabbed by the elbow of a stern and proselytizing girl, sitting beside him. She offered immediate apricots and nuts for his sugar level, spoke to him sharply, and took him home.

She had heard of him and his work and she herself published, edited, and wrote a competitive journal called *Man Does Live By Bread Alone.* In the organic heat of her continuous presence he could not help but become interested once more in his muscles, his arteries, and nerve connections. In fact he began to love them, treasure them, praise them with funny little songs in *Man Does Live . . .*

the fingers of my flesh transcend
my transcendental soul
the tightness in my shouders end
my teeth have made me whole

To the mouth of his head (that glory of will and determination) he brought hard apples, nuts, wheat germ, and soybean oil. He said to his old friends, From now on, I guess I'll keep my wits about me. I'm going on the natch. He said he was about to begin a spiritual deep-breathing journey. How about you too, Mom? he asked kindly.

His conversion was so radiant, splendid, that neighborhood kids his age began to say that he had never been a real addict at all, only a journalist along for the smell of the story. The mother tried several times to give up what had become without her son and his friends a lonely habit. This effort only brought it to supportable levels. The boy and his girl took their electronic mimeograph and moved to the bushy edge of another borough. They were very strict. They said they would not see her again until she had been off drugs for sixty days.

At home alone in the evening, weeping, the mother read and reread the seven issues of *Oh! Golden Horse!* They seemed to her as truthful as ever. We often crossed the street to visit and console. But if we mentioned any of our children who were at college or in the hospital or dropouts at home, she would cry out, My baby! My baby! and burst into terrible, face-scarring, time-consuming tears. The End.

First my father was silent, then he said, "Number One: You have a nice sense of humor. Number Two: I see you can't tell a plain story. So don't waste time." Then he said sadly, "Number Three: I suppose that means she was alone, she was left like that, his mother. Alone. Probably sick?"

I said, "Yes."

"Poor woman. Poor girl, to be born in a time of fools, to live among fools. The end. The end. You were right to put that down. The end."

I didn't want to argue, but I had to say, "Well, it is not necessarily the end, Pa."

"Yes," he said, "what a tragedy. The end of a person."

"No, Pa," I begged him. "It doesn't have to be. She's only about forty. She could be a hundred different things in this world as time goes on. A teacher or a social worker. An ex-junkie! Sometimes it's better than having a master's in education."

"Jokes," he said. "As a writer that's your main trouble. You don't want to recognize it. Tragedy! Plain tragedy! Historical tragedy! No hope. The end."

"Oh, Pa," I said. "She could change."

"In your own life, too, you have to look it in the face." He took a couple of nitroglycerin. "Turn to five," he said, pointing to the dial on the oxygen tank. He inserted the tubes into his nostrils and breathed deep. He closed his eyes and said, "No."

I had promised the family to always let him have the last word when arguing, but in this case I had a different responsibility. That woman lives across the street. She's my knowledge and my invention. I'm sorry for her. I'm not going to leave her there in that house crying. (Actually neither would Life, which unlike me has no pity.)

Therefore: She did change. Of course her son never came home again. But right now, she's the receptionist in a storefront community clinic in the East

Village. Most of the customers are young people, some old friends. The head doctor has said to her, "If we only had three people in this clinic with your experiences . . ."

"The doctor said that?" My father took the oxygen tubes out of his nostrils and said, "Jokes. Jokes again."

"No, Pa, it could really happen that way, it's a funny world nowadays."

"No," he said. "Truth first. She will slide back. A person must have character. She does not."

"No, Pa," I said. "That's it. She's got a job. Forget it. She's in that storefront working."

"How long will it be?" he asked. "Tragedy! You too. When will you look it in the face?"

Enormous Changes at the Last Minute

A young man said he wanted to go to bed with Alexandra because she had an interesting mind. He was a cabdriver and she *had* admired the curly back of his head. Still, she was surprised. He said he would pick her up again in about an hour and a half. Because she was fair and a responsible person, she placed between them a barrier of truthful information. She said, I suppose you don't know many middle-aged women.

You don't look so middle-aged to me. I mean, everyone likes what they like. That is, I'm interested in your point of view, your way of life. Anyway, he said, peering into the mirror, your face is nice and your eyebrows are out of sight.

Make it two hours, she said. I'm visiting my father whom I happen to love.

I love mine too, he said. He just doesn't love me. Too too bad.

O.K. That's enough, she said. Because they had already *had* the following factual and introductory conversation.

How old are your kids?

I have none.

Sorry. Then what do you do for a living?

Children. Early teenage. Adoptions, foster homes. Probation. Troubles—well . . .

Where'd you go to school?

City colleges. What about you?

Oh, me. Lots of places. Antioch. Wisconsin. California. I might go back someday. Some place else though. Maybe Harvard. Why not?

He leaned on his horn to move a sixteen-wheel trailer truck delivering Kleenex to the A & P.

I wish you'd stop that, she said. I hate that kind of driving.

Why? Oh! You're an idealist! He looked through his rearview mirror straight into her eyes. But were you married? Ever?

Once. For years.

Who to?

It's hard to describe. A revolutionist.

Really? Could I know him? What's his name? We say revolutionary nowadays.

Oh?

By the way, my name's Dennis. I probably like you, he said.

You do, do you? Well, why should you? And let me ask you something. What do you mean by nowadays?

By the birdseed of St. Francis, he said, taking a tiny brogue to the tip of his tongue. I meant no harm.

Nowadays! she said. What does that mean? I guess you think you're kind of brand-new. You're not so brand-new. The telephone was brand-new. The airplane was brand-new. *You've* been seen on earth before.

Wow! he said. He stopped the cab just short of the hospital entrance. He turned to look at her and make decisions. But you're right, he said sweetly. You know the mind *is* an astonishing, long-living, erotic thing.

Is it? she asked. Then she wondered: What is the life expectancy of the mind?

Eighty years, said her father, glad to be useful. Once he had explained electrical storms before you could find the Book of Knowledge. Now in the cave of old age, he continued to amass wonderful information. But he was sick with oldness. His arteries had a hopeless future, and conversation about all the obsolescent tubing often displaced very interesting subjects.

One day he said, Alexandra! Don't show me the sunset again. I'm not interested any more. You know that. She had just pointed to a simple sunset happening outside his hospital window. It was a red ball—all alone, without its evening streaking clouds—a red ball falling hopelessly west, just missing the Hudson River, Jersey City, Chicago, the Great Plains, the Golden Gate—falling, falling.

Then in Russian he sighed some Pushkin. Not for me, the spring. *Nye dyla menya . . .* He slept. She read the large-print edition of *The Guns of August.* A half hour later, he opened his eyes and told her how, in that morning's *Times,* the Phoenicians had sailed to Brazil in about 500 B.C. A remarkable people. The Vikings too were remarkable. He spoke well of the Chinese, the Jews, the Greeks, the Indians—all the old commercial people. Actually he had never knocked an entire nation. International generosity had been started in him during the late nineteenth century by his young mother and father, candleholders inside the dark tyranny of the czars. It was childhood training. Thoughtfully, he passed it on.

In the hospital bed next to him, a sufferer named John feared the imminent rise of the blacks of South Africa, the desperate blacks of Chicago, the yellow Chinese, and the Ottoman Turks. He had more reason than Alexandra's father to dread the future because his heart was strong. He would probably live to see it all. He believed the Turks when they came would bring to New York City diseases like cholera, virulent scarlet fever, and particularly leprosy.

Leprosy! for God's sakes! said Alexandra. John! Upset yourself with reality for once! She read aloud from the *Times* about the bombed, burned lepers' colonies in North Vietnam. Her father said, Please, Alexandra, today, no propaganda. Why do you constantly pick on the United States? He remembered the first time he'd seen the American flag on wild Ellis Island. Under its protection and working like a horse, he'd read Dickens, gone to medical school, and shot like a surface-to-air missile right into the middle class.

Then he said, But they shouldn't put a flag in the middle of the chocolate pudding. It's ridiculous.

It's Memorial Day, said the nurse's aide, removing his tray.

In the early evening Dennis stood at the door of each room of Alexandra's apartment. He looked this way and that. Underuse in a time of population stress, he muttered. He entered the kitchen and sniffed the kitchen air. It doesn't matter, he said aloud. He took a fingerful of gravy out of the pot on the stove. Beef stew, he whispered. Then he opened the door to the freezer compartment and said, Sweet Jesus! because there were eleven batches of the same, neatly stacked and frozen. They were for Alexandra's junkies, whose methadone required lots of protein and carbohydrates.

I wouldn't have them in my house. It's a wonder you got a cup and a saucer left. Creeps, said Dennis. However, yes indeed, I will eat this stuff. Why? Does it make me think of home or of something else? he asked. I think, a movie I once saw.

Apple turnovers! You know I have to admit it, our commune isn't working too well. Probably because it's in Brooklyn and the food coop isn't together. But it's cool, they've accepted the criticism.

You have lots of junk in here, he pointed out after dinner. He had decided to give the place some respectful attention. He meant armchairs, lamps, desk sets, her grandmother's wedding portrait, and an umbrella stand with two of her father's canes.

Um, said Alexandra, it's rent-controlled.

You know what I like to do, Alexandra? I like to sit with a girl and look at a late movie, he said. It's an experience common to Americans at this hour. It's important to be like others, to dig the average dude, you have to be him. Be HIM. It's groovier than a lot of phony gab. You'd be surprised how friendly you get.

I'm not against friendliness, she said, I'm not even against Americans.

They watched half of *A Day at the Races.* This is very relaxing, he said. It's kind of long though, isn't it? Then he began to undress. He held out his arms. He said, Alexandra I really can't wait any more. I'm a sunrise person. I like to go to bed early. Can I stay a few days?

He gave reasons: 1. It was a Memorial Day weekend, and the house in Brooklyn was full of tripping visitors. 2. He was disgusted with them anyway because they'd given up the most beautiful batik work for fashionable tie-dying. 3. He and Alexandra could take some good walks in the morning because all the parks to walk in were the lightest green. He had noticed that the tree on the corner though dying of buses was green at the beginning of many twigs. 4. He could talk to her about the kids, help her to understand their hangups, their incredible virtues. He had missed being one of them by about seven useless years.

So many reasons are not essential, Alexandra said. She offered him a brandy. Holy toads! he said furiously. You *know* I'm not into that. Touched by gloom, he began to remove the heavy shoes he wore for mountain walking. He dropped his pants and stamped on them a couple of times to make sure he and they were disengaged.

Alexandra, in the first summer dress of spring, stood still and watched. She breathed deeply because of having been alone for a year or two. She put her two hands over her ribs to hold her heart in place and also out of modesty to quiet its immodest thud. Then they went to bed in the bedroom and made love until that noisy disturbance ended. She couldn't hear one interior sound. Therefore they slept.

In the morning she became interested in reality again, which she had always liked. She wanted to talk about it. She began with a description of John, her father's neighbor in the hospital.

Turks? Far out! Well he's right. And another thing. Leprosy *is* coming. It's coming to the Forest Hills County Fair, the Rikers Island Jamboree, the Fillmore East, and the Ecolocountry Gardens in Westchester. In August.

Reality? A lesson in reality? Am I a cabdriver? No. I drive a cab but I am not a cabdriver. I'm a song hawk. A songmaker. I'm a poet, in other words. Do you know that every black man walking down the street today is a poet? But only one white honky devil in ten. One in ten.

Nowadays I write for the Lepers all the time. Fuck poetry. The Lepers dig me. I dig them.

The Lepers? Alexandra said.

Cool! You know them? No? Well, you may have known them under their old name. They used to be called The Split Atom. But they became too popular and their thing is anonymity. That's what they're known for. They'll probably change their name after the summer festivals. They might move to the country and call themselves Winter Moss.

Do you really make a living now?

Oh yes. I do. I do. Among technicians like myself I do.

Now: I financially carry one third of a twelve-person, three-children commune. I only drive a cab to keep on top of the world of illusion, you know, Alexandra, to rap with the bourgeoisies, the fancy whores, the straight ladies visiting their daddies. Oh, excuse me, he said.

Now, Alexandra, imagine this: two bass guitars, a country violin, one piccolo, and drums. The Lepers' theme song! He sat up in bed. The sun shone on his chest. He had begun to think of breakfast, but he sang so that Alexandra could know him better and dig his substantialness.

ooooh
first my finger goes   goes   goes
then my nose
then baby   my toes

if you love me this way   anyway   any day
I'll go your way
my Little Neck rose

Well? he asked. He looked at Alexandra. Was she going to cry? I thought you were such a reality freak, Alexandra. That's the way it is in the real world. Anyway! He then said a small prose essay to explain and buttress the poem:

> The kids! the kids! Though terrible troubles hang over them, such as the absolute end of the known world quickly by detonation or slowly through the easygoing destruction of natural resources, they are still, even now, optimistic, humorous and brave. In fact, they intend enormous changes at the last minute.

Come on, said Alexandra, hardhearted, an enemy of generalization, there are all kinds. My boys aren't like that.

Yes, they are, he said, angry. You bring them around. I'll prove it. Anyway, I love them. He tried for about twenty minutes, forgetting breakfast, to show Alexandra how to look at things in this powerful last-half-of-the-century way. She tried. She had always had a progressive if sometimes reformist disposition, but at that moment, listening to him talk, she could see straight ahead over the thick hot rod of love to solitary age and lonesome death.

But there's nothing to fear my dear girl, her father said. When you get there you will not want to live a hell of a lot. Nothing to fear at all. You will be used up. You are like a coal burning, smoldering. Then there's nothing left to burn. Finished. Believe me, he said, although he hadn't been there yet himself, at that moment you won't mind. Alexandra's face was a bit rumpled, listening.

Don't look at me like that! he said. He was too sensitive to her appearance. He hated her to begin to look older the way she'd had to in the last twenty years. He said, Now *I* have seen people die. A large number. Not one or two. Many. They are good and ready. Pain. Despair. Unconsciousness, nightmares. Perfectly good comas, wrecked by nightmares. They are ready. You will be too, Sashka. Don't worry so much.

Ho ho ho, said John in the next bed listening through the curtains. Doc, I'm not ready. I feel terrible, I got lousy nightmares. I don't sleep a wink. But I'm not ready. I can't piss without this tube. Lonesomeness! Boy! Did you ever see *one* of my kids visiting? No! Still I am *not* ready. N O T   R E A D Y. He spelled it out, looking at the ceiling or through it, to the roof garden for incurables, and from there to God.

The next morning Dennis said, I would rather die than go to the hospital.

For God's sakes why?

Why? Because I hate to be in the hands of strangers. They don't let you take the pills you got that you know work, then if you need one of their pills, even if you buzz, they don't come. The nurse and three interns are making out in the information booth. I've seen it. It's a high counter, she's answering questions, and they're taking turns banging her from behind.

Dennis! You're too dumb. You sound like some superstitious old lady with rape dreams.

That's cool, he said. I *am* an old lady about my health. I mean I like it. I want my teeth to go right on. Right on sister. He began to sing, then stopped. Listen! Your destiny's in their hands. It's up to them. Do you live? Or are you a hippie crawling creep from their point of view? Then die!

Really. Nobody ever decides to let you die. In fact, that's what's wrong. They decide to keep people alive for years after death has set in.

You mean like your father?

Alexandra leaped out of bed stark naked. My father! Why he's got twenty times your zip.

Cool it! he said. Come back. I was just starting to fuck you and you get so freaked.

And another thing. Don't use that word. I hate it. When you're with a woman you have to use the language that's right for her.

What do you want me to say?

I want you to say, I was just starting to make love to you, etc.

Well, that's true, said Dennis, I was. When she returned to him, he only touched the tips of her fingers, though all of her was present. He kissed each finger and said right after each kiss, I want to make love to you. He did this sweetly, not sarcastically.

Dennis, Alexandra said in an embarrassment of recognition, you look like one of my placements, in fact you look like a kid, Billy Platoon. His real name is Platon but he calls himself Platoon so he can go to Vietnam and get killed like his stepbrother. He's a dreamy boy.

Alexandra, you talk a lot, now hush, no politics.

Alexandra continued for a sentence or two. He carries a stick with a ball full of nails attached, like some medieval weapon, in case an enemy from Suffolk Street CIA's him. That's what they call it.

Never heard that before. Besides I'm jealous. And also I'm the enemy from Suffolk Street.

No, no, said Alexandra. Then she noticed in her mother's bedroom bureau mirror across the room a small piece of her naked self. She said, Ugh!

There, there! said Dennis lovingly, caressing what he thought she'd looked at, a couple of rippled inches between her breast and belly. It's natural, Alexandra. Men don't change as much as women. Among all the animals, human females are the only ones to lose estrogen as they get older.

Is that it? she said.

Then there was nothing to talk about for half an hour.

But how come you knew that? she asked. The things you know, Dennis. What for?

Why—for my art, he said. And despite his youth he rested from love the way artists often do in order to sing. He sang:

Camp out
    out in the forest daisy
    under the gallows tree
with the
        ace of pentacles
        and me

            daisy flower

What of the
        earth's ecology
you're drivin too fast
Daisy you're drivin alone
    Hey Daisy cut the ignition
                let the oil
                back in the stone.

Oh, I like that one. I admire it! Alexandra said. But in fact, *is* ecology a good word for a song? It's technical . . .

Any word is good, it's the big word today anyway, said Dennis. It's what you do with the word. The language and the idea, they work it out together.

Really? Where do you get most of your ideas?

I don't know if I want to eat or sleep, he said, I think I just want to nuzzle your titty. Talk talk talk. Most? Well, I would say the majority are from a magazine, the *Scientific American.*

During breakfast, language remained on his mind. Because of this, he was silent. After the pancakes, he said, Actually Alexandra, I *can* use any words I want. And I have. I proved it last week in a conversation just like this one. I asked these blue-eyed cats to give me a dictionary. I just flipped the pages and jabbed and the word I hit was *ophidious.* But I did it, because the word does the dreaming for you. The WORD.

To a tune that was probably "On Top of Old Smoky" he sang:

The ophidious garden
was invented by Freud

where three ladies murdered
oh three ladies murdered

the pricks of the birds

the cobra is buried
the rattlesnake writhes

in the black snaky garden
in the blue snaky garden

in the hairs of my wives.

More coffee, please, he said with pride and modesty.

It's better than most of your songs, Alexandra said. It's a poem, isn't it? It *is* better.

What? What? It is *not* better, it is not, goddamn. It is not . . . It just isn't . . . oh, excuse me for losing my cool like that.

Forget it sonny, Alexandra said respectfully. I only meant I liked it, but I know, I'm too frank from living alone so much I think. Anyway, how come you always think about wives? Wives, mothers?

Because that's me, said peaceful Dennis. Haven't you noticed it yet? That's my bag. I'm a motherfucker.

Oh, she said, I see. But I'm not a mother, Dennis.

Yes, you are, Alexandra. I've figured out a lot about you. I know. I act like the weekend stud sometimes. But I wrote you a song. Just last night in the cab. I think about you. The Lepers'll never dig it. They don't know too much about life. They're still baby bees trying to make it to the next flower, but some old-timer'll tape it, some sore dude who's been out of it for a couple of years who wants to grow. He'll smell the shit in it.

Oh
I know something about you baby

that's sad
don't be mad
baby

That you will never have children at
rest
at that beautiful breast
my love

But see
everywhere you go, children follow you
for more
many more

are the children of your life
than the children of the married wife.

That one is out of the Bible, he said.

Pa, Alexandra said, don't you think a woman in this life ought to have at least one child?

No doubt about it, he said, You should have when you were married to Granofsky, the Communist. We disagreed. He had no sense of humor. He's probably boring the Cubans to death this minute. But he was an intelligent person otherwise. I would have brilliant grandchildren. They would not necessarily have the same politics.

Then he looked at her, her age and possibilities. He softened. You don't look so bad. You could still marry, dear girl. Then he softened further, thinking of hopeless statistics he had just read about the ratio of women to men. Actually! So what! It's not important, Alexandra. According to the Torah, only the man is commanded to multiply. You are not commanded. You have a child, you don't have, God doesn't care. You don't have one, you call in the maid. You say to your husband, Sweetie, get my maid with child. O.K. Well, your husband has anyway been fooling around with the maid for a couple of years, but now it's a respectable business. Good. You don't have to go through the whole thing, nine months, complications, maybe a Caesarean, no no pronto, a child for the Lord, Hosanna.

Pa, she said, several weeks later, but what if I did have a baby?

Don't be a fool, he said. Then he gave her a terrible long medical look, which included her entire body. He said, Why do you ask this question? He became red in the face, which had never happened. He took hold of his chest with his right hand, the hospital buzzer with the left. First, he said, I want the nurse! Now! Then he ordered Alexandra: marry!

Dennis said, I don't know how I got into this shit. It's not right, but because your habits and culture are different, I will compromise. What I suggest is this, Alexandra. The three children in our commune belong to us all. No one knows who the father is. It's far out. I swear—by the cock of our hard-up gods, I swear it's beautiful. One of them might be mine. But she doesn't have any distinguishing marks. Why don't you come and live with us and we'll all raise that kid up to be a decent human and humane being in this world. We need a slightly older person, we really do, with a historic sense. We lack that.

Thank you, Alexandra replied. No.

Her father said, Explain it to me, please. For what purpose did you act out this nonsense? For love? At your age. Money? Some conniver flattered you. You probably made him supper. Some starving ne'er-do-well probably wanted a few meals and said, Why not? This middle-aged fool is an easy mark. She'll give me a pot roast at night, bacon and eggs in the morning.

No Pa, no, Alexandra said. Please, you'll get sicker.

John in the next bed dying with a strong heart wrote a little note to him. Doc, you're crazy. Don't leave enemies. That girl is loyal! She hasn't missed a Tues., Thurs., or Sat. Did you ever see *one* of my kids visit? Something else? I feel worse and worse. But I'm still *not ready.*

I want to tell you one more thing, her father said. You are going to embitter my last days and ruin my life.

After that, Alexandra hoped every day for her father's death, so that she could have a child without ruining his interesting life at the very end of it when ruin is absolutely retroactive.

Finally, Dennis said, then let me at least share the pad with you. It'll be to *your* advantage.

No, Alexandra said. Please, Dennis. I've got to go to work early. I'm sleepy.

I dig. I've been a joke to you. You've used me in a bad way. That's not cool. That smells under heaven.

No, Alexandra said. Please, shut up. Anyway, how do you know you're the father?

Come on, he said, who else would be?

Alexandra smiled, bit her lip to the edge of blood to show pain politely. She was thinking about the continuity of her work, how to be proud and not lose a productive minute. She thought about the members of her case load one by one.

She said, Dennis, I know exactly what I'm going to do.

In that case, this is it, I'm splitting.

This is what Alexandra did in order to make good use of the events of her life. She invited three pregnant clients who were fifteen and sixteen years old to live with her. She visited each one and explained to them that she was pregnant too, and that her apartment was very large. Although they had disliked her because she'd always worried more about the boys, they moved out of the homes of their bad-tempered parents within a week. At the very first evening meal they began to give Alexandra good advice about men, which she did appreciate years later. She ensured their health and her own and she took notes as well. She established a precedent in social work which would not be followed or even mentioned in state journals for about five years.

Alexandra's father's life was not ruined, nor did he have to die. Shortly before the baby's birth, he fell hard on the bathroom tiles, cracked his skull, dipped the wires of his brain into his heart's blood. Short circuit! He lost twenty, thirty years in the flood, the faces of nephews, in-laws, the names of two Presidents, and a war. His eyes were rounder, he was often awestruck, but he was smart as ever, and able to begin again with fewer scruples to notice and appreciate.

The baby was born and named Dennis for his father. Of course his last name was Granofsky because of Alexandra's husband, Granofsky the Communist.

The Lepers, who had changed their name to the Edible Amanita, taped the following song in his tiny honor. It was called "Who? I."

The lyrics are simple. They are:

Who is the father?
Who is the father
Who is the father

I! I! I! I!

I am the father
I am the father
I am the father.

Dennis himself sang the solo which was I! I! I! I! in a hoarse enraged prophetic voice. He had been brave to acknowledge the lyrics. After a thirty-eight-hour marathon encounter at his commune, he was asked to leave. The next afternoon he moved to a better brownstone about four blocks away where occasional fatherhood was expected.

On the baby's third birthday, Dennis and the Fair Fields of Corn produced a folk-rock album because that was the new sound and exciting. It was called *For Our Son.* Tuned-in listeners could hear how taps played by the piccolo about forty times a verse flitted in and out of the long dark drum rolls, the ordinary banjo chords, and the fiddle tune which was something but not exactly like "Lullaby and Good Night."

Will you come to see me Jack
When I'm old and very shaky?
Yes I will for you're my dad
And you've lost your last old lady
Though you traveled very far
To the highlands and the badlands
And ripped off the family car
Still, old dad, I won't forsake you.

Will you come to see me Jack?
Though I'm really not alone.
Still I'd like to see my boy
For we're lonesome for our own.
Yes I will for you're my dad

Though you dumped me and my brothers
And you sizzled down the road
Loving other fellows' mothers.

Will you come to see me Jack?
Though I look like time boiled over.
Growing old is not a lark.
Yes I will for you're my dad
Though we never saw a nickel
As we struggled up life's ladder
I will call you and together
We will cuddle up and see
What the weather's like in Key West
On the old-age home TV.

This song was sung coast to coast and became famous from the dark Maine woods to Texas's shining gulf. It was responsible for a statistical increase in visitors to old-age homes by the apprehensive middle-aged and the astonished young.

FLANNERY O'CONNOR

1925–1964

Flannery O'Connor saw in her native Georgia the violence that results when people are immersed in a culture that offers them a conception of life too narrow to accommodate their innermost longings. It is not that her South is overtly repressive to the lower middle-class and poor whites about whom O'Connor writes: her characters do not live in fear of lynch mobs, the police, or any external force for that matter. Their trouble is that they have internalized a set of attitudes that assume their world is a gentle, easy-going place where folksy wisdom and Bible-belt theology suffice to explain all the human experience "good country people" will ever undergo. These attitudes, although they constitute the common man's simple myth of the South, simply cannot contain the reality of the people they are supposed to describe.

In an atmosphere in which myth and simplistic concepts of personality are assumed to be valid, people either reduce the scope of their lives to live comfortably or invent private hypocrisies that let them do whatever it is they want to do. In either case, their conventional exterior becomes grotesquely unrepresentative of their interior. Stock comic characters whose very comicness results from such a discrepancy of thought and appearance have always abounded in popular fiction: think of the small-town con-man, the pious-sounding traveling salesman. But Flannery O'Connor catches in the disjunction between the ordinariness of her characters' vocabulary and intonation and the extraordinariness of their passions a deeper kind of hypocrisy, one that is at least partly unconscious and that over a period of time distorts the self and sets up the conditions for some violent explosion. If the explosion comes, the characters confront a range of experience far beyond the comfortable confines of the myth by which they live: they suddenly face their hidden capacity—for cruelty, violence, even murder.

There is little in Flannery O'Connor's life (except her perceptiveness and sensitivity to common people) that would account for the grotesqueness of the characters and the violence of the events in her stories. She was born and grew up in Savannah, Georgia, of all southern cities perhaps the one most eager to preserve its pre-Civil War traditions. As a devout Roman Catholic in a predominantly Fundamentalist society, O'Connor was especially attracted to the Church's emphasis on mysteries and revelations—the mystical experience at the limits of human cognition. She was therefore especially sensitive to society's attempt to imagine itself too narrowly, too materialistically. On the death of her father when she was thirteen, she and her mother moved to a farmhouse in Milledgeville, Georgia. She attended the local college for women, and later won a scholarship to study for an M.A. in creative writing at the University of Iowa. For a brief time she lived in New York, and then in Connecticut with the family of Robert Fitzgerald, the poet and translator, who had taken a warm interest in her and her writing. About the time that her first novel, *Wise Blood* (1952), was published and widely admired, she learned that she was suffering from the same chronic illness that had killed her father. She thereupon returned to live with her mother in rural Georgia, making speaking trips when she was well enough, but mostly working on the perfectly controlled fiction of which the stories that follow are fine examples. "Everything That Rises Must Converge" is the title story of the collection she finished only a few weeks before her death in 1964.

Everything That Rises Must Converge

Her doctor had told Julian's mother that she must lose twenty pounds on account of her blood pressure, so on Wednesday nights Julian had to take her downtown on the bus for a reducing class at the Y. The reducing class was designed for working girls over fifty, who weighed from 165 to 200 pounds. His mother was one of the slimmer ones, but she said ladies did not tell their age or weight. She would not ride the buses by herself at night since they had been integrated, and because the reducing class was one of her few pleasures, necessary for her health, and *free,* she said Julian could at least put himself out to take her, considering all she did for him. Julian did not like to consider all she did for him, but every Wednesday night he braced himself and took her.

She was almost ready to go, standing before the hall mirror, putting on her hat, while he, his hands behind him, appeared pinned to the door frame, waiting like Saint Sebastian for the arrows to begin piercing him. The hat was new and had cost her seven dollars and a half. She kept saying. "Maybe I shouldn't have paid that for it. No, I shouldn't have. I'll take it off and return it tomorrow. I shouldn't have bought it."

Julian raised his eyes to heaven. "Yes, you should have bought it," he said. "Put it on and let's go." It was a hideous hat. A purple velvet flap came down on one side of it and stood up on the other; the rest of it was green and looked like a cushion with the stuffing out. He decided it was less comical than jaunty and pathetic. Everything that gave her pleasure was small and depressed him.

She lifted the hat one more time and set it down slowly on top of her head. Two wings of gray hair protruded on either side of her florid face, but her eyes, sky-blue, were as innocent and untouched by experience as they must have been when she was ten. Were it not that she was a widow who had struggled fiercely to feed and clothe and put him through school and who was supporting him still, "until he got on his feet," she might have been a little girl that he had to take to town.

"It's all right, it's all right," he said. "Let's go." He opened the door himself and started down the walk to get her going. The sky was a dying violet and the houses stood out darkly against it, bulbous liver-colored monstrosities of a uniform ugliness though no two were alike. Since this had been a fashionable neighborhood forty years ago, his mother persisted in thinking they did well to have an apartment in it. Each house had a narrow collar of dirt around it in which sat, usually, a grubby child. Julian walked with his hands in his pockets, his head down and thrust forward and his eyes glazed with the determination to make himself completely numb during the time he would be sacrificed to her pleasure.

The door closed and he turned to find the dumpy figure, surmounted by the atrocious hat, coming toward him. "Well," she said, "you only live once and paying a little more for it, I at least won't meet myself coming and going."

"Some day I'll start making money," Julian said gloomily—he knew he never would—"and you can have one of those jokes whenever you take the fit." But first they would move. He visualized a place where the nearest neighbors would be three miles away on either side.

"I think you're doing fine," she said, drawing on her gloves. "You've only been out of school a year. Rome wasn't built in a day."

She was one of the few members of the Y reducing class who arrived in hat and gloves and who had a son who had been to college. "It takes time," she said "and the world is in such a mess. This hat looked better on me than any of the others, though when she brought it out I said, 'Take that thing back. I wouldn't have it on my head,' and she said, 'Now wait till you see it on,' and then she put it on me, I said, 'We-ull,' and she said, 'If you ask me, that hat does something for you and you do something for the hat, and besides,' she said, 'with that hat, you won't meet yourself coming and going.' "

Julian thought he could have stood his lot better if she had been selfish, if she had been an old hag who drank and screamed at him. He walked along, saturated in depression, as if in the midst of his martyrdom he had lost his faith. Catching sight of his long, hopeless, irritated face, she stopped suddenly with a grief-stricken look, and pulled back on his arm. "Wait on me," she said. "I'm going to the house and take this thing off and tomorrow I'm going to return it. I was out of my head. I can pay the gas bill with that seven-fifty."

He caught her arm in a vicious grip. "You are not going to take it back," he said. "I like it."

"Well," she said, "I don't think I ought . . ."

"Shut up and enjoy it," he muttered, more depressed than ever.

"With the world in the mess it's in," she said, "it's a wonder we can enjoy anything. I tell you, the bottom rail is on the top."

Julian sighed.

"Of course," she said, "if you know who you are, you can go anywhere." She said this every time he took her to the reducing class. "Most of them in it are not our kind of people," she said, "but I can be gracious to anybody. I know who I am."

"They don't give a damn for your graciousness," Julian said savagely. "Knowing who you are is good for one generation only. You haven't the foggiest idea where you stand now or who you are."

She stopped and allowed her eyes to flash at him. "I most certainly do know who I am," she said, "and if you don't know who you are, I'm ashamed of you."

"Oh hell," Julian said.

"Your great-grandfather was a former governor of this state," she said. "Your grandfather was a prosperous landowner. Your grandmother was a Godhigh."

"Will you look around you," he said tensely, "and see where you are now?" and he swept his arm jerkily out to indicate the neighborhood, which the growing darkness at least made less dingy.

"You remain what you are," she said. "Your great-grandfather had a plantation and two hundred slaves."

"There are no more slaves," he said irritably.

"They were better off when they were," she said. He groaned to see that she was off on that topic. She rolled onto it every few days like a train on an open track. He knew every stop, every junction, every swamp along the way, and knew the exact point at which her conclusion would roll majestically into the station: "It's ridiculous. It's simply not realistic. They should rise, yes, but on their own side of the fence."

"Let's skip it," Julian said.

"The ones I feel sorry for," she said, "are the ones that are half white. They're tragic."

"Will you skip it?"

"Suppose we were half white. We would certainly have mixed feelings."

"I have mixed feelings now," he groaned.

"Well let's talk about something pleasant," she said. "I remember going to Grandpa's when I was a little girl. Then the house had double stairways that went up to what was really the second floor—all the cooking was done on the first. I used to like to stay down in the kitchen on account of the way the walls smelled. I would sit with my nose pressed against the plaster and take deep breaths. Actually the place belonged to the Godhighs but your grandfather Chestny paid the mortgage and saved it for them. They were in reduced circumstances." she said, "but reduced or not, they never forgot who they were."

"Doubtless that decayed mansion reminded them," Julian muttered. He never spoke of it without contempt or thought of it without longing. He had seen it once when he was a child before it had been sold. The double stairways had rotted and been torn down. Negroes were living in it. But it remained in his mind as his mother had known it. It appeared in his dreams regularly. He would stand on the wide porch, listening to the rustle of oak leaves, then wander through the high-ceilinged hall into the parlor that opened onto it and gaze at the worn rugs and faded draperies. It occurred to him that it was he, not she, who could have appreciated it. He preferred its threadbare elegance to anything he could name and it was because of it that all the neighborhoods they had lived in had been a torment to him—whereas she had hardly known the difference. She called her insensitivity "being adjustable."

"And I remember the old darky who was my nurse, Caroline. There was no better person in the world. I've always had a great respect for my colored friends," she said. "I'd do anything in the world for them and they'd . . ."

"Will you for God's sake get off that subject?" Julian said. When he got on a bus by himself, he made it a point to sit down beside a Negro, in reparation as it were for his mother's sins.

"You're mighty touchy tonight," she said. "Do you feel all right?"

"Yes I feel all right," he said. "Now lay off."

She pursed her lips. "Well, you certainly are in a vile humor," she observed. "I just won't speak to you at all."

They had reached the bus stop. There was no bus in sight and Julian, his hands still jammed in his pockets and his head thrust forward, scowled down the empty street. The frustration of having to wait on the bus as well as ride on it began to creep up his neck like a hot hand. The presence of his mother was borne in upon him as she gave a pained sigh. He looked at her bleakly. She was holding herself very erect under the preposterous hat, wearing it like a banner of her imaginary dignity. There was in him an evil urge to break her spirit. He suddenly unloosened his tie and pulled it off and put it in his pocket.

She stiffened. "Why must you look like *that* when you take me to town? she said. "Why must you deliberately embarrass me?"

"If you'll never learn where you are," he said, "you can at least learn where I am."

"You look like a—thug," she said.

"Then I must be one," he murmured.

"I'll just go home," she said. "I will not bother you. If you can't do a little thing like that for me . . ."

Rolling his eyes upward, he put his tie back on. "Restored to my class," he muttered. He thrust his face toward her and hissed, "True culture is in the mind, the *mind,*" he said, and tapped his head, "the mind."

"It's in the heart," she said, "and in how you do things and how you do things is because of who you *are.*"

"Nobody in the damn bus cares who you are."

"I care who I am," she said icily.

The lighted bus appeared on top of the next hill and as it approached, they moved out into the street to meet it. He put his hand under her elbow and hoisted her up on the creaking step. She entered with a little smile, as if she were going into a drawing room where everyone had been waiting for her. While he put in the tokens, she sat down on one of the broad front seats for three which faced the aisle. A thin woman with protruding teeth and long yellow hair was sitting on the end of it. His mother moved up beside her and left room for Julian beside herself. He sat down and looked at the floor across the aisle where a pair of thin feet in red and white canvas sandals were planted.

His mother immediately began a general conversation meant to attract anyone who felt like talking. "Can it get any hotter?" she said and removed from her purse a folding fan, black with a Japanese scene on it, which she began to flutter before her.

"I reckon it might could," the woman with the protruding teeth said, "but I know for a fact my apartment couldn't get no hotter."

"It must get the afternoon sun," his mother said. She sat forward and looked up and down the bus. It was half filled. Everybody was white. "I see we have the bus to ourselves," she said. Julian cringed.

"For a change," said the woman across the aisle, the owner of the red and white canvas sandals. "I come on one the other day and they were thick as fleas—up front and all through."

"The world is in a mess everywhere," his mother said. "I don't know how we've let it get in this fix."

"What gets my goat is all those boys from good families stealing automobile tires," the woman with the protruding teeth said. "I told my boy, I said you may not be rich but you been raised right and if I ever catch you in any such mess, they can send you on to the reformatory. Be exactly where you belong."

"Training tells," his mother said. "Is your boy in high school?"

"Ninth grade," the woman said.

"My son just finished college last year. He wants to write but he's selling typewriters until he gets started," his mother said.

The woman leaned forward and peered at Julian. He threw her such a malevolent look that she subsided against the seat. On the floor across the aisle there was an abandoned newspaper. He got up and got it and opened it out in front of him. His mother discreetly continued the conversation in a lower tone but the woman across the aisle said in a loud voice, "Well that's nice. Selling typewriters is close to writing. He can go right from one to the other."

"I tell him," his mother said, "that Rome wasn't built in a day."

Behind the newspaper Julian was withdrawing into the inner compartment of his mind where he spent most of his time. This was a kind of mental bubble in which he established himself when he could not bear to be a part of what was going on around him. From it he could see out and judge but in it he was safe from any kind of penetration from without. It was the only place where he felt free of the general idiocy of his fellows. His mother had never entered it but from it he could see her with absolute clarity.

The old lady was clever enough and he thought that if she had started from any of the right premises, more might have been expected of her. She lived according to the laws of her own fantasy world, outside of which he had never seen her set foot. The law of it was to sacrifice herself for him after she had first created the necessity to do so by making a mess of things. If he had permitted her sacrifices, it was only because her lack of foresight had made them necessary. All of her life had been a struggle to act like a Chestny without the Chestny goods, and to give him everything she thought a Chestny ought to have; but since, said she, it was fun to struggle, why complain? And when you had won, as she had won, what fun to look back on the hard times! He could not forgive her that she had enjoyed the struggle and that she thought *she* had won.

What she meant when she said she had won was that she had brought him up successfully and had sent him to college and that he had turned out so well—good looking (her teeth had gone unfilled so that his could be straightened), intelligent (he realized he was too intelligent to be a success), and with a future ahead of him (there was of course no future ahead of him). She excused his gloominess on the grounds that he was still growing up and his radical ideas on his lack of practical experience. She said he didn't yet know a thing about "life," that he hadn't even entered the real world—when already he was as disenchanted with it as a man of fifty.

The further irony of all this was that in spite of her, he had turned out so well. In spite of going to only a third-rate college, he had, on his own initiative, come out with a first-rate education; in spite of growing up dominated by a small mind, he had ended up with a large one; in spite of all her foolish views, he was free of prejudice and unafraid to face facts. Most miraculous of all, instead of being blinded by love for her as she was for him, he had cut himself emotionally free of her and could see her with complete objectivity. He was not dominated by his mother.

The bus stopped with a sudden jerk and shook him from his meditation. A woman from the back lurched forward with little steps and barely escaped falling in his newspaper as she righted herself. She got off and a large Negro got on. Julian kept his paper lowered to watch. It gave him a certain satisfaction to see injustice in daily operation. It confirmed his view that with a few exceptions there was no one worth knowing within a radius of three hundred miles. The Negro was well dressed and carried a briefcase. He looked around and then sat down on the other end of the seat where the woman with the red and white canvas sandals was sitting. He immediately unfolded a newspaper and obscured himself behind it. Julian's mother's elbow at once prodded insistently into his ribs. "Now you see why I won't ride on these buses by myself," she whispered.

The woman with the red and white canvas sandals had risen at the same time the Negro sat down and had gone further back in the bus and taken the seat of the woman who had got off. His mother leaned forward and cast her an approving look.

Julian rose, crossed the aisle, and sat down in the place of the woman with the canvas sandals. From this position, he looked serenely across at his mother.

Her face had turned an angry red. He stared at her, making his eyes the eyes of a stranger. He felt his tension suddenly lift as if he had openly declared war on her.

He would have liked to get in conversation with the Negro and to talk with him about art or politics or any subject that would be above the comprehension of those around them, but the man remained entrenched behind his paper. He was either ignoring the change of seating or had never noticed it. There was no way for Julian to convey his sympathy.

His mother kept her eyes fixed reproachfully on his face. The woman with the protruding teeth was looking at him avidly as if he were a type of monster new to her.

"Do you have a light?" he asked the Negro.

Without looking away from his paper, the man reached in his pocket and handed him a packet of matches.

"Thanks," Julian said. For a moment he held the matches foolishly. A NO SMOKING sign looked down upon him from over the door. This alone would not have deterred him; he had no cigarettes. He had quit smoking some months before because he could not afford it. "Sorry," he muttered and handed back the matches. The Negro lowered the paper and gave him an annoyed look. He took the matches and raised the paper again.

His mother continued to gaze at him but she did not take advantage of his momentary discomfort. Her eyes retained their battered look. Her face seemed to be unnaturally red, as if her blood pressure had risen. Julian allowed no glimmer of sympathy to show on his face. Having got the advantage, he wanted desperately to keep it and carry it through. He would have liked to teach her a lesson that would last her a while, but there seemed no way to continue the point. The Negro refused to come out from behind his paper.

Julian folded his arms and looked stolidly before him, facing her but as if he did not see her, as if he had ceased to recognize her existence. He visualized a scene in which, the bus having reached their stop, he would remain in his seat and when she said, "Aren't you going to get off?" he would look at her as at a stranger who had rashly addressed him. The corner they got off on was usually deserted, but it was well lighted and it would not hurt her to walk by herself the four blocks to the Y. He decided to wait until the time came and then decide whether or not he would let her get off by herself. He would have to be at the Y at ten to bring her back, but he could leave her wondering if he was going to show up. There was no reason for her to think she could always depend on him.

He retired again into the high-ceilinged room sparsely settled with large pieces of antique furniture. His soul expanded momentarily but then he became aware of his mother across from him and the vision shriveled. He studied her coldly. Her feet in little pumps dangled like a child's and did not quite reach the floor. She was training on him an exaggerated look of reproach. He felt completely detached from her. At that moment he could with pleasure have slapped her as he would have slapped a particularly obnoxious child in his charge.

He began to imagine various unlikely ways by which he could teach her a lesson. He might make friends with some distinguished Negro professor or lawyer and bring him home to spend the evening. He would be entirely justified but her blood pressure would rise to 300. He could not push her to the extent of making her have a stroke, and moreover, he had never been successful at making any Negro friends. He had tried to strike up an acquaintance on the bus with some of the better types, with ones that looked like professors or ministers or lawyers. One morning he had sat down next to a distinguished-looking dark brown man who had answered his questions with a sonorous solemnity but who had turned out to be an undertaker. Another day he had sat down beside a cigar-smoking Negro with a diamond ring on his finger, but after a few stilted pleasantries, the Negro had rung the buzzer and risen, slipping two lottery tickets into Julian's hand as he climbed over him to leave.

He imagined his mother lying desperately ill and his being able to secure only a Negro doctor for her. He toyed with that idea for a few minutes and then dropped it for a momentary vision of himself participating as a sympathizer in a sit-in demonstration. This was possible but he did not linger with it. Instead, he approached the ultimate horror. He brought home a beautiful suspiciously Negroid woman. Prepare yourself, he said. There is nothing you can do about it. This is the woman I've chosen. She's intelligent, dignified, even good, and she's suffered and she hasn't thought it *fun*. Now persecute us, go ahead and persecute us. Drive her out of here, but remember, you're driving me too. His eyes were narrowed and through the indignation he had generated, he saw his mother across the aisle, purple-faced, shrunken to the dwarf-like proportions of her moral nature, sitting like a mummy beneath the ridiculous banner of her hat.

He was tilted out of his fantasy again as the bus stopped. The door opened with a sucking hiss and out of the dark a large, gaily dressed, sullen-looking colored woman got on with a little boy. The child, who might have been four, had on a short plaid suit and a Tyrolean hat with a blue feather in it. Julian hoped that he would sit down beside him and that the woman would push in beside his mother. He could think of no better arrangement.

As she waited for her tokens, the woman was surveying the seating possibilities—he hoped with the idea of sitting where she was least wanted. There was something familiar-looking about her but Julian could not place what it was. She was a giant of a woman. Her face was set not only to meet opposition but to seek it out. The downward tilt of her large lower lip was like a warning sign: DON'T TAMPER WITH ME. Her bulging figure was encased in a green crepe dress and her feet overflowed in red shoes. She had on a hideous hat. A purple velvet flap came down on one side of it and stood up on the other; the rest of it was green and looked like a cushion with the stuffing out. She carried a mammoth red pocketbook that bulged throughout as if it were stuffed with rocks.

To Julian's disappointment, the little boy climbed up on the empty seat beside his mother. His mother lumped all children, black and white, into the common category, "cute," and she thought little Negroes were on the whole cuter than little white children. She smiled at the little boy as he climbed on the seat.

Meanwhile the woman was bearing down upon the empty seat beside Julian. To his annoyance, she squeezed herself into it. He saw his mother's face change as the woman settled herself next to him and he realized with satisfaction that this was more objectionable to her than it was to him. Her face seemed almost gray and there was a look of dull recognition in her eyes, as if suddenly she had sickened at some awful confrontation. Julian saw that it was because she and the woman had, in a sense, swapped sons. Though his mother would not realize the symbolic significance of this, she would feel it. His amusement showed plainly on his face.

The woman next to him muttered something unintelligible to herself. He was conscious of a kind of bristling next to him, a muted growling like that of an angry cat. He could not see anything but the red pocketbook upright on the bulging green thighs. He visualized the woman as she had stood waiting for her tokens—the ponderous figure, rising from the red shoes upward over the solid hips, the mammoth bosom, the haughty face, to the green and purple hat.

His eyes widened.

The vision of the two hats, identical, broke upon him with the radiance of a brilliant sunrise. His face was suddenly lit with joy. He could not believe that Fate had thrust upon his mother such a lesson. He gave a loud chuckle so that she would look at him and see that he saw. She turned her eyes on him slowly. The blue in them seemed to have turned a bruised purple. For a moment he had an uncomfortable sense of her innocence, but it lasted only a second before principle rescued him. Justice entitled him to laugh. His grin hardened until it said to her as plainly as if he were saying aloud: Your punishment exactly fits your pettiness. This should teach you a permanent lesson.

Her eyes shifted to the woman. She seemed unable to bear looking at him and to find the woman preferable. He became conscious again of the bristling presence at his side. The woman was rumbling like a volcano about to become active. His mother's mouth began to twitch slightly at one corner. With a sinking heart, he saw incipient signs of recovery on her face and realized that this was going to strike her suddenly as funny and was going to be no lesson at all. She kept her eyes on the woman and an amused smile came over her face as if the woman were a monkey that had stolen her hat. The little Negro was looking up at her with large fascinated eyes. He had been trying to attract her attention for some time.

"Carver!" the woman said suddenly. "Come heah!"

When he saw that the spotlight was on him at last, Carver drew his feet up and turned himself toward Julian's mother and giggled.

"Carver!" the woman said. "You heah me? Come heah!"

Carver slid down from the seat but remained squatting with his back against the base of it, his head turned slyly around toward Julian's mother, who was smiling at him. The woman reached a hand across the aisle and snatched him to her. He righted himself and hung backwards on her knees, grinning at Julian's mother. "Isn't he cute?" Julian's mother said to the woman with the protruding teeth.

"I reckon he is," the woman said without conviction.

The Negress yanked him upright but he eased out of her grip and shot across the aisle and scrambled, giggling wildly, onto the seat beside his love.

"I think he likes me," Julian's mother said, and smiled at the woman. It was the smile she used when she was being particularly gracious to an inferior. Julian saw everything lost. The lesson had rolled off her like rain on a roof.

The woman stood up and yanked the little boy off the seat as if she were snatching him from contagion. Julian could feel the rage in her at having no weapon like his mother's smile. She gave the child a sharp slap across his leg. He howled once and then thrust his head into her stomach and kicked his feet against her shins. "Be-have," she said vehemently.

The bus stopped and the Negro who had been reading the newspaper got off. The woman moved over and set the little boy down with a thump between herself and Julian. She held him firmly by the knee. In a moment he put his hands in front of his face and peeped at Julian's mother through his fingers.

"I see yoooooooo!" she said and put her hand in front of her face and peeped at him.

The woman slapped his hand down. "Quit yo' foolishness," she said, "before I knock the living Jesus out of you!"

Julian was thankful that the next stop was theirs. He reached up and pulled the cord. The woman reached up and pulled it at the same time. Oh my God, he thought. He had the terrible intuition that when they got off the bus together, his mother would open her purse and give the little boy a nickel. The gesture would be as natural to her as breathing. The bus stopped and the woman got up and lunged to the front, dragging the child, who wished to stay on, after her. Julian and his mother got up and followed. As they neared the door, Julian tried to relieve her of her pocketbook.

"No," she murmured, "I want to give the little boy a nickel."

"No!" Julian hissed. "No!"

She smiled down at the child and opened her bag. The bus door opened and the woman picked him up by the arm and descended with him, hanging at her hip. Once in the street she set him down and shook him.

Julian's mother had to close her purse while she got down the bus step but as soon as her feet were on the ground, she opened it again and began to rummage inside. "I can't find but a penny," she whispered, "but it looks like a new one."

"Don't do it!" Julian said fiercely between his teeth. There was a streetlight on the corner and she hurried to get under it so that she could better see into her pocketbook. The woman was heading off rapidly down the street with the child still hanging backward on her hand.

"Oh little boy!" Julian's nother called and took a few quick steps and caught up with them just beyond the lamppost. "Here's a bright new penny for you." and she held out the coin, which shone bronze in the dim light.

The huge woman turned and for a moment stood, her shoulders lifted and her face frozen with frustrated rage, and stared at Julian's mother. Then all at once she seemed to explode like a piece of machinery that had been given one ounce of pressure too much. Julian saw the black fist swing out with the red pocketbook. He shut his eyes and cringed as he heard the woman shout, "He don't take nobody's pennies!" When he opened his eyes, the woman was disappearing down the street with the little boy staring wide-eyed over her shoulder. Julian's mother was sitting on the sidewalk.

"I told you not to do that," Julian said angrily. "I told you not to do that!"

He stood over her for a minute, gritting his teeth. Her legs were stretched out in front of her and her hat was on her lap. He squatted down and looked her in the face. It was totally expressionless. "You got exactly what you deserved." he said. "Now get up."

He picked up her pocketbook and put what had fallen out back in it. He picked the hat up off her lap. The penny caught his eye on the sidewalk and he picked that up and let it drop before her eyes into the purse. Then he stood up and leaned over and held his hands out to pull her up. She remained immobile. He sighed. Rising above them on either side were black apartment buildings, marked with irregular rectangles of light. At the end of the block a man came out of a door and walked off in the opposite direction. "All right," he said. "suppose somebody happens by and wants to know why you're sitting on the sidewalk?"

She took the hand and, breathing hard, pulled heavily up on it and then stood for a moment, swaying slightly as if the spots of light in the darkness were circling around her. Her eyes, shadowed and confused, finally settled on his face. He did not try to conceal his irritation. "I hope this teaches you a lesson," he said. She leaned forward and her eyes raked his face. She seemed trying to determine his identity. Then, as if she found nothing familiar about him, she started off with a headlong movement in the wrong direction.

"Aren't you going on to the Y?" he asked.

"Home," she muttered.

"Well, are we walking?"

For answer she kept going. Julian followed along, his hands behind him. He saw no reason to let the lesson she had had go without backing it up with an explanation of its meaning. She might as well be made to understand what had happened to her. "Don't think that was just an uppity Negro woman," he said. "That was the whole colored race which will no longer take your condescending pennies. That was your black double. She can wear the same hat as you, and to be sure," he added gratuitously (because he thought it was funny), "it looked better on her than it did on you. What all this means," he said, "is that the old world is gone. The old manners are obsolete and your graciousness is not worth a damn." He thought bitterly of the house that had been lost for him. "You aren't who you think you are," he said.

She continued to plow ahead, paying no attention to him. Her hair had come undone on one side. She dropped her pocketbook and took no notice. He stooped and picked it up and handed it to her but she did not take it.

"You needn't act as if the world had come to an end," he said, "because it hasn't. From now on you've got to live in a new world and face a few realities for a change. Buck up," he said, "it won't kill you."

She was breathing fast.

"Let's wait on the bus," he said.

"Home," she said thickly.

"I hate to see you behave like this," he said. "Just like a child. I should be able to expect more of you." He decided to stop where he was and make her stop and wait for a bus. "I'm not going any farther," he said, stopping. "We're going on the bus."

She continued to go on as if she had not heard him. He took a few steps and caught her arm and stopped her. He looked into her face and caught his breath. He was looking into a face he had never seen before. "Tell Grandpa to come get me," she said.

He stared, stricken.

"Tell Caroline to come get me," she said.

Stunned, he let her go and she lurched forward again, walking as if one leg were shorter than the other. A tide of darkness seemed to be sweeping her from him. "Mother!" he cried. "Darling, sweetheart, wait!" Crumpling, she fell to the pavement. He dashed forward and fell at her side, crying, "Mamma, Mamma!" He turned her over. Her face was fiercely distorted. One eye, large and staring, moved slightly to the left as if it had become unmoored. The other remained fixed on him, raked his face again, found nothing and closed.

"Wait here, wait here!" he cried and jumped up and began to run for help toward a cluster of lights he saw in the distance ahead of him. "Help, help!" he shouted, but his voice was thin, scarcely a thread of sound. The lights drifted farther away the faster he ran and his feet moved numbly as if they carried him nowhere. The tide of darkness seemed to sweep him back to her, postponing from moment to moment his entry into the world of guilt and sorrow.

Good Country People

Besides the neutral expression that she wore when she was alone, Mrs. Freeman had two others, forward and reverse, that she used for all her human dealings. Her forward expression was steady and driving like the advance of a heavy truck. Her eyes never swerved to left or right but turned as the story turned as if they followed a yellow line down the center of it. She seldom used the other expression because it was not often necessary for her to retract a statement, but when she did, her face came to a complete stop, there was an almost imperceptible movement of her black eyes, during which they seemed to be receding, and then the observer would see that Mrs. Freeman, though she might stand there as real as several grain sacks thrown on top of each other, was no longer there in spirit. As for getting anything across to her when this was the case, Mrs. Hopewell had given it up. She might talk her head off. Mrs. Freeman could never be brought to admit herself wrong on any point. She would stand there and if she could be brought to say anything, it was something like, "Well, I wouldn't of said it was and I wouldn't of said it wasn't" or letting her gaze range over the top kitchen shelf where there was an assortment of dusty bottles, she might remark, "I see you ain't ate many of them figs you put up last summer."

They carried on their most important business in the kitchen at breakfast. Every morning Mrs. Hopewell got up at seven o'clock and lit her gas heater and Joy's. Joy was her daughter, a large blonde girl who had an artificial leg. Mrs. Hopewell thought of her as a child though she was thirty-two years old and highly educated. Joy would get up while her mother was eating and lumber into the bathroom and slam the door, and before long, Mrs. Freeman would arrive at the back door. Joy would hear her mother call, "Come on in," and then they would talk for a while in low voices that were indistinguishable in the bathroom. By the time Joy came in, they had usually finished the weather report and were on one or the other of Mrs. Freeman's daughters, Glynese or Carramae. Joy called them Glycerin and Caramel. Glynese, a redhead, was eighteen and had many admirers; Carramae, a blonde, was only fifteen but already married and pregnant. She could not keep anything on her stomach. Every morning Mrs. Freeman told Mrs. Hopewell how many times she had vomited since the last report.

Mrs. Hopewell liked to tell people that Glynese and Carramae were two of the finest girls she knew and that Mrs. Freeman was a *lady* and that she was never ashamed to take her anywhere or introduce her to anybody they might meet. Then she would tell how she had happened to hire the Freemans in the first place and how they were a godsend to her and how she had had them four years. The reason for her keeping them so long was that they were not trash.

They were good country people. She had telephoned the man whose name they had given as reference and he had told her that Mr. Freeman was a good farmer but that his wife was the nosiest woman ever to walk the earth. "She's got to be into everything," the man said. "If she don't get there before the dust settles, you can bet she's dead, that's all. She'll want to know all your business. I can stand him real good," he had said, "but me nor my wife neither could have stood that woman one more minute on this place." That had put Mrs. Hopewell off for a few days.

She had hired them in the end because there were no other applicants but she had made up her mind beforehand exactly how she would handle the woman. Since she was the type who had to be into everything, then, Mrs. Hopewell had decided, she would not only let her be into everything, she would *see to it* that she was into everything—she would give her the responsibility of everything, she would put her in charge. Mrs. Hopewell had no bad qualities of her own but she was able to use other people's in such a constructive way that she had kept them four years.

Nothing is perfect. This was one of Mrs. Hopewell's favorite sayings. Another was: that is life! And still another, the most important, was: well, other people have their opinions too. She would make these statements, usually at the table, in a tone of gentle insistence as if no one held them but her, and the large hulking Joy, whose constant outrage obliterated every expression from her face, would stare just a little to the side of her, her eyes icy blue, with the look of someone who has achieved blindness by an act of will and means to keep it.

When Mrs. Hopewell said to Mrs. Freeman that life was like that, Mrs. Freeman would say, "I always said so myself." Nothing had been arrived at by anyone that had not first been arrived at by her. She was quicker than Mr. Freeman. When Mrs. Hopewell said to her after they had been on the place a while, "You know, you're the wheel behind the wheel," and winked, Mrs. Freeman had said, "I know it. I've always been quick. It's some that are quicker than others."

"Everybody is different," Mrs. Hopewell said.

"Yes, most people is," Mrs. Freeman said.

"It takes all kinds to make the world."

"I always said it did myself."

The girl was used to this kind of dialogue for breakfast and more of it for dinner; sometimes they had it for supper too. When they had no guest they ate in the kitchen because that was easier. Mrs. Freeman always managed to arrive at some point during the meal and to watch them finish it. She would stand in the doorway if it were summer but in the winter she would stand with one elbow on top of the refrigerator and look down on them, or she would stand by the gas heater, lifting the back of her skirt slightly. Occasionally she would stand against the wall and roll her head from side to side. At no time was she in any hurry to leave. All this was very trying on Mrs. Hopewell but she was a woman of great patience. She realized that nothing is perfect and that in the Freemans she had good country people and that if, in this day and age, you get good country people, you had better hang onto them.

She had had plenty of experience with trash. Before the Freemans she had averaged one tenant family a year. The wives of these farmers were not the kind you would want to be around you for very long. Mrs. Hopewell, who had divorced her husband long ago, needed someone to walk over the fields with her; and when Joy had to be impressed for these services, her remarks were usually so ugly and her face so glum that Mrs. Hopewell would say, "If you can't come pleasantly, I don't want you at all," to which the girl, standing square and rigid-shouldered with her neck thrust slightly forward, would reply, "If you want me, here I am—LIKE I AM."

Mrs. Hopewell excused this attitude because of the leg (which had been shot off in a hunting accident when Joy was ten). It was hard for Mrs. Hopewell to realize that her child was thirty-two now and that for more than twenty years she had had only one leg. She thought of her still as a child because it tore her heart to think instead of the poor stout girl in her thirties who had never danced a step or had any *normal* good times. Her name was really Joy but as soon as she was twenty-one and away from home, she had it legally changed. Mrs. Hopewell was certain that she had thought and thought until she had hit upon the ugliest name in any language. Then she had gone and had the beautiful name, Joy, changed without telling her mother until after she had done it. Her legal name was Hulga.

When Mrs. Hopewell thought the name, Hulga, she thought of the broad blank hull of a battleship. She would not use it. She continued to call her Joy to which the girl responded but in a purely mechanical way.

Hulga had learned to tolerate Mrs. Freeman who saved her from taking walks with her mother. Even Glynese and Carramae were useful when they occupied attention that might otherwise have been directed at her. At first she had thought she could not stand Mrs. Freeman for she had found that it was not possible to be rude to her. Mrs. Freeman would take on strange resentments and for days together she would be sullen but the source of her displeasure was always obscure; a direct attack, a positive leer, blatant ugliness to her face—these never touched her. And without warning one day, she began calling her Hulga.

She did not call her that in front of Mrs. Hopewell who would have been incensed but when she and the girl happened to be out of the house together, she would say something and add the name Hulga to the end of it, and the big spectacled Joy-Hulga would scowl and redden as if her privacy had been intruded upon. She considered the name her personal affair. She had arrived at it first purely on the basis of its ugly sound and then the full genius of its fitness had struck her. She had a vision of the name working like the ugly sweating Vulcan who stayed in the furnace and to whom, presumably, the goddess had to come when called. She saw it as the name of her highest creative act. One of her major triumphs was that her mother had not been able to turn her dust into Joy, but the greater one was that she had been able to turn it herself into Hulga. However, Mrs. Freeman's relish for using the name only irritated her. It was as if Mrs. Freeman's beady steel-pointed eyes had penetrated far enough behind her face to reach some secret fact. Something about her seemed to fascinate Mrs. Freeman and then one day Hulga realized that it was the artificial leg. Mrs. Freeman had a special fondness for the details of secret infections, hidden deformities, assaults upon children. Of diseases, she preferred the lingering or incurable. Hulga had heard Mrs. Hopewell give her the details of the hunting accident, how the leg had been literally blasted off, how she had never lost consciousness. Mrs. Freeman could listen to it any time as if it had happened an hour ago.

When Hulga stumped into the kitchen in the morning (she could walk without making the awful noise but she made it—Mrs. Hopewell was certain—because it was ugly-sounding), she glanced at them and did not speak. Mrs. Hopewell would be in her red kimono with her hair tied around her head in rags. She would be sitting at the table, finishing her breakfast and Mrs. Freeman would be hanging by her elbow outward from the refrigerator, looking down at the table. Hulga always put her eggs on the stove to boil and then stood over them with her arms folded, and Mrs. Hopewell would look at her—a kind of indirect gaze divided between her and Mrs. Freeman—and would think that if she would only keep herself up a little, she wouldn't be so bad looking. There was nothing wrong with her face that a pleasant expression wouldn't help. Mrs. Hopewell said that people who looked on the bright side of things would be beautiful even if they were not.

Whenever she looked at Joy this way, she could not help but feel that it would have been better if the child had not taken the Ph.D. It had certainly not brought her out any and now that she had it, there was no more excuse for her to go to school again. Mrs. Hopewell thought it was nice for girls to go to school to have a good time but Joy had "gone through." Anyhow, she would not have been strong enough to go again. The doctors had told Mrs. Hopewell that with the best of care, Joy might see forty-five. She had a weak heart. Joy had made it plain that if it had not been for this condition, she would be far from these red hills and good country people. She would be in a university lecturing to people who knew what she was talking about. And Mrs. Hopewell could very well picture her there, looking like a scarecrow and lecturing to more of the same. Here she went about all day in a six-year-old skirt and a yellow sweat shirt with a faded cowboy on a horse embossed on it. She thought this was funny; Mrs. Hopewell thought it was idiotic and showed simply that she was still a child. She was brilliant but she didn't have a grain of sense. It seemed to Mrs. Hopewell that every year she grew less like other people and more like herself—bloated, rude, and squint-eyed. And she said such strange things! To her own mother she had said—without warning, without excuse, standing up in the middle of a meal with her face purple and her mouth half full—"Woman! do you ever look inside? Do you ever look inside and see what you are *not?* God!" she had cried sinking down again and staring at her plate, "Malebranche was right: we are not our own light. We are not our own light!" Mrs. Hopewell had no idea to this day what brought that on. She had only made the remark, hoping Joy would take it in, that a smile never hurt anyone.

The girl had taken the Ph.D. in philosophy and this left Mrs. Hopewell at a complete loss. You could say, "My daughter is a nurse," or "My daughter is a school teacher," or even, "My daughter is a chemical engineer." You could not say, "My daughter is a philosopher." That was something that had ended with the Greeks and Romans. All day Joy sat on her neck in a deep chair, reading. Sometimes she went for walks but she didn't like dogs or cats or birds or flowers or nature or nice young men. She looked at nice young men as if she could smell their stupidity.

One day Mrs. Hopewell had picked up one of the books the girl had just put down and opening it at random, she read, "Science, on the other hand, has to assert its soberness and seriousness afresh and declare that it is concerned solely with what-is. Nothing—how can it be for science anything but a horror and a phantasm? If science is right, then one thing stands firm: science wishes to know nothing of nothing. Such is after all the strictly scientific approach to Nothing. We know it by wishing to know nothing of Nothing." These words had been underlined with a blue pencil and they worked on Mrs. Hopewell like some evil incantation in gibberish. She shut the book quickly and went out of the room as if she were having a chill.

This morning when the girl came in, Mrs. Freeman was on Carramae. "She thrown up four times after supper," she said, "and was up twict in the night after three o'clock. Yesterday she didn't do nothing but ramble in the bureau drawer. All she did. Stand up there and see what she could run up on."

"She's got to eat," Mrs. Hopewell muttered, sipping her coffee, while she watched Joy's back at the stove. She was wondering what the child had said to the Bible salesman. She could not imagine what kind of a conversation she could possibly have had with him.

He was a tall gaunt hatless youth who had called yesterday to sell them a Bible. He had appeared at the door, carrying a large black suitcase that weighted him so heavily on one side that he had to brace himself against the door facing. He seemed on the point of collapse but he said in a cheerful voice, "Good morning, Mrs. Cedars!" and set the suitcase down on the mat. He was not a bad-looking young man though he had on a bright blue suit and yellow socks that were not pulled up far enough. He had prominent face bones and a streak of sticky-looking brown hair falling across his forehead.

"I'm Mrs. Hopewell," she said.

"Oh!" he said, pretending to look puzzled but with his eyes sparkling, "I saw it said 'The Cedars,' on the mailbox so I thought you was Mrs. Cedars!" and he burst out in a pleasant laugh. He picked up the satchel and under cover of a pant, he fell forward into her hall. It was rather as if the suitcase had moved first, jerking him after it. "Mrs. Hopewell!" he said and grabbed her hand. "I hope you are well!" and he laughed again and then all at once his face sobered completely. He paused and gave her a straight earnest look and said, "Lady, I've come to speak of serious things."

"Well, come in," she muttered, none too pleased because her dinner was almost ready. He came into the parlor and sat down on the edge of a straight chair and put the suitcase between his feet and glanced around the room as if he were sizing her up by it. Her silver gleamed on the two sideboards; she decided he had never been in a room as elegant as this.

"Mrs. Hopewell," he began, using her name in a way that sounded almost intimate, "I know you believe in Chrustian service."

"Well yes," she murmured.

"I know," he said and paused, looking very wise with his head cocked on one side, "that you're a good woman. Friends have told me."

Mrs. Hopewell never liked to be taken for a fool. "What are you selling?" she asked.

"Bibles," the young man said and his eye raced around the room before he added, "I see you have no family Bible in your parlor, I see that is the one lack you got!"

Mrs. Hopewell could not say, "My daughter is an atheist and won't let me keep the Bible in the parlor." She said, stiffening slightly, "I keep my Bible by my bedside." This was not the truth. It was in the attic somewhere.

"Lady," he said, "the word of God ought to be in the parlor."

"Well, I think that's a matter of taste," she began. "I think . . ."

"Lady," he said, "for a Chrustian, the word of God ought to be in every room in the house besides in his heart. I know you're a Chrustian because I can see it in every line of your face."

She stood up and said, "Well, young man, I don't want to buy a Bible and I smell my dinner burning."

He didn't get up. He began to twist his hands and looking down at them, he said softly, "Well lady, I'll tell you the truth—not many people want to buy one nowadays and besides, I know I'm real simple. I don't know how to say a thing but to say it. I'm just a country boy." He glanced up into her unfriendly face. "People like you don't like to fool with country people like me!"

"Why!" she cried, "good country people are the salt of the earth! Besides, we all have different ways of doing, it takes all kinds to make the world go 'round. That's life!"

"You said a mouthful," he said.

"Why, I think there aren't enough good country people in the world!" she said, stirred. "I think that's what's wrong with it!"

His face had brightened. "I didn't intraduce myself," he said. "I'm Manley Pointer from out in the country around Willohobie, not even from a place, just from near a place."

"You wait a minute," she said. "I have to see about my dinner." She went out to the kitchen and found Joy standing near the door where she had been listening.

"Get rid of the salt of the earth," she said, "and let's eat."

Mrs. Hopewell gave her a pained look and turned the heat down under the vegetables. "*I* can't be rude to anybody," she murmured and went back into the parlor.

He had opened the suitcase and was sitting with a Bible on each knee.

"You might as well put those up," she told him. "I don't want one."

"I appreciate your honesty," he said. "You don't see any more real honest people unless you go way out in the country."

"I know," she said, "real genuine folks!" Through the crack in the door she heard a groan.

"I guess a lot of boys come telling you they're working their way through college," he said, "but I'm not going to tell you that. Somehow," he said, "I don't want to go to college. I want to devote my life to Chrustian service. See," he said, lowering his voice, "I got this heart condition. I may not live long. When you know it's something wrong with you and you may not live long, well then lady . . ." He paused, with his mouth open, and stared at her.

He and Joy had the same condition! She knew that her eyes were filling with tears but she collected herself quickly and murmured, "Won't you stay for dinner? We'd love to have you!" and was sorry the instant she heard herself say it.

"Yes mam," he said in an abashed voice. "I would sher love to do that!"

Joy had given him one look on being introduced to him and then throughout the meal had not glanced at him again. He had addressed several remarks to her, which she had pretended not to hear. Mrs. Hopewell could not understand deliberate rudeness, although she lived with it, and she felt she had always to overflow with hospitality to make up for Joy's lack of courtesy. She urged him to talk about himself and he did. He said he was the seventh child of twelve and that his father had been crushed under a tree when he himself was eight year old. He had been crushed very badly, in fact, almost cut in two and was practically not recognizable. His mother had got along the best she could by hard working and she had always seen that her children went to Sunday School and that they read the Bible every evening. He was now nineteen year old and he had been selling Bibles for four months. In that time he had sold seventy-seven Bibles and had the promise of two more sales. He wanted to become a missionary because he thought that was the way you could do most for people. "He who losest his life shall find it," he said simply and he was so sincere, so genuine and earnest that Mrs. Hopewell would not for the world have smiled. He prevented his peas from sliding onto the table by blocking them with a piece of bread which he later cleaned his plate with. She could see Joy observing sidewise how he handled his knife and fork and she saw too that every few minutes, the boy would dart a keen appraising glance at the girl as if he were trying to attract her attention.

After dinner Joy cleared the dishes off the table and disappeared and Mrs. Hopewell was left to talk with him. He told her again about his childhood and his father's accident and about various things that had happened to him. Every five minutes or so she would stifle a yawn. He sat for two hours until finally she told him she must go because she had an appointment in town. He packed his Bibles and thanked her and prepared to leave, but in the doorway he stopped and wrung her hand and said that not on any of his trips had he met a lady as nice as her and he asked if he could come again. She had said she would always be happy to see him.

Joy had been standing in the road, apparently looking at something in the distance, when he came down the steps toward her, bent to the side with his heavy valise. He stopped where she was standing and confronted her directly. Mrs. Hopewell could not hear what he said but she trembled to think what Joy would say to him. She could see that after a minute Joy said something and that then the boy began to speak again, making an excited gesture with his free hand. After a minute Joy said something else at which the boy began to speak once more. Then to her amazement, Mrs. Hopewell saw the two of them walk off together, toward the gate. Joy had walked all the way to the gate with him and Mrs. Hopewell could not imagine what they had said to each other, and she had not yet dared to ask.

Mrs. Freeman was insisting upon her attention. She had moved from the refrigerator to the heater so that Mrs. Hopewell had to turn and face her in order to seem to be listening. "Glynese gone out with Harvey Hill again last night," she said. "She had this sty."

"Hill," Mrs. Hopewell said absently, "is that the one who works in the garage?"

"Nome, he's the one that goes to chiropracter school," Mrs. Freeman said.

"She had this sty. Been had it two days. So she says when he brought her in the other night he says, 'Lemme get rid of that sty for you,' and she says, 'How?' and he says, 'You just lay yourself down acrost the seat of that car and I'll show you.' So she done it and he popped her neck. Kept on a-popping it several times until she made him quit. This morning," Mrs. Freeman said, "she ain't got no sty. She ain't got no traces of a sty."

"I never heard of that before," Mrs. Hopewell said.

"He ast her to marry him before the Ordinary," Mrs. Freeman went on, "and she told him she wasn't going to be married in no *office.*"

"Well, Glynese is a fine girl," Mrs. Hopewell said. "Glynese and Carramae are both fine girls."

"Carramae said when her and Lyman was married Lyman said it sure felt sacred to him. She said he said he wouldn't take five hundred dollars for being married by a preacher."

"How much would he take?" the girl asked from the stove.

"He said he wouldn't take five hundred dollars," Mrs. Freeman repeated.

"Well we all have work to do," Mrs. Hopewell said.

"Lyman said it just felt more sacred to him," Mrs. Freeman said. "The doctor wants Carramae to eat prunes. Says instead of medicine. Says them cramps is coming from pressure. You know what I think it is?"

"She'll be better in a few weeks," Mrs. Hopewell said.

"In the tube," Mrs. Freeman said. "Else she wouldn't be as sick as she is."

Hulga had cracked her two eggs into a saucer and was bringing them to the table along with a cup of coffee that she had filled too full. She sat down carefully and began to eat, meaning to keep Mrs. Freeman there by questions if for any reason she showed an inclination to leave. She could perceive her mother's eye on her. The first round-about question would be about the Bible salesman and she did not wish to bring it on. "How did he pop her neck?" she asked.

Mrs. Freeman went into a description of how he had popped her neck. She said he owned a '55 Mercury but that Glynese said she would rather marry a man with only a '36 Plymouth who would be married by a preacher. The girl asked what if he had a '32 Plymouth and Mrs. Freeman said what Glynese had said was a '36 Plymouth.

Mrs. Hopewell said there were not many girls with Glynese's common sense. She said what she admired in those girls was their common sense. She said that reminded her that they had had a nice visitor yesterday, a young man selling Bibles. "Lord," she said, "he bored me to death but he was so sincere and genuine I couldn't be rude to him. He was just good country people, you know," she said, "—just the salt of the earth."

"I seen him walk up," Mrs. Freeman said, "and then later—I seen him walk off," and Hulga could feel the slight shift in her voice, the slight insinuation, that he had not walked off alone, had he? Her face remained expressionless but the color rose into her neck and she seemed to swallow it down with the next spoonful of egg. Mrs. Freeman was looking at her as if they had a secret together.

"Well, it takes all kinds of people to make the world go 'round," Mrs. Hopewell said. "It's very good we aren't all alike."

"Some people are more alike than others," Mrs. Freeman said.

Hulga got up and stumped, with about twice the noise that was necessary, into her room and locked the door. She was to meet the Bible salesman at ten o'clock at the gate. She had thought about it half the night. She had started thinking of it as a great joke and then she had begun to see profound implications in it. She had lain in bed imagining dialogues for them that were inane on the surface but that reached below to depths that no Bible salesman would be aware of. Their conversation yesterday had been of this kind.

He had stopped in front of her and had simply stood there. His face was bony and sweaty and bright, with a little pointed nose in the center of it, and his look was different from what it had been at the dinner table. He was gazing at her with open curiosity, with fascination, like a child watching a new fantastic animal at the zoo, and he was breathing as if he had run a great distance to reach her. His gaze seemed somehow familiar but she could not think where she had been regarded with it before. For almost a minute he didn't say anything. Then on what seemed an insuck of breath, he whispered. "You ever ate a chicken that was two days old?"

The girl looked at him stonily. He might have just put this question up for consideration at the meeting of a philosophical association. "Yes," she presently replied as if she had considered it from all angles.

"It must have been mighty small!" he said trumphantly and shook all over with little nervous giggles, getting very red in the face, and subsiding finally into his gaze of complete admiration, while the girl's expression remained exactly the same.

"How old are you?" he asked softly.

She waited some time before she answered. Then in a flat voice she said, "Seventeen."

His smiles came in succession like waves breaking on the surface of a little lake. "I see you got a wooden leg," he said. "I think you're real brave. I think you're real sweet."

The girl stood blank and solid and silent.

"Walk to the gate with me," he said. "You're a brave sweet little thing and I liked you the minute I seen you walk in the door."

Hulga began to move forward.

"What's your name?" he asked, smiling down on the top of her head.

"Hulga," she said.

"Hulga," he murmured, "Hulga. Hulga. I never heard of anybody name Hulga before. You're shy, aren't you, Hulga?" he asked.

She nodded, watching his large red hand on the handle of the giant valise.

"I like girls that wear glasses," he said. "I think a lot. I'm not like these people that a serious thought don't ever enter their heads. It's because I may die."

"I may die too," she said suddenly and looked up at him. His eyes were very small and brown, glittering feverishly.

"Listen," he said, "don't you think some people was meant to meet on account of what all they got in common and all? Like they both think serious thoughts and all?" He shifted the valise to his other hand so that the hand nearest her was free. He caught hold of her elbow and shook it a little. "I don't work on Saturday," he said. "I like to walk in the woods and see what Mother Nature is wearing. O'er the hills and far away. Pic-nics and things. Couldn't we go on a pic-nic tomorrow? Say yes, Hulga," he said and gave her a dying look as if he felt his insides about to drop out of him. He had even seemed to sway slightly toward her.

During the night she had imagined that she seduced him. She imagined that the two of them walked on the place until they came to the storage barn beyond the two back fields and there, she imagined, that things came to such a pass that she very easily seduced him and that then, of course, she had to reckon with his remorse. True genius can get an idea across even to an inferior mind. She imagined that she took his remorse in hand and changed it into a deeper understanding of life. She took all his shame away and turned it into something useful.

She set off for the gate at exactly ten o'clock, escaping without drawing Mrs. Hopewell's attention. She didn't take anything to eat, forgetting that food is usually taken on a picnic. She wore a pair of slacks and a dirty white shirt, and as an afterthought, she had put some Vapex on the collar of it since she did not own any perfume. When she reached the gate no one was there.

She looked up and down the empty highway and had the furious feeling that she had been tricked, that he had only meant to make her walk to the gate after the idea of him. Then suddenly he stood up, very tall, from behind a bush on the opposite embankment. Smiling, he lifted his hat which was new and wide-brimmed. He had not worn it yesterday and she wondered if he had bought it for the occasion. It was toast-colored with a red and white band around it and was slightly too large for him. He stepped from behind the bush still carrying the black valise. He had on the same suit and the same yellow socks sucked down in his shoes from walking. He crossed the highway and said, "I knew you'd come!"

The girl wondered acidly how he had known this. She pointed to the valise and asked, "Why did you bring your Bibles?"

He took her elbow, smiling down on her as if he could not stop. "You can never tell when you'll need the word of God, Hulga," he said. She had a moment in which she doubted that this was actually happening and then they began to climb the embankment. They went down into the pasture toward the woods. The boy walked lightly by her side, bouncing on his toes. The valise did not seem to be heavy today; he even swung it. They crossed half the pasture without saying anything and then, putting his hand easily on the small of her back, he asked softly, "Where does your wooden leg join on?"

She turned an ugly red and glared at him and for an instant the boy looked abashed. "I didn't mean you no harm," he said. "I only meant you're so brave and all. I guess God takes care of you."

"No," she said, looking forward and walking fast, "I don't even believe in God."

At this he stopped and whistled. "No!" he exclaimed as if he were too astonished to say anything else.

She walked on and in a second he was bouncing at her side, fanning with his hat. "That's very unusual for a girl," he remarked, watching her out of the corner of his eye. When they reached the edge of the wood, he put his hand on her back again and drew her against him without a word and kissed her heavily.

The kiss, which had more pressure than feeling behind it, produced that extra surge of adrenalin in the girl that enables one to carry a packed trunk out of a burning house, but in her, the power went at once to the brain. Even before he released her, her mind, clear and detached and ironic anyway, was regarding him from a great distance, with amusement but with pity. She had never been kissed before and she was pleased to discover that it was an unexceptional experience and all a matter of the mind's control. Some people might enjoy drain water if they were told it was vodka. When the boy, looking expectant but uncertain, pushed her gently away, she turned and walked on, saying nothing as if such business, for her, were common enough.

He came along panting at her side, trying to help her when he saw a root that she might trip over. He caught and held back the long swaying blades of thorn vine until she had passed beyond them. She led the way and he came breathing heavily behind her. Then they came out on a sunlit hillside, sloping softly into another one a little smaller. Beyond, they could see the rusted top of the old barn where the extra hay was stored.

The hill was sprinkled with small pink weeds. "Then you ain't saved?" he asked suddenly, stopping.

The girl smiled. It was the first time she had smiled at him at all. "In my economy," she said, "I'm saved and you are damned but I told you I didn't believe in God."

Nothing seemed to destroy the boy's look of admiration. He gazed at her now as if the fantasic animal at the zoo had put its paw through the bars and given him a loving poke. She thought he looked as if he wanted to kiss her again and she walked on before he had the chance.

"Ain't there somewheres we can sit down sometime?" he murmured, his voice softening toward the end of the sentence.

"In that barn," she said.

They made for it rapidly as if it might slide away like a train. It was a large two-story barn, cool and dark inside. The boy pointed up the ladder that led into the loft and said, "It's too bad we can't go up there."

"Why can't we?" she asked.

"Yer leg," he said reverently.

The girl gave him a contemptuous look and putting both hands on the ladder, she climbed it while he stood below, apparently awestruck. She pulled herself expertly through the opening and then looked down at him and said, "Well, come on if you're coming," and he began to climb the ladder, awkwardly bringing the suitcase with him.

"We won't need the Bible," she observed.

"You never can tell," he said, panting. After he had got into the loft, he was a few seconds catching his breath. She had sat down in a pile of straw. A wide sheath of sunlight, filled with dust particles, slanted over her. She lay back against a bale, her face turned away, looking out the front opening of the barn where hay was thrown from a wagon into the loft. The two pin-speckled hillsides lay back against a dark ridge of woods. The sky was cloudless and cold blue. The boy dropped down by her side and put one arm under her and the other over her and began methodically kissing her face, making little noises like a fish. He did not remove his hat but it was pushed far enough back not to interfere. When her glasses got in his way, he took them off of her and slipped them into his pocket.

The girl at first did not return any of the kisses but presently she began to and after she had put several on his cheek, she reached his lips and remained there, kissing him again and again as if she were trying to draw all the breath out of him. His breath was clear and sweet like a child's and the kisses were sticky like a child's. He mumbled about loving her and about knowing when he first seen her that he loved her, but the mumbling was like the sleepy fretting of a child being put to sleep by his mother. Her mind, throughout this, never stopped or lost itself for a second to her feelings. "You ain't said you loved me none," he whispered finally, pulling back from her. "You got to say that."

She looked away from him off into the hollow sky and then down at a black ridge and then down farther into what appeared to be two green swelling lakes. She didn't realize he had taken her glasses but this landscape could not seem exceptional to her for she seldom paid any close attention to her surroundings.

"You got to say it," he repeated. "You got to say you love me."

She was always careful how she committed herself. "In a sense," she began, "if you use the word loosely, you might say that. But it's not a word I use. I don't have illusions. I'm one of those people who see *through* to nothing."

The boy was frowning. "You got to say it. I said it and you got to say it," he said.

The girl looked at him almost tenderly. "You poor baby," she murmured. "It's just as well you don't understand," and she pulled him by the neck, face-down, against her. "We are all damned," she said, "but some of us have taken off our blindfolds and see that there's nothing to see. It's a kind of salvation."

The boy's astonished eyes looked blankly through the ends of her hair. "Okay," he almost whined, "but do you love me or don'tcher?"

"Yes," she said and added, "in a sense. But I must tell you something. There mustn't be anything dishonest between us." She lifted his head and looked him in the eye. "I am thirty years old," she said. "I have a number of degrees."

The boy's look was irritated but dogged. "I don't care," he said. "I don't care a thing about what all you done. I just want to know if you love me or don'tcher?" and he caught her to him and wildly planted her face with kisses until she said, "Yes, yes."

"Okay then," he said, letting her go. "Prove it."

She smiled, looking dreamily out on the shifty landscape. She had seduced him without even making up her mind to try. "How?" she asked, feeling that he should be delayed a little.

He leaned over and put his lips to her ear. "Show me where your wooden leg joins on," he whispered.

The girl uttered a sharp little cry and her face instantly drained of color. The obscenity of the suggestion was not what shocked her. As a child she had sometimes been subject to feelings of shame but education had removed the last traces of that as a good surgeon scrapes for cancer; she would no more have felt it over what he was asking than she would have believed in his Bible. But she was as sensitive about the artificial leg as a peacock about his tail. No one ever touched it but her. She took care of it as someone else would his soul, in private and almost with her own eyes turned away. "No," she said.

"I known it," he muttered, sitting up. "You're just playing me for a sucker."

"Oh no no!" she cried. "It joins on at the knee. Only at the knee. Why do you want to see it?"

The boy gave her a long penetrating look. "Because," he said, "it's what makes you different. You ain't like anybody else."

She sat staring at him. There was nothing about her face or her round freezing-blue eyes to indicate that this had moved her; but she felt as if her heart had stopped and left her mind to pump her blood. She decided that for the first time in her life she was face to face with real innocence. This boy, with an instinct that came from beyond wisdom, had touched the truth about her. When after a minute, she said in a hoarse high voice, "All right," it was like surrendering to him completely. It was like losing her own life and finding it again, miraculously, in his.

Very gently he began to roll the slack leg up. The artificial limb, in a white sock and brown flat shoe, was bound in a heavy material like canvas and ended in an ugly jointure where it was attached to the stump. The boy's face and his voice were entirely reverent as he uncovered it and said, "Now show me how to take it off and on."

She took it off for him and put it back on again and then he took it off himself, handling it as tenderly as if it were a real one. "See!" he said with a delighted child's face. "Now I can do it myself!"

"Put it back on," she said. She was thinking that she would run away with him and that every night he would take the leg off and every morning put it back on again. "Put it back on," she said.

"Not yet," he murmured, setting it on its foot out of her reach. "Leave it off for awhile. You got me instead."

She gave a little cry of alarm but he pushed her down and began to kiss her again. Without the leg she felt entirely dependent on him. Her brain seemed to have stopped thinking altogether and to be about some other function that it was not very good at. Different expressions raced back and forth over her face. Every now and then the boy, his eyes like two steel spikes, would glance behind him, where the leg stood. Finally she pushed him off and said, "Put it back on me now."

"Wait," he said. He leaned the other way and pulled the valise toward him and opened it. It had a pale blue spotted lining and there were only two Bibles in it. He took one of these out and opened the cover of it. It was hollow and contained a pocket flask of whiskey, a pack of cards, and a small blue box with printing on it. He laid these out in front of her one at a time in an evenly-spaced row, like one presenting offerings at the shrine of a goddess. He put the blue box in her hand. THIS PRODUCT TO BE USED ONLY FOR THE PREVENTION OF DISEASE, she read, and dropped it. The boy was unscrewing the top of the flask. He stopped and pointed, with a smile, to the deck of cards. It was not an ordinary deck but one with an obscene picture on the back of each card. "Take a swig," he said, offering her the bottle first. He held it in front of her, but like one mesmerized, she did not move.

Her voice when she spoke had an almost pleading sound. "Aren't you," she murmured, "aren't you just good country people?"

The boy cocked his head. He looked as if he were just beginning to understand that she might be trying to insult him. "Yeah," he said, curling his lip slightly, "but it ain't held me back none. I'm as good as you any day in the week."

"Give me my leg," she said.

He pushed it farther away with his foot. "Come on now, let's begin to have us a good time," he said coaxingly. "We ain't got to know one another good yet."

"Give me my leg!" she screamed and tried to lunge for it but he pushed her down easily.

"What's the matter with you all of a sudden?" he asked, frowning as he screwed the top on the flask and put it quickly back inside the Bible. "You just a while ago said you didn't believe in nothing. I thought you was some girl!"

Her face was almost purple. "You're a Christian!" she hissed. "You're a fine Christian! You're just like them all—say one thing and do another. You're a perfect Christian, you're . . ."

The boy's mouth was set angrily. "I hope you don't think," he said in a lofty indignant tone, "that I believe in that crap! I may sell Bibles but I know which end is up and I wasn't born yesterday and I know where I'm going!"

"Give me my leg!" she screeched. He jumped up so quickly that she barely saw him sweep the cards and the blue box back into the Bible and throw the Bible into the valise. She saw him grab the leg and then she saw it for an instant slanted forlornly across the inside of the suitcase with a Bible at either side of its opposite ends. He slammed the lid shut and snatched up the valise and swung it down the hole and then stepped through himself.

When all of him had passed but his head, he turned and regarded her with a look that no longer had any admiration in it. "I've gotten a lot of interesting things," he said. "One time I got a woman's glass eye this way. And you needn't to think you'll catch me because Pointer ain't really my name. I use a different name at every house I call at and don't stay nowhere long. And I'll tell you another thing, Hulga," he said, using the name as if he didn't think much of it, "you ain't so smart. I been believing in nothing ever since I was born!" And then the toast-colored hat disappeared down the hole and the girl was left, sitting on the straw in the dusty sunlight. When she turned her churning face toward the opening, she saw his blue figure struggling successfully over the green speckled lake.

Mrs. Hopewell and Mrs. Freeman, who were in the back pasture, digging up onions, saw him emerge a little later from the woods and head across the meadow toward the highway. "Why, that looks like that nice dull young man that tried to sell me a Bible yesterday," Mrs. Hopewell said, squinting. "He must have been selling them to the Negroes back in there. He was so simple," she said, "but I guess the world would be better off if we were all that simple."

Mrs. Freeman's gaze drove forward and just touched him before he disappeared under the hill. Then she returned her attention to the evil-smelling onion shoot she was lifting from the ground. "Some can't be that simple," she said. "I know I never could."

JOHN BARTH

b. 1930

Barth shares with Barthelme a vision of the modern world as a fantastic place. An observer of Barth's world may begin by seeing it as a "realistic" enough fictional locus—as in the specifically described car-ride of "Lost in the Funhouse"—but very quickly he is levitated into a kind of fantasy that belies all down-to-earth detail. A funhouse, a riverboat on which an old-time minstrel show is put on (in *The Floating Opera,* 1956), or a hospital run by a mad psychiatrist (in *The End of the Road,* 1958) are some of the metaphors for the giddy world that Barth creates. His characters find themselves in varying states of inaction, wild and whirling action, precise intellection, total emotionalism—all without very much relation to their circumstances. Behind them they sense systems of control over their lives that they can't possibly understand: their past, the pattern of history, somebody else's hypnotizing will—who knows? All they know is that they feel caught up by something bigger than they are.

Barth was born in Cambridge, Maryland, a locale that he frequently uses in his fiction. He went to college in Baltimore, at Johns Hopkins, and stayed on to take a master's degree in English. After teaching English for a number of years at Pennsylvania State University and at the State University of New York at Buffalo, Barth returned to teach at Johns Hopkins in 1972, and was a visiting professor at Boston University in 1972–1973.

Unlike other authors who are learned in literature, Barth does not write about books, though his work is marked by a constant appropriation of other writers' styles and techniques for his own purposes. An example is his novel *The Sot-Weed Factor* (1960). On one level it reads like a rollicking eighteenth-century novel by Smollett, but in fact what Barth is doing in it is setting up a world of fast-moving and apparently purposeful action in which characters actually flounder as much as in the paralyzed nonaction of *The Floating Opera.*

Lost in the Funhouse

For whom is the funhouse fun? Perhaps for lovers. For Ambrose it is *a place of fear and confusion.* He has come to the seashore with his family for the holiday, *the occasion of their visit is Independence Day, the most important secular holiday of the United States of America.* A single straight underline is the manuscript mark for italic type, *which in turn* is the printed equivalent to oral emphasis of words and phrases as well as the customary type for titles of complete works, not to mention. Italics are also employed, in fiction-stories especially, for "outside," intrusive, or artificial voices, such as radio announcements, the texts of telegrams and newspaper articles, *et cetera.* They should be used *sparingly.* If passages originally in roman type are italicized by someone repeating them, it's customary to acknowledge the fact. *Italics mine.*

Ambrose was "at that awkward age." His voice came out high-pitched as a child's if he let himself get carried away; to be on the safe side, therefore, he moved and spoke with *deliberate calm* and *adult gravity.* Talking soberly of unimportant or irrelevant matters and listening consciously to the sound of your own voice are useful habits for maintaining control in this difficult interval. *En route* to Ocean City he sat in the back seat of the family car with his brother, Peter, age fifteen, and Magda G——, age fourteen, a pretty girl an exquisite young lady, who lived not far from them on B—— Street in the town of D——, Maryland. Initials, blanks, or both were often substituted for proper names in nineteenth-century fiction to enhance the illusion of reality. It is as if the author felt it necessary to delete the names for reasons of tact or legal liability. Interestingly, as with other aspects of realism, it is an *illusion* that is being enhanced, by purely artificial means. Is it likely, does it violate the principle of verisimilitude, that a thirteen-year-old boy could make such a sophisticated observation? A girl of fourteen is *the psychological coeval* of a boy of fifteen or sixteen; a thirteen-year-old boy, therefore, even one precocious in some other respects, might be three years *her emotional junior.*

Thrice a year—on Memorial, Independence, and Labor Days—the family visits Ocean City for the afternoon and evening. When Ambrose and Peter's father was their age the excursion was made by train, as mentioned in the novel *The 42nd Parallel* by John Dos Passos. Many families from the same neighborhood used to travel together, with dependent relatives and often with Negro servants; schoolfuls of children swarmed through the railway cars; everyone shared everyone else's Maryland fried chicken, Virginia ham, deviled eggs, potato salad, beaten biscuits, iced tea. Nowadays (that is, in 19——, the year of our story) the journey is made by automobile—more comfortably and quickly though without the extra fun though without the *camaraderie* of a general excursion. It's all part of the deterioration of American life, their father declares; Uncle Karl supposes that when the boys take *their* families to Ocean City for the holidays, they'll fly in Autogiros. Their mother, sitting in the middle of the front seat like Magda in the second, only with her arms on the seat-back behind the men's shoulders, wouldn't want the good old days back again, the steaming trains and stuffy long dresses; on the other hand, she can do without Autogiros, too, if she has to become a grandmother to fly in them.

Description of physical appearance and mannerisms is one of several standard methods of characterization used by writers of fiction. It is also important to "keep the senses operating"; when a detail from one of the five senses, say visual, is "crossed" with a detail from another, say auditory, the reader's imagination is oriented to the scene, perhaps unconsciously. This procedure may be compared to the way surveyors and navigators determine their positions by two or more compass-bearings, a process known as triangulation. The brown hair on Ambrose's mother's forearms gleamed in the sunlight. Though right-handed, she took her left arm from the seat-back to press the dashboard cigar-lighter for Uncle Karl. When the glass bead in its handle glowed red, the lighter was ready for use. The smell of Uncle Karl's cigar-smoke reminded one of. The fragrance of the ocean came strong to the picnic-ground where they always stopped for lunch, two miles inland from Ocean City. Having to pause for a full hour almost within sound of the breakers was difficult for Peter and Ambrose when they were younger; even at their present age it was not easy to keep their anticipation, *stimulated by the briny spume,* from turning into short temper. The Irish author James Joyce, in his unusual novel entitled *Ulysses,* now available in this country, uses the adjectives *snot-green* and *scrotum-tightening* to describe the sea. Visual, auditory, tactile, olfactory, gustatory. Peter and Ambrose's father, while steering their black 1936 LaSalle sedan with one hand, could with the other remove the first cigarette from a white pack of Lucky Strikes and, more remarkably, light it with a match forefingered from its book and thumbed against the flint-paper without being detached. The matchbook cover merely advertised U.S. War Bonds and Stamps. A fine metaphor, simile, or other figure of speech, in addition to its obvious "first-order" relevance to the thing it describes, will be seen upon reflection to have a second order of significance: it may be drawn from the *milieu* of the action, for example, or be particularly appropriate to the sensibility of the narrator, even hinting to the reader things of which the narrator is unaware; or it may cast further and subtler lights upon the thing it describes, sometimes ironically qualifying the more evident sense of the comparison.

To say that Ambrose and Peter's mother was *pretty* is to accomplish nothing; the reader may acknowledge the proposition, but his imagination is not engaged. Besides, Magda was pretty, yet in an altogether different way. Although she lived on B—— Street, she had very good manners and did better than average in school. Her figure was very well developed for her age. Her right hand lay casually on the plush upholstery of the seat, very near Ambrose's left leg, on which his own hand rested. The space between their legs, between her right and his left leg, was out of the line of sight of anyone sitting on the other side of Magda, as well as anyone glancing into the rearview mirror. Uncle Karl's face resembled Peter's—rather, vice versa. Both had dark hair and eyes, short husky statures, deep voices. Magda's left hand was probably in a similar position on her left side. The boy's father is difficult to describe; no particular feature of his appearance or manner stood out. He wore glasses and taught English in the T—— County High School. Uncle Karl was a masonry contractor.

Although Peter must have known as well as Ambrose that the latter, because of his position in the car, would be the first to see the electrical towers of the power plant at V——, the halfway point of their trip, he leaned forward and slightly toward the center of the car and pretended to be looking for them through the flat pinewoods and tuckahoe creeks along the highways. For as long as the boys could remember, "looking for the Towers" had been a feature of the first half of their excursions to Ocean City, "looking for the standpipe" of the second. Though the game was childish, their mother preserved the tradition of rewarding the first to see the Towers with a candybar or piece of fruit. She insisted now that Magda play the game; the prize, she said, was "something hard to get nowadays." Ambrose decided not to join in; he sat back in his seat. Magda, like Peter, leaned forward. Two sets of straps were discernible through the shoulders of her sun-dress; the inside right one, a brassiere-strap, was fastened or shortened with a small safety-pin. The right armpit of her dress, presumably the left as well, was damp with perspiration. The simple strategy for being first to espy the Towers, which Ambrose had understood by the age of four, was to sit on the right-hand side of the car. Whoever sat there, however, had also to put up with the worst of the sun, and so Ambrose, without mentioning the matter, chose sometimes the one and sometimes the other. Not impossibly, Peter had never caught on to the trick, or thought that his brother hadn't, simply because Ambrose on occasion preferred shade to a Baby Ruth or tangerine.

The shade-sun situation didn't apply to the front seat, owing to the windshield; if anything the driver got more sun, since the person on the passenger side not only was shaded below by the door and dashboard but might swing down his sun visor all the way too.

"Is that them?" Magda asked. Ambrose's mother teased the boys for letting Magda win, insinuating that "somebody [had] a girlfriend." Peter and Ambrose's father reached a long thin arm across their mother to butt his cigarette in the dashboard ashtray, under the lighter. The prize this time for seeing the Towers first was a banana. Their mother bestowed it after chiding their father for wasting a half-smoked cigarette when everything was so scarce. Magda, to take the prize, moved her hand from so near Ambrose's that he could have touched it as though accidentally. She offered to share the prize, things like that were so hard to find; but everyone insisted it was hers alone. Ambrose's mother sang an iambic trimeter couplet from a popular song, femininely rhymed:

What's good is in the Army;
What's left will never harm me.[1]

Uncle Karl tapped his cigar-ash out the ventilator window; some particles were sucked by the slip-stream back into the car through the rear window on the passenger side. Magda demonstrated her ability to hold a banana in one hand and peel it with her teeth. She still sat forward; Ambrose pushed his glasses back onto the bridge of his nose with his left hand, which he then negligently let fall to the seat-cushion immediately behind her. He even permitted the single hair, gold, on the second joint of his thumb to brush the fabric of her skirt. Should she have sat back at that instant, his hand would have been caught under her.

Plush upholstery prickles uncomfortably through gabardine slacks in the July sun. The function of the *beginning* of a story is to introduce the principal characters, establish their initial relationships, set the scene for the main action, expose the background of the situation if necessary, plant motifs and foreshadowings where appropriate, and initiate the first complication or whatever of the "rising action." Actually, if one imagines a story called "The Funhouse," or "Lost in the Funhouse," the details of the drive to Ocean City don't seem especially relevant. The *beginning* should recount the events between Ambrose's first sight of the funhouse early in the afternoon and his entering it with Magda and Peter in the evening. The *middle* would narrate all relevant events from the time he goes in to the time he loses his way; middles have the double and contradictory function of delaying the climax while at the same time preparing the reader for it and fetching him to it. Then the *ending* would tell what Ambrose does while he's lost, how he finally finds his way out, and what everybody makes of the experience. So far there's been no real dialogue, very little sensory detail, and nothing in the way of a *theme.* And a long time has gone by already without anything happening; it makes a person wonder. We haven't even reached Ocean City yet: we will never get out of the funhouse.

The more closely an author identifies with the narrator, literally or metaphorically, the less advisable it is as a rule to use the first-person narrative viewpoint. Once five years previously the three young people *aforementioned* played Niggers and Masters in the backyard; when it was Ambrose's turn to

[1]They're Either Too Young or Too Old" (Schwartz-Loesser). © 1943 by M. Whitmark & Sons, renewed by Warner Bros. Music. All rights reserved. Used by permission.

be Master and theirs to be Niggers, Peter had to go serve his evening papers; Ambrose was afraid to punish Magda alone, but she led him to the whitewashed Torture Chamber between the woodshed and the privy in the Slaves Quarters; there she knelt sweating among bamboo rakes and dusty mason jars, pleadingly embraced his knees, and while bumblebees droned in the lattice as if on an ordinary summer afternoon, purchased clemency at a surprising price set by herself. Doubtless she remembered nothing of this event; Ambrose on the other hand seemed unable to forget the least detail of his life. He even recalled how, standing beside himself with awed impersonality in the reeky heat, he'd stared the while at an empty cigar-box in which Uncle Karl kept stonecutting chisels: beneath the words *El Producto,* a laureled, loose-toga'd lady regarded the sea from a marble bench; beside her, forgotten or not yet turned to, was a five-stringed lute. Her chin reposed on the back of her right hand: her left depended negligently from the bench-arm. The lower half of scene and lady was peeled away; the words EXAMINED BY—were inked there into the wood. Nowadays cigar boxes are made of pasteboard. Ambrose wondered what Magda would have done, Ambrose wondered what Magda would do when she sat back on his hand as he resolved she should. Be angry. Make a teasing joke of it. Give no sign at all. For a long time she leaned forward, playing cow-poker with Peter against Uncle Karl and Mother and watching for the first sign of Ocean City. At nearly the same instant picnic-ground and Ocean-City-standpipe hove into view; an Amoco filling station on their side of the road cost Mother and Uncle Karl fifty cows and the game; Magda bounced back, clapping her right hand on Mother's right arm; Ambrose moved clear "in the nick of time."

At this rate our hero, at this rate our protagonist will remain in the funhouse forever. Narrative ordinarily consists of alternating dramatization and summarization. One symptom of nervous tension, paradoxically, is repeated and violent yawning; neither Peter nor Magda nor Uncle Karl nor Mother reacted in this manner. Although they were no longer small children, Peter and Ambrose were each given a dollar to spend on boardwalk amusements in addition to what money of their own they'd brought along. Magda too, though she protested she had ample spending money. The boy's mother made a little scene out of distributing the bills; she pretended that her sons and Magda were small children and cautioned them not to spend the sum too quickly or in one place. Magda promised with a merry laugh, and having both hands free, took the bill with her left. Peter laughed also and pledged in a falsetto to be a good boy. His imitation of a child was not clever. The boys' father was tall and thin, balding, fair-complexioned. Assertions of that sort are not effective; the reader may acknowledge the proposition, but. We should be much further along than we are; something has gone wrong; not much of this preliminary rambling seems relevant. Yet everyone begins in the same place; how is it that most go along without difficulty but a few lose their way?

"Stay out from under the boardwalk," Uncle Karl growled from the side of his mouth. The boys' mother pushed his shoulder *in mock annoyance.* They were all standing before Fat May the Laughing Lady, who advertised the funhouse. Larger than life, Fat May mechanically shook, rocked on her heels, slapped her thighs while recorded laughter—uproarious, female—came amplified from a hidden loudspeaker. It chuckled, wheezed, wept; tried in vain to catch its breath; tittered, groaned, exploded raucous and anew. You couldn't hear it without laughing yourself, no matter how you felt. Father came back from talking to a Coast-Guardsman on duty and reported that the surf was spoiled with crude oil from tankers recently torpedoed offshore. Lumps of it, difficult to remove, made tarry tidelines on the beach and stuck on swimmers. Many bathed in the surf nevertheless and came out speckled; others paid to use a municipal pool and only sunbathed on the beach. We would do the latter. We would do the latter. We would do the latter.

Under the boardwalk, cold sand littered with cigar-butts, treasured with cigarette-stubs, Coca-Cola caps, cardboard lollipop-sticks, matchbook-covers warning that A Slip of the Lip Can Sink a Ship, grainy other things. What is the story's point? Ambrose is ill. He perspires in the dark passages; candied apples-on-a-stick, delicious-looking, disappointing to eat. Funhouses need men's and ladies' rooms at intervals.

Magda's teeth. She *was* left-handed. Perspiration. They've gone all the way, through, Magda and Peter, they've been waiting for hours with Mother and Uncle Karl while Father searches for his lost son; they draw french-fried potatoes from a paper cup and shake their heads. They've named the children they'll one day have and bring to Ocean City on holidays. Can spermatozoa properly be thought of as male animalcules when there are no female spermatozoa? They grope through hot dark windings, past Love's Tunnel's fearsome obstacles. Some perhaps lose their way.

Peter suggested then and there that they do the funhouse; he had been through it before, so had Magda, Ambrose hadn't and suggested, his voice cracking on account of Fat May's laughter, that they swim first. All were chuckling, couldn't help it; Ambrose's father, Ambrose and Peter's father came up grinning like a lunatic with two boxes of syrup-coated popcorn, one for Mother, one for Magda; the men were to help themselves. Ambrose walked on Magda's right; being by nature left-handed, she carried the box in her left hand. Up front the situation was reversed.

"What are you limping for?" Magda inquired of Ambrose. He supposed in a husky tone that his foot had gone to sleep in the car. Her teeth flashed.

"Pins and needles?" It was the honeysuckle on the lattice of the former privy that drew the bees. Imagine being stung there. How long is this going to take?

The adults decided to forgo the pool, but Uncle Karl insisted they change into swimsuits and do the beach. "He wants to watch the pretty girls," Peter teased, and ducked behind Magda from Uncle Karl's pretended wrath. "You've got all the pretty girls you need right here," Magda declared, and Mother said: "Now that's the gospel truth." Magda scolded Peter, who reached over her shoulder to sneak some popcorn. "Your brother and father aren't getting any." Uncle Karl wondered if they were going to have fireworks that night, what with the shortages. It wasn't the shortages, Mr. M.—— replied; Ocean City had fireworks from pre-war. But it was too risky on account of the enemy submarines, some people thought.

"Don't seem like Fourth of July without fireworks," said Uncle Karl. The inverted tag in dialogue-writing is still considered permissible with proper names or epithets, but sounds old-fashioned with personal pronouns. "We'll have 'em again soon enough," predicted the boys' father. Their mother declared she could do without fireworks: they reminded her too much of the real thing. Their father said all the more reason to shoot off a few now and again. Uncle Karl asked *rhetorically* who needed reminding, just look at people's hair and skin.

"The oil, yes," said Mrs. M——.

Ambrose had a pain in his stomach and so didn't swim but enjoyed watching the others. He and his father burned red easily. Magda's figure was exceedingly well developed for her age. She too declined to swim, and got mad, and became angry when Peter attempted to drag her into the pool. She always swam, he insisted; what did she mean not swim? Why did a person come to Ocean City?

"Maybe I want to lay here with Ambrose," Magda teased.

Nobody likes a pedant.

"Aha," said Mother. Peter grabbed Magda by one ankle and ordered Ambrose to grab the other. She squealed and rolled over on the beach blanket. Ambrose pretended to help hold her back. Her tan was darker than even Mother's and Peter's. "Help out, Uncle Karl!" Peter cried. Uncle Karl went to seize the other ankle. Inside the top of her swimsuit, however, you could see the line where the sunburn ended and, when she hunched her shoulders and squealed again, one nipple's auburn edge. Mother made them behave themselves. "*You* should certainly know," she said to Uncle Karl. Archly. "that when a lady says she doesn't feel like swimming, a gentleman doesn't ask questions." Uncle Karl said excuse *him;* Mother winked at Magda; Ambrose blushed; stupid Peter kept saying "Phooey on *feel like!*" and tugging at Magda's ankle; then even he got the point, and cannon-balled with a holler into the pool.

"I swear," Magda said, in mock *in feigned* exasperation.

The diving would make a suitable literary symbol. To go off the high board you had to wait in a line along the poolside and up the ladder. Fellows tickled girls and goosed one another and shouted to the ones at the top to hurry up, or razzed them for bellyfloppers. Once on the springboard some took a great while posing or clowning or deciding on a dive or getting up their nerve; others ran right off. Especially among the younger fellows the idea was to strike the funniest pose or do the craziest stunt as you fell, a thing that got harder to do as you kept on and kept on. But whether you hollered *Geronimo!* or *Sieg heil!*, held your nose or "rode a bicycle," pretended to be shot or did a perfect jackknife or changed your mind halfway down and ended up with nothing, it was over in two seconds, after all that wait. Spring, pose, splash. Spring, neat-o, splash. Spring, aw shit, splash.

The grown-ups had gone on; Ambrose wanted to converse with Magda; she was remarkably well developed for her age; it was said that that came from rubbing with a Turkish towel, and there were other theories. Ambrose could think of nothing to say except how good a diver Peter was, who was showing off for her benefit. You could pretty well tell by looking at their bathing-suits and arm-muscles how far along the different fellows were. Ambrose was glad he hadn't gone in swimming, the cold water shrank you up so. Magda pretended not to be interested in the diving; she probably weighed as much as he did. If you knew your way around in the funhouse like your own bedroom you could wait until a girl came along and then slip away without ever getting caught, even if her boyfriend was right with her. She'd think *he* did it! It would be better to be the boyfriend, and act outraged, and tear the funhouse apart. Not act; *be*.

"He's a master diver," Ambrose said. In feigned admiration. "You really have to slave away at it to get that good." What would it matter anyhow if he asked her right out whether she remembered, even teased her with it as Peter would have?

There's no point in going farther; this isn't getting anybody anywhere; they haven't even come to the funhouse yet. Ambrose is off the track, in some new or old part of the place that's not supposed to be used; he strayed into it by some one-in-a-million chance, like the time the roller-coaster-car left the tracks in the nineteen-teens against all the laws of physics and sailed over the boardwalk in the dark. And they can't locate him because they don't know where to look. Even the designer and operator has forgotten this other part, that winds around on itself like a whelk-shell. That winds around the right part like the snakes on Mercury's caduceus. Some people, perhaps, don't "hit their stride" until their twenties, when the growing-up business is over and women appreciate other things besides wisecracks and teasing and strutting. Peter didn't have one-tenth the imagination *he* had, not one-tenth. Peter did this naming-their-children thing as a joke, making up names like Aloysius and Murgatroyd, but Ambrose knew *exactly* how it would feel to be married and have children of your own, and be a loving husband and father, and go comfortably to work in the mornings and to bed with your wife at night, and wake up with her there. With a breeze coming through the sash and birds and mockingbirds singing in the chinese-cigar trees. His eyes watered, there aren't enough ways to say that. He would be quite famous in his line of work. Whether Magda was his wife or not, one evening when he was wise-lined and gray at the temples, he'd smile gravely, at a fashionable dinner-party, and remind her of his youthful passion. The time they went with his family to Ocean City; the *erotic fantasies* he used to have about her. How long ago it seemed, and childish! Yet tender, too, *n'est-ce pas?* Would she have imagined that the world-renowned whatever remembered how many strings were on the lute on the bench beside the girl on the label of the cigar-box he'd stared at in the toolshed at age eight while she, age nine. Even then he had felt *wise beyond his years;* he'd stroked her hair and said in his deepest voice and correctest English, as to a dear child: "I shall never forget this moment."

But though he had breathed heavily, groaned as if ecstatic, what he'd really felt throughout was an odd detachment, as though someone else were Master. Strive as he might to be transported, he heard his mind take notes upon the scene: *This is what they call* passion. *I am experiencing it.* Many of the digger-machines were out of order in the penny arcades and could not be repaired or replaced for the duration. Moreover, the prizes, made now in USA, were less interesting than formerly, pasteboard items for the most part, and some of the machines wouldn't work on white pennies. The gypsy-fortuneteller machine might have provided a foreshadowing of the climax of this story if Ambrose had operated it. It was even dilapidateder than most: the silver coating was worn off the brown metal handles, the glass windows around the dummy were cracked and taped, her kerchiefs and silks long faded. If a man lived by himself he could take a department-store mannequin with flexible joints and modify her in certain ways. *However:* by the time he was that old he'd have a real woman. There was a machine that stamped your name around a white-metal coin with a star in the middle: A——. His son would be the Third, and when the lad reached thirteen or so he would put a strong arm around his shoulder and tell him calmly: "It is perfectly normal. We have all been through it. It will not last forever." Nobody knew how to be what they were right. He'd smoke a pipe, teach his son how to fish and softcrab, assure him he needn't worry about himself. Magda would certainly give, Magda would certainly yield a great deal of milk, although guilty of occasional solecisms. It don't taste so bad. Suppose the lights came on now!

The day wore on. You think you're yourself, but there are other persons in you. Ambrose gets an erection when Ambrose doesn't want one, *and ob-*

versely. Ambrose watches them disagreeing; Ambrose watches him watch. In the funhouse mirror-room you can't see yourself go on forever, because no matter how you stand your head gets in the way. Even if you had a glass periscope, the image of your eye would cover up the thing you really wanted to see. The police will come; there'll be a story in the papers. That must be where it happened. Unless he can find a surprise exit, an unofficial backdoor or escape-hatch opening on an alley, say, and then stroll up to the family in front of the funhouse and ask where everybody's been; *he's* been out of the place for ages. That's just where it happened, in that last lighted room: Peter and Magda found the right exit; he found one that you weren't supposed to find and strayed off into the works somewhere. In a perfect funhouse you'd be able to go only one way, like the divers off the high board; getting lost would be impossible; the doors and halls would work like minnow-traps or the valves in veins.

On account of German U-boats Ocean City was "browned out": street-lights were shaded on the seaward side; shopwindows and boardwalk amusement-places were kept dim, not to silhouette tankers and Liberty-ships for torpedoing. In a short-story about Ocean City, Maryland, during World War II the author could make use of the image of sailors on leave in the penny arcades and shooting-galleries, sighting through the cross hairs to toy machine-guns at swastika'd subs, while out in the black Atlantic a U-boat skipper squints through his periscope at real ships outlined by the glow of penny arcades. After dinner the family strolled back to the amusement end of the boardwalk. The boys' father had burnt red as always and was masked with Noxzema, a minstrel in reverse. The grown-ups stood at the end of the boardwalk where the Hurricane of '33 had cut an inlet from the ocean to Assawoman Bay.

"Pronounced with a long *o,*" Uncle Karl reminded Magda with a wink. His shirt-sleeves were rolled up; Mother punched his brown biceps with the arrowed heart on it and said his mind was naughty. Fat May's laugh came suddenly from the funhouse, as if she'd just got the joke; the family laughed too at the coincidence. Ambrose went under the boardwalk to search for out-of-town matchbook-covers with the aid of his pocket flashlight; he looked out from the edge of the North American continent and wondered how far their laughter carried over the water. Spies in rubber rafts; survivors in life-boats. If the joke had been beyond his understanding, he could have said: "*The laughter was over his head.*" And let the reader see the serious wordplay on second reading.

He turned the flashlight on and then off at once even before the woman whooped. He sprang away, heart athud, dropping the light. The man had snarled: "Cut da friggin' light!" Perspiration drenched and chilled him by the time he scrambled up to the family. "See anything?" his father asked. His voice wouldn't come; he shrugged and violently brushed sand from his pantslegs.

"Let's ride the old flying-horses!" Magda cried. I'll never be an author. It's been forever already, everybody's gone home, Ocean City's deserted, the ghost-crabs are tickling across the beach and down the littered cold streets. And the empty halls of clapboard hotels and abandoned funhouses. A tidal wave; an enemy air raid; a monster-crab swelling like an island from the sea. *The Inhabitants fled in terror.* Magda clung to his trouserleg; he alone knew the maze's secret. "He gave his life that we might live," said Uncle Karl with a scowl of pain, as he. The woman's legs had been twined behind the man's neck; he'd spread her fat cheeks with tatooed hands and pumped like a whipper. *An astonishing coincidence.* He yearned to tell Peter. He wanted to throw up for excitement. They hadn't even chased him. He wished he were dead.

One possible ending would be to have Ambrose come across another lost person in the dark. They'd match their wits together against the funhouse, struggle like Ulysses past obstacle after obstacle, help and encourage each other. Or a girl. By the time they found the exit they'd be closest friends, sweethearts if it were a girl; they'd know each other's inmost souls, be bound together *by the cement of shared adventure;* then they'd emerge into the light, and it would turn out that his friend was a Negro. A blind girl. President Roosevelt's son. Ambrose's former arch-enemy.

Shortly after the mirror-room he'd groped along a musty corridor, his heart already misgiving him at the absence of phosphorescent arrows and other signs. He'd found a crack of light—not a door, it turned out, but a seam between the plyboard wall-panels—and squinting up to it, espied a small old man nodding upon a stool beneath a bare speckled bulb. A crude panel of toggle- and knife-switches hung beside the open fuse-box near his head; elsewhere in the little room were wooden levers and ropes belayed to boat-cleats. At the time, Ambrose wasn't lost enough to rap or call; later he couldn't find that crack. Now it seemed to him that he'd possibly dozed off for a few minutes somewhere along the way; certainly he was exhausted from the afternoon's sunshine and the evening's problems; he couldn't be sure he hadn't dreamed part or all of the sight. Had an old black wall fan droned like bumble-bees and shimmied two flypaper streamers? Had the funhouse operator—gentle, somewhat sad and tired-appearing—murmured in his sleep? Is there really such a person as Ambrose, or is he a figment of the author's imagination? Was it Assawoman Bay or Sinepuxent? Are there other errors of fact in this fiction? Was there another sound besides the little slap slap of thigh on ham, like water sucking at the chineboards of a skiff?

When you're lost, the smartest thing to do is stay put till you're found, hollering if necessary. But to holler guarantees humiliation as well as rescue; keeping silent permits some saving of face—you can act surprised at the fuss when your rescuers find you and swear you weren't lost, if they do. What's more you might find your own way yet, *however belatedly.*

"Don't tell me your foot's still asleep!" Magda exclaimed as the three young people walked from the inlet to the area set aside for ferris-wheels, carrousels, and other carnival rides, they having decided in favor of the vast and ancient merry-go-round instead of the funhouse. What a sentence, everything was wrong from the outset. People don't know what to make of him, he doesn't know what to make of himself, he's only thirteen, *athletically and socially inept,* not astonishingly bright, but there are antennae; he has . . . some sort of receivers in his head; things speak to him, he understands more than he should, the world winks at him through its objects, grabs grinning at his coat. Everybody else is in on some secret he doesn't know; they've forgotten to tell him. Through simple *procrastination* his mother put off his baptism until this year. Everyone else had it done as a baby; he'd assumed the same of himself, as had his mother so she claimed, until it was time for him to join Grace Methodist-Protestant and the oversight came out. He was mortified, but pitched sleepless through his private catechizing, intimidated by the ancient mysteries, a thirteen-year-old would never say that, resolved to experience conversion like St. Augustine. When the water touched his brow and Adam's sin left him, he contrived by a strain like defecation to bring tears into his eyes—but felt nothing. There was some simple, radical difference about him; he hoped it was genius, feared it was madness, devoted himself to amiability and inconspicuousness. Alone on the seawall near his house he was seized by the terrifying transports he'd thought to find in summershed, in Communion-cup. The grass was alive! The town, the river, himself, were not imaginary; time roared in his ears like wind; the world was *going on!* This part ought to be dramatized. The Irish author James Joyce once wrote. Ambrose M—— is going to scream.

There is no *texture of rendered sensory detail,* for one thing. The faded distorting mirrors beside Fat May; the impossibility of choosing a mount when one had but a single ride on the great carrousel; the *vertigo attendant on his recognition* that Ocean City was worn out, the place of fathers and grandfathers, straw-boatered men and parasoled ladies survived by their amusements. Money spent, the three paused at Peter's insistence beside Fat May to watch the girls get their skirts blown up. The object was to tease Magda, who said, "I swear, Peter M——, you've got a one-track mind! Amby and me aren't *interested* in such things." In the tumbling-barrel, too, just inside the Devil's-mouth entrance to the funhouse, the girls were up-ended, and their boyfriends and others could see up their dresses if they cared to. Which was the whole point, Ambrose realized. Of the entire funhouse! If you looked around, you noticed that almost all the people on the boardwalk were paired off into couples except the small children; in a way, that was the whole point of Ocean City! If you had X-ray eyes and could see everything going on at that instant under the boardwalk and in all the hotel-rooms and cars and alleyways, you'd realize that all that normally *showed,* like restaurants and dance-halls and clothing and test-your-strength machines, was merely preparation and intermission. Fat May screamed.

Because he watched the goings-on from the corner of his eye, it was Ambrose who spied the half-dollar on the boardwalk near the tumbling-barrel. Losers weepers. The first time he'd heard some people moving through a corridor not far away, just after he'd lost sight of the crack of light, he'd decided not to call to them, for fear they'd guess he was scared and poke fun; it sounded like roughnecks; he'd hoped they'd come by and he could follow in the dark without their knowing. Another time he'd heard just one person, unless he imagined it, bumping along as if on the other side of the plywood; perhaps Peter coming back for him, or Father, or Magda lost too. Or the owner and operator of the funhouse. He'd called out once, as though merrily: "Anybody know where the heck we are?" But the query was too stiff, his voice cracked when the sounds stopped he was terrified: maybe it was a queer who waited for fellows to get lost, or a longhaired filthy monster that lived in some cranny of the funhouse. He stood rigid for hours it seemed like, scarcely respiring. His future was shockingly clear, in outline. He tried holding his breath to the point of unconsciousness. There ought to be a button you could push to end your life absolutely without pain; disappear in a flick, like turning out a light. He would push it instantly! He despised Uncle Karl. But he despised his father too, for not being what he was supposed to be. Perhaps his father hated *his* father, and so on, and his son would hate him, and so on. Instantly!

Naturally he didn't have nerve enough to ask Magda to go through the funhouse with him. With incredible nerve and to everyone's surprise he invited Magda, quietly and politely, to go through the funhouse with him. "I warn you, I've never been through it before," he added, *laughing easily;* "but I reckon we can manage somehow. The important thing to remember, after all, is that it's meant to be a *fun*house; that is, a place of amusement. If people really got lost or injured or too badly frightened in it, the owner'd go out of business. There'd even be lawsuits. No character in a work of fiction can make a speech this long without interruption or acknowledgment from the other characters."

Mother teased Uncle Karl: "Three's a crowd, I always heard." But actually Ambrose was relieved that Peter now had a quarter too. Nothing was what it looked like. Every instant, under the surface of the Atlantic Ocean, millions of living animals devoured one another. Pilots were falling in flames over Europe; women were being forcibly raped in the South Pacific. His father should have taken him aside and said: "There is a simple secret to getting through the funhouse, as simple as being first to see the Towers. Here it is. Peter does not know it; neither does your Uncle Karl. You and I are different. Not surprisingly, you've often wished you weren't. Don't think I haven't noticed how unhappy your childhood has been! But you'll understand, when I tell you, why it had to be kept secret until now. And you won't regret not being like your brother and your uncle. *On the contrary.*" If you knew all the stories behind all the people on the boardwalk you'd see that *nothing* was what it looked like. Husbands and wives often hated each other; parents didn't necessarily love their children; et cetera. A child took things for granted because he had nothing to compare his life to, and everybody acted as if things were as they should be. Therefore each saw himself as the hero of the story, when the truth might turn out to be that he's the villain, or the coward. And there wasn't one thing you could do about it!

Hunchbacks, fat ladies, fools—that no one chose what they were was unbearable. In the movies he'd meet a beautiful young girl in the funhouse; they'd have hairsbreadth escapes from real dangers; he'd do and say the right things; she also; in the end they'd be lovers; their dialogue-lines would match up; he'd be perfectly at ease; she'd not only like him well enough, she'd think he was *marvelous;* she'd lie awake thinking about *him,* instead of vice versa—the way *his* face looked in different lights and how he stood and exactly what he'd said—and yet that would be only one small episode in his wonderful life, among many many others. Not a *turning-point* at all. What had happened in the toolshed was nothing. He hated, he loathed his parents! One reason for not writing a lost-in-the-funhouse story is that either everybody's felt what Ambrose feels, in which case it goes without saying, or else no normal person feels such things, in which case Ambrose is a freak. "Is anything more tiresome, in fiction, than the problems of sensitive adolescents?" And it's all too long and rambling, as if the author. For all a person knows the first time through, the end could be just around any corner; perhaps, *not impossibly* it's been within reach any number of times. On the other hand he may be scarcely past the start, with everything yet to get through, an intolerable idea.

Fill in: His father's raised eyebrows when he announced his decision to do the funhouse with Magda. Ambrose understands now, but didn't then, that his father was wondering whether he knew what the funhouse was *for*—especially since he didn't object, as he should have, when Peter decided to come along too. The ticket-woman, witchlike, mortifying him when inadvertently he gave her his name-coin instead of the half-dollar, then unkindly calling Magda's attention to the birthmark on his temple: "Watch out for him, girlie, he's a marked man!" She wasn't even cruel, he understood, only vulgar and insensitive. Somewhere in the world there was a young woman with such splendid understanding that she'd see him entire, like a poem or story, and find his words so valuable after all that when he confessed his apprehensions she would explain why they were in fact the very things that made him precious to her . . . and to Western Civilization! There was no such girl, the simple truth being. Violent yawns as they approached the mouth. Whispered advice from an old-timer on a bench near the barrel: "Go crabwise and ye'll get an eyeful without upsetting!" Composure vanished at the first pitch: Peter hollered joyously, Magda tumbled, shrieked, clutched her skirt, Ambrose scrambled crabwise, tightlipped with terror, was soon out, watched his dropped name-coin slide among the couples. Shamefaced he saw that to get through expeditiously was not the point; Peter feigned assistance in order to trip Magda up, shouted "I see Christmas!" when her legs went flying. The old man, his latest betrayer, cackled approval. A dim hall then of blackthread cobwebs and recorded gibber: he took Magda's elbow to steady her against revolving discs set in the slanted floor to throw your feet out from under, and explained to her in a calm deep voice his theory that each phase of the funhouse was triggered either automatically, by a series of photoelectric devices, or else manually by operators stationed at peepholes. But he lost his voice thrice as the discs unbalanced him; Magda was anyhow squealing; but at one point she clutched him about the waist to keep from falling, and her right cheek pressed for a moment against his belt-buckle. Heroically he drew her up, it was his chance to clutch her close as if for support and say: "I love you." He even put an arm lightly about the small of her back before a sailor-and-girl pitched into them from behind, sorely treading his left big toe and knocking Magda asprawl with them. The sailor's girl was a string-haired hussy with a loud laugh and light-blue drawers; Ambrose realized that he wouldn't have said "I love you" anyhow, and was smitten with self-contempt. How much better it would be to be that common sailor! A wiry little Seaman 3rd, the fellow squeezed a girl to each side and stumbled hilarious into the mirror-room, closer to Magda in thirty seconds than Ambrose had got in thirteen years. She giggled at something the fellow said to Peter; she drew her hair from her eyes with a movement so womanly it struck Ambrose's heart; Peter's smacking her backside then seemed particularly coarse. But Magda made a pleased indignant face and cried, "All right for *you,* mister!" and pursued Peter into the maze without a backward glance. The sailor followed after, leisurely drawing his girl against his hip; Ambrose understood not only that they were all so relieved to be rid of his burdensome company that they didn't even notice his absence, but that he himself shared their relief. Stepping from the treacherous passage at last into the mirror-maze, he saw once again, more clearly than ever, how readily he deceived himself into supposing he was a person. He even foresaw, wincing at his dreadful self-knowledge, that he would repeat the deception, at ever-rarer intervals, all his wretched life, so fearful were the alternatives. Fame, madness, suicide; perhaps all three. It's not believable that so young a boy could articulate that reflection, and in fiction the merely true must always yield to the plausible. Yet Ambrose M—— understood, as few adults do, that the famous loneliness of the great was no popular myth but a general truth—and moreover, that it was as much cause as effect.

All the preceding except the last few sentences is exposition that should've been done earlier or interspersed with the present action instead of lumped together. No reader would put up with so much with such *prolixity.* It's interesting that Ambrose's father, though presumably an intelligent man (as indicated by his role as high-school teacher), neither encouraged nor discouraged his children at all in any way—as if he either didn't care about them or cared all right but didn't know how to act. If this fact should contribute to one of his children's becoming a celebrated but wretchedly unhappy scientist, was it a good thing or not? He too might someday face that question; it would be useful to know whether it had tortured his father for years, for example, or never once crossed his mind.

In the mirror-maze two important things happened. First, our hero found a name-coin someone else had lost or discarded: *AMBROSE,* suggestive of the famous lightship and of his father's favorite dessert, which his mother prepared on special occasions out of coconut, oranges, grapes, and what else. Second, as he wondered at the endless replication of his image in the mirrors—second, as he *lost himself in the reflection* that the necessity for an observer makes perfect observation impossible, better make him eighteen at least, yet that would render other things unlikely, he heard Peter and Magda chuckling somewhere in the maze. "Here!" "No, here!" they shouted to each other; Peter said, "Where's Amby?" Magda murmured. "Amb?" Peter called. In a pleased, friendly voice. He didn't reply. The truth was, his brother was a *happy-go-lucky youngster* who'd've been better off with a regular brother of his own, but who seldom complained of his lot and was generally cordial. Ambrose's throat ached; there aren't enough different ways to say that. He stood quietly while the two young people giggled and thumped through the glittering maze, hurrah'd their discovery of its exit, cried out in joyful alarm at what next beset them. Then he set his mouth and followed after, as he supposed, took a wrong turn, strayed into the pass *wherein he lingers yet.*

The action of conventional dramatic narrative may be represented by a diagram called Freitag's Triangle

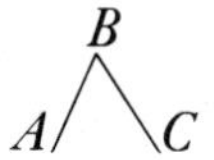

or more accurately by a variant of that diagram

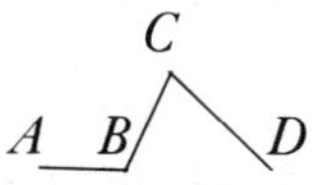

in which *AB* represents the exposition, *B* the introduction of conflict, *BC* the "rising action," complication, or development of the conflict, *C* the climax or turn of the action, *CD* the *dénouement* or resolution of the conflict.

While there is no reason to regard this pattern as an absolute necessity, like many other conventions it became conventional because great numbers of people over great numbers of years learned by trial and error that it was effective; one ought not to forsake it, therefore, unless one wishes to forsake as well the effect of drama or has clear cause to feel that deliberate violation of the "normal" pattern can better effect that effect. This can't go on much longer; it can go on forever. He died telling stories to himself in the dark; years later, when that vast unsuspected area of the funhouse came to light, the first expedition found his skeleton in one of its labyrinthine corridors and mistook it for part of the entertainment. He died of starvation telling himself stories in the dark; but unbeknownst unbeknownst to him, an assistant operator of the funhouse, happening to overhear him, crouched just behind the plyboard partition and wrote down his every word. The operator's daughter, an exquisite young woman with a figure unusually well developed for her age, crouched just behind the partition and transcribed his every word. Though she had never laid eyes on him, she recognized that here was one of Western Culture's truly great imaginations, the eloquence of whose suffering would be an inspiration to unnumbered. And her heart was torn between her love for the misfortunate young man (yes, she loved him, though she had never laid though she knew him only—but how well!—through his words, and the deep, calm voice in which he spoke them) between her love et cetera and her woman's intuition that only in suffering and isolation could he give voice et cetera. Lone dark dying. Quietly she kissed the rough plyboard, and a tear fell upon the page. Where she had written in shorthand *Where she had written in shorthand* Where she had written in shorthand *Where she* et cetera. A long time ago we should have passed the apex of Freitag's Triangle and made brief work of the *dénouement;* the plot doesn't rise by meaningful steps but winds upon itself, digresses, retreats, hesitates, sighs, collapses, expires. The climax of the story must be its protagonist's discovery of a way to get through the funhouse. But he has found none, may have ceased to search.

What relevance does the war have to the story? Should there be fireworks outside or not?

Ambrose wandered, languished, dozed. Now and then he fell into his habit of rehearsing to himself the unadventurous story of his life, narrated from the third-person point of view, from his earliest memory parenthesis of maple-leaves stirring in the summer breath of tidewater Maryland end of parenthesis to the present moment. Its principal events, on this telling, would appear to have been *A, B, C, and D.*

He imagined himself years hence, successful, married, at ease in the world, the trials of his adolescence far behind him. He has come to the seashore with his family for the holiday: how Ocean City has changed! But at one seldom at one ill-frequented end of the boardwalk a few derelict amusements survive from times gone by: the great carrousel from the turn of the century, with its monstrous griffins and mechanical concert-band; the roller-coaster rumored since 1916 to have been condemned; the mechanical shooting-gallery in which only the image of our enemies changed. His own son laughs with Fat May and wants to know what a funhouse is; Ambrose hugs the sturdy lad close and smiles around his pipestem at his wife.

The family's going home. Mother sits between Father and Uncle Karl, who teases him good-naturedly who chuckles over the fact that the comrade with whom he'd fought his way shoulder to shouder through the funhouse had turned out to be a colored boy—to their mutual discomfort, as they'd opened their souls. But such are the walls of custom, which even. Whose arm is where? How must it feel. He dreams of a funhouse vaster by far than any yet constructed; but by then they may be out of fashion, like steamboats and excursion-trains. Already quaint and seedy: the draperied ladies on the frieze of the carrousel are his father's father's mooncheeked dreams; if he thinks of it more he will vomit his apple-on-a-stick.

He wonders: will he become a regular person? Something has gone wrong; his vaccination didn't take; at the Boy-Scout initiation campfire he only pretended to be deeply moved, as he pretends to this hour that it is not so bad after all in the funhouse, and that he has a little limp. How long will it last? He envisions a truly astonishing funhouse, incredibly complex yet utterly controlled from a great central switchboard like the console of a pipeorgan. Nobody had enough imagination. He could design such a place himself, wiring and all, and he's only thirteen years old. He would be its operator: panel-lights would show what was up in every cranny of its cunning of its multifarious vastness; a switchflick would ease this fellow's way, complicate that's, to balance things out; if anyone seemed lost or frightened, all the operator had to do was.

He wishes he had never entered the funhouse. No: he wishes he had never been born. But he was. Then he wishes he were dead. But he's not. Therefore he will construct funhouses for others and be their secret operator—though he would rather be among the lovers for whom funhouses are designed.

Life-Story

I

Without discarding what he'd already written he began his story afresh in a somewhat different manner. Whereas his earlier version had opened a straight-forward documentary fashion and then degenerated or at least modulated intentionally into irrealism and dissonance he decided this time to tell his tale from start to finish in a conservative, "realistic," unself-conscious way. He being by vocation an author of novels and stories it was perhaps inevitable that one afternoon the possibility would occur to the writer of these lines that his own life might be a fiction, in which he was the leading or an accessory character. He happened at the time[1] to be in his study attempting to draft the opening pages of a new short story; its general idea had preoccupied him for some months along with other general ideas, but certain elements of the conceit, without which he could scarcely proceed, remained unclear. More specifically: narrative plots may be imagined as consisting of a "ground-situation" (Scheherazade desires not to die) focused and dramatized by a "vehicle-situation" (Scheherazade beguiles the King with endless stories), the several incidents of which have their final value in terms of their bearing upon the "ground-situation." In our author's case it was the "vehicle" that had vouchsafed itself, first as a germinal proposition in his commonplace book—D comes to suspect that the world is a novel, himself a fictional personage—subsequently as an articulated conceit explored over several pages of the workbook in which he elaborated more systematically his casual inspirations: since D is writing a fictional account of this conviction he has indisputably a fictional existence in his account, replicating what he suspects to be his own situation. Moreover E, hero of D's account, is said to be writing a similar account, and so the replication is in both ontological directions, et cetera. But the "ground-situation"—some state of affairs on D's part which would give dramatic resonance to his attempts to prove himself factual, assuming he made such attempts—obstinately withheld itself from his imagination. As is commonly the case the question reduced to one of stakes: what were to be the consequences of D's —and finally E's—disproving or verifying his suspicion, and why should a reader be interested?

What a dreary way to begin a story he said to himself upon reviewing his long introduction. Not only is there no "ground-situation," but the prose style is heavy and somewhat old-fashioned, like an English translation of Thomas Mann, and the so-called "vehicle" itself is at least questionable: self-conscious, vertiginously arch, fashionably solipsistic, unoriginal—in fact a convention of

[1] 9:00 A.M., Monday, June 20, 1966.

twentieth-century literature. Another story about a writer writing a story! Another regressus in infinitum! Who doesn't prefer art that at least overtly imitates something other than its own processes? That doesn't continually proclaim "Don't forget I'm an artifice!"? That takes for granted its mimetic nature instead of asserting it in order (not so slyly after all) to deny it, or vice-versa? Though his critics sympathetic and otherwise described his own work as avant-garde, in his heart of hearts he disliked literature of an experimental, self-despising, or overtly metaphysical character, like Samuel Beckett's, Marian Cutler's, Jorge Borges's. The logical fantasies of Lewis Carroll pleased him less than straight-forward tales of adventure, subtly sentimental romances, even densely circumstantial realisms like Tolstoy's. His favorite contemporary authors were John Updike, Georges Simenon, Nicole Riboud. He had no use for the theater of absurdity, for "black humor," for allegory in any form, for apocalypic preachments meretriciously tricked out in dramatic garb.

Neither had his wife and adolescent daughters, who for that matter preferred life to literature and read fiction when at all for entertainment. Their kind of story (his too, finally) would begin if not once upon a time at least with arresting circumstance, bold character, trenchant action. C flung away the whining manuscript and pushed impatiently through the french doors leading to the terrace from his oak-wainscoted study. Pausing at the stone balustrade to light his briar he remarked through a lavender cascade of wisteria that lithe-limbed Gloria, Gloria of timorous eye and militant breast, had once again chosen his boat-wharf as her basking-place.

By Jove he exclaimed to himself. It's particularly disquieting to suspect not only that one is a fictional character but that the fiction one's in—the fiction one is—is quite the sort one least prefers. His wife entered the study with coffee and an apple-pastry, set them at his elbow on his work table, returned to the living room. Ed' pelut' kondo nedode; nyoing; nyoing nyang. One manifestation of schizophrenia as everyone knows is the movement from reality toward fantasy, a progress which not infrequently takes the form of distorted and fragmented representation, abstract formalism, an increasing preoccupation, even obsession, with pattern and design for their own sakes—especially patterns of a baroque, enormously detailed character—to the (virtual) exclusion of representative "content." There are other manifestations. Ironically, in the case of graphic and plastic artists for example the work produced in the advanced stages of their affliction may be more powerful and interesting than the realistic productions of their earlier "sanity." Whether the artists themselves are gratified by this possibility is not reported.

B called upon a literary acquaintance, B——, summering with Mrs. B and children on the Eastern Shore of Maryland. "You say you lack a ground-situation. Has it occurred to you that that circumstance may be your ground-situation? What occurs to me is that if it is it isn't. And conversely. The case being thus, what's really wanting after all is a well-articulated vehicle, a foreground or upstage situation to dramatize the narrator's or author's grundlage. His what. To write merely C comes to suspect that the world is a novel, himself a fictional personage is but to introduce the vehicle; the next step must be to initiate its uphill motion by establishing and complicating some conflict. I would advise in addition the eschewal of overt and self-conscious discussion of the narrative process. I would advise in addition the eschewal of overt and self-conscious discussion of the narrative process. The via negativa and its positive counterpart are it is to be remembered poles after all of the same cell. Returning to his study.

If I'm going to be a fictional character G declared to himself I want to be in a rousing good yarn as they say, not some piece of avant-garde preciousness. I want passion and bravura action in my plot, heroes I can admire, heroines I can love, memorable speeches, colorful accessory characters, poetical language. It doesn't matter to me how naively linear the anecdote is; never mind modernity! How reactionary J appears to be. How will such nonsense sound thirty-six years from now?[2] As if. If he can only get K through his story I reflected grimly; if he can only retain his self-possession to the end of this sentence; not go mad; not destroy himself and/or others. Then what I wondered grimly. Another sentence fast, another story. Scheherazade my only love! All those nights you kept your secret from the King my rival, that after your defloration he was unnecessary, you'd have killed yourself in any case when your invention failed.

Why could he not begin his story afresh X wondered, for example with the words why could he not begin his story afresh et cetera? Y's wife came into the study as he was about to throw out the baby with the bathwater. "Not for an instant to throw out the baby while every instant discarding the bathwater is perhaps a chief task of civilized people at this hour of the world."[3] I used to tell B—— that without success. What makes you so sure it's not a film he's in or a theater-piece?

Because U responded while he certainly felt rather often that he was merely acting his own role or roles he had no idea who the actor was, whereas even the most Stanislavsky methodist would presumably if questioned closely recollect his offstage identity even onstage in mid-act. Moreover a great part of T's "drama," most of his life in fact, was non-visual, consisting entirely in introspection, which the visual dramatic media couldn't manage easily. He had for example mentioned to no one his growing conviction that he was a fictional character, and since he was not given to audible soliloquizing a "spectator" would take him for a cheerful, conventional fellow, little suspecting that et

[2] 10:00 A.M., Monday, June 20, 1966.

[3] 11:00 A.M. Monday, June 20, 1966.

cetera. It was of course imaginable that much goes on in the mind of King Oedipus in addition to his spoken sentiments; any number of interior dramas might be being played out in the actors' or characters' minds, dramas of which the audience is as unaware as are V's wife and friends of his growing conviction that he's a fictional character. But everything suggested that the medium of his life was prose fiction—moreover a fiction narrated from either the first-person or the third-person-omniscient point of view.

Why is it L wondered with mild disgust that both K and M for example choose to write such stuff when life is so sweet and painful and full of such a variety of people, places, situations, and activities other than self-conscious and after all rather blank introspection? Why is it N wondered et cetera that both M and O et cetera when the world is in such parlous explosive case? Why et cetera et cetera et cetera when the world, which was in the beginning, is now evidently nearing the end of its road? Am I being strung out in this ad libitum fashion I wondered merely to keep my author from the pistol? What sort of story is it whose drama lies always in the next frame out? If Sinbad sinks it's Scheherazade who drowns; whose neck one wonders is on her line?

II

Discarding what he'd already written as he could wish to discard the mumbling pages of his life he began his story afresh, resolved this time to eschew overt and self-conscious discussion of his narrative process and to recount instead in the straight-forwardest manner possible the several complications of his character's conviction that he was a character in a work of fiction, arranging them into dramatically ascending stages if he could for his readers' sake and leading them (the stages) to an exciting climax and denouement if he could.

He rather suspected that the medium and genre in which he worked—the only ones for which he felt any vocation—were moribund if not already dead. The idea pleased him. One of the successfullest men he knew was a blacksmith of the old school who et cetera. He meditated upon the grandest sailing-vessel ever built, the *France II,* constructed in Bordeaux in 1911 not only when but because the age of sail had passed. Other phenomena that consoled and inspired him were the great flying-boat *Hercules,* the zeppelin *Hindenburg,* the *Tsar Pushka* cannon, the then-record Dow-Jones industrial average of 381.17 attained on September 3, 1929.

He rather suspected that the society in which he persisted—the only one with which he felt any degree of identification—was moribund if not et cetera. He knew beyond any doubt that the body which he inhabited—the only one et cetera—was et cetera. The idea et cetera. He had for thirty-six years lacking a few hours been one of our dustmote's three billion tenants give or take five hundred million, and happening to be as well a white male citizen of the United

States of America he had thirty-six years plus a few hours more to cope with one way or another unless the actuarial tables were mistaken, not bloody likely, or his term was unexpectedly reduced.

Had he written for his readers' sake? The phrase implied a thitherto-unappreciated metaphysical dimension. Suspense. If his life was a fictional narrative it consisted of three terms—teller, tale, told—each dependent on the other two but not in the same ways. His author could as well tell some other character's tale or some other tale of the same character as the one being told as he himself could in his own character as author; his "reader" could as easily read some other story, would be well advised to; but his own "life" depended absolutely on a particular author's original persistence, thereafter upon some reader's. From this consideration any number of things followed, some less tiresome than others. No use appealing to his author, of whom he'd come to dislike even to think. The idea of his playing with his characters' and his own self-consciousness! He himself tended in that direction and despised the tendency. The idea of his or her smiling smugly to himself as the "words" flowed from his "pen" in which his protagonist's unhappy inner life was exposed! Ah he had mistaken the nature of his narrative; he had thought it very long, longer than Proust's, longer than any German's, longer than *The Thousand Nights and a Night* in ten quarto volumes. Moreover he'd thought it the most prolix and pedestrian *tranche-de-vie* realism, unredeemed by even the limited virtues of colorful squalor, solid specification, an engaging variety of scenes and characters—in a word a bore, of the sort he himself not only would not write but would not read either. Now he understood that his author might as probably resemble himself and the protagonist of his own story-in-progress. Like himself, like his character aforementioned, his author not impossibly deplored the obsolescence of humanism, the passing of *savoir-vivre,* et cetera; admired the outmoded values of fidelity, courage, tact, restraint, amiability, self-discipline, et cetera; preferred fictions in which were to be found stirring actions, characters to love as well as ditto to despise, speeches and deeds to affect us strongly, et cetera. He too might wish to make some final effort to put by his fictional character and achieve factuality or at least to figure in if not be hero of a more attractive fiction, but be caught like the writer of these lines in some more or less desperate tour de force. For him to attempt to come to an understanding with such an author were as futile as for one of his own creations to et cetera.

But the reader! Even if his author were his only reader as was he himself of his work-in-progress as of the sentence-in-progress and his protagonist of his, et cetera, his character as reader was not the same as his character as author, a fact which might be turned to account. What suspense.

As he prepared to explore this possibility one of his mistresses whereof he had none entered his brown study unannounced. "The passion of love," she announced, "which I regard as no less essential to a satisfying life than those values itemized above and which I infer from my presence here that you too esteem highly, does not in fact play in your life a role of sufficient importance to sustain my presence here. It plays in fact little role at all outside your imaginative and/or ary life. I tell you this not in a criticizing spirit, for I judge you to be as capable of the sentiment aforementioned as any other imagin[a-tive], deep-feeling man in good physical health more or less precisely in the middle of the road of our life. What hampers, even cripples you in this regard is your final preference, which I refrain from analyzing, for the sedater, more responsible pleasures of monogamous fidelity and the serener affections of domesticity, notwithstanding the fact that your enjoyment of these is correspondingly inhibited though not altogether spoiled by an essentially romantical, unstable, irresponsible, death-wishing fancy. V. S. Pritchett, English critic and author, will put the matter succinctly in a soon-to-be-written essay on Flaubert, whose work he'll say depicts the course of ardent longings and violent desires that rise from the horrible, the sensual, and the sadistic. They turn into the virginal and mystical, only to become numb by satiety. At this point pathological boredom leads to a final desire for death and nothingness—the Romantic syndrome. If, not to be unfair, we qualify somewhat the terms horrible and sadistic and understand satiety to include a large measure of vicariousness, this description undeniably applies to one aspect of yourself and your work; and while your ditto has other, even contrary aspects, the net fact is that you have elected familial responsibilities and rewards—indeed, straight-laced middle-classness in general—over the higher expanses of spirit and wastes of shame attendant upon a less regular, more glamorous style of life. So to elect is surely admirable for the layman, even essential if the social fabric, without which there can be no culture, is to be preserved. For the artist, however, and in particular the writer, whose traditional material has been the passions of men and women, the choice is fatal. You having made it I bid you goodnight probably forever."

Even as she left he reached for the sleeping pills cached conveniently in his writing desk and was restrained from their administration only by his being in the process of completing a sentence, which he cravenly strung out at some sacrifice of rhetorical effect upon realizing that he was et cetera. Moreover he added hastily he had not described the intruder for his readers' vicarious satiety: a lovely woman she was, whom he did not after all describe for his readers' et cetera inasmuch as her appearance and character were inconstant. Her interruption of his work inspired a few sentences about the extent to which his fiction inevitably made public his private life, though the trespasses in this particular were as nothing beside those of most of his profession. That is to say, while he did not draw his characters and situations directly from life nor permit his author-protagonist to do so, any moderately attentive reader of his oeuvre, his what, could infer for example that its author feared for example schizophrenia, impotence creative and sexual, suicide—in short living and dying. His fictions were preoccupied with these fears among their other, more serious preoccupations. Hot dog. As of the sentence-in-progress he was not in fact unmanageably schizophrenic, impotent in either respect, or dead by his own hand, but there was always the next sentence to worry about. But there was always the next sentence to worry about. In sum he concluded hastily such limited self-exposure did not constitute a misdemeanor, representing or mis as it did so small an aspect of his total self, negligible a portion of his total life —even which totalities were they made public would be found remarkable only for their being so unremarkable. Well shall he continue.

Bearing in mind that he had not developed what he'd mentioned earlier about turning to advantage his situation vis-à-vis his "reader" (in fact he deliberately now postponed his return to that subject, sensing that it might well constitute the climax of his story) he elaborated one or two ancillary questions, perfectly aware that he was trying, even exhausting, whatever patience might remain to whatever readers might remain to whoever elaborated yet another ancillary question. Was the novel of his life for example a *roman à clef.*? Of that genre he was as contemptuous as of the others aforementioned; but while in the introductory adverbial clause it seemed obvious to him that he didn't "stand for" anyone else, any more than he was an actor playing the role of himself, by the time he reached the main clause he had to admit that the question was unanswerable, since the "real" man to whom he'd correspond in a *roman à clef* would not be also in the *roman à clef* and the characters in such works were not themselves aware of their irritating correspondences.

Similarly unanswerable were such questions as when "his" story (so he regarded it for convenience and consolement though for all he knew he might be not the central character; it might be his wife's story, one of his daughter's, his imaginary mistress's, the man-who-once-cleaned-his-chimney's) began. Not impossibly at his birth or even generations earlier: a *Bildungsroman*, an *Erziehungsroman, a roman fleuve.*! More likely at the moment he became convinced of his fictional nature: that's where he'd have begun it, as he'd begun the piece currently under his pen. If so it followed that the years of his childhood and younger manhood weren't "real," he'd suspected as much, in the first-order sense, but a mere "background" consisting of a few well-placed expository insinuations, perhaps misleading, or inferences, perhaps unwarranted, from strategic hints in his present reflections. God so to speak spare his readers from heavyfooted force expositions of the sort that begin in the countryside near —— in May of the year —— it occurred to the novelist —— that his own life might be a —— , in which he was the leading or an accessory character. He happened at the time to be in the oak-wainscoted study of the old family summer residence; through a lavender cascade of hysteria he observed that his wife had once again chosen to be the subject of this clause, itself the direct object of his observation. A lovely woman she was, whom he did not describe in keeping with his policy against drawing characters from life as who should draw a condemnee to the gallows. Begging his pardon. Flinging his tiresome tale away he pushed impatiently through the French windows leading from his study to a sheer drop from the then-record high into a nearly fatal depression.

He clung onto his narrative depressed by the disproportion of its ratiocination to its dramatization, reflection to action. One had heard *Hamlet* criticized as a collection of soliloquies for which the implausible plot was a mere excuse; witnessed Italian operas whose dramatic portions were no more than interstitial relief and arbitrary continuity between the arias. If it was true that he didn't take his "real" life seriously enough even when it had him by the throat, the fact didn't lead him to consider whether the fact was a cause or a consequence of his tale's tedium or both.

Concluding these reflections he concluded these reflections: that there was at this advancèd page still apparently no ground-situation suggested that his story was dramatically meaningless. If one regarded the absence and his vain endeavors to supply the defect, as itself a sort of ground-situation, did his life-story thereby take on a kind of meaning? A "dramatic" sort he supposed, though of so sophistical a character as more likely to annoy than to engage.

III

The reader! You, dogged, uninsultable, print-oriented bastard, it's you I'm addressing, who else, from inside this monstrous fiction. You've read me this far then? Even this far? For what discreditable motive? How is it you don't go to a movie, watch TV, stare at a wall, play tennis with a friend, make amorous advances to the person who comes to your mind when I speak of amorous advances? Can nothing surfeit, saturate you, turn you off? Where's your shame?

Having let go this barrage of rhetorical or at least unanswered questions and observing himself nevertheless in midst of yet another sentence he concluded and caused the "hero" of his story to conclude that one or more of three things must be true: 1) his author was his sole and indefatigable reader; 2) he was in a sense his own author, telling his story to himself, in which case in which case; and/or 3) his reader was not only tireless and shameless but sadistic, masochistic if he was himself.

For why do you suppose—you! you!—he's gone on so, so relentlessly refusing to entertain you as he might have at a less desperate than this hour of the world[4] with felicitous language, exciting situation, unforgettable character and image? Why has he as it were ruthlessly set about not to win you over but to turn you away? Because your own author bless and damn you his life is in

[4] 11:00 P.M.; Monday, June 20, 1966.

your hands! He writes and reads himself; don't you think he knows who gives his creatures their lives and deaths? Do they exist except as he or others read their words? Age except we turn their pages? And can he die until you have no more of him? Time was obviously when his author could have turned the trick; his pen had once to left-to-right it through these words as does your kindless eye and might have ceased at any one. This. This. And did not as you see but went on like an Oriental torturemaster to the end.

But you needn't! He exclaimed to you. In vain. Had he petitioned you instead to read slowly in the happy parts, what happy parts, swiftly in the painful no doubt you'd have done the contrary or cut him off entirely. But as he longs to die and can't without your help you force him on, force him on. Will you deny you've read this sentence? This? To get away with murder doesn't appeal to you, is that it? As if your hands weren't inky with other dyings! As if he'd know you'd killed him! Come on. He dares you.

In vain. You haven't: the burden of his knowledge. That he continues means that he continues, a fortiori you too. Suicide's impossible: he can't kill himself without your help. Those petitions aforementioned, even his silly plea for death—don't you think he understands their sophistry, having authored their like for the wretches he's authored? Read him fast or slow, intermittently, continuously, repeatedly, backward, not at all, he won't know it; he only guesses someone's reading or composing sentences such as this one; the net effect is that there's a net effect, of continuity and an apparently consistent flow of time, though his pages do seem to pass more swiftly as they near his end.

To what conclusion will he come? He'd been about to append to his own tale inasmuch as the old analogy between Author and God, novel and world, can no longer be employed unless deliberately as a false analogy, certain things follow: 1) fiction must acknowledge its fictitiousness and metaphoric invalidity or 2) choose to ignore the question or deny its relevance or 3) establish some other, acceptable relation between itself, its author, its reader. Just as he finished doing so however his real wife and imaginary mistresses entered his study; "It's a little past midnight" she announced with a smile; "do you know what that means?"

Though she'd come into his story unannounced at a critical moment he did not describe her, for even as he recollected that he'd seen his first light just thirty-six years before the night incumbent he saw his last: that he could not after all be a character in a work of fiction inasmuch as such a fiction would be of an entirely different character from what he thought of as fiction. Fiction consisted of such monuments of the imagination as Cutler's *Morganfield*, Riboud's *Tales Within Tales*, his own creations; fact of such as for example read those fictions. More, he could demonstrate by syllogism that the story of his life was a work of fact: though assaults upon the boundary between life and art, reality and dream, were undeniably a staple of his own and his century's literature as they'd been of Shakespeare's and Cervante's, yet it was a fact that in the corpus of fiction as far as he knew no fictional character had become convinced as had he that he was a character in a work of fiction. This being the case and he having in fact become thus convinced it followed that his conviction was false. "Happy birthday," said his wife et cetera, kissing him et cetera to obstruct his view of the end of the sentence he was nearing the end of, playfully refusing to be nay-said so that in fact he did at last as did his fictional character end his ending story endless by interruption cap his pen.

TONI MORRISON

b. 1931

Morrison made her entrance into the literary world in 1970 with the publication of her novel *The Bluest Eye,* a beautifully crafted story of her hometown of Lorain, Ohio. Her father a laborer, she felt the full impact of the Depression, and expressed it in its particularity.

Like Katherine Anne Porter she never meant to be a writer, and even now does it part-time while being a senior editor at Random House. The profession found her, and gives her such satisfaction when she "gets it right" that it's unlikely that the two will ever be parted. Morrison is an extremely busy person: in addition to her position as a senior editor, she is the mother of two teenaged boys, and teaches creative writing at Yale and Breadloaf. She loves language, and has the artist's respect for the integrity of her characters, who are usually strong people who live their lives (not uncomically) with iron determination to be themselves. Always at stake in a Morrison novel is a question of maintaining one's identity, because if it is not discovered and projected, the harsh realities of economics and social stereotypes will sweep it away.

Although Morrison's first two novels move beautifully as groups of episodes, they do constitute portraits of an historical time and connected characters; in that sense, they are novels rather than groups of independent short stories. But unlike her last novel, *Song of Solomon* (1977), the earlier ones rely very little on plot to bind them together. They are more like Joyce's collection of short stories, *Dubliners,* or Hemingway's *In Our Time,* fictions that circle around particular events and locales rather than tell a consecutive story. It is this quality that prompted the editor of this anthology to print "1919" apart from its context in the novel. That it means more as part of the novel is certainly true, but so do Joyce's and Hemingway's in the context of their collections.

1919

Except for World War II, nothing ever interfered with the celebration of National Suicide Day. It had taken place every January third since 1920, although Shadrack, its founder, was for many years the only celebrant. Blasted and permanently astonished by the events of 1917, he had returned to Medallion handsome but ravaged, and even the most fastidious people in the town sometimes caught themselves dreaming of what he must have been like a few years back before he went off to war. A young man of hardly twenty, his head full of nothing and his mouth recalling the taste of lipstick, Shadrack had found himself in December, 1917, running with his comrades across a field in France. It was his first encounter with the enemy and he didn't know whether his company was running toward them or away. For several days they had been marching, keeping close to a stream that was frozen at its edges. At one point they crossed it, and no sooner had he stepped foot on the other side than the day was adangle with shouts and explosions. Shellfire was all around him, and though he knew that this was something called *it,* he could not muster up the proper feeling—the feeling that would accommodate *it.* He expected to be terrified or exhilarated—to feel *something* very strong. In fact, he felt only the bite of a nail in his boot, which pierced the ball of his foot whenever he came down on it. The day was cold enough to make his breath visible, and he wondered for a moment at the purity and whiteness of his own breath among the dirty, gray explosions surrounding him. He ran, bayonet fixed, deep in the great sweep of men flying across this field. Wincing at the pain in his foot, he turned his head a little to the right and saw the face of a soldier near him fly off. Before he could register shock, the rest of the soldier's head disappeared under the inverted soup bowl of his helmet. But stubbornly, taking no direction from the brain, the body of the headless soldier ran on, with energy and grace, ignoring altogether the drip and slide of brain tissue down its back.

When Shadrack opened his eyes he was propped up in a small bed. Before him on a tray was a large tin plate divided into three triangles. In one triangle was rice, in another meat, and in the third stewed tomatoes. A small round depression held a cup of whitish liquid. Shadrack stared at the soft colors that filled these triangles: the lumpy whiteness of rice, the quivering blood tomatoes, the grayish-brown meat. All their repugnance was contained in the neat balance of the triangles—a balance that soothed him, transferred some of its equilibrium to him. Thus reassured that the white, the red and the brown would stay where they were—would not explode or burst forth from their restricted zones—he suddenly felt hungry and looked around for his hands. His glance was cautious at first, for he had to be very careful—anything could be anywhere.

Then he noticed two lumps beneath the beige blanket on either side of his hips. With extreme care he lifted one arm and was relieved to find his hand attached to his wrist. He tried the other and found it also. Slowly he directed one hand toward the cup and, just as he was about to spread his fingers, they began to grow in higgledy-piggledy fashion like Jack's beanstalk all over the tray and the bed. With a shriek he closed his eyes and thrust his huge growing hands under the covers. Once out of sight they seemed to shrink back to their normal size. But the yell had brought a male nurse.

"Private? We're not going to have any trouble today, are we? Are we, Private?"

Shadrack looked up at a balding man dressed in a green-cotton jacket and trousers. His hair was parted low on the right side so that some twenty or thirty yellow hairs could discreetly cover the nakedness of his head.

"Come on. Pick up that spoon. Pick it up, Private. Nobody is going to feed you forever."

Sweat slid from Shadrack's armpits down his sides. He could not bear to see his hands grow again and he was frightened of the voice in the apple-green suit.

"Pick it up, I said. There's no point to this . . ." The nurse reached under the cover for Shadrack's wrist to pull out the monstrous hand. Shadrack jerked it back and overturned the tray. In panic he raised himself to his knees and tried to fling off and away his terrible fingers, but succeeded only in knocking the nurse into the next bed.

When they bound Shadrack into a straitjacket, he was both relieved and grateful, for his hands were at last hidden and confined to whatever size they had attained.

Laced and silent in his small bed, he tried to tie the loose cords in his mind. He wanted desperately to see his own face and connect it with the word "private"—the word the nurse (and the others who helped bind him) had called him. "Private" he thought was something secret, and he wondered why they looked at him and called him a secret. Still, if his hands behaved as they had done, what might he expect from his face? The fear and longing were too much for him, so he began to think of other things. That is, he let his mind slip into whatever cave mouths of memory it chose.

He saw a window that looked out on a river which he knew was full of fish. Someone was speaking softly just outside the door . . .

Shadrack's earlier violence had coincided with a memorandum from the hospital executive staff in reference to the distribution of patients in high-risk areas. There was clearly a demand for space. The priority or the violence earned Shadrack his release, $217 in cash, a full suit of clothes and copies of very official-looking papers.

When he stepped out of the hospital door the grounds overwhelmed him: the cropped shrubbery, the edged lawns, the undeviating walks. Shadrack looked at the cement stretches: each one leading clearheadedly to some presumably desirable destination. There were no fences, no warnings, no obstacles at all between concrete and green grass, so one could easily ignore the tidy sweep of stone and cut out in another direction—a direction of one's own.

Shadrack stood at the foot of the hospital steps watching the heads of trees tossing ruefully but harmlessly, since their trunks were rooted too deeply in the earth to threaten him. Only the walks made him uneasy. He shifted his weight, wondering how he could get to the gate without stepping on the concrete. While plotting his course—where he would have to leap, where to skirt a clump of bushes—a loud guffaw startled him. Two men were going up the steps. Then he noticed that there were many people about, and that he was just now seeing them, or else they had just materialized. They were thin slips, like paper dolls floating down the walks. Some were seated in chairs with wheels, propelled by other paper figures from behind. All seemed to be smoking, and their arms and legs curved in the breeze. A good high wind would pull them up and away and they would land perhaps among the tops of the trees.

Shadrack took the plunge. Four steps and he was on the grass heading for the gate. He kept his head down to avoid seeing the paper people swerving and bending here and there, and he lost his way. When he looked up, he was standing by a low red building separated from the main building by a covered walkway. From somewhere came a sweetish smell which reminded him of something painful. He looked around for the gate and saw that he had gone directly away from it in his complicated journey over the grass. Just to the left of the low building was a graveled driveway that appeared to lead outside the grounds. He trotted quickly to it and left, at last, a haven of more than a year, only eight days of which he fully recollected.

Once on the road, he headed west. The long stay in the hospital had left him weak—too weak to walk steadily on the gravel shoulders of the road. He shuffled, grew dizzy, stopped for breath, started again, stumbling and sweating but refusing to wipe his temples, still afraid to look at his hands. Passengers in dark, square cars shuttered their eyes at what they took to be a drunken man.

The sun was already directly over his head when he came to a town. A few blocks of shaded streets and he was already at its heart—a pretty, quietly regulated downtown.

Exhausted, his feet clotted with pain, he sat down at the curbside to take off his shoes. He closed his eyes to avoid seeing his hands and fumbled with the laces of the heavy high-topped shoes. The nurse had tied them into a double knot, the way one does for children, and Shadrack, long unaccustomed to the manipulation of intricate things, could not get them loose. Uncoordinated, his fingernails tore away at the knots. He fought a rising hysteria that was not merely anxiety to free his aching feet; his very life depended on the release of the knots. Suddenly without raising his eyelids, he began to cry. Twenty-two years old, weak, hot, frightened, not daring to acknowledge the fact that he didn't even know who or what he was . . . with no past, no language, no tribe, no source, no address book, no comb, no pencil, no clock, no pocket handkerchief, no rug, no bed, no can opener, no faded postcard, no soap, no key, no tobacco pouch, no soiled underwear and nothing nothing nothing to do . . . he was sure of one thing only: the unchecked monstrosity of his hands. He cried soundlessly at the curbside of a small Midwestern town wondering where the window was, and the river, and the soft voices just outside the door . . .

Through his tears he saw the fingers joining the laces, tentatively at first, then rapidly. The four fingers of each hand fused into the fabric, knotted themselves and zig-zagged in and out of the tiny eyeholes.

By the time the police drove up, Shadrack was suffering from a blinding headache, which was not abated by the comfort he felt when the policemen pulled his hands away from what he thought was a permanent entanglement with his shoelaces. They took him to jail, booked him for vagrancy and intoxication, and locked him in a cell. Lying on a cot, Shadrack could only stare helplessly at the wall, so paralyzing was the pain in his head. He lay in this agony for a long while and then realized he was staring at the painted-over letters of a command to fuck himself. He studied the phrase as the pain in his head subsided.

Like moonlight stealing under a window shade an idea insinuated itself: his earlier desire to see his own face. He looked for a mirror; there was none. Finally, keeping his hands carefully behind his back he made his way to the toilet bowl and peeped in. The water was unevenly lit by the sun so he could make nothing out. Returning to his cot he took the blanket and covered his head, rendering the water dark enough to see his reflection. There in the toilet water he saw a grave black face. A black so definite, so unequivocal, it astonished him. He had been harboring a skittish apprehension that he was not real —that he didn't exist at all. But when the blackness greeted him with its indisputable presence, he wanted nothing more. In his joy he took the risk of letting one edge of the blanket drop and glanced at his hands. They were still. Courteously still.

Shadrack rose and returned to the cot, where he fell into the first sleep of his new life. A sleep deeper than the hospital drugs; deeper than the pits of plums, steadier than the condor's wing; more tranquil than the curve of eggs.

The sheriff looked through the bars at the young man with the matted hair. He had read through his prisoner's papers and hailed a farmer. When Shadrack awoke, the sheriff handed him back his papers and escorted him to the back of a wagon. Shadrack got in and in less than three hours he was back in Medallion, for he had been only twenty-two miles from his window, his river, and his soft voices just outside the door.

In the back of the wagon, supported by sacks of squash and hills of pumpkins, Shadrack began a struggle that was to last for twelve days, a struggle to order and focus experience. It had to do with making a place for fear as a way of controlling it. He knew the smell of death and was terrified of it, for he could not anticipate it. It was not death or dying that frightened him, but the unexpectedness of both. In sorting it all out, he hit on the notion that if one day a year were devoted to it, everybody could get it out of the way and the rest of the year would be safe and free. In this manner he instituted National Suicide Day.

On the third day of the new year, he walked through the Bottom down Carpenter's Road with a cowbell and a hangman's rope calling the people together. Telling them that this was their only chance to kill themselves or each other.

At first the people in the town were frightened; they knew Shadrack was crazy but that did not mean that he didn't have any sense or, even more important, that he had no power. His eyes were so wild, his hair so long and matted, his voice was so full of authority and thunder that he caused panic on the first, or Charter, National Suicide Day in 1920. The next one, in 1921, was less frightening but still worrisome. The people had seen him a year now in between. He lived in a shack on the riverbank that had once belonged to his grandfather long time dead. On Tuesday and Friday he sold the fish he had caught that morning, the rest of the week he was drunk, loud, obscene, funny and outrageous. But he never touched anybody, never fought, never caressed. Once the people understood the boundaries and nature of his madness, they could fit him, so to speak, into the scheme of things.

Then, on subsequent National Suicide Days, the grown people looked out from behind curtains as he rang his bell; a few stragglers increased their speed, and little children screamed and ran. The tetter heads tried goading him (although he was only four or five years older then they) but not for long, for his curses were stingingly personal.

As time went along, the people took less notice of these January thirds, or rather they thought they did, thought they had no attitudes or feelings one way or another about Shadrack's annual solitary parade. In fact they had simply stopped remarking on the holiday because they had absorbed it into their thoughts, into their language, into their lives.

Someone said to a friend, "You sure was a long time delivering that baby. How long was you in labor?"

And the friend answered, " 'Bout three days. The pains started on Suicide Day and kept up till the following Sunday. All my boys is Sunday boys."

Some lover said to his bride-to-be, "Let's do it after New Years, 'stead of before. I get paid New Year's Eve."

And his sweetheart answered, "OK, but make sure it ain't on Suicide Day. I ain't 'bout to be listening to no cowbells whilst the weddin's going on."

Somebody's grandmother said her hens always started a laying of double yolks right after Suicide Day.

The Reverend Deal took it up, saying the same folks who had sense enough to avoid Shadrack's call were the ones who insisted on drinking themselves to death or womanizing themselves to death. "May's well go on with Shad and save the Lamb the trouble of redemption."

Easily, quietly, Suicide Day became a part of the fabric of life up in the Bottom of Medallion, Ohio.

JOHN UPDIKE

b. 1932

Updike was born and grew up in a small town in Pennsylvania-Dutch country. Undoubtedly it was there that he developed the sensibility that characterizes and forms his fiction: that of a sensitive small-town American boy, very much down-to-earth, curious, observant, and accepting of different life styles. Updike went to Harvard, where he had ample opportunity to employ these qualities in reacting to an urbane, intellectual environment in which (in the early fifties anyway) everyone seemed busy copying, creating, or maintaining any of a multitude of different life styles. The seemingly assured Old Boston or Main Line types, the would-be executives demonstrating efficiency and open-mindedness, the esthetes, the gifted scientists more or less untouched by the society around them—Updike observed them all, without committing himself very deeply to any. He soon knew that he wanted to be a writer, probably a poet; but he had impressive talents in art too, and after leaving Harvard he won a place at the Ruskin School of Drawing in Oxford. When he returned from England he decided to give himself five years to make it as a writer; but after only a few months it was clear that he was headed for a career that most undergraduate writers dare not let themselves dream of. At twenty-four he began publishing in *The New Yorker,* and soon he was one of that magazine's most valued writers. His first novel, *The Poorhouse Fair* (1959), was marked by a highly developed, "poetic" prose style and a warm appreciation of the small-town values that had been part of his boyhood and adolescence. Many other novels have followed, plus collections of his short stories from *The New Yorker* and a few volumes of verse.

The characteristic note produced by the intersection of Updike's basic sensibility with one or more sophisticated ways of life is one of gentle, ironic self-awareness. Updike is sometimes attacked as precious, because of his evident love of the sound and arrangement of language, and as too narrow in the spectrum of experience with which he is willing to deal; but no one in contemporary fiction is better at representing the special feelings of guilt and quasi-involvement of those who see clearly but are not themselves committed.

A & P

In walks these three girls in nothing but bathing suits. I'm in the third checkout slot, with my back to the door, so I don't see them until they're over by the bread. The one that caught my eye first was the one in the plaid green two-piece. She was a chunky kid, with a good tan and a sweet broad soft-looking can with those two crescents of white just under it, where the sun never seems to hit, at the top of the backs of her legs. I stood there with my hand on a box of HiHo crackers trying to remember if I rang it up or not. I ring it up again and the customer starts giving me hell. She's one of these cash-register-watchers, a witch about fifty with rouge on her cheekbones and no eyebrows, and I know it made her day to trip me up. She'd been watching cash registers for fifty years and probably never seen a mistake before.

By the time I got her feathers smoothed and her goodies into a bag—she gives me a little snort in passing, if she'd been born at the right time they would have burned her over in Salem—by the time I get her on her way the girls had circled around the bread and were coming back, without a pushcart, back my way along the counters, in the aisle between the checkouts and the Special bins. They didn't even have shoes on. There was this chunky one, with the two-piece —it was bright green and the seams on the bra were still sharp and her belly was still pretty pale so I guessed she just got it (the suit)—there was this one, with one of those chubby berry-faces, the lips all bunched together under her nose, this one, and a tall one, with black hair that hadn't quite frizzed right, and one of these sunburns right across the eyes, and a chin that was too long—you know, the kind of girl other girls think is very "striking" and "attractive" but never quite makes it, as they very well know, which is why they like her so much—and then the third one, that wasn't quite so tall. She was the queen. She kind of led them, the other two peeking around and making their shoulders round. She didn't look around, not this queen, she just walked straight on slowly, on these long white prima-donna legs. She came down a little hard on her heels, as if she didn't walk in her bare feet that much, putting down her heels and then letting the weight move along to her toes as if she was testing the floor with every step, putting a little deliberate extra action into it. You never know for sure how girls' minds work (do you really think it's a mind in there or just a little buzz like a bee in a glass jar?) but you got the idea she had talked the other two into coming in here with her, and now she was showing them how to do it, walk slow and hold yourself straight.

She had on a kind of dirty-pink—beige maybe, I don't know—bathing suit with a little nubble all over it and, what got me, the straps were down. They were off her shoulders looped loose around the cool tops of her arms, and I guess as a result the suit had slipped a little on her, so all around the top of the cloth there was this shining rim. If it hadn't been there you wouldn't have known there could have been anything whiter than those shoulders. With the straps pushed off, there was nothing between the top of the suit and the top of her head except just *her*, this clean bare plane of the top of her chest down from the shoulder bones like a dented sheet of metal tilted in the light. I mean, it was more than pretty.

She had sort of oaky hair that the sun and salt had bleached, done up in a bun that was unravelling, and a kind of prim face. Walking into the A & P with your straps down, I suppose it's the only kind of face you *can* have. She held her head so high her neck, coming up out of those white shoulders, looked kind of stretched, but I didn't mind. The longer her neck was, the more of her there was.

She must have felt in the corner of her eye me and over my shoulder Stokesie in the second slot watching, but she didn't tip. Not this queen. She kept her eyes moving across the racks, and stopped, and turned so slow it made my stomach rub the inside of my apron, and buzzed to the other two, who kind of huddled against her for relief, and they all three of them went up the cat-and-dog-food-breakfast-cereal-macaroni-rice-raisins-seasonings-spreads-spaghetti-soft drinks-crackers-and-cookies aisle. From the third slot I look straight up this aisle to the meat counter, and I watched them all the way. The fat one with the tan sort of fumbled with the cookies, but on second thought she put the packages back. The sheep pushing their carts down the aisle—the girls were walking against the usual traffic (not that we have one-way signs or anything)—were pretty hilarious. You could see them, when Queenie's white shoulders dawned on them, kind of jerk, or hop, or hiccup, but their eyes snapped back to their own baskets and on they pushed. I bet you could set off dynamite in an A & P and the people would by and large keep reaching and checking oatmeal off their lists and muttering "Let me see, there was a third thing, began with A, asparagus, no, ah, yes, applesauce!" or whatever it is they do mutter. But there was no doubt, this jiggled them. A few houseslaves in pin curlers even looked around after pushing their carts past to make sure what they had seen was correct.

You know, it's one thing to have a girl in a bathing suit down on the beach, where what with the glare nobody can look at each other much anyway, and another thing in the cool of the A & P, under the fluorescent lights, against all those stacked packages, with her feet paddling along naked over our checkerboard green-and-cream rubber-tile floor.

"Oh Daddy," Stokesie said beside me. "I feel so faint."

"Darling," I said. "Hold me tight." Stokesie's married, with two babies chalked up on his fuselage already, but as far as I can tell that's the only difference. He's twenty-two, and I was nineteen this April.

"Is it done?" he asks, the responsible married man finding his voice. I forgot to say he thinks he's going to be manager some sunny day, maybe in 1990 when it's called the Great Alexandrov and Petrooshki Tea Company or something.

What he meant was, our town is five miles from a beach, with a big summer colony out on the Point, but we're right in the middle of town, and the women generally put on a shirt or shorts or something before they get out of the car into the street. And anyway these are usually women with six children and varicose veins mapping their legs and nobody, including them, could care less. As I say, we're right in the middle of town, and if you stand at our front doors you can see two banks and the Congregational church and the newspaper store and three real-estate offices and about twenty-seven old freeloaders tearing up Central Street because the sewer broke again. It's not as if we're on the Cape; we're north of Boston and there's people in this town haven't seen the ocean for twenty years.

The girls had reached the meat counter and were asking McMahon something. He pointed, they pointed, and they shuffled out of sight behind a pyramid of Diet Delight peaches. All that was left for us to see was old McMahon patting his mouth and looking after them sizing up their joints. Poor kids, I began to feel sorry for them, they couldn't help it.

. . .

Now here comes the sad part of the story, at least my family says it's sad, but I don't think it's sad myself. The store's pretty empty, it being Thursday afternoon, so there was nothing much to do except lean on the register and wait for the girls to show up again. The whole store was like a pinball machine and I didn't know which tunnel they'd come out of. After a while they come around out of the far aisle, around the light bulbs, records at discount of the Caribbean Six or Tony Martin Sings or some such gunk you wonder they waste the wax on, sixpacks of candy bars, and plastic toys done up in cellophane that fall apart when a kid looks at them anyway. Around they come. Queenie still leading the way, and holding a little gray jar in her hand. Slots Three through Seven are unmanned and I could see her wondering between Stokes and me, but Stokesie with his usual luck draws an old party in baggy gray pants who stumbles up with four giant cans of pineapple juice (what do these bums *do* with all that pineapple juice? I've often asked myself) so the girls come to me. Queenie puts down the jar and I take it into my fingers icy cold. Kingfish Fancy Herring Snacks in Pure Sour Cream: 49¢. Now her hands are empty, not a ring or a bracelet, bare as God made them, and I wonder where the money's coming from. Still with that prim look she lifts a folded dollar bill out of the hollow at the center of her nubbled pink top. The jar went heavy in my hand. Really, I thought that was so cute.

Then everybody's luck begins to run out. Lengel comes in from haggling with a truck full of cabbages on the lot and is about to scuttle into that door marked MANAGER behind which he hides all day when the girls touch his eye. Lengel's pretty dreary, teaches Sunday school and the rest, but he doesn't miss that much. He comes over and says, "Girls, this isn't the beach."

Queenie blushes, though maybe it's just a brush of sunburn I was noticing for the first time, now that she was so close. "My mother asked me to pick up a jar of herring snacks." Her voice kind of startled me, the way voices do when you see the people first, coming out so flat and dumb yet kind of tony, too, the way it ticked over "pick up" and "snacks." All of a sudden I slid right down her voice into her living room. Her father and the other men were standing around in ice-cream coats and bow ties and the women were in sandals picking up herring snacks on toothpicks off a big plate and they were all holding drinks the color of water with olives and sprigs of mint in them. When my parents have somebody over they get lemonade and if it's a real racy affair Schlitz in tall glasses with "They'll Do It Every Time" cartoons stencilled on.

"That's all right," Lengel said. "But this isn't the beach." His repeating this struck me as funny, as if it had just occurred to him, and he had been thinking all these years the A & P was a great big dune and he was the head lifeguard. He didn't like my smiling—as I say he doesn't miss much—but he concentrates on giving the girls that sad Sunday-school-superintendent stare.

Queenie's blush is no sunburn now, and the plump one in plaid, that I liked better from the back—a really sweet can—pipes up, "We weren't doing any shopping. We just came in for the one thing."

"That makes no difference," Lengel tells her, and I could see from the way his eyes went that he hadn't noticed she was wearing a two-piece before. "We want you decently dressed when you come in here."

"We *are* decent," Queenie says suddenly, her lower lip pushing, getting sore now that she remembers her place, a place from which the crowd that runs the A & P must look pretty crummy. Fancy Herring Snacks flashed in her very blue eyes.

"Girls, I don't want to argue with you. After this come in here with your shoulders covered. It's our policy." He turns his back. That's policy for you. Policy is what the kingpins want. What the others want is juvenile delinquency.

All this while, the customers had been showing up with their carts but, you know, sheep, seeing a scene, they had all bunched up on Stokesie, who shook open a paper bag as gently as peeling a peach, not wanting to miss a word. I could feel in the silence everybody getting nervous, most of all Lengel, who asks me, "Sammy, have you rung up their purchases?"

I thought and said "No" but it wasn't about that I was thinking. I go through the punches, 4, 9, GROC, TOT—it's more complicated than you think, and after you do it often enough, it begins to make a little song, that you hear words to, in my case "Hello (*bing*) there, you (*gung*) hap-py *pee*-pul (*splat*)!"

—the *splat* being the drawer flying out. I uncrease the bill, tenderly as you may imagine, it just having come from between the two smoothest scoops of vanilla I had ever known were there, and pass a half and a penny into her narrow pink palm, and nestle the herrings in a bag and twist its neck and hand it over, all the time thinking.

The girls, and who'd blame them, are in a hurry to get out, so I say "I quit" to Lengel quick enough for them to hear, hoping they'll stop and watch me, their unsuspected hero. They keep right on going, into the electric eye; the door flies open and they flicker across the lot to their car, Queenie and Plaid and Big Tall Goony-Goony (not that as raw material she was so bad), leaving me with Lengel and a kink in his eyebrow.

"Did you say something, Sammy?"

"I said I quit."

"I thought you did."

"You didn't have to embarrass them."

"It was they who were embarrassing us."

I started to say something that came out "Fiddle-de-doo." It's a saying of my grandmother's, and I know she would have been pleased.

"I don't think you know what you're saying," Lengel said.

"I know you don't," I said. "But I do." I pull the bow at the back of my apron and start shrugging it off my shoulders. A couple customers that had been heading for my slot begin to knock against each other, like scared pigs in a chute.

Lengel sighs and begins to look very patient and old and gray. He's been a friend of my parents for years. "Sammy, you don't want to do this to your Mom and Dad," he tells me. It's true, I don't. But it seems to me that once you begin a gesture it's fatal not to go through with it. I fold the apron, "Sammy" stitched in red on the pocket, and put it on the counter, and drop the bow tie on top of it. The bow tie is theirs, if you've ever wondered. "You'll feel this for the rest of your life," Lengel says, and I know that's true, too, but remembering how he made that pretty girl blush makes me so scrunchy inside I punch the No Sale tab and the machine whirs "pee-pul" and the drawer splats out. One advantage to this scene taking place in summer, I can follow this up with a clean exit, there's no fumbling around getting your coat and galoshes, I just saunter into the electric eye in my white shirt that my mother ironed the night before, and the door heaves itself open, and outside the sunshine is skating around on the asphalt.

I look around for my girls, but they're gone, of course. There wasn't anybody but some young married screaming with her children about some candy they didn't get by the door of a powder-blue Falcon station wagon. Looking back in the big windows, over the bags of peat moss and aluminum lawn furniture stacked on the pavement, I could see Lengel in my place in the slot, checking the sheep through. His face was dark gray and his back stiff, as if he'd just had an injection of iron, and my stomach kind of fell as I felt how hard the world was going to be to me hereafter.

Tomorrow and Tomorrow and So Forth

Whirling, talking, 11D began to enter Room 109. From the quality of their excitement Mark Prosser guessed it would rain. He had been teaching high school for three years, yet his students still impressed him; they were such sensitive animals. They reacted so infallibly to merely barometric pressure.

In the doorway, Brute Young paused while little Barry Snyder giggled at his elbow. Barry's stagy laugh rose and fell, dipping down toward some vile secret that had to be tasted and retasted, then soaring artificially to proclaim that he, little Barry, shared such a secret with the school's fullback. Being Brute's stooge was precious to Barry. The fullback paid no attention to him; he twisted his neck to stare at something not yet coming through the door. He yielded heavily to the procession pressing him forward.

Right under Prosser's eyes, like a murder suddenly appearing in an annalistic frieze of kings and queens, someone stabbed a girl in the back with a pencil. She ignored the assault saucily. Another hand yanked out Geoffrey Langer's shirt-tail. Geoffrey, a bright student, was uncertain whether to laugh it off or defend himself with anger, and made a weak, half-turning gesture of compromise, wearing an expression of distant arrogance that Prosser instantly coördinated with feelings of fear he used to have. All along the line, in the glitter of key chains and the acute angles of turned-back shirt cuffs, an electricity was expressed which simple weather couldn't generate.

Mark wondered if today Gloria Angstrom wore that sweater, an ember-pink angora, with very brief sleeves. The virtual sleevelessness was the disturbing factor: the exposure of those two serene arms to the air, white as thighs against the delicate wool.

His guess was correct. A vivid pink patch flashed through the jiggle of arms and shoulders as the final knot of youngsters entered the room.

"Take your seats," Mr. Prosser said. "Come on. Let's go."

Most obeyed, but Peter Forrester, who had been at the center of the group around Gloria, still lingered in the doorway with her, finishing some story, apparently determined to make her laugh or gasp. When she did gasp, he tossed his head with satisfaction. His orange hair bobbed. Redheads are all alike, Mark thought, with their white eyelashes and pale puffy faces and thyroid eyes, their mouths always twisted with preposterous self-confidence. Bluffers, the whole bunch.

When Gloria, moving in a considered, stately way, had taken her seat, and Peter had swerved into his, Mr. Prosser said, "Peter Forrester."

"Yes?" Peter rose, scrabbling through his book for the right place.

"Kindly tell the class the exact meaning of the words 'Tomorrow, and tomorrow, and tomorrow/Creeps in this petty pace from day to day.' "

Peter glanced down at the high-school edition of *Macbeth* lying open on his desk. One of the duller girls tittered expectantly from the back of the room. Peter was popular with the girls; girls that age had minds like moths.

"Peter. With your book shut. We have all memorized this passage for today. Remember?" The girl in the back of the room squealed in delight. Gloria laid her own book face-open on her desk, where Peter could see it.

Peter shut his book with a bang and stared into Gloria's. "Why," he said at last, "I think it means pretty much what it says."

"Which is?"

"Why, that tomorrow is something we often think about. It creeps into our conversation all the time. We couldn't make any plans without thinking about tomorrow."

"I see. Then you would say that Macbeth is here referring to the, the date-book aspect of life?"

Geoffrey Langer laughed, no doubt to please Mr. Prosser. For a moment, he *was* pleased. Then he realized he had been playing for laughs at a student's expense.

His paraphrase had made Peter's reading of the lines seem more ridiculous than it was. He began to retract. "I admit—"

But Peter was going on; redheads never know when to quit. "Macbeth means that if we quit worrying about tomorrow, and just lived for today, we could appreciate all the wonderful things that are going on under our noses."

Mark considered this a moment before he spoke. He would not be sarcastic. "Uh, without denying that there is truth in what you say, Peter, do you think it likely that Macbeth, in his situation, would be expressing such"—he couldn't help himself—"such sunny sentiments?"

Geoffrey laughed again. Peter's neck reddened; he studied the floor. Gloria glared at Mr. Prosser, the anger in her face clearly meant for him to see.

Mark hurried to undo his mistake. "Don't misunderstand me, please," he told Peter. "I don't have all the answers myself. But it seems to me the whole speech, down to 'Signifying nothing,' is saying that life is—well, a *fraud.* Nothing wonderful about it."

"Did Shakespeare really think that?" Geoffrey Langer asked, a nervous quickness pitching his voice high.

Mark read into Geoffrey's question his own adolescent premonitions of the terrible truth. The attempt he must make was plain. He told Peter he could sit down and looked through the window toward the steadying sky. The clouds were gaining intensity. "There is," Mr. Prosser slowly began, "much darkness in Shakespeare's work, and no play is darker than 'Macbeth.' The atmosphere is poisonous, oppressive. One critic has said that in this play, humanity suffocates." This was too fancy.

"In the middle of his career, Shakespeare wrote plays about men like

Hamlet and Othello and Macbeth—men who aren't allowed by their society, or bad luck, or some minor flaw in themselves, to become the great men they might have been. Even Shakespeare's comedies of this period deal with a world gone sour. It is as if he had seen through the bright, bold surface of his earlier comedies and histories and had looked upon something terrible. It frightened him, just as some day it may frighten some of you." In his determination to find the right words, he had been staring at Gloria, without meaning to. Embarrassed, she nodded, and, realizing what had happened, he smiled at her.

He tried to make his remarks gentler, even diffident. "But then I think Shakespeare sensed a redeeming truth. His last plays are serene and symbolical, as if he had pierced through the ugly facts and reached a realm where the facts are again beautiful. In this way, Shakespeare's total work is a more complete image of life than that of any other writer, except perhaps for Dante, an Italian poet who wrote several centuries earlier." He had been taken far from the Macbeth soliloquy. Other teachers had been happy to tell him how the kids made a game of getting him talking. He looked toward Geoffrey. The boy was doodling on his tablet, indifferent. Mr. Prosser concluded, "The last play Shakespeare wrote is an extraordinary poem called 'The Tempest.' Some of you may want to read it for your next book reports—the ones due May 10th. It's a short play."

The class had been taking a holiday. Barry Snyder was snicking BBs off the blackboard and glancing over at Brute Young to see if he noticed. "Once more, Barry," Mr. Prosser said, "and out you go." Barry blushed, and grinned to cover the blush, his eyeballs sliding toward Brute. The dull girl in the rear of the room was putting on lipstick. "Put that away, Alice," Mr. Prosser commanded. She giggled and obeyed. Sejak, the Polish boy who worked nights was asleep at his desk, his cheek white with pressure against the varnished wood, his mouth sagging sidewise. Mr. Prosser had an impulse to let him sleep. But the impulse might not be true kindness, but just the self-congratulatory, kindly pose in which he sometimes discovered himself. Besides, one breach of discipline encouraged others. He strode down the aisle and shook Sejak awake. Then he turned his attention to the mumble growing at the front of the room.

Peter Forrester was whispering to Gloria, trying to make her laugh. The girl's face, though, was cool and solemn, as if a thought had been provoked in her head. Perhaps at least *she* had been listening to what Mr. Prosser had been saying. With a bracing sense of chivalrous intercession, Mark said, "Peter. I gather from this noise that you have something to add to your theories."

Peter responded courteously. "No, sir. I honestly don't understand the speech. Please, sir, what *does* it mean?"

This candid admission and odd request stunned the class. Every white, round face, eager, for once, to learn, turned toward Mark. He said, "I don't know. I was hoping *you* would tell *me.*"

In college, when a professor made such a remark, it was with grand effect. The professor's humility, the necessity for creative interplay between teacher and student were dramatically impressed upon the group. But to 11D, ignorance in an instructor was as wrong as a hole in a roof. It was as if he had held forty strings pulling forty faces taut toward him and then had slashed the strings. Heads waggled, eyes dropped, voices buzzed. Some of the discipline problems, like Peter Forrester, smirked signals to one another.

"Quiet!" Mr. Prosser shouted. "All of you. Poetry isn't arithmetic. There's no single right answer. I don't want to force my own impression on you, even if I *have* had much more experience with literature." He made this last clause very loud and distinct, and some of the weaker students seemed reassured. "I know none of *you* want that," he told them.

Whether or not they believed him, they subsided, somewhat. Mark judged he could safely reassume his human-among-humans attitude again. He perched on the edge of the desk and leaned forward beseechingly. "Now, honestly. Don't any of you have some personal feeling about the lines that you would like to share with the class and me?"

One hand, with a flowered handkerchief balled in it, unsteadily rose. "Go ahead, Teresa," Mr. Prosser said encouragingly. She was a timid, clumsy girl whose mother was a Jehovah's Witness.

"It makes me think of cloud shadows," Teresa said.

Geoffrey Langer laughed. "Don't be rude, Geoff," Mr. Prosser said sideways, softly, before throwing his voice forward: "Thank you, Teresa. I think that's an interesting and valid impression. Cloud movement has something in it of the slow, monotonous rhythm one feels in the line 'Tomorrow, and tomorrow, and tomorrow.' It's a very gray line, isn't it, class?" No one agreed or disagreed.

Beyond the windows actual clouds were bunching rapidly, and erratic sections of sunlight slid around the room. Gloria's arm, crooked gracefully above her head, turned gold. "Gloria?" Mr. Prosser asked.

She looked up from something on her desk with a face of sullen radiance. "I think what Teresa said was very good," she said, glaring in the direction of Geoffrey Langer. Geoffrey chuckled defiantly. "And I have a question. What does 'petty pace' mean?"

"It means the trivial day-to-day sort of life that, say, a bookkeeper or a bank clerk leads. Or a schoolteacher," he added, smiling.

She did not smile back. Thought wrinkles irritated her perfect brow. "But Macbeth has been fighting wars, and killing kings, and being a king himself, and all," she pointed out.

"Yes, but it's just these acts Macbeth is condemning as 'nothing.' Can you see that?"

Gloria shook her head. "Another thing I worry about—isn't it silly for

Macbeth to be talking to himself right in the middle of this war, with his wife just dead, and all?"

"I don't think so, Gloria. No matter how fast events happen, thought is faster."

His answer was weak; everyone knew it, even if Gloria hadn't mused, supposedly to herself, but in a voice the entire class could hear, "It seems so *stupid.*"

Mark winced, pierced by the awful clarity with which his students saw him. Through their eyes, how queer he looked, with his long hands, and his horn-rimmed glasses, and his hair never slicked down, all wrapped up in "literature," where, when things get rough, the king mumbles a poem nobody understands. The delight Mr. Prosser took in such crazy junk made not only his good sense but his masculinity a matter of doubt. It was gentle of them not to laugh him out of the room. He looked down and rubbed his fingertips together, trying to erase the chalk dust. The class noise sifted into unnatural quiet. "It's getting late," he said finally. "Let's start the recitations of the memorized passage. Bernard Amilson, you begin."

Bernard had trouble enunciating, and his rendition began " 'T'mau 'n' t'mau 'n' t'mau.' " It was reassuring, the extent to which the class tried to repress its laughter. Mr. Prosser wrote "A" in his marking book opposite Bernard's name. He always gave Bernard A on recitations, despite the school nurse, who claimed there was nothing organically wrong with the boy's mouth.

It was the custom, cruel but traditional, to deliver recitations from the front of the room. Alice, when her turn came, was reduced to a helpless state by the first funny face Peter Forrester made at her. Mark let her hang up there a good minute while her face ripened to cherry redness, and at last forgave her. She may try it later. Many of the youngsters knew the passage gratifyingly well, though there was a tendency to leave out the line "To the last syllable of recorded time" and to turn "struts and frets" into "frets and struts" or simply "struts and struts." Even Sejak, who couldn't have looked at the passage before he came to class, got through it as far as "And then is heard no more."

Geoffrey Langer showed off, as he always did, by interrupting his own recitation with bright questions. " 'Tomorrow, and tomorrow, and tomorrow,' " he said, " 'creeps in'—shouldn't that be '*creep* in,' Mr. Prosser?"

"It is 'creep*s*.' The trio is in effect singular. Go on." Mr. Prosser was tired of coddling Langer. If you let them, these smart students will run away with the class. "Without the footnotes."

" 'Creep*sss* in this petty pace from day to day, to the last syllable of recorded time, and all our yesterdays have lighted fools the way to dusty death. Out, out—' "

"No, no!" Mr. Prosser jumped out of his chair. "This is poetry. Don't mushmouth it! Pause a little after 'fools.' " Geoffrey looked genuinely startled this time, and Mark himself did not quite understand his annoyance and, mentally turning to see what was behind him, seemed to glimpse in the humid undergrowth the two stern eyes of the indignant look Gloria had thrown Geoffrey. He glimpsed himself in the absurd position of acting as Gloria's champion in her private war with this intelligent boy. He sighed apologetically. "Poetry is made up of lines," he began, turning to the class. Gloria was passing a note to Peter Forrester.

The rudeness of it! To pass notes during a scolding that she herself had caused! Mark caged in his hand the girl's frail wrist and ripped the note from her fingers. He read it to himself, letting the class see he was reading it, though he despised such methods of discipline. The note went:

> Pete—I think you're *wrong* about Mr. Prosser. I think he's wonderful and I get a lot out of his class. He's heavenly with poetry. I think I love him. I really do *love* him. So there.

Mr. Prosser folded the note once and slipped it into his side coat pocket. "See me after class, Gloria," he said. Then, to Geoffrey, "Let's try it again. Begin at the beginning."

While the boy was reciting the passage, the buzzer sounded the end of the period. It was the last class of the day. The room quickly emptied, except for Gloria. The noise of lockers slamming open and books being thrown against metal and shouts drifted in.

"Who has a car?"

"Lend me a cig, pig."

"We can't have practice in this slop."

Mark hadn't noticed exactly when the rain started, but it was coming down fast now. He moved around the room with the window pole, closing windows and pulling down shades. Spray bounced in on his hands. He began to talk to Gloria in a crisp voice that, like his device of shutting the windows, was intended to protect them both from embarrassment.

"About note passing." She sat motionless at her desk in the front of the room, her short, brushed-up hair like a cool torch. From the way she sat, her naked arms folded at her breasts and her shoulders hunched, he felt she was chilly. "It is not only rude to scribble when a teacher is talking, it is stupid to put one's words down on paper, where they look much more foolish than they might have sounded if spoken." He leaned the window pole in its corner and walked toward his desk.

"And about love. 'Love' is one of those words that illustrate what happens to an old, overworked language. These days, with movie stars and crooners and preachers and psychiatrists all pronouncing the word, it's come to mean nothing but a vague fondness for something. In this sense, I love the rain, this blackboard, these desks, you. It means nothing, you see, whereas once the word signified a quite explicit thing—a desire to share all you own and are with someone else. It is time we coined a new word to mean that, and when you think up the word *you* want to use, I suggest that you be economical with it. Treat it as something you can spend only once—if not for your own sake, for the good of the language." He walked over to his own desk and dropped two pencils on it, as if to say, "That's all."

"I'm sorry," Gloria said.

Rather surprised, Mr. Prosser said, "Don't be."

"But you don't understand."

"Of course I don't. I probably never did. At your age, I was like Geoffrey Langer."

"I bet you weren't." The girl was almost crying; he was sure of that.

"Come on, Gloria. Run along. Forget it." She slowly cradled her books between her bare arm and her sweater, and left the room with that melancholy shuffling teen-age gait, so that her body above her thighs seemed to float over the desks.

What was it, Mark asked himself, these kids were after? What did they want? Glide, he decided, the quality of glide. To slip along, always in rhythm, always cool, the little wheels humming under you, going nowhere special. If Heaven existed, that's the way it would be there. "He's heavenly with poetry." They loved the word. Heaven was in half their songs.

"Christ, he's humming." Strunk, the physical ed teacher, had come into the room without Mark's noticing. Gloria had left the door ajar.

"Ah," Mark said, "a fallen angel, full of grit."

"What the hell makes you so happy?"

"I'm not happy, I'm just serene. I don't know why you don't appreciate me."

"Say." Strunk came up an aisle with a disagreeably effeminate waddle, pregnant with gossip. "Did you hear about Murchison?"

"No." Mark mimicked Strunk's whisper.

"He got the pants kidded off him today."

"Oh dear."

Strunk started to laugh, as he always did before beginning a story. "You know what a goddam lady's man he thinks he is?"

"You bet," Mark said, although Strunk said that about every male member of the faculty.

"You have Gloria Angstrom, don't you?"

"You bet."

"Well, this morning Murky intercepts a note she was writing, and the note says what a damn neat guy she thinks Murchison is and how she *loves* him!"

Strunk waited for Mark to say something, and then, when he didn't, continued, "You could see he was tickled pink. But—get this—it turns out at lunch that the same damn thing happened to Fryeburg in history yesterday!" Strunk laughed and cracked his knuckles viciously. "The girl's too dumb to have thought it up herself. We all think it was Peter Forrester's idea."

"Probably was," Mark agreed. Strunk followed him out to his locker, describing Murchison's expression when Fryeburg (in all innocence, mind you) told what had happened to him.

Mark turned the combination of his locker, 18–24–3. "Would you excuse me, Dave?" he said. "My wife's in town waiting."

Strunk was too thick to catch Mark's anger. "I got to get over to the gym. Can't take the little darlings outside in the rain; their mommies'll write notes to teacher." He clattered down the hall and wheeled at the far end, shouting, "Now don't tell You-know-who!"

Mr. Prosser took his coat from the locker and shrugged it on. He placed his hat upon his head. He fitted his rubbers over his shoes, pinching his fingers painfully, and lifted his umbrella off the hook. He thought of opening it right there in the vacant hall, as a kind of joke, and decided not to. The girl had been almost crying; he was sure of that.

DONALD BARTHELME

b.1933

The world of Barthelme's fiction seems so strange because he confines it within one time plane—the present. Whatever has produced the present circumstances in a Barthelme story is irrelevant. Characters cannot comfort themselves with historical explanations of how they got to where they are; they are made to confront their problems totally in the present. This lack of history allows Barthelme to present with great sharpness his sense of disparity, inconsequence, and incongruity in modern life—the way it feels to live rather than to think about living and try to explain life to yourself.

Barthelme's characters confront a present that is saturated with the debris of our civilization: bits and pieces of language from TV ads and billboards, politicians' speeches, literary criticism, popular science, computer printouts, debased psychology, and everything else that makes up our verbal junk pile. They have to "communicate" with this stuff, and the trouble is that they sound like somebody else, or the person they are talking to hears them as somebody else. "Honesty" is an overwhelming problem, and relationships seem to happen because of either a momentary harmony of discord or a sudden flash of violence that is, in effect, a throwing over of the burden of language.

Barthelme was born in Philadelphia, grew up in Texas, and went to the University of Houston. His sense, not unpleasant, of displacement in Texas was intensified by his father's practice of modernist architecture—"an anomaly in Texas in the thirties," Barthelme says. The family lived in a house designed by his father, "wonderful to live in but strange to see on the Texas prairie. On Sundays people used to park their cars out on the street and stare. We had a routine, the family on Sundays. We used to get up from Sunday dinner, if enough cars had parked, and run out in front of the house in a sort of chorus line, doing high kicks."[1]

In addition to a continuing interest in architecture, Barthelme loves book design and typography; in fact, in one of his best-known statements he asserted that "the principle of collage is the central principle of all art in the

[1]Joe David Bellamy, *The New Fiction: Interviews with Innovative American Writers* (Urbana, Ill.: University of Illinois Press, 1974), p. 47.

twentieth century in all media." His imagination is especially visual, and informed by the playful childish joy that won the National Book Award for Children's Literature for his book *The Slightly Irregular Fire Engine.* He has written one novel, *Snow White,* and has collected in book form about half of more than one hundred short stories and pieces, almost all of which first appeared in *The New Yorker.* For the last ten years he has made his home in New York.

Me and Miss Mandible

13 September

Miss Mandible wants to make love to me but she hesitates because I am officially a child; I am, according to the records, according to the gradebook on her desk, according to the card index in the principal's office, eleven years old. There is a misconception here, one that I haven't quite managed to get cleared up yet. I am in fact thirty-five, I've been in the Army, I am six feet one, I have hair in the appropriate places, my voice is a baritone, I know very well what to do with Miss Mandible if she ever makes up her mind.

In the meantime we are studying common fractions. I could, of course, answer all the questions, or at least most of them (there are things I don't remember). But I prefer to sit in this too-small seat with the desktop cramping my thighs and examine the life around me. There are thirty-two in the class, which is launched every morning with the pledge of allegiance to the flag. My own allegiance, at the moment, is divided between Miss Mandible and Sue Ann Brownly, who sits across the aisle from me all day long and is, like Miss Mandible, a fool for love. Of the two I prefer, today, Sue Ann; although between eleven and eleven and a half (she refuses to reveal her exact age) she is clearly a woman, with a woman's disguised aggression and woman's peculiar contradictions. Strangely neither she nor any of the other children seem to see any incongruity in my presence here.

15 September

Happily our geography text, which contains maps of all the principal land-masses of the world, is large enough to conceal my clandestine journal-keeping, accomplished in an ordinary black composition book. Every day I must wait until Geography to put down such thoughts as I may have had during the morning about my situation and my fellows. I have tried writing at other times and it does not work. Either the teacher is walking up and down the aisles (during this period, luckily, she sticks close to the map rack in the front of the room) or Bobby Vanderbilt, who sits behind me, is punching me in the kidneys and wanting to know what I am doing. Vanderbilt, I have found out from certain desultory conversations on the playground, is hung up on sports cars, a veteran consumer of *Road & Track.* This explains the continual roaring sounds which seem to emanate from his desk; he is reproducing a record album called *Sounds of Sebring.*

19 September

Only, I, at times (only at times), understand that somehow a mistake has been made, that I am in a place where I don't belong. It may be that Miss

Mandible also knows this, at some level, but for reasons not fully understood by me she is going along with the game. When I was first assigned to this room I wanted to protest, the error seemed obvious, the stupidest principal could have seen it; but I have come to believe it was deliberate, that I have been betrayed again.

Now it seems to make little difference. This life-role is as interesting as my former life-role, which was that of a claims adjuster for the Great Northern Insurance Company, a position which compelled me to spend my time amid the debris of our civilization: rumpled fenders, roofless sheds, gutted warehouses, smashed arms and legs. After ten years of this one has a tendency to see the world as a vast junkyard, looking at a man and seeing only his (potentially) mangled parts, entering a house only to trace the path of the inevitable fire. Therefore when I was installed here, although I knew an error had been made, I countenanced it, I was shrewd; I was aware that there might well be some kind of advantage to be gained from what seemed a disaster. The role of The Adjuster teaches one much.

22 September

I am being solicited for the volleyball team. I decline, refusing to take unfair profit from my height.

23 September

Every morning the roll is called: Bestvina, Bokenfohr, Broan, Brownly, Cone, Coyle, Crecelius, Darin, Durbin, Geiger, Guiswite, Heckler, Jacobs, Kleinschmidt, Lay, Logan, Masei, Mitgang, Pfeilsticker. It is like the litany chanted in the dim miserable dawns of Texas by the cadre sergeant of our basic training company.

In the Army, too, I was ever so slightly awry. It took me a fantastically long time to realize what the others grasped almost at once: that much of what we were doing was absolutely pointless, to no purpose. I kept wondering why. Then something happened that proposed a new question. One day we were commanded to whitewash, from the ground to the topmost leaves, all of the trees in our training area. The corporal who relayed the order was nervous and apologetic. Later an off-duty captain sauntered by and watched us, white-splashed and totally weary, strung out among the freakish shapes we had created. He walked away swearing. I understood the principle (orders are orders), but I wondered: Who decides?

29 September

Sue Ann is a wonder. Yesterday she viciously kicked my ankle for not paying attention when she was attempting to pass me a note during History. It is swollen still. But Miss Mandible was watching me, there was nothing I could do. Oddly enough Sue Ann reminds me of the wife I had in my former role, while Miss Mandible seems to be a child. She watches me constantly, trying to keep sexual significance out of her look; I am afraid the other children have noticed. I have already heard, on that ghostly frequency that is the medium of classroom communication, the words "*Teacher's pet!*"

2 October

Sometimes I speculate on the exact nature of the conspiracy which brought me here. At times I believe it was instigated by my wife of former days, whose name was . . . I am only pretending to forget. I know her name very well, as well as I know the name of my former motor oil (Quaker State) or my old Army serial number (US 54109268). Her name was Brenda, and the conversation I recall best, the one which makes me suspicious now, took place on the day we parted. "You have the soul of a whore," I said on that occasion, stating nothing less than literal, unvarnished fact. "You," she replied, "are a pimp, a poop, and a child. I am leaving you forever and I trust that without me you will perish of your own inadequacies. Which are considerable."

I squirm in my seat at the memory of this conversation, and Sue Ann watches me with malign compassion. She has noticed the discrepancy between the size of my desk and my own size, but apparently sees it only as a token of my glamour, my dark man-of-the-world-ness.

7 October

Once I tiptoed up to Miss Mandible's desk (when there was no one else in the room) and examined its surface. Miss Mandible is a clean-desk teacher, I discovered. There was nothing except her gradebook (the one in which I exist as a sixth-grader) and a text, which was open at a page headed *Making the Processes Meaningful.* I read: "Many pupils enjoy working fractions when they understand what they are doing. They have confidence in their ability to take the right steps, and to obtain correct answers. However, to give the subject full social significance, it is necessary that many realistic situations requiring the processes be found. Many interesting and lifelike problems involving the use of fractions should be solved . . ."

8 October

I am not irritated by the feeling of having been through all this before. Things are done differently now. The children, moreover, are in some ways different from those who accompanied me on my first voyage through the elementary schools: "*They have confidence in their ability to take the right steps and to obtain correct answers.*" This is surely true. When Bobby Vanderbilt, who sits behind me and has the great tactical advantage of being able to maneuver in my disproportionate shadow, wishes to bust a classmate in the mouth he first asks Miss Mandible to lower the blind, saying that the sun hurts his eyes. When she does so, *bip!* My generation would never have been able to con authority so easily.

13 October

It may be that on my first trip through the schools I was too much under the impression that what the authorities (who decides?) had ordained for me was right and proper, that I confused authority with life itself. My path was not particularly of my own choosing. My career stretched out in front of me like a paper chase, and my role was to pick up the clues. When I got out of school, the first time, I felt that this estimate was substantially correct, and eagerly entered the hunt. I found clues abundant: diplomas, membership cards, campaign buttons, a marriage license, insurance forms, discharge papers, tax returns, Certificates of Merit. They seemed to prove, at the very least, that I was *in the running.* But that was before my tragic mistake on the Mrs. Anton Bichek claim.

I misread a clue. Do not misunderstand me: it was a tragedy only from the point of view of the authorities. I conceived that it was my duty to obtain satisfaction for the injured, for this elderly lady (not even one of our policyholders, but a claimant against Big Ben Transfer & Storage, Inc.) from the company. The settlement was $165,000; the claim, I still believe, was just. But without my encouragement Mrs. Bichek would never have had the self-love to prize her injury so highly. The company paid, but its faith in me, in my efficacy in the role, was broken. Henry Goodykind, the district manager, expressed this thought in a few not altogether unsympathetic words, and told me at the same time that I was to have a new role. The next thing I knew I was here, at Horace Greeley Elementary, under the lubricious eye of Miss Mandible.

17 October

Today we are to have a fire drill. I know this because I am a Fire Marshal, not only for our room but for the entire right wing of the second floor. This distinction, which was awarded shortly after my arrival, is interpreted by some as another mark of my somewhat dubious relations with our teacher. My armband, which is red and decorated with white felt letters reading FIRE, sits on the little shelf under my desk, next to the brown paper bag containing the lunch I carefully make for myself each morning. One of the advantages of packing my own lunch (I have no one to pack it for me) is that I am able to fill it with things I enjoy. The peanut butter sandwiches that my mother made in my former existence, many years ago, have been banished in favor of ham and cheese. I have found that my diet has mysteriously adjusted to my new situation; I no longer drink, for instance, and when I smoke, it is in the boys' john, like everybody else. When school is out I hardly smoke at all. It is only in the matter of sex that I feel my own true age; this is apparently something that, once learned, can never be forgotten. I live in fear that Miss Mandible will one day keep me after school, and when we are alone, create a compromising situation. To avoid this I have become a model pupil: another reason for the pronounced dislike I have encountered in certain quarters. But I cannot deny that I am singled by those long glances from the vicinity of the chalkboard; Miss Mandible is in many ways, notably about the bust, a very tasty piece.

24 October

There are isolated challenges to my largeness, to my dimly realized position in the class as Gulliver. Most of my classmates are polite about this matter, as they would be if I had only one eye, or wasted, metal-wrapped legs. I am viewed as a mutation of some sort but essentially a peer. However Harry Broan, whose father has made himself rich manufacturing the Broan Bathroom Vent (with which Harry is frequently reproached; he is always being asked how things are in Ventsville), today inquired if I wanted to fight. An interested group of his followers had gathered to observe this suicidal undertaking. I replied that I didn't feel quite up to it, for which he was obviously grateful. We are now friends forever. He has given me to understand privately that he can get me all the bathroom vents I will ever need, at a ridiculously modest figure.

25 October

"*Many interesting and lifelike problems involving the use of fractions should be solved . . .*" The theorists fail to realize that everything that is either interesting or lifelike in the classroom proceeds from what they would probably call interpersonal relations: Sue Ann Brownly kicking me in the ankle. How lifelike, how womanlike, is her tender solicitude after the deed! Her pride in my newly acquired limp is transparent; everyone knows that she has set her mark upon me, that it is a victory in her unequal struggle with Miss Mandible for my great, overgrown heart. Even Miss Mandible knows, and counters in perhaps the only way she can, with sarcasm. "Are you wounded, Joseph?" Conflagrations smolder behind her eyelids, yearning for the Fire Marshal clouds her eyes. I mumble that I have bumped my leg.

30 October

I return again and again to the problem of my future.

4 November

The underground circulating library has brought me a copy of *Movie—TV Secrets,* the multicolor cover blazoned with the headline, "Debbie's Date Insults Liz!" It is a gift from Frankie Randolph, a rather plain girl who until today has had not one word for me, passed on via Bobby Vanderbilt. I nod and smile over my shoulder in acknowledgment; Frankie hides her head under her desk. I have seen these magazines being passed around among the girls (sometimes one of the boys will condescend to inspect a particularly lurid cover). Miss Mandible confiscates them whenever she finds one. I leaf through *Movie—TV Secrets* and get an eyeful. "The exclusive picture on these pages isn't what it seems. We know how it looks and we know what the gossipers will do. So in the interests of a nice guy, we're publishing the facts first. Here's what really happened!" The picture shows a rising young movie idol in bed, pajama-ed and bleary-eyed, while an equally blowzy young woman looks startled beside him. I am happy to know that the picture is not really what it seems; it seems to be nothing less than divorce evidence.

What do these hipless eleven-year-olds think when they come across, in the same magazine, the full-page ad for Maurice de Paree, which features "Hip Helpers" or what appear to be padded rumps? ("A real undercover agent that adds appeal to those hips and derriere, both!") If they cannot decipher the language the illustrations leave nothing to the imagination. "Drive him frantic . . ." the copy continues. Perhaps this explains Bobby Vanderbilt's preoccupation with Lancias and Maseratis; it is a defense against being driven frantic.

Sue Ann has observed Frankie Randolph's overture, and catching my eye, she pulls from her satchel no less than seventeen of these magazines, thrusting them at me as if to prove that anything any of her rivals has to offer, she can top. I shuffle through them quickly, noting the broad editorial perspective:

"Debbie's Kids Are Crying"
"Eddie Asks Debbie. Will You . . . ?"
"The Nightmares Liz Has About Eddie!"
"The Things Debbie Can Tell About Eddie"
"The Private Life of Eddie and Liz"
"Debbie Gets Her Man Back?"
"A New Life for Liz"
"Love Is a Tricky Affair"
"Eddie's Taylor-Made Love Nest"
"How Liz Made a Man of Eddie"
"Are They Planning to Live Together?"
"Isn't It Time to Stop Kicking Debbie Around?"
"Debbie's Dilemma"
"Eddie Becomes a Father Again"
"Is Debbie Planning to Re-wed?"
"Can Liz Fulfill Herself?"
"Why Debbie Is Sick of Hollywood"

Who are these people, Debbie, Eddie, Liz, and how did they get themselves in such a terrible predicament? Sue Ann knows, I am sure; it is obvious that she has been studying their history as a guide to what she may expect when she is suddenly freed from this drab, flat classroom.

I am angry and I shove the magazines back at her with not even a whisper of thanks.

5 November

The sixth grade at Horace Greeley Elementary is a furnace of love, love, love. Today it is raining, but inside the air is heavy and tense with passion. Sue Ann is absent; I suspect that yesterday's exchange has driven her to her bed. Guilt hangs about me. She is not responsible, I know, for what she reads, for the models proposed to her by a venal publishing industry; I should not have been so harsh. Perhaps it is only the flu.

Nowhere have I encountered an atmosphere as charged with aborted sexuality as this. Miss Mandible is helpless; nothing goes right today. Amos Darin has been found drawing a dirty picture in the cloakroom. Sad and inaccurate, it was offered not as a sign of something else but as an act of love in itself. It has excited even those who have not seen it, even those who saw but understood only that it was dirty. The room buzzes with imperfectly comprehended titillation. Amos stands by the door, waiting to be taken to the principal's office. He wavers between fear and enjoyment of his temporary celebrity. From time to time Miss Mandible looks at me reproachfully, as if blaming me for the uproar. But I did not create this atmosphere, I am caught in it like all the others.

8 November

Everything is promised my classmates and I, most of all the future. We accept the outrageous assurances without blinking.

9 November

I have finally found the nerve to petition for a larger desk. At recess I can hardly walk; my legs do not wish to uncoil themselves. Miss Mandible says she will take it up with the custodian. She is worried about the excellence of my themes. Have I, she asks, been receiving help? For an instant I am on the brink of telling her my story. Something, however, warns me not to attempt it. Here I am safe, I have a place; I do not wish to entrust myself once more to the whimsy of authority. I resolve to make my themes less excellent in the future.

11 November

A ruined marriage, a ruined adjusting career, a grim interlude in the Army when I was almost not a person. This is the sum of my existence to date, a dismal total. Small wonder that re-education seemed my only hope. It is clear even to me that I need reworking in some fundamental way. How efficient is the society that provides thus for the salvage of its clinkers!

Plucked from my unexamined life among other pleasant, desperate, money-making young Americans, thrown backward in space and time, I am beginning to understand how I went wrong, how we all go wrong. (Although this was far from the intention of those who sent me here; they require only that I *get right.)*

14 November

The distinction between children and adults, while probably useful for some purposes, is at bottom a specious one, I feel. There are only individual egos, crazy for love.

15 November

The custodian has informed Miss Mandible that our desks are all the correct size for sixth-graders, as specified by the Board of Estimate and furnished the schools by the Nu-Art Educational Supply Corporation of Englewood, California. He has pointed out that if the desk size is correct, then the pupil size must be incorrect. Miss Mandible, who has already arrived at this conclusion, refuses to press the matter further. I think I know why. An appeal to the administration might result in my removal from the class, in a transfer to some sort of setup for "exceptional children." This would be a disaster of the first magnitude. To sit in a room with child genuises (or, more likely, children who are "retarded") would shrivel me in a week. Let my experience here be that of the common run, I say; let me be, please God, typical.

20 November

We read signs as promises. Miss Mandible understands by my great height, by my resonant vowels, that I will one day carry her off to bed. Sue Ann interprets these same signs to mean that I am unique among her male acquaintances, therefore most desirable, therefore her special property as is everything that is Most Desirable. If neither of these propositions work out then life has broken faith with them.

I myself, in my former existence, read the company motto ("Here to Help in Time of Need") as a description of the duty of the adjuster, drastically mislocating the company's deepest concerns. I believed that because I had obtained a wife who was made up of wife-signs (beauty, charm, softness, perfume, cookery) I had found love. Brenda, reading the same signs that have now misled Miss Mandible and Sue Ann Brownly, felt she had been promised that she would never be bored again. All of us, Miss Mandible, Sue Ann, myself,

Brenda, Mr. Goodykind, still believe that the American flag betokens a kind of general righteousness.

But I say, looking about me in this incubator of future citizens, that signs are signs, and that some of them are lies. This is the great discovery of my time here.

23 November

It may be that my experience as a child will save me after all. If only I can remain quietly in this classroom, making my notes while Napoleon plods through Russia in the droning voice of Harry Broan, reading aloud from our History text. All of the mysteries that perplexed me as an adult have their origins here, and one by one I am numbering them, exposing their roots.

2 December

Miss Mandible will refuse to permit me to remain ungrown. Her hands rest on my shoulders too warmly, and for too long.

7 December

It is the pledges that this place makes to me, pledges that cannot be redeemed, that confuse me later and make me feel I am not *getting anywhere.* Everything is presented as the result of some knowable process; if I wish to arrive at four I get there by way of two and two. If I wish to burn Moscow the route I must travel has already been marked out by another visitor. If, like Bobby Vanderbilt, I yearn for the wheel of the Lancia 2.4-liter coupé, I have only to go through the appropriate process, that is, get the money. And if it is money itself that I desire, I have only to make it. All of these goals are equally beautiful in the sight of the Board of Estimate; the proof is all around us, in the no-nonsense ugliness of this steel and glass building, in the straightline matter-of-factness with which Miss Mandible handles some of our less reputable wars. Who points out that arrangements sometimes slip, that errors are made, that signs are misread? *"They have confidence in their ability to take the right steps and to obtain correct answers."* I take the right steps, obtain correct answers, and my wife leaves me for another man.

8 December

My enlightenment is proceeding wonderfully.

9 December

Disaster once again. Tomorrow I am to be sent to a doctor, for observation. Sue Ann Brownly caught Miss Mandible and me in the cloakroom, during recess, and immediately threw a fit. For a moment I thought she was actually going to choke. She ran out of the room weeping, straight for the principal's office, certain now which of us was Debbie, which Eddie, which Liz. I am sorry to be the cause of her disillusionment, but I know that she will recover. Miss Mandible is ruined but fulfilled. Although she will be charged with contributing to the delinquency of a minor, she seems at peace; *her* promise has been kept. She knows now that everything she has been told about life, about America, is true.

I have tried to convince the school authorities that I am a minor only in a very special sense, that I am in fact mostly to blame—but it does no good. They are as dense as ever. My contemporaries are astounded that I present myself as anything other than an innocent victim. Like the Old Guard marching through the Russian drifts, the class marches to the conclusion that truth is punishment.

Bobby Vanderbilt has given me his copy of *Sounds of Sebring,* in farewell.

The Indian Uprising

We defended the city as best we could. The arrows of the Comanches came in clouds. The war clubs of the Comanches clattered on the soft, yellow pavements. There were earthworks along the Boulevard Mark Clark and the hedges had been laced with sparkling wire. People were trying to understand. I spoke to Sylvia. "Do you think this a good life?" The table held apples, books, long-playing records. She looked up. "No."

Patrols of paras and volunteers with armbands guarded the tall, flat buildings. We interrogated the captured Comanche. Two of us forced his head back while another poured water into his nostrils. His body jerked, he choked and wept. Not believing a hurried, careless, and exaggerated report of the number of casualties in the outer districts where trees, lamps, swans had been reduced to clear fields of fire we issued entrenching tools to those who seemed trustworthy and turned the heavy-weapons companies so that we could not be surprised from that direction. And I sat there getting drunker and drunker and more in love and more in love. We talked.

"Do you know Fauré's 'Dolly'?"

"Would that be Gabriel Fauré?"

"It would."

"Then I know it," she said. "May I say that I play it at certain times, when I am sad, or happy, although it requires four hands."

"How is that managed?"

"I accelerate," she said, "ignoring the time signature."

And when they shot the scene in the bed I wondered how you felt under the eyes of the cameramen, grips, juicers, men in the mixing booth: excited? stimulated? And when they shot the scene in the shower I sanded a hollow-core door working carefully against the illustrations in texts and whispered instructions from one who had already solved the problem. I had made after all other tables, one while living with Nancy, one while living with Alice, one while living with Eunice, one while living with Marianne.

Red men in waves like people scattering in a square startled by something tragic or a sudden, loud noise accumulated against the barricades we had made of window dummies, silk, thoughtfully planned job descriptions (including scales for the orderly progress of other colors), wine in demijohns, and robes. I analyzed the composition of the barricade nearest me and found two ashtrays, ceramic, one dark brown and one dark brown with an orange blur at the lip; a tin frying pan; two-litre bottles of red wine; three-quarter-litre bottles of Black & White, aquavit, cognac, vodka, gin, Fad #6 sherry; a hollow-core door in birch veneer on black wrought-iron legs; a blanket, red-orange with faint blue stripes; a red pillow and a blue pillow; a woven straw wastebasket; two glass jars for flowers; corkscrews and can openers; two plates and two cups, ceramic, dark brown; a yellow-and-purple poster; a Yugoslavian carved flute, wood, dark brown; and other items. I decided I knew nothing.

The hospitals dusted wounds with powders the worth of which was not quite established, other supplies having been exhausted early in the first day. I decided I knew nothing. Friends put me in touch with a Miss R., a teacher, unorthodox they said, excellent they said, successful with difficult cases, steel shutters on the windows made the house safe. I had just learned via an International Distress Coupon that Jane had been beaten up by a dwarf in a bar on Tenerife but Miss R. did not allow me to speak of it. "You know nothing," she said, "you feel nothing, you are locked in a most savage and terrible ignorance, I despise you, my boy, *mon cher,* my heart. You may attend but you must not attend now, you must attend later, a day or a week or an hour, you are making me ill. . . ." I nonevaluated these remarks as Korzybski instructed. But it was difficult. Then they pulled back in a feint near the river and we rushed into that sector with a reinforced battalion hastily formed among the Zouaves and cabdrivers. This unit was crushed in the afternoon of a day that began with spoons and letters in hallways and under windows where men tasted the history of the heart, cone-shaped muscular organ that maintains *circulation of the blood.*

But it is you I want now, here in the middle of this Uprising, with the streets yellow and threatening, short, ugly lances with fur at the throat and inexplicable shell money lying in the grass. It is when I am with you that I am happiest, and it is for you that I am making this hollow-core door table with black wrought-iron legs. I held Sylvia by her bear-claw necklace. "Call off your braves," I said. "We have many years left to live." There was a sort of muck running in the gutters, yellowish, filthy stream suggesting excrement, or nervousness, a city that does not know what it has done to deserve baldness, errors, infidelity. "With luck you will survive until matins," Sylvia said. She ran off down the Rue Chester Nimitz, uttering shrill cries.

Then it was learned that they had infiltrated our ghetto and that the people of the ghetto instead of resisting had joined the smooth, well-coördinated attack with zipguns, telegrams, lockets, causing that portion of the line held by the I.R.A. to swell and collapse. We sent more heroin into the ghetto, and hyacinths, ordering another hundred thousand of the pale, delicate flowers. On the map we considered the situation with its strung-out inhabitants and merely personal emotions. Our parts were blue and their parts were green. I showed the blue-and-green map to Sylvia. "Your parts are green," I said. "You gave me heroin first a year ago," Sylvia said. She ran off down George C. Marshall Allée, uttering shrill cries. Miss R. pushed me into a large room painted white (jolting and dancing in the soft light, and I was excited! and there were people watching!) in which there were two chairs. I sat in one chair and Miss R. sat in the other. She wore a blue dress containing a red figure. There was nothing exceptional about her. I was disappointed by her plainness, by the bareness of the room, by the absence of books.

The girls of my quarter wore long blue mufflers that reached to their knees. Sometimes the girls hid Comanches in their rooms, the blue mufflers together in a room creating a great blue fog. Block opened the door. He was carrying weapons, flowers, loaves of bread. And he was friendly, kind, enthusiastic, so I related a little of the history of torture, reviewing the technical literature quoting the best modern sources, French, German, and American, and pointing out the flies which had gathered in anticipation of some new, cool color.

"What is the situation?" I asked.

"The situation is liquid," he said. "We hold the south quarter and they hold the north quarter. The rest is silence."

"And Kenneth?"

"That girl is not in love with Kenneth," Block said frankly. "She is in love with his coat. When she is not wearing it she is huddling under it. Once I caught it going down the stairs by itself. I looked inside. Sylvia."

Once I caught Kenneth's coat going down the stairs by itself but the coat was a trap and inside a Comanche who made a thrust with his short, ugly knife at my leg which buckled and tossed me over the balustrade through a window and into another situation. Not believing that your body brilliant as it was and your fat, liquid spirit distinguished and angry as it was were stable quantities to which one could return on wires more than once, twice, or another number of times I said: "See the table?"

In Skinny Wainwright Square the forces of green and blue swayed and struggled. The referees ran out on the field trailing chains. And then the blue part would be enlarged, the green diminished. Miss R. began to speak. "A former king of Spain, a Bonaparte, lived for a time in Bordentown, New Jersey. But that's no good." She paused. "The ardor aroused in men by the beauty of women can only be satisfied by God. That is *very* good (it is Valéry) but it is not what I have to teach you, goat, muck, filth, heart of my heart." I showed the table to Nancy. "See the table?" She stuck out her tongue red as a cardinal's hat. "I made such a table once," Block said frankly. "People all over America have made such tables. I doubt very much whether one can enter an American home without finding at least one such table, or traces of its having been there, such as faded places in the carpet." And afterward in the garden the men of the 7th Cavalry played Gabrieli, Albinoni, Marcello, Vivaldi, Boccherini. I saw Sylvia. She wore a yellow ribbon, under a long blue muffler. "Which side are you on," I cried, "after all?"

"The only form of discourse of which I approve," Miss R. said in her dry, tense voice, "is the litany. I believe our masters and teachers as well as plain citizens should confine themselves to what can safely be said. Thus when I hear the words *pewter, snake, tea, Fad #6 sherry, serviette, fenestration, crown, blue* coming from the mouth of some public official, or some raw youth, I am not disappointed. Vertical organization is also possible," Miss R. said, "as in

pewter
snake
tea
Fad #6 sherry
serviette
fenestration
crown
blue.

I run to liquids and colors," she said, "but you, you may run to something else, my virgin, my darling, my thistle, my poppet, my own. Young people," Miss R. said, "run to more and more unpleasant combinations as they sense the nature of our society. Some people," Miss R. said, "run to conceits or wisdom but I hold to the hard, brown, nutlike word. I might point out that there is enough aesthetic excitement here to satisfy anyone but a damned fool." I sat in solemn silence.

Fire arrows lit my way to the post office in Patton Place where members of the Abraham Lincoln Brigade offered their last, exhausted letters, postcards, calendars. I opened a letter but inside was a Comanche flint arrowhead played by Frank Wedekind in an elegant gold chain and congratulations. Your earring rattled against my spectacles when I leaned forward to touch the soft, ruined place where the hearing aid had been. "Pack it in! Pack it in!" I urged, but the men in charge of the Uprising refused to listen to reason or to understand that it was real and that our water supply had evaporated and that our credit was no longer what it had been, once.

We attached wires to the testicles of the captured Comanche. And I sat there getting drunker and drunker and more in love and more in love. When we threw the switch he spoke. His name, he said, was Gustave Aschenbach. He was born at L——, a country town in the province of Silesia. He was the son of an upper official in the judicature, and his forebears had all been officers, judges, departmental functionaries. . . . And you can never touch a girl in the same way more than once, twice, or another number of times however much you may wish to hold, wrap, or otherwise fix her hand, or look, or some other quality, or incident, known to you previously. In Sweden the little Swedish children cheered when we managed nothing more remarkable than getting off a bus burdened with packages, bread and liver-paste and beer. We went to an old church and sat in the royal box. The organist was practicing. And then into the graveyard next to the church. *Here lies Anna Pedersen, a good woman.* I threw a mushroom on the grave. The officer commanding the garbage dump reported by radio that the garbage had begun to move.

Jane! I heard via an International Distress Coupon that you were beaten up by a dwarf in a bar on Tenerife. That doesn't sound like you, Jane. Mostly you kick the dwarf in his little dwarf groin before he can get his teeth into your tasty and nice-looking leg, don't you, Jane? Your affair with Harold is reprehensible, you know that, don't you, Jane? Harold is married to Nancy. And there is Paula to think about (Harold's kid), and Billy (Harold's other kid). I think your values are peculiar, Jane! Strings of language extend in every direction to bind the world into a rushing, ribald whole.

And you can never return to felicities in the same way, the brilliant body, the distinguished spirit recapitulating moments that occur once, twice, or another number of times in rebellions, or water. The rolling consensus of the Comanche nation smashed our inner defenses on three sides. Block was firing a greasegun from the upper floor of a building designed by Emery Roth & Sons. "See the table?" "Oh, pack it in with your bloody table!" The city officials were tied to trees. Dusky warriors padded with their forest tread into the mouth of the mayor. "Who do you want to be?" I asked Kenneth and he said he wanted to be Jean-Luc Godard but later when time permitted conversations in large, lighted rooms, whispering galleries with black-and-white Spanish rugs and problematic sculpture on calm, red catafalques. The sickness of the quarrel lay thick in the bed. I touched your back, the white, raised scars.

We killed a great many in the south suddenly with helicopters and rockets but we found that those we had killed were children and more came from the north and from the east and from other places where there are children preparing to live. "Skin," Miss R. said softly in the white, yellow room. "This is the Clemency Committee. And would you remove your belt and shoelaces." I removed my belt and shoelaces and looked (rain shattering from a great height the prospects of silence and clear, neat rows of houses in the subdivisions) into their savage black eyes, paint, feathers, beads.

JOYCE CAROL OATES

b. 1938

In the 1970 collection of the *O. Henry Prize Stories,* the editor William Abrahams invented a new prize category, "Special Award for Continuing Achievement." It was a fitting tribute to Joyce Carol Oates, and also an anticipation of the need that her writing was to create for some new way to acknowledge a writer so good and so productive (and so remarkably young), that beginning in 1963 and excepting in 1966 her short stories were *always* in the annual O. Henry prize collection. During the same period she was writing four novels (of which one, *Them,* won the 1970 National Book Award), two Off-Broadway plays, and a collection of poems. Since 1970 her output has been equally prodigious.

Because Oates has always read widely and sensitively, it is hard to cite especially powerful influences on her writing. She was an English major at Syracuse, the valedictorian of her class; then she took an M.A. at Wisconsin, and was proceeding toward a Ph.D. at Rice before she gave up studying literature for writing it. Thus, in a sense, because she is so well-read, all traditional writers are behind her; and while sometimes in her work we are reminded of Faulkner's ear for the interaction of many voices strained by various personal repressions, or of Kafka's haunting presentation of a detailed and seemingly ordinary reality that gently floats into nightmare, still the realism of Flaubert and the lyrical introspection of Proust are there too. In fact, Oates' fiction is of all kinds the most original and distinctive: not free of influences but fully assimilative of the suggestions of a wide and rich tradition.

In an interview in *Commonweal* (December 5, 1969) Oates said that although she had once thought that she was much indebted to Flannery O'Connor she now saw that in O'Connor's fiction there is always a religious dimension, a glimmer of revelation beyond the purely natural, whereas in hers "there is only the natural world." The two writers obviously have a lot in common, but Oates is right in pointing to exactly that area as the one that distinguishes her from O'Connor.

Like Flannery O'Connor, Oates was born a Roman Catholic. She grew up in a rural area near Lockport, N.Y., a small upstate town. Her characters are typically immersed in a middle-class culture full of TV and radio announcers' clichés; all of them have appropriated a jumble of styles from old movies, the business establishment, black society, etc. The styles don't fit, singly or in combination, and Oates explores the pressure that builds up (particularly in our money-dominated world), and presents the violent collisions that occur when people with different images of themselves try to relate to one another.

Oates now teaches literature at the University of Windsor, Canada.

Where Are You Going, Where Have You Been?

For Bob Dylan

Her name was Connie. She was fifteen and she had a quick nervous giggling habit of craning her neck to glance into mirrors, or checking other people's faces to make sure her own was all right. Her mother, who noticed everything and knew everything and who hadn't much reason any longer to look at her own face, always scolded Connie about it. "Stop gawking at yourself, who are you? You think you're so pretty?" she would say. Connie would raise her eyebrows at these familiar complaints and look right through her mother, into a shadowy vision of herself as she was right at that moment: she knew she was pretty and that was everything. Her mother had been pretty once too, if you could believe those old snapshots in the album, but now her looks were gone and that was why she was always after Connie.

"Why don't you keep your room clean like your sister? How've you got your hair fixed—what the hell stinks? Hair spray? You don't see your sister using that junk."

Her sister June was twenty-four and still lived at home. She was a secretary in the high school Connie attended, and if that wasn't bad enough—with her in the same building—she was so plain and chunky and steady that Connie had to hear her praised all the time by her mother and her mother's sisters. June did this, June did that, she saved money and helped clean the house and cooked and Connie couldn't do a thing, her mind was all filled with trashy daydreams. Their father was away at work most of the time and when he came home he wanted supper and he read the newspaper at supper and after supper he went to bed. He didn't bother talking much to them, but around his bent head Connie's mother kept picking at her until Connie wished her mother was dead and she herself was dead and it was all over. "She makes me want to throw up sometimes," she complained to her friends. She had a high, breathless, amused voice which made everything she said sound a little forced, whether it was sincere or not.

There was one good thing: June went places with girl friends of hers, girls who were just as plain and steady as she, and so when Connie wanted to do that her mother had no objections. The father of Connie's best girl friend drove the girls the three miles to town and left them off at a shopping plaza, so that they could walk through the stores or go to a movie, and when he came to pick them up again at eleven he never bothered to ask what they had done.

They must have been familiar sights, walking around that shopping plaza in their shorts and flat ballerina slippers that always scuffed the sidewalk, with charm bracelets jingling on their thin wrists; they would lean together to whisper and laugh secretly if someone passed by who amused or interested them. Connie had long dark blond hair that drew anyone's eye to it, and she wore part of it pulled up on her head and puffed out and the rest of it she let fall down her back. She wore a pull-over jersey blouse that looked one way when she was at home and another way when she was away from home. Everything about her had two sides to it, one for home and one for anywhere that was not home: her walk that could be childlike and bobbing, or languid enough to make anyone think she was hearing music in her head, her mouth which was pale and smirking most of the time, but bright and pink on these evenings out, her laugh which was cynical and drawling at home—"Ha, ha, very funny"—but high-pitched and nervous anywhere else, like the jingling of the charms on her bracelet.

Sometimes they did go shopping or to a movie, but sometimes they went across the highway, ducking fast across the busy road, to a drive-in restaurant where older kids hung out. The restaurant was shaped like a big bottle, though squatter than a real bottle, and on its cap was a revolving figure of a grinning boy who held a hamburger aloft. One night in mid-summer they ran across, breathless with daring, and right away someone leaned out a car window and invited them over, but it was just a boy from high school they didn't like. It made them feel good to be able to ignore him. They went up through the maze of parked and cruising cars to the bright-lit, fly-infested restaurant, their faces pleased and expectant as if they were entering a sacred building that loomed out of the night to give them what haven and what blessing they yearned for. They sat at the counter and crossed their legs at the ankles, their thin shoulders rigid with excitement, and listened to the music that made everything so good: the music was always in the background like music at a church service, it was something to depend upon.

A boy named Eddie came in to talk with them. He sat backwards on his stool, turning himself jerkily around in semi-circles and then stopping and turning again, and after a while he asked Connie if she would like something to eat. She said she did and so she tapped her friend's arm on her way out—her friend pulled her face up into a brave droll look—and Connie said she would meet her at eleven, across the way. "I just hate to leave her like that," Connie said earnestly, but the boy said that she wouldn't be alone for long. So they went out to his car and on the way Connie couldn't help but let her eyes wander over the windshields and faces all around her, her face gleaming with a joy that had nothing to do with Eddie or even this place; it might have been the music. She drew her shoulders up and sucked in her breath with the pure pleasure of being alive, and just at that moment she happened to glance at a face just a few feet from hers. It was a boy with shaggy black hair, in a convertible jalopy painted gold. He stared at her and then his lips widened into a grin. Connie slit her eyes at him and turned away, but she couldn't help glancing back and there he was still watching her. He wagged a finger and laughed and said, "Gonna get you, baby," and Connie turned away again without Eddie noticing anything.

She spent three hours with him, at the restaurant where they ate hamburgers and drank Cokes in wax cups that were always sweating, and then down an alley a mile or so away, and when he left her off at five to eleven only the movie house was still open at the plaza. Her girl friend was there, talking with a boy. When Connie came up the two girls smiled at each other and Connie said, "How was the movie?" and the girl said, "*You* should know." They rode off with the girl's father, sleepy and pleased, and Connie couldn't help but look at the darkened shopping plaza with its big empty parking lot and its signs that were faded and ghostly now, and over at the drive-in restaurant where cars were still circling tirelessly. She couldn't hear the music at this distance.

Next morning June asked her how the movie was and Connie said, "So-so."

She and that girl and occasionally another girl went out several times a week that way, and the rest of the time Connie spent around the house—it was summer vacation—getting in her mother's way and thinking, dreaming, about the boys she met. But all the boys fell back and dissolved into a single face that was not even a face, but an idea, a feeling, mixed up with the urgent insistent pounding of the music and the humid night air of July. Connie's mother kept dragging her back to the daylight by finding things for her to do or saying, suddenly, "What's this about the Pettinger girl?"

And Connie would say nervously, "Oh, her. That dope." She always drew thick clear lines between herself and such girls, and her mother was simple and kindly enough to believe her. Her mother was so simple, Connie thought, that it was maybe cruel to fool her so much. Her mother went scuffling around the house in old bedroom slippers and complained over the telephone to one sister about the other, then the other called up and the two of them complained about the third one. If June's name was mentioned her mother's tone was approving, and if Connie's name was mentioned it was disapproving. This did not really mean she disliked Connie and actually Connie thought that her mother preferred her to June because she was prettier, but the two of them kept up a pretense of exasperation, a sense that they were tugging and struggling over something of little value to either of them. Sometimes, over coffee, they were almost friends, but something would come up—some vexation that was like a fly buzzing suddenly around their heads—and their faces went hard with contempt.

One Sunday Connie got up at eleven—none of them bothered with church—and washed her hair so that it could dry all day long, in the sun. Her parents and sister were going to a barbecue at an aunt's house and Connie said no, she wasn't interested, rolling her eyes to let mother know just what she thought of it. "Stay home alone then," her mother said sharply. Connie sat out back in a lawn chair and watched them drive away, her father quiet and bald, hunched around so that he could back the car out, her mother with a look that was still angry and not at all softened through the windshield, and in the back seat poor old June all dressed up as if she didn't know what a barbecue was, with all the running yelling kids and the flies. Connie sat with her eyes closed in the sun, dreaming and dazed with the warmth about her as if this were a kind of love, the caresses of love, and her mind slipped over onto thoughts of the boy she had been with the night before and how nice he had been, how sweet it always was, not the way someone like June would suppose but sweet, gentle, the way it was in movies and promised in songs; and when she opened her eyes she hardly knew where she was, the back yard ran off into weeds and a fence-line of trees and behind it the sky was perfectly blue and still. The asbestos "ranch house" that was now three years old startled her—it looked small. She shook her head as if to get awake.

It was too hot. She went inside the house and turned on the radio to drown out the quiet. She sat on the edge of her bed, barefoot, and listened for an hour and a half to a program called XYZ Sunday Jamboree, record after record of hard, fast, shrieking songs she sang along with, interspersed by exclamations from "Bobby King": "An' look here you girls at Napoleon's—Son and Charley want you to pay real close attention to this song coming up!"

And Connie paid close attention herself, bathed in a glow of slow-pulsed joy that seemed to rise mysteriously out of the music itself and lay languidly about the airless little room, breathed in and breathed out with each gentle rise and fall of her chest.

After a while she heard a car coming up the drive. She sat up at once, startled, because it couldn't be her father so soon. The gravel kept crunching all the way in from the road—the driveway was long—and Connie ran to the window. It was a car she didn't know. It was an open jalopy, painted a bright gold that caught the sunlight opaquely. Her heart began to pound and her fingers snatched at her hair, checking it, and she whispered "Christ. Christ," wondering how bad she looked. The car came to a stop at the side door and the horn sounded four short taps as if this were a signal Connie knew.

She went into the kitchen and approached the door slowly, then hung out the screen door, her bare toes curling down off the step. There were two boys in the car and now she recognized the driver: he had shaggy, shabby black hair that looked crazy as a wig and he was grinning at her.

"I ain't late, am I?" he said.

"Who the hell do you think you are?" Connie said.

"Toldja I'd be out, didn't I?"

"I don't even know who you are."

She spoke sullenly, careful to show no interest or pleasure, and he spoke in a fast bright monotone. Connie looked past him to the other boy, taking her time. He had fair brown hair, with a lock that fell onto his forehead. His sideburns gave him a fierce, embarrassed look, but so far he hadn't even bothered to glance at her. Both boys wore sunglasses. The driver's glasses were metallic and mirrored everything in miniature.

"You wanta come for a ride?" he said.

Connie smirked and let her hair fall loose over one shoulder.

"Don'tcha like my car? New paint job," he said. "Hey."

"What?"

"You're cute."

She pretended to fidget, chasing flies away from the door.

"Don'tcha believe me, or what?" he said.

"Look, I don't even know who you are," Connie said in disgust.

"Hey, Ellie's got a radio, see. Mine's broke down." He lifted his friend's arm and showed her the little transistor the boy was holding, and now Connie began to hear the music. It was the same program that was playing inside the house.

"Bobby King?" she said.

"I listen to him all the time. I think he's great."

"He's kind of great," Connie said reluctantly.

"Listen, that guy's *great.* He knows where the action is."

Connie blushed a little, because the glasses made it impossible for her to see just what this boy was looking at. She couldn't decide if she liked him or if he was just a jerk, and so she dawdled in the doorway and wouldn't come down or go back inside. She said, "What's all that stuff painted on your car?"

"Can'tcha read it?" He opened the door very carefully, as if he was afraid it might fall off. He slid out just as carefully, planting his feet firmly on the ground, the tiny metallic world in his glasses slowing down like gelatine hardening and in the midst of it Connie's bright green blouse. "This here is my name, to begin with," he said. ARNOLD FRIEND was written in tarlike black letters on the side, with a drawing of a round grinning face that reminded Connie of a pumpkin, except it wore sunglasses. "I wanta introduce myself, I'm Arnold Friend and that's my real name and I'm gonna be your friend, honey, and inside the car's Ellie Oscar, he's kinda shy." Ellie brought his transistor radio up to his shoulder and balanced it there. "Now these numbers are a secret code, honey," Arnold Friend explained. He read off the numbers 33, 19, 17 and raised his eyebrows at her to see what she thought of that, but she didn't think much of it. The left rear fender had been smashed and around it was written, on the gleaming gold background: DONE BY CRAZY WOMAN DRIVER. Connie had to laugh at that. Arnold Friend was pleased at her laughter and looked up at her. "Around the other side's a lot more—you wanta come and see them?"

"No."

"Why not?"

"Why should I?"

"Don'tcha wanta see what's on the car? Don'tcha wanta go for a ride?"

"I don't know."

"Why not?"

"I got things to do."

"Like what?"

"Things."

He laughed as if she had said something funny. He slapped his thighs. He was standing in a strange way, leaning back against the car as if he were balancing himself. He wasn't tall, only an inch or so taller than she would be if she came down to him. Connie liked the way he was dressed, which was the way all of them dressed: tight faded jeans stuffed into black, scuffed boots, a belt that pulled his waist in and showed how lean he was, and a white pull-over shirt that was a little soiled and showed the hard small muscles of his arms and shoulders. He looked as if he probably did hard work, lifting and carrying things. Even his neck looked muscular. And his face was a familiar face, somehow: the jaw and chin and cheeks slightly darkened, because he hadn't shaved for a day or two, and the nose long and hawk-like, sniffing as if she were a treat he was going to gobble up and it was all a joke.

"Connie, you ain't telling the truth. This is your day set aside for a ride with me and you know it," he said, still laughing. The way he straightened and recovered from his fit of laughing showed that it had been all fake.

"How do you know what my name is?" she said suspiciously.

"It's Connie."

"Maybe and maybe not."

"I know my Connie," he said, wagging his finger. Now she remembered him even better, back at the restaurant, and her cheeks warmed at the thought of how she sucked in her breath just at the moment she passed him—how she must have looked to him. And he had remembered her. "Ellie and I come out here especially for you," he said. "Ellie can sit in back. How about it?"

"Where?"

"Where what?"

"Where're we going?"

He looked at her. He took off the sunglasses and she saw how pale the skin around his eyes was, like holes that were not in shadow but instead in light. His eyes were like chips of broken glass that catch the light in an amiable way. He smiled. It was as if the idea of going for a ride somewhere, to some place, was a new idea to him.

"Just for a ride, Connie sweetheart."

"I never said my name was Connie," she said.

"But I know what it is. I know your name and all about you, lots of things,"

Arnold Friend said. He had not moved yet but stood still leaning back against the side of his jalopy. "I took a special interest in you, such a pretty girl, and found out all about you like I know your parents and sister are gone somewheres and I know where and how long they're going to be gone, and I know who you were with last night, and your best girl friend's name is Betty. Right?"

He spoke in a simple lilting voice, exactly as if he were reciting the words to a song. His smile assured her that everything was fine. In the car Ellie turned up the volume on his radio and did not bother to look around at them.

"Ellie can sit in the back seat," Arnold Friend said. He indicated his friend with a casual jerk of his chin, as if Ellie did not count and she should not bother with him.

"How'd you find out all that stuff?" Connie said.

"Listen: Betty Schultz and Tony Fitch and Jimmy Pettinger and Nancy Pettinger," he said, in a chant. "Raymond Stanley and Bob Hutter—"

"Do you know all those kids?"

"I know everybody."

"Look, you're kidding. You're not from around here."

"Sure."

"But—how come we never saw you before?"

"Sure you saw me before," he said. He looked down at his boots, as if he were a little offended. "You just don't remember."

"I guess I'd remember you," Connie said.

"Yeah?" He looked up at this, beaming. He was pleased. He began to mark time with the music from Ellie's radio, tapping his fists lightly together. Connie looked away from his smile to the car, which was painted so bright it almost hurt her eyes to look at it. She looked at that name, ARNOLD FRIEND. And up at the front fender was an expression that was familiar—MAN THE FLYING SAUCERS. It was an expression kids had used the year before, but didn't use this year. She looked at it for a while as if the words meant something to her that she did not yet know.

"What're you thinking about? Huh?" Arnold Friend demanded. "Not worried about your hair blowing around in the car, are you?"

"No."

"Think I maybe can't drive good?"

"How do I know?"

"You're a hard girl to handle. How come?" he said. "Don't you know I'm your friend? Didn't you see me put my sign in the air when you walked by?"

"What sign?"

"My sign." And he drew an X in the air, leaning out toward her. They were maybe ten feet apart. After his hand fell back to his side the X was still in the air, almost visible. Connie let the screen door close and stood perfectly still inside it, listening to the music from her radio and the boy's blend together.

She stared at Arnold Friend. He stood there so stiffly relaxed, pretending to be relaxed, with one hand idly on the door handle as if he were keeping himself up that way and had no intention of ever moving again. She recognized most things about him, the tight jeans that showed his thighs and buttocks and the greasy leather boots and the tight shirt, and even that slippery friendly smile of his, that sleepy dreamy smile that all the boys used to get across ideas they didn't want to put into words. She recognized all this and also the singsong way he talked, slightly mocking, kidding, but serious and a little melancholy, and she recognized the way he tapped one fist against the other in homage to the perpetual music behind him. But all these things did not come together.

She said suddenly, "Hey, how old are you?"

His smile faded. She could see then that he wasn't a kid, he was much older —thirty, maybe more. At this knowledge her heart began to pound faster.

"That's a crazy thing to ask. Can'tcha see I'm your own age?"

"Like hell you are."

"Or maybe a coupla years older, I'm eighteen."

"Eighteen?" she said doubtfully.

He grinned to reassure her and lines appeared at the corners of his mouth. His teeth were big and white. He grinned so broadly his eyes became slits and she saw how thick the lashes were, thick and black as if painted with a black tar-like material. Then he seemed to become embarrassed, abruptly, and looked over his shoulder at Ellie. "*Him,* he's crazy," he said. "Ain't he a riot, he's a nut, a real character." Ellie was still listening to the music. His sunglasses told nothing about what he was thinking. He wore a bright orange shirt unbuttoned halfway to show his chest, which was a pale, bluish chest and not muscular like Arnold Friend's. His shirt collar was turned up all around and the very tips of the collar pointed out past his chin as if they were protecting him. He was pressing the transistor radio up against his ear and sat there in a kind of daze, right in the sun.

"He's kinda strange," Connie said.

"Hey, she says you're kinda strange! Kinda strange!" Arnold Friend cried. He pounded on the car to get Ellie's attention. Ellie turned for the first time and Connie saw with shock that he wasn't a kid either—he had a fair, hairless face, cheeks reddened slightly as if the veins grew too close to the surface of his skin, the face of a forty-year-old baby. Connie felt a wave of dizziness rise in her at this sight and she stared at him as if waiting for something to change the shock of the moment, make it all right again. Ellie's lips kept shaping words, mumbling along with the words blasting in his ear.

"Maybe you two better go away," Connie said faintly.

"What? How come?" Arnold Friend cried. "We come out here to take you for a ride. It's Sunday." He had the voice of the man on the radio now. It was the same voice, Connie thought. "Don'tcha know it's Sunday all day and honey, no matter who you were with last night today you're with Arnold Friend and don't you forget it!—Maybe you better step out here," he said, and this last was in a different voice. It was a little flatter, as if the heat was finally getting to him.

"No. I got things to do."

"Hey."

"You two better leave."

"We ain't leaving until you come with us."

"Like hell I am—"

"Connie, don't fool around with me. I mean, I mean, don't fool *around,*" he said, shaking his head. He laughed incredulously. He placed his sunglasses on top of his head, carefully, as if he were indeed wearing a wig, and brought the stems down behind his ears. Connie stared at him, another wave of dizziness and fear rising in her so that for a moment he wasn't even in focus but was just a blur, standing there against his gold car, and she had the idea that he had driven up the driveway all right but had come from nowhere before that and belonged nowhere and that everything about him and even about the music that was so familiar to her was only half real.

"If my father comes and sees you—"

"He ain't coming. He's at a barbecue."

"How do you know that?"

"Aunt Tillie's. Right now they're—uh—they're drinking. Sitting around," he said vaguely, squinting as if he were staring all the way to town and over to Aunt Tillie's back yard. Then the vision seemed to get clear and he nodded energetically. "Yeah. Sitting around. There's your sister in a blue dress, huh? And high heels, the poor sad bitch—nothing like you, sweetheart! And your mother's helping some fat woman with the corn, they're cleaning the corn—husking the corn—"

"What fat woman?" Connie cried.

"How do I know what fat woman. I don't know every goddam fat woman in the world!" Arnold Friend laughed.

"Oh, that's Mrs. Hornby. . . . Who invited her?" Connie said. She felt a little light-headed. Her breath was coming quickly.

"She's too fat. I don't like them fat. I like them the way you are, honey," he said, smiling sleepily at her. They stared at each other for a while, through the screen door. He said softly, "Now what you're going to do is this: you're going to come out that door. You're going to sit up front with me and Ellie's going to sit in the back, the hell with Ellie, right? This isn't Ellie's date. You're my date. I'm your lover, honey."

"What? You're crazy—"

"Yes, I'm your lover. You don't know what that is but you will," he said. "I know that too. I know all about you. But look: it's real nice and you couldn't ask for nobody better than me, or more polite. I always keep my word. I'll tell you how it is, I'm always nice at first, the first time. I'll hold you so tight you won't think you have to try to get away or pretend anything because you'll know you can't. And I'll come inside you where it's all secret and you'll give in to me and you'll love me—"

"Shut up! You're crazy!" Connie said. She backed away from the door. She put her hands against her ears as if she'd heard something terrible, something not meant for her. "People don't talk like that, you're crazy," she muttered. Her heart was almost too big now for her chest and its pumping made sweat break out all over her. She looked out to see Arnold Friend pause and then take a step toward the porch lurching. He almost fell. But, like a clever drunken man, he managed to catch his balance. He wobbled in his high boots and grabbed hold of one of the porch posts.

"Honey?" he said. "You still listening?"

"Get the hell out of here!"

"Be nice, honey. Listen."

"I'm going to call the police—"

He wobbled again and out of the side of his mouth came a fast spat curse, an aside not meant for her to hear. But even this "Christ!" sounded forced. Then he began to smile again. She watched this smile come, awkward as if he were smiling from inside a mask. His whole face was a mask, she thought wildly, tanned down onto his throat but then running out as if he had plastered make-up on his face but had forgotten about his throat.

"Honey—? Listen, here's how it is. I always tell the truth and I promise you this: I ain't coming in that house after you."

"You better not! I'm going to call the police if you—if you don't—"

"Honey," he said, talking right through her voice, "honey, I'm not coming in there but you are coming out here. You know why?"

She was panting. The kitchen looked like a place she had never seen before, some room she had run inside but which wasn't good enough, wasn't going to help her. The kitchen window had never had a curtain, after three years, and there were dishes in the sink for her to do—probably—and if you ran your hand across the table you'd probably feel something sticky there.

"You listening, honey? Hey?"

"—going to call the police—"

"Soon as you touch the phone I don't need to keep my promise and can come inside. You won't want that."

She rushed forward and tried to lock the door. Her fingers were shaking. "But why lock it," Arnold Friend said gently, talking right into her face. "It's just a screen door. It's just nothing." One of his boots was at a strange angle, as if his foot wasn't in it. It pointed out to the left, bent at the ankle. "I mean, anybody can break through a screen door and glass and wood and iron or anything else if he needs to, anybody at all and specially Arnold Friend. If the place got lit up with a fire honey you'd come running out into my arms, right into my arms and safe at home—like you knew I was your lover and'd stopped fooling around. I don't mind a nice shy girl but I don't like no fooling around." Part of those words were spoken with a slight rhythmic lilt, and Connie somehow recognized them—the echo of a song from last year, about a girl rushing into her boy friend's arms and coming home again—

Connie stood barefoot on the linoleum floor, staring at him. "What do you want?" she whispered.

"I want you," he said.

"What?"

"Seen you that night and thought, that's the one, yes sir. I never needed to look any more."

"But my father's coming back. He's coming to get me. I had to wash my hair first—" She spoke in a dry, rapid voice, hardly raising it for him to hear.

"No, your daddy is not coming and yes, you had to wash your hair and you washed it for me. It's nice and shining and all for me, I thank you, sweetheart," he said, with a mock bow, but again he almost lost his balance. He had to bend and adjust his boots. Evidently his feet did not go all the way down; the boots must have been stuffed with something so that he would seem taller. Connie stared out at him and behind him Ellie in the car, who seemed to be looking off toward Connie's right, into nothing. This Ellie said, pulling the words out of the air one after another as if he were just discovering them, "You want me to pull out the phone?"

"Shut your mouth and keep it shut," Arnold Friend said, his face red from bending over or maybe from embarrassment because Connie had seen his boots. "This ain't none of your business."

"What—what are you doing? What do you want?" Connie said. "If I call the police they'll get you, they'll arrest you—"

"Promise was not to come in unless you touch that phone, and I'll keep that promise," he said. He resumed his erect position and tried to force his shoulders back. He sounded like a hero in a movie, declaring something important. He spoke too loudly and it was as if he were speaking to someone behind Connie. "I ain't made plans for coming in that house where I don't belong but just for you to come out to me, the way you should. Don't you know who I am?"

"You're crazy," she whispered. She backed away from the door but did not want to go into another part of the house, as if this would give him permission to come through the door. "What do you. . . . You're crazy, you . . ."

"Huh? What're you saying, honey?"

Her eyes darted everywhere in the kitchen. She could not remember what it was, this room.

"This is how it is, honey: you come out and we'll drive away, have a nice ride. But if you don't come out we're gonna wait till your people come home and then they're all going to get it."

"You want that telephone pulled out?" Ellie said. He held the radio away from his ear and grimaced, as if without the radio the air was too much for him.

"I toldja shut up, Ellie," Arnold Friend said, "you're deaf, get a hearing aid, right? Fix yourself up. This little girl's no trouble and's gonna be nice to me, so Ellie keep to yourself, this ain't your date—right? Don't hem in on me. Don't hog. Don't crush. Don't bird dog. Don't trail me," he said in a rapid meaningless voice, as if he were running through all the expressions he'd learned but was no longer sure which one of them was in style, then rushing on to new ones, making them up with his eyes closed, "Don't crawl under my fence, don't squeeze in my chipmunk hole, don't sniff my glue, suck my popsicle, keep your own greasy fingers on yourself!" He shaded his eyes and peered in at Connie, who was backed against the kitchen table. "Don't mind him honey he's just a creep. He's a dope. Right? I'm the boy for you and like I said you come out here nice like a lady and give me your hand, and nobody else gets hurt, I mean, your nice old bald-headed daddy and your mummy and your sister in her high heels. Because listen: why bring them in this?"

"Leave me alone," Connie whispered.

"Hey, you know that old woman down the road, the one with the chickens and stuff—you know her?"

"She's dead!"

"Dead? What? You know her?" Arnold Friend said.

"She's dead—"

"Don't you like her?"

"She's dead—she's—she isn't here any more—"

"But don't you like her, I mean, you got something against her? Some grudge or something?" Then his voice dipped as if he were conscious of a rudeness. He touched the sunglasses perched on top of his head as if to make sure they were still there. "Now you be a good girl."

"What are you going to do?"

"Just two things, or maybe three," Arnold Friend said. "But I promise it won't last long and you'll like me that way you get to like people you're close to. You will. It's all over for you here, so come on out. You don't want your people in any trouble, do you?"

She turned and bumped against a chair or something, hurting her leg, but she ran into the back room and picked up the telephone. Something roared in her ear, a tiny roaring, and she was so sick with fear that she could do nothing but listen to it—the telephone was clammy and very heavy and her fingers groped down to the dial but were too weak to touch it. She began to scream into the phone, into the roaring. She cried out, she cried for her mother, she felt her breath start jerking back and forth in her lungs as if it were something Arnold Friend were stabbing her with again and again with no tenderness. A noisy sorrowful wailing rose all about her and she was locked inside it the way she was locked inside the house.

After a while she could hear again. She was sitting on the floor with her wet back against the wall.

Arnold Friend was saying from the door, "That's a good girl. Put the phone back."

She kicked the phone away from her.

"No, honey. Pick it up. Put it back right."

She picked it up and put it back. The dial tone stopped.

"That's a good girl. Now you come outside."

She was hollow with what had been fear, but what was now just an emptiness. All that screaming had blasted it out of her. She sat, one leg cramped under her, and deep inside her brain was something like a pinpoint of light that kept going and would not let her relax. She thought, I'm not going to see my mother again. She thought, I'm not going to sleep in my bed again. Her bright green blouse was all wet.

Arnold Friend said, in a gentle-loud voice that was like a stage voice, "The place where you came from ain't there any more, and where you had in mind to go is cancelled out. This place you are now—inside your daddy's house—is nothing but a cardboard box I can knock down any time. You know that and always did know it. You hear me?"

She thought, I have got to think. I have to know what to do.

"We'll go out to a nice field, out in the country here where it smells so nice and it's sunny," Arnold Friend said. "I'll have my arms around you so you won't need to try to get away and I'll show you what love is like, what it does. The hell with this house! It looks solid all right," he said. He ran a fingernail down the screen and the noise did not make Connie shiver, as it would have the day before. "Now put your hand on your heart, honey. Feel that? That feels solid too but we know better, be nice to me, be sweet like you can because what else is there for a girl like you but to be sweet and pretty and give in? —and get away before her people come back?"

She felt her pounding heart. Her hand seemed to enclose it. She thought for the first time in her life that it was nothing that was hers, that belonged to her, but just a pounding, living thing inside this body that wasn't really hers either.

"You don't want them to get hurt," Arnold Friend went on. "Now get up, honey. Get up all by yourself."

She stood.

"Now turn this way. That's right. Come over here to me—Ellie, put that away, didn't I tell you? You dope. You miserable creepy dope," Arnold Friend said. His words were not angry but only part of an incantation. The incantation was kindly. "Now come out through the kitchen to me honey and let's see a smile, try it, you're a brave sweet little girl and now they're eating corn and hotdogs cooked to bursting over an outdoor fire, and they don't know one thing about you and never did and honey you're better than them because not a one of them would have done this for you."

Connie felt the linoleum under her feet; it was cool. She brushed her hair back out of her eyes. Arnold Friend let go of the post tentatively and opened his arms for her, his elbows pointing in toward each other and his wrists limp, to show that this was an embarrassed embrace and a little mocking, he didn't want to make her self-conscious.

She put out her hand against the screen. She watched herself push the door slowly open as if she were safe back somewhere in the other doorway, watching this body and this head of long hair moving out into the sunlight where Arnold Friend waited.

"My sweet little blue-eyed girl," he said, in a half-sung sigh that had nothing to do with her brown eyes but was taken up just the same by the vast sunlit reaches of the land behind him and on all sides of him, so much land that Connie had never seen before and did not recognize except to know that she was going to it.

In the Region of Ice

Sister Irene was a tall, deft woman in her early thirties. What one could see of her face made a striking impression—serious, hard gray eyes, a long slender nose, a face waxen with thought. Seen at the right time, from the right angle, she was almost handsome. In her past teaching positions she had drawn a little upon the fact of her being young and brilliant and also a nun, but she was beginning to grow out of that.

This was a new university and an entirely new world. She had heard—of course it was true—that the Jesuit administration of this school had hired her at the last moment to save money and to head off the appointment of a man of dubious religious commitment. She had prayed for the necessary energy to get her through this first semester. She had no trouble with teaching itself; once she stood before a classroom she felt herself capable of anything. It was the world immediately outside the classroom that confused and alarmed her, though she let none of this show—the cynicism of her colleagues, the indifference of many of the students, and, above all, the looks she got that told her nothing much would be expected of her because she was a nun. This took energy, strength. At times she had the idea that she was on trial and that the excuses she made to herself about her discomfort were only the common excuses made by guilty people. But in front of a class she had no time to worry about herself or the conflicts in her mind. She became, once and for all, a figure existing only for the benefit of others, an instrument by which facts were communicated.

About two weeks after the semester began, Sister Irene noticed a new student in her class. He was slight and fair-haired, and his face was blank, but not blank by accident, blank on purpose, suppressed and restricted into a dumbness that looked hysterical. She was prepared for him before he raised his hand, and when she saw his arm jerk, as if he had at last lost control of it, she nodded to him without hesitation.

"Sister, how can this be reconciled with Shakespeare's vision in *Hamlet*? How can these opposing views be in the same mind?"

Students glanced at him, mildly surprised. He did not belong in the class, and this was mysterious, but his manner was urgent and blind.

"There is no need to reconcile opposing views," Sister Irene said, leaning forward against the podium. "In one play Shakespeare suggests one vision, in another play another; the plays are not simultaneous creations, and even if they were, we never demand a logical—"

"We must demand a logical consistency," the young man said. "The idea of education is itself predicated upon consistency, order, sanity—"

He had interrupted her, and she hardened her face against him—for his sake, not her own, since she did not really care. But he noticed nothing. "Please see me after class," she said.

After class the young man hurried up to her.

"Sister Irene, I hope you didn't mind my visiting today. I'd heard some things, interesting things," he said. He stared at her, and something in her face allowed him to smile. "I . . . could we talk in your office? Do you have time?"

They walked down to her office. Sister Irene sat at her desk, and the young man sat facing her; for a moment they were self-conscious and silent.

"Well, I suppose you know—I'm a Jew," he said.

Sister Irene stared at him. "Yes?" she said.

"What am I doing at a Catholic university, huh?" He grinned. "That's what you want to know."

She made a vague movement of her hand to show that she had no thoughts on this, nothing at all, but he seemed not to catch it. He was sitting on the edge of the straight-backed chair. She saw that he was young but did not really look young. There were harsh lines on either side of his mouth, as if he had misused that youthful mouth somehow. His skin was almost as pale as hers, his eyes were dark and not quite in focus. He looked at her and through her and around her, as his voice surrounded them both. His voice was a little shrill at times.

"Listen, I did the right thing today—visiting your class! God, what a lucky accident it was; some jerk mentioned you, said you were a good teacher—I thought, what a laugh! These people know about good teachers here? But yes, listen, yes, I'm not kidding—you are good. I mean that."

Sister Irene frowned. "I don't quite understand what all this means."

He smiled and waved aside her formality, as if he knew better. "Listen, I got my B.A. at Columbia, then I came back here to this crappy city. I mean, I did it on purpose, I wanted to come back. I wanted to. I have my reasons for doing things. I'm on a three-thousand-dollar fellowship," he said, and waited for that to impress her. "You know, I could have gone almost anywhere with that fellowship, and I came back home here—my home's in the city—and enrolled here. This was last year. This is my second year. I'm working on a thesis, I mean I was, my master's thesis—but the hell with that. What I want to ask you is this: Can I enroll in your class, is it too late? We have to get special permission if we're late."

Sister Irene felt something nudging her, some uneasiness in him that was pleading with her not to be offended by his abrupt, familiar manner. He seemed to be promising another self, a better self, as if his fair, childish, almost cherubic face were doing tricks to distract her from what his words said.

"Are you in English studies?" she asked.

"I was in history. Listen," he said, and his mouth did something odd, drawing itself down into a smile that made the lines about it deepen like knives, "listen, they kicked me out."

He sat back, watching her. He crossed his legs. He took out a package of cigarettes and offered her one. Sister Irene shook her head, staring at his hands. They were small and stubby and might have belonged to a ten-year-old, and the nails were a strange near-violet color. It took him awhile to extract a cigarette.

"Yeah, kicked me out. What do you think of that?"

"I don't understand."

"My master's thesis was coming along beautifully, and then this bastard —I mean, excuse me, this professor, I won't pollute your office with his name —he started making criticisms, he said some things were unacceptable, he—" The boy leaned forward and hunched his narrow shoulders in a parody of secrecy. "We had an argument. I told him some frank things, things only a broad-minded person could hear about himself. That takes courage, right? He didn't have it! He kicked me out of the master's program, so now I'm coming into English. Literature is greater than history; European history is one big pile of garbage. Sky-high. Filth and rotting corpses, right? Aristotle says that poetry is higher than history; he's right; in your class today I suddenly realized that this is my field, Shakespeare, only Shakespeare is—"

Sister Irene guessed that he was going to say that only Shakespeare was equal to him, and she caught the moment of recognition and hesitation, the half-raised arm, the keen, frowning forehead, the narrowed eyes; then he thought better of it and did not end the sentence. "The students in your class are mainly negligible, I can tell you that. You're new here, and I've been here a year—I would have finished my studies last year but my father got sick, he was hospitalized, I couldn't take exams and it was a mess—but I'll make it through English in one year or drop dead. I can do it, I can do anything. I'll take six courses at once—" He broke off, breathless. Sister Irene tried to smile. "All right then, it's settled? You'll let me in? Have I missed anything so far?"

He had no idea of the rudeness of his question. Sister Irene, feeling suddenly exhausted, said, "I'll give you a syllabus of the course."

"Fine! Wonderful!"

He got to his feet eagerly. He looked through the schedule, muttering to himself, making favorable noises. It struck Sister Irene that she was making a mistake to let him in. There were these moments when one had to make an intelligent decision. . . . But she was sympathetic with him, yes. She was sympathetic with something about him.

She found out his name the next day: Allen Weinstein.

After this she came to her Shakespeare class with a sense of excitement. It became clear to her at once that Weinstein was the most intelligent student in the class. Until he had enrolled, she had not understood what was lacking, a mind that could appreciate her own. Within a week his jagged, protean mind had alienated the other students, and though he sat in the center of the class, he seemed totally alone, encased by a miniature world of his own. When he spoke of the "frenetic humanism of the High Renaissance," Sister Irene dreaded the raised eyebrows and mocking smiles of the other students, who no longer bothered to look at Weinstein. She wanted to defend him, but she never did, because there was something rude and dismal about his knowledge; he used it like a weapon, talking passionately of Nietzsche and Goethe and Freud until Sister Irene would be forced to close discussion.

In meditation, alone, she often thought of him. When she tried to talk about him to a young nun, Sister Carlotta, everything sounded gross. "But no, he's an excellent student," she insisted. "I'm very grateful to have him in class. It's just that . . . he thinks ideas are real." Sister Carlotta, who loved literature also, had been forced to teach grade-school arithmetic for the last four years. That might have been why she said, a little sharply, "You don't think ideas are real?"

Sister Irene acquiesced with a smile, but of course she did not think so: only reality is real.

When Weinstein did not show up for class on the day the first paper was due, Sister Irene's heart sank, and the sensation was somehow a familiar one. She began her lecture and kept waiting for the door to open and for him to hurry noisily back to his seat, grinning an apology toward her—but nothing happened.

If she had been deceived by him, she made herself think angrily, it was as a teacher and not as a woman. He had promised her nothing.

Weinstein appeared the next day near the steps of the liberal arts building. She heard someone running behind her, a breathless exclamation: "Sister Irene!" She turned and saw him, panting and grinning in embarrassment. He wore a dark-blue suit with a necktie, and he looked, despite his childish face, like a little old man; there was something oddly precarious and fragile about him. "Sister Irene, I owe you an apology, right?" He raised his eyebrows and smiled a sad, forlorn, yet irritatingly conspiratorial smile. "The first paper—not in on time, and I know what your rules are. . . . You won't accept late papers, I know—that's good discipline, I'll do that when I teach too. But, unavoidably, I was unable to come to school yesterday. There are many—many—" He gulped for breath, and Sister Irene had the startling sense of seeing the real Weinstein stare out at her, a terrified prisoner behind the confident voice. "There are many complications in family life. Perhaps you are unaware—I mean—"

She did not like him, but she felt this sympathy, something tugging and nagging at her the way her parents had competed for her love so many years before. They had been whining, weak people, and out of their wet need for affection, the girl she had been (her name was Yvonne) had emerged stronger than either of them, contemptuous of tears because she had seen so many. But Weinstein was different; he was not simply weak—perhaps he was not weak at all—but his strength was confused and hysterical. She felt her customary rigidity as a teacher begin to falter. "You may turn your paper in today if you have it," she said, frowning.

Weinstein's mouth jerked into an incredulous grin. "Wonderful! Marvelous!" he said. "You are very understanding, Sister Irene, I must say. I must say . . . I didn't expect, really . . . " He was fumbling in a shabby old briefcase for the paper. Sister Irene waited. She was prepared for another of his excuses, certain that he did not have the paper, when he suddenly straightened up and handed her something. "Here! I took the liberty of writing thirty pages instead of just fifteen," he said. He was obviously quite excited; his cheeks were mottled pink and white. "You may disagree violently with my interpretation —I expect you to, in fact I'm counting on it—but let me warn you, I have the exact proof, right here in the play itself!" He was thumping at a book, his voice growing louder and shriller. Sister Irene, startled, wanted to put her hand over his mouth and soothe him.

"Look," he said breathlessly, "may I talk with you? I have a class now I hate, I loathe, I can't bear to sit through! Can I talk with you instead?"

Because she was nervous, she stared at the title page of the paper: " 'Erotic Melodies in *Romeo and Juliet*' by Allen Weinstein, Jr."

"All right?" he said. "Can we walk around here? Is it all right? I've been anxious to talk with you about some things you said in class."

She was reluctant, but he seemed not to notice. They walked slowly along the shaded campus paths. Weinstein did all the talking, of course, and Sister Irene recognized nothing in his cascade of words that she had mentioned in class. "The humanist must be committed to the totality of life," he said passionately. "This is the failing one finds everywhere in the academic world! I found it in New York and I found it here and I'm no ingénu, I don't go around with my mouth hanging open—I'm experienced, look, I've been to Europe, I've lived in Rome! I went everywhere in Europe except Germany, I don't talk about Germany . . . Sister Irene, think of the significant men in the last century, the men who've changed the world! Jews, right? Marx, Freud, Einstein! Not that I believe Marx, Marx is a madman . . . and Freud, no, my sympathies are with spiritual humanism. I believe that the Jewish race is the exclusive . . . the exclusive, what's the word, the exclusive means by which humanism will be extended . . . Humanism begins by excluding the Jew, and now," he said with a high, surprised laugh, "the Jew will perfect it. After the Nazis, only the Jew is authorized to understand humanism, its limitations and its possibilities. So, I say that the humanist is committed to life in its totality and not just to his profession! The religious person is totally religious, he is his religion! What else? I recognize in you a humanist and a religious person—"

But he did not seem to be talking to her or even looking at her.

"Here, read this," he said. "I wrote it last night." It was a long free-verse poem, typed on a typewriter whose ribbon was worn out.

"There's this trouble with my father, a wonderful man, a lovely man, but his health—his strength is fading, do you see? What must it be to him to see his son growing up? I mean, I'm a man now, he's getting old, weak, his health is bad—it's hell, right? I sympathize with him. I'd do anything for him, I'd cut open my veins, anything for a father—right? That's why I wasn't in school yesterday," he said, and his voice dropped for the last sentence, as if he had been dragged back to earth by a fact.

Sister Irene tried to read the poem, then pretended to read it. A jumble of words dealing with "life" and "death" and "darkness" and "love." "What do you think?" Weinstein said nervously, trying to read it over her shoulder and crowding against her.

"It's very . . . passionate," Sister Irene said.

This was the right comment; he took the poem back from her in silence, his face flushed with excitement. "Here, at this school, I have few people to talk with. I haven't shown anyone else that poem." He looked at her with his dark, intense eyes, and Sister Irene felt them focus upon her. She was terrified at what he was trying to do—he was trying to force her into a human relationship.

"Thank you for your paper," she said, turning away.

When he came the next day, ten minutes late, he was haughty and disdainful. He had nothing to say and sat with his arms folded. Sister Irene took back with her to the convent a feeling of betrayal and confusion. She had been hurt. It was absurd, and yet— She spent too much time thinking about him, as if he were somehow a kind of crystallization of her own loneliness; but she had no right to think so much of him. She did not want to think of him or of her loneliness. But Weinstein did so much more than think of his predicament: he embodied it, he acted it out, and that was perhaps why he fascinated her. It was as if he were doing a dance for her, a dance of shame and agony and delight, and so long as he did it, she was safe. She felt embarrassment for him, but also anxiety; she wanted to protect him. When the dean of the graduate school questioned her about Weinstein's work, she insisted that he was an "excellent" student, though she knew the dean had not wanted to hear that.

She prayed for guidance, she spent hours on her devotions, she was closer to her vocation than she had been for some years. Life at the convent became tinged with unreality, a misty distortion that took its tone from the glowering skies of the city at night, identical smokestacks ranged against the clouds and giving to the sky the excrement of the populated and successful earth. This city was not her city, this world was not her world. She felt no pride in knowing this, it was a fact. The little convent was not like an island in the center of this noisy world, but rather a kind of hole or crevice the world did not bother with, something of no interest. The convent's rhythm of life had nothing to do with the world's rhythm, it did not violate or alarm it in any way. Sister Irene tried to draw together the fragments of her life and synthesize them somehow in her vocation as a nun: she was a nun, she was recognized as a nun and had given herself happily to that life, she had a name, a place, she had dedicated her superior intelligence to the Church, she worked without pay and without expecting gratitude, she had given up pride, she did not think of herself but only of her work and her vocation, she did not think of anything external to these, she saturated herself daily in the knowledge that she was involved in the mystery of Christianity.

A daily terror attended this knowledge, however, for she sensed herself being drawn by that student, that Jewish boy, into a relationship she was not ready for. She wanted to cry out in fear that she was being forced into the role of a Christian, and what did that mean? What could her studies tell her? What could the other nuns tell her? She was alone, no one could help; he was making her into a Christian, and to her that was a mystery, a thing of terror, something others slipped on the way they slipped on their clothes, casually and thoughtlessly, but to her a magnificent and terrifying wonder.

For days she carried Weinstein's paper, marked A, around with her; he did not come to class. One day she checked with the graduate office and was told that Weinstein had called in to say his father was ill and that he would not be able to attend classes for a while. "He's strange, I remember him," the secretary said. "He missed all his exams last spring and made a lot of trouble. He was in and out of here every day."

So there was no more of Weinstein for a while, and Sister Irene stopped expecting him to hurry into class. Then, one morning, she found a letter from him in her mailbox.

He had printed it in black ink, very carefully, as if he had not trusted handwriting. The return address was in bold letters that, like his voice, tried to grab onto her: Birchcrest Manor. Somewhere north of the city. "Dear Sister Irene," the block letters said, "I am doing well here and have time for reading and relaxing. The Manor is delightful. My doctor here is an excellent, intelligent man who has time for me, unlike my former doctor. If you have time, you might drop in on my father, who worries about me too much I think, and explain to him what my condition is. He doesn't seem to understand. I feel about this new life the way that boy, what's his name, in *Measure for Measure,* feels about the prospects of a different life; you remember what he says to his sister when she visits him in prison, how he is looking forward to an escape into another world. Perhaps you could *explain* this to my father and he would stop worrying." The letter ended with the father's name and address, in letters that were just a little too big. Sister Irene, walking slowly down the corridor as she read the letter, felt her eyes cloud over with tears. She was cold with fear, it was something she had never experienced before. She knew what Weinstein was trying to tell her, and the desperation of his attempt made it all the more pathetic; he did not deserve this, why did God allow him to suffer so?

She read through Claudio's speech to his sister, in *Measure for Measure:*

Ay, but to die, and go we know not where;
To lie in cold obstruction and to rot;
This sensible warm motion to become
A kneaded clod; and the delighted spirit
To bathe in fiery floods, or to reside
In thrilling region of thick-ribbed ice,
To be imprison'd in the viewless winds
And blown with restless violence round about
The pendent world; or to be worse than worst
Of those that lawless and incertain thought
Imagines howling! 'Tis too horrible!
The weariest and most loathed worldly life
That age, ache, penury, and imprisonment
Can lay on nature is a paradise
To what we fear of death.

Sister Irene called the father's number that day. "Allen Weinstein residence, who may I say is calling?" a woman said, bored. "May I speak to Mr. Weinstein? It's urgent—about his son," Sister Irene said. There was a pause at the other end. "You want to talk to his mother, maybe?" the woman said. "His mother? Yes, his mother, then. Please. It's very important."

She talked with this strange, unsuspected woman, a disembodied voice that suggested absolutely no face, and insisted upon going over that afternoon. The woman was nervous, but Sister Irene, who was a university professor, after all, knew enough to hide her own nervousness. She kept waiting for the woman to say, "Yes, Allen has mentioned you . . ." but nothing happened.

She persuaded Sister Carlotta to ride over with her. This urgency of hers was something they were all amazed by. They hadn't suspected that the set of her gray eyes could change to this blurred, distracted alarm, this sense of mission that seemed to have come to her from nowhere. Sister Irene drove across the city in the late afternoon traffic, with the high whining noises from residential streets where trees were being sawed down in pieces. She understood now the secret, sweet wildness that Christ must have felt, giving himself for man, dying for the billions of men who would never know of him and never understand the sacrifice. For the first time she approached the realization of that great act. In her troubled mind the city traffic was jumbled and yet oddly coherent, an image of the world that was always out of joint with what was happening in it, its inner history struggling with its external spectacle. This sacrifice of Christ's, so mysterious and legendary now, almost lost in time—it was that by which Christ transcended both God and man at one moment, more than man because of his fate to do what no other man could do, and more than God because no god could suffer as he did. She felt a flicker of something close to madness.

She drove nervously, uncertainly, afraid of missing the street and afraid of finding it too, for while one part of her rushed forward to confront these people who had betrayed their son, another part of her would have liked nothing so much as to be waiting as usual for the summons to dinner, safe in her room. . . . When she found the street and turned onto it, she was in a state of breathless excitement. Here lawns were bright green and marred with only a few leaves, magically clean, and the houses were enormous and pompous, a mixture of styles: ranch houses, colonial houses, French country houses, white-bricked wonders with curving glass and clumps of birch trees somehow encircled by white concrete. Sister Irene stared as if she had blundered into another world. This was a kind of heaven, and she was too shabby for it.

The Weinsteins' house was the strangest one of all: it looked like a small Alpine lodge, with an inverted-V-shaped front entrance. Sister Irene drove up the black-topped driveway and let the car slow to a stop; she told Sister Carlotta she would not be long.

At the door she was met by Weinstein's mother, a small, nervous woman with hands like her son's. "Come in, come in," the woman said. She had once been beautiful, that was clear, but now in missing beauty she was not handsome or even attractive but looked ruined and perplexed, the misshapen swelling of her white-blond professionally set hair like a cap lifting up from her surprised face. "He'll be right in. Allen?" she called, "our visitor is here." They went into the living room. There was a grand piano at one end and an organ at the other. In between were scatterings of brilliant modern furniture in conversational groups, and several puffed-up white rugs on the polished floor. Sister Irene could not stop shivering.

"Professor, it's so strange, but let me say when the phone rang I had a feeling—I had a feeling," the woman said, with damp eyes. Sister Irene sat, and the woman hovered about her. "Should I call you Professor? We don't . . . you know . . . we don't understand the technicalities that go with—Allen, my son, wanted to go here to the Catholic school; I told my husband why not? Why fight? It's the thing these days, they do anything they want for knowledge. And he had to come home, you know. He couldn't take care of himself in New York, that was the beginning of the trouble. . . . Should I call you Professor?"

"You can call me Sister Irene."

"Sister Irene?" the woman said, touching her throat in awe, as if something intimate and unexpected had happened.

Then Weinstein's father appeared, hurrying. He took long, impatient strides. Sister Irene stared at him and in that instant doubted everything—he was in his fifties, a tall, sharply handsome man, heavy but not fat, holding his shoulders back with what looked like an effort, but holding them back just the same. He wore a dark suit and his face was flushed, as if he had run a long distance.

"Now," he said, coming to Sister Irene and with a precise wave of his hand motioning his wife off, "now, let's straighten this out. A lot of confusion over that kid, eh?" He pulled a chair over, scraping it across a rug and pulling one corner over, so that its brown underside was exposed. "I came home early just for this, Libby phoned me. Sister, you got a letter from him, right?"

The wife looked at Sister Irene over her husband's head as if trying somehow to coach her, knowing that this man was so loud and impatient that no one could remember anything in his presence.

"A letter—yes—today—"

"He says what in it? You got the letter, eh? Can I see it?"

She gave it to him and wanted to explain, but he silenced her with a flick of his hand. He read through the letter so quickly that Sister Irene thought perhaps he was trying to impress her with his skill at reading. "So?" he said, raising his eyes, smiling, "so what is this? He's happy out there, he says. He doesn't communicate with us any more, but he writes to you and says he's happy—what's that? I mean, what the hell is that?"

"But he isn't happy. He wants to come home," Sister Irene said. It was so important that she make him understand that she could not trust her voice; goaded by this man, it might suddenly turn shrill, as his son's did. "Someone must read their letters before they're mailed, so he tried to tell me something by making an allusion to—"

"What?"

"—an allusion to a play, so that I would know. He may be thinking suicide, he must be very unhappy—"

She ran out of breath. Weinstein's mother had begun to cry, but the father was shaking his head jerkily back and forth. "Forgive me, Sister, but it's a lot of crap, he needs the hospital, he needs help—right? It costs me fifty a day out there, and they've got the best place in the state, I figure it's worth it. He needs help, that kid, what do I care if he's unhappy? He's unbalanced!" he said angrily. "You want us to get him out again? We argued with the judge for two hours to get him in, an acquaintance of mine. Look, he can't control himself—he was smashing things here, he was hysterical. They need help, lady, and you do something about it fast! You do something! We made up our minds to do something and we did it! This letter—what the hell is this letter? He never talked like that to us!"

"But he means the opposite of what he says—"

"Then he's crazy! I'm the first to admit it." He was perspiring, and his face had darkened. "I've got no pride left this late. He's a little bastard, you want to know? He calls me names, he's filthy, got a filthy mouth—that's being smart, huh? They give him a big scholarship for his filthy mouth? I went to college too, and I got out and knew something, and I for Christ's sake did something with it; my wife is an intelligent woman, a learned woman, would you guess she does book reviews for the little newspaper out here? Intelligent isn't crazy—crazy isn't intelligent. Maybe for you at the school he writes nice papers and gets an A, but out here, around the house, he can't control himself, and we got him committed!"

"But—"

"We're fixing him up, don't worry about it!" He turned to his wife. "Libby, get out of here, I mean it. I'm sorry, but get out of here, you're making a fool of yourself, go stand in the kitchen or something, you and the goddamn maid can cry on each other's shoulders. That one in the kitchen is nuts too, they're all nuts. Sister," he said, his voice lowering, "I thank you immensely for coming out here. This is wonderful, your interest in my son. And I see he admires you—that letter there. But what about that letter? If he did want to get out, which I don't admit—he was willing to be committed, in the end he said okay himself—if he wanted out I wouldn't do it. Why? So what if he wants to come back? The next day he wants something else, what then? He's a sick kid, and I'm the first to admit it."

Sister Irene felt that sickness spread to her. She stood. The room was so big it seemed it must be a public place; there had been nothing personal or private about their conversation. Weinstein's mother was standing by the fireplace, sobbing. The father jumped to his feet and wiped his forehead in a gesture that was meant to help Sister Irene on her way out. "God, what a day," he said, his eyes snatching at hers for understanding, "you know—one of those days all day long? Sister, I thank you a lot. There should be more people in the world who care about others, like you. I mean that."

On the way back to the convent, the man's words returned to her, and she could not get control of them; she could not even feel anger. She had been pressed down, forced back, what could she do? Weinstein might have been watching her somehow from a barred window, and he surely would have understood. The strange idea she had had on the way over, something about understanding Christ, came back to her now and sickened her. But the sickness was small. It could be contained.

About a month after her visit to his father, Weinstein himself showed up. He was dressed in a suit as before, even the necktie was the same. He came right into her office as if he had been pushed and could not stop.

"Sister," he said, and shook her hand. He must have seen fear in her because he smiled ironically. "Look, I'm released. I'm let out of the nut house. Can I sit down?"

He sat. Sister Irene was breathing quickly, as if in the presence of an enemy who does not know he is an enemy.

"So, they finally let me out. I heard what you did. You talked with him, that was all I wanted. You're the only one who gave a damn. Because you're a humanist and a religious person, you respect . . . the individual. Listen," he said, whispering, "it was hell out there! Hell Birchcrest Manor! All fixed up with fancy chairs and *Life* magazines lying around—and what do they do to you? They locked me up, they gave me shock treatments! Shock treatments, how do you like that, it's discredited by everybody now—they're crazy out there themselves, sadists. They locked me up, they gave me hypodermic shots, they didn't treat me like a human being! Do you know what that is," Weinstein demanded savagely, "not to be treated like a human being? They made me an animal—for fifty dollars a day! Dirty filthy swine! Now I'm an outpatient because I stopped swearing at them. I found somebody's bobby pin, and when I wanted to scream I pressed it under my fingernail and it stopped me—the screaming went inside and not out—so they gave me good reports, those sick bastards. Now I'm an outpatient and I can walk along the street and breathe in the same filthy exhaust from the buses like all you normal people! Christ," he said, and threw himself back against the chair.

Sister Irene stared at him. She wanted to take his hand, to make some gesture that would close the aching distance between them. "Mr. Weinstein—"

"Call me Allen!" he said sharply.

"I'm very sorry—I'm terribly sorry—"

"My own parents committed me, but of course they didn't know what it was like. It was hell," he said thickly, "and there isn't any hell except what other people do to you. The psychiatrist out there, the main shrink, he hates Jews too, some of us were positive of that, and he's got a bigger nose than I do, a real beak." He made a noise of disgust. "A dirty bastard, a sick, dirty, pathetic bastard—all of them. Anyway, I'm getting out of here, and I came to ask you a favor."

"What do you mean?"

"I'm getting out. I'm leaving. I'm going up to Canada and lose myself. I'll get a job, I'll forget everything, I'll kill myself maybe—what's the difference? Look, can you lend me some money?"

"Money?"

"Just a little! I have to get to the border, I'm going to take a bus."

"But I don't have any money—"

"No money?" He stared at her. "You mean—you don't have any? Sure you have some!"

She stared at him as if he had asked her to do something obscene. Everything was splotched and uncertain before her eyes.

"You must . . . you must go back," she said, "you're making a—"

"I'll pay it back. Look, I'll pay it back, can you go to where you live or something and get it? I'm in a hurry. My friends are sons of bitches: one of them pretended he didn't see me yesterday—I stood right in the middle of the sidewalk and yelled at him, I called him some appropriate names! So he didn't see me, huh? You're the only one who understands me, you understand me like a poet, you—"

"I can't help you, I'm sorry—I . . ."

He looked to one side of her and flashed his gaze back, as if he could control it. He seemed to be trying to clear his vision.

"You have the soul of a poet," he whispered, "you're the only one. Everybody else is rotten! Can't you lend me some money, ten dollars maybe? I have three thousand in the bank, and I can't touch it! They take everything away from me, they make me into an animal. . . . You know I'm not an animal, don't you? Don't you?"

"Of course," Sister Irene whispered.

"You could get money. Help me. Give me your hand or something, touch me, help me—please. . . ." He reached for her hand and she drew back. He stared at her and his face seemed about to crumble, like a child's. "I want something from you, but I don't know what—I want something!" he cried. "Something real! I want you to look at me like I was a human being, is that too much to ask? I have a brain, I'm alive, I'm suffering—what does that mean? Does that mean nothing? I want something real and not this phony Christian love garbage—it's all in the books, it isn't personal—I want something real—look. . . ."

He tried to take her hand again, and this time she jerked away. She got to her feet. "Mr. Weinstein," she said, "please—"

"You! You nun!" he said scornfully, his mouth twisted into a mock grin. "You nun! There's nothing under that ugly outfit, right? And you're not particularly smart even though you think you are; my father has more brains in his foot than you—"

He got to his feet and kicked the chair.

"You bitch!" he cried.

She shrank back against her desk as if she thought he might hit her, but he only ran out of the office.

Weinstein: the name was to become disembodied from the figure, as time went on. The semester passed, the autumn drizzle turned into snow, Sister Irene rode to school in the morning and left in the afternoon, four days a week, anonymous in her black winter cloak, quiet and stunned. University teaching was an anonymous task, each day dissociated from the rest, with no necessary sense of unity among the teachers: they came and went separately and might for a year just miss a colleague who left his office five minutes before they arrived, and it did not matter.

She heard of Weinstein's death, his suicide by drowning, from the English Department secretary, a handsome white-haired woman who kept a transistor radio on her desk. Sister Irene was not surprised; she had been thinking of him as dead for months. "They identified him by some special television way they have now," the secretary said. "They're shipping the body back. It was up in Quebec. . . ."

Sister Irene could feel a part of herself drifting off, lured by the plains of white snow to the north, the quiet, the emptiness, the sweep of the Great Lakes up to the silence of Canada. But she called that part of herself back. She could only be one person in her lifetime. That was the ugly truth, she thought, that she could not really regret Weinstein's suffering and death; she had only one life and had already given it to someone else. He had come too late to her. Fifteen years ago, perhaps, but not now.

She was only one person, she thought, walking down the corridor in a dream. Was she safe in this single person, or was she trapped? She had only one identity. She could make only one choice. What she had done or hadn't done was the result of that choice, and how was she guilty? If she could have felt guilt, she thought, she might at least have been able to feel something.

Student Questionnaire

Part of our job as educational publishers is to try to improve the textbooks we publish. Thus, when revising we take into account the experiences of both instructors and students with the previous edition. At some time your instructor will be asked to comment extensively on THE MODERN TRADITION, 4th Edition, but right now we want to hear from you. After all, although instructors assign texts, students are the ones who pay for them.

Please help us by completing this questionnaire and returning it to College English Developmental Group, Little, Brown and Company, 34 Beacon Street, Boston, Mass. 02106.

School ______________________ Course title ______________________

Instructor's name ____

Please give us your reaction to the following selections.

		Keep	Drop	Didn't read
Hawthorne	Young Goodman Brown	□	□	□
Poe	The Cask of Amontillado	□	□	□
James	My Friend Bingham	□	□	□
de Maupassant	The Necklace	□	□	□
Conrad	The Secret Sharer	□	□	□
Chekhov	Misery	□	□	□
Cather	Paul's Case	□	□	□
Joyce	Araby	□	□	□
	The Dead	□	□	□
Kafka	The Metamorphosis	□	□	□
	A Hunger Artist	□	□	□
Lawrence	The Prussian Officer	□	□	□
	Odour of Chrysanthemums	□	□	□
Porter	Flowering Judas	□	□	□
	The Grave	□	□	□
Fitzgerald	Babylon Revisited	□	□	□
Faulkner	Dry September	□	□	□
	Barn Burning	□	□	□
Hemingway	Big Two-Hearted River: Part I	□	□	□
	Big Two-Hearted River: Part II	□	□	□
Borges	Funes, The Memorious	□	□	□
	The Secret Miracle	□	□	□
Nabokov	First Love	□	□	□
	"That in Aleppo Once . . ."	□	□	□
Wright	Big Boy Leaves Home	□	□	□
	The Man Who Lived Underground	□	□	□
Welty	Why I Live at the P.O.	□	□	□
	Death of a Travelling Salesman	□	□	□

		Keep	Drop	Didn't read
Olsen	Tell Me a Riddle	□	□	□
	I Stand Here Ironing	□	□	□
Ellison	Battle Royal	□	□	□
	Flying Home	□	□	□
Malamud	Black Is My Favorite Color	□	□	□
	The Magic Barrel	□	□	□
Lessing	He	□	□	□
	To Room Nineteen	□	□	□
Paley	A Conversation with My Father	□	□	□
	Enormous Changes at the Last Minute	□	□	□
O'Connor	Everything That Rises Must Converge	□	□	□
	Good Country People	□	□	□
Morrison	1919	□	□	□
Updike	A & P	□	□	□
	Tomorrow and Tomorrow and So Forth	□	□	□
Barthelme	Me and Miss Mandible	□	□	□
	The Indian Uprising	□	□	□
Oates	Where Are You Going, Where Have You Been?	□	□	□
	In the Region of Ice	□	□	□

Are there any authors not included whom you would like to see represented?

____

Will you keep this book for your library? ____________________

Please add any comments or suggestions ____________________

____

____

Date ____________ Name ____________________

Address ________________________________